The Earthrin Stones

Book 1 of 3

Inheritance of a Sword and a Path

(A novel set in the realm of Dhea Loral)

Douglas Van Dyke Jr.

The Earthrin Stones

Book 1 of 3

Inheritance of a Sword and a Path

©2021 by Douglas Van Dyke

Originally published 2006, 2015, 2019
This edition published through Ingram 2021

ISBN: 978-1-949060-03-4
BISAC FIC009020 Fiction: Fantasy – Epic
       FIC002000 Fiction: Action & Adventure

PUBLISHED BY Douglas Van Dyke Jr
Please Visit:
http://dhealoral.com
Retail Price: $20.00

"If I ever meet my time, I want you to take care of my sword for me."

Trestan turned towards the tents and saw that the closest man had been alerted. The mercenary grabbed his scimitar and moved to attack. He looked to be close to Trestan's father's age. A patch covered one eye, giving him a tough appearance. Trestan had to reach for his other weapon, though he had never hoped to actually have a need for it when it became his to wield.

He drew the Sword of the Spirit from its scabbard, holding the elvish blade of Sir Wilhelm before him in both hands. The bastard sword gleamed in the morning light, though the sun had yet to rise. The hilt accommodated both hands easily. The other man weaved his scimitar back and forth as they faced each other. Trestan accepted the challenge with a bit of fear, but fully accepting of whatever destiny chose. It was time to find out what kind of a swordsman he really was.

Acknowledgements

I wish to thank all those who have helped me, not only in the making of this book, but also in shaping me into the person I am today.

I'm grateful to my mother and father, for their support and trust in me.

I'm thankful to have such a great brother as Brian, who has supported me. My sister-in-law Carrie as well, for the journal she gave me that helped my work. I've also enjoyed the companionship of those who walked the roads of Epos Goth with us.

My expressions of gratitude go out to Joshua Scott for the time and effort put into designing the cover.

To those people at October Skies who helped me with internet advice and are hosting my website, your work and time is greatly appreciated.

I have been blessed to know many friends who have enjoyed role-playing games with me, and offered their support in my endeavors.

And my most profound thanks to the woman who believes in me and makes me feel like the most wonderful man in the world…my wife, Jennifer.

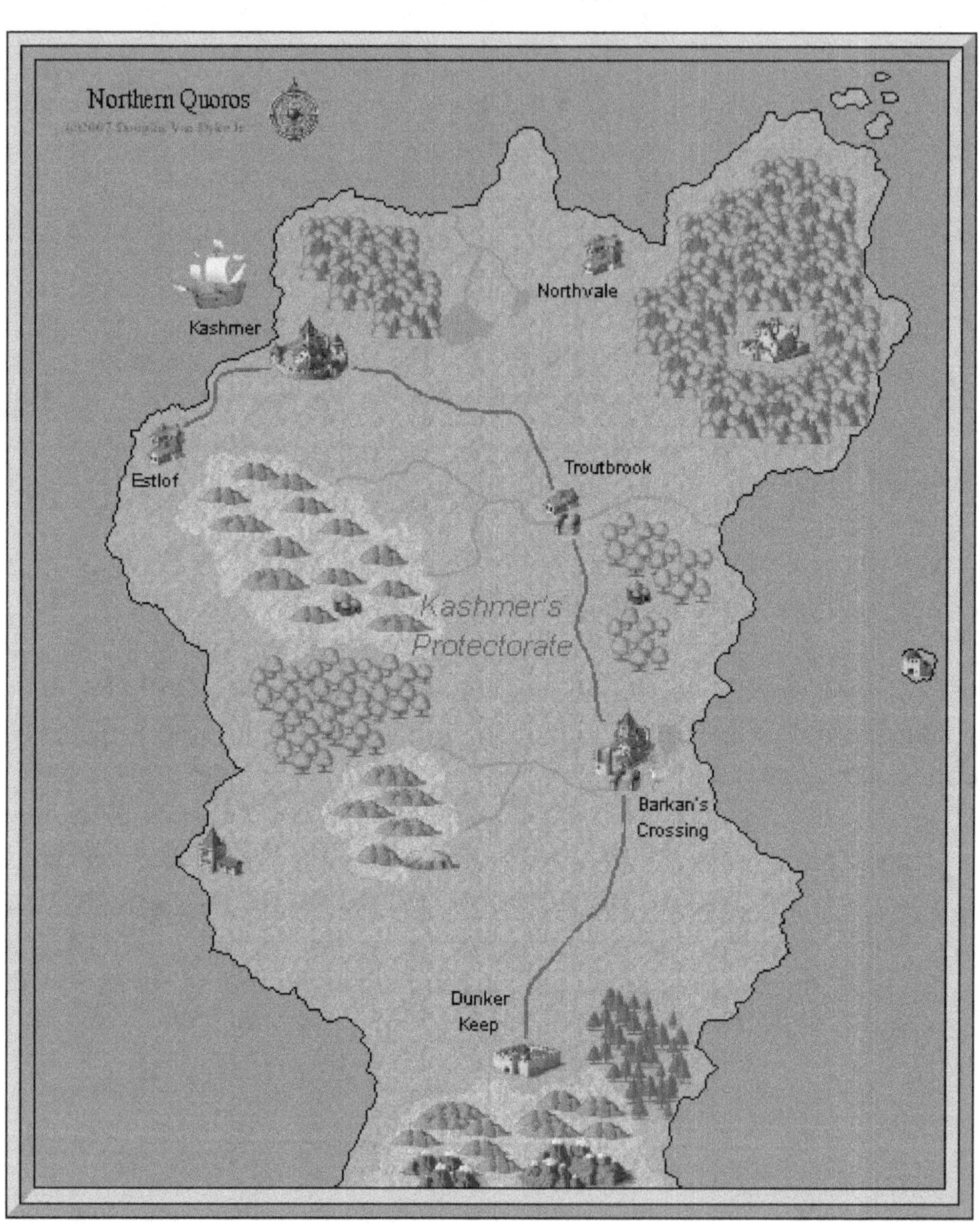

Northern Quoros
Kashmer
Northvale
Estlof
Troutbrook
Kashmer's
Protectorate
Barkan's
Crossing
Dunker
Keep

PROLOGUE

Dhea Loral is an ancient phrase meaning "Hero's Table". Centuries ago, magic was very commonplace in the realm. Most ordinary folk enjoyed magical lighting and a variety of medicinal potions. Empires ruled continents amidst large armies, but their soldiers spent more time patrolling quiet borders than marching for conquest. The bounty of the land fed the masses and the gods blessed the soil of their worshippers. But these same gods stood by as proud, ambitious demigods and immortals worked to change the lands in their own ways. These lesser powers threatened the balance of nature and order while expanding their influence. They pushed armies into motion. Though the gods sensed danger in the escalating conflicts, they could not help but interfere to favor a champion or defeat a rival. At times the common people enjoyed overflowing gifts, and other times the onslaught of wars left them oppressed.

Over time, war and hatred generated more chaos. The world fell from its pinnacle of prosperity. The divine powers became more interested in revenge and dominance than the balance of the world. Pacts between deities were called into play, expanding their involvement in the ongoing conflict. The wars eventually raged so wildly that the gods sundered continents and cast down cities in their destruction. When events were at their most cataclysmic, the gods realized with shock what their disputes had wrought.

Great cities were lost, empires broken, continents torn and reformed. Small villages clung to whatever scraps they could nurture out of the wounded ground. The balance of things natural had been tipped to the point of making some species extinct. The gods had been so consumed in petty disputes that they forgot their role as caretakers.

The major divine powers assembled to bring a lasting peace and balance back to the world. They provided miracles to bring back some growth where needed, saving some civilizations from the brink of death. They agreed to sign a binding Covenant, so that future wars would never reach that scale of destruction again. On the first of Primus, in the year now called 1 AC, (After Covenant), the gods and demigods sealed a pact regarding the involvement of the deities in the future of the world. Restrictions were placed and honored by all. They voluntarily gave up several privileges and bound their oaths. Even the most chaotic of gods can never break the Covenant.

Thus also began the modern priests and clerics. They now became their gods' influence in the world. The gods controlled their dominions from farther away, being careful not to touch the new balance of the realm. Those mortals they favored carried the strength of their power, but only enough to assist in small ways. Though demigods and immortals still walked the realms, they were limited in what they could do. Nevertheless, the major heavenly powers now became more of a watchdog over minor powers. Any divine mandates intended for the world of mortals were now carried out exclusively by mortals who worshipped them.

The year is now 1250 AC, (After Covenant). The oldest elves are too young to remember the time of the Covenant, yet the races are still recovering from that dark time. The first few centuries were simply an attempt at survival. Cities slowly rose across the landscape once again, carved by hearty folk. Ships ventured into the seas to explore nearby lands, discover lost ones, and update obsolete maps. Barbarians and raiders became a common hazard in the vast stretches of wilderness and sea. Many mages go on expeditions to lost cities in search of forgotten lore. Old ways of magic have been sought and uncovered. Legendary cities have faded into the mists of time, waiting to be discovered and their secrets opened for all to see. The races of the world once again fight wars and struggle, as well as grow and prosper, but the gods stay aloft in the heavens. Only their clerics and paladins interfere in the lands. Now that the dark years are hopefully in the past, nations and cities once again struggle to realize their potential.

But deities have long memories and immense patience. Some gods have not forgotten old rivalries or deeds inflicted upon them during the Godswars. Some feel the world has recovered enough to set forth plans into motion once again, testing the limits of the Covenant. As they are forbidden to enter the world of Dhea Loral directly, they begin to whisper into the dreams of those mortals who serve them. Agents of the gods set forth secretively, working in subtle ways to once again participate in the gods' struggle for power.

One does not have to go far for adventure; sometimes it is thrust upon the most unlikely of heroes…

CHAPTER 1

On the 24th day of Florum, the planting season was old enough to see the green forests alive and mostly recovered from the winter season. Common folk across the continent of Quoros pursued their interests in fishing, agriculture, brewing, needlework, or simply enjoyed a lazy day. Lifestyles had improved from the dark years old ones spoke of during evening fireside chats. Elders still lectured of days when farms suffered, caravans between lands faced frequent ambush, and many a winter night passed with scarce food. Life seemed so calm and serene in most small villages, a far cry from the tales of war in other parts of the realms. One might expect to find a young man collecting firewood, going about his farm chores, or collecting wild flowers for the maiden of choice.

The day sparkled with the promise of sunshine and the soft wind brought forth the fragrance of the early flowers. Outside of one these many small hamlets, morning sunlight filtered through a cover of leaves into the waiting ferns and plants below. A place of serene beauty existed in those woods, blessed by a goddess. Stones and wood planks made up a tiered garden, no more than ten feet each side, as part of a humble shrine. A young man stood nearby, his worship interrupted. While others enjoyed the weather and calm tidings that the morning brought, this man found peaceful thoughts far from his mind.

"You dare interrupt my prayers and defile this place of worship? Have you nay respect? Nay good conscience to guide your blades? Worldly treasures will not save your souls in the next life!"

The young man stood defiant, blade in hands and legs spread slightly. He held his sword in a two-handed grip that allowed strength and control. Three silent attackers would test him this day. The young man looked back angrily on their impassive visages: fire staring down ice. The odds weren't good but he steadied his resolve. He determined to fight bravely for his ideals and hope to survive the battle with more than his morals intact. Like a coiled spring ready to pounce, his legs stood ready and balanced. His brown eyes measured his foes to determine where the first threat would come. They issued forth no explanation for their aggression yet made their intent clear through bared blades. The young man decided it was time to force a move, then pray for the best. He picked the enemy most eager, (one with a sword cocked back for a swing), and intentionally turned part of his back towards the attacker. In doing so, he seemed to be diverting his attention and left an opening for the impetuous one to attack.

The attacker fell for the bait, seeing an opportunity to strike. Expecting the attack, the young man spun off to the side and parried the sword strike. He caught and pushed the attacker's sword away. The young man continued the motion, keeping the arc constant as he used both hands on the hilt to try a swing of his own. The opponent's shield blocked the counterstrike. The easy feint and strike had missed, and now the young man worked his sword fast as the action exploded around him. The other two opponents advanced and attempted to once again surround him in their circle of blades. Right and left the young man parried the swords coming at him. With no shield at hand, his sword served both offense and defense. Not relying solely on strength alone, he controlled the momentum of his sword with the counterbalances of both wrists and forearms. What it lacked in hitting

3

power it made up for in speed and control. His spinning blade circles deterred any opening, while his feet kept moving to avoid getting encircled. In the initial lunges from his attackers, none of their blades could penetrate past the blocking sword.

There was little enough room to maneuver between the garden shrine and the surrounding trees. One attacker, shafts of sunlight outlining his tall frame, brushed against the young man. Aware of the trap closing, the lone defender reversed his direction of travel. He swung his sword up while he ducked low to run his body between the middle of his opponents. Spinning his blade as he went, he blocked a couple attacks but also sliced at the side of one aggressor. The young man felt the blade skim along an opponent's torso. Slipping behind them, he continued another swing from the reverse direction to strike the same foe. The two hits from his sword struck hard and drew wounds, but were mostly absorbed by the attacker's armor. The young man paid for the move, feeling a sword slide along his side as well. Too occupied to worry about any wound, he pushed the attack against the two remaining opponents before they could reorganize. The third stumbled a bit apart after getting wounded. The defender's temporary gain failed to bring any break in the fighting. Left and right and spinning from side to side, he blocked two enemy swords as they pressed at him again. The sounds of clashing weapons mixed with hard breathing, while dust kicked up to obscure parts of the wood.

Bad chance struck. As the young man moved around to one side, his foot caught a root. He fell down to his knees. The sword came loose from his hands and tumbled a few feet away. Trying to quickly dive for it, he felt a sword tip scratch into his back as he moved. There he lay after the strike, sword still out of reach but two opponents standing above him quietly.

"Cursed tree root! If this had been in the open I would have fared much better. As it is, I swear I bravely outfought you three!" Trestan declared from the dirt.

The young man slowly regained his feet, for the most part unhindered. One offending tree limb, (which played the part of a sword in his imagination), brushed him as he stood, a reminder he had lost this one. He staggered past his unmoving attackers to retrieve the short wooden pole which served as his practice sword. Turning back, he once again looked over his three opponents. They mutely stood, soaking in the sun's light and the soil's nutrients, unmoving as the trees they had always been. Those three formed a nice triangle, with low branches serving as swords or shields to the youth's imagination. He worked to catch his breath even as he relaxed in the cool morning air. The small glade remained a peaceful place, where a young man could simply imagine himself as a legendary knight from myth.

Trestan tucked the practice stick into the simple rope-belt that held up his trousers. He inspected himself where one branch had brushed him, and was glad to see it hadn't torn his garb prior to the day's work. He had few enough tunics and couldn't afford to tear them. He had a handsome, compassionate face, with dark hair atop his head. His mustache could be called a thick collection of whiskers, though the rest was clean-shaven. Trestan was muscular and solidly built, thanks to hard work at his father's smithy. The young man kept energetic and friends knew he was quick to smile. The rest of his appearance caused some to overlook those good traits. There was little he could do about the black, sooty areas on

4

his hands, face and garb. He washed often, but a hot day at the forge replaced everything he tried to clean off. Patches covered the loose-fitting tunic and trousers. He only had three tunics to his name: the festival one, the work one, and the evening one. A length of old rope was the only belt he ever needed. His shoes were black and soot-covered; each sporting a hole or two in them. A wooden stick served as practice sword. Trestan's only weapon was a quarterstaff; the weapon of choice to most peasants, as it was all they could afford. Simple and humble, he went about many days dreaming of other worlds and other places he could be, if only he had the chance.

As Trestan stood there contemplating his fight, he heard someone coming down the path towards the beautiful glade. He didn't need to look to know who it was. Few enough folks came here, yet the clinking steel plates and jostling leather accouterments heralded the approach and identified the armored owner.

Trestan gave the impassive stand of trees a firm glare as he spoke. "Gloat over your unfair victory if you will. Not a fair fight. I'd easily beat any of you one-on-one. I don't care if you spent a hundred years growing that root to trip me. It's a rather dirty way to win. Next time will be different."

The armored man's deep voice offered, "Young knight, I witnessed your demise. I assume evil has won the day and some fair maiden in her castle will be weeping. I shall grieve in your memory, good sir. Gods curse the sneaky root."

Trestan turned around and smiled at his longtime friend. Sir Wilhelm Jareth's brownish-gray mix of hair extended to his mustache and well-trimmed beard, announcing his fifty-plus years. The retired adventurer's movements exuded experience and confidence, adding charm to his persona. The old warrior wore plate armor decorated with religious symbols. Polished and battle ready, some permanent scratches testified to its share of battles. Armor seemed needless in this quiet countryside, as there had been no calls to war or defense of the nearby hamlet in more years than many could remember. Despite the peace, Sir Wilhelm's bastard sword, (also known as a hand-and-a-half sword), hung by his side. When unsheathed, the sword displayed remarkable craftsmanship. The elvish design left it slimmer than human-crafted swords of the region. The hilt had been lengthened so that a person could easily fit two hands on it, but the weapon obviously had not been designed as a heavy cleaver. Trestan recalled seeing Sir Wilhelm amaze others with how effortlessly he could cut complex patterns in the air using it.

Armor and weapon aside, Trestan came to know the aging warrior from his wit and personality. They had spent many hours at this very shrine discussing philosophy and matters that one would think a smith's boy would have no interest studying.

They exchanged a handshake in greeting. The young man commented on the older man's observation. "Nay, the pity is nay fair maiden awaits me. More is the pity if I don't find one before I die valiantly defending anything. But I'll gladly die in peace if I ever find such a lady worth championing."

Sir Wilhelm looked upon the young man but seemed to smile elsewhere. Perhaps a memory? "My boy, the pursuit of women is a dangerous hobby. The right one will find you when you aren't looking. Until then, better to live your life in the pursuit of something greater for yourself and others. Live so that one day, when death finds you, you'll look to the heavens and exclaim, 'Thank thee gods for the wonderful gift of life which you have given me.' Such has been my pursuit." The old warrior glanced at the shrine. "If you'll excuse me, I shall tend some prayers and thanks to Abriana now so that I might properly start the day."

Sir Wilhelm Jareth approached the shrine and knelt in reverent prayer. Trestan stood quietly, bowing his head in reverence. Built by Sir Wilhelm's own hands, the shrine stood in a quiet spot in the woods not far from the village. Stones and wood planks created a tiered garden with bordering benches for quiet reflection. Plants and flowers from some local gardeners and farmers added colors to it. It occupied a small clearing within a small copse of trees. It appeased the Goddess of Love and Healing, Abriana. Her tenets offered friendship and comfort to the lonely, assistance for those in peril, and the healing powers of the mind and body to cure all ills. Trestan knew of paladins and other such holy warriors in the world who bore devotion of their chosen gods into battle, but he couldn't be sure if Sir Wilhelm was among such men. After all, in Trestan's limited exposure to the world, he had no way to tell for sure.

The aging warrior ended his prayers and took a seat at one of the benches, motioning for Trestan to join him. The young man accepted. When no immediate words issued forth from the old adventurer, Trestan offered a few of his own. "They were a sorry lot, despicable." He motioned to indicate the trees that had been his sparring partners. "They pick out a poor man like me and wish to steal my humble worth for their own selfish pursuits. They would have left me dead only to drink and laugh over my stolen coin."

Sir Wilhelm responded, "Surely a tragedy to lose such a young lad. You are a good boy and may find the afterlife that suits you, but their deeds condemn them. It is enough to feel sorry for them." The veteran warrior grinned.

The young man returned the grin. "This is one of your oddities of looking at life and death."

Jareth motioned to his holy symbols on his fine armor, "Oddities? I am a servant of Abriana. Although she is a peaceful and loving goddess, many warriors follow her tenets to protect that which we love. There is much to be fought for in this world, but how we face life decides the next one. Grieve for a lost love who meets their death prematurely, but at least know they go to a better place. Feel sorry for the attackers, even if you are the one to end their lives. Their path condemns them to an afterlife of torment. If they could only be turned to something good, the world and their souls would be much better off. Yet many die in their selfish pursuits, and their souls are lost for good. A good man shouldn't fear an early death."

"I've never experienced a loved one under the threat of the sword. I'm guessing it isn't easy to hold your blade back and try to redeem a person that just killed someone you loved." Trestan's tone wasn't offering argument. He showed interest in learning Jareth's reasoning.

"Well," the older man murmured, measuring an honest response. "If my loved one were still alive, I would indeed fight fiercely to save them. That shows Abriana the measure of my love: willing to risk my own life and limb to protect another. Even a downed or surrendered opponent deserves mercy, if they ask for it, and so Abriana offers it. A saved soul is worth as much as a faithful one."

Sir Wilhelm sat in quiet contemplation when Trestan prodded him again. "But, if blood was spilled, and they stood defiant…" He left the sentence unfinished.

The warrior drew his sword from the scabbard. The steel reflected the light of the morning sun, highlighting unknown symbols etched along the length of the blade. Sleek and balanced, it promised a skilled fight against any who would test it. The young smith had never seen a more impressive weapon.

The warrior held the naked blade before them. "Abriana's devotees do not replace courts and judges. If the man is unrepentant, my sorrow for his soul will not stay my blade. A hateful killer is the enemy of love and healing. There are evil men that actually pay homage to gods who terrorize decent folk. I imagine their afterlife only offers some of the same strife and sadness they have infected into in this world. Am I to feel sorry for them? That will not stop my blade."

Sir Wilhelm replaced the valuable sword in his scabbard. Seeing Trestan's eyes still on the sword, he changed the subject. "I saw part of your practice fight. You are imitating my style."

The young man blushed, though one could hardly tell from the ash and dust on his face. "Oh that. Well, I took some of what I saw you doing and I thought I'd practice it. I felt it wasn't the smoothest, but I'm getting fast. Hopefully I impressed."

The seasoned warrior smiled, "It was good. You are still a novice, but probably one of the better swordsmen in the village. Well, not that it seems a big compliment."

Trestan's blush didn't have the chance to abate, but he protested the observation, "Surely you jest!"

"I am quite serious my boy! Aside from myself and Sahbin, I doubt there is a man around here that could match your abilities. The guards look tough and can hold a sword, but I've seen how poorly they wield their blades. Without the discipline Sahbin instills in them, they'd be little more than ruffians."

Trestan's mind flitted briefly to Sahbin. The local lord hired her a few years ago to train his retainers. Under her direction, the soldiers served as both village constables and guards for the keep.

Sir Wilhelm further remarked, "I hope you don't take my compliments and start an argument with a sword someday. It's better to go through life never having the need to use one."

Trestan saw the opportunity to ask a question he hadn't inquired from his mentor before, "You say that most knights who use such swords put all their strength into a strong blow, yet you use the handle and a lighter blade to use speed and control instead. Where did you learn this from?"

"I observed warriors up north, in the Empire of Tariyka. Their fighting styles are amazing to behold. They tend to fight with less armor, so their styles represent speed and grace over physical strength. Most opponents you face will not be as armored as I am, so you don't need powerful blows to knock them down. It is useful to be able to switch from offense to defense, right and left, with speed and precision." Sir Wilhelm demonstrated the arm movements. "I saw your spinning style and the way you turn your blade around with simple hand and wrist movements. Many sword warriors need to reset their hips a different way each time and roll their whole body around. My method benefits from a light sword, for I couldn't wield a heavy one and use that same style." At that thought Sir Wilhelm saw the young man's gaze drift back to the sword. He saw the next question before it was asked.

He offered the scabbarded sword for Trestan to hold. The young man, (dirty, poor, and with little chance of pursuing his boyish adventures), looked to the old knight as if he offered a dream come true. Trestan gingerly took it. Once it settled in his hands, he marveled at how light it was compared to its look. The blacksmith's son could feel the exceptionally good craftsmanship involved. "It feels so light! It must have magic in it, right? Mind if I draw the blade?"

The older man laughed, "My boy, I wouldn't give you the sword and forbid you to admire the blade. Have a look and wave it around a bit…not too close to a tree root mind you."

Trestan displayed the greatest reverence for the blade as he slowly drew it out. Trestan gingerly set the scabbard on the bench before he waved it in the air. His concern ensured that the polished blade touched nothing.

Sir Wilhelm Jareth continued to talk about the blade while the lad reveled in holding it. "Its origin is of elvish make. I tried to acquire a Tariykan sword, but they protect the secrets of their crafted weapons closely. Their swords are more respected than most anything a family could own; it is the pride of the house. This elvish sword serves well enough for my purpose. The elves also value skill and grace over raw strength."

The aging warrior watched Trestan, though his gaze looked intently into qualities that existed deep within the young man. As the young smith continued to stare slack-jawed at the sword, Sir Wilhelm's gentle words startled him, "Boy, I have nay sons or daughters. Much as I have loved some women in my life, I was never blessed with a child. Among all the villagers, you are the only other person that comes to Abriana's shrine on a regular basis. I don't count Lord Verantir Tessald, for he comes out only to pay lip service to all the shrines and temples as part of his political position. You, on the other hand, share my ideals and seem to respect the goddess in your own way. I've seen how much compassion and help you've given to the others of the village. It's rare that I hear an angry tone from your lips." Sir Wilhelm drew a deep breath and declared, "If I ever meet my time, I want you to take care of my sword for me."

Trestan's shock allowed the sword to drop low enough to make a solid noise on a rock. He stammered out an apology and quickly re-sheathed the blade. Jareth laughed as the youth hastily returned it to him, hilt first as was proper custom.

"I meant it boy…I mean…young man. It wouldn't be proper to call you a boy anymore; you have grown so much. I hope you shall never have to use a sword, I hope it rusts to nothing before it is ever needed again. Nevertheless, when I pass on, I can think of nay others better suited to take care of it for me."

Trestan tried to recover his composure, "I…uh…don't know what to say. I hope to have you around forever. You'll be a wise guide to my children if I ever get the blessing and curse of having some."

The retired warrior laughed, "Well, that may be a long time yet, I'm not dead. Although, you may be once you finally get to work and your father gets a hold of you!"

"Uh oh," Trestan looked towards the sun, "I've been playing way too long, my father is going to be upset. I better run, but I'll see you tonight if I'm able!"

Sir Wilhelm saluted using the sword, "You know where I live; the door is always open,"

Trestan got up and bowed in respect. He dashed off down the trail back to the village. A couple seconds later, he turned around and raced back because he had forgotten his quarterstaff at the shrine. He retrieved it with an embarrassed smile. Then the young man bowed a second time then ran off again.

After he was gone the older warrior looked up to the heavens and spoke. "That young man could be a smith forever in a small hamlet and be content. I think, however, he could be much more in your service if given the chance. The lad is capable of more than what fate's lot has dealt him so far."

Sir Wilhelm looked down to the rock on which Trestan had dropped the blade. It was a thin rock, the kind one might skip across a pond. Nevertheless, the small drop of the sword sundered it into two halves without nicking the weapon. Trestan had been too preoccupied to notice.

"A curse on all Tariykan sword smiths anyway," noted Sir Wilhelm Jareth. "Elven magic makes for a much better blade!"

*   *   *   *   *

Trestan ran along a path through a sparse wood. A brook ran along his right side directly towards the rising sun. The bountiful fishing along the brook provided the nearby village its name: Troutbrook. Water drifted lazily past, deep enough for the fish, but not so deep as to be a major deterrent for anyone wanting to cross. Freshly planted farm fields bordered the woods along the north side where Trestan ran. The cattle and sheep herders occupied the south side of the brook, which avoided land disputes. It was a good time of the year to enjoy an outdoor run along that peaceful waterway. The breeze carried the scents from many breakfast cook fires. Flowers started blooming in the trees. Some of the village men were fishing along the brook, awake before dawn to enjoy it. Trestan passed them with a wave but didn't stop for conversation.

From the village, a person could take a canoe and be at the ocean within a day. Many villages up and down the coastline traded deep-sea fish and crabs with Troutbrook for other supplies, so there was no shortage of seafood around Trestan's home. Despite the trade, fishing was simply part of the heritage.

Trestan finally came over a slight rise where the riverbank turned steep and gazed upon the buildings of his home. A small stone bridge, just wide enough for a single wagon, straddled the brook just south of the village. Three main streets composed Troutbrook, the widest one traveled in a straight line north from the old stone bridge. This main road had the most important merchant locales on it: the inn, pub, a couple of dry goods stores, carpenter shop, stable, church, bakery, butcher, tailor and the blacksmith. Both ends of the main street had open-air markets on the outskirts for merchants and farmers who couldn't afford a building. The smaller two streets paralleled either side of the main one. They accessed the merchants' back doors and some houses. A few unnamed cross streets and alleys provided thoroughfare between the three roads.

The most dominant building on the main street, The Church of the Sacred Harvest, reflected the large farmer population of the area. Based on the tenets of Yestreal, God of Sun and Weather, it appealed to humble folk of the land. Farmers prayed for their livelihood and crops, others paid homage to respect the cycle of the seasons and nature. The general populace disliked the only other god that held sway over the ground and crops. Mothrok, Goddess of Earth and Stone linked to the land but her clergy tended to raise unliving servant skeletons. Due to that nature, most farmers offered her prayers only out of fear and to guard against misfortune. On the other hand, The Church of the Sacred Harvest was the only church in Troutbrook actively tended by clergy, and it drew many worshippers. There were shrines to other gods outside of town, (like Sir Wilhelm Jareth's shrine to Abriana), but no other buildings of organized worship. Yestreal's church included a shrine built in the middle of the main street in front of the church. A green stone etched with strange markings occupied a column of marble, and this formed a part of the central well in the village. The stone reportedly possessed magical properties: a gift from the god to promote the growth of crops and the prosperity of the region. People often prayed to it for good weather in lean times.

Trestan glanced farther north, along the ridge and slightly off the road from the village. Even the church seemed a small and insignificant building compared to the manor where Lord Verantir Tessald lived and ruled over the immediate area. Both the lord's keep and the stone church dated back to around the Godswars and had been tended well during the dark years. The manor also housed the most beautiful young lady in the village. Lady Shauntay Tessald still sought a suitor. The local boys, Trestan included, fancied her despite knowing they would never win her father's approval.

Closer to town, Trestan headed straight across field trails to the smithy. He did his best to avoid the newly seeded rows. His father's hammer rang out clearly among the other village noise. Trestan faced the humble home that he lived in with his father. The front of the house faced one of the small side streets, while the back of the house connected to the smith yard, and the blacksmith stall faced the main street. It wasn't a very far distance to walk to work, unless you had a care to go play in the woods that morning. The side street passing by the front of their house wasn't anything grand to look at. Two stumps sat outside the front door where father and son could sit and enjoy a quiet sunset after a hard day's work. A few houses belonging to other village folk dotted the west side of street. Other than that, it was rather open space with some small farms and unused land. The row of houses and merchant back doors looked drab and plain, yet it had been the only home Trestan had ever known. The house itself had one level and boasted only three rooms. One room was a common room and kitchen combined. The next was his father's bedroom. The third was part Trestan's bedroom and part storage. An enclosed yard sat between the house and the smithy, bordered on either side by other buildings. In the yard, metal stock piled next to a large metal tub which served as the sunlit bath for father and son. The back wall of the smithy and a line of hanging laundry offered the bath some privacy.

He ran into the house and dropped off his quarterstaff and practice sword. Using a water basin in the common room, he splashed his face and hands a bit to refresh himself before the facing the ash of the forge. Trestan's mind remained distracted on Sir Wilhem's offer regarding the sword. His mentor had shown quite a bit of his heart that morning. It was something the young man wouldn't soon forget. He took a deep breath to steady himself. It was time to put in a hard day of work.

Trestan saw his father, Hebden Karok, pound away to finish last night's project. Glancing around, he noted someone missing. "Mikhael isn't here?" Mikhael, son of the owner of the dry goods store, worked in the smithy from time to time in exchange for deals for his father.

Hebden glanced up, a reflection of how Trestan might look when older. The older smith sported thicker arms, gray hairs, and an extra layer of soot. Trestan saw a slight frown on his father's face. He got the feeling he would have been a more welcome sight if he had gotten there earlier.

Hebden Karok set down the hammer, standing tall and proper to address his son. "Glad to see you found your way here. I hope your morning walk got you fresh and ready for the day. Mikhael can't join us; his folks had some chores for him."

Trestan grabbed a leather apron to protect his patched work clothes. "What have we got waiting? You look like you've got something big on your mind."

Hebden nodded a forced smile. "Lord Verantir himself sent word this morning. He has a tiny little job for us to do."

A slight pause informed the young smith the job wasn't exactly tiny, or easy. "I'm ready, what is it?"

Hebden nodded to the stall used to shoe horses. "His lordship would like us to shoe several of his horses that are overdue. I've already seen them. Big warhorses, with only one exception! It promises to take up a lot of time today on top of some items I'd like to get repaired for friends."

Trestan acknowledged his readiness to get started. As he did, a glance around the street turned up something that pulled at his attention. Fairest among any flowers in the valley, the Lady Shauntay Tessald could catch any young man's eyes across the length of the village street. Silver clasps adorned braided, long, blonde hair. Her perfume usually wielded the power to entice many a man swept up in her blue eyes. The lady's corset accentuated her already ample bosom; the neckline just low enough to show the beginning of her cleavage. In a fashion unladylike to nobles she wore a ruffle skirt, which stopped at the knees, and her knee-high heeled boots. Men could get a forbidden glance at her thighs when she positioned herself to "accidentally" reveal anything. While such apparel was not uncommon among most women, the nobility formed its own intricate codes of dress. The older townswomen frowned and whispered at her style. Despite the allure of her figure and attire, her smile remained her most captivating weapon. Trestan knew she had a skill of persuading favors from people while only compensating them with her gratitude. Indeed, men fawned over her and bent over backwards to win her admiration. She was actually quite the scandal to the well-respected women of the village. She neither cared nor listened, and like it or not she could do what she pleased as the lord's only child.

Two escorts accompanied Lady Shauntay. Trestan knew little about the first, a young woman hailing from the city of Kashmer to the north. Supposedly the lady's riding instructor, the two acted more as friends rather than a mentor/apprentice relationship. When the lady's parents weren't around the two eschewed the side-saddle riding that female nobility favored. The second escort always guarded her employer's daughter. Sahbin, the only female guard employed at the Tessald mansion, possessed muscles and scars that would shame many adventurer visitors to the town. The bodyguard dressed in chain armor with plates over vulnerable areas, short hair tucked under a helm. Aside from the aging Sir Wilhelm, Sahbin was the most dangerous fighter in the village.

Hebden followed Trestan's eyes to the sight down the street. He gave a snort in amusement as he realized the distraction and the nature in which she dressed. "Her mother must be out of town for her ladyship to appear like that. Probably trying to find a proper suitor for her and marry her off." The smith shook his head. "Lady Shauntay is out flaunting and flirting favors again most likely. She must have ridden in with the other two when they delivered the horses to the stable, though I didn't see her."

Trestan half turned to reply, but his eyes stayed focused down the street. "Horses? Stable…huh?"

His father gave a laugh and elbowed his son to get the young man's attention. "The warhorses that I just told you needed new shoes. They are in the stables waiting for us to start working for a living."

Trestan blushed, "I'm sorry, lost track of things there for a moment."

"Well," Hebden Karok glanced at the forge before turning back to his son, "I think you'll be alright holding the shop by yourself while I grab the first horse. It's not like her ladyship has any reason to come by a soot pile. I'll be right back with our first victim."

Trestan attended to the coals of the forge. He gathered a few supplies together and arranged his tools. He became aware of someone walking by the smithy, but his mind was in his work until a voice addressed him.

"I couldn't help but notice those hairpieces you have hanging there. Nice design."

Soft, gentle and female, it was a pleasant voice. Trestan set his tools down in a hurry. The young smith turned about to look at the voice's owner, then almost stepped back in shock. Lady Shauntay stood before him: silky blonde hair, curvaceous figure, intoxicating perfume and ruffled skirt. She trapped him with her soft blue eyes from only a few feet away. He hardly registered the bodyguard and the young woman from Kashmer standing slightly behind her. All his attention narrowed to every village boy's dream, belatedly realizing she had just complimented him.

Trestan went through a moment of stunned indecision, then bought time for his response by bowing. It felt hurried and clumsy, though it widened the smile on the noble's daughter. "My thanks for such kind words, um, regarding my humble work, milady. I toyed with some designs with some leftover copper stock. Would you like to inspect one closer?" Trestan felt heat in his cheeks he could not attribute to the forge.

12

Lady Shauntay nodded her approval. Trestan turned to retrieve the hairpieces in question, trying to move calmly despite a galloping heart and nervous fingers. Shiny copper loops and stylish intersections wove a pattern that might accentuate any lady's hair. Trestan had crafted them just to practice his skills rather than any thought of actually selling them. It awed him to hand those pieces over to the most desirable woman in the village. Typically, the Tessald family bought high quality silver and gold items from Kashmer in the north, or even shipped the best stuff from the distant city of Orlaun. The local lord's family only dealt with the blacksmith when some menial task like horseshoes came up.

He stood silent and nervous as the lady and her riding instructor stepped just far away for some private chat over the items. They shared some girlish giggles, while the bodyguard Sahbin held a rigid hand-on-her-sword stance nearby. Trestan strained to listen to the conversation, slightly distracted by the perfume scent of the lovely lady. He overheard, "…this looks good. It will work out well…" and felt comforted that the giggles weren't a mockery of his work.

Trestan tried to casually smooth down his helplessly immature mustache. By the time Lady Shauntay turned back to him, Trestan made every attempt to stand tall, keep his stomach tucked, and rest a fist pose-like on his hip. There was no disguising his overall dirty clothing, but he smiled in confidence as if he bore a lord's outfit. She looked him up and down. The lady ran soft fingers over the polished copper pieces slowly, shining her warm smile into the young man's heart.

"We are blessed to have such a skilled young smith in our midst," she began. "I would love to have jewelry such as these for my own. You truly master bending metal to your desire! What price do you set on owning such wonderful works of art?"

Trestan had never considered a value, nor someone actually wanting to buy them. He collected his thoughts. "Um…uh. Well, your ladyship…the ingots cost me very little. Nothing much really." In truth, they cost a lot to a smith's boy. In the face of such radiant beauty, he found it hard to ask her for anything. "I wouldn't charge you for them, milady, I'd be proud to just let you have them."

Lady Shauntay appeared flattered. "That is so benevolent of you. I won't have these for free. I don't carry money on me when I am in the village, but I can see to it that my father can stop by and pay for these properly. I wouldn't want your hard work to go to waste. May I have these three then?"

He just couldn't refuse. "Take them and enjoy, milady. You honor me by your praise. Just remember if anyone else admires them as much as you do, be sure to let them know where you got them."

"Aye, I will indeed. Bye for now. Good fortune follow you." Lady Shauntay Tessald slowly turned away from the smithy and continued to walk down the street. Sahbin never even cracked a smile with her iron jaw, yet nodded politely to Trestan before she followed her charge. The young Tessald noble paused and turned in an alluring way, flirting one last smile at the poor smith's boy.

Trestan thought his heart skipped a beat. He gawked as she walked away, studying her curves and movements very closely. The young man remembered to take in a deep breath as Lady Shauntay's attention wandered elsewhere. His throat felt very dry. Trestan replayed the scene in his head. He started to think of a few things he could have said better. Trestan's mind dwelt on every movement the young lady had made, as well as the scent of her perfume. During the whole conversation he had struggled to keep his eyes off the start of her gifted cleavage, though temptation proved a worthy adversary. Sahbin's intimidating frown and solid muscles had helped keep the young man's eyes focused honorably.

His daydreams broke apart when his father walked up to the smithy leading the first horse. Trestan recognized the well-known mount. Sahbin's large warhorse had a mean temper and vicious kick. The horse stood seventeen hands high and packed with muscle. It mirrored the danger of its owner. The young smith recalled an incident on the main street where Sahbin had reacted instinctively to a drunk causing trouble with the noble family. The bodyguard's horse kicked backwards and seriously wounding the drunkard. Although Lord Tessald chided her for overreacting, the injured man never recovered the full use of one arm. The horse looked fearsome enough without the rider.

Hebden Karok looked at his son and shrugged, "Might as well get the bad one out of the way first thing, aye?"

Trestan nodded grimly, but his eyes retained a sparkle when he started work that morning.

*   *   *   *   *

The sun and forge combination were tempered by a cool, early season breeze originating from the eastern ocean. Both Trestan and his father took a break for noonmeal. Hebden Karok ate some bread and cheese inside their house. In the blacksmith shop, Trestan sat in a cool corner opposite the forge and patted a content stomach. He grabbed a clay water jug and proceeded to walk to the well outside the church. Trestan wasn't worried about guarding anything in the smithy; it was within sight and they never had problems with thieves.

Trestan glanced at a relic the church of Yestreal displayed upon a brick extension of the well. The green stone, with its strange markings, was said to be a sacred gift from the god in ancient times. Traveling mages confirmed it radiated magic of some kind. The clergy residing in the Church of the Sacred Harvest claimed Yestreal's stone helped the crops grow and fended off droughts and other disasters. Trestan and the majority of villagers attended services here, but he always felt his heart belonged elsewhere. The more he talked to Sir Wilhelm Jareth, the more Abriana's ways appealed to him. Therefore, he paid little regard to the stone.

A youth named Petrow, brown hair conflicting with his blue eyes, dipped his cup into the water bucket at the well. At twenty years he was only a year older than Trestan. Petrow's frayed, stained garb appeared as impoverished as Trestan's, and simple laced sandals cushioned his feet. He also wore a leather utility harness with numerous tools and implements strapped to it. His trademark woodcutter's axe propped against the well. He stood muscular, tanned, and never excused himself from a day of hard work. Petrow worked as a jack-of-all-trades in the village to support an income. He supplied wood to both inn and pub, repaired thatch roofs for others when asked, ran errands for the local shopkeepers and worked as an extra hand on farms or ranches. He knew enough about so many jobs that he often irked Trestan with his 'vast' knowledge.

He saw Trestan approach and smiled in greeting to his lifetime friend. "You look like you've been putting in tough hours today my friend! What has your father got you doing now?"

The young smith lowered the bucket back into the well. "We're putting new shoes on several of Lord Tessald's horses. It's going about as well as can be expected. After that we have several smaller chores to fill. But, my day is the brightest day in a long time."

Petrow cast a glance at his friend, but Trestan ignored him, even started humming a tune. It seemed a game, but the older youth quickly lost patience. "Ok, don't keep me in suspense. I've got a full list of jobs calling me today. This village can't run itself without me! That scruff of lip-whiskers doesn't cover your ear-to-ear grin."

Trestan was in too good a mood to banter about his mustache. "Someone important came by the smithy today and paid me a compliment."

Once again, a period of silence followed. The jack-of-all-trades felt as if the smith switched roles on him. Usually Petrow kept Trestan in suspense whenever there was big news. "Important? Was it the Priest Gerloch? Maybe Sahbin? Lord Tessald himself? Ok, spit it out, I give up already!"

"Her Ladyship Shauntay Tessald," Trestan enjoyed the shock on Petrow's face. "She came by and admired those copper hairpieces I made. She even bought them. Well, I gave them to her."

"*Gave* them? Those must have cost you a few good coins just for the metal. Did she offer to pay or just sweet talk you into handing them over?"

Trestan responded, "She offered. She said her father would pay when he came by but I told her he didn't need to. Hey! The most beautiful girl in the village was standing right there asking for my trinkets. It was an honor!"

A sudden smug look and upward tilt of Petrow's nose discomforted the young smith. "I used to be infatuated with her too. I hate to say it; all her good points are on the outside."

"But…"

"Let me explain, Tres." Petrow liked to condense his friend's name. The way he shook his head, Trestan felt Petrow once again adopted his superior-knowledge-role. "Do you know how many merchants to whom she owes money? You're not the only young man from whom she has acquired some item and didn't pay. She arrives so sweet and dresses to display rather than hide. She promises her father will pay, but he never does. I dare you to go up to Lord Tessald when he's in town and ask for money to pay for those pieces. I'd like to see his reaction. You can bet if he asks her about it, she'll deny owing anything, or she'll remind you that you offered it as a present. She uses people Tres, I wish you'd see that."

Trestan poured the bucket of water into the clay jug with a sigh. "I don't get it. I had a pleasant encounter with the most desirable woman in town, and you treat it like you are sympathetic over some loss of mine."

Petrow looked past Trestan into the street, his eyebrows raised. "Well, maybe second most desirable now." Trestan followed Petrow's glance.

A woman rode into town from the south, having already crossed the lone bridge over the river. She sat astride a small warhorse armored with leather barding and laden with packs, such as might carry provisions for a long ride, or maybe even a treasure of ill-gotten bounty. Her femininity could be easily seen by her lovely shape, though the young men couldn't see more details until she rode past them. The rider wore black leather armor; a dark steel helm protected her head and covered a small portion of her face though it left her ears open. Her ears were slightly pointed, and the face angular, proclaiming elvish blood mixed with human ancestry. What the men could see of her beyond the helmet added some exotic beauty to this stranger. Long, black hair cascaded out from beneath the helm, catching the breeze. Green eyes surveyed the village, studying everything as she traveled. The young men admired the athletic curves of her figure. As she passed, they could see she was armed for dangerous business. A crossbow strapped across her back, with a second crossbow on the side of the horse. Numerous quivers held many crossbow bolts, including one on her left side and one on her right lower leg. Her rapier hung on her left side, opposite the young men, but the glare of the midday sun revealed a glint of silver on the basket hilt. Despite the harshness of her war implements, she grinned and gave a nod to the two men as she passed them. They gave respectful bows in return, though neither man seized the opportunity to speak.

Whether adventuress or mercenary, she dismounted in front of the inn and tied her horse to the railing. Slightly short compared to a normal human woman, and a bit slender, her walk was quick and graceful. She took off her helmet and shook out her hair a bit before entering the inn, though neither of the young men could see anything more revealing of her face from where they stood. Once inside the inn and out of view, both men regained their breathing. They forgot their previous conversation.

Petrow said to the young smith, "When you get done with your chores this evening, meet me for a few drinks and let's splurge some copper pennies, maybe even a full drab."

Trestan responded, "I plan to see Sir Jareth later this evening, but I'll definitely join you for a round. Meet at the pub or the inn?"

Petrow grinned widely in reply, as if the answer should have been obvious. He indicated the armored warhorse, "At the inn. Assuming she stays, I'd be interested to see what develops there tonight."

The young smith reclaimed his water jug and headed back to the smithy. Already he could see his father resuming his place near the forge. He turned about as he walked and called back to Petrow. "I shall see you there tonight, with my good shirt."

Upon returning, father and son shared a drink before Hebden asked Trestan to get the next horse. Trestan obliged, even half-hoping the lady of elvish blood would pick that moment to stable her mount. Despite longing for it, he didn't find her there. Looking around the stable pens, he spotted the obvious choice. In one of the stalls stood one of the few horses Lady Shauntay favored on her rides. The expensive saddle and reins hung nearby, both objects of fine colors and ornamentation. As he coaxed the horse out of the stall, Trestan couldn't help but notice the horse's mane. It had been combed and braided as

16

fashionably as its owner's hair. In fact, the smith was taken aback as he noticed three very familiar copper hairpieces holding the braids in place.

Trestan hung his head low and laughed to himself. His passionately designed work was the adornment upon her ladyship's favorite horse. He hadn't told his father yet of the exchange that morning between him and the flirtatious noble, but there would be no concealing it when his father saw that braided mane. Petrow would certainly laugh once he heard about it.

The humble young smith, feeling poor indeed in his patched trousers and dirty shirt, hitched his rope-belt a bit higher and led the ornamented horse out to the smithy.

CHAPTER 2

The mild chill of a Florum twilight leeched away the day's warmth. Lights lit up windows as families shared an evening meal or talked around comfortable hearth fires. Village lanterns blazed in regular spacing along the entire street all the way down to the stone bridge. Yestreal's church began to shine with divine illumination, as the ever-present miracle became more noticeable in the dark hours. Only the pub and the inn drew a crowd at this hour. The rest of the merchant shops shuttered and locked. The open-air markets were packed up and dismantled for the night. The appointed time arrived to unwind and relax from a hard day of work or an easy day of fishing.

Trestan readied himself for the night's entertainment. He bathed in a metal tub located in the small yard between his house and the smithy. Heated rocks from the forge warmed the water and fended off chills. He loved taking a long bath out under the open sky. The shops on either side had no windows into this yard, and the smithy had a back wall blocking the view from the street. There was a decent cake of soap handy, supplied by Mikhael and the dry goods store. The young smith scrubbed the soot layers and sweat from his body. He even used a cracked mirror, burning candle, and self-crafted scissors to trim his mustache a bit.

Trestan dressed in his good tunic. He had worked hard to keep soot and dirt off of it during the years he had worn it around the yard. The shirt was a light green color, made with good quality dyes, and excellent stitching compared to his other two shirts. He wore a spare pair of trousers which didn't fit his father anymore. They had less patches than Trestan's leggings. The simple length of rope still did the job of a belt well enough. He didn't have a spare set of shoes, so he tried to clean his as best as he could. He admired himself in the mirror, satisfied that a clean face finally showed. Some of his fingernails were still stained dark, but a good shade of pink returned to them again. Working over forge and iron was dirty work.

The door to his home cracked open, Hebden's voice called, "Are you decent?"

"Aye, father." Trestan felt he was ready to enjoy the evening.

Hebden took a step into the yard, glancing up at the dark sky. "Not sure this is one of those nights you and Petrow should be out."

Trestan hung his head to one side, his shoulders drooped rather exaggeratingly. "I've been working for this all day. That was a lot of effort."

"Normally I wouldn't suggest the pub," Hebden nodded northward, up the street, "but tonight that might be the better place to enjoy your drink."

Trestan's head perked up, "I thought you hated me going there. Said it yourself, it's for serious drinkers and smokers."

"Aye," Hebden took a deep breath. "More adventurer-types rode into town when you were in your room earlier."

"Adventurers bring good entertainment!"

"Not tonight." Hebden's sudden firmness interrupted the rest of Trestan's thoughts. "They gave mistrustful glances to everyone as they rode up the street. One of

18

them looked so fierce as to set my heart racing. Didn't get a proper look to understand *what* I was looking at."

Trestan had to prompt his father, "What do you mean?"

"Wasn't really a he or she, more like an *it*. Large humanoid, riding one of those large steeds from the south that would make Lord Verantir's horses seem the runts of the litter. Its face was…" Hebden had to pause. His hands rose and waved about his ears. "It either had an unusual, horned helm, or it really did have actual horns extending from a misshapen face. I heard grunts that could have been it or its horse."

Trestan glanced over his shoulder, but he didn't have a view of the inn due to the blacksmith store's back wall. "And the others of the group?"

Hebden extended his open hands to his sides, exasperated. "I didn't pay them much mind after trying to figure out the big one. One was cloaked, neither displayed armor…weren't them that concerned me!" Hebden sighed. "Just consider going to the pub tonight. The inn may not be a good idea." After offering the advice, Hebden went back inside.

Trestan finished his preparations and headed toward the inn. Despite his father's warnings, he looked forward to meeting these mysterious characters. Trestan discounted Hebden's spook as merely someone wearing a helmet decoration. Adventurers always proved to be interesting. They often brought tales with them, many hard to believe, and sometimes paid extravagantly for their meals and drinks. Sometimes a minstrel accompanied such bands, and would provide extra entertainment for the locals. The evening promised to be stimulating however it ended.

When the young smith crossed the street, his eye caught sight of three riders down to the south by the bridge. A glance identified Lady Shauntay and her escorts enjoying an evening ride; certainly not something that her mother would have approved. The younger two laughed and talked, their giggles carrying across the darkened end of the main street. Sahbin rode composed and quiet. The three women wheeled their horses to the south and galloped over the bridge into the woods on the other side of the river. Trestan shook his head and turned his attention back to the merriment coming from the inn.

The Fishing Hole Inn prospered from its location. The road the village sat on ran from the large capital city of Kashmer on the northwest coast down to Dunker Keep on the southern border. Travelers headed north or south along the main road stopped at this inn. Visitors included merchant caravans, solitary traders, messengers and occasionally adventurers. Kashmer had thriving guilds for daring warriors and explorers and the southern mountains called to many. Soldiers used the road as well, patrolling the land or replacing guards at Dunker Keep. When unoccupied by travelers, the inn still did business as a place where you could share a good, reasonably-priced meal with neighbors without having to cook it yourself. Everyone in the village knew most everybody else. Not a very different atmosphere than the local pub, except much quieter due to possible sleeping guests upstairs. A grand hearth marked a part of the common room where storytellers or the rare performer could entertain. A bar ran along the opposite wall. Along each of the walls were boards etched with the records of the biggest fish caught in the nearby brook.

Even though many residents of the town weren't very literate, anyone seemed able to read the length and weight of the prize fish catches.

Trestan scanned the common room. As he looked around all he could really make out was the familiar faces of the village. More than a few waved or greeted him with words. Even as Trestan walked in, however, a few comments launched from some of the men old enough to see him grow from a baby.

"Hey Trestan! A few coppers for your thoughts! Maybe three loopy ones?"

"Lad, were you trying to impress the woman, or her horse?"

"He was after the horse. After the wedding they can ride into the sunset together!"

"You forgot to give that horse some copper shoes to match the hair decorations!"

"Boy, I always imagined you wanted to get below a woman's beltline…but I didn't figure you were aiming low enough to hit the horse she rode."

Trestan rolled his eyes. Much as he wanted entertainment, it seemed he was the choice of amusement for the night. He wondered how much had been passed along by his father, and how much spread by his best friend. In either case, he hoped the merriment would die down sooner rather than later.

After exchanging polite salutations of his own he saw Petrow at the far side of the bar. Anyone coming down the stairs from the rooms would have to squeeze by that spot. Petrow even made sure he had a seat open on both sides of him, gesturing to one for Trestan.

The young smith sat down next to the village handyman, noting his blue-eyed friend wore a big smile and tried hard to contain laughter. Trestan ordered a drink, whispering to Petrow, "Oh, one day I'll get you back somehow. Don't doubt it for one minute." Trestan glanced at the empty seat on Petrow's other side. "Foot of the stairs, as always?"

Petrow, finally getting control over a straight face, replied, "Most accessible spot for anyone coming down from their room!"

The young blacksmith decided to switch focus to a more interesting topic, "Seen or heard anything?"

"Well, I haven't seen the dark lady we saw riding in, but this is what I heard so far," Petrow leaned forward, eager to share information. "The lady rider has ventured down to the common room a few times, glanced around for a bit, and then went back up to her room. Her room faces the street out front. She's been seen looking out the window quite often. She hasn't been down since the other three arrived…did you know about them?" Trestan nodded as he finally received his drink. Petrow continued, "All of whom look to be adventurers as well from what I've seen. The men around the bar here were also quite taken in by the lady elf's good looks, but I'm hoping she finds this empty chair next to me. It's been a good spot in the past."

Petrow needed a moment to wet his whistle and gather his thoughts. He downed a swallow before continuing. "I saw the other three, one of them must have been hit with the ugly stick. They weren't a pretty spectacle, however; you've been the only thing worth a good laugh so far." Trestan rolled his eyes again, noting the occasional comments regarding him were still being whispered in parts of the room. Petrow continued, "Those three weren't kind at all, though one spoke eloquently enough. I guess I'll describe him first. I think he's a magic user. He had a decorated staff, several pouches attached to his belt, a bandolier and a simple dagger. No armor either, just robes. Full-blooded elf, I think. Wiry fellow but his eyes…" Petrow's hands moved as if to grab the proper words from the air. "We had brief eye contact, and I found myself quickly averting my eyes. I felt like my stare was treading on forbidden ground. Oh, he had silver-colored hair too, long and braided like a girl."

Trestan interrupted, "That doesn't sound like the one hit by the ugly stick."

"Nay, I'm saving that one for last," the smith grunted as his friend continued. "The second one, human, also didn't wear any armor. In fact, his silk shirt opened wide at the chest. Pale skin, slanted eyes, maybe Tariykan or such. Held a strange weapon: a handle with a blade bending forward from it at a near-right angle. A length of chain wrapped around the handle. His walk was…he glided across the floor as if flowing smoothly through a dance."

Head propped on one hand, Trestan proved disinterested in the group so far. "Tell me about the ugly one! Father said one wore horns or something?"

Petrow took another drink before he talked again. "Aye, that odd one could scare you to death in a dark alley. A cloak covered most of his face and body. Probably stood over eight feet tall and bent over to walk through the door. Biggest axe you ever saw on his back! I couldn't tell you whether his bull-like horns are from a helmet or if he really has horns on his head, the cloak partly covered them. He gave me the shivers."

The smith also finished a drink and confronted his friend, "Wait a moment! You talk about him being an ugly one, and you didn't even see his face?"

"I didn't need to see it! When they went by me to go upstairs, I got the impression I better not take a peek. I kept my eyes on the bar and pretended I didn't notice them. That tall one reeked like musk or wet fur. Why was he all covered up? If you ask me he's probably an ugly sight to behold. I could see one set of fingers as he held his cloak. Dark skin color, thicker fingers than a human. By the way, those fellers didn't stay upstairs for long before coming back down. Both times they walked through this common room the conversation took a dive only to liven up afterwards. Despite the late hour, they are back out on the streets for some reason."

Trestan got a few more details from Petrow, but only guesses about where the adventurers were going or why they here. The two parties seemingly stayed separate, and none of the outsiders had talked any more than necessary. Some inn rumors focused on the fact that both groups came from the south. Then again, there were only two directions anyone came from in order to arrive in the village, unless they stumbled out of the wilds. As the two young friends socialized over drinks, Trestan noticed a figure creeping down the stairs.

The lady rider from that afternoon stood on the lower portion of the stairs, only a few steps away from their spot at the bar. The two young friends usually heard the stairs creak when someone came down to the common area, despite the other distracting inn noises. The lone adventuress had snuck to the very bottom without making a sound and now surveyed the common room. Her penetrating gaze betrayed strong determination to find someone…or something? Trestan gave Petrow a slight nudge. The young jack-of-all-trades got the hint and turned to view the stairs.

She wore no helmet, thus offering the first good view of her head and face. The two young men sat transfixed in order to drink in her image: raven black tresses, searching green eyes, and the narrower, angular face and ears betraying elvish blood. She wore the same dark leather armor, which provocatively hugged her petite frame. The silver-hued rapier hung at her side, the polished basket of the hilt reflected a dance of candle lights. Worn swords were common enough among travelers for their defense. The weapon drew more attention from Trestan than it did from Petrow, as the smith studied the work and care that had gone into it. Some creatures of myth could only be slain by weapons of silver; few people but nobles and adventurers actually had the money and reason to buy such a weapon. Now that the men had a closer look, Trestan also noticed the pommel of her sword formed the head of a hunting cat baring its teeth. The rapier displayed grace and danger, sharing those traits with its eye-catching wielder. For a long breath the young men sat entranced at her face and figure. The beauty of the prettiest local girls seemed rather homely in the face of this unknown and exotic woman of adventure. At some point they realized she studied them as well. Her eyes fixed on them, without any visible offense at their stares. Instead, she unexpectedly turned her lips into a smile and approached.

The dark lady took the open seat next to Petrow for herself. The two young men waited for her to initiate a question, but she only looked expectantly at them. It played like a game. The adventuress sat there smiling quietly, awaiting their greeting. Trestan wouldn't have been surprised if she planned to sit there in silence for some time.

Petrow belatedly seized his chance to impress her. His hands gestured openly in friendship, putting his best charm into his voice. "Greetings fair maiden, you must have traveled far. Let the dust of the road be washed away by the fine vintages we might offer you here. As two members of the village's appointed welcoming ambassadors, we invite you to have fun and share tales whilst you visit our town."

Her smile widened as she responded. Her voice proved teasingly pleasant, but the firm nature of her well-crafted blade hinted at hidden steel within her. She spoke with a warm and confidant tone, "Pleasant evening to you, good sirs. It is a delight indeed to dwell with some cheery company after riding the miles to get here. You are the welcome representatives, you say? Are you here to tend to my needs and make me feel at home?"

Petrow nodded, "Aye fine lady, we are yours to serve."

Her expression changed to amusement. "Well, good sirs, I'm surprised this small village can afford the eighteen of them that have greeted me so far."

The sound of Trestan actually snorting in laughter quickly deflated Petrow's smile. Petrow tried his best to humbly nod defeat to the traveler, then tried to keep the conversation flowing. "Nevertheless, we are at your disposal. Indulge us with a tale or two and we shall share some tales of our own. May we get you a drink and hear what brings you through our quiet town?"

"I'm wondering if you saw the other travelers in the village. They entered here earlier by the rumors I'm overhearing. Allow *me* to buy *you* the drinks in appreciation for being my eyes and ears."

Petrow and Trestan refused at first, trying to be gentleman about it. However, the strange lady favored some of the finer vintages and actually had the silver to pay for it. The bartender had a few dusty bottles of renowned wines aging on his shelf, having seen many a night without a traveler having the taste or money to spend on them. The two young men knew of them and had wondered what their taste might be like, and before they realized it the lady specifically called for one of those rare bottles. Trestan savored his first taste of really good wine, yet he hadn't learned the name of their generous benefactor. It was past time that proper introductions should be made.

Trestan leaned forward to offer a good view of himself, as Petrow sat back and savored a drink of the wine. "My thanks, milady. My name is Trestan Karok and this is my friend, Petrow. Both born and raised here, yet never have we enjoyed such a sweet drink and generous company. May we have the pleasure of knowing who to thank?"

She brushed her hair back from her alluring green eyes, nestling the strands behind her slightly pointed ears. "My name is Katressa Bilil, though many call me Cat." Trestan self-consciously glanced at the rapier's pommel as she answered. The growling lion stared back at him. She caught his glance. "Aye, I do admire wild hunting cats. The sword was custom made for me."

Petrow decided to steal the conversation to a different topic, one that would put him back on the stage with this lady adventuress. "You wanted to know about any strangers? Well, it just so happens that three others entered the village this day and are staying here. They checked in and went up to their rooms, but then came back down and went back into the street. I haven't seen them coming or going for some time now."

A puzzled look came over her expression. "Only three? I seek four: two males, an armored woman, and a…an 'It'?"

Petrow and Trestan almost felt the room get colder when she also used the term 'It'. They looked at Cat in their own puzzled expressions, but she waited patiently for them to respond. The village handyman volunteered, "We saw a robed elf, a human male, and…a horned 'It', but nay woman. Other than you that is, though lovely swordmaidens as fine as you seldom grace these parts."

Katressa laughed again. The young men certainly enjoyed her company. She smiled easily, presented a fine sight to the eyes, and presented herself more casually than they would have guessed earlier. "You never quit, do you Petrow? The woman I speak off wears black armor, with the dreariest ornamentation." Cat's visage turned serious as she continued, "You'll know her when you see her cold eyes and dismal manner. But you've told me what I needed to know already. So, as the latest representatives to have an interest in my welfare here, tell me a bit about the village and the area."

Trestan managed to get in a word before his friend, "Katressa, Troutbrook boasts…"

She winked at them, "You can both call me Cat if you prefer. Nay need to be so formal."

The young men looked at each other with a smile. Certainly this would be an entertaining night! They didn't know why she shadowed this group, and neither of them proved eager to press the issue. Katressa stayed and chatted for a decent part of the evening.

23

She warmed up to them, and they stayed glued to her every word. They found out she was indeed a half-elf, and from her stories of far-off places it was obvious she traveled a lot.

She told them more than they had ever known about the ruling capital city of Kashmer to the north. Neither young man had ever been there. The port city of Kashmer had its own king and government; it also exercised some rule over the nearby towns and villages in an agreement that satisfied mutual protection and strengthened trade. Troutbrook generally earned much from caravans, while the military arm of the city protected the borders of the civilized areas from less friendly inhabitants.

Cat treated the young men with stories about other kingdoms and cities as well, including elvish lands they didn't know existed. Sometimes the conversation blended with jokes, disagreements on whether the drinks they had went better with crackers or bread, and sometimes they laughed over nothing. The two young men didn't question why she traveled or what kind of life she lived. Trestan and Petrow enjoyed simply talking with her.

*   *   *   *   *

The jovial mood soured immediately when something powerful thrust the inn door open. It slammed against the wall with enough clatter to wake anyone sleeping in the upstairs guest rooms. The conversations in the common room abruptly silenced. Raised eyebrows jerked towards the door. The biggest stranger, "It", filled the opening of the doorway. The cloaked giant bent over to squeeze past the doorframe, and once inside it almost brushed the ceiling as it straightened to full height. Trestan couldn't take his eyes off the peculiar horns coming out of the sides of the cloak hood. Each horn stretched easily as long as a short sword, sporting several notches along their yellowish lengths. The face remained hidden, though the hood turned and scanned the room. Petrow was right: the biggest axe Trestan ever laid eyes on hung from its back. It stopped and stared in Trestan's direction, and the young smith averted his eyes in a hurry. Only after it moved again did Trestan venture a peek from beneath his brows. The large humanoid grabbed a barrel near the door that was used for waste. The elf and human adventurers entered, walking past their companion to a nearby table. "It" upended the barrel, tossing garbage into the street, then carried it with him. The three strangers walked calmly, nonchalant, despite the silent stares. The smaller two casually sat in their chosen chairs. The larger one used the upended barrel for his own seat.

Petrow's descriptions didn't do justice to their real appearance. The elf's robes contained vibrant dyes and perfectly fit their bearer. He did have the look of a spellcaster about him, complete with decorated staff and well-tailored, leather pouches of mysterious contents on his belt. His long, silver hair was braided back and set with gems. The elf's yellow eyes swept across the room and took note of everything.

The human at his side wore imported silk garments adorned with nature designs. His black hair, narrow eyes and pale skin revealed lineage from the foreign lands north of this continent. Soft leather moccasins covered his feet.

The tension broke when the elf snapped his fingers and ordered a simple soup and bread for him and his companions. The serving people, all family that owned the inn,

24

moved to fulfill the request as the conversations began to start anew. Voices remained hushed compared to before, and many eyes lingered on the three strangers whenever a subtle glimpse seemed possible.

Trestan and Petrow talked quietly, barely murmuring between themselves and Cat. She became more aloof compared to the fun, easy-going spirit displayed earlier. Cat only nodded to their comments and didn't respond back. Her emerald eyes focused on the other group over the rim of her glass. In that moment, she seemed every bit a crouched hunting cat, watching her prey. Trestan could not help but glance at the band of three often. Adventurers were usually sources of entertainment. These three acted different, separating themselves from the lesser people with looks and actions. When their food arrived, they promptly waved the serving girl away. Aside from the fact they ate in the inn's common room, they seemed as eccentric as visiting nobility. Trestan noted with alarm that in the midst of the strangers' conversation they threw looks towards his end of the bar. The young smith wondered if his stares had been that rude. Without warning or provocation, the big one stood up and turned towards Trestan's vicinity. The elf and human stopped eating and stared in the smith's direction. Slowly and powerfully 'It' rumbled to the end of the bar. The young smith heard Cat set her glass down with a loud clink. One of her hands dropped out of sight, possibly to the hilt of the rapier she carried. Trestan realized it wasn't his stares, but something about the adventuress that drew the ire of the three. He and Petrow were sitting in the worst spot at that moment.

Trestan kept his face down and tried to remain calm. Looking down, he saw the giant's cloak slip upwards to reveal cloven hooves instead of boots. The cloaked one stopped near them. Trestan could have tried to get a look at his face, but his fear overruled curiosity. That musky smell reached him for the first time and he grimaced. It was as bad as the smell of a dead animal. The common room went silent.

In a deep guttural voice mixed with grunts, It spoke to Katressa, "Why do you choose to follow us? Poking into other people's affairs is not only rude, it is unhealthy."

Trestan watched Cat calmly sip her drink with her left hand, while her right stayed out of sight and hidden behind Petrow. He visualized her right hand poised to draw the silver rapier. If the woman feared this creature, she hid it well.

Cat spoke in a calm voice. "Oh, Bortun, I could claim you were following me. I arrived here at midday, long before your group rode into the village. I am a free, traveling spirit. After seeing how your group acted two days ago in that other town, I'm surprised you have the gall to call me rude."

The tall figure, Bortun, tossed his cloak wide open. Others in the tavern cursed and stepped back. The two young men could swear that he grew another foot even as his true nature was revealed. Bortun was physically man-like over only a small portion of his body. Muscles bunched up on leathery arms. Large animal-like legs ended in the cloven hooves Trestan had glimpsed. Armor composed of animal hides provided cover over hairy skin that looked just as tough. The short brown fur covering much of his upper body was nothing compared to his head and face. The nature of the minotaur, (a half-bull, half-man abomination) painted wide-eyed fright on the scared inn patrons. Steer's horns protruded from the sides of his bullish head. The creature's eyes appeared like inky black pools, and animal grunts issued from his throat. The minotaur moved closer to the much smaller half-elf. She didn't flinch, not even when that gruesome snout exhaled a blast of air in her face. "Small fool, we like to keep our business to ourselves. What right do you have to watch our every move?"

The elf companion of the minotaur voiced his own opinion, "It is obvious. The way she dresses, the way she moves, her quiet and inquisitive demeanor, and her disarming smile give her away."

Although the elf did not speak loudly, his voice carried over the hushed room. "My name is Revwar. My poor, cursed companion over there is Bortun. My other friend at the table here is Loung Chao, from far off Tariyka. We've survived many adventures, and we'd like to keep to ourselves. We may not be the strongest on social graces but we pay well for food and drink, then we move on the next day. I'd be more worried about this lone traveler in your midst. She follows us whether she admits it or not. The only real motive that presents itself in my mind is a rather lucrative robbery if we let down our guard. I would keep a close eye on your purses."

Katressa was about to make a reply of her own, but Petrow cut her off. Even to Trestan's surprise, the handyman jumped to her defense, despite the intimidating minotaur standing over them. "She didn't come in here laying down accusations, sir! It doesn't sound like she has done anything to you, so don't be labeling her a thief in public without proof."

Trestan felt Petrow went too far trying to impress a woman. His friend's rash actions courted danger. The confidence displayed by the elf wizard and his companions, backed by Bortun's intimidation, put fear into Trestan's heart. The young smith placed a restraining hand on his friend's shoulder and gave him a warning glare.

Cat's sour expression suggested she didn't welcome Petrow's intervention. She spoke immediately, "I assure you I am also an adventurer that sometimes likes to keep to myself. I won't have any reason to interfere with your journey, as long as you don't interfere with mine. Why would I attempt to incite your wrath after seeing the amusing way you dealt with that dwarf in Barkan's Crossing? Leave me be and we won't have a problem down the road."

Bortun actually stepped closer and flexed his arms a bit. The creature's sneer betrayed his eagerness to trade more than words. Revwar called him back, "It is not in our best interests to cause any problems here, Bortun. We shall let the young lady go on her way. If she misbehaves, I am sure some misfortune will befall her soon enough. I think it's time to retire for the night."

Revwar and Loung Chao left their unfinished meal and proceeded to the stairs. The minotaur did not easily back down, nor lower its muscular arms until after snorting a blast of fetid breath in their direction. Bortun brushed hard against the half-elf as he went by. Cat's hand tightened on her rapier handle, but she calmed down and let the unwanted contact go unanswered. Bortun probably hoped to provoke a response. She disappointed him by remaining calm as he lumbered past, finding the willpower to turn away from him and take another sip of her drink. The stair boards groaned heavily as the abomination climbed them. His two companions followed. Revwar briefly paused at the top of the stairs

26

and looked back at the half-elf. "We ride to Kashmer in the morning, see that you don't infringe upon our privacy again."

Katressa waited until the room's conversation levels resumed before she downed the remainder of her glass. Trestan and Petrow looked at their drinking companion in silence. Neither young man knew what to say after such a tense encounter.

The half-elf resumed a charming smile, "Well, wherever they are going next, it sure isn't Kashmer. I'm curious about the disappearance of their fourth companion." Turning to Petrow, she offered, "I thank you for sticking up for a stranger, but it's best not to get them upset. I suggest you both go straight home and get a cozy sleep tonight. Perhaps we shall meet again in the morning."

Katressa "Cat" Bilil then turned back to the staircase and headed up to her own room. Her footsteps left no noise on the aged stairs. She left a lot of unanswered questions behind her.

*   *   *   *   *

The night deepened until the inn was empty of its crowd and the pub's patrons were falling off their chairs. Lanterns lit parts of the street and the southern bridge, but few figures moved about. Troutbrook quietly surrendered to peaceful slumber.

On the inn's side of the main street, south of the church, one of Troutbrook's largest houses still had candles lit. Inside, Sir Wilhelm Jareth stirred a hot cup of tea. He wore drab-colored clothes of good tailoring. He took two cups of tea to his upstairs common room. At different times it could be a meditation chamber or a reception room for guests, but above all it was the heart of his home. His suit of armor stood supported on a stand on one side of the room. The elvish sword occupied a place of honor over a hearth that contained only dying embers. Candles provided illumination for the room. Tables and shelves displayed many odds and ends discovered during the old warrior's career, though of some he never spoke.

Sir Wilhelm set down the cups of tea and gently reached out to wake his friend. "Trestan, you seem to have fallen asleep. Wake up and share some hot tea with me, then off to bed in your own home."

Trestan yawned and stretched in one of Jareth's padded chairs. He blushed as he accepted the tea. "I'm sorry, it was such a long day. What were we talking about?"

Sir Wilhelm chuckled. The aged warrior settled into an older padded chair which had long ago conformed to his shape. "You asked me if I wouldn't mind a little sparring session to practice your sword skills. Of all things, you yearned for more activity while falling asleep in the chair. You didn't want this day to end."

Trestan smiled. His quarterstaff and his wooden sword-pole leaned near the chair. He didn't think he would seriously get in a practice session, but it never hurt to be prepared.

Jareth sipped from his tea. "Your father has never mentioned it, but I'm guessing he doesn't know you have been practicing your skills with a weapon."

The young man shrugged. "He expects me to know how to use a quarterstaff well enough to protect myself. I secretly practice swordplay, but I wouldn't be surprised if he knew. He's seen me wield swords that we forged together. I have to treat them carefully and proper so as not to tarnish or nick them. But, all boys practice like they have a real sword right? I can remember when I was younger; Petrow and I sometimes knocked our brains out with our wooden ones!"

Sir Wilhelm chuckled at some recollection. "I remember the time you two fought on that bridge for over an hour. Smacked your heads until both of you walked off complaining of headaches. A few bruises too, I recall."

The young smith laughed at the memory. They quietly chuckled a bit longer before Jareth switched the subject back to an earlier conversation. "So, what did you think about those strangers in the inn? Not just the three at the table, but the woman also."

Trestan thought about it for a moment. "It's hard to know someone when you have only just met them. Cat seemed nice and fun, but I can see how she might be a thief. I wonder why she followed them, if she did indeed. The minotaur scared me to the bone but I guess that's a normal reaction. I've never seen a creature like that before. The other two, well…they also felt intimidating but I couldn't tell you if they were bad or good."

The older man nodded. "Good and evil are not always so clear. Anyone could follow one path for most of his life, but in a frantic moment take an action they can't undo. In the long run it shapes our lives."

"But people do tend to follow a course in life right?"

"True," Sir Wilhelm agreed. "Most of life is built on how we react to it. We can choose to be despondent and contemplate retribution, or we can choose to ignore the bad and focus on the good."

Sir Wilhelm put his hands out like he was weighing options on a scale. "I tend to prefer the easy way of living. Get over it and move on when possible. In the great scheme of things, it truly does not matter. I fancy that better than some people I have seen who overreact to the most trivial of circumstances."

Trestan nodded, "I hope to take life easy as well, while not letting important responsibilities pass by."

Sir Wilhelm spoke again, "People might blame the God of Trickery or someone else, but they are victims of their own temptations and loose morals. A person can always change their course, even if they don't think they can. So, it's hard to judge someone else because of that. You never know their history and what kind of life they've faced."

The young man sat back and thought to himself a bit, "I've seen people who were lifelong friends spar over an angry incident, then never talk to each other again. Stubborn! I guess you get to know people and just accept them for who they are or let them go their own way."

Outside the shuttered window, they heard a dog barking in the alley below. Jareth nodded agreement. "You shouldn't judge people. You get to know them better, then accept them for all their good qualities and faults. That's a thing about love; you love a person for who they are, including faults."

Jareth leaned back farther in his favorite chair. He laughed at some seemingly inside joke before speaking again. "I'm sorry, the whole point was simply that you can never know all about a person in a glance. Here I was asking about the people at the inn, and instead I dragged you into another of my lectures."

Trestan looked to the older man, "I should be sorry, for keeping you up this late and infringing on your hospitality."

"Oh nonsense!" Sir Wilhelm glanced towards the window. The dog's barking had become a distraction. The older warrior spoke again, "It is nay bother at all! I have all the time in the world on my hands. I am happy to relax after all the adventures in my life, and spread my wisdom with appreciative youngsters."

Trestan Karok reached over and patted the strong sword arm of his mentor. "I do like talking to you and hearing your philosophies. It gives me a lot to think…"

In mid-sentence Trestan was interrupted by a flash of light beyond the shuttered windows, as if lightning had struck just outside. The dog in the alley whined pitifully. A moment later, its last yelp was cut short. The two men sat in silence for a few moments listening for outside noises. The only thing they made out was the sound of someone running.

"What was that?" whispered Trestan. He looked to his mentor with wide eyes, but Jareth seemed just as confused.

Sir Wilhelm set his cup down and crept towards the window. "Blow out the candles."

Trestan snuffed the candles, while Jareth worked at the shutter latches. Most of the light now came from the large moon Aburis through the opening window. Sir Wilhelm looked upon the alley below, taking every bit of care to move quietly. The old warrior's ensuing reaction surprised Trestan. He withdrew to a crouch behind the window's lower frame. Only his eyes peeked over the window ledge at the scene below. Whatever he had seen, the man did not wish to be spotted by anyone outside.

Sir Wilhelm turned to the young man. The look on his face, backlit by the window, revealed worry. "Something burned the dog. When that didn't kill it, an edged weapon nearly halved it. Foul deeds are at work outside. I don't see anyone down there, but I can't really see the street from here."

It didn't take long for Sir Wilhelm to decide upon a course of action. Trestan saw the firmness in his purpose as he moved. The older man strode across the room and snapped his sword and scabbard up from its resting place over the mantle. He glanced back at his armor stand, momentarily considering it. The metal and chain protection would take time to don properly.

He whispered, "Abriana guide me."

They heard a few horses gallop past. Sahbin's voice shouted from the street, "Hold right there! Stop what you are doing!"

Although Sahbin was the protector of the noble's daughter, she still held the rank of captain of the guard as well. Whatever the situation, the swordswoman's horse raced to deal with some perceived threat.

Upon hearing the urgent manner of that shout, Sir Wilhelm shook his head, "Nay, not enough time."

Trestan watched his friend leave his armor unattended on its stand. Sir Wilhelm rushed to the downstairs door with only his sword. Since he preferred to swing his elvish sword with both hands, he didn't even possess a shield for protection. Alarmed, Trestan jumped to his own feet. He grabbed his staff and tucked his practice sword in his belt. He wasn't really thinking about what might lie ahead, but he wasn't about to sit in Jareth's house and simply pass the time in worry. Both men dashed for the exit, unsure of what awaited outside on the street.

CHAPTER 3

Guard Captain Sahbin, dressed in her fine armor with sword in hand, looked down from horseback on the odd scene on the street. The three strangers tarried in front of the Church of the Sacred Harvest, perhaps twenty meters away. Her scarred face examined each with a stern, professional gaze. Bortun held his great axe in hand as if ready to use it. It was hard to read the facial expressions of the minotaur. The Tariykan named Loung Chao did not have his bladed weapon readied, though he calmly leaned against a bamboo staff. Revwar the elf stood with staff handy, standing tall and defiant. They watched and awaited the guard's reaction. Sahbin surveyed the rest of the scene. The holy relic of the church, the green stone, lay in the street near the shrine that normally held it. She noticed the three adventurers' horses hitched in front of the church, saddled and ready for a ride. Few people had good reason to ride into the wilds during the dark of night, except maybe her own wild charges.

Lady Shauntay and the young lady from Kashmer, also mounted, flanked the swordswoman. It was Sahbin's responsibility to Lord Tessald to serve as the village watch when not guarding the young noble. It concerned her that Lady Shauntay took charge instead of letting Sahbin handle it. The Tessald noble seemed to have witnessed something, calling out the questionable activities of the trio from the end of the street. The guard had plenty of experience defusing hostile situations while asserting her own authority. She wished Lady Shauntay would ride for help and safety, but the noble's daughter outranked her.

Lady Shauntay shouted at Revwar, "Surrender now! My father will have words with you. You will explain your actions and why you threaten me with drawn weapons."

Despite Sahbin's intimidating presence and Lady Shauntay's firmness, Revwar gave a half-shrug. He nonchalantly spread his arms open as he spoke. "We mean nay harm. Much as we would like to see your father and thank him for his hospitality in this town, we really must be going. I ask that your bodyguard put her sword away, as there is nay need for violence."

This infuriated Lady Shauntay further. "Put her sword away? Ask the creature to put away his axe and drop your staff too! I saw what you did! You will be held accountable!"

Bortun stepped closer to the horsewomen, tossing his head and snorting in anger. Sahbin guided her warhorse between the young noble and the minotaur. Her sword straightened threateningly towards the abomination's horned head.

Revwar's expression hardened to a tight-lipped frown. His yellow eyes glared at the young noble, while his outstretched hands clenched the empty air in front of him. "We would have preferred more secrecy, but it sounds like it's time for a certain wealthy lady's kidnapping. *Gaezel Kuostal!*"

At those mystical words, the mage pulled at the air with his fists. A half-circle of sand and dirt kicked up as something unseen originated behind the horsewomen. An invisible chain whipped across the surface of the street towards the wizard. All three horses ridden by the noble's party stumbled as the unseen force tripped them from behind.

31

Frightened screams came from horses and women alike. Sahbin tumbled free as her horse fell over. Lady Shauntay barely missed getting rolled over by her own horse as she hit the ground hard. Somehow, the horse trainer from Kashmer did not go down. The dust kicked up a choking cloud in the street. The first two horses rolled on the ground, frantically trying to regain their footing. Sahbin retained the grip on her sword and quickly struggled to her feet. Lady Shauntay writhed on the ground, making no effort to stand up. The other woman turned her horse to flee.

Loung Chao raised the hollow bamboo staff to his lips, firing the blowgun. A long, needle-like blade flew across the couple dozen meters separating him from the rider. The Kashmer woman jerked as the dart buried itself in a vital spot. She fell from her horse, the animal heedlessly galloped down the street. The horses of the noble and her guard staggered up and bolted from the scene.

Sahbin swore at her horse, expecting better training from it. She got her sword up and ready, for the minotaur spun his axe in lazy circles as its cloven hooves closed the distance. His muscles alone made him an intimidating foe. Sahbin had to decide how best to fight these three opponents, conscious of the fact her assigned charge still rolled in the street near her. "Milady please get up! Run across the street; just get out of here!" Lady Shauntay, blood in her hair, seemed too disoriented to stay balanced even on all fours.

Loung Chao didn't even draw his blade weapon, instead grabbing another long needle to load into his blowgun. Revwar reached into a pouch on his belt, calling to Bortun, "We have nay time for a weapon duel. I shall take care of her quickly and we can ride out before townsfolk investigate." The silver-haired wizard threw a cold glance at the guard. "You are outmatched."

Loung Chao held the next dart in hand, but stopped to allow the wizard to deal with Sahbin. Bortun snarled but reluctantly gave way so the elf would have a clear line of sight to his target. The minotaur stepped closer to where Lady Shauntay struggled. Sahbin would not be intimidated or run in the face of her duty. She shouted a war cry and lunged at the minotaur, making herself a harder target for the other two opponents. Revwar held some arcane reagent in his hands, cursing as the swordswoman moved to the other side of the imposing creature. Something zipped through the air, followed by a pained grunt from the wizard. Loung looked over to Revwar. A crossbow bolt stuck out of the elf's side, blood already soaking his robes. The mage toppled on the raised wooden walkway in front of the church. The Tariykan human looked across the street. He spotted the assailant on the roof of the carpenter shop, directly facing the church across the main street.

Katressa "Cat" Bilil perched on the roof, outfitted in her black leather armor and metal helm. The half-elf used a claw attached to her belt to pull back the string for another shot. Loung realized he would have to deal with this new opponent. Up there she was no easy target for the minotaur, and the wizard was down, leaving the owner of the blowgun as her next target. Loung Chao fit the needle into place for a shot.

Sahbin and the minotaur exchanged a few swift swings. The massive axe blocked her attacks, yet at the same time she did well to avoid the deadly blade. She saw the spell caster fall and the other human distracted, so she pressed the attack while she could. Never had she faced an opponent so physically challenging. Sahbin often beat male warriors in

32

physical competitions, yet this creature towered over her. There was no way she could parry the great axe, so she focused on evading the swings. They circled a bit as they fought. Both combatants glimpsed two other townspeople approaching. Sir Wilhelm and Trestan ran from the far south end of the street. The time it would take them join the battle left a lot of time for something to go bad for the guard or the noble. Sahbin tried to get in close to the minotaur for a hit but he had a much longer reach with his axe. She avoided one long swing after another, but couldn't gain enough time to get close between swings.

The blowgun swung upwards as Loung aimed at the half-elf. She was about ready to fire, but the human beat her to the draw. A burst of breath and the dart sailed towards its target. The distance and elevation proved a little more than Loung had guessed. The dart fell short and stabbed into the front wall of the carpenter's shop. Now he faced a loaded crossbow pointed in his direction. The human warrior summoned his mental disciplines and martial prowess. He didn't attempt to reload the blowgun, instead focusing on the tip of the bolt aimed at him. Cat fired straight and true towards the warrior's heart. At the last instant he turned an arm in front of him and spun around. Amazed at his speed, Cat wasn't even sure if she hit or not. A moment later he completed his spin, holding the blowgun in one hand and Cat's bolt in the other! The man clenched his fist with a grin, snapped the bolt and dropped it at his feet. One creative curse escaped her lips as she reached for her belt claw to reload. Loung reached for another dart.

Sahbin attempted some new tricks as she circled the minotaur. She tried a foot sweep to trip him, but her leg lacked the reach to connect before she backpedaled to avoid a flurry of swings. She taunted him to swing and then aimed a blow at one of the hands holding the axe. Her blade barely nicked the hardwood handle but missed flesh. She succeeded in getting the minotaur to fight more defensively, which caused Bortun to shorten his reach. Sahbin got in closer and stabbed with her sword at his midsection. She fell short of drawing blood. The guard captain began breathing heavy as she continued to avoid the heavy axe.

Sahbin glanced at Lady Shauntay, distressed to see the noble sitting nearby, hands on her head. The Kashmer riding instructor showed no sign of movement, apparently dead or unconscious. Bortun took advantage of Sahbin's distraction and spun around twice, which forced her to evade again. Sahbin thought she might be able to stab past his defense. She feigned exhaustion and pretended to be off balance from the constant evasion. Bortun took the bait. Holding the axe high over his left shoulder, he brought it across and down. Sahbin dropped prone to avoid the swing, bounced back up and lunged forward. Her sword finally pierced the minotaur in his side, stabbing through his thick animal-hide armor. Bortun let loose a pained rumble. The great axe harmlessly bit into the street off to Sahbin's left side.

Displaying typical minotaur resilience, he shrugged off the hit and swung while the swordswoman was still vulnerable. From its position on her left he swung the axe upwards and across, the reverse of his last swing. A shocked Sahbin raised her left arm protectively, but had no shield to block the blow. The axe blade sliced into her arm and launched her several feet away. She somehow retained her grip on her sword even as she landed in a heap. She weakly raised her head to look about and saw her severed left arm lying at the hooves of the minotaur. Blood gushed freely from a deep gash in the side of her chest. Her chain mail sleeve had been shorn and her breastplate sundered. She looked over to the noble. Lady Shauntay, still wobbly, returned a shocked expression.

Sahbin's words came out as a whisper, "I'm sorry I failed you, milady. I tried my best..."

Bodyguard and constable, Sahbin dropped her head back to the street and died.

*   *   *   *   *

A new, female figure appeared from an alley alongside the church grounds. She possessed a flail at her side ending in a heavy, spiked, metal ball. The human wore blackened chain mail, partly plated, displaying runes and depictions of death. The scariest design included the holy symbol of DeLaris, Goddess of Death.

Many who regarded the Goddess of Death did not exactly view her as evil, but she served as constant warning to those whose life actions left them forsaken by other gods. Many people who lived the wrong kind of life, whether evil, misguided, rich or poor, all shared an afterlife of torment at her hands. Her followers preach death as eternal and inevitable. The goddess once played a major part in the cataclysms of the ancient war, until even she realized that such out-of-control death brought chaos upon her as well. DeLaris merely reaped the souls of the dead now, and passed them on to the afterlife they deserved, for good or bad. Her highest clerics could bring the dead back to life, but only to show the goddess' control over death. At other times, her clerics used the power to simply bring forth the dead as mindless servants.

The abbess representing the Death Goddess displayed her dark holy symbol from a chain upon her neck. Wizards used arcane magic, but priestesses channeled divine miracles. Pouches attached to her belt promised a number of dark miracles in store for her enemies. A dark-gray half-cape around her shoulders was the lightest colored clothing she wore. Short, blonde locks appeared at the base of the skull-shaped helm on her head. Cold, blue eyes scanned the street and appraised the conflict.

The elf wizard bleeding to death near her required the most obvious need for her talents. She held up her holy symbol and mouthed a few words of prayer to her goddess. Kneeling by Revwar, she grabbed the bolt and pulled it out with a quick jerk. The elf writhed and screamed, but her prayers continued. Unseen beneath his robes, the wound closed and mended. The effect became plain to see: he took in a deep breath and pulled himself back to his feet. Drying blood still soaked a portion of his robes, but the wound miraculously vanished.

Revwar retrieved his staff and bowed respectfully, "My thanks, Savannah. I'm indebted again."

Midway across the street, Loung Chao stood closer to the carpenter shop and prepared to fire another round from his blowgun. Once again, he was ready just before Katressa could fire. The dart flew at the half-elf and she attempted to dodge. Fast and agile, she moved out of the way just in time as it sailed past. She brought up her own crossbow for a shot, and the martial artist steeled himself to concentrate on the bolt. A click and twang of the bowstring sent the missile on its deadly course. Loung watched it and spun again, his head whipping around hard.

Even as he spun Katressa moved to reload her weapon. When she looked in his direction Loung retrieved another dart…with her bolt clenched between his teeth. With an amused grin on his face, he bit down and snapped that bolt in two as well. Cat gaped and cursed, "Who are you? Nobody can do that!"

Sir Wilhelm Jareth and Trestan ran forward as fast as they could, concerned for Lady Shauntay. Sir Wilhelm drew his elvish sword and tossed the empty scabbard aside. Trestan held his quarterstaff aloft as he advanced, but wasn't sure how he was going to use it. They paused in their charge to examine the downed Kashmer woman. Sir Jareth observed her open, staring eyes, the dart's position and lack of blood from the wound. "It's too late for her."

The minotaur stood closest to them, standing defiantly over poor Sahbin's corpse. Bortun checked the wound at his side, judging it inadequate to cause worry. He took half a step forward, but stopped to glance at Revwar. He knew enough to avoid catching the edge of a spell.

Revwar raised his staff and glared at the two late arrivals. "We must end this before any more problems arise. Loung, stop playing and kill her! I'll work on these two."

Sir Wilhelm held a hand up for Trestan to stop. The elf aimed his staff at them and spoke in a strange tongue. Without further delay Jareth shoved Trestan away and dodged whatever was coming. A ball of fire shot forth from the staff, leaving a smoke streak behind it. The flaming sphere narrowly missed Trestan and instead landed harmlessly in the dusty street just beyond him. Its fire quickly died out. Seeing the ineffectiveness of the spell, the abbess of the Goddess of Death pulled another miracle from her devotion. Savannah said a prayer then stepped forward. She passed into something unseen and disappeared.

Sir Wilhelm Jareth advanced upon the minotaur. The creature had one arm hidden behind its back, so the aging warrior watched for some kind of trick. Bortun held the great axe easily in one hand. His second hand snapped forward and flung a small throwing axe at the warrior. Jareth flew into motion, two hands on the hilt of the sword as he swung it defensively. Abriana's fighter knocked the axe aside in mid-flight then stepped forward to strike the minotaur. The creature had to raise its own axe up to block the blow. Sparks flew from the head of the blade as the sword edge collided with it.

The flying axe spun into the strangers' three horses hitched at the church post. Completely unintentional by Jareth, the deflected axe lamed Loung's horse.

Sir Wilhelm launched into a bold attack against Bortun. Using wrist and forearms, twisting his hips as needed but never turning very far, his sword spun in vicious circles. Bortun had his axe in front of him, yet in order for a swing he needed to draw it back and make use of his reach. The elvish bastard sword spun very fast, attacked left then right and occasionally switched to a straight downward swing. The magical weapon focused on speed and did not require much power behind the blows. The minotaur couldn't risk cocking the axe back for a blow without risking a serious cut himself, so instead he withdrew to get out of the human's reach. The head of the axe was demoted to a shield to block the swinging sword. Sparks flew each time the weapons connected. Sir Wilhelm gradually forced the slow, lumbering creature back. The aging knight began appreciating his lack of armor. One hit from the minotaur might kill him anyway, and without armor he could move faster and not tire as easily.

Bortun typically used power and reach to keep opponents at bay, yet this human practically bumped into him. He had to try a new tactic. Confident in his weapon and superior strength, he decided to simply shove the axe head forward, perhaps knock the human down and get back an advantage. When the moment came, he thrust his axe forward as planned but the human stepped aside quickly. Jareth's sword switched to a new attack, swinging up from below and knocking the axe up high. The next swing by the human came parallel to the ground and across his opponent's midsection. Bortun couldn't block; he had to hop back or be disemboweled. The blade ripped a line of blood through the thick hides he wore for protection; however, the scratch only served to remind him how narrowly he'd avoided serious injury. The eight-foot-tall creature brought the axe back close to protect himself, backing into the hitching post in front of the church. He was trapped.

*   *   *   *   *

When Sir Wilhelm first leapt at the creature, Trestan hovered several paces behind the fight. He wasn't sure how he could help. Even if the minotaur's axe didn't scare him, he could be hit by Sir Wilhelm's spinning blade. He avoided the elf wizard's line-of-sight for fear of an attack from that direction. Standing rather impotently at the edge of the action, he felt a light touch on his back. Trestan heard a prayer uttered in a cold feminine voice.

"DeLaris, please stop this soul from moving. Relax his limbs like the coldness of death."

Trestan reflexively turned to attack. Even as he tried, tingling and numbness overcame his body. His vision spun as he fell. No matter how much he willed it, his limbs simply refused to work. He couldn't feel his quarterstaff. Instead, he heard it clatter to the ground. Only his ears and eyes were left to him, as he lay helpless in the street.

Trestan could only stare helplessly as the abbess knelt beside him, staring through her skull-helm. Her blue eyes were filled with cold loathing. Trestan felt terrified. The dark cleric held the flail beside his head. He tried with all his will to move, but he couldn't even feel his body. Trestan mourned his apparent fate. She lifted her weapon slowly and gently set the spiked ball on his forehead.

She spoke to him in a faraway tone. "In a tradition of my goddess that we observe on occasions, your life is claimed and spared. My goddess is the master of death, and she chooses or refuses it as she demands. This day your life was deemed over, until the goddess' servant touched you with mercy. It is not mercy in the true sense, it is simply mastery over whether you live or die. This day is your lucky day, for she will allow you to live. Remember the control she has over your fate."

Savannah lifted her weapon away from its threatening place on his forehead. She grabbed the dropped quarterstaff and rose back to her feet. The dark abbess threw the staff onto the roof of the building next to the church. Trestan still had the practice pole-sword tucked in his belt, but knew it would do him little good even if he could move again before

36

the battle concluded. Savannah stepped away, and he couldn't move his head enough to see where she had gone. The young smith could barely turn his head towards the rest of the battle. He watched Jareth and the minotaur at the point when Bortun backed into the hitching post.

*　　　　*　　　　*　　　　*　　　　*

Loung heard Revwar's request to kill the roof archer while reloading his blowgun for another shot. Cat slid her bolt into place first and brought her weapon in line. Loung had both hands on the hollow bamboo rod as she fired. The Tariykan let go with one hand and caught the missile once again. With a snap, it broke and fell to his feet to rest among the other broken bolts. Cat sighed and chided herself for not switching to an easier target. The next dart came and the half-elf dodged. She felt it skim off her helmet.

She grabbed her belt claw and once again brought back the string on her crossbow. It fell into place with a click. Once done, she reached to the quiver strapped to her right calf and withdrew another bolt. As her agile fingers started to slide the bolt home, she looked toward the street to see how her opponent fared. All she saw in his former spot was a discarded bamboo stick as well as the small pile of broken bolts.

More than a little worried, she finished loading and got her finger on the trigger. She crouched closer to the front of the roof. Below, she looked over the scene as the other combatants moved about. She watched the minotaur backing up under an assault from a human warrior. Not far away, closer to the still Kashmer woman, Cat saw the young smith she had met earlier. He lie supine while the dark cleric's weapon rest on his brow, though she seemed to be only talking with him. Cat scanned the street looking for the Tariykan. She sighted another danger. Lady Shauntay had feebly crawled closer to her downed guardian. Unnoticed by her, the wizard was approaching her from behind with his hands holding another magical trick. Cat raised the crossbow, aiming for the spellcaster.

The half-elf began tightening her pull on the trigger when interrupted by an attack from below. Two legs rose at the edge of the roof and scissor-kicked the missile weapon from her hands. The crossbow dropped into the street. The martial artist performed a handstand on the sign over the door of the carpenter shop. Katressa stepped back a couple paces to draw her silver, custom-made rapier. In front of her, Loung vaulted with a twist to land in a well-balanced stance on the roof. He pulled out a short-handled stick: a sickle-blade on one end, a fine chain dangling from the other end. Loung held the wood handle while his other hand spun the weighted chain in a lazy circle. Katressa changed her grip slightly on the slender rapier, ready to use all her wits and agility. They locked glares for a moment, facing each other across the wood-shingles roof.

They began a dance of weapons.

*　　　　*　　　　*　　　　*　　　　*

Lady Shauntay fought through the blurry vision from the tears rolling down her perfumed cheeks. Her eyes had no other focus other than her guardian and friend, Sahbin,

37

lying in a pool of blood. The noble's daughter lost all shallow concerns at that moment. Her world had taken a sudden horrible turn, and she only wished for her protector to stand tall again. Sahbin did not move. The horrific injury appalled Shauntay, shocking the noble girl into fright. She felt the need to get up and run.

Somehow the young woman found the strength to climb to her feet. Her mansion and father were to the north, so she turned for home. Revwar stood in the way, holding a snake in one hand. "A kidnapping for you, my princess, for I would rather the residents of your village not know what you saw. *Reptiliath Nosutrum!*"

The elf threw the snake. Lady Shauntay screamed and threw her hands up for protection. The enchanted snake's body hit and started to coil around her. It took on the image of a rope, but squirmed and moved as a real snake. It pinned her arms and tightened around her legs. Lady Shauntay screamed once, before the elf tied a gag around her mouth. Soon, she was helpless.

*   *   *   *   *

Bortun moved his axe wildly, trying to pick off every swing that came at him. Sir Wilhelm attacked relentlessly. The minotaur would have been seriously wounded if the human hadn't cared about the safety of the nearby horses. The minotaur tried to push forward, but the keen elvish sword moved too efficiently to allow the creature any room without endangering a limb. Bortun risked launching a kick while the weapons were joined, receiving a slash on the leg for his effort. Needing room, he tried a risky move to put the hitch post between them. The creature pushed forward, working hard to not get hit again for his trouble, and then dropped and rolled backward. Bortun's heavy bulk evaded under the hitch post and onto the wooden boardwalk of the church.

From a short distance away, Trestan watched Jareth perform an amazing feat. The human warrior launched a furious downward strike that cleaved through the hitch post, severed in a spray of splinters. It continued its descent by wounding the minotaur again, and even chopped a large fragment of wood out of the boardwalk. The blow seemed worthy of the minotaur itself. Trestan realized the sword must have strong magical properties.

Jareth stepped forward to end it, but the minotaur thrashed in a frenzy. A lucky, frantic swing from a well-muscled arm connected and sent Jareth to the ground as well. Human and minotaur rolled apart as both clambered to their feet. Sir Wilhelm would have been open to an attack by Revwar, but the wizard was still occupied with the young noble. The warriors regained to their feet on opposite sides of a muscular draft horse, freed from the damaged hitch post. Jareth guessed by its size that it could carry the minotaur when he chose to ride. Large horses were bred in the mountains to the south to accommodate riders from large races. Neither Bortun nor Jareth wanted to injure the beast between them. As each maneuvered, both sought a way to gain a fighting advantage.

Sir Wilhelm got near the front of the mount and caught its attention. He extended one hand off the hilt of his sword and spoke some words softly. "Dear Abriana, free this creature's mind of hostility and fear. Let it run wild and free."

38

Trestan gaped, (as much as the miracle allowed), at seeing the miracle blessed by the warrior's goddess. The large horse turned to run free in the nearby meadows. It frolicked like a young foal as it scampered to the fields. Bortun cursed as it ran off.

Sir Wilhelm stood without protection, without armor, and the minotaur could finally use his reach. Bortun pulled back his axe. Jareth didn't run, only shifting a bit to one side. The axe swept across with all the minotaur's power. Jareth jumped up and landed on the top of the empty relic's stand on the village well. The great axe hit the side of the stand, chips of cracked stone fell onto the street next to the relic. From the marble stand, Sir Wilhelm launched through the air at the creature. The elvish sword flashed at Bortun's head. The minotaur stumbled back and roared in anger at the sight of one of its horns lying in the street.

*   *   *   *   *

On the roof across the street from the church, a silver rapier snaked in and out, trying to twist past the foreign weapon. Loung's sickle-like blade constantly hooked and swept Cat's rapier aside. His other hand whipped the weighted chain on the other end of the handle as a counterattack. The half-elf worked to uphold her balance on the loose roof as the chain alternated between her head and legs. Cat felt as if she fought two different weapons. The attacks backed her away from the main street end of the roof.

She tried to parry the weighted chain end, only to face Loung's sickle swung in a wide arc using the remainder of the chain. She attacked again when he attempted to regrip the sickle's handle. Loung's move appeared well-practiced; his hand slid back to the wood handle and the chain deflected her rapier. Cat repeatedly tried to angle the rapier around his weapon to pierce him. The man worked hard but managed to block all her strikes.

She tried to draw a dagger from behind her back. Sensing her distraction, Loung feigned an attack with his blade. Katressa parried as he anticipated. His chain whipped around the rapier's basket hilt to disarm her. Cat held for a moment but was pulled off balance. Loung snapped a kick into her right hand. The rapier, caught up in the chain, yanked free of her injured hand. Not wasting a moment, Katressa dropped low and spun around in a foot sweep. This time, Loung was surprised as she knocked his feet out from under him. Still in a low crouch, she reversed the direction of her foot to kick him in the face. Loung lost the grip on his weapon as blood ran from his nose. Both combatants rolled apart and regained their footing.

They sought their weapons. The sickle blade barely clung to a roof shingle. The handle's chain stretched taut over the edge of the roof to where it twisted around the rapier's hilt. The silver rapier hung in midair over the yard between Trestan's house and smithy. A tenuous hold existed where both weapons could easily fall. Loung dived for his weapon while Cat drew the dagger from behind her back. He got the fingers of one hand on the handle but was forced to block her dagger strike with his other forearm. She pulled her dagger straight back and made a shallow cut across his arm. He yelled and rolled away, which dislodged the hanging weapons. Both sickle blade and rapier dropped to the ground.

*　　　　*　　　　*　　　　*　　　　*

Jareth fought close to the minotaur again, moving as a blur. He attacked left and right while the wounded minotaur retreated. The axe head parried the first few strikes. Bortun thrust the axe forward again and the human batted it down. Sir Wilhelm went for the creature's weakness. Only moving his forearms, one over the other, he spun the sword from axe handle to right shoulder in a fast movement. Bleeding from the new wound, the minotaur did not quite pull his axe in before the flat of the blade smacked his left hand. A follow-up swing sliced a new cut in the creature's left arm. Resilient and tough, minotaurs were still flesh and blood. The hides he wore over his naturally hard skin couldn't withstand the magical edge of the elvish sword. Bleeding from half a dozen wounds, Bortun staggered and called for help. Sir Wilhelm struck the minotaur's right hand, sending his axe tumbling to the ground.

The paladin of Abriana spun full circle in his movement and stabbed hard. The sword impaled the creature through the upper abdomen. Bortun let loose an agonizing, animal-like groan and fell to the ground. The quarter-ton, eight-feet tall minotaur squirmed at the human's feet.

Trestan saw the next threat coming at his mentor, but had barely begun to feel objects and twitch his muscles. He tried shouting a warning. A gurgle came out of his throat instead of words, but the older warrior heard. Sir Wilhelm raised his sword and turned to deal with the mage or abbess.

The elven mage stood to the side, watching but not threatening him yet. At his feet the young noble struggled in the bonds of the snake-rope.

The abbess Savannah had eyes on Jareth: hands outstretched in the throes of a spell. Using her goddess-given miracle of life over death, she willed a new soldier to attack the human. As her summoning ended, she spat a quick spell and once again disappeared.

The unliving creature lurched towards Jareth with its own two feet. One arm held high a sword; the other was still lying where the minotaur had severed it. The animated body of Sahbin approached. It bore no memories of its previous life, nor soul. A destructive spirit that had no use for air, food, or other sustenance controlled the body. Only the thoughts of its creator burned in its essence. It was to kill Jareth by any means possible.

*　　　　*　　　　*　　　　*　　　　*

Katressa launched at Loung with her dagger. Loung Chao avoided the first couple strikes, and then swept a low kick to force his opponent back. She also kicked but it lacked strength due to her balance. She realized the man looked confident even though unarmed. His hands moved in some kind of pattern, waiting for Katressa to try another swing.

Cat changed her dagger grip: blade pointed up. She feinted to one side then redirected at his chest. Loung grabbed her arm with his left hand and rolled behind it so that her dagger arm stretched past him. He brought his right elbow into her ribs. Her leather armor deflected some of the blow but Cat knew she was in trouble. They turned as they fought, trying to outmaneuver each other. Loung elbowed her hard a few more times. Cat's

40

weapon arm remained stretched upwards and behind his back, held by his left hand. Loung twisted, his open-hand thrust hitting her jaw as his leg tripped her to the roof shingles. The dagger fell free.

She kicked up and scored a hit, then tried to regain her feet. The human wouldn't give her the chance. A punch and a spinning kick sent her rolling further down the roof, away from the main street. She attempted another foot sweep but he vaulted it into a flying kick. Katressa reeled but flung herself further from him and rolled back to her feet. Not far behind her, the roof ended over one of the parallel side streets.

Katressa tasted blood and knew she'd have significant bruises. She gasped for breath despite complaints from her sore ribs. It was no comfort that Loung sported a bloody nose. Without her weapons she was nowhere near as deadly. The Tariykan calmly flexed in loose clothing and looked confidant that his fists were the only weapons he needed. Cat knew she was outmatched. In her young adventuring career she had been forced to run a few times to live another day.

There was no room to run, but she hoped to create one if she could back him away. She lunged with her fists, but he set to work showing his skill at unarmed combat. Painful hits and kicks hammered Katressa so fast that she had no time to react. Her helmet flew off her head just before a spinning kick from the man knocked her back down. The half-elf lie in a daze, unable to focus her eyes on her opponent. Her strength was gone.

The man bowed to her before assuming a fighting stance again. "Very brave. A worthy adversary. Now, to make sure you can't follow us again…"

*   *   *   *   *

The walking corpse of Sahbin advanced on Jareth and swung its blade. Its moves were rather basic. The warrior woman had muscles and flexibility but it was a shadow of the guard's previous abilities. Sir Wilhelm scowled his disgust at the defilement of Sahbin's corpse. He knew such creatures had few weaknesses and did not feel pain. Damage to certain areas of the corpse would greatly inhibit the creature and cause the occupying spirit to leave.

Jareth blocked the clumsy sword strikes and delivered a few of his own in reply. "Abriana forgive me for what needs to be done."

The old warrior spun and delivered the blow he needed. Sahbin's head fell away. The evil spirit controlling the corpse departed, which allowed the body to collapse.

The time and distraction were enough for the other two spell users to prepare themselves. Jareth turned to face them. Savannah's prayers had restored Bortun, and he climbed back to his feet. Sir Wilhelm's efforts up to that point seemed worthless now that his opponent had been brought back to health. Revwar proved to be the more immediate threat. Waving his hands and speaking, he hurled a spell towards Abriana's chosen. Three sword shapes emerged near the elf, flying through the air to their target. Trailing bright flames as they went, each looked to be a menacing weapon.

Sir Wilhelm spun his sword and tried to parry. He knocked one aside, dodged another. The third sliced into the old warrior and flared brightly. All three swords disappeared afterward, regardless of whether they hit or missed. Sir Wilhelm Jareth, stumbling and hurt, attempted to charge the wizard before another spell could be cast. The elf touched a portion of his staff and extended a finger towards the warrior. A beam, crackling with energy, shot out from the elf's hand and struck the brave man in the chest.

Behind Jareth, Trestan could see a portion of the beam cut through his mentor. The young man watched in despair as Sir Wilhelm fell. The elvish sword dropped from weakened fingers. The noise it made clattering to the ground stood out in Trestan's ears. Trestan did not want to believe his eyes. He tried to get up, but his muscles only twitched meekly. He looked to Sir Wilhelm for some sign that a fight was left in him. From what Trestan could see of the wounds inflicted by the magic, they looked mortal.

Revwar reached down and picked up the fine elvish sword. "Might as well collect a few trophies of our visit." He motioned to Bortun. "Carry the young woman. She has seen too much."

Revwar went to where the scabbard lay and picked it up as well. He then walked back towards his horse. On his way he observed the young smith still struggling to move. That confused the elf, having assumed Savannah had finished him off earlier. Watching the human twitch and try to move brought understanding. Revwar had seen that miracle before. He smiled wickedly and raised a hand.

"Don't hurt him, or you face my goddess' wrath! At least for now, his life has been granted by DeLaris!" Savannah stared hard at the elf.

Revwar lowered his hand and shook his head. "You really must stop granting people their lives back, I really much prefer when you take them."

The minotaur easily hoisted the noble girl over his shoulder, ignoring her muffled screams. His other hand held his axe. Weary but standing, Bortun looked around came to the conclusion its horse wouldn't be returning any time soon. It resigned itself to jogging, for horse riding was a luxury and not required for his travel. He watched Savannah slip down a side alley. Her horse was tied on the next street over.

The elf wizard returned to his horse to tie the sword and its scabbard beside the saddle. He realized one of their companions was missing. He turned about in the street and called out, "Loung! We are heading out! Get back here!" The elf noted the wound on the Tariykan's horse. "You are going to need a new horse."

*   *   *   *   *

Loung stood over Katressa. He was ready to reach down and end her life when he heard the yell from the street. Almost on reflex he looked back, but there was nothing to see over the edge of the roof, except the top of the church. While distracted, he heard a small grunt and movement right beside him. He jumped back to avoid an attack.

He had nothing to fear. Cat tried to get away in the only direction she had left…down. The half-elf exerted the effort she needed to drop over the rear end of the carpenter's shop. Loung Chao looked over the edge and saw her crawling on the side street below, badly hurt. He gave another bow and decided it wasn't worth going down to finish her. They had to leave and complete what they came to do.

42

Running back along the roof, he dropped lightly into the yard between the smithy and Trestan's house. He found his weapon and untangled it from the rapier. He simply discarded the half-elf's blade. Rewrapping the chain around his weapon handle, he ran through the smithy and back into the main street.

He looked around at the carnage on the street. He was relieved that none of his companions seemed to be down. Loung saw the blood on his horse and mouthed a Tariykan curse. He went to the nearby stable for another one.

.   *   *   *   *   *

Trestan ached to do something, but his muscles would not cooperate enough. Even if he could get up and try to fight, his quarterstaff was thrown away. His practice sword-pole would not make a difference. Lady Shauntay looked his direction with a silent plea in her eyes. She was even more helpless, bound and thrown over the shoulder of the minotaur.

He caught movement from Sir Wilhelm. The warrior brought one of his hands close to his side and uttered prayers. Trestan couldn't hear what was said. The warrior spoke softly, his eyes closed in reverence.

Nervously, the young smith glanced back to the elf wizard. Revwar had finished strapping the sword to his mount and was heading towards the village well. The village's holy relic still sat in the dirt of the street, next to the well. That sight disturbed Trestan. Did they come to steal the relic for its magic? Was that what started the confrontation? Even as he watched, Revwar picked up the holy item. His staff leaned inside the crook of his arm as he dusted off the stone. Trestan looked between Revwar and Sir Wilhelm as events hastened. The old warrior's prayers to his goddess somehow healed some of his wounds. Sir Wilhelm staggered to his feet. Revwar didn't pocket the stone as the young smith feared. Surprisingly, the elf placed it back on the altar, exactly how it was before. Trestan wondered why the stone had been on the ground in the first place, but maybe it had been an accident. Trestan's mentor moved very quietly as he stooped to pick up Sahbin's sword. The warrior then charged after the mage.

"Look out!" Barked Bortun's deep voice.

The great axe launched following the minotaur's bellow. Sir Wilhelm was forced to stop and step back as the large weapon sailed past him. Revwar saw the threat and acted quickly. Once again, the deadly beam lanced out at the warrior. Abriana's champion grunted in pain from the new wounds. The elf didn't hold back after that first spell. Sir Wilhelm dropped to his knees, but Revwar adopted the motions of another destructive incantation. The old warrior looked towards Trestan with sorrow.

He held his head high and spoke to the heavens. "Thank you goddess for the life you have given me! I die without fear of my soul's destination."

Suddenly the next spell launched out at him. A light show illuminated the area as crackling energy struck out at Sir Wilhelm. Electric sparks lanced out from elvish hands to burn at the old warrior. The human dropped to the ground, yet the elf still kept up the attack for a few moments longer. Tears fell from Trestan's eyes as he watched. There was no doubt the elf mage was making sure the human would not rise again.

Once the deed was done, Revwar turned away and left the holy stone sitting on top of its marble stand. He vaulted into the saddle and turned to face the south part of town. The minotaur retrieved his axe from where it landed. Bortun roughly jostled his prisoner as he prepared for the run ahead of him.

Trestan heard noise from the south. He managed to turn his head and witness a figure at the far end of the street. The abbess of the Goddess of Death waited on her horse for the others to catch up.

Another horse whinnied from the north. Loung Chao rode out of the stable on Katressa's own horse. He approached the elf and minotaur. The elf raised his eyebrows in a silent question. The Tariykan answered, "Not dead. But she is in rough shape, certainly nay condition for traveling. I'll take her horse so she doesn't follow us again."

The three then headed southward. Trestan found the strength to roll aside from Revwar's path as his horse's hooves thundered past. Trestan's muscles were returning to their old strength at a faster rate than before. He rested his eyes his fallen mentor. Wisps of smoke rose from black marks all over the body. A good man had been lost. The young smith could recall the words Sir Wilhelm had spoken only that morning: "A good man has nothing to fear from an early death."

A commotion to the south pulled his attention. A human yell mixed with a horse's shrill scream, followed by the sound of something large hitting the ground. Trestan looked over in time to see a downed horse and a couple people rolling in the street closer by the bridge. Savannah and Loung were still on their mounts; Bortun stood nearby with Lady Shauntay over his shoulder. Revwar, however, was getting back to his feet after tumbling off of his horse. His horse seemed unable get back upright. Another humanoid figure rolled on the ground near the horse. Bortun walked over and stomped one heavy hoof down hard on the person. The downed person curled up in a ball and didn't provide any more resistance. Loung reached out a hand and helped Revwar on the back of his stolen horse. Together they resumed their ride south. The band of adventurers crossed the bridge over the nearby brook and stole off into the night.

Trestan slowly forced himself to sit up and look around. Blood stained the street. A couple people he had known for years lie dead near him. The half-elf adventuress was likely hurt somewhere, as well as the person writhing down the street. The most beautiful girl in town had been kidnapped. He could count two wounded horses, but several more had run riderless into the night. The young man felt sorrowful and angry. Somewhere in the back of his mind, it nagged him that he didn't even know why the fight erupted in the first place.

CHAPTER 4

A few moments went by before Trestan could stagger to his fallen friend. He checked for signs of life, even though he feared he'd find none. Not a single precious breath moved past Sir Wilhelm's proud and handsome face, nor did his strong heart beat anymore. Sir Wilhelm's visage reflected serenity, as if he died peacefully. The paladin's soul probably rest in the loving arms of his goddess. Trestan tried not to cry, but moonlit trails of sorrow ran down the surface of his cheeks.

Sahbin's body lingered at the edge of his vision. He could not face looking at such mutilation. He preferred to remember Sahbin and Sir Wilhelm Jareth as they had once been. Random memories welled up of both in better times. He walked down visions of laughs, conversations, stern words, and village festivals. Both had been around this village for most of his remembered life. Of course he was never close to Sahbin, but he had seen her laugh and smile in those rare times when she wasn't absorbed in her duties. Jareth had been a second father to him, offering him a helping hand and guidance since he was small. Just this morning he had told Jareth he wanted the man to help be a teacher and guide to his children. Now that day would never come. Growing up in a small village, Trestan took for granted that his friends would be there the next day, certain faces would be around for a long time, and tomorrow would dawn as uneventfully as any other morning.

The young man felt a swell of hatred within him at that moment, born from the losses and the lack of reasoning. He fumed at those who came and took away the life that could have been. It angered him that Sahbin's dead, animated body fought for her enemies after the brave woman had stood her ground. He experienced raw anger for being a witness to the terrible deeds that night and being unable to do anything about it. The young smith wanted to retaliate or somehow alter the history of those events. Trestan tried to bring some measure of calm back to his mind as he sat brooding. He realized that his anger would not change what happened.

The young man looked about the street. The wounded horse tied to the hitch post wouldn't carry a rider anytime soon, but it would mend. The body of the Kashmer woman lie as he had first seen her. The long dart that took her life stood untouched upon her back, stained with her blood. Further away, Revwar's horse still struggled on its side. Trestan saw the person lying injured down the shadowy street, and resolved that somehow he should get help for the wounded man.

An unexpected sight appeared of a side alley across the street. The adventuress ran out of a small gap between two merchant buildings, approaching the scene of the battle. Trestan remembered how Loung described her: "…rough shape, certainly nay condition for traveling."

Cat jogged at an easy pace towards the church. She didn't appear to be suffering or handicapped by wounds. Quite the contrary, when she got close she displayed nothing more than dried blood near the corners of her mouth. Cat seemed about as beautiful and healthy as when he had seen her at the inn. The half-elf did lack her rapier and helmet, and her crossbow still rested on the ground near the carpentry shop. Trestan noticed she held a small bottle in one of her hands. The half-elf studied the scene of the battle outside the church, but she made a straight run for Trestan.

She looked upon the young man with concern evident in her eyes. "Young sir, are you injured somewhere? Bleeding or hurt in any way?"

Trestan shook his head. "Nay milady, I was under a spell most of the time. My wounds are only in my heart and memories."

He noticed Cat examining him, perhaps looking for injury. She glanced down, and he caught the briefest hint of amusement in her eyes. He wasn't sure if he imagined it or not, for she looked over to Sir Wilhelm next. Her solemn frown suggested she knew the man was dead. Trestan, studying her face, noticed the slight remains of healed cuts and small bruises. "Milady Cat, the Tariykan with them mentioned you before he rode off. Umm…I should add he was on your horse when he left. Anyway, he told them you were in bad shape and unfit to travel. He seems to be incorrect."

Katressa Bilil opened her hand so he could see the holy symbol on the bottle. "I travel with healing draughts when I can. A little drink of those healing miracles put me back on my feet. I was wondering if more might be needed here…" She trailed off as she glanced again at Sir Wilhelm.

Trestan shook his head, "It's too late for my good friend here. I'm glad he fought bravely and good against such odds. In fact, when he knew death was at hand he actually praised his goddess for the life she had given him. He told me only this morning he hoped he could meet death that way. How rare is that? But, milady, you can still be of help. Down closer to the bridge, lies another man who was in the path of those strangers. I didn't see what happened but they rode him down and lost a horse doing it."

She patted the smith on the shoulder, "I'll take care of him and then you can fill me in on the rest of what happened."

As she ran off, Trestan wondered about that brief look of amusement on the woman's face. He hadn't simply imagined it. With nerves and feeling returned to his limbs he soon realized the focus of her mirth in the midst of that terrible scene. His trousers were noticeably wet between the legs. Shocked, Trestan tried to recall the point in the battle that his bladder relaxed, but he soon understood. Apparently, the abbess' spell relaxed more muscles than the young smith had initially realized. The young man chuckled over the realization, a laugh burst forth more from madness than mirth. He had thought that despite the loss he had at least retained his dignity…now he lost even that. It felt like the lowest moment of his life. In one day he lost so much he had loved.

Loved? Love and healing were the specialties of Sir Wilhelm's goddess, Abriana. He remembered Jareth saying that love and hate couldn't exist without each other. It was only in the darkest times suffered under hate that you truly appreciated love's value. Jareth had also talked to him about death, and the healing process after one experienced it firsthand. His thoughts on Sir Wilhelm's words and memories, the sum of the man's faith, helped Trestan find some firm ground in that tumultuous moment. Trestan felt full of grief, but he still lived and must find a way to move onward.

Trestan Karok kneeled by the side of Sir Wilhelm Jareth, placing one hand over his own heart and the other hand over the heart of his teacher. He bowed his head and prayed. "Revered Abriana, Goddess of Love and Healing, I pray to you now in my moment of suffering. Carry this soul, who has fallen while in your service, to the paradise he has earned. Thank you for the guidance and knowledge he has brought me in the time I've known him. I beseech that through such knowledge and the healing strength of your love, my heart and mind will heal from the blow dealt to my senses this night."

The young smith had to pause and consider his next words, "Guide me in what path I choose next in this life. The 'enemies of love and healing', as Jareth would have called them, have struck and rode off into the night with a prisoner. The dark ripples that started tonight will spread outward from the ones who created them. I am a humble smith; I don't know what I might do to change things. At the same time, I consider myself your servant. If there is anything I can do to heal my heart and others, I ask that you make me your instrument in this world. I pray my path will further the course of love and healing to those around me. I do not want others to experience the pain I have felt tonight. I would not wish the same on anybody."

A call came from down the street. Cat yelled for Trestan's attention. He slowly got up and turned his head that way, listening for the words. Her voice drifted to him over the empty, silent street. "It's your friend Petrow! He's hurt."

The young man brushed the tears from his eyes. He started to walk back to the south end of town, slowly testing his legs. His muscles felt as good as ever. The damnable miracle had finally worn off. He noticed a welcome sight near the end of the church boardwalk. His quarterstaff hung off the edge of the roof of the next building. He jumped up and grabbed it. Trestan felt some small relief at getting his weapon back, even though the need had passed.

He passed window after window that remained dark. Not all merchants lived right next to their shops, but there should have been people who heard the noise on the street. No one came outside to investigate. No one wanted to be involved. There should have been one constable on duty at night, walking the main street, but they were nowhere to be seen. Trestan guessed Sahbin had taken that duty when she knew she'd be in town with the horses and the noble. If that were so, then no help would come until someone got up the courage to run to Lord Tessald's mansion and wake the barracks. It appalled Trestan that no one offered help. Then again, he couldn't expect them to risk their lives.

Katressa had trouble forcing Petrow to drink the healing draught. The young handyman, dazed and angered, fought any attempt to help him. The half-elf did not seem surprised. Mindful of his injuries, she subdued him in a position whereby she could force the drink down his throat. Once the blue-eyed man finally swallowed, he calmed a bit. The potion acted fast. Petrow regained both strength and clarity. He drained the miraculous draught down while Cat released her hold on him. Petrow drew several deep breaths. Trestan ran up as he thanked the half-elf, both still sitting in the dusty street. Though Petrow was healed, Trestan saw Revwar's horse suffered a leg injury, unable to get up. Petrow's wood axe lie nearby.

Petrow looked from Katressa to Trestan, rubbing his abdomen from the remembered effects of the minotaur's heavy stomp. Katressa put away the empty vial, speaking to Petrow, "Good sir, you are not the worse for wear now. I didn't expect to run into someone who would give me a few more bruises tonight, but I'll heal. What happened to put you in the way of the mage's horse?"

Petrow looked up the street at the battle scene while collecting his thoughts. "I peeked out to investigate the noise up the street. I saw the battle during Sir Wilhelm's last moments. I recognized Lady Shauntay being held by the minotaur. I saw Trestan rolling on the ground hurt. I guess when they finally rode my direction I wasn't thinking. I had my woodcutter's axe with me, and I thought to somehow do something. I was angry…probably wasn't thinking the brightest."

Petrow reached over to his axe and pulled it closer to him. "They were riding right towards my spot. I ran out into the street so I could hit the elf with my axe. Somewhere out there I think my courage wore off. I realized what a dangerous thing I was doing! I remember the shock on the elf's face, some uncertainty on my part as far as what to do next, and then smack! It was such a shock, I don't know if we collided by accident or not. After that I vaguely recall something hard landing on my stomach."

"The minotaur stomped you pretty good," provided Trestan. "Nay more brave or foolish than what I did. I ran right up to them with Sir Wilhelm thinking to somehow help. Their cleric cast a miracle, which put me out of the fight. I'm lucky she didn't kill me. Sahbin and Sir Wilhelm died while I watched. That woman from Kashmer who instructed Lady Shauntay is also dead back there. I don't even know what they were fighting over. I saw the holy stone from the church on the ground, but they put that back in its place and kidnapped Lady Shauntay."

Trestan and Petrow both cast a glance at Katressa. She returned a puzzled expression at them, until she realized their unspoken questions. "I followed them from the south because I figured they were up to something. I didn't know what. I was on the next street over when I first heard shouting. I climbed the carpenter's shop to get a safe look. I didn't see anything until the moment the mage cast a spell that tripped the horses."

Petrow glanced back at Trestan. "Tres, you must feel terrible right now over Jareth's death. I swear before the gods, such a murder will someday be avenged. Why, I've half a mind right now to go down that road and go a second round with them. I'd love to plant my axe into one of those trespassers."

Petrow noticed something; his eyes widened a bit. He smirked at Trestan, "Ok, my friend. That must have scared you more than I thought. I mean, I was scared…but I didn't wet my pants!"

Trestan flushed red; even Katressa couldn't hide another grin at that moment. The young smith shouted, "It was the miracle the cleric cast on me! It relaxed my muscles and made me helpless. I swear I didn't lose control like that! Milady, is that so rare an occurrence?"

Katressa nodded in amused agreement, "Such things like that have been known to happen under some restraining spells and miracles."

The handyman wouldn't let it rest. "Oh nay, I know Trestan! He may practice swordplay, but he's a soft guy inside that shell. Couldn't handle the terror, eh?"

48

Trestan shook his head. "Ok, believe what you want. I hope you get hit with the same power someday and see for yourself what it's like. I tell you, it's the scariest thing you can imagine to be so helpless in the face of such opponents."

Petrow hefted his axe. "Well, I guess it won't happen. I wouldn't mind trying an axe out on them after the way this night went. Too bad they're running; I'd have liked one whack at that elf or his creature pet."

"They are running, but to what?" The smith was looking down the south road into the darkness beyond.

Cat stood and straightened her leather outfit. Although her wounds were healed, her hair was tangled, and she looked like she had been through a rough tumble. She turned her attention on Trestan. The woman silently considered Trestan's words before she spoke. "What are you thinking, young man?"

Trestan considered his feelings for a moment. "They have two horses carrying three riders, one of those riders wearing heavy armor. The minotaur is forced to run, carrying a burden. They aren't getting away too fast. It might not be the brightest move on my part, but I'm thinking I want to follow them."

Petrow looked at him incredulously, "Tres, you know I was partly kidding about wanting to try my axe on them?"

The young smith ran his hands over his quarterstaff, aware that it had been useless during the battle. "They kidnapped young Lady Shauntay, whose scared eyes touched mine as she was carried off. I knew that look; I wore it when I was helpless and at their mercy. They spilled blood on our streets. They killed someone very dear to me. Now, I'm not one to go for vengeance, it's against what Jareth taught me. But, I'm scared for what they might have done that we don't know about. I'm also fearful for Lady Shauntay."

Noticing Katressa standing there, weighing the young man against his words, the smith asked her, "What were you planning on doing?"

Cat smiled a weary smile. "I want to get my horse back. They are a tough, well-seasoned band, despite that I can't give up. I followed them before and I can again. I can get real sneaky if I need to. I have to try following them, but I do not wish for you to misinterpret my words. I have nay intention of fighting them! I watched all my bolts get caught by that man and then lost every weapon I had on me before he nearly killed me. Maybe, if I find a way, I can do something to stop them. There are more subtle ways of dealing with an enemy."

Trestan nodded, "They are 'enemies of love and healing,' as Sir Wilhelm would say. They have a prisoner, but they can't go much faster than we can. I may get myself killed down that road, but I feel my conscience tugging me that direction."

Petrow got to his feet. He looked between Cat and Trestan, aware that both seemed set on their course. "I think this is foolish and dumb. The sad part is that I want in on it too. Tres, you've been my best friend since I can remember. I'm not letting you go at this alone. You need someone to watch over you, at least until you lose heart in this and turn home."

Trestan set his jaw firm, "I'm not coming back until I've done all I could or I'm unable to follow. After that, I hope to come back and pick up my life again."

Katressa glanced back up the street. "Well, after I get my weapons and some food, we might catch them. There are plenty of the lord's horses still in the stable, we can borrow…"

"NAY!" Trestan planted himself in front of her and put his hands up to wave off the idea. "We are not stealing off into the night as they did. I'm walking, and if you touch a horse that doesn't belong to you…well…don't. I'm not into stealing."

The half-elf looked aghast, she tilted her head to the side. "I didn't know you felt so strongly. I don't know if we can make a difference, but I hoped we could journey faster. You'll have to work hard to keep up with my pace."

The smith finally found a grin, though a small one, make its way to his face, "That should be easy. Loung Chao said you were unfit for traveling."

Katressa scoffed, glanced down at herself, and looked back at him. "I'm glad he would be surprised at my resourcefulness. It's about time I got one up on him."

Petrow interrupted, "Speaking of horses as you were a moment ago, we have one here that we need to deal with soon. The leg is bad. We have to, well, we have to end its suffering."

Trestan glanced at Katressa. She opened her arms wide. "Nay, my healing draughts are all used up."

The horse no longer thrashed about. It was lying still, watching them. A bone protruded from an unnatural bend in the leg, and the silent consensus among the three was to end its life in the most humane way possible. Katressa considered it for a bit before speaking, "Even if I grabbed my weapons, I don't know that I could make a quick, painless strike. I know where to hit, but neither my rapier nor my crossbow would be fast for such a large animal."

She looked to Petrow. He looked at his axe and then cringed. "I'm sorry Lady Cat, I don't think I could either. Killing a chicken is easy, but I don't see how I could do a fast job with a horse."

Trestan looked sadly at his quarterstaff. It was obviously not the weapon for the job. He looked back to the horse and the answer came to him. The elvish sword of Sir Wilhelm remained tied to the back of the saddle. Revwar must have forgotten it after the collision. The image of Jareth cutting through a hitching post, minotaur, and the wooden boardwalk planks was clear in his mind. A part of him didn't want to touch the sword. It was Sir Wilhelm's, though it had been willed to Trestan after his death. Trestan had every right to claim it, yet he felt reluctant to do so. He heard his own voice betray him. "I can do it, with that sword."

Petrow glanced at the sword, noticing it for the first time. "Isn't that Sir Wilhelm's? How did it get… never mind. I guess I know how."

Trestan felt he had to put some thoughts into words, "He wanted me to have the sword after his death. I was honored, but surprised. I wanted him to be alive to see my children grow. I'm not ready to accept this." Trestan sighed, "I do it now, only for what must be done."

The young smith hesitated. His limbs wouldn't respond and move him closer to the sword. He whispered, very quietly. "Abriana, guide me."

50

Whether Cat's half-elf ears picked up his prayer or not, she slowly and calmly walked around to the horse's head. The horse turned to keep its eyes on her. Cat spoke gently to it, using soothing words. She whispered to Trestan as she moved. "I'll distract it; you untie the sword."

She lulled the horse with her words. She even hummed some melancholy melody from another land. Trestan moved very slowly, pausing several times when he thought the horse might be trying to watch him. It listened to Cat, but its eyes were wide with fright. Petrow stood as still as a statue off to the side. Trestan reached out to touch the drawstrings holding the sword in place. The half-elf's humming and gentle words had a soothing effect, despite the chilling reality of their situation. She kept the horse enthralled. Trestan finally released the last knot, freeing the sheathed sword. He backed away from the horse a bit, aware that it still glanced in his direction. He moved slowly closer to its head and neck. He drew the sword out of its scabbard, trying to be as quiet as possible as the sound of the sliding metal came to his ears. With the blade free of the scabbard, he just stood there holding it. The edge still shined magnificent as ever, the runes of the elven craftsmen decorating the shiny surface. Trestan allowed himself to be mesmerized by the etched knots that twisted along the blade, delaying the deed. As he stood there studying it, he listened to Cat speaking softly in Elvish.

Grabbing the handle firmly with both hands, the young smith willed courage and conviction to his arms, "Come on Trestan. Compared to what you have already seen tonight, this should be nowhere near as horrible. Do it."

He lifted the sword high above his head. Concentrating on where he needed to strike the blow, he cleaved down. Sir Wilhelm's sword proved as magically keen as one could imagine.

*   *   *   *   *

He jogged through the smithy in the dark, almost tripping over some of the materials and tools. Trestan spotted the rapier he needed to retrieve for Cat. He didn't immediately grab it; he focused on the back door to his home. Before entering, he set his staff and the elvish sword by the door. Across and up the street, he knew Cat would be heading to her inn room to grab her equipment. The last he had seen of her was when she picked up her crossbow in the street and checked it for damage. Petrow ran his own errand. They needed supplies before departing.

No one had gone out to the streets yet, though voices had been heard in the night air. He wondered if his father might be up and about. If so, Trestan didn't know what to say about his decision to leave. He slowly opened the door. Moonlight partly illuminated the dark hallway. He saw a crack of flickering candle light underneath the closed bedroom door of his father. The young smith crept to his room. Every noise resonated like a shout. He went into his dark room without hearing any sounds coming from his father's room. His blind fingers found a burlap bag, so he grabbed it. Spare shirt, trousers, all the coins he had…stuffed into the bag.

"Trestan! Is that you?"

51

Startled by the familiar voice, the young man froze. Looking back, his father's door was still shut tightly. Everything remained very quiet and still for what seemed like the longest moment. Trestan found it hard to swallow. He wanted to reply; yet to do so would inevitably bring about a discussion Trestan wanted to avoid. Working quietly, he stuffed some metal eating utensils that were bundled in a cloth wrap into the bag next. One good thing about working in a smithy: never a lack of metal tools. A few candles. A thin blanket. When Trestan finished there, the only thing left was to get some food for the trip.

"Trestan? Answer me if it is you, boy! Who is out there?"

Trestan's heart pounded, but could imagine his father more scared at that moment. Hebden Karok must have been awakened by the sounds of battle. Cat and Loung had battled on the roof next door. It must have been frightening for his father to hear the fighting and not know what was going on. Trestan wouldn't have been surprised if the bedroom door was blocked by objects on the inside to stall any forced entry.

Feeling guilty about betraying his father by his own silence, the young man moved into the room that served as both kitchen and common area. He quickly scavenged some bread and cured meat. He took a quick drink of water, for he lacked a suitable container such as a canteen. He did take the metal cup that he had used since boyhood. He was looking about one last time when his father's voice changed.

"Whoever you are, get out! I have a weapon in here! There is nay money or valuables to be found, you are only looking for trouble if you stay!"

Trestan felt guilty and ashamed. He was scaring his father and leaving in the night. He wanted to put his father's mind at ease. Unfortunately, everything wasn't all right. Hebden's son was about to leave home and go on a fool's errand. Trestan was scared enough about this journey. If his father had the chance, he would talk Trestan out of it. The young man didn't doubt that any of his logic would fail in the face of his father. It was the hardest choice the young man had ever made in his life. He quietly walked out the door, into the moonlit yard.

In the yard behind the house, he paused only long enough to change into his old set of trousers. He wasn't about to take another step in wet pants. Once done, he strapped on Sir Wilhelm's sword, feeling awkward about it. He shouldered the burlap bag and retrieved Cat's rapier. Trestan grabbed his quarterstaff but paused again.

It was hard to leave his home. He had every hope and dream of coming back, but he had to be realistic with himself on the seriousness of the quest before him. He closed his eyes, and whispered, "Abriana, fair goddess to whom I have opened my devotion, I need your counsel. My path before me is hard, and maybe more than I can handle. I need your guidance again."

Trestan turned a bit, randomly, and opened his eyes. There before him, on the ground by some discarded junk, lay Cat's helmet. It had been knocked from her during the battle, and seemed to fall in a place where Abriana could send him a message. Trestan actually smiled when he looked up to the heavens. "I was afraid you would answer my query as such. I pray you watch over my friends and me. I try not to dwell on how ill-advised this whole course of action is, but I go forth anyways, hoping this will find a good ending."

52

Trestan stared at the old wooden boards of his lifelong home. His mind envisioned the flicker of candlelight under his father's door. "Watch over my father. I fear he will worry too much."

Trestan picked up the helmet, and took off into the night.

*   *   *   *   *

In the still quiet of the night the three of them jogged down the south road. The moons, (Aburis, Nirahha and Liijay), lit the path under a thin cover of trees. At times they walked through more open spaces, viewing distant ranches of people that did business in Troutbrook. The first few miles were familiar to the two young men, but no one talked much. They were all self-absorbed in their thoughts. The weariness of the night and its events weighed down on them. They focused on simply pushing onward at a fast pace.

Cat had gotten several supplies from her room for the journey. She retained a backpack and much of her equipment. Most of her dry rations were in her stolen saddlebags, but she managed to sneak some food from the inn. She brought a full waterskin, some blankets and a basic tent. The tent only consisted a canvas covering, as well as ropes and pitons. One had to find wood to serve as a support beam and the uprights, or fasten it between trees to provide some shelter. Her original crossbow had been damaged during the fight. She now carried her spare, which had been stored in her room at the time. Her boots were well made for walking as well as riding. Though smaller and more heavily laden with equipment than the two men, Cat carried herself lightly. The two young men had offered to help her carry some things, but she politely refused. Trestan and Petrow benefited from a hard working lifestyle, but Cat was used to traveling long distances with a load on her back. Her elven heritage kept her from stumbling in the dark.

Petrow grabbed more food as well and, unlike Trestan, had actually found a canteen for carrying water. He easily leaned the woodcutter's axe over his shoulder as he walked. Petrow also carried a knife tucked into his leather harness of tools. A wool blanket, guaranteed warmth on any cool Florum night, slung over a shoulder. Other than that, he had little more than Trestan. He carried some coins, no utensils or candles, and two torches. Cat advised against using torches this night. It would only attract attention if they got near their quarry and wouldn't burn very long, so it was good to conserve. On this night all three moons provided ample light to see the road.

The nighttime walk went by at a brisk pace. Petrow and Trestan were surprised at how fast and easily the smaller half-elf walked despite the weight she carried. Neither Trestan's shoes nor Petrow's sandals were the best comfort on the long walk. They hoped the adventurers and their hostage hadn't diverged on one of the smaller paths they passed. Cat wasn't a tracker and the light wasn't sufficient to see details on the road. All were weary in some way, whether from the fight or the knowledge of those lost. They put a few miles under their feet out of sheer determination. At some early hour in the morning, Petrow sat down on the side of the road, calling for a rest. Before long, all three were asleep, wrapped up in what blankets they had.

*   *   *   *   *

A gentle shake woke Trestan. He opened his eyes to rays of sunlight filtering through the leaves above. Cat called his name, though it took a moment to adjust to his surroundings. The young smith normally woke in a dark room, on a bed slightly softer and much warmer than the cold ground. When his eyes focused on Cat, the vision before him brought him fully awake. Her long, raven-black hair fell about her shoulders as her green eyes fixed on his, and that exotic, half-elf face smiled above him. Even more noticeable, she was slightly underdressed. She wore a light brown chemise, and short, knee length pantaloons. It wasn't as form fitting to her slim frame as her armor, but it was certainly more intimate looking. Glancing to the side, he saw her dark leather armor on her backpack. Her blanket had been rolled up and tied to the bottom of her pack already.

He looked back at her questioningly. A man normally only saw as much of a lady's underclothes when during the act of passion. Cat took offense to his stare: her eyes narrowed and her lips frowned. "Good morn. Don't go looking for something I'm not offering. The elves have been known to dance under full moons with much less covering them than this. I have a morning routine of stretching and relaxing following a night spent on the hard ground; it helps the muscles for the day ahead. It's time to wake up and get ready to travel again. We won't tarry long. I'd be pleased if you and Petrow could dig up a decent, if cold, meal. My rations are in the large sack next to my backpack."

With that, she walked barefoot a few steps to the side and closed her eyes in silent meditation. Trestan sat up and looked about their campsite: a disarray of sleeping blankets, weapons, and packs strewn randomly. Petrow slept on grass a short distance away from his blanket, curled up from the night's chill. The young smith kneeled by his own burlap bag and started to shake out his thin blanket. He felt several sore spots throughout his body as he moved. Whether they originated from his sleeping position or the efforts of last night, he had no clue. Trestan put his blanket away. Although a fresh shirt appealed to him, there was no bath and a long road in sight. Having only two shirts handy, he decided to save the other one for when he had a chance to clean up.

He woke Petrow. The slightly older man got up after a series of yawns, stretching and scratching. Trestan passed on the message to clean up the camp and help scrounge up a good meal. The young smith also nodded his head to where Cat performed her morning routine. Petrow's eyes widened almost comically and his jaw dropped. Cat stretched, but some of the positions she assumed seemed unachievable by most humans. The young adventuress went about the routine like no one watched, and eventually the young men pulled their eyes away. Each silently admitted the woman was extremely flexible.

They prepared a meager, cold meal of salted meat and day-old bread. Both looked forward to satisfying their stomach growls. Trestan found a container of jelly from the Fishing Hole Inn; swiped during the previous evening and stored in Cat's food sack. Trestan didn't complain about the questionable theft. His stomach convinced him how much better the old bread would be with jelly on it. When the men had most of their belongings put away, they ate. Trestan grabbed Cat's portion before Petrow could get his

54

hands on it. Petrow looked to Trestan and whispered, "I thought you were set on Lady Shauntay? Have you changed your mind in the face of our traveling companion?"

Trestan shrugged, "Every young man has his heart on Lady Shauntay, and I only dream she might pick me. Likely just a fantasy, I know. Until then, I'm going to take breakfast to our lovely traveling companion."

Cat finished her routine as Trestan approached with her meal. When she accepted, her eyes remained stern. The half-elf reprimanded, "You two were staring. I'd like a little respect regardless of how I choose to walk about."

Trestan kept his eyes respectfully in line with Cat's. "I ask forgiveness, milady. I truly mean nay disrespect, my eyes betray my admiration of a beautiful woman. If I didn't stop for at least one moment to savor the sight of such exotic beauty, I fear it would mean my heart was dead."

Cat betrayed a hint of a smile, "You're as charismatic as the ballad minstrels of faraway Orlaun. I shall forgive you for painting me in such a desirable image, as long as you don't forget my wishes of respect for my own habits. I shall eat and dress fast, and once I do you better be ready to outrun a horse with the pace I shall set for the day."

*   *   *   *   *

The sun still burned low to the horizon on their left as they hurried along the road. Cat walked fast and effortless, black armor and silver rapier giving her a formidable appearance. Trestan and Petrow, following in their modest peasant garb, looked more like servants than anything else. Petrow carried his wood axe in hand, while Trestan held his quarterstaff, leaving Sir Wilhelm's sword strapped over his back. The two young men breathed harder and sweat more than the woman.

As it was, few eyes would have observed them in this countryside. Occasional homes or shacks dotted the horizon, but most were in a bad state of abandonment. Although the roads through Kashmer's Protectorate generally boasted safety, the routes passed through lands claimed by less civilized creatures. Orc tribes were known to inhabit the hills west of their path. Several times a year, armed patrols searched parts of the countryside near the roads to root out rumored beasts and other creatures that staked out homes too close to villages. In return for such protection, the city of Kashmer to the north collected taxes and increased its wealth through the trade of goods from the local towns. Many would say the protection extended only to the roads. The wilds were still too vast and untouched, allowing many things to hide away from the beaten path.

The newfound companions walked in a more talkative mood than the night before. Katressa and Trestan filled Petrow in on the details of the battle. Trestan had seen more, being forced to watch from the middle of the street as the fight raged around him. It didn't seem that Petrow seriously believed some of what they told him, but they spoke truthfully. Trestan and Petrow turned the subject towards Katressa, trying to learn more about how she came to be in Troutbrook and what role she played in events.

Katressa took off her helm and straightened her hair a bit as they continued to walk. "I work as a privateer for Kashmer. The city hires out adventurers as extra militia, using their talents to root out homeland threats. The biggest concern of Kashmer is that they remain the leaders of trade for this region, bringing in wealth and business. To stay on top, they use a sizeable navy to protect their fleets of mercantile ships from pirates and such. They also hire out private ships to hunt pirates for them, hence the origin of the word privateers. However, they also see the need in keeping their eyes on the land as well. This countryside is not tamed, and threats from these wildlands are every bit as much danger to their prosperity.

"So that is where fate finds me these days. I only get paid if I do anything useful and can prove it. I also get deals from certain merchants, with the discount paid by the Guild of Mercantile, or by the local lords. Other than those few perks, I might as well find excitement and pay elsewhere. There are certainly better paying jobs out there, but I'm nay unscrupulous mercenary. I prefer to help people when I can. Even searching around for rumors and information can lead to its own rewards. I passed through Barkan's Crossing to the south of here just a few days ago. Nothing much going on, I just walked around listening for rumors and such. While there, a group of adventurers came out of the countryside and started poking around. They arrived on foot, except for the minotaur's steed. They bought horses yet only light provisions, for it seemed they were mostly well stocked. The minotaur, Bortun, caused quite a stir. I'm not surprised that he covered up his appearance a bit by the time he got to Troutbrook."

Katressa turned and saw the two young men listening attentively, even as they struggled to keep the pace. "Revwar spoke very well to the locals, calming them a bit, even though he himself kept a certain mystery and aloofness. Savannah, like all clerics of Death, naturally caused some nervousness. Nay commoners like to deal with DeLaris' chosen. On the last night there, they caused a bit too much trouble with some locals. I should say, however, the locals were asking for it. Local tempers and fear flared into a mob at an inn. As things got heated a dwarf bouncer tried to separate the sides before anything bad broke out. He asked the band of strangers to leave. Revwar tried more sweet-talking, laced with contempt, and the dwarf made known his dislike of weak and cowardly spell casters."

She sighed at the memory, "Well, the elf made an example of the dwarf in the face of the angry mob. He cast a few spells, including some snake-rope, which immobilized and embarrassed the dwarf. The mob shrank back. The adventurers didn't kill the dwarf, or cause any physical wounds that I could see, but it left everyone shaken. The crowd gave way fearfully when the band left the town. Other strong arms working at the tavern cut the dwarf free and carried him to a back room. After that incident, being the privateer that I am, I decided they were up to nay good and worth tailing to see what they might do next. I still find myself wondering what their real purpose was. They kidnapped the noble's daughter, but in such a way that I think it was unplanned."

More conversation passed without yielding more insight on the motives of the strangers. Meanwhile, their feet continued to push the road and Troutbrook behind them. The countryside grew rich with grasslands and pockets of forests. Low rolling hills dominated the horizon, hiding streams, pastures, hermits, and possibly inhuman eyes. Whenever the road passed through woods or crested a hill the party hoped they would gain sight of their quarry on the other side. When the road opened once again into endless grass and hills, they simply trudged on.

Near midday Petrow spotted a valuable clue. They walked by a soft, muddy area bordering a thick copse of trees. Imprinted in the mud were footprints belonging to a large hoofed creature. After looking about the area for some time, Katressa ventured a guess.

"Well, I'm nay more a tracker than you two. I see several footprints, large and small. Bortun certainly might have made those large ones; I'd even bet on it. I couldn't tell you how many people were here, but in places the large hooves cover the small ones, and in other places the small prints mar the large ones. You can tell if a group passed by at the same time if their tracks overlap each other. I think I'll check through this slight gap in the bushes."

Before she could move far, Petrow and Trestan had already pushed ahead. Petrow spoke tough and confident as he said, "I'll take a look too!" Then Trestan simply stated, "Stay back for safety milady!"

Before she could say anything, Cat found herself being outdistanced by the two young men as they crashed through the trees. Her plan to sneak up the trail was ruined as the other two blundered through the woods towards whatever dangers might lie within. Muttering a curse, she ducked into the underbrush and continued forward in stealth.

Petrow and Trestan charged from the encircling trees into a small clearing. Sunlight filtered through a leafy canopy to illuminate an empty campsite. Ash and blackened tinder remained of a fire pit in the center. The grass and small plants had been trampled around the area of the camp. Both men looked about for some sign that anyone might still be around. They held axe and quarterstaff close, fearing and yet defending against any angry minotaurs. Even the rustling of small animals in the underbrush kept the two young men on their toes. As they moved deeper into the empty camp, they saw the remains of food and other trash.

Cat's voice called out, startling them. "You two realize how dead you are? How dangerous your actions could have been?"

Both men looked around. They could not see her in the woods, and they weren't even sure which direction her voice came from. They felt very vulnerable standing in a sunlit, open camp, while shadows filled the woods around them.

From out of the bushes came her voice again, "Trestan, look left."

The young smith raised his quarterstaff in defense and faced to his left as commanded. He jumped back as he heard the click of a crossbow. A bolt zipped through the air to smack squarely into a branch at eye level, five feet from him. He stared at the bolt for a moment, not seeing any obvious danger. He then looked around for Katressa, but could not tell where she was.

The half-elf called out again, "Where am I? Did you not see where the bolt attacked from? That tree branch is a smaller target than you."

Trestan hated to admit that his knees nearly shook. "Cat, you're scaring me. My nerves are on edge as it is. Was it wrong to feel protective of you? I'd rather nay harm came to you while I'm here." Trestan spotted Katressa once she arose from the bushes at the edge of the clearing, her empty crossbow in hand.

Petrow, his axe gripped tightly, furtively looked about for more danger. It was unlike Petrow to give the appearance that he wasn't in control of a situation. The young smith wondered what made Cat upset enough to scare them both like that. She met Trestan's eyes, and he saw genuine concern there. She motioned for Petrow to come closer and hear what she had to say.

Cat kept mindful that they were simple folk and not veterans. A lesson needed to be taught. "Remember your limitations and your enemies' strengths. I am nay maiden stuck at a farm and content to knit blankets. Was your axe or quarterstaff really going to be of much use against that band? If it comes to battle, I think we will lose. I followed them from Barkan's Crossing to Troutbrook for two days without them seeing me…and I even passed them on the road. I work as a scout and infiltrator. For many years I served my elf homeland well against trespassing monsters. I watch, sneak, plan, and strike when I can win. Even then, sometimes I lose, like I did last night. The healing potion took away most of the damage, but I still hurt. It does not protect me when you run where the enemy might be, making noise and charging openly. I'd be safer if I quietly moved in and observed them without raising an alarm. If we rush in head first, we lose. We're lucky this camp appears to have been deserted."

As she finished, they heard the sound of horses on the unseen road. They wanted to rush out and see what was there, yet Cat's lesson burned in the young men's thoughts. She turned and motioned for them to stay and then ran into the bushes closer to the road. Within moments, neither man could see her. A short amount of time passed as the horses thundered by and left. Cat returned to the clearing before all the noise had faded.

She described the appearance of the riders. They traveled from the north, wearing the livery of the guards from Troutbrook. They had not seen Cat, instead focusing their minds on the road before them as they rode hard and fast southward. Apparently, Lord Tessald's men rode to catch the kidnappers. When the news sunk in, the young men stood there wondering what course they should take next. For all they knew, they might walk into Barkan's Crossing just as Lady Shauntay and her guards rode back to her father.

Trestan looked to Katressa, "I may never be a warrior, but I didn't choose this course lightly. I didn't come all this way to turn back now."

Petrow looked at his lifetime friend, "Nor would I turn back so soon. I'll go if you are, Tres."

Katressa nodded, "Brave or foolish, I'm pleased to see you do not get discouraged easily. But follow my lead more, I beg you. Let us return Lady Shauntay to Troutbrook if it is in our power, not end up as unnamed corpses on some back road."

*   *   *   *   *

Miles passed as the day started to wane. The countryside transitioned to steeper hills and valleys. In the distance, far south on the horizon, they could see the mountain peaks marking the end of Kashmer's Protectorate. Giant creatures roamed the wild mountains. There were areas east of the road that one could descend to sea level and find scattered fishing villages. At times they stood on high enough plateaus that they could see the ocean against the eastern horizon. Occasional, seldom-used trails carved into the land off to that side, used only by the fishermen and a few merchants. Much of this land remained wild, and could be claimed by less civilized creatures.

They stopped for a brief drink and meal at a well next to some ruins. Although the well proved workable and had good water, the castle it once supplied decayed in ruins and partial collapse around the hilltop. Moss-covered stones and overgrown paths remained of someone's long-forgotten legacy. Trestan assumed cataclysms and wars pre-dating the Covenant may have brought down whoever once lived here. He gazed upon the old fort and crumbling towers with a bit of wanderlust. He imagined climbing around inside it, perchance finding some age old treasure. Likely it had either been picked over or, even worse, guarded by the souls of those forever trapped inside. It was hard to imagine the surrounding hills as they must have appeared ages ago. He wondered if there had been houses and stores perched on this hilltop as well? Had there once been a jousting field where the road now treads? The knowledge of the past, like the occupants of the castle, was long out of reach and forgotten. The ruins only served as a landmark now. The well had become a stopping point for caravans and merchants, kept serviceable by Kashmer soldiers, but no one seemed to lay claim to this once grand structure.

They continued along the trail, hoping to cover a lot more ground before night forced them to camp again. Katressa professed confidence they might reach the next town by afternoon of the next day. During their conversation she complimented the young men on how well they had kept up with her. Trestan hadn't missed the fact that Petrow had washed his feet a bit at the well. The young handyman had not said anything, but on the sides of the sandals Trestan could see traces of blood. The young smith also suffered sore feet, and dreaded what he might find left of his soles once they camped. Though the pain was a constant discomfort, they distracted themselves with scenery and chats. Conversation flowed as smoothly as it had the previous night at the inn. They actually found things to smile and laugh about, keeping their minds calm in face of the hard road ahead of them.

At one point, Katressa pointed to the sword on Trestan's back. "You've laid claim to that sword, but you haven't taken it off your back yet. You favored your quarterstaff when you charged into that empty camp. Have you used a sword before?"

She spoke as Trestan used his staff as a walking stick. "I think a part of my heart doesn't yet want to lay claim to this sword milady, though Sir Wilhelm wanted me to have it. I am more accustomed to carrying this staff."

When Trestan said no more on the subject, Petrow added in, "Pardon my answering on behalf of Trestan's sake, as he seems to keep quiet on the subject. He has practiced with a sword; he keeps it a secret from his father."

Trestan bristled a bit at Petrow's comment. The young smith turned to give him a warning stare. "Please don't speak of that to anyone! I don't want my father to know!"

Petrow would not be intimidated. He knew Trestan was not as mad as he appeared. He pointed to the blade as he said to Cat, "From what I've heard and seen, I think Tres is getting pretty good with a sword."

The half-elf read into the words and learned a bit more of Trestan's past. "So, the warrior with you on the street was your secret trainer? Did you take to his lessons well?"

Trestan walked a bit in silence. He favored humility, but the lady had asked him directly the measure of his skills. "I've pretended at being a swordsman and Sir Wilhelm gave me praise. He said I was probably one of the better swordsmen in the village, but that isn't a big compliment. I have practiced milady, but I am untested, and perhaps unready."

Petrow smiled, "You're too humble, my friend. You're a better man than Tessald's armsmen even if they possess better skill with the sword than you, and I'm not saying that they *do* have better training. I couldn't honestly tell you whether they have any skill. I've seen them staggering drunk, and I compare them to the adventurers that visit town. Now, Sahbin could handle herself, but the rest sometimes acted like thugs themselves, or were bested when passing warriors put them to shame."

Trestan stroked his young mustache, "I wasn't saying I was better than any of them. So what if they've rarely used a sword themselves? When have I wielded one in battle?"

Cat's eyes passed back and forth as the young men talked, guessing more than either revealed. Petrow spoke next, "The threat of a sword is enough for the village folk. That noble house on the hill has always been the law, but life goes merrily on regardless of whatever decrees come from there. Nothing real exciting ever comes to that town. I'm just saying they aren't as good as you might think they are."

Cat interrupted before Trestan could reply, "You mean aside from Sahbin, there were nay veteran warriors among Lord Tessald's ranks?"

Trestan replied, "There are two that settled there for more years than I can count easily. I think they were once guards or soldiers from Kashmer's navy. They helped train the others, but they don't even carry swords themselves."

A snicker came from Petrow, "They are old and trying to enjoy a quieter life. They don't use swords because they can't really handle them anymore. Instead, they arm themselves with crossbows and keep a distance from any potential trouble. Crossbows are easy, people joke about them as being the old warrior's weapon."

Petrow missed the sudden warning on Trestan's face. The smith tried clearing his throat as well to stop the older man from completing the sentence, but it was too late. Petrow saw Cat smile, and realized his error as she lovingly patted the crossbow slung across her back. She tilted her exotic face to one side and answered, "I love the sting of my deadly crossbow. I don't mind if you see it that way. After all, at thirty-seven years I am definitely the old warrior here."

The age shocked Trestan and Petrow, who had never given thought to such aspects of a half-elf's lifespan. Katressa Bilil seemed as youthful and energetic as the two of them, if not more so. Half-elves enjoyed a much longer life expectancy than pure humans. It didn't sit well that their beautiful traveling companion was old enough by human terms to be their mother. If someday Trestan and Petrow lived to be grandfathers, Katressa would barely age by comparison.

Seeing the look on their faces, Cat obviously regretted bringing her age into the conversation. Silence reigned for several steps. They still walked at a fast pace along the road, Trestan and Petrow kept exchanging glances. Cat stepped ahead and began fidgeting with her rapier and scabbard. "Forget I brought that up. It's time to see what my companions are made from."

60

She unhooked her scabbard from her baldric. The scabbard still covered the rapier blade and thus blunted the weapon. Cat turned to face them, still walking backwards to cover ground. She withdrew in a guard position and motioned to Trestan. "Draw your blade, swordsman. Leave scabbard covering the steel, like mine. Let's see what you can do."

Trestan found himself eager to try a friendly practice swordfight against the half-elf. He handed his quarterstaff to Petrow, and then took hold of the elvish bastard sword. Trestan bowed to the woman even as he moved forward. Scabbard clashed against scabbard, though neither participant tried to hit or swing very hard. It was more a test of parrying strikes and seeing how the other reacted to the attacks. They still strode up the trail, but now the pace was accentuated by sword swings and thrusts.

Trestan found it hard to guard against Cat's skill. She never had to draw back for a large swing; the thin rapier's thrusting blade only needed to sneak around an opponent's defenses well enough to make a hit. Her method displayed efficiency, and she kept her balance even while backing along the road. Trestan's attacks still focused on spinning the sword in tight circles to block what should have been swings by heavier swords. Over time the young smith thought he perceived weaknesses in Cat's style, and his moves changed accordingly. The young smith attempted maneuvers which Sir Wilhelm had taught him in regards to trying to "trap" Cat's blade. He even learned a few moves from her and used them as well, which impressed her. The road passed by as they advanced and guarded along every step of the way.

Eventually Trestan tired out and Petrow got his chance to spar. Petrow used a heavy tree branch to substitute for his axe. His style left more openings than Trestan's, but Cat assured him that if he wasn't afraid of suffering a minor wound, his return blow would end the resistance of any foe. As she worked with him, she offered advice on his style. Both men took turns fencing and sparring with Cat for some time.

After they finished sparring, Cat finally felt as exhausted as the two young men. She still set a fast pace down the road. Cat admitted Trestan might be a novice, but he had been well-trained by his former mentor. She didn't expect a young smith to fight as well as he did, though she didn't hand out too much praise. It wouldn't do any good to swell the young man's head when there were many dangerous people in the world.

When Petrow asked Cat what she thought about his skill, she teasingly smiled. "Well, if I were you I still wouldn't try standing your ground against any wizards on horseback anytime soon."

*   *   *   *   *

The sun dropped behind the hills to the west. In the distance, red rays of sunlight glinted off the tops of the mountains ahead of them. The valleys they walked through became bathed in shadow. Night sounds started, while the daytime animals sought shelter for the evening. Aburis, the largest moon as well as the strongest pull of the tides at this time of year, was well on the rise. In another part of the sky, Nirahha barely peeked over the ridge tops.

61

Cat tried to continue a fast pace, but Trestan and Petrow couldn't match her anymore. Both men proudly resisted a call for a rest, but they plodded along in a sleepy haze. The adventuress felt the weariness of the trail, and she imagined how the same effect multiplied on her two companions. Though strong-willed and physically capable, neither man had walked so far in his life. Cat knew they were at their limit.

They cleared the top of another ridge. The road dropped down from the heights into another dark valley. Cat stopped abruptly and held out her hands. The two dazed men promptly bumped into her. Before they could get in a word, she shushed them and pointed a short distance into the valley. Both men strained to focus on the object of her attention. It wasn't far away, but through the canopy of trees they saw a flicker of light and a thin trail of smoke rise from it.

They were overlooking a campfire.

CHAPTER 5

As tired as they had been on the trail, the sight of someone else on the road refreshed their senses. This time, Petrow and Trestan followed Katressa's instructions, staying behind while she scouted. The two men stayed alert and watchful during her absence. Nevertheless, both men jumped when her whispered voice proceeded her. "I'm back."

Petrow already had his axe ready, "Is it them?"

"Nay," Cat replied, deflating their enthusiasm. "A gnome, tending a fire and reading a manuscript. I believe he's alone."

After some discussion, the three decided to approach the gnome openly and inquire whether he had seen anyone on the road. Petrow led, holding up a lit torch so as to approach the campfire in a friendly way. The camp sat within some trees, yet quite visible to the road. As they rounded some trunk shadows the gnome could see them as well as they could see him. He peered at them in the dark and then put away the scroll he had been reading. They saw the gnome glance at his small crossbow. The gnome didn't make any moves towards the weapon or show much alarm; he simply exercised caution due to the unknown intent of his surprise visitors. Cat waved and he returned the gesture with a smile.

As they drew closer, they got a better look at the small humanoid. From his little boots to the crown of his head, his height didn't top three feet. He was rather handsome as far as gnomes go. His dark brown hair included a thin, well-tended mustache and goatee. The lines on his cheeks suggested he smiled a lot. His fashion included colorful clothes; straps and bags criss-crossed his tunic. Aside from the small crossbow, he wore a light mace upon his belt. He held a smoking pipe, which provided a sweet aroma that pervaded the camp. They suspected a short, carved piece of wood tucked away in the gnome's belt could be a wand. The gnome didn't have a pony, dog or other visible mount. The companions looked for signs that anyone else might be sharing the camp but only one blanket stretched out near the fire.

He greeted them as they entered his camp. He spoke warmly, with an easy smile, "Greetings and fair eve, travelers. I trust your intentions are honorable, if so you are welcome to enter my camp in peace. If your intent is something more rash, I assure you I have magic at my disposal to protect myself."

Cat answered on behalf of the three, "We come with peaceful intentions. We've journeyed from Troutbrook and seek news on other groups who may have passed you on the road today. This is all we desire. Although we'd also be honored to share your campfire and be your guests for a bit."

"I am glad to hear of it," the gnome responded, "Have a seat with me and let us trade introductions."

The companions arranged themselves around the fire, their host sat on a stump. Cat made a formal introduction for the group. She gave the gnome their names and professions, labeling herself as a privateer in the service of Kashmer. Trestan and Petrow nodded to their host as she introduced them. The young men felt out of place considering how ragged they looked compared to Cat and the gnome.

The gnome's meek voice spoke eloquently and kindly. "A good evening to meet such nice people. I am known by many names, as is the nature of my folk. I will give you the name I use around human settlements. Call me Mel Bellringer! I am from the Bellringer family: makers of fine bells, chimes, gongs, and other acoustical instruments. However, I am not into the family business. I had magic flowing in my blood and sought to develop it. I present myself before you as a sorcerer and traveler. What brings you out on the road at so late an hour?"

Trestan answered, "We're following a band of adventurers who caused mischief in Troutbrook. They kidnapped a lady of the nobility."

Mel looked shocked, "You don't say! Describe them to me."

Trestan started with Bortun's description, figuring that a minotaur passing by on the road would certainly stand out. Then he described Loung Chao as the gnome nodded his head.

Mel spoke, "Aye, I saw that band! They were walking along, not enough horses to share between them. They weren't friendly either."

"Did they have a woman with them? She is fair and beautiful, wearing a skirt and displaying some expensive jewelry on her?" Trestan asked.

Mel paused to recall what he had seen earlier that day. "There were two women with them. One was as you described. She looked sad and tired, definitely nay condition to be traveling like that. She looked at me as if she had something to say, but the minotaur pushed her along. Interesting minotaur, he had one horn broken." Trestan smiled, remembering when Sir Wilhelm had chopped it off.

Cat leaned closer to Mel, "About what time of the day did you see them, good sir?"

The gnome drummed his finger against the side of the nose as he gathered his memories, "Let's see. I've been buried in my reading. I've been here all day, and thus I had to adjust my sitting a lot as the reading light changed. Nothing beats sunlight for illuminating an old script or a new book. It may have been a few hours after the sun's peak in the sky. It wasn't quite close to evening yet, but the sun was descending."

While Cat worked out the time difference in her head, Petrow prompted the gnome with a question. "You just sat around here all day? Reading? What about the dangers in the woods?"

Mel dismissed the notion with a wave of his hand. "Oh, I'm not too worried about these woods. I'm what your people call a forest gnome. I have kin in there. They weren't too receptive my visit or I'd be staying with them, but let us not dwell on that. The only other creatures that wander by this area are goblins, and occasional wild beasts, but they are generally as afraid of us as we are of them."

Cat started to think out loud, "So if they really pushed it they might have made it to Barkan's Crossing this evening. I doubt they would have been able to march Lady Shauntay, unless they put her on a horse. That would be risking an escape. Too much 'if' and 'maybe'; we can't just assume. I'm guessing they rested for the night, but they are still a good few hours ahead of us." She raised her head to look at the gnome. "Did you see a company of guards ride by today? There were men dispatched out of Troutbrook to catch that band."

64

"Indeed, Lady Katressa," The gnome picked up another manuscript, "I was reading this when the first band came by, and had nearly completed it by the time the guards appeared. I had to spend time deciphering and figuring out some of the strange handwriting, but maybe another hour or two had gone by. They rode past about ten strong. They were dressed in bright colors, very lovely if you ask me. Light blue colors they wore, arranged in waves, with the symbol of a fish under the water. Does that not sound like the standard that a town named Troutbrook would use?"

The three friends looked at each other. Cat finally voiced her thoughts. "The guards should have overtaken the others by now. When daylight comes, will we see them going back to town? If not, what shall we assume? In the morning, we may find a scene of battle on the road ahead."

Mel Bellringer looked them over as he smoked his pipe. He noted the two young men watching parts of the conversation through heavy eyelids. "There is nothing more you can do this night. I assume you are honestly trying to help that poor lady. Enjoy my campfire tonight. In the morning, you will be refreshed and ready to continue on with a clear mind and a renewed body. I don't want to pressure you into staying, though I certainly have enjoyed having someone to share conversation with out here in the countryside. Set your bedrolls and get your rest. May Daerkfyre watch over us all!"

Petrow and Trestan started to set out their blankets and loosen their footwear. Cat watched their host with renewed interest and a bit of confusion. She had caught something odd that the two men had missed. Mel could tell that her eyes were on him. He met her gaze, "Something troubles you?"

Cat asked, "Isn't Daerkfyre the Valorous a dwarven deity? A gnome paying homage to a dwarven god?"

Mel blushed, "Oh…heh…well. I'm asked that often enough. Dwarves tend to threaten me when they find out. Imagine! Offended that I honor them by worshipping one of their gods! It's a long story in itself, but I helped a dwarven nation some time back in retrieving a relic dear to them. During that time I was on bad terms with my own god. In order to help those dwarves, I had to face a vision of one of their deities. It was part of a test. In my case I faced Daerkfyre, and I had to be judged worthy by him to continue. I put forth my plea before him, and even to my astonishment he judged me worthy! Since then I have turned to him for my devotion. It was Daerkfyre that showed trust and faith in me, when my own god had abandoned me. Now I may be told by others that I can't be worshipping a dwarven god, but I'll let him decide that and not mortals."

Cat smiled at him, "You certainly are an interesting person, Mel Bellringer! Also, a fine host!"

From off to the side, Trestan and Petrow held their own conversation. The smith grunted in pain, "Three on the right, two on the left. Hells this will hurt."

"I'm jealous of your shoes! My sandals left me with three on the right, and four on the left!"

Cat and Mel turned to see the young men sitting on their blankets, each rubbing their feet. Cat asked, "What are you two talking about?"

Trestan stopped rubbing and quieted, but Petrow answered directly, "Counting the blisters on our feet! It's been a long walk."

Cat recoiled at seeing Petrow flash the blood-tinged sole of one foot in her direction. She stated, "Oh gods! When we get to a town I have to buy you both a pair of good shoes. That reminds me of my early days of traveling, but worse."

Mel Bellringer actually looked over both sets of feet with an odd fascination. Dabbling in sometimes disgusting reagents for spells and potions, he was not disturbed in the least examining the blisters and even commented on how well or bad they looked. "Aye, this one is still weeping some fluid. You should get that taken care of by a healer."

Katressa turned away and prepared her own blanket for the night. "Ok, I know I've seen some worse injuries, but this is just making me sick. I feel sorry for rushing both of you along like I did today. I certainly have pushed you hard and we've not made much progress in catching them. I don't see how you will travel too well tomorrow."

Mel retrieved a jar out of one of the many pouches on his torso straps. The straps and pouches were in a confusing array, some overlapping others over the gnome's chest. One had to wonder how Mel kept track of where he stored various items. "Here, spread a dab of this on those sores. By morning they should be a lot better. They are my own herbal remedy: created by alchemical magic and a bit of ma's home recipe. Use it and sleep well."

The two men rubbed some onto the blisters after soaking their feet with water. The half-elf felt guilty when she looked over at the sores, especially when Trestan winced in pain as he applied the ointment. Katressa admired how well they had carried on without complaint. She remembered days of her youth when her feet felt as bad as theirs looked. So much time she had spent under the sun and stars running through forests or over plains. Her feet got used to long distances at an early age.

She worried that they should post a guard, but both men looked very tired. She had to trust Mel that this was a relatively safe area. The half-elf started to succumb to her weariness. She set all her weapons within easy reach around her blanket. This night she stayed on top of one blanket, using a dark gray cloak from her pack to cover her and warm away the chills of the night. The adventuress relaxed as Petrow and Trestan thanked the gnome through their yawns. Eventually, sleep caught up with her.

*   *   *   *   *

When Trestan first opened his sleepy eyes, the third and smallest moon, Liijay, hovered at the pinnacle of the starlit sky. Figuring dawn would be a couple hours away, Trestan turned to find a more comfortable position. Any useful light from the campfire had died out, but the stars and moons illuminated Cat's form nearby. She had already been upright and watched him as he turned over. He half-buried his face in his traveling sack. It wasn't the softest thing to lie on, but it served its purpose.

Wondering about Cat's wakefulness, he whispered quietly, "Bad dream? Or light sleeper?"

She leaned close to him, speaking softly. "Light sleeper, always have been. I heard some odd noise in the woods a short time ago. The night sounds have returned, so I'm not as worried anymore. When you walk the adventurer's road as long as I have, you adjust to less sleep and more watchfulness."

Though Trestan still felt half-asleep, he whispered again, "I wish you would tell me something of your adventures. I would love to hear a tale."

Although Trestan sounded sluggish, Cat started a tale from her past. The young man listened in, even though his eyes slowly dropped closed and then snapped back open a few times. She kept her voice low so that she wouldn't wake anyone else.

"It was maybe twenty years ago…and especially for a half-elf, it was a young age. Up until then my scouting and fighting skills had been limited to games in the woods with the other elves of my community. My human mother mostly stayed in the elf city where my father lived. It wasn't a grand city of stone and manors like human cities. Elves build in the boughs as well as around the bases of huge, ancient trees. Wooden walkways stretched across the treetops, offering a grand view of all of the forest. Gardens cultivated over several elf generations were a paradise to tread.

"Then one day, demons attacked the city. Somehow, beyond explanation, a portal to another dimension opened up and the evil spawn poured through. I know not whether they intended anything specific, but during the battle several of them raided a sacred vault of our people. While several of the defenders rallied around our most sacred treasures, others tried to protect and save their families. The demons were everywhere and my surprised kinsmen tried to form a defense as best as they could. My poor mother, already ill and weakened by age, died valiantly against the creatures. She bought time for me to flee, but I couldn't simply run into the forest and abandon my people. I turned around and snuck back towards the sound of the fighting. I was small and afraid back then. I saw demons and elves alike slaughtered as I made my way quietly through the bushes.

"When I found the fiercest portion of the battle, I was only in time to see the leader of the demons flee back through the portal with several followers. I later found out the creature was a coldast: a mix of earth element and undead spirit. The creature and its brethren bore away several items of the highest value. I only learned more of the theft after the battle. Though I had almost reached my twentieth year, to elves I was a child.

"But I must return to the events of that day to speak of what happened next. I saw an argument between my father and several elders near the portal. There were still demons about, but the elves had won the ground around the portal after the leading demons had fled back through it. I couldn't hear much, but they were clearly arguing over the portal itself. My father was concerned about the holy items that had been stolen, while various elders were more concerned with shutting the portal and ending the threat of the demons. Eventually, several stepped forth to brave the portal and retrieve the stolen goods. Reatheneus Bilil, my father, proclaimed loudly, 'Yestreal's gift was a relic, it should not be abandoned so easily!' He looked to me and touched a hand to his ear, whereupon he wore a gold unicorn earring I had given him as a gift. He and those brave few went into the portal. We waited for hours. More demons attacked from the forest around us as well as through the portal itself. Finally, the elders conceded they could wait nay longer. I watched numbly as they called forth a miracle and closed the passage between dimensions.

"I screamed, I cried, I denied everything that had happened. Swords and weapons all over the ground, yet the portal was closed and I couldn't charge through to help my father. I never saw him again. I had lost my mother, friends, kinsmen, and my father was trapped in another world. That day I grew out of my childhood for good. I became a scout and an expert shot with a crossbow and bow. It wasn't very long before I started down the adventurer's path."

Cat finished her sad tale and watched Trestan's breathing, unsure if the young man remained awake. He seemed to keep his ear turn toward her, though his eyes were closed. Cat explained, "And that is why I support your decision to go after this group. I was unable to follow and I felt helpless. You have a choice, and I will be there to help you for the loss you suffered that night. Be careful and don't throw your life away if you can help it. I loved my father, but I felt he threw his life away needlessly in the end. He disappeared to some evil, uncertain fate, and left me alone to face the future by myself. Learn from this story, to strike when you know you can win and accomplish your goals and live. Don't leave any little girls crying as they face life alone."

Tears trailed down Cat's cheek from such painful memories. She wiped them away as her nose sniffled. The half-elf wondered why she had told Trestan all that, but she felt it was the right message to give him. She looked at the young man and wondered what fate would lie in store for him. Could he make enough of a difference to heal the wounds in his heart? Cat used one finger to brush a strand of hair out of Trestan's face as she added, "Goodnight Trestan."

Barely audible and half-muffled by the sack his face rested on, Trestan responded through closed eyes, "Goodnight Cat." His breathing resumed a steady rhythm as he succumbed to sleep.

*   *   *   *   *

Petrow faced the morning with a yawn and a stretch. Cat hovered by the rekindled fire, her attention on breakfast. There were no stretches or exercises today as far as Petrow could tell; she was already dressed in her armor. Mel Bellringer's manuscripts were packed away neatly in wood and leather tubes. The gnome straightened out some of his packs while striking up a quiet conversation with Cat. The half-elf just nodded her head as the gnome did all of the talking. Gnomes had a reputation for being talkative, and Mel seemed no exception. Off to one side, Trestan stirred on his blanket. Petrow considered stashing his blanket and pack, but decided to heed the call of nature first. He donned his work harness and knife, but left the axe. Slipping sandals on, he was amazed at how good the gnome's salve worked. The gnome's remedy mostly erased the blisters on his feet. He knew he still had a long walk ahead of him, but his feet would be more up to the task than he could have hoped for during the previous evening. The human stretched and basked in the morning light as he walked into the thicker treeline.

He wondered what they would find in Barkan's Crossing. He heard it was the largest town in the southern reaches of Kashmer's Protectorate. It was also the last real patch of civilization before the fort, Dunker Keep, that marked the southern border. Dunker

Keep's small village satisfied the needs of miners, a few farms, and the fort's garrison. Likely Troutbrook and Dunker Keep combined couldn't match Barkan's Crossing. Barkan's Crossing was said to be a bustling place, where tradesmen gathered to make use of the raw materials flowing into the town. Petrow doubted they would easily find one group of people in a town as busy and sprawling as that. The young man looked forward to visiting a larger city, though he would have preferred it under different circumstances.

Petrow turned his mind to the task at hand. He stood out of sight of the camp. A lot of underbrush grew around the remains of a fallen tree. Branches and dead wood crisscrossed the area. Green moss and small plants added color to the dark corpse of the tree. Trees and leaves blocked most of the sun's light this early in the day. In the distance, he heard the songs of morning birds. Finding a spot in which to do his business, he started lowering his leggings.

A frantic scream, followed by chattering noises, erupted from right under him. Something he thought was a tree root under his sandal moved, yanking him off balance. Stepping back in surprise, he stared as a smaller humanoid creature got to its feet. Black and green skin identified the goblin, as well as the yellow eyes staring back at Petrow in surprise. The creature's dark skin colors had camouflaged it well among the dead branches. Both the goblin and Petrow let out a scream. It occurred to Petrow he was without axe, face to face with a creature known to have an evil disposition. The goblin wore animal hides and carried a long dagger at its side. Though this one stood only half his height, they were renowned for attacking in large numbers and committing acts of cruelty to any prisoners. Another goblin rose out of the brush. The second creature moved several branches as it got to its feet, appearing to Petrow as if a larger number jumped up from that spot. The first goblin started to scramble away from him, but Petrow, screaming while terrified, ran back toward the camp.

At the first scream, Cat dropped the pan beside the fire and Mel looked up from his breakfast. They couldn't immediately identify the direction from which it originated. Cat sprang her crossbow and started loading it. Mel stood there dumbfounded, momentarily torn between the dropped pan or his own crossbow. Trestan sat up from his blanket, looking about with half open eyes.

Petrow stumbled out of the trees, a scream on his lips and his trousers wrapped around his knees. Everyone in the camp got a good look at his manhood as he ran for his axe. "Goblins! Goblins! A whole bunch of them…"

A goblin ran out of the woods to one side, moving away from Petrow. This was the one the young man had stepped on and frightened. It unintentionally came rather close to Trestan. Trestan's eyes opened in alarm at the sudden threat. The young smith grabbed his quarterstaff, ignoring the elvish sword lying right next to it. He got to his feet and actually charged the goblin barefoot, "Abriana! Guide my weapon!"

Mel Bellringer ignored the pan of food at the sight of the goblin running through the edge of the camp. Daerkfyre the Valorous would want him to smite evil goblins without mercy. The gnome started to go for his crossbow. Halfway to having it loaded he stopped, changed his mind and reached into one of his many pouches for spell items. He had something better to use against a "bunch" of goblins. He pulled out an item and looked for an opportunity to use it.

Cat loaded her crossbow fast. She ignored Petrow as he hopped and pulled at his leggings. She aimed at the one running by Trestan, though he nearly blocked her line of sight. Cat fired a shot that passed within two feet of Trestan's arm. The bolt hit the goblin and sent it tumbling. A moment later, it scrambled along the ground, still very much alive. The bolt stuck out from a pack the goblin carried, not even touching flesh. The scrambling creature yelled and screamed frantically, yellow eyes wide with fright. The companions feared he was calling out for reinforcements.

Petrow held axe in hand. He looked about the edge of the clearing for more enemies. He tried recalling if it had been three more goblins in the bushes or a full-grown troll. Although he couldn't see any opponents, he could hear more movement in the bushes. He kept his axe cocked back for a swing as he looked for an attacker.

The smith came within melee range of the first goblin. Trestan gave a yell and swung his quarterstaff at the dark creature. A low-hanging branch blocked the blow. The goblin scrambled underneath the lowest boughs of a tree as it searched for cover. Behind Trestan, Cat anxiously reloaded her crossbow. The smith's muscular arms swung his staff back and forth, thrashing the low branches of the tree as he attempted to hit the goblin or flush it out. The smaller creature cowered. Leaves and broken twigs rained on it as Trestan continued to pummel the tree. Suddenly, the goblin pulled out a long dagger and tried a few strikes of its own. The young smith used the advantage that his longer weapon gave him. The goblin stabbed with the dagger, but mostly tried to keep cover between itself and the larger attacker. It continued to yell for help. Just as loudly, Trestan continued to yell war cries, "For Abriana! For Jareth! I defend my friends!"

While Petrow scanned the woods, he heard a foreign voice bark in an unknown language. He saw where this newest opponent squatted, half concealed by bushes. It was another goblin at the edge of the foliage. It spent its attention on the plight of its companion, not watching Petrow. Petrow had no way to know whether it talked to more goblins in the woods or answered the calls of the first goblin. The handyman reacted in what he thought was a heroic way. He had won some axe-throwing competitions for copper wagers behind the inn at Troutbrook. Judging the distance, and the goblin's unawareness of the danger, he hefted the simple axe with both hands and prepared to throw it. With a mighty heave, he launched the axe towards its target.

The axe flew four feet over the goblin's head and crashed harmlessly into the trees beyond.

With a gaped mouth and awed look the young human realized how stupid that action had been. Petrow drew his knife from its sheath. Keeping his eyes on the scared goblin he pointed it out to the others. "Help! I got a goblin right here!"

The goblin was spooked by the presence of the human, but it looked with terror at something behind Petrow. The creature turned and ran into the woods. Another of Cat's bolts zipped past the would-be-axe-throwing-champion towards the fleeing creature. Everyone in the clearing heard a yelp from within the trees as Cat's bolt found its mark. The original yelp was followed by other unknown words and curses spouted from a hidden

70

source beyond the leaves. More movement and branch rustling could be heard, but the origin remained hidden.

Mel watched Trestan's fight. He saw the young man drop to the ground with a pained scream. The goblin, wielding its dagger, ran out from the tree to make a break for the relative safety of the woods. The creature's pack jostled along, the large crossbow bolt still stuck in it. Cat and Petrow turned to watch but could do nothing quickly enough to prevent its escape. Mel Bellringer cast his spell, filling the item in his hand with the power of destructive magic. As the others watched, he threw a ball of clay at the goblin. The clay ball landed in front of the fleeing creature but the monster ran past while the ensorcelled item rolled to a stop. Trestan staggered to his feet and started after the goblin. Mel yelled a warning, "Don't chase! Get down NOW!"

Trestan, Cat and Petrow hit the ground without much time to spare. The clay ball exploded into a mass of smoke and heat. The audible wave, louder than anything they'd ever heard, hammered their ears and left them stunned. Leaves, sticks and debris flung out from the expanding cloud. Mel had a brief glimpse of the goblin flying through the air before he was knocked on his own butt by the force of the blast. The others clapped their hands to their ears, but the worst of the noise had already passed. The explosion echoed for some time alongside the sounds of raining debris. Everyone cowered until the noises finally settled. The companions from Troutbrook slowly lifted their heads and looked around to see the results. Charred leaves floated back to the ground in a dusty mist. Although the goblin couldn't be seen, there were sounds in the woods of more than one goblin fleeing in fear.

At that point, the most animated form in the clearing was their small sorcerer. The gnome cheered loudly in delight at the destructiveness of his spell. "Timed Boomy!"

Mel Bellringer strode forward, confident that any goblins left alive were probably running until they dropped from exhaustion. He carried the wand in hand in case he needed to use it. The three companions could only guess at what damage the wand might unleash if it had been needed. As the gnome congratulated himself and excitedly moved about, the rest shifted position every time the wand swung their direction.

"That had an official name penned by some important mage, but I messed up the recipe and ended up with something better." Mel did a dance and struck a pose, "Timed Boomy! I set the time with a word when I throw it, and I'm usually quite accurate, and it ticks away the time a bit so I can throw it and run or I just leave it somewhere, and it has come in quite handy, and it really surprises some opponents like this one time…"

As Mel rambled on about his spell, Cat and Petrow slowly got to their feet. They looked about to make sure no other goblins offered a threat. No enemies were visible. Mel's magical blast had scared off whatever was still out there. Amidst the falling leaves and the haziness of settling dust, they realized Trestan sat while cradling one leg in pain. It dawned on them the goblin might have done a nasty thing with its dagger before it ran off. Cat and Petrow both ran to Trestan, with Mel not far behind. The young smith waved them off as they bombarded him with questions and looked for the injury. They were concerned until he finally explained why he held his bare foot.

"Nay, he didn't stab me; he didn't even get close. I was fighting barefoot and stepped on a sharp rock or something. It's quite painful but I think I'll live if you all can just give me room to breathe."

At this statement, the tension of the encounter vanished. Mel, Petrow and Cat started to share a laugh. Before long, Trestan had difficulty stifling a laugh as well.

Troutbrook's handyman felt exhilarated about his brush with death. Petrow started to explain, "I was so scared. But we won! Here I was in the woods, alone, surrounded by seven goblins…"

Trestan opened his eyes wide, "Seven?"

"Well, give or take some, I didn't stop to count…"

Cat added, "Nor did you stop to pull your pants up."

Petrow looked at the half-elf slyly, "I'm sure you weren't complaining. Anyway, I wasn't about to give them that as a target. But look what we did! We got attacked by surprise and we killed over half of them! That's a point of pride…"

"Ok, wait…wait a second," Cat interrupted through her own giggles, "I only saw two goblins. There might have been more, but I only saw two."

Petrow's voice declared adamantly, "We killed four!"

"Four? How did you count four?"

Petrow tried to count them off on his fingers, "Well, you shot two with your crossbow, and I think Mel got two with his spell."

Katressa "Cat" Bilil let out a hearty laugh, "In the name of the gods, Petrow! The first one I shot didn't die. His pack stopped the bolt, and then he was the one thrown by Mel's explosion. I didn't see any other goblins get hit by that burst, though granted one might have. The second one I shot gave out a yelp, but that doesn't mean I struck him a fatal blow."

Trestan limped over to his blanket to grab his shoes. The young smith stared at the elf-crafted sword briefly, wondering why he had chosen to use the quarterstaff when the fighting began. Petrow called out to him, "Tres, help me out here. She is taking away from our moment of glory!"

Trestan sat down on his blanket with an astonished look towards Petrow, "Moment of glory? I fought off a goblin that looked as scared as I was, then I stepped on something sharp and went down! He could have just stabbed me then and there! I'm glad we're alive, that's enough for me. Cat is right about what she said yesterday: if we fight the likes of those other adventurers, we would lose."

Petrow said, "None of you is going to even try a body count before we continue? They might have had money on them. Let's at least check before we go on."

Cat stated, "Fine, you can start checking when you go back into the woods."

Petrow cast a nervous glance at the trees, "What do you mean? Why just me?"

Cat replied sarcastically, "What? Oh master axe wielder, do you want to leave your blade all by itself in the woods, or do you think you might need a throwing weapon again later on?"

*   *   *   *   *

The only two goblins that had even been in the valley that morning staggered towards their distant village. They had seen the scariest thing ever in their young lives, and were glad to simply be alive. They leaned on each other for support, step by painful step.

The first one walked stiffly. Its scorched back burned a deeper shade of black. Small abrasions marked his skin in spots where flying dirt and rocks scoured small portions of his flesh. His pack had a human-sized crossbow bolt embedded in it.

The other walked with a pained limp. It fared slightly better, though another one of those large crossbow bolts had pierced the muscles of his skinny posterior. He walked with a pained limp, but at least the wound was not very life-threatening. He almost fainted whenever he looked around at the sharp weapon protruding from the rear of his loincloth.

One young goblin looked at the other. He then spoke in his native language. Though the goblin tongue was not as well-developed as that of humans, the message translated similar to: "That's the last time I run away from chores. When pa sees our mess, we'll be in deep trouble for sure!"

*   *   *   *   *

Before the companions left camp that morning, Mel reapplied his salve to the feet of both men. They agreed it was working wonders for easing their sores. Even Cat took off her boots to get some relief from the gnome's concoction. They didn't stay at the camp for long, believing more goblins might be nearby. When the three from Troutbrook continued their journey south, Mel Bellringer of the Bellringer family shouldered his packs and scroll tubes and joined them.

"I want to come along and help any way I can! I can finish my research later. The thought of participating in a rescue excites me!" Apparently, Cat had told the gnome a little more of their story during the preparation of breakfast. Thus, Mel was more informed about what they faced and the nature of their quest. He confidently declared, "I have all sorts of nasty surprises for any elf wizard that crosses my path."

With the morning sun shining down, they continued southward into the higher country. They walked over the foothills of the southern region of Kashmer's Protectorate. The views of the land were breathtaking in the Florum month. Flowers blossomed on the ground and in the trees, the wind tasted of the eastern sea breeze. Occasionally, baby animals could be seen following their parents. Trestan and Petrow felt as if they had passed their first real test of the adventure, though only Trestan appreciated how close they had come to injury. They hiked over more hills than they could count.

The gnome talked frequently and had stories about everything. He discussed customs of far off Tariyka, though all his knowledge came from books and hearsay. Mel promoted the arts and songs from far off Orlaun. He talked about delicacies in foreign lands. As the stomachs of the two young humans made known the displeasure of the journey's diet, Mel tempted them with recipes from interesting places. While the two young men recoiled at how centaurs could turn a wyvern's bladder into a delicacy, they were just as tortured when he told them of tasty foreign dishes that made their mouths water.

Cat once again brought her rapier out to play and the men practiced as they walked. They welcomed the distraction. Trestan and Petrow took turns trying to get past Cat's impressive swordplay. Mel watched and commented on the fighting, even using the subject to talk about coliseum fights and famous battles in history…many of which he had only heard stories but never witnessed himself. After a long period of time, the group sat down for another rest. Trestan and Petrow had gotten in their share of swordplay, and at least for a moment enjoyed sitting in the trees by the roadside. The four passed around water under the shade of a large tree.

Mel talked with few pauses, "…and after this incident Baron Lichter changed his standard to a nice blue color, stating he'd sooner give up his lands rather than display colors similar to his rival. It was a blue similar to those armsmen from Troutbrook I believe…"

Cat finally interrupted, "Of which we have seen nay sign. I'd thought we might have seen a battle by now, or maybe even seen the guards riding back towards their hometown with Lady Shauntay in tow."

"Indeed," Mel continued, as if he hadn't been interrupted, "And a similar blue emblem was worn by the merchant guards of…"

"Mel," Cat paused as the gnome turned his attention to her. She very much liked the gnome but knew how members of his race could talk for hours without a break. She tried a polite way to get the gnome to quiet down. "Better get some water in you while we are resting."

Mel reached for his waterskin, "You are so right. My mouth is uncommonly dry. I can't help it. You three have been contributing to one of the nicest conversations I have had in a long time."

As the gnome drank, the other three looked at him incredulously, each one wondering what they had contributed to the one-sided conversation. Cat enjoyed a quiet moment. The half-elf commented on the task before them, "Anyway, we aren't very far from Barkan's Crossing right now. I've seen more buildings along the hills, though most seem abandoned. In the next hour or two we should be entering the farms on the outskirts of the town."

Cat sat with her knees against her chest, arms folded around her legs. "The question is what next? If we get to town with nay sign of them, we'll just have to start asking around. I doubt that group would want to go through town openly again, but if they left the road I may have missed it."

Mel finished his drink, "Well, one thing is for sure. You will need help in dealing with them. I don't know how you planned on just the three of you taking on all eight of them to rescue the woman. Count me in to help with whatever you need!"

Trestan, Petrow and Cat turned their heads towards the gnome so fast it left the small man wondering what he said wrong. Trestan asked, "We asked if you had seen a party go by: a minotaur, elf wizard…"

"Aye, I did," interrupted Mel, "You described a few of them. That was the group that went past me on the road."

Trestan counted the numbers on his fingers to reassure himself that his count was not wrong, "We were following a party of five, including the captured lady. They had only two horses. You are saying they were with others?"

Mel nodded his head, "Well, aye! You described some of them, but there were nine in all if you include that noble lady. They did have only two horses. The ones you didn't describe were human and had the look of thugs or hired sellswords. I think a couple of them looked kind of like sailors, judging by their jewelry, tattoos and their gait."

Trestan sat back against a tree, absorbing the ill news. Petrow also looked stunned. Cat frowned and paced around the tree. For a minute or two, not even the gnome disturbed the quietness lingering around the companions. Private thoughts preoccupied all of them. Mel realized the group hadn't been prepared to deal with the extra enemies he saw. Petrow threw a few glances down the trail leading back home. Trestan pulled the elvish sword from its scabbard, and looked for an answer in the runes carved into the blade.

Cat looked at them one-by-one. She kept a straight face, leaving her thoughts unreadable. The half-elf was no novice to the road's hazards. She privately wondered if she was better off trying any kind of rescue alone or…if it came to it…dying alone without taking them with her. She felt uneasy about the risk involved. Her attitude changed somewhat when she saw Trestan close his eyes in silent prayer to his goddess. This was not the face of a scared young man. He looked to be a simple man dressed in patched, dirty clothes, wearing a rope belt. Yet she could see the resolve in his face and feel his love for others, even as he prayed for guidance. She assumed he planned to go forward.

Cat spoke softly, "Sword of the Spirit."

Trestan's eyes popped open and he looked at Cat. Petrow and Mel also wondered what the half-elf referenced. The privateer's exotic green eyes focused on the runes of the elf sword. She indicated the blade's symbols and explained to Trestan, *"Fa Iblearol re fa Dolingomo re fa sen-Salustrel.* That's what the legible runes on the blade say. Other runes merely reflect the magical enchantments placed on it. The longer version translates to 'The sword, of the spirit of the soul'. But the short version names it Sword of the Spirit."

Trestan looked over the foreign markings, though of course he could not make out the elf writing. Petrow and Mel were momentarily shaken from the thoughts going through their minds. Katressa Bilil had seen their course for the near future in the determination of the young smith. She looked south and spotted some haze originating from some smoke.

"Look there," she pointed, though the others were not gifted as her with the keen sight of elven heritage. "It is maybe two or three ridges over. Barkan's Crossing awaits us. We came this far, so we shouldn't turn back without stepping foot into the town. We shall see what we can find out once we get there."

The companions got up and hefted their packs. They set forth again towards their goal, but the hopes of success at their quest waned further. Trestan doubted they would succeed, but he found himself relying more and more on the faith in the goddess his mentor worshipped. His sorrow turned into an almost single-minded determination to carry this quest to some kind of logical conclusion. He was well aware of the danger and risk to his new friends, but he felt he had to walk this path.

They followed the path south.

CHAPTER 6

A busy community of craftsmen and artisans made Barkan's Crossing the largest town in the southern part of Kashmer's Protectorate. Dunker Keep shipped a plentiful supply of metal ore. An abundance of wools and leathers came from the local grasslands. A few mills harvested lumber in the nearby hills. These goods shipped far and wide, either as raw supplies or as skilled laborers shaped them. Many items went up the road to supply Kashmer, the trade center of the country. The northern trade delivered to Tariyka and other more distant lands. Merchant caravans also journeyed southward down the road, going past Dunker Keep to trade with items from Cloudview. The large races inhabiting the mountains rarely purchased human goods, though any successful trade originated from Kashmer's Protectorate. In return, many nice foreign goods, some rare, traveled by road or ship into Barkan's Crossing. The town boasted numerous shops and trades, providing all basic needs of those who live there and the needs of others trading with the town. The core of the town developed at the beginning of steeper foothills at the base of the mountain range. An old tower, large but crumbled into ruin, featured along the road, marked some old kingdom's domain. The main part of town spread out along a ridgeline, beside the old tower. A stone bridge spanned the mountain river on the south side of town, though more houses and buildings had sprung up on the far side of the river.

Since Barkan's Crossing dominated a ridge, it didn't sit directly on the ocean water. A mountain river waterfall on the edge of the ridge and the town dropped a few hundred feet to the lake below. A long ramp had been carved into the ridge to support a means for wagon passage, bending back and forth as it made its gradual descent to the lake below town. The lake attached to the ocean by a wide river, good enough for shallow bottom boats to operate. From there, they could sail north to Kashmer or south to distant Orlaun. A modest harbor nicknamed Lowtown formed around the lake.

As the past few decades rolled by, people from the distant country regions settled closer to Barkan's Crossing out of protection. Some settled in fortified ranches in the nearby hills. The town continued to grow and spread outward, until the city walls simply divided the old town from the new. Creatures of the wild avoided the outskirts of the town, though the ranches often found guards useful against intelligent pests that sought to steal during the night. Families established houses further and further out of the town. A period of expansion would sometimes be halted by a period of fortifying. This type of change happened whenever a creature or the threat of them became serious enough on the outskirts that people wouldn't dare build out further until fears were settled again. All of this simply combined to an abundance of fenced dwellings on the roads into town.

The party from Troutbrook walked past many of these outer dwellings as they gradually ascended the ridge to town. Trestan and Petrow felt soreness returning to their feet, but it was not as bad as the previous night. Seeing the distant rooftops of the town, they felt less burdened. In fact, they were looking forward to their first trip to this renowned town. Katressa vowed to make good on her promise to buy the men new shoes. She had the coin and was willing to help them out, since they had willingly gone on this dangerous quest. At that time Mel tried starting a discussion about how some new shoes would suit him well. Cat pointedly told him he could afford to pay for his own shoes.

Looking ahead during their conversations, Trestan commented, "Barkan's Crossing! I've never been here, despite father telling me he would take me some day. He gets his metal from here after it is mined further south. He's done business in this town, but as far back as I can remember I was too young for those trips. I'm sure he knows some of the local smiths."

Cat nodded, "There are several smithies here. Several more of everything, so I guess that isn't saying much. There is more competition between craftsmen. You'll buy their wares cheaper here than anything they send overseas." A moment later, she amended her comment, "Well, unless they think you are a foreigner. They have a tendency to raise the rates if that happens. They tried that on me but I figure I drove a hard bargain."

Mel found his entry into the conversation, as he often did, "I came through here a little while back. They have a way of charging me three times as much as any humans passing through town. I found an inn that seemed well worth what I paid for it. The place was well-furnished, wonderful meals, warm baths. Let me see if I can recall the name."

Even as Trestan and Petrow entertained thoughts of a good inn, Cat spoke, "I can think of some really luxurious places to stay in town, but we aren't going to any of those spots. The first time the adventurers went through town they caused confrontation at the Eagle's Nest. That is where we may stay; for I think it unlikely they would go there. I'd prefer to avoid a chance encounter with them until we have a plan. That place is nice if you pay for a private room, just for the view from the windows. The inn is close enough to the ridge that you can see the falls and a good part of the lower lands east to the ocean."

Trestan said, "Any warm bed and bath would be great. I've had hard days at work, but never such a long and fast walk as this. I only hope I can afford this trip with the coins I have on me. I set out to rescue a maiden, and it would look bad if I ended up penniless and having to walk back. Though you sound like you are charitable milady, I can't ask for you to pay our way."

"I already told you I can and will help out a lot in regards to money," responded Cat, "Even though you both would prefer to be humble and refuse it. Have nay worries if this seems against chivalry. Around the types of people I have known, chivalry is considered dead. I spend a lot of adventures not earning much coin, but every so now and then I really hit it big. I tell you my purse is deep enough for the three of us and I am not lying. That doesn't include you, Mel, you have your own means. Trestan and Petrow are here for noble purpose but simple enough beginnings, I plan to help them out accordingly with…my horse!"

Trestan stopped on the trail even as the others did, "With your horse?"

Cat halted on the trail, looking off to the side. "That's my horse over there!"

Inside a fence-enclosed pasture, an excited horse pawed the ground and trotted a fence line as it observed them. Without the dark leather saddle and bridle neither of the two young men recognized it, but Cat recognized her horse just as easily as it seemed to recognize her. She started to run up to the fence as if rejoining a long lost friend. Cat slowed, looked nervously up and down the road, worried that the presence of the horse also meant the presence of the other adventuring party. The horse stood unguarded in someone's pasture, with no danger in sight. Cat hugged her horse over the fence, and it nuzzled her in return. It also sniffed her over for food and she found some to satisfy its begging.

"Well, this is an odd turn. How did you get here?" Cat talked to her horse as she rubbed the neck. "I have been worried about you!"

While Cat attended the horse, Trestan noticed a horseman in the same meadow riding towards them. The young smith quietly pointed him out to Cat. Cat continued giving her horse attention, but said she would do the talking when the rider arrived. She made sure to stress that point to Mel. Whether the gnome really understood or not he nodded and stood back a bit. When the horseman trotted alongside the fence, they could see he was a middle-aged man who spent a lot of years in the sun. He acted friendly enough, though he had a crossbow over his back as a normal precaution.

The rider tipped his wide-brimmed, straw hat to Cat in a manner of greeting, "Fair day to you people. I am Fahjol, and I claim ownership to this ranch. Are you finding my horse interesting?"

Katressa flashed him a warm smile, often the one weapon the infiltrator ever needed. "My name is Larona. We were traveling by and I thought I recognized this horse as belonging to an acquaintance of mine. I should mention that it was stolen some days ago. You don't look to be the type who would do that."

The rider seemed taken aback by the news, "Why…er…nay Lady Larona. I just purchased this horse and one other from some men this morning. They rode up and claimed to have some gambling debts, and were looking for a quick and cheap sale. That aroused suspicion in me, but they were fine horses and I'd been looking to buy. So I paid them after looking the horses over to make sure I wasn't getting sick animals or anything. I feel sorry for your friend, but I already paid good gold on these animals."

Katressa seemed to pout a bit, "Well, I'll just tell him who he can talk to if he wants to get his horse back. I'm sure he can propose something; it's not my affair." Her face brightened a bit, and fixed pleading eyes on Fahjol. "I would be interested in a description of these men who sold you the horses. Might be someone we know and then we can find out who it was."

Trestan listened as rancher eagerly obliged. He described two men, dressed in light armor and with short swords, down to a style of earring on one and an accent on another. It was no one they recognized. Either way, Cat's horse had arrived in Barkan's Crossing, even if the main portion of the elf's party hadn't. While Cat chatted with the rancher, Trestan wondered why they might sell the two horses. The action suggested the other party had arrived at their destination, had other transport ready, or might be going somewhere horses couldn't. His thoughts returned to the present as Cat and the rider bid each other farewell and good luck.

After a friendly handshake with Fahjol, Katressa turned her back on her horse and walked back towards the path. There was a moment's hesitation as Trestan and Petrow cast glances between the retreating half-elf and her seemingly abandoned mount. Mel simply followed Katressa, keeping his mouth shut. The rider stayed near the horse a bit longer, watching them as they moved away from the ranch. The party from Troutbrook was well out of earshot when Trestan spoke next.

"Milady, you do realize you left your horse behind?" Trestan asked, "Are you not going to reclaim it?"

Cat smiled slyly, "The town is right up ahead on the ridge. The way I see things, I now know where my horse is, and it has free room and board."

Mel interpreted that as a cue to once again speak freely, as he was much accustomed to doing, "The men he described could be some of the men that passed me yesterday. It has me wondering where the more obvious ones were hiding. This group may have a habit of splitting and reforming considering what you also told me."

Cat thought about it. "I guess with the attention they drew to themselves last time, it was best not to have the minotaur and the cleric give them away to anyone asking about them. That's logical enough, considering they had to know someone would follow them. I don't know where they may have left the trail, but we know they came this far. The fact that they nay longer needed the horses provides an interesting clue to the mystery and puzzle of where they are heading. We'll ask if anyone at the entry to town saw them, but I know what they are going to say."

*   *   *   *   *

"Nay, none meeting that description passed this way," the guard assured them. "I was made known of their appearance a few days ago, and am well aware of the commotion they caused within our town limits. They will not be allowed re-entry, unless they gave up the elf for questioning and left the minotaur behind."

With the sun hovering around its highest point in the sky, the companions stood before the guards in sparse shade offered by the overhanging roof and nearby trees. The North Road guard station consisted of a ramshackle building serving as a temporary post. Due to the city's expansion, the government frequently had to build new guard stations further and further out. The companions counted five guards, flanking an official tax collector. Trestan and Petrow felt their stomachs growl at the sight of the noonmeal the guards enjoyed. The gray-bearded taxman sat at his own small table in the shade, a box and ledger before him. He wore no armor nor weapon except the quill in his hand. He had the habit of fanning himself with a peacock-feather fan, despite his costly robes being lighter than the leather armor in which the guards perspired. The lieutenant in charge, bearing ringmail and a large mace, addressed their questions. Trestan and Petrow gave their feet a rest by sitting on some hay bales used to supply mounted militia. Mel actually started poking into the guards' food, until their protests caused him to sulk beside the two humans. So far, Katressa had done most of the talking.

She nodded as the lieutenant answered, expecting that somehow the adventurers bypassed the town. "Some guards from Troutbrook used horses to try to catch up with them. Did you see those guards pass through?"

The lieutenant paused a bit before answering. He looked the half-elf up and down before deciding there was no harm in the question. "They arrived at a late hour last night.

They got the same reply we gave you. Nay sign of the ones you are talking about. So, that band caused some trouble up north as well?"

Cat nodded, "I'm not sure their intent, but they ended up kidnapping Lord Tessald's daughter. They rode this way and are somewhere in this area. This gnome saw her with them last afternoon, and she was still their hostage."

Up to that point the guards ate their lunch with their eyes on the road. At the mention of a kidnapped noble, all ears perked up and took notice. That was certainly big news and a potential high reward to rescue such a prize. The lieutenant looked on with amazement. "The Troutbrook guards didn't mention that! Nay wonder there was such a large pursuit. They may have mentioned it to my superiors. After we were unable to provide clues to those villains' whereabouts, they continued into town to rest for the night."

Cat replied, "Fair enough, sir, and I thank you for enlightening me. I had a personal interest in this as they stole from me as well." She half-turned to include the other guards in her gaze. "Should you find any more news, or rumors, I would be interested. I know you have your duty to perform, but I would also try to offer a bonus that is worth your while."

She started to move past the post. Trestan, Petrow and Mel rose to follow. The taxman cleared his throat pointedly loud. The lieutenant and the guards blocked their passage. The lieutenant spoke, "As with many people entering town, we charge an entry fee. But the details of that fee I leave to the representative of our local government." He nodded to indicate the collector.

Cat turned to regard the lushly dressed graybeard. "Entry fee? But privateers in the employ of the Protectorate are charged nay such fees!"

The taxman pointed to indicate each of them in turn. "You have shown me your writ of employ, but I have not seen one from the others. My supervisors make it very clear on which parties I can and can't accept taxes. The gnome looks the part of a privateer as well, therefore I can accept him free just by the weight of your writ, young lady. However, we have problems with local lads tagging along with adventuring groups just to get into town free and drink themselves to excess in our taverns. This is not welcomed by the fathers or the rest of the community. These two look the part of farmer lads, and unless they have writs they must pay a traveler's fee of a copper drab each. That is standard fare for most that enter the gates."

Katressa did not argue, instead she nodded and fished in her own pouch for the change needed. Trestan and Petrow tried to move quickly to pay for themselves, but the half-elf proved faster. The taxman nodded his satisfaction. They were allowed to head into town as he scrawled the new total into the ledger. The companions left the guardhouse behind as they entered the fringes of the town. Trestan frowned at his own ragged and dirty clothes as they walked. It amazed him that the two poor boys in the group had to pay to get into town, as opposed to getting left outside with the goblins, yet the richer members of the group were allowed in with few questions asked.

Several minutes later they indulged a meal under the pavilion tent of a farmers' market. There wasn't much of a selection that early in the growing season, but it was a good change from the bland food they had on the road. It gave them a chance to sit and discuss their options. Trestan enjoyed the sights of the town, but the urgency of their quest pushed at the back of his mind. He was eager to hear Cat's suggestions, though she was interrupted and annoyed by their gnome companion. Somehow the gnome went from talking about the foot sores on the two young men, into a talk about various ugly battle wounds he had seen. The discussion soured their taste of the food. It also served to scare Petrow a bit, though he tried hard to ignore to the gnome.

Trestan finally interrupted before Cat said anything rash, "I think we need to decide our next move. We have to ask around a bit right? Maybe someone else has seen anything out of the ordinary."

Petrow nodded, "There is the matter of our hometown guards. Are they still around or did they find any clues?"

Cat thought it over. "We do need to ask around, though if we tarry too long we may lose their trail anyway. We will need to split up to cover more ground faster. I figure the Eagle's Nest would be a good meeting spot, since it would be ridiculous of them to go around that place again."

Mel looked at Cat. "What would you like me to do?"

Trestan imagined Cat had been waiting for that moment all day. The half-elf answered, "First, you can head over to the south gate and find out if the Troutbrook guards left town by that route or not. See if the guards at that gate had a clue where the armsmen were going. Find out if the other party headed that way, and if they haven't, ask around at the pubs and other public places. We'll meet at the Eagle's Nest, or leave a message there if either of us finds anything."

Mel nodded eagerly, "I sure can do that, nay problem. Just start a conversation and work some questions into it somehow." At this, the two young men watched Cat roll her eyes. Certainly she had just unleashed a talkative gnome into an unsuspecting town. Mel continued, "What will you do?"

Cat answered, "Find these two young men some new shoes and maybe some other clothing as well. They are embarking to rescue a lady of nobility, so they should look the part. Or, if the worst happens, be well dressed for their funeral."

Trestan and Petrow both expressed smiles at the idea of new tunics and trousers. That excitement was short lived as they realized Cat spoke seriously about the possibility of them being buried in their new clothes. Cat continued, "The Eagle's Nest has some rooms sizeable for four people if someone is willing to pay their price, and I will. Hopefully one is available. We'll secure a room there and leave your name with the tavern keeper. I think formal baths may have to wait, but we can wash up a bit before we venture out again. A trip around the merchants will also give us a chance to garner information."

*   *   *   *   *

After parting ways with the gnome sorcerer, the other three went to the inn and procured a room. Cat admitted Mel was irritating her with his constant talking and his varied but useless subjects. Upon arrival at the inn they discovered, to Cat's delight, a large room available for the night. The companions didn't stay long enough for any drinks or food. They rented the room and washed their hands, feet and faces clean of roadside dirt.

81

They opened the shutters to observe a breathtaking view of the lands below the high ridge. The saw the lake well below their window; a wide river exiting out through the lowlands and to the sea. Numerous ships occupied the lake. They could not see the waterfall from their window, just the mist coming from it as it plunged down. They could hear a distant roar from the thundering falls. After standing there and reflecting the beauty of it, for the two young humans had never seen such a spectacle, they pulled away from the window to get on with their plans. There was a lock on the room door, but Cat advised they leave nothing valuable behind while they were out. She informed them that many thieves could make a living "investigating" what adventurers leave in their rooms.

The three of them visited merchant after merchant. Some vendors operated from rented spots in open markets, hawking wares from bulging carts; others were established inside large buildings. The inner hub of the town contained the biggest market area, surrounded by the old, innermost walls. Trestan and Petrow were amazed and flattered at the amount of gold Cat spent. She not only gave them a fair amount of coins, but also dropped several silvers towards information that seemed to yield nothing in regards to the other adventuring party. They discovered that the guards from Troutbrook rode southwards out of the town gates that morning. While this news discouraged the companions, the person who had given them the information had no clue as to what the guards had been doing, and thus if they had any trail on their prey.

Cat insisted on doing the talking and bribing. While she questioned, Trestan and Petrow were free to set their minds to shopping. They soon focused on little else, as if they were children let loose to play. For both, shopping for clothes was not commonly done unless they needed to or had the extra cash. A chest full of clothes would have been a luxury for either one. They tried forestalling Cat's attempts at charity, but she pushed gold into their hands while they stood among the nicest wardrobes they had ever seen. Leather vests and boots, metal studded coats, velvet shirts, silks from Tariyka and rings of gold with exquisite designs conspired to melt their resolve. Trestan and Petrow held on to some frugality, passing up some wondrous clothes Cat offered to buy. They walked down long lines of merchant stalls displaying the best that the local tradesmen had to offer. All the while, Cat chatted and dug up information in the background, while the two young men laughed as they looked at items.

Trestan searched for a sturdy leather belt to replace the length of rope he used. Petrow looked over shoes and boots to comfort his weary feet. Both men purchased those items and gawked at the next luxury. When they returned to denying Cat's generosity, she assured them it wasn't hurting her purse at all. She often bought new clothes just as they were doing, as adventures wore down her old garments and new coins came her way after the hard work. Even as they shopped, the half-elf stopped to purchase a hair clasp.

She stated, "It's too much time and effort to mess with my hairstyle when I often wear a helmet. Hair clasps and similar jewelry are easy options."

Although Cat never seemed to lose focus on their mission, the young men relaxed and indulged themselves. Cat smiled secretly at their enjoyment. Helping these two men buy the best outfits they had ever owned, talking and laughing as they did, was medicine for her own soul. Trestan and Petrow lived for the moment, buying things they couldn't afford before, and laughing at the items they decided not to buy.

"Good gods, Petrow," exclaimed Trestan, "You can buy several good shirts and another pair of shoes for the price of that coat! Summer is coming, and you want to wear that?"

Petrow held the colorful coat up and inspected it. "I'm just looking and imagining. It would be nice to wear when I go out and chop firewood in the winter months."

The young smith looked over the other garments Petrow bought and one other set he considered buying. "How many colors have you accumulated in one outfit anyhow? In what time of the season do orange, light green, tan, blue and dark red actually look good when arranged like that?"

"It's better than the drab outfits I've been wearing. It's practical too; this one has an abundance of pockets." Petrow took a last look at the coat, sighed, and returned it to the merchant. "I see what you mean. It's nothing I need, but it looks good."

Cat sidled up to them, appearing quietly by their sides like she often did. "You two picked out good items. Do you have everything you need? Good shirts? New packs?"

Trestan hefted the leather backpack that replaced his burlap bag. Inside were more trousers, shirts and other garments. He still wore his old shoes, though a new pair was tied to his pack. Petrow carried as many items as Trestan did; yet his were more elaborate or excessive. Petrow craved stunning colors, plentiful decorations, lacy shirtsleeves, even colorful trim on the pants and vest. They stood together going over what they had bought, even as the waning sunlight painted the clouds in evening shades. They pulled the edges of clothing out of their packs to let their generous companion see the different colors and nice materials. They had expended a lot of silver and gold in their eyes, though if Cat minded, she did not show it. The half-elf must have wanted it, as she had pushed the coins right into their hands at every turn.

She listened to their excitement and looked at their equipment as they described it. They shared a laugh over some of the selections, particularly Petrow's. When they were done, she posed one question. "What are you missing?"

The young men of Troutbrook looked to her and then to themselves for an answer. Both tallied their equipment in their minds, thinking if they had forgotten anything of importance. Petrow ventured a guess after some thought. "Well, we could stock up on more rations. Oh! I wanted to get my own mug! There was a tent over by the wall selling some with nice patterns."

Trestan shook his head. "I don't think that's what she meant. I have everything I could ever have wanted on me right now. I would be a fashionable figure walking down the streets of my hometown with these garments."

Katressa Bilil nodded her agreement, "You would make a fine, handsome figure on the streets of your hometown…but you are not heading to a fanciful affair. You may be going into more battles, in your rescue of someone in distress. Everything you could have wanted as a smith or laborer you might own, but to play the part of a warrior, you need protection."

The half-elf allowed that thought to sink into the heads of her two human companions. She pointed over one street, towards the sound of a ringing hammer and the heat of a forge's fire. "We need to find you some good leather armor at the very least. You might consider some metal chain; though I assure you the lightest chain tunic actually tends to get quite heavy on a long walk."

Trestan had tried on metal armor at his father's smithy. Petrow had even modeled a suit or two. Both knew how to don it, though neither had ever worn it for anything other than modeling it for Hebden Karok. Now they both moved to pick out a suit of armor that would be their own protection against the battles that might follow.

*   *   *   *   *

Katressa spent the extra coin to have a tub pulled into their private room for her use. Petrow and Trestan bathed in a common bathing room on the first floor of the inn. A serving boy brought warmed water and soap. Trestan used a small mirror to shave the stubble on his cheeks. Humble as his mustache was, he took some vanity in trimming around it and trying to make it look better. Both men eagerly soaked their suffering feet. Eventually, Cat sent word she finished her bath and that the rented room was available. Petrow finished his quick bath, donned a towel and disappeared up the private stairs connecting the bath room to the upstairs beds. Petrow declared his eagerness to Trestan to wear one of his new outfits for dinner. Trestan had many thoughts from his journey on the road, and so lingered in the tub to sort them out.

He thought back to the places he had passed during the last two days. Despite the task before them and the hard pace they followed, there had been an abundance of wonderful landscapes to admire. Blooming flowers, lush meadows, animals, and creeks full of fish. In other circumstances, it would have been an unquestionably beautiful trip.

As Trestan thought back to those scenic places, he tried to imagine them from Lady Shauntay's eyes. He tried to imagine her being dragged or carried across the same terrain. He could picture the soles of her feet bloody, or her arms bruised from restraints. Her eyes might have even been closed to shut away the nightmare around her, while she hoped for a rescue. His heart went out to her plight, for if anything he felt further away from helping her than he had in Troutbrook.

He thought back to every resting point along the road, when he could lay his head down to rest and pause the long walk. Even as he remembered the quiet moments on the road, his mind brought forth images of the torment Lady Shauntay must have endured. Like him, she would forever see the face of a dear friend frozen in death. Trestan could only assume she saw Sahbin as a good friend, such as he viewed Sir Wilhelm. The young man often found the image of his dead mentor's face lingering on his thoughts. He could only imagine how Lady Shauntay felt after losing Sahbin in such a terrible way. Trestan recoiled at the thought of being tied and thrown over a minotaur's shoulder. Even when she walked, she must have been forced along at a fast pace, without a gnomish salve to heal her feet. Trestan sat staring at the far wall, alone in his thoughts.

Had she been beaten? Had she been raped?

The young smith almost cried at the thought. Despite their pursuit, the young noble had been at the mercy of her captors for most of two days. Had it really been only two days? Katressa had ridden into town on the 24th of Florum. The fight on the street had been at a point when Nirahha was in the pinnacle of the night sky, signifying midnight. On the 25th of Florum they walked until finding the gnome's camp. Today, the 26th day of the month, they fought the goblins and eventually arrived in Barkan's Crossing. So much had happened in so little time.

During much of the walk, when Trestan had not spoken, his mind traveled to the next hill or turn. He had visualized coming upon the other band around every blind hill, catching them unprepared. Trestan imagined the battle before him several times during the journey. Cat's bolts would speed past his head to hit a vital spot on the minotaur. The young smith would swing a blow with the elf sword to behead the dark cleric that had paralyzed him. He imagined completing the turn, and coming face to face with the elven wizard. Yelling, "For Abriana and Jareth", he would stab through the heart. Revwar would not thank his gods; he would merely die cursing on the end of the sharp elvish blade. Then Trestan imagined a grateful lady of noble blood, running to him and kissing her hero. Trestan replayed the battle at least five different ways and with five different endings, but the final kiss remained in each outcome. The way Trestan remembered many good ballads, all good stories ended with the kiss of a lovely lady.

Yet, every turn and valley did not yield the opposing band. Miles went by and events showed him the truth of his inexperience. The past two days he had looked up to Cat as his new mentor and instructor, as well as his friend. The half-elf bonded with them. He could see it in her eyes when she tried to hide her fears of what would happen to him and Petrow if they actually faced that band. Trestan's misadventures charging the clearing and stepping on a rock during battle forced him to think realistically. He had to admit courage alone did not make the hero. His muscles and stamina couldn't match the minotaur. His will alone wouldn't shield him from spells or dark miracles.

The minor injuries of his past seemed trivial when he recalled the image of Sahbin catapulted through the air, away from her severed arm. Sir Wilhelm had been severely injured as well, yet regained his feet to fight again. Even Cat displayed a reservoir of strength Trestan wasn't sure he could claim. She fought the Tariykan one on one and by her own admission lost. If it hadn't been for the miraculous healing potions, she could have been dying in the streets of Troutbrook hoping clerics would get to her in time.

He imagined facing Loung Chao over a short distance, with the Tariykan pointing his blowgun and ready to fire. Could Trestan avoid that deadly missile and beat an opponent who nearly killed Cat? The cleric of the Goddess of Death had been very formidable. How could he make sure of a strike against a cleric that needed only a touch to render him helpless? If the minotaur charged him, would he be able to stand toe-to-toe against its muscles like Jareth did? He could imagine Revwar, silver hair whipping about his shoulders as his yellow eyes stared coldly at the young smith. A trio of phantom swords would fly at him, or a shaft of energy would cut through the air. Trestan faced the question of whether he could take a hit from any one of these four enemies or their unknown henchmen. With the young man's own blood pouring out, could he still find the energy to strike the killing blow that would save the day?

Trestan had been sitting in the cold water of the tub for some time. The water sent a shiver through him, a cold reminder of the fears whispering in his mind. Whether it was grief or vengeance, the wounds in his heart remained unhealed until drawn to a proper conclusion. Trestan could only hope that if the moment came, he could find the strength to accomplish whatever needed to be done. Whatever the outcome, he held the goodness of Sir Wilhelm's teachings close to heart. His brown eyes looked up to the dark rafters of the ceiling, heart reaching out to one far above him. He asked Abriana for guidance. Trestan prayed some good would come of his dangerous path. He found it hard to bear the thought of Cat or Petrow dying, and realized he would give his own life if it came to saving one of them. The young man took comfort in his willingness to die for a good cause. As the quality of metal was judged by the consuming power of fire, his life could be weighed by facing danger. Sir Wilhelm often viewed life as merely a test for the next realm. Trestan didn't intend to fail it by shying away.

Trestan tried to push bad thoughts away. Tonight may be the only chance he'd get to wear fine clothes out to supper. He clothed himself in fresh new garments for the first time in over a year. The colors were plain, but the fabric was extravagant. An eye-catching, dark-red shirt went on first. Gray pants and black leather shoes followed. Trestan went up the back stairs to finish dressing in his room. Petrow opened the door for him. After being so poor for so long, Petrow's newly bought outfit stood out with bright colors. He even had elaborate peacock feathers coming out of a hat. His lace and ruffles could have been accused of imitating the nobility, if only he had jewelry to complete the appearance. Although the blue-eyed man also bought simpler travel clothes, he dressed as fine as could be for tonight.

Trestan considered the gray vest that matched the pants, but he decided to abandon it in favor of wearing something more important to him. For once in his life, Trestan could dress like the adventurers passing through Troutbrook. The young smith had bought some armor that started with basic leather, yet also had metal pieces to protect key areas of the body. Wearing a vest underneath would add to the heat of the outfit, and with the armor the vest would not even be seen. Trestan donned the armor piece by piece, from the torso protection to the strap-on bracers and greaves. Trestan simply tucked his rawhide gloves into his new, sturdy belt. The young smith hoped he would never again be dependent on a simple rope to hold up his trousers. The armor came with a metal helmet, featuring a thin visor that lowered to protect the lower parts of the face. Trestan decided to forgo the helm, preferring to spend some time fussing about his hair to make sure he looked as handsome as ever. Trestan put on a baldric, which held Sword of the Spirit over his back. The handle of the elven blade stood visible over Trestan's shoulder, ready for action should he ever need it. The young smith wasn't about to let his most important possession be left behind in an unguarded room.

Petrow often asked Trestan his opinion on his own look, and he offered suggestions and help with the young smith's armor. The two of them fussed and changed their minds many times. Petrow considered taking his brand new axe down to the dining room as well,

86

but he eventually changed his mind. It was a well-made waraxe, with a handle as long as his old axe, but Petrow did not have a covering for the blade. It rest on the bed next to Petrow's old axe. Petrow also bought armor: a simple leather jerkin and bracers. He hadn't felt comfortable with the heavier metal armor. One other addition to Petrow's arsenal was a quartet of small, balanced throwing axes. Cat had giggled when she saw them, remembering the goblin incident. To the two young men a crossbow was as unfamiliar to them as most other weapons. Petrow had thrown small axes before in friendly competition, so it seemed a logical choice for him. Petrow decided that for dinner, he would take nothing more than his simple knife, belted on a new harness.

When the two men finished, they walked into the upper hallway of the inn, facing a mirror mounted on the wall. Only candlelight illuminated the image, but the two men stared at their reflections with wonder. They felt such a transition in their appearance from the new clothes. The young humans felt that even their facial expressions had changed in some subtle way.

Petrow straightened out some imagined wrinkle in his sleeves and summed up what both were thinking, "Tres, there are two strangers staring back at us."

"Aye, Petrow," Trestan replied, "And if you recall, we laughed over people dressed like you are right now."

The handyman playfully slapped his friend while the smith chuckled. Petrow considered the reflections in the mirror as he spoke again. "This was a short journey compared to what adventurers go through, Tres. Imagine, how changed we might be if we walked all the way to far-off Orlaun?"

Trestan dropped his head slightly, "Who says we won't walk all the way to Orlaun? Tonight we might find out, depending on if the gnome found anything."

Petrow paused a moment, contemplating his thoughts. "If this has all been for naught, then we might as well enjoy this night before walking back to face our hometown."

Trestan nodded, "I hope Mel found something. Even if he did, I'll be wondering what we could possibly hope to do to change things. It seems like we can't win either way, but I try to think the effort we put forth must be worth something. I'd hate to come this far for naught."

Petrow turned a grin to his friend, "Dwell not on the dark possibilities. We're here, Tres! We've had all day to travel the shops of one of the biggest towns in this part of the country! Even better, led by a hostess with a bottomless purse, willing to pay our way. I can see concerns in your eyes. Believe me, I've had my doubts a good part of this trip. I will not let you take this moment away from me. This day has been one of the best that either of us could have asked! After being the boy who works for coppers all my life in my hometown, I finally walked through a rich town and picked what I wanted from the merchants. This is luxury!"

Trestan's face went unreadable, "So we enjoyed luxuries today? We shopped like nobles?"

Petrow thought he caught sarcasm in his friend's voice, but continued with genuine happiness, "Aye my friend!"

"And where is the noble?" Trestan retorted sharply, with more venom than intended, "Lady Shauntay spends the days as a slave, if she even still draws breath. For all we know…she might be laying injured or worse! She might even…"

Trestan's raised tone suddenly faltered. He stifled any forthcoming words and tried to choke back his fears. Petrow stood back from Trestan, unsure how to respond to the outburst. The childhood friends had come on a hard journey from the home they had known all their lives. Even as they looked at each other and stared at their reflections in the mirror, they saw their old friend. There were differences, evidenced in the clothes they wore and attitudes after the long road. At the same time, under those layers of expensive clothing, they were young men growing up in ways they didn't expect.

Petrow put an arm around Trestan's shoulder. The younger man welcomed the contact. "I'm not saying you can't grieve or worry. But life comes on two sides of a coin, Tres. You can't have the lucky side without the unlucky side, and if the lucky side happens to shine in your favor and brightens one day, you should live that day to the fullest."

Trestan put his face in his hands, rubbing tired eyes. After drawing a deep breath, he raised his face looking more collected, though not completely at peace. "I still feel guilty for some reason. One of my good friends, a man I really respected, was murdered in front of me. Others died that night. All of those people had goals in life. A woman, most beautiful, was taken against her will. She may still draw breath, but if so, she is likely living a harder life than you and I ever had as 'commoners'. How can I be so close to such events and yet feel relaxed and at peace?"

It took Petrow a moment to collect his thoughts and answer his friend's query. "Well, you just have to realize and face the fact there is nothing you can do *at this moment*. You don't have to soften your resolve, but instead you have to be reasonable with yourself. Let me tell you a story."

Petrow drew himself up straighter, recalling something from many years ago. "I can't help but be happy that I could dress up today. Neither of us has ever had it so well. But I do remember when someone showed me a lot of charity at a time when my world looked dark. You may remember my parents both died one winter when I was young. There were nay relatives to take care of me. The house reduced to burnt cinders in the snow. Troutbrook as a whole adopted me and made sure I had a roof over my head every night. In return, I grew up helping people with chores and their jobs. The church took me in some nights and made use of my labor, but they wouldn't keep me and I wouldn't stay there. That path wasn't for me. I guess the other labor set me up to be the town's handyman, seeing as I had already been there my whole life helping with one job or another."

Trestan patiently listened to his friend's story. The older youth continued, "Growing older, it wasn't as easy for folks to let me sleep over some nights. Sometimes I spent the night sleeping in a store; the guard on watch, I guess. Sometimes I put in my work for the day, and those I helped got me a room at the inn those nights. The village always put a roof over my head, but I grew tired of going from place to place like that. One day my mind settled on the task to build a new house on the cleared, blackened area where the old house once stood. I swore I would spend nay more nights under any roof but my own.

88

Maybe I was thirteen back then, yet I stubbornly set out to build the supports and planned to at least have a roof over my head that night.

"After a day of walking around the village and working for people to gather junk to use as supplies, I had about eight pieces of wood that were all different lengths, several used nails but nay hammer, and a monster headache. I was lying out on the ground next to my haphazard pile of supplies as evening came. Sir Wilhelm brought out some blankets and camped with me under the stars. I felt miserable, yet he visited my spot, started a fire, and over my protests he roasted some meat and shared a meal with me. My mind couldn't calm down due to my frustration. He told me to relax and share the food with him. He was a great man, Tres, and while I fretted he acted like a father to me and got me to enjoy a fire under an open night sky. Guess what he told me that helped to settle my nerves?"

Trestan shook his head, "I have nay clue what he said or where this is all going."

Petrow took out a copper penny, "He tossed a coin into the air, but didn't show me whether it landed crown or castle. He looked at me and said, 'Life comes on two sides of a coin, Petrow. You can't have the lucky side without the unlucky side, and you can't control which one turns up at a flick of the wrist. Most important though, if the lucky side shines in your favor and brightens one evening by sharing a warm blanket and meat under a scenic starlit sky, you need to relax and enjoy it.'"

Trestan cracked a smile, "So that's where you came up with that bit of lucky coin wisdom!"

"Aye, told by one of the wisest men we ever knew. I'm glad I finally relaxed and shared laughs with him that night; I needed my strength the next day. Jareth grabbed a bunch of strong townsmen and supplies. After a hard day of work I spent the next night and every night thereafter under my own roof. That first night about all I had was a roof and some beams holding it up, but it was a roof. If Jareth were here right now, he wouldn't want us to suffer with worries. Tonight, you have a chance to eat well and sleep in a soft bed. We have this chance to rest up, for tomorrow we may need to run or fight, and we'll need our strength. I bet you never swing that smithy hammer so well when your strength is taxed by lack of sleep, or your mind weighted by worry. We should take what the night offers us. It may be the gods giving us this gift to regain our will for the task ahead."

Trestan nodded, smiling over Petrow's tale, "You're right. Give me a moment to collect myself and I shall go down."

Petrow considered Trestan's motives, deciding to give his friend the time he needed. "Ok, I'll head down. You follow as soon as you can, my friend."

Trestan wore a restored grin when Petrow turned to head down the stairs to the common room of the inn. The young smith took a moment to study his reflection in the mirror. He straightened his outfit, brushed away specks of dust. Looking every bit a gentleman, he turned and strode down the stairs with renewed vigor.

CHAPTER 7

Trestan walked downstairs into a light veil of smoke. Apparently, the locals in this pub favored smoking as much as Troutbrook's residents liked fishing. The heavy aromas of different pipe weeds saturated the air, assaulting the noses of anyone unused to the smell. Some of the scents were quite enticing and sweet, but the overall barrage forced Trestan to choke and clear his throat before he could go further. The smith had never been a smoker, figuring he got enough in his lungs from furnaces and other fires. Looking past the wisps of pipe smoke he could see patrons filling the room. From his vantage he could not spot his friends, but he couldn't see into all the dark corners from the stairway. The candles and hearth fire offered barely enough light to reveal anything in the dim room. The young man moved to the crowded bar instead, planning to resume his search after proper refreshment. He found a spot and ordered from the barkeep.

From out of Cat's description, Trestan spotted the dwarf bouncer who must have suffered the indignities of Revwar's cruel spells. He was the only dwarf in the bar. If a name had been mentioned, Trestan had forgotten it. The dwarf certainly looked as if he could crush any elf with his bare hands if given the chance. He stood maybe four feet tall yet seemed every bit as wide. The short figure wore no armor over his chest, just a shirt with short sleeves to show off his arms. The young smith had never seen such well-muscled arms in his life, with the exception of the minotaur. The dwarf's brown eyes complimented his thick, brown beard. Hair on the side of his head had been braided down to the level of his beard, ending in charms resembling a hammer and axe. Though his chest was unprotected by anything more than cloth and muscle, he did have a helm and wore metal bracers on his arms. He occasionally spared a quick grin to regular guests of the inn, though mostly his eyes stayed stern and serious. The dwarf constantly scanned the room for anything that might disrupt the peaceful nature of the evening. Trestan met his gaze for a moment and found himself on the receiving end of a challenging glare. It occurred to the young man the dwarf remained angry at being the public recipient of Revwar's incapacitating spells. With such being the case, the blatant stare of a newcomer was probably someone who came to see the dwarf and enjoy mirth over the half-week-old incident. The young man quickly turned his attention elsewhere.

Trestan found a suitable distraction in another corner of the bar. A richly dressed dandy entertained the folk in one corner with a rhyming tale of an old hero of Kashmer. The man seemed talented, though he wasn't putting on a public performance for the sake of the whole bar. He would play a familiar tune on a panpipe between song verses, to the delight of several ladies and a few gentlemen. Trestan's attention focused more on the selected song than the man and his audience.

The young smith jumped when Petrow came up and clapped him on the shoulder. "There you are! You might want to join us sooner than later, we are over in that corner," Petrow indicated the direction, though Trestan could not see Cat or Mel.

"Soon enough, I was entranced by the tale being told over there," Trestan nodded towards the singer, "It's the song about Sir Halruth rescuing Princess Miawycke from the pirates. You and I have heard this one sung in Troutbrook before."

Petrow turned to regard the story, listening in silence for some time before talking again. "Appropriate subject, don't you think? If we rescue that noble lady, do you think they would sing a song about us?"

Trestan smirked, "I doubt it. Minstrels find it easier to write a song about the knight of noble blood rescuing a lady of equally noble blood, especially when they eventually married and had many children together."

Petrow nodded, turning his attention back to the song. The local musician finished, to the applause of several people. Despite calls for more tales, the singer indulged his dry throat with wine, then flirted with a local maid. The handyman of Troutbrook took that as a cue they should get back to the table. "Still, one must be allowed to indulge certain fantasies. Let us continue our night with the others."

Trestan picked up his drink and made ready to follow. The young smith shrugged sadly, "I have been fantasizing since we left town, but I am mired in reality too many times. What I should be doing now is bugging you about if Mel found any information."

"That's a dumb question," Petrow replied, "The gnome is a fountain of information, most of it useless and irrelevant! I'll tell you right now though, he didn't get any farther than we did."

Trestan felt his shoulders sink and his look of disappointment must have showed. Petrow added, "But he did learn the Troutbrook guards didn't find anything either. They simply rode south hoping to pick up the trail. For all we know, the other party may still be anywhere in the area. Mel thought they might be hoping to catch a ship due to the presumed sailors joining them. A talk with the harbormaster down by the lake revealed nothing odd. You might want to be more worried about…well…"

"Aye?"

Petrow led Trestan through the crowd, though the smith pushed Petrow in a way that gave a wide berth around the dwarf bouncer. The handyman continued, "When I left to find you Mel was grinding Cat's nerves. He talked on and on and got off subject a few times. You could see Cat was getting ready to say or do something nasty."

They came within sight of their two companions; Trestan saw immediately that the situation seemed tense at the booth where they waited. Cat sat on Mel's side of the booth, but stuck against the wall where there was no escape from his talking. She held a hand up to cover her face, and was pointedly staring away from the gnome. Trestan saw the hint of a frown in the corner of her mouth. Mel Bellringer, of the Bellringer family, talked animatedly, waving his arms, and displayed an angry scowl. At times it seemed as if he wasn't talking to Cat, but rather directing his comments to someone unseen above him, loud enough that the half-elf could not help but hear him.

They overheard part of the gnome's rant as they approached, "…but if you have good advice, or you go about doing as she asks, I guess don't bother talking to her. NAY! She likes her silence and privacy! Nay cares in the world about a helpful gnome that spent the whole day scurrying about and trying to find the answer to her questions! I guess it is just, 'Shut up until I give you permission to speak', that is how she is!"

Cat interrupted, still facing away from the gnome, her expression hidden by her hand. "That is not what I said!"

91

The gnome wheeled about in his seat and pointed an accusing finger at her, though she didn't see it. "But you meant it, you meant it! Let's all ignore the lonely soul who came along to help because we don't want to listen to his helpful information. You just use me for my magic skills. You don't give one wit about any advice I offer freely."

Petrow glanced back at Trestan to make sure he noticed what was going on at the booth. The young smith nodded with a frown. Both could tell that the evening wasn't promising to go well. The smith whispered to his friend, "Tell me when the coin flips back to the lucky side again."

Mel quieted momentarily when the two young men approached the table. Petrow sat first, squeezing up against the wall and allowing Trestan the open portion of the booth, leaving him straight across from the gnome. The young men settled into their seats without a word. Uncomfortable silence dominated for a few breaths as they faced each other over the narrow table surface. Cat lifted an imploring look at them as if she needed support. Her fine-angled elf features were drawn into a frown. Neither human was sure what she expected of them. Trestan searched for something to say, but couldn't think of anything appropriate.

Mel took the initiative during the silent period. He looked up at Trestan and asked straightforward, "Do you think I prattle on too much?"

Trestan sat stunned, pinned by the direct question and scrambling for a polite response. The small gnome just stared with hurt eyes. The smith put on a nice smile and stumbled on trying to find some words. Mel didn't wait for an answer; the awkward moment of silence had given him the answer he feared.

"You do! You do think I talk too much!" Mel exclaimed, throwing his arms up. "I can see you have a hard time trying to answer me, but your opinion is clear on your face!"

The gnome pouted, taking a big drink of ale. Trestan shifted uncomfortably in his seat, not sure how to respond. Petrow's reaction was less than helpful: he turned his head to some interesting cracks in the wall and quietly sipped his drink. The young handyman tried to blend in with the seat, though the bright colors of his clothes would have made that impossible. Cat still covered her face from the gnome's view, but it was obvious she regretted whatever she said to upset him. The evening had looked to be full of promise in regards to nice clothes and food, but the tension within the companions spoiled the atmosphere.

The smith attempted to cheer the gnome. "You're a valuable part of the party, Mel. Sure, you have quite a few tales to spin, but I've learned a lot from listening. I'm glad to have you with us."

The gnome let loose a sniffle before responding, "Sure, you say that now! I can see what's coming. It's the story of my life. Nay person wants my company. My god abandoned me, my family exiled me, and nothing has gone right!"

Trestan put a hand on the gnome's, "Oh come now! I can't believe nay people or family would want you around. Why would your family exile you?"

As soon as he asked it, Cat sent a sharp glare in his direction. Trestan felt he understood the meaning, "Thanks, now he's going to answer that with a big, long story again!" She was right.

Mel began reminiscing, and to the embarrassment of the trio from Troutbrook he started to cry as he spoke. "My family brought me up to continue the Bellringer name. I spent time with my pa trying to make bells and chimes, but I never got good at it. Every time I thought I had a nice one, it was a little bent, out of tune, or some other flaw. I couldn't make a decent bell to save my life!"

Mel paused to draw a handkerchief from a pouch and blow his sorrows into it. This attracted some attention from the other people at nearby tables. With tears in his eyes, he continued, "So here I was a failure at the family name. An embarrassment to my father! One day, another curse found its way to my doorstep. It wasn't my choice to be gifted with magic, and to make it worse there were times when some raw power would be channeled accidentally. A rat chased my sister on top of a stool one day. She screamed for me to kill it. Rats are nothing to you humans, but to a gnome child those vermin can be a real monster! I tried to shoo it away when suddenly a bolt of power shot from my hands and splattered rat pieces all over the living room! I have nay clue what I even said; I was just trying to make scary noises."

Tavern patrons snuck glances as the gnome outright bawled at the table. Trestan tried to keep a polite, friendly smile, despite the spectacle. Mel continued, "You think my sister would listen to me and help clean up before my parents found out, but nay! She ran to them to tell them what happened. My father came in and I was still trying to clean rat blood off of mom's favorite seat cushion. I'm not sure if he knew how he should react but he didn't take the news well. I had a few other magical 'accidents' and before you know it my father is giving me supplies and kicking me out the door to go find my future elsewhere. Oh, he tried to make it sound like he was just pushing me to find my career as a magic man, but he kicked me out of the house.

Mel's arms waved as fast as his tongue waggled. "I went and learned from the teachers I could find. When I first met adventure I proved unready for the task. Nothing went right for me for a long time. I remember getting knocked on the ground by a goblin in a fight one day, then healed by a cleric and back on my feet, then knocked on my butt again by the same goblin! I tell you, when sorcerers end up within reach of an enemy sword, we need something better on our side to keep us from getting split in two! Anyway, I got robbed shortly after…despite being so helpful giving directions to that seemingly nice, old lady. One day I tried to rescue a dwarf trapped in a collapsed tunnel. Let me tell you, a shrink potion got him unstuck, but they don't take kindly to such magic! I don't think my kneecaps have ever recovered!"

Trestan noticed that Cat had her second hand covering her mouth, trying to hold back laughter. He didn't turn his head to see Petrow, but he could feel his friend next to him quivering as he too tried to stifle a laugh. Trestan tried his best to keep a straight face while he consoled Mel Bellringer in the midst of the confusingly abbreviated tale. The nearby inn patrons, astonished and staring at the crying gnome, weren't sure how to react to him. Oblivious to the rest; Mel struggled to lay bare his whole sad story.

Mel brightened a bit at this point, "But that same adventure with the dwarves brought me to a new deity. A strong dwarven god blessed me and showed faith in me! Ever since, my life has been better! I stand firm in the belief placed in me by the warrior god,

93

Daerkfyre. My family still won't take me in, I found that out when I tried visiting them recently, but life is looking better."

Mel managed a small smile through his teary face at his proclamation. Trestan felt some relief that this had been a short story compared to most of the ones the gnome told over the last day. Even as Trestan and the gnome traded relieved smiles, the dwarf bouncer stood one foot away from Bellringer with a big frown upon his face.

"Nay it isn't a bad minstrel nor a drunk sailor that disturbs this portion of the pub room!" The dwarf shouted in Mel's ear, "Tis nothing more than a prattling gnome who has less hold on his tongue than on his right to go about his affairs privately! The whole pub couldn't care one bit about your sorrows, gnome. We appreciate your patronage but would prefer you not distract our other customers with unwanted blathering."

The dwarf's harsh tone drew attention from everyone in the vicinity. The short yet muscular bouncer gave Mel a stern look. Trestan had not seen a lot of dwarves, but he was aware they took less kindly to gnomes than most other races did. If Mel Bellringer took offense to the dwarf's message, he didn't show it. Quite the opposite, the gnome visibly brightened a bit at the dwarf's presence. The others at the table thought it odd until they remembered that Mel worshipped a dwarven god, and likely was very fond of the race. At such realization, they hoped that the gnome wouldn't say anything else to upset their less-than-polite host.

Mel quickly greeted the bearded one, "Hello and fair eve! I am Mel Bellringer of the Bellringer family, makers of fine bells, chimes, gongs, and other…"

"I don't care if you are the head ding-a-ling o' clan tinklebells! My name is Salgor Bandago and I keep the peace around here. That means if you are going to cry off a river, do it far away and downhill from the rest o' the patrons."

Salgor rested clenched fists on his hips and broadened his scowl further than most humans could manage. Mel simply nodded his head, seemingly unswayed by the dwarf's show of muscle. Undaunted, the small sorcerer started to say more, "Oh aye, I forgot how straightforward and gruff dwarves are. It's been so long since I last had the pleasure of journeying with one. Adding my spells to their muscle, beating back enemies, drinking strong ale, passing out after half a mug; what wonderful memories those were! Ah, to adventure and fight with dwarves again!"

Salgor muttered, "Gods bless that time will never come, for the sake o' the dwarf!"

For the first time Mel seemed ruffled. "I'm surprised you haven't been more sociable to me. Dwarves are like a second family!"

An incredulous look came over the dwarf's face, "Second family? While gnomes are like the bit o' sandstone that occasionally pops up in our best mines? Look shorty, you have two marks against you: you are a gnome, and by your own admission you are a mage as well. That's two combinations that don't mix well with me. You want to go for a third?"

Even as he said it, Trestan and Mel seemed to notice the same tattoo on the dwarf's left arm. The design bore a fist holding up a fiery hammer, the whole thing surrounded by a field of flames. While Trestan couldn't tell one dwarven symbol from another, he noticed by the look of recognition on Mel's face that it might be the symbol of Daerkfyre, dwarven

God of Valor. The young smith had to come up with an interruption quickly, or the gnome might come up with the lucky third combination that would really anger the dwarf.

"You're the dwarf that got hurt by the elf wizard a few days ago, aren't you?"

Trestan could have hit himself for blurting out such poor choice of words. The dwarf whipped a scowl towards him so fast that he felt the blood drain from his face. The overly strong muscles in the dwarf's arms tensed. Petrow, next to him, suddenly went rigid from the expectation of trouble. Cat's eyes and jaw stretched wide open, looking at Trestan with a mixture of shock and pity.

The young man tried to add to his statement, though his mouth became very dry in the face of Salgor's stare. "The same…elf wizard…that we're hunting. Uh…he caused a disturbance up north in Troutbrook, and we're trying to follow him."

Salgor clenched a fist in front of him as he talked. "That rotten, cowardly cur! I helped stop a bunch of rioters from tearing apart this place to get to him! I told him that he and his bunch were unwelcome, and had to leave. He turned on me then, used his cowardly spells. Never should a dwarf have to endure such embarrassment!"

Katressa gave a look of relief at Trestan, using the opening he had provided in the conversation. "We thought you'd be interested in helping us because of that. After what they did in Troutbrook we journeyed to catch him and his band."

Salgor turned an inquisitive look upon the half-elf. "I remember seeing you here that night. So what did the pointy-eared pile of sand do up in Troutbrook anyway?"

Cat leaned over Mel to respond. The gnome had momentarily forgotten the tattoo and listened attentively to the new conversation. "He attacked some townspeople on the main street at night. I don't know what he was after, if anything, but when the fight was over he took off with a noble's daughter as a hostage."

"And you followed him back here? He's back in this area?"

Cat nodded, and the dwarf's response not only surprised them, it shook the whole common room. "I WANT MY AXE BURIED IN THAT DIRTY PIECE O' WATERED DOWN ALE!"

Veins visibly popping out off his arms and neck, the dwarf brought his fist down hard on the edge of the table. A sharp crack sounded as splinters flew and drinks toppled. The impact broke off the end of one of the boards. The roar of his voice and crunch of the table boomed through the smoky air of the tavern.

A hush descended on the common room as faces turned to regard the angry dwarf and broken table. Men paused in smoking their pipes. Raised glasses froze halfway to the parched mouths that desired them. A couple dozen eyes focused on them. The broken piece of tabletop hung precariously from a splinter a moment longer before falling to the floor, echoing through the quieted room. Salgor's frown disappeared as he turned to face the patrons staring at him. The dwarf then glanced over at the innkeeper, watching under raised eyebrows. Salgor spoke calmly, "I'll pay for that Miek. I'm good for it."

The barkeep nodded, but the attention of the rest of the bar focused on the dwarf for the second time that week. Since the first time was when the dwarf suffered under Revwar's spells, Salgor didn't take kindly to the renewed attention. The frown returned to the bouncer and he gave an ugly stare back at the common room.

"What? You've never seen an angry dwarf before? And do you really want to see one?"

Faces hurriedly turned away, resuming a focus on anything but the volatile dwarf. Commotion and conversation gradually returned to the room once Salgor turned back to face the booth. Even talkative Mel offered no words. Petrow was too scared to even put a hand out and pick up his toppled mug from the table. Salgor reached out and straightened the glasses and mugs so as not to waste good drinks. "So", the dwarf continued as he grabbed a rag and wiped up the stains. His efforts seemed silly given the wrecked state of the end of the table, "You said you followed 'em back here?"

Cat skillfully replaced her disarming smile, "The group swelled in numbers somewhat. They were seen riding towards here, and they sold two of their horses just outside of town this very morning. So wherever they are going next, they aren't planning on riding. I don't imagine that certain members of their group will want to be seen around this town again, but that doesn't help tell us where they might go."

Salgor thought it out a bit. "They might be heading in to the mountains, but if so I would expect a group to keep their horses at least until Dunker Keep. They might be heading west into the less populated lands, through hill country. I think it likely they might be boarding a ship and heading out to sea. We have a sizeable port here. If they snuck on a ship and sailed away, they would have the whole wide world to pick a destination."

The bouncer tugged at his sizeable beard a bit while thinking things over in his mind. Eventually he spoke again, with a nod towards the other customers in the bar. "Someone here is bound to know something o' know someone who does. Many people here hail from outlying ranches and farms. Someone from a big ranch is always drinking the night away around here. Any o' these people might have seen that group pass through, even if they didn't see them for what they are. I bet if I was to start asking around, I could learn more than the town guards."

Cat replied, "If you could find out anything we'd be grateful. We aren't necessarily looking for a fight, but we do need to rescue their prisoner."

Salgor Bandago pounded one fist against the other, "You may not, but I sure wish to lop off their fingers and use 'em to clean the wax out o' me ears! I can think of a hundred other nasty things I could do to that wizard if I see him again."

He turned to regard Trestan, and it momentarily scared the smith wondering what the dwarf might say. "Lad, if you ever be held helpless by one such as that, you'd not suffer that indignity to go unanswered! Your blood would scream for revenge also."

Trestan answered the dwarf evenly, recalling his treatment by the dark cleric, "I suffered too, held motionless and helpless by that cleric accompanying them. I bear nay overwhelming hatred, but it was a serious hurt to my heart."

Salgor nodded and actually gave a smile of condolence. The dwarf's hand followed with a warm slap on Trestan's shoulder. "Then you understand me well. I'll help find 'em if I can, and if they still be about we'll give 'em a lesson in respect!"

Salgor took his leave of the booth. He looked over the tavern locals until he saw some from an outlying farm. He promptly marched over to talk to them. It amused the companions to observe the targeted patrons appearing skittish. The locals only knew Salgor just broke a table in anger, and for whatever reason was striding straight over to them. They squirmed in their seats.

Mel wasn't above yelling for another wine to replace his spilt one as soon as the dwarf left. The gnome looked to be in a good mood, as if the whole encounter brought a breath of fresh air. "Did you see his tattoo? I forgot to ask him about it, but that's the holy symbol of Daerkfyre the Valorous. Imagine! To meet another dwarf and he shares the same god I do. We are privileged, he and I, to be brothers of the same faith! Not that dwarves always welcome that news. I still don't know what they have against a gnome brother. I feel honored to have met such a strong associate."

Petrow addressed Mel, trying to find a way to keep the gnome's mouth occupied by something other than talking. "I'm surprised you aren't following local custom, since you have a similar hobby."

The short sorcerer regarded him, "What do you mean?"

Petrow reached into one of his colorful pockets and produced a small bag. "While shopping around this morning, I didn't forget you. There were lots of leaves from local and distant ports waiting to be smoked and enjoyed. I got you a pouch originating from Pluetlo's Island, a traditional home of many halflings and gnomes. Go ahead and enjoy the flavor, much as many of these locals enjoy doing here. It was Cat's money I used, she deserves any thanks as much as I."

The gnome's eyes widened in pleasant surprise at the sight of the pouch. Mel took it with one hand, even as he reached into a pocket for his pipe. "My thanks, all of you. I'm sorry if I offended anyone earlier, seeing the dwarf and this gift more than make up for anything else."

Trestan put on a smile and addressed Mel as the latter began stuffing his pipe, "Don't worry, you found out as much as we did. I sympathize with your story, Mel. It seems all adventurers have a sad tale of how they got into treading unknown roads. From what Sir Wilhelm told me, I believe if you stick to your ideals, life can be a great adventure regardless of the hardships in your path."

Mel nodded, prepared to light the end of his pipe. He brought his bare finger up to the rim of the bowl. Trestan watched, not surprised that the gnome would use a minor spell to light the pipeweed. The gnome did surprise him when the flame not only lit the pipe, but shot outwards more than five feet from the booth. Even as Mel began to puff on the pipe, the locals at the closest table finally decided their choice of seating that night had been more excitement than they planned. They left hurriedly.

As Mel sat back and smoked his pipe in contentment, Cat silently appraised the two young men for the first time that evening. Her eyes roamed judgmentally over Trestan and Petrow. Trestan tried to sit up straighter and strike a pose. Katressa smiled at them both. "You young men look quite handsome, I must say. Your clothes are nice and you wear them well. You appear as true gentlemen, through and through."

Trestan and Petrow got a little red in the face from Cat's praise, though Mel had to slip in a statement of his own. "I believe Petrow is looking to pass himself off as nobility; he's certainly dressed for the part. Nice colors lad!"

Although the gnome meant it as an honest compliment, Trestan actually stifled a laugh at Petrow's expense. Petrow caught Trestan's reaction. "Mock me as you will young smith, and I do mean young. You are still younger than me by a year! But if we die tomorrow, I will be the one dressed in style."

The mood sobered after that. When full drinks were once again available at their table, and the gnome finished smoking for the time being, Trestan felt the need to ask a question.

"So, what do we do now? Search the harbor for the right ship? Ask around at more pubs? We could even patrol the street ourselves in case they try to sneak through town, but we would more likely waste the night and be half-asleep most of tomorrow."

Katressa nodded, "I may ask around in a few places. Alone. I don't mean to exclude anyone, I'm used to handling my own 'interrogations' and questions. The harbor might be a good spot to try tomorrow, if the dwarf is unsuccessful. He has the same urgency we do, and he knows the town, so he might get farther than we would. Take a look at him now, he seems to be going somewhere."

The four at the booth turned their eyes to search for the dwarf. They saw him, but now Salgor sported a suit of chain armor. Salgor Bandago looked every bit a veteran adventurer. The dwarf wore a number of armaments he hadn't worn as a bouncer. He held a heavy waraxe in one hand; his left carried a metal shield engraved with his personal crest. The centerpiece was a large ale cask, supported by a dwarvish temple, a hammer poised to tap the cask. A solid mace dangled from his belt. Even the dwarf's boots reflected a change, from his old ale-stained pair to what looked to be an even older, muddied set. A large pack bulged outward and upwards from his back, sizeable enough to stuff another dwarf in if needed. With all this weight burdening him, he still walked steadily towards the table where the companions sat.

Mel looked the dwarf up and down, "Are you planning on going somewhere?"

Salgor stopped next to the damaged table and looked Mel in the eye. "Nay, dwarves sleep like this. And drink like this. We pretty much always wear this stuff, though when we take a bath we tend to leave the axe to the side so it doesn't get rusty."

Mel nodded his head, though he furrowed his eyebrows in thought. Obviously he couldn't remember dwarves always dressing like that. Salgor ignored him and directed his conversation to Trestan and Katressa. "Can't say I found 'em, but I did find something worth checking. Maybe just a farmer's worries, but I'm heading out to investigate some odd activities. If I find anything, I'll be back to tell you. That is, unless I run into that wizard first, and teach him a thing o' my own."

Trestan answered, "We appreciate your help, good sir. I wish the best for you, and a safe journey back. We would be eager for anything you can find out."

Salgor nodded and then walked towards the exit. "Miek! You already got plenty o' muscles around tonight. I'm heading out and getting some fresh air!"

The barkeep frowned but didn't make any comments as the dwarf left. Trestan, Cat, Petrow and Mel had their eyes on the door for some time after Salgor exited. Petrow spoke first, "Well, any clue is promising at this point. We know they're somewhere around, but it is so hard to find a group in such a large, unknown area. Is this adventure, Cat?"

Cat finished a sip of her wine, her green eyes looked at Petrow over the rim of her goblet. She held his gaze as she set down her drink and thought about an answer. "Long, dreary moments of wait and uncertainty, of long walks, of endless worrying. Then you are interrupted by brief but intense moments of blood, screams and fast heartbeats. That's adventure alright"

Trestan asked, "But this is the life you choose? A life of helping others and searching for hidden treasures of the world?"

Cat nodded, "You'd have a hard time dragging me away from it. I get scared too, but there are times that are well worth it."

*   *   *   *   *

The night air carried a bit of a chill. Petrow and Mel Bellringer had already made their way to the upstairs room to settle into their beds. Trestan Karok and Katressa Bilil dallied outside the Eagle's Nest, standing quietly in the light of a flickering street lantern. Cat readjusted her cloak, ready to disappear into the cool night to see what other information she might discover. Trestan quietly waited beside her, unsure what he wanted to say next. He didn't want to see her go off on her own this evening, even though he knew she preferred working alone. The half-elf had certainly proved her independence and self-reliance, but the young man didn't want her taking this upon herself while his only option would then be to go back to his room and try to sleep. Trestan found the woman to be very enjoyable company. He might have only known her for three days, but they had shared a lot of conversations and traded ideas in that time.

Cat complimented him yet again on his looks and wardrobe. He replied, "I still pale in comparison to your grace and beauty."

The young man surprised himself by his choice of words. Cat merely smiled and adjusted her cloak. The young smith shifted uncomfortably from one foot to the next trying to think of something to break the silence. Cat finished fidgeting with her outfit and turned a smile his way. Her eyebrows raised slightly, as if asking him how good she looked. Trestan only glanced over her and smiled, still unsure what to say, yet impressed by the qualities in the woman before him.

"Well," she said at last, "don't wait up for me. I'm not sure how long I'll be out."

Trestan's face reflected concern, "You realize how this doesn't sit well with me. I hate to see you doing this alone. I know you do well on your own, but I feel left out. Useless."

Cat pulled a strand of stray hair away from her face. "'Tis not just concern for me that cautions your words? Nay, I understand your heart. I can relate if you feel the need to do something. I would be thankful for the help, but I believe I am better at doing this alone."

Cat reached out and took his hand in hers, Trestan's hand tingled at her touch. Trestan felt something stirring within him. It was as if the more he looked at her the more he found himself thinking about her. There was no doubt she was a lovely adventuring companion and fun to be around. The half-elf had become a close friend, to both he and Petrow.

99

Unaware of the young man's thoughts, Cat released his hand and drew the hood of her cloak over her hair, shielding her face better from the cool breeze. She stepped towards the next inn, but Trestan spoke again, "Cat?"

Green eyes turned his way under the hood. She waited quietly to hear what he would say. Trestan wasn't sure what he had originally wanted to say either. Finally a question tumbled out of his mind, "What happens if we find the other group near here somewhere? Somewhere outside of town where we might be on our own?"

Katressa replied, "Whatever we do, we won't barge right in. The dwarf might do that if he were with us, so I prefer finding something on my own. Without his help we have a better chance of quietly sneaking up on them. We need to be stealthy and steal her back. That is our best chance."

Cat started to walk backwards, away from Trestan, moving further up the street even as she kept his gaze, "Find some sleep tonight if you can. We never know what the next day brings."

Then she walked into the night, a black figure on a dark street.

*   *   *   *   *

It was still dark when Trestan awoke from a dream. He faced the wall next to his bed. Though probably very early morning, it remained quite dark. As Trestan lay quietly, getting reacquainted with his locale, he could hear things through the thin walls of the inn. A man snored, probably in the next room over. The walls were thin enough that the sound reached Trestan as if he was on the other side of the same room. Somewhere from outside the sounds of a distant dog's bark mixed with the wind blowing past the shutters. It seemed there might be a drizzle of rain outside, for the young man could hear drops of water hitting the roof. For a short time young Karok just relaxed and listened to the night sounds, hoping he might return to dreaming.

A floorboard squeak interrupted his reverie. By itself it didn't alarm Trestan, as it blended in with all the other night sounds he heard. Trestan shifted a little on his mattress. He had been sleeping on his stomach, and though he continued to do so he turned his head to face into the rented room instead of the enclosing wall. It was hard to see much in the dark, though light spilled around the worn shutter from a nearby street lantern. The partly open shutter let in a fair amount of cool night air as well. Mel slept on the mattress at the foot of Trestan's. The gnome had cracked open the shutter quite a bit earlier, stating that forest gnomes were used to a bit of open breeze and skies. In the still darkness Trestan could hear the gnome's quiet breathing, as well as breathing coming from the other side of the room where Petrow slept. The handyman had shed his expensive clothes and was resting peacefully.

When Trestan settled his eyes on Katressa's mattress, he became fully awake. The bed was empty, save some of her packs set on top of it. The young human wondered what time it was, and how long the half-elf's bed had remained unused. A quick glance around the room did not reveal the half-elf anywhere. Where was their companion?

Right after such thoughts came to him, he heard another floorboard squeak. It was done slowly, which tripped an alarm in the man's head. Someone must be sneaking around the hallway outside the door. Trestan looked towards the draw bolt holding the door shut. In the dark, he wondered if his imagination was playing tricks on him. A small scratching or clicking came from the general area of the door. Despite the dark, his brown eyes could make out the handle of the draw bolt turn and move. The lock barring their room was somehow being manipulated by someone outside the door!

Trestan almost gave way to panic. He'd heard stories from traveling adventurers about surprises in the night when half the party might be killed before an alarm could be raised. He was tempted to shout and raise an alarm then, but a part of him wanted to keep his mouth shut for other reasons. This could be Katressa returning to their suite. It could also be someone of ill intent, who would charge in slaying if anyone shouted in alarm. Trestan dropped his right hand over the side of his mattress and felt about. The bedding was not very high off of the floor, and Trestan purposely left the sword lying right next to his blankets. His fingers quickly found the handle, lying ready if he needed it. His mind frantically considered several courses of action. A part of him still wanted to spring up and shout a warning. Another part of him advised that staying still and pretending to sleep might be the better course, until he could see the intruder's intent. He could try to get to his own feet and quietly sneak up on the door, but he doubted his movements would go undetected.

The door opened, swinging his way and obscuring the intruder. Time had run out while Trestan remained undecided, so the course was chosen for him. He relaxed his hand within easy grasping range of his sword. Trestan narrowed his eyelids a bit in case whoever entered was of a race that had exceptional night vision. He wanted to appear asleep, and he forced himself to breathe slowly to further complete the illusion. For a quiet, tense moment he saw nothing passing the door. A hand, small by human standards, wrapped around the edge of the doorframe and quietly pulled it closed. Trestan saw the general outline of a humanoid frame, slightly smaller than a normal human. It was hard to make out details due to a cloak covering the person. The figure at the door turned to face the interior of the room, slowly scanning the beds and occupants. Trestan tensed. He wasn't sure if he continued to breathe evenly when the intruder looked his direction. The figure seemed to take little notice of him, reaching up to remove the hood of its cloak.

Cat's long hair tumbled free as Trestan breathed a sigh of relief. He continued to feign sleep. Cat seemed unaware of his observation as she tiptoed over to her bedside. She dropped the cloak from around her shoulders, revealing different clothes than earlier that evening. The chemise and pantaloons that made up her undergarments were all she wore under the dark cloak. He quietly watched as she went over to her packs and dug out items in the dark. Though it was hard for Trestan to see much more than outlines, he knew her elven blood would allow her to see in that darkness very well. She turned and he saw her from a profile view, as she fidgeted with her top. Cat suddenly reached down and pulled her chemise off. He had that one instant where he saw her feminine curves outlined in the dim light, and it engraved a wonderful image upon his memory he would always treasure.

He closed his eyes. As much as any man would have liked to watch Cat at that moment, the smith had too much respect for her to sneak such a peek. With his eyes closed, he trained his ears on every sound and movement. He could hear a pair of heavy boots moving somewhere downstairs, but he concentrated on the sounds across the room. Clothes and packs made soft rustling noises. Cat occasionally breathed different, adding slight grunts and groans. The young man realized she wasn't simply getting undressed and slipping into bed…she was dressing in something different. He cracked open his eyelids. Cat stood nearly fully dressed in her black adventuring leathers, her spare stuff packed away like she was ready to travel. He watched as she belted on the silver rapier. She slung crossbow over shoulder, her bolt quivers strapped to her as usual. She paused for a moment, wearing or carrying all her equipment. She gazed over the sleeping occupants of the room, hesitation apparent in her actions.

Trestan raised his head and shoulders a bit from the bed. Cat raised a single finger to her lips to signal Trestan he should not wake the others. The half-elf stepped lightly to his bedside and knelt to put their faces close. She asked him, "How long have you been awake, my friend?"

Seeing her unspoken question, Trestan answered, "I closed my eyes, I swear."

Cat grinned and trusted the answer, though Trestan imagined she might be blushing. She put a hand on his shoulder and whispered, "I know this must look odd. You must get your sleep. We move again in the morning."

The human looked her with new understanding. Even as he spoke his next words, he heard the noise of those same heavy boots walking the hallway on their floor of the inn. "Then you found out something? If we're moving, you must know where we need to look."

Katressa nodded again. She tilted her head to indicate the sound of those heavy boots. "The dwarf, Salgor, seems to have found their trail. That sounds like him heading to his room. I heard him approach the inn, at which point I hastily threw on my cloak and went out the door to talk to him. He found an interesting story regarding one of the ranches outside town. In the morning, have everyone grab a quick but sustaining breakfast and he'll lead you in the right direction."

She started to rise, but Trestan grabbed her arm softly, "But where are you going?"

She leaned close to his ear, "I'm not leaving my horse behind. It's time to reclaim my property. Worry not about anything right now, Trestan. You should get your sleep, for you will need it before a very boisterous dwarf bangs on this door in the morning. Sleep well."

Satisfied, he released his gentle grip on her arm. She rose and went to the door. He laid in bed watching her depart. Once she was through the door, she used whatever skills and tools she had to reset the draw bolt from outside in the hallway. The young man watched the bolt settle into place. Trestan wondered how Jareth would have felt about his close friendship with someone who displayed such thieving prowess. His mentor had always treated everyone fairly, however, and surely the old man would have recognized the good in her heart and her willingness to risk all to help others.

Trestan put his head on his pillow and tried to force himself to sleep. The heavy dwarven footsteps in the hallway receded to the point where he could no longer hear their

102

owner. For a long time he listened to the other night sounds: drizzle of rain hitting the roof, the gnome's breathing, and the snores of some unknown man next door. The young smith was too excited to go to sleep as of yet, but he did his best to relax.

A new sound came to his ears. Straining to sort it out from the other night sounds, he found it originated from the general direction he had last heard the dwarf's heavy boots. It was very unclear at first and intermittent. The sound resembled that of two smooth stones being rubbed across each other. The slow, rhythmic grinding noise continued until Trestan realized with a start what it was. At the realization, the young human didn't rest very well for the remainder of that night.

The sound was that of a sharpening stone, slowly being dragged across an axe blade to hone it for an upcoming battle.

CHAPTER 8

They awoke to a sound that resembled a battering ram smashing a castle's gates, though it was only a dwarf banging on their door. "Get your lazy carcasses out o' those beds! You can rest as long as you want when death claims you! We got that cowardly elf caster to go after, and you can bet he's already finished his breakfast!"

Petrow and Mel almost fell out of their beds as the door rattled. Trestan rolled out of his bed in a panic, making an attempt to grab his sword in his sleepy state. Mel sputtered, "What? What? Who is that? More goblins?"

Listening to the sudden ruckus inside the room, Salgor was confident he had sufficiently awakened the group. He yelled through the door one last time. "Me and my full belly will be waiting for you downstairs. Oh, and I'm not easily forgetting that you just called me a goblin, 'Bell-boy', so watch that mouth o' yours from here out."

Over the sound of Petrow's yawning and Mel's excited exclamations, Trestan heard the heavy dwarven boots recede down the hall. The young smith once again felt the fool, laying spread out in a tumbled heap on the floor. Even as he tried to sort himself upright, his companions fired away questions at their rude awakening and Cat's absence. Trestan shared the events of the previous night as he dressed. Petrow and Mel showered him with questions. Trestan replied they'd have to ask Salgor what clues he found.

Mel received the news as if someone mentioned a party. He smiled as he packed his things. Petrow dressed in his more conservative road clothes: garments that were still rather colorful compared to what most might consider good taste. Together, the three packed their belongings and belted on weapons. Petrow had a holster for each axe. The woodcutter's axe strapped on to his back, but the waraxe hung from his belt. Mel fussed and straightened his many pouches and straps, making each one accessible. Trestan used Petrow's help to put on his armor. Trestan needed to get used to the weight. All three headed down to the inn's common room when they were ready.

Salgor Bandago stood at the bar alone, drinking a pint of ale. On his back he still wore the oversized backpack. Axe and mace hung from his belt, while the shield rested against the bar near him. At the closest table sat three meager plates of eggs and meat. The three sat down to eat, glancing at the dwarf in disappointment over the size of their portions. The dwarf sneered at them, even as trickles of ale dripped down his braided beard. "Be happy I'm letting you eat. It's not much but that's all you really need. Nay warriors can run too far or fight too well on a bulging stomach. I fixed it up only because you needed a little muscle on those arms."

Trestan and Petrow were muscular by human standards from the hard work done during their lives. Their biceps were small in comparison to the dwarf's arms. Trestan avoided comments, especially since off to the side he could see the broken table from last night's conversation. The dwarf continued scowling and speaking as they poked at their food. "I'm eager to get on the road. The sooner we get moving the better, on behalf o' our cause and my temper. I have a score to settle with that mage. A dwarf doesn't like an enemy to get the best o' him and live to boast about it."

They ate quickly under the dwarf's watching eyes. Salgor emptied the pint and slammed it down on the bar when they were ready to leave. Mel's stomach grumbled. They spoke little as they walked out of the bar. Trestan and Petrow felt intimidated about discussing anything in front of the dwarf. Mel simply observed Salgor in quiet fascination, reflecting his happiness at seeing a dwarven face. Salgor was not one for small talk. The dwarf gestured and pointed more than he spoke.

They left the bar and turned north in silence. The humans and gnome retraced the route that brought them into town. Salgor didn't go all the way back to the north guard gate before turning eastward on a new street. After walking down a rather wide street containing warehouses, they arrived at the start of the long ramp that wound its way down to sea level. They marched down the twisting wagonway, avoiding merchants and carts traveling to and from the harbor below. The ramp offered their best view of the waterfall. They looked in awe as it cascaded down a very long drop, with even smaller falls and drop-offs around the cliff's side. It was a long walk to reach the bottom of the ramp, partly due to the winding nature of the wagonway.

Trestan and Petrow assumed their destination to be the harbor or one of the many shipping vessels moored there. At the bottom of the ramp, Salgor turned away from the harbor in a generally northern direction again. The line of buildings ended at another guard post. This one stood larger and older than the one they had seen on the road. They passed by it without incident, following a trail that wound its way through a growth of tall brush. The simple dirt trail featured no more than wagon ruts and trampled grass. Mel started talking again: asking about the harbor, comments on the local flowers, and questions about some of the outlying farms and ranches.

Salgor finally responded to one of Mel's statements with an irritated tone. Even as he spoke, he still continued marching at a fast pace. His heavy boots seemed bent on slamming any loose pebbles deep into the dirt and mud as he went. "I work bars and I fight monsters. I've only lived here less than a year, so don't think o' me as a tour guide!"

Mel smiled and looked appreciative to have finally gotten some words out of the dwarf, "You seem to know where you are headed. I just assumed you knew this area well."

The dwarf sighed, "Every now and then someone my size has to get some space away from a human town. A walk can do the soul good and builds the leg muscles. During my time here, I happened to meet several locals in the bar and I've gotten to visit some out at their homes."

Mel offered his insight, "And one of those locals saw or heard something? Ooh, ooh, I want to know!"

Salgor scowled at the gnome, and not for the first time, "I will tell you all when Katressa rejoins us. I'd rather say things once and not repeat myself. I didn't tell her the whole story, but I'm certain we are on the right path."

Some time passed before they arrived at a small crossroads between trails. They figured they were a good couple miles northeast of the town. Wagon ruts intersected within sight of a farmhouse. Salgor stopped and slowly scanned the area around them. Low hills and some woods marked the landscape, though it was mostly rather open. To their backs they could see the ridge rising up to rendezvous with Barkan's Crossing.

Mel looked towards the distant farmhouse, "Are we there yet?"

Salgor bellowed, "Aye!"

Mel took a step back, surprised at the answer and the dwarf's booming voice. He beamed a smile and looked at the house. "They are holed up in there eh? Hmm, what kind of spell to prepare? Maybe if I do a bit of…wait a moment, if they are here why are we standing in the open?"

Salgor shook his head slowly, "I didn't say they were here. This is merely the place where we have to be."

Trestan and Petrow looked around to get a better perspective on their surroundings. They saw no other homes within sight, and there was no one else using the trails. Both men did notice something odd in the thick weeds near the intersection. An overgrowth of vines covered the base of an ancient, broken statue. Pieces of the stone figure lay in the tall grass nearby. Salgor took off his large backpack and set it on the path. He opened a flap in the side to reveal a few small ale casks. He reached within but pulled out a bottle instead. Popping the cork, he leaned against his pack and started to drink. Trestan and Petrow took the cue to sit down and take a break from walking. Mel scratched his head in confusion.

Salgor took another swig from the bottle and enjoyed the taste as it burned down his throat. At Petrow's look, he handed the container to the young man and offered a drink. Petrow accepted with a thankful nod. He bravely took a swig…and promptly made a face. He coughed and turned a red shade as he tried to hand the bottle back to the dwarf. Salgor laughed: a deep, rumbling, belly laugh that showed a line of yellow teeth, minus one. "Those humans can't make a drink that kicks like dwarven whiskey! You're a strong lad to be sitting upright after that gulp."

He set the bottle away as Petrow recovered. The handyman got out his canteen to wash out the taste. Mel chuckled, having firsthand tried a similar drink in younger days. Salgor still grinned as he spoke. "This is the rendezvous spot with Katressa. I expect we still have a march to go, though I don't know exactly where they are. I do know they turned northeast and went up the coastline for whatever reason. For more than that you will have to wait for your friend to get here."

*   *   *   *   *

When horse and rider came within sight, she rode in from the northeast. The dark leather clothes gave her away at a distance. Salgor shouldered his bulging pack easily and the rest gathered their packs as well. The young men had been expecting to see Cat riding in from the western road. The half-elf dismounted when they got close. She was dressed as armored and ready for action as she could be. Cat even wore her helm, a crossbow on her back, and a spare on her horse. Cat's horse bore no ill marks. It felt good to rescue one kidnap victim of the other band, and one that looked like it had been treated well.

Salgor greeted her, "Figured you might be riding up ahead to scout. I hoped you were planning on saving some action for the rest o' the group here. We certainly gave you a good head start. You would think the races that don't have as much longevity wouldn't spend so much time sleeping, but they like their beds."

106

Cat looked the dwarf up and down. Her green eyes studied the dwarf's armaments and the eagerness of battle. Trestan spotted a frown at the corners of her mouth and it wasn't hard to guess why. She had hoped to sneak in and steal the noble, then get away from trouble. The dwarf, carrying shield and heavy weapons, displayed no intention of letting the elf wizard get away without a fight. The raven-haired adventuress sighed and responded to Salgor's words. "It was still dark when I rode away from the ranch. You gave me good directions to the statue here, but I figured I would have a lot of time on my hands waiting. A little tour through the countryside wouldn't hurt. I didn't find anything suspicious."

Salgor nodded, "I know the trails a bit further out, but after that I will be giving my best guesses as well. All I know so far is a general direction. They came close to Barkan's Crossing, maybe some of their accomplices entered it, but the elf and minotaur turned northeast up the coast."

They resumed their walk up the trail that Cat had just traveled. She led her horse, content to walk alongside her companions. It wasn't long before the adventuress offered the saddle to Mel if he wanted a ride. Though Mel and Salgor both had short legs, the dwarf moved along at a pace that left Mel struggling. The gnome accepted, despite trepidation at the size of the horse. Soon he rode easily on its back as the other four marched on. Mel voiced his delight of the horse ride, but hoped it didn't do anything unexpected.

As they went, Salgor divulged what he learned the previous night. His deep voice set the pace as they walked, "I know a rancher up this path. He and his hired hands usually rotate nights that they visit the pub. None of them were present last night, but a neighbor was. The neighbor told me something had them scared out at their ranch, even had them holed up like they were worried about being attacked by something. Last night I ran out here and had a talk with him."

Salgor pointed up ahead to a cattle ranch. Trestan looked and saw none of the cattle outside the barn, nor was anyone visible. There were lowland gullies and small woods around the area. "I don't think we have reason to stop, but this is what he told me. One of their ranch hands thought he saw a bull's horns down in the wooded areas outside the fence. They had some animals acting strange too. Dogs barking, skittish cows and horses, deer running scared. They didn't put it all together at once, nor really suspect any danger. Anyways two o' 'em went down into a wooded gully to retrieve what they thought was an escaped bull."

The dwarf shook his head sadly, "Those poor boys never were prepared for what they would find. Later that afternoon someone saw a smoke trail rising from those same woods. The rest o' the ranchers realized the other two were still missing, and by that time they confirmed they weren't missing any o' the bulls from their ranch. A group o' 'em set out to take care o' the fire and see what was going on down there. They found the first two boys…what was left o' 'em. One was sliced into two pieces; the other was a burning pile o' bones. A lot o' things could slice a man or burn, but not too many could also be mistaken for a bull in the woods. I'd say the elf's group is trying to sneak off in a new direction."

Trestan voiced one of his thoughts to the group. "They could have cut across terrain earlier if they had another destination in mind. Why did they risk going so close to town?"

107

The dwarf shrugged. To him the answer did not matter, only vengeance. "Maybe it could have been something as trivial as supplies, but for whatever reason they turned and I'm ready to follow. By the time I talked to the ranchers last night, they had heard a neighbor who had seen individuals running across his fields. He said there was a band of armed strangers, one large and misshapen. They also mentioned one person was being carried. Those country folk weren't about to go out and ask the group's business. They shut and barred their place until the group was out o' sight. The direction is even further up this trail."

Katressa nodded at the dwarf. "One was being carried…so hopefully she is still alive."

Salgor questioned, "If they killed her they couldn't collect the ransom could they? Well, I suppose they could but they would need her as a secure bargaining chip right?"

Trestan shook his head, "I'm not sure if that was their intent."

The others looked to him, but he had no answers. "I don't know what they want. I doubt the street fight in Troutbrook was planned. I don't know why the wizard's band was out that evening."

Salgor looked to each of them. "None of you has told me much about that yet. What happened in Troutbrook?"

*   *   *   *   *

The company relaxed in a sandy clearing as the sun passed its zenith. Partially eaten meals sat unattended on rocks as the group members enjoyed other activities. Mel had finished his meal, despite eating larger portions than either of the humans, and sat down on a fallen tree. He watched the others as he puffed away on his pipe. The rest had decided on impulse to do more weapon training. Salgor and Petrow went through the combat motions with axes. Trestan and Cat started their own training duel with swords. Petrow learned a lot from the dwarven axe-wielder. Salgor called on him to try different strikes, and the dwarf used his shield to block while in comparison Cat had originally been dodging. The human tried figuring how to get in good strikes when dealing with a shield. Salgor offered lots of good advice, showing the young man a better grip and how to avoid overextending himself. Across the clearing, Trestan and Cat practiced with naked steel. The elvish sword ringed against the cat's-head-pommel rapier several times, though never very hard. Neither one wanted to nick their weapons or draw blood, so they swung polite and easy.

Mel gave his own comments, though he never practiced with his own small mace. He watched Salgor with a lot of attention, admiring the dwarven warrior's moves. Mel would have loved to swing an axe like the dwarf, but his muscles were never suited for such a task. Despite Mel worshipping a warrior dwarven god, he never did try to master melee weapons. He preferred the magic gift within him, or the trusty crossbow by his side. Mel felt a true warrior used any weapons at his disposal. The magic that had tormented his younger years remained the best weapon he had.

108

Cat would have liked to watch the axe battle, but she found herself trying hard to match Trestan's improved skills. The agile half-elf was amazed that the blacksmith had tutored so well under Sir Wilhelm. She could still beat back his attacks easily, but even in practice the keen edge of his blade commanded her complete attention, lest she accidentally get a deep cut performing a bad move. One of the young smith's strengths was the speed at which he maneuvered his sizeable weapon. Sir Wilhelm had taught him how to use such a blade fast and to react quickly.

The half-elf called out to Trestan as she attacked, seeing how well he could defend from different attacks. "High then low."

Cat brought her rapier up high to force his sword high in a block. After two strikes, she circled the blade into a low cut designed to cripple the legs. He moved wrist over wrist to switch the sword from a high block, into a downward pointing low block. Weapons connected, though Cat knew she would have scored a hit if this had been for real.

"Low leg stabs."

Keeping her blade low, she snaked the rapier left and right trying to stab at either of Trestan's legs. She forced him to move as well as block in order to keep his legs safe. Trestan blocked and dodged, continuing to learn how to keep his balance and fight defensively.

"A feint towards your chest."

Cat threatened his chest with the strike of her rapier. He blocked and blocked again as she kept the weapon dancing at chest level. As she had warned him, she was feinting towards his chest to distract him from a surprise attack. Cat had to watch the elvish sword carefully, for she intended to move very close without getting cut. She seized the moment when the opportunity arrived. The silver rapier blade snuck under the bastard sword, yet part of the rapier's basket hilt came down on the top of the blade. A twisting pressure of her wrist allowed Cat to trap the blade in place and even push it away from her. Trestan set his stance different to gain leverage, but he didn't see the other attack coming. Katressa reached her left arm around the human's side. Trestan felt the handle of her dagger touch him in the back near a vulnerable spot. The hit done, they stood frozen for a moment as Trestan studied the move and figured where he could have improved.

"Beware the tricks and cunning of your opponents. I don't think you could retaliate after being stabbed back here." Cat relaxed her stance a bit. "But you are getting good and fast, and you…"

"Oh my!" Trestan exclaimed, looking beyond the half-elf, "Petrow got hurt."

Even as Cat reflexively half-turned to look, her instincts suspected her human friend played a trick. She could still hear the ringing of axe on shield as if nothing wrong happened. Trestan applied the leverage of his larger muscles to pop the rapier out of Cat's grasp. She tried to step back quickly to gain room. She delivered another hit with the dagger handle. Trestan dropped his sword to get his hands on her fast enough. He locked onto her wrist. A spin and a pull, and the human yanked Cat over his back to land in a heap on the ground. The dagger went flying away, but the adventuress thought it better for safety. Her mind tried to adjust to her opponent's bold move. Dust kicked up as she scrambled away.

Trestan grabbed at her as she moved to get back to her feet. She only got as far as her knees before a tackle sent her sprawling to the ground.

Cat smiled and laughed as she struggled. Now here was a surprise! Trestan rolled her onto her back and worked to pin her arms. Her instincts almost made her lash out and kick him between the legs, but she reminded herself this was all in good fun. Without the dirty tricks she would normally employ, the woman found herself held down as he sat on top of her thighs. He succeeded in pinning her arms. He didn't hurt her, but his weight and muscles kept her trapped underneath him.

There was a moment of silence except for heavy breathing from the both of them. The dust floated between their eyes, but Cat could make out Trestan's face despite the sunshine over his shoulder. He smiled, quite happy about his little victory. His surprise move had been fun, though she felt awkward being pinned by the young man she had been training.

"Now that you have me, what are you going to do with me?" She asked, her soft voice flirted.

Mel's voice called out from his viewpoint, "Nice job taking her down lad! I think you passed the training lesson!"

Trestan, normally so respectful and shy around women, suddenly blushed and realized the position he placed her in. He stammered an apology as he got off, then offered a hand to help her up. They dusted themselves, Trestan brushing away some of the sand on Cat's shoulders and back. Cat took off her helmet and shook out her hair a bit. The young smith turned around to see Salgor and Petrow observe what had been going on.

He turned back to Cat and said, "Pardon, milady. I wanted to demonstrate I could be tricky and cunning also. I hope you didn't take offense."

Cat put her helm back on her head, a smile still on her face. "Trestan, you did not offend me. It was a pleasant surprise and well done. You don't have to always address me as 'milady' you know. I'm your friend."

Trestan smiled back, "Old habit. My father and Sir Wilhelm brought me up to always be honorable and respectful. I'm glad to see you liked my little trick and that I didn't hurt you."

"I'm glad I restrained myself from hurting *you*." Cat recovered her rapier and sheathed it. "I grew up learning to fight dirty."

They all ended the training, passed around the unfinished food and drank to quench their thirst. While they packed away their lunch, Salgor motioned to Trestan that he wanted to look at the elvish sword. Trestan handed it over proudly. Trestan guessed the dwarf had probably seen a variety of good weapons. Salgor seemed to look over the sword with a knowledgeable eye. When he was done examining the blade, the dwarf handed it back without comment.

Trestan was interested in what the dwarf thought. The young man was proud of the weapon, though he could not yet accept it as his, "There is quite an enchantment upon it, the blade cuts through items unlike any weapons I've ever seen."

"Bah," Salgor scoffed, "Don't take this personally, lad. It's a good blade for one o' small skill to have in his defense. I've never been impressed with elf-made weapons that require a magical spell to give 'em a good edge."

The group started up the road, though Salgor continued to comment on the blade. "If you want the true measure o' a warrior, it lies within muscle, steel, and the heart. No silver-piece conjuror can replace that!"

Katressa, leading her mount alongside them, addressed the dwarf, "Respectfully, dwarves enchant weapons too. I'm just commenting, not trying to argue."

"Well, it is an enchantment of a natural type," responded Salgor. "We put meat on our bones and use our muscles to dig ore out o' the deepest parts of the mountains. Hard forged steel and mithril…hammered and folded more than any human master would attempt in order to achieve a strong blade. If anything else, is it the miraculous blessings o' our gods. Many a dwarven priest has consecrated weapons to be used to great effect against our enemies."

They walked on more, though the dwarf noticed a frown on Trestan's face. He clapped the human on the back and spoke again. "Be neither insulted nor shamed lad, dwarves say it like they see it. I judge you by the way you act, not by the weapon you wield."

Trestan nodded, "I'm not really an adventurer. I'm a smith hoping to make some small difference where I can. I carry this sword because it was left to me by a good and noble man, who strongly upheld his ideals."

Salgor smiled then, "Now that sounds like something worth toasting!" Still walking, he reached back into a pocket of his pack and pulled out a different alcohol flask.

The dwarf took a big swig and invited the others to do the same. Everyone politely and timidly sipped it, nodding their appreciation even if it burned their throats. Trestan finished his sip and returned it to Salgor, then asked, "What about you, Salgor? What does the adventuring life hold for you?"

Salgor shrugged, "You see lad, I don't really see myself as an adventurer though many would call me one. I follow the natural course o' my people, which often includes bashing in goblin skulls and hacking orcs apart. In have my ambitions in life just like everyone else. Someday I seek to open my own tavern. I'm a brewer by hobby you know! I work these taverns and inns just to know the business better and sample what other people consider good ale. It brings in some money to help me get by. I've already created my own special brand, Bandago's Brew! Someday I'll want to settle down and be a host to many a drink lover such as myself."

Trestan prodded the dwarf further, "And your axe? It seems a fine weapon that has seen a lot of use."

"Indeed!" Salgor agreed, as pride glowed in his eyes. "Made by our natural dwarven magic, craft and ores. My uncle forged it before I left home to wander. Another relative o' mine performed the blessings o' my god to keep the blade sharp and strong. Divine miracles, not unpredictable arcana. Daerkfyre the Valorous offered his strength for me to be his tool in the world!"

Mel piped in, and the moment the others had dreaded arrived. "What a coincidence! I'm a blessed tool of Daerkfyre in this world too!"

Salgor scowled at the gnome, "What makes you say that gnome?"

"When my god abandoned me, I found a new one that would watch over me," Mel fished through his pockets and pulled out a crude metal symbol, identical to Salgor's tattoo. "Daerkfyre took me in and made me the warrior I am today!"

"O' all the preposterous…" Salgor started sputtering nonsense, apparently having trouble saying anything clearly. The warrior stopped in his tracks, bringing rest of the party to a halt. Cat, Petrow, and Trestan all tensed, unsure what would develop between their companions.

Mel mistook Salgor's reaction as the joy of meeting another Daerkfyre worshipper in a land where it wasn't as common. After all, Mel was always jolly and happy to meet a fellow worshipper. "I know it's rare to see a fellow brother in this land."

"Brother? Brother?!" Salgor's expression walked the line between disbelief and anger. "If Daerkfyre touched you he sure made you deaf and dumb! Don't ever insult me by calling me your brother again, and never again blaspheme a dwarven god. Especially my own! I'll bury you right next to the elf wizard if you do! A mix o' body parts that people won't know which part belonged to which person!"

Mel looked shocked, "Why are dwarves upset that I honor their god? I would think you would be privileged to know me!"

"Privileged?" Salgor shook his head, "More like embarrassed! A gnome worshipping a dwarven god is a mockery o' that god. How dare you speak homage to a deity promoting strength and courage! You have nay muscles! You wear that tiny mace that I don't think you can use well, and you are a caster as well as a gnome. You aren't fit to worship a young dwarf maiden's beard stubble!"

Mel fought back a sniffle, drew a breath and tried his best to stand tall again. "Well say what you may, my heart and soul walk the path which I was led to follow. I'm strong in battle and courageous. I've sent enemies running before me! You watch! I'll show you that I won't embarrass our god."

Salgor shook his head, facing Mel with a terrible scowl, "You already have. Step warily around me, gnome. You would be wise not to invoke my anger. If you do, I'll give you a lesson on Daerkfyre's strength."

The party resumed their walk, though they marched on silently.

*   *   *   *   *

The path faded to almost nothing, becoming more of a game trail. The group hadn't seen any structures, even ruined ones, in the last couple hours. They could feel the salty air blowing in from the east, indicating they approached the Sea of Krakus. At times they could see the blue expanse of water just to their right side, drawing closer. Salgor admitted he could not track, but this seemed to be the general direction the other band had been heading.

Cat's excellent vision spotted smoke from a campfire near the setting sun. She pointed to a bluff some distance away that ran close to the shoreline. It had a peculiar rock formation: from the side it jutted as the head and curved beak of a bird of prey. Trees and brush crowned the bluff, but the rest of the party could see the smoke as well. They displayed their elation quietly, in smiles and pounding fists into palms. They hoped this was their opponent at last.

From this point Cat led them, finding a path to bring them closer without coming within view of any sentries that might be up there. Trestan and Petrow led the horse, trying their best to guide it and keep it hidden from view. Her chosen route brought them down a ravine that channeled a river during the thaw. For now, only a stream trickled a winding path to the nearby sea. They laid their packs in a spot where foliage overshadowed a dry section. The horse grazed on some long grass, though they hitched it to a tree to keep it from wandering into eyesight of the bluff.

Everyone eyed the campfire smoke. The sun hid behind the hills, covering the low areas in shadow. Trestan hated breaking the silence. "What now? Do we sneak right up or scout it out?"

Salgor spoke his mind, "We walk right in. If they are friendly they won't attack. If it's our quarry or bandits, we slay 'em all fast."

Mel went through his packs, "Let's see, I have materials for 'Timed Boomy', 'Rat Blaster', and…will we need a pack of 'Twirly Lights' for some illumination?"

Cat shook her head and sighed. "If it's our prey, they are well-trained killers. If we make a mistake, we'll die. They don't know we're here, so I'll scout them out."

Salgor threw up his arms, "Bah! Sneaking and skulking; that is the elf way."

Cat narrowed her eyes at the dwarf. "Have you forgotten their hostage? Above all, the best thing we can do is rescue their prisoner. If we do nothing else, we have achieved a victory."

Trestan and Petrow looked to each other and the plateau where the unknown camp was located. They both thought of Lady Shauntay. Each wondered if she was indeed this close, or whether she even lived at all.

Cat interrupted their thoughts. "I'll scout. You all make camp here. Build nay fire, for that elf will see it as surely as I see theirs if he is up there."

Salgor scowled again, "Who put you in charge anyway?"

Trestan and Petrow both raised their arms in response to supporting Cat. Salgor was not too happy that his only support came from the gnome's pointing finger. The dwarf spoke again, "Fine…sneak around in the dark. But, I insist on this: you take one of us with you. That way when you see the elf or find out it isn't him; that extra person can run back and grab the rest o' us."

The half-elf frowned at the idea. She trusted in her abilities, and doubted the others could stay as well hidden. Finally she nodded her head, seeing the dwarf's determination. "I will take one of you."

Trestan watched as Cat looked them over and struggled with the decision. Petrow volunteered to go, but Cat didn't answer his pleas. Even as she looked him up and down, Trestan saw the answer in her eyes. Petrow was inexperienced, though he probably could attempt it. Yet, Petrow's flashy clothes stood out against any backdrop. Cat then looked to the dwarf, and the Cat's frown appeared as plain as day. Cat would not take Salgor. Not only was he more of a straightforward person, he wanted a fight with the elf wizard. For all the adventuress knew Salgor might rush forth and attack. For their safety and the noble's own good, she could not take the dwarf. Mel stood tall as she looked at him. Even though Cat judged silently, Mel talked about how he used to play games of hide and seek as a kid. Although gnomes might be good scouts in the woods on that plateau, Mel's personality was a big strike against him. Trestan knew Cat would feel Mel might be talkative and not very keyed in on the task at hand. The half-elf would not ask Mel to go with her.

Cat turned her green eyes towards Trestan. Trestan was young and inexperienced, though he felt he handled himself thoughtfully. The young man wasn't very apt to do something rash, other than leaving home to start the quest in the first place. From the very beginning the young smith wanted to make a difference, but he never got very distracted or went against Cat's wishes. As she looked into his eyes, he saw the answer.

She planned to pick him.

CHAPTER 9

In the blackness, Trestan tried hard to follow the dark figure ahead of him without breaking the silence. Every now and then Cat would wave for him to stop, or crawl forward, but mostly Trestan stayed several paces behind her. She occasionally whispered, keeping him informed about their surroundings. She told him this plateau overlooked a beach along the seashore. Cat also spotted more than one campfire, but she hadn't yet seen details of the camp. Although Trestan was a little disoriented due to the darkness, he figured they had swung towards the north side of the bluff before circling south and climbing.

Once again Cat waved for him to wait where he was, then crawled ahead and out of sight. This left Trestan alone in the dark, lying on his belly amidst some trees and bushes. The elvish sword weighed on his back, though he had left his quarterstaff behind. Petrow had pointed out to him that the long staff could more likely snag and make noise. Trestan hoped he would have no need of the sword this night. He listened as he waited. Off to his left, waves crashed against the beach. An owl hooted from somewhere above. Trestan heard sneezes from the unseen camp. Trestan hoped the owner of the sneezes was human. He heard a light tap of a stick, in a pattern that signaled Trestan to crawl forward again. As he did, he became aware the trees thinned out slightly. He began seeing more stars through the leaves above. One of the moons reflected light on the area, though it was poor.

Trestan didn't mind the darkness in some ways. It kept them hidden enough to sneak close. At the same time, he was frightened to be out here almost alone when faced with unknown danger. When charging the strange group in Troutbrook alongside Sir Wilhelm, there had been little time for apprehension. On this night he had plenty of time to feel nervous. As the young human snuck forward, he winced at every little sound he made. His hands and feet always seemed to dislodge a pebble or push one leafy branch into another. Cat moved with much less noise than he could achieve. Trestan got to see Cat in her infiltrator element, scouting out enemy camps with utmost secrecy. As Trestan listened, he heard voices from the area up ahead. He crawled beside Cat as she peered over a fallen log. The distant campfire light accentuated her elvish features. Trestan could make out a frown on her face.

Cat lowered herself behind the log and looked at him. "Gods, Trestan. What are we dealing with here?"

Trestan frowned also, not sure what she meant, but knowing she should be able to read his expressions in the dim light. She motioned with her hands that he should rise and take a look for himself. Trestan pushed his head above the log. He did it painfully slow, afraid that whoever was out there might see him.

There was a larger party here than what they expected. Six tents of mixed sizes and shapes sat amongst a break in the trees. A couple of tents were large enough to sleep small groups of people comfortably. Three fires lit the area; two existed as small cooking fires. The largest, a bonfire, could be visible for some distance at night. To the east of camp, a steep bank led to the shoreline below. The bluff offered a good view of the beach and the sea. They saw no horses or animals, but there were several people scattered around the camp.

Trestan counted the occupants of the camp. He could see at least four men moving about the clearing. They didn't seem to be doing anything except chatting around the fires. They had the look of hard men, each one armed to some degree, though none wore armor. He examined each one; sure that Cat did the same. The two silent observers sought any symbols or trappings indicating to whom the residents of the camp declared fealty.

Some of the men passed a bottle between themselves as they chatted. The closest two talked about the women in some tavern. The little bit of conversation that reached the woods didn't offer enough details. Another man cleaned cookware at the far campfire. He scrubbed at some pots with a small amount of clean water and a large amount of spit. Another played the part of sentry, throwing wood on the already large, main fire. Their weapons consisted of daggers and small, curved blades. Cat noted something about the way they talked and moved, so she leaned closer to Trestan and whispered.

"They are mostly sailors." Katressa observed. "They might be working as mercenaries or such, but they walk like they spend most of their time on a boat."

"Maybe pirates? Or smugglers?" Offered Trestan.

A person emerged from one of the tents. He dressed in finer clothes than the others. A saber at his side looked like it had been conscripted by some country as a naval officer's side arm, though the man wearing it did not look to be from any organized militia. His bright red hair and confidant movements marked him. The men around camp took a respectful notice of him, though they didn't interrupt anything they were doing. One offered a bottle but the red-haired man declined. Cat and Trestan watched as the man went to another tent and entered it. Whatever his purpose in this new tent, the two nearer men sharing the bottle chuckled over some kind of 'privileges of rank'.

A short time later he re-emerged from the tent, and this time he had someone with him. Trestan and Cat both looked with wide eyes as the dark cleric of DeLaris, Savannah, stepped from the tent and shared some words with the red-haired man. Both eavesdroppers shared a small grin at finding the group they had spent the past few days tracking. That grin was quickly erased. As Red-hair and the abbess talked, the saber wielder held a length of rope. The rope stretched to something still inside the tent. He gave it a rough tug, and from the other end someone stepped into view.

Trestan stared with startled sadness. Lady Shauntay stumbled out barefoot on blistered feet. Scratches from walking through tall grass and brush marked her from knees to ankles. Her corset and ruffled skirt were the same clothes worn since the day the battle took place. Her garb hung unkempt and muddy. Her blonde hair hung unbraided; missing the silver clasps that once held it in place. Her tangled locks still displayed flecks of dried blood from when she had fallen off her horse that same dreadful night. The rope Red-hair held connected to her bound hands, though her feet were not bound at all. The young noble gazed downward, avoiding any direct looks with her captors. Trestan and Cat could not hear the conversation between Red-hair and Savannah. Red-hair seemed to be enjoying himself, laughing often and jerking hard on Lady Shauntay's rope. The young woman winced at the rough treatment.

Trestan unconsciously rose. He wanted to charge right across and test the sword's magical blade on that evil face. Cat placed a restraining hand on his shoulder, bringing him

116

back to the reality of the situation. Charging alone into that camp would just be foolish. He lowered himself back to where he could barely peer over the fallen log. Trestan wanted to wish all sorts of bad things upon that man. The young smith admitted such thoughts of revenge and violence weren't really in line with Abriana's philosophies. It was better to hope the young noble would not have to endure this hardship much longer.

It appeared she had one person watching over her. Savannah pointed a finger threateningly at Red-hair right after he had his fun tugging on the rope. His laughter died and he seemed to shrink from Savannah. The abbess of DeLaris gestured to one of the cooking fires, accentuating one more threat before turning her back on the man and re-entering the tent.

More respectful with how he treated his prisoner, but still less than nice, the saber wielder led the young noble towards the cook fire on the far end of camp. The two eavesdroppers from Troutbrook watched as he sat her down near the fire and handed her a plate of food. Red-hair tied off the trailing length of rope to the trunk of a young tree. They showed a lot of confidence in their watchfulness by allowing her hands bound in front; they likely had a number of people to dissuade any attempt at escape. Lady Shauntay tore into the food with her tied, bare hands to feed her hunger. The way she gobbled the food indicated to the others that she may have been underfed in the last few days. Red-hair sat down next to the spit-and-polish pot washer and they talked. Soon both men broke out a set of dice and started tossing them on the ground, taking turns keeping an eye on their captive. She continued to do nothing more than eat her fill.

Trestan looked to Cat for guidance. On a night such as this, they might have a chance to grab the noble and flee into the woods if they acted quick and quiet. There was no way to tell what surprises the rest of the tents held. Trestan also realized, as Cat did, they would have to take out several guards quickly in order to get her out without rousing the whole camp. Cat seemed to change expressions as she looked over the camp and went over several plans in her mind.

Suddenly, the half-elf stiffened in surprise. Cat stared intently at something, pondering some curiosity. Trestan tried to follow her gaze, but he didn't see anything at first. He threw a questioning look at Cat and she responded, "From where Lady Shauntay and the others are sitting, look to the right. There is a depression with some thick bushes in it. Someone is there."

Trestan looked and saw movement coming from where she indicated, but his eyes couldn't see as well as hers. The young human saw a flash of color but he couldn't make out a shape. The figure rose a bit, watching the cooking fire where the noble and her two guards sat.

"Oh gods!" Cat hissed, "Its Petrow! What's he doing?"

Trestan saw Petrow move closer to the campfire. Petrow wasn't very far from where the noble and her captors sat. The smith saw his lifelong friend raise a throwing axe, preparing for a shot. Trestan reached over his shoulder to the hilt of the elvish sword. He looked to Cat and whispered, "I can't believe he's that stupid. We have to help, it's now or never."

Cat already had rapier in hand, but Trestan sensed she didn't share his feelings. Cat stuttered a response. Suddenly, she looked past Trestan with shock. "Look there!"

Trestan turned his head to face the trees on the other side of him. He saw and heard nothing, but he froze with his hand on the hilt, ready to draw the sword if anything appeared. A sharp pain exploded in the back of his head and neck. He slumped over, his vision and thoughts slipping as he lost consciousness.

*   *   *   *   *

Petrow had no idea where Katressa and Trestan hid, but luck was with him. He had crept up the hill and into the brush at a spot near where Lady Shauntay sat. A short distance away, Red-hair and the pot washer started a game of dice as the noble's daughter ate. Petrow could see the other men of the camp, though it appeared they drank and minded their own business. The handyman feared who might be in the tents, but he had the opportunity of a lifetime in front of him. Lady Shauntay was tied to a small tree with only her hands bound. Only two guards were on this side of the camp, and yet they sat with their backs to him. If the young man could hit both men fast, all he needed to do was sever the rope binding the noble to the sapling, then run off into the dark with her. It could be quick and easy. Petrow didn't really care as much for the lady herself. He sympathized with her, but he never liked how she had used all the young men of the village. He wanted to be the hero. He didn't care to be the one to whom the young lady would be indebted; however, her rich father would also be indebted. Petrow relied on the fact that Cat and Trestan had to be somewhere around the camp. The adventuress was deadly enough with her crossbow.

It seemed simple when Petrow thought it over. He would have liked to do something to the minotaur or elf as well, but he respected them enough to fear their capabilities. Ahead were only two mercenaries. They might run rather than face a surprise charge. Petrow had hit targets the size of the Red-hair's head in axe-throwing competitions. The young man merely needed to take a breath and focus his shot. He laid the waraxe in front of him, ready to pick it up after the throw. He took out one of his four throwing axes, and then took out a second. For a short while he tested the heft of each, making sure he had a good feel of the weight.

Petrow raised one overhead to prepare the first throw. His left held the second, ready to switch hands for another throw as he charged. He picked a spot on Red-hair's head and focused on it as the target. Out of the corner of his eyes he saw Lady Shauntay lick the last scraps from her plate. Red-hair handed the dice back to the other man for the next throw. While the other man shook it, Red-hair sat still…making a nice target.

Petrow threw the axe in a smooth, practiced motion. He switched the other throwing axe to his right hand even as the other flew in the air. His aim seemed good.

"Oww!"

The throwing axe hit the center of the red mass of hair with the blade and then bounced off into the grass behind him. The other dice roller looked on dumbfounded as Red-hair clutched his head and fell into a curled-up position. He and Lady Shauntay spotted blood seeping through the clutched hands. From the main fire, one of the other men looked to the source of the exclamation with no particular alarm. He had trouble seeing in the dark after looking directly into the large bonfire.

Petrow charged, waraxe held in the left hand even as the right hand cocked back for another throw. The pot washer dropped the dice in surprise as he saw the threat coming, too shocked to utter a sound. Petrow slowed only long enough to throw a second axe. The other man panicked and threw up his arms for protection. The axe hit a flailing arm but only with the handle and deflected off harmlessly. The man lost his seating and fell on his back as Petrow rushed in. So far, hardly a sound had been raised to wake the camp.

Until a startled Lady Shauntay screamed in terror at the sight of this strange man attacking so near to her.

Voices called out from the tents. The two drinking sentries drew weapons and looked toward the source of the scream. Various shouts and questions echoed from the camp.

Petrow held the axe in both hands and hurried to finish the job so he could run screaming for his own life. Red-hair rolled on the ground, but he seemed unable to put up a fight. The wounded man groaned in pain as he pressed against his bloody wound. The fallen pot washer grabbed a pan but rolled aside as Petrow's axe came down. The waraxe bit into the earth and the young man yanked it loose. The pan swung around and nailed Petrow with a loud clang. The young handyman stumbled and went to his knees, but he swung blindly at the other man. Another loud clang rang as the axe knocked the pan from the ruffian's hand. Both men scrambled about on their knees as the noble continued to scream. Petrow readied his axe for another swing even as the other man grabbed the only other weapon within reach: a pot with a handle. This seemed a small weapon in the face of Petrow's axe. Weapons collided as Petrow tried to smash through the other man's arsenal of cookware. The blow backed the other man up into a bad spot. The pot washer only had sandals to protect his feet, which didn't offer much protection when he stepped back and slipped on the burning logs of the campfire. The man screamed and fell, kicking about with his flaming sandal.

Petrow saw several camp people looking his way. Tent flaps opened as armed men ran out or peeked out at the commotion. Loung Chao stepped out of a tent. The Tariykan stood imposing even without weapons. The threat of the martial artist paled when Petrow saw who stepped out of one of the other tents. His remaining horn gouged a hole in the tent flap as Bortun the minotaur emerged. Neither wore armor, though the minotaur carried the large battleaxe that dwarfed Petrow's axe.

Petrow hoped a bolt from Cat's crossbow would fly in and take out any of these new opponents. He panicked at the growing danger he now faced. He turned towards Lady Shauntay as she continued screaming and yelled in her face. "Shut up! I'm trying to rescue you! Let me cut this rope and run into those trees. Run like your life depends on it, because it does!"

The young noble quieted but turned a worried look towards the gathering enemies. She breathed heavy and appeared in shock from the suddenness of the whole ordeal. She hadn't even stood up yet. Petrow lined up a swing where the rope was tied around the small tree. He swung the axe but ended up hitting the tree too high on the first try. The young man tried to rally his courage despite the shouts of alarm only several steps away from him. He feared a big minotaur was going to hit him awfully hard with a huge axe if he didn't hurry. He steadied his shaking limbs and swung a second time.

The axe blade cut the rope from the tree. "Run, run, run!"

Lady Shauntay got to her feet a little too slowly for Petrow's liking. The blisters, cuts, and pains inflicted upon her on the road from Troutbrook slowed her down as she escaped. Hands still bound, she trailed the length of rope behind her. Through the darkness, she stumbled blindly as tree limbs and brush clawed at her. Her messed hair and rumpled dress snagged a few times.

Petrow glanced back at the camp as she started to run. The most obvious threat came in the shape of the Tariykan martial artist running right at him. Other humans and mercenaries were near, but Loung Chao moved swift as the wind. Petrow readied his axe for a swing. It would be too late to outrun the Tariykan, but if he got in a lucky hit then at least the chances for both of them escaping would be better. Loung Chao showed no fear nor hint of slowing as he bore down on Petrow. The young handyman yelled, "Troutbrook!" and promptly lamented his lack of battle cry ingenuity.

He swung the axe horizontally at Loung. The man jumped over the swing, disappearing from Petrow's field of vision. The young handyman dropped to one knee and reversed his swing. Again he connected to nothing but air, but looking behind him the tactics became clear. Loung hit the ground running after diving over the swing. The Tariykan focused on recapturing the fleeing noblewoman.

That left someone else to deal with Petrow. That someone snorted its musky stench down the back of Petrow's neck.

Petrow barely held on to his bladder as he slowly turned to face his challenger. Bortun the minotaur stood with his axe casually held in front of him. A ring of human mercenaries, much more than Mel's count, formed a wide circle around both adversaries. The armed men appeared threatening enough, but Bortun dominated Petrow's field of vision. Petrow had to look about two feet up to meet those inky black eyes. The minotaur's inky eyes glared at the rash human. Beyond the minotaur Petrow could see the other familiar faces he dreaded. The skull-faced helm of the abbess moved through the edge of the crowd. The handyman worried about what she might do to him, but she only stopped at the side of Red-hair and inspected the man's wound. He resisted weakly. She laid a hand on his head and began her healing prayers. As her miracle restored the health of Petrow's first victim, the second one coddled his burned foot. In another direction, Petrow felt the yellow eyes of Revwar the elf boring into him. The wizard looked at the intruder with undisguised scorn.

Revwar broke the uneasy silence, "As I am a gracious host to unexpected company, I think we should let this one live until he's answered a few questions."

Petrow sighed in relief, though he feared captivity at the hands of this group. Bortun frowned at the elf, clear disapproval at being deprived of its sport. Even as Petrow smirked at the creature, the dark cleric dispelled his courage with her next few words. Savannah stood after healing Red-hair and spoke coldly, "I will have plenty of healing left after I take care of our two men. Let Bortun have some fun and teach a lesson."

The smirk transferred from Petrow to Bortun as the elf nodded his approval. Bortun looked at the waraxe Petrow carried and nodded towards it. "Nice toy you got there."

The minotaur hefted his axe, but allowed Petrow time to make the first move. Petrow pretended to look over his axe, delaying before he actually had to fight the creature. Where were Trestan and Cat? If they were out there why didn't they help him? Petrow looked around the ring of men. He searched for an opening to run for his life, but at the same time he wondered about the noble. He was disappointed to see Loung walking back, the unconscious Lady Shauntay slung over his shoulder.

A cheer from the men was the only warning Petrow received. A solid hit with the flat part of the massive axe sent an explosion of pain through Petrow even as it knocked him aside. His breath rushed out in a huff. The youth rolled into the circle of men, though they quickly moved out of the way as Bortun followed. Petrow used rage to retaliate, even though he knew he had been seriously hurt. He swung his axe towards the minotaur, but there wasn't much strength behind it. Bortun brought a cloven hoof down hard on the waraxe and pinned it to the ground. The young handyman let go of the handle as the larger battle-axe came down and sundered his weapon. He gasped for air as he crawled away from its splintered remnants. The minotaur tossed aside his own axe and reached down to pick up the human. Bortun held him upright and steady, then punched him hard with one muscular arm. Petrow's breath burst out for a second time. Bortun spun around once with the human lifted over his head, then slammed Petrow's body down on the ground.

The young man was in no condition to fight back. He hurt from broken bones and bled from the mouth. He glanced up and saw a couple figures through a haze of blurred vision. Loung dumped Lady Shauntay to the ground at the edge of the circle. Revwar playfully scolded Loung, "A pity you knocked her out, Loung. She might have had some entertainment watching this."

Large, rough hands grabbed Petrow and flipped him onto his back. Bortun leaned over the bruised human and spoke, snorting through some of the words. "I recognize you, human. You stood up for the half-elf back in that bar, and you tried rather badly to stop us from riding out of town. You might remember this from the streets of your hometown."

Then the minotaur raised one muscular leg over Petrow and stomped down hard.

*   *   *   *   *

The light slowly invaded his vision, only for him to close his eyes tightly against the brightness. He awoke rather disoriented. He floated on the edge of his dreams, trying vainly to return to them. He vaguely remembered the sensation of pain, which assaulted him once again. Trying to sneak a look, the light again proved too much and he tried to cover himself with the warm blanket he felt covering him. His body sought the surrender of sleep.

A voice came from nearby, "Look at him! He's finally waking up."

Another, deeper voice answered in return, "Finally we'll get some answers. I was getting sick and tired o' waiting to find out what happened up there. To hell with the half-elf and her story."

Trestan returned to some awareness. He laid under a warm blanket; a bright sun glared overhead. He heard movement nearby and recognized Mel's and Salgor's voices. He tried to sit up, though tiredness and a headache held him back. His senses barely registered Mel as the gnome sat next to him..

"Easy lad," Mel said in his tiny voice, "Whatever happened gave you bad welt on the head. I used up my home recipe trying to ease the swelling. No more salve left until I get to mix some up."

Mel and Salgor helped Trestan rise. Salgor's strong arms forced the young smith into a sitting position. The young man felt the nozzle of a bottle near his lips and drank a large gulp. It burned down his throat. Trestan coughed and spat the fiery liquid out.

The gnome sounded aghast, "Salgor! You have to give him water! Don't give dwarven spirits to a human in this shape!"

"Bah!" The dwarf huffed, "Dwarven spirits will put fire in his belly."

Trestan felt worse but also more awake. The young man took in his surroundings. He saw the ravine where they had made camp. Mel and Salgor were beside him helping the smith sit upright, each one looking a little concerned about his health. Cat and Petrow were nowhere to be seen. Cat's horse grazed in the shade. The sun shone midway through its heavenly course. It seemed odd to wake up so late in the day, and Trestan found his memory of the previous night to be incomplete.

"How did I get back here?" Trestan asked.

Salgor held out a hand to silence Mel's inevitable and lengthy response, then spoke, "I dragged you down partway after Katressa came back for me. She had already dragged you a good distance off o' that bluff. What I am wondering is what happened up there that you got hit in the head and Petrow ended up missing?"

"Oh gods," Trestan recalled the image of Petrow getting ready to throw an axe into the enemy camp. "I remember Petrow was getting ready to stir up a hornets' nest. I wish I knew what happened. What did Cat say?"

Mel and Salgor exchanged confused looks. The gnome replied, "She didn't say anything about a hornets' nest did she? I thought it was a larger animal."

"Animal?" Now Trestan wore the confused expression. "What are you talking about? What animal?"

Salgor wore the customary scowl that indicated he didn't like something that was going on. His eyes narrowed as he looked at Trestan. "She told us the two of you were almost to the camp when you ran into Petrow. She was vague, but said you had somehow enraged some animal the size o' a large boar. She didn't answer direct questions, but by the time it ended you got butted in the back o' the head and Petrow ran off into the woods. She said she took out the creature with her crossbow. I found her explanation odd since she wasn't willing to show me the spot when I asked her. I told her I wanted to help find Petrow. She waved me off and said wait 'til it was light, after I had taken care o' you back here at camp. She kind o' departed quickly and said she would look while we guarded you."

Trestan's confused look showed. He recalled all the events leading up to his loss of consciousness, which were nothing like the tale told to Salgor. The young man wondered why Cat had made up such a thing. Salgor saw the look in Trestan's eyes and his own

122

suspicions were confirmed that the half-elf had been lying. The dwarf looked sternly into the eyes of the young human. "Lad, tell me exactly what happened during the night."

Trestan related what they had seen in the camp. As soon as he mentioned spotting the cleric Savannah and mentioned the hostage Lady Shauntay, Salgor stomped his feet in disgust. The dwarf roared in rage, "I knew it! She lied! She didn't want me running in there and taking my vengeance out on the sorry bunch o' worthless bone weapons. That darned half-elf lied and I missed out on my revenge last night."

Mel interrupted, gesturing wildly with his little hands as he awaited answers. "Well what happened next? What did you see? And where is Petrow?"

Trestan told them about how they had spotted Petrow getting ready to attack a couple men in the camp. Even as he said it he became extremely worried about the fate of his old friend. What had happened after he had been knocked out?

While Salgor still fumed, Mel spoke out loud. "Petrow shouldn't have done that by himself. We were all waiting here ready to help. Did anything happen to him?"

Trestan answered, "I don't know. I didn't see what happened. I saw him about to attack, I told Cat we should help. Cat looked like she was reluctant to do so, but she had her rapier out and ready. Then she saw something, I turned around." Trestan tried to remember everything that came next. "Something hit me and I went out."

Salgor scowled, "That was when you got hit on the back of your head?" At Trestan's nod, Salgor spoke again, "So, what did Cat see? Who hit you?"

Trestan shrugged helplessly. "I'm not sure. She looked past me and said 'Look there'. I turned around and didn't see anything, but then I got hit in the back of the head."

Salgor growled and took up his axe. He paced furiously back and forth, though the young smith watched silently. Mel observed quietly for a short period of time, but eventually he made an observation. "There was a mark on the back of your head. Aside from the swelling, there were a few straight red lines from whatever hit you."

Salgor stopped and answered. "You figured out who hit you yet? She was reluctant to fight, even thought it was suicide to do so. The half-elf has been against any straight fight against that group since they almost killed her in the last fight. She's scared like the rest o' you. She turned your attention away when she saw you were about to charge in with your friend. Then the basket hilt of her rapier left that bruise Mel saw."

Trestan shook his head, then winced when that brought back some of his headache. "Nay, I don't believe it."

Salgor leaned on his axe and stared straight at the young smith. The dwarf's eyes scowled at the young human. "You know who hit you."

Trestan thought it over, as well as the lies Cat told to his two companions. He remembered the reluctant look on Cat's face, and thought it odd that she had drawn out her rapier instead of her crossbow. The young man had to get past his feelings for Cat and admit what his logic had figured out. "Cat knocked me out."

CHAPTER 10

The three companions sat impatiently around the camp waiting for Katressa to return. As much as the dwarf wanted to roar up the hill and find out what happened, even he admitted it would be better to wait for the half-elf's appearance and find out more. Trestan rested quite a bit while they waited. Mel's healing salve helped his head but a lingering headache remained. During this time Mel still talked about anything and everything, but his audience didn't pay much attention.

Before much time had passed they saw a familiar figure walking down the hill from the bluff. Although she picked a course that hid her from above, she didn't try to avoid the eyes of the companions in the ravine. Cat slowed when she saw Trestan awake and all three staring at her. Cat hesitated but didn't stop. The half-elf knew the others would know she lied to them. She had trouble looking at any of them in the eye. Since her attitude already conveyed her guilt and wrongdoing, Trestan dropped his gaze as well. The young smith stared blankly into the sand and dirt of the ravine. Trestan felt a sting of betrayal from Cat's actions. He tried to remember all the good Cat had done for them, but his mind lingered on questions of Petrow's fate.

Salgor had his axe across his lap when he addressed the half-elf. "You lied to me you worthless sneak! My enemy is sitting up on that bluff, waiting for the sharp side o' my axe, and yet he lived to breathe the air o' another dawn."

Trestan had his eyes down, but he could see Cat's boots at the edge of his vision. He had the urge to say something harsh, but he couldn't bring himself to voice any words yet. Cat replied to the dwarf's accusation. "It's not like I thought you all wouldn't find out. Some story was needed to delay you from doing something rash. I apologize for making up a tale about last night but everything I did was for your own good."

Mel started to speak, but Salgor drowned the gnome's words with his own tirade. "And was it for Petrow's own good? Was it for the good of the lady they still hold captive? We dwarves don't mix words and step lightly! If there is a problem we stand right up and take care of it. Don't worry about protecting me next time."

Cat angrily shot back, "Fine, you could have charged in last night. It would have been without me! I knew the truth would send you storming right up there to get yourself killed. I might have had a chance to snatch her from their captivity last night, alone and easily. Thanks to Petrow's foolishness I know how that would have ended! She screamed when she saw him and woke the whole camp. What good would we have done if we charged in blindly, especially after they were awakened to the possible danger? They are tough, organized, and they outnumber us by several. I counted heads last night. There were quite a few more than what Mel saw on the road. It broke my heart to stop Trestan from helping his friend, but I wasn't about to see him get killed foolishly."

Trestan raised his face to Cat and she caught his eyes. She saw the sadness and tears welling up, and she had to avert her gaze. "And what happened to my friend?"

The half-elf also started to water at the eyes. He could see that she cared for Petrow as well. Trestan felt sympathy for her, but did not believe that she had a right to deny him the chance to help his friend. She spoke through strained words, trying to keep a steady

124

voice as she recalled the scene of torture. "He's alive. He actually put up a good fight before they caught him. They hurt him but then they healed him after. They stuffed Petrow and Lady Shauntay into the same tent under guards. I think they questioned him a bit. Apparently he hasn't told them where our camp is."

Trestan muttered, "So at least I have a chance to save him. You shouldn't have stopped me, Cat. I respected you. I trusted you at every turn. It was my choice to get involved last night."

"And accomplish what?" Some of the iron returned to her voice as Katressa replied, "To get yourself killed for nothing? To charge and die gloriously for what you believe, even if that doesn't free the noble? To help a friend that bit off more than he could chew? I saved your life last night!"

Salgor scoffed, "Bah! We'll head up right now and get those kids out o' there."

Cat turned to Salgor, but before she could speak Trestan interrupted, "This is about your father isn't it?"

Everyone, especially Cat, turned curiously to Trestan. Cat asked with a slight tremor to her voice, "What do you mean, about my father?"

Trestan told her, "I remember the story that night before the goblin attack, even though I was almost asleep…

"My father was concerned about the holy items that had been stolen, while various elders were more concerned with shutting the portal and ending the threat of the demons. Eventually, several stepped forth to brave the portal and retrieve the stolen goods. Reatheneus Bilil, my father, proclaimed loudly, 'Yestreal's gift was a relic, it should not be abandoned so easily!' He looked to me and touched a hand to his ear, whereupon he wore a gold unicorn earring I had given him as a gift. He and those brave few went into the portal. We waited for hours. More demons attacked from the forest around us as well as through the portal itself. Finally, the elders conceded they could wait nay longer. I watched numbly as they called forth a miracle and closed the passage between dimensions.

"I screamed, I cried, I denied everything that had happened. Swords and weapons all over the ground, yet the portal was closed and I couldn't charge through to help my father. I never saw him again. I had lost my mother, friends, kinsmen, and my father was trapped in another world. That day I grew out of my childhood for good."

Trestan finished recounting Cat's story and weighed the visible effect that it had on her. A tear fell from her eyes as she remembered the events from her tale. Trestan continued, "That day changed your whole life and it still haunts you. You were worried I would charge into a losing battle, just like you fear your father did. You already lost one battle to them and nearly died. You are as scared as the rest of us." Trestan glanced at the dwarf. "Well, almost all of us. You want to stand up for what is right but you refuse to do so if the odds are against you."

The raven-haired adventuress spoke again, her tone and pace picking up as the words tumbled out. "I try to be realistic. What good is it if one dies for a goal they never accomplish? What good is it to throw your life away for nothing? I pray I could go back to that day and tell that to my father, and damn you Trestan for bringing it up!"

She turned away from them all. Her head lowered, Trestan could see her shoulders shake as she cried. Mel broke the silence, "So, do I prepare to unleash my array of boom spells on the camp or are we just going to walk away here?"

Trestan choked back his own tears and stood up. He was angry at Cat, but he could never hate her for her reasons. He walked over to the half-elf and placed his hands on her small shoulders. She roughly shook them off, but then he grabbed her hard and spun her around. The smith took a weak fist in the gut before he pulled her close into a hug. Her resistance dropped and she sobbed into his chest. Trestan himself wasn't sure if he wanted to scream or cry. The young man looked to Abriana's philosophies for guidance. He remembered the words of his mentor over the years.

"Cat," Trestan started. "Your friends call you Cat, and we are your friends. You've been there for us all this time, and we are all a part of this nay matter how we feel."

Cat stayed silent, but Trestan knew she listened. "Petrow and I knew we were taking a big risk, but we chose to take it. My friend Jareth told me once, a good man has nothing to fear from an early death. Nobody wants to die, but when the time came for Jareth he thanked his goddess even in the face of his enemies. Sometimes people have to be willing to fight and die for something. Abriana expects us to fight for what we love."

Trestan paused a moment, unsure what to say next. Mel and Salgor offered no comments. With the half-elf held in his embrace, the young smith finally spoke again. "You hurt me so much by your actions last night, but I forgive you. You were thinking of our safety, and the tragic loss of a loved one in your past. But you have to forgive us for being willing to face long odds and death to set things right. I feel angry with the people up there, though I try to guide my actions on behalf of their captives, not vengeance. Don't tell us you won't join us. Don't tell me that Petrow isn't worth attempting a rescue. Mel, Salgor and I are going to try to free Petrow and Lady Shauntay from that camp. You want to help too, because sometimes you have to be willing to risk it all for those you love. Sir Wilhelm and Reatheneus Bilil both taught us that."

A few heartbeats of silence passed. Cat nodded her head against his chest. Salgor didn't like one of the things Trestan said and had to set the record straight. "You may not be interested in vengeance, but I am! I'll shove my fist so far up that wizard's ass that I'll be able to move his mouth like a puppet and have him beg for mercy..."

Trestan shook his head, "Ok, I didn't need that image in my head."

Mel laughed and joined in, "Yeah! And I get to play with my new wand!" Mel indicated the wand that had been tucked into his belt since he joined. "I hear it is supposed to work real well. It should send some of them running."

Cat gently eased herself from Trestan's hug and shook her head, "Wait, wait. If you all are determined to do this I'll go, but there is something you have to know first."

Salgor replied, "What could be worse? What more is there to know?"

Cat looked up at Trestan with tears on her cheeks and concern in her eyes, "I came back when I saw something new around the camp. A ship moored offshore from the bluff, and there were men rowing ashore to be greeted by the members of that band. Now we know why they built the large fire last night. It was for their friends to find them."

* * * * *

Petrow stared through a small hole in their tent at the furled masts of the ship anchored offshore. "Well this can't be good news. They have a ship out there. Nay wonder they ditched the horses back around Barkan's Crossing."

No reply answered him, so he glanced back to check on his partner in captivity. Both of them had arms and hands tied tightly behind their backs. About a foot and a half of rope existed between each ankle, allowing them to walk but not run. Lady Shauntay sat against one of the uprights supporting the tent. She didn't acknowledge him or speak, nor had she given him much notice at all during the whole time they were stuck together. The young noble sometimes looked at him like he might be nothing more than an insolent fly on the wall, but mostly she stared blankly at thin air. Petrow had never respected the spoiled noble much, though he felt some sympathy for the rough treatment she endured. The road had battered and dirtied her. He judged that she was trying to shut away the world, and maybe even retreat from the pains of her mind and body. Petrow shuddered thinking she might have endured a torture session under the minotaur and cleric. They beat, healed, and beat him again, in one of the longest nights he could ever recall.

He pulled his thoughts away from the memory. Not having anything else to do, he paced the small tent in short steps and spoke out loud. "Barkan's Crossing has a good harbor. Cat said they had appeared from nowhere without horses except for the minotaur. I bet the ship secretly dropped them off and waited to take them back to wherever they wanted."

No reply came from the noble's lips, though she glanced at him. She didn't seem to see him as a real person, but he continued his one-sided conversation. "They made a big scene when they traveled through that town before. That group knew someone would pursue them. They must have sent one of their lackeys into town to arrange a meeting spot with the ship rather than enter and deal with the guards. Seems logical. They sold their horses and came close to Barkan's before turning and heading up the shore a bit. That's a lot of trouble to kidnap a minor noble from a village; I didn't think you were worth that much. You must be proud."

A whisper finally broke past her lips, "I'm not."

Petrow stopped and looked at her but she wouldn't meet his eyes. He shuffled so he could get in front of her again and spoke, "Well, it is alive. I see they didn't harm your ability to speak. You certainly screamed loud enough last night when I tried to rescue you."

She glared. Her voice came through a little stronger. "That was a rescue? You should have just ended my life for me. That would have been more merciful." She looked him up and down, which was the only time she had studied him at all. Her brows knitted together and her mouth opened a couple times wordlessly. Lady Shauntay admitted, "I've seen you before, but I can't remember where."

Petrow sarcastically attempted a flourish, but the ropes prevented him from doing any kind of dance. "I'm just one of your local hometown heroes. Petrow the handyman, any service at your request. I chop firewood, kill chickens, collect eggs, farm fields, patch roofs…anything done really well, except rescue a damsel."

"Humph," She snorted, "I remember you now. Just another lovesick commoner from my little hole in a hole village. So where did you come up with the money to buy that mismatched assortment of outdated fashions?"

Petrow frowned. He witnessed more of her selfish attitude than her 'lovesick commoners' of the village could see. "I'll have you know this was a nice mix of colors before they got dirt and blood all over them. Blood spilled for *you*, my spoiled lady. A few of us came out to save your hide. I can at least say, after seeing how you have retained your uppity attitude and standoffish behavior, that you weren't worth the trouble."

She turned away from him again and offered a flat reply, "I guess I should be honored, you have my thanks."

Petrow was about to respond with something harsh, but he saw a change in her face. She softened somewhat and blinked away tears. The handyman paused to consider the noble. He never had liked her much, and even now she didn't seem a very good person. She was only human, however, and hurt in one way or another by the events of the past few days. He pushed away the temptation to remain spiteful in the light of her attitudes.

"Look, I didn't come out here because anyone asked me to. Well, my friend Trestan wanted to help you. Do you remember Trestan?"

She looked up at him with the same perplexed look she used when trying to remember him. It stung Petrow to remember how it had brightened Trestan's day when she had flirted with him, and apparently the young woman couldn't even remember his name. "He is the smith's son. You used his attention and flirted with him for some copper hairpieces. Trestan fell under your influence, as all young men in town seem to do, and he gave you those copper pieces free. They must have cost him a bundle to buy and make and you used them as a horse decoration and then promptly forgot he ever existed."

Lady Shauntay frowned and turned away without a reply. Petrow was so mad he didn't try to say anything else right away. It hurt knowing they had gone through all this trouble for someone who would never appreciate it.

Finally Petrow simply sighed as he said, "Well, I know you've had a terrible ordeal. I hope we both get out of this and get a chance to live our lives again."

Lady Shauntay spoke through quivering lips, "I want Sahbin to rescue me. I want her sword at my side. I want to go on late moonlit rides through the countryside. I want my servants to bring me new clothes. I want to interact with people who treat me with respect. I want my old life back."

Petrow stood silent for a bit. "That's a lot of wanting from others. Well I don't know what they plan to do with us, but maybe if we get these ropes untied we can still get out of here. I don't know what happened to my friend but I've learned to depend on myself. We can get back to back and maybe loosen them."

Lady Shauntay didn't answer. She sat with her blank stare on the tent walls. Petrow spoke a little louder, "If we want to escape we have to work on it ourselves. There are plenty of guards outside but we might have a running chance. I don't want to be sold somewhere as a slave."

"They won't let me live. I'm alive now only as a bargaining piece in case someone found us before they got far enough away."

Petrow got in front of her face again, "They were just here to ransom you right? I suppose you have nothing to fear as long as your folks come up with the money."

The noble stared right back at him. "You just stated something like, that was a lot of trouble to kidnap a young noble from a village. And then something about me not being worth that much. 'You must be proud.' To which I replied, 'I'm not.' You thought I was saying I'm not proud. I'm saying I'm not worth that much trouble."

Petrow wore a mask of confusion at that moment. "Then why are you here?"

"I am here because I saw what they were really after. I saw them trying to get away with a crime and cover it up. They needed to silence me. Instead of killing me outright on the street, they took me hostage as insurance since they knew someone might follow. When they depart on that ship, there will be nay more threat. They'll kill me and you so that nay person will be left to talk about what they were really after."

Petrow looked her right in the face. "All the more reason to earn our freedom. Now tell me, what did you see that night? What was this whole thing about?"

Lady Shauntay told him, and Petrow was surprised to learn what she witnessed.

*　　*　　*　　*　　*

Revwar cast one look back at the anchored ship. Rowboats ferried supplies between ship and shore. He could make out Savannah's form on the deck, making her way to the captain's quarters. The elf turned and strode through camp. He looked for Orthymbar and found the redheaded man smoking a pipe with some of his mates. Petrow's throwing axe left a bad cut on his scalp the previous evening, but the cleric healed the damage. The man nodded to acknowledge the wizard's approach. "Hail friend, I'm wondering if we will have nice weather tonight before setting sail."

The men near Orthymbar didn't realize the red-haired man and the elf were having a coded conversation. Revwar replied. "I believe it shall be a good moonlit night. It is getting warmer, and Aburis' reign is coming to a close. Soon Nirahha will command the sky."

The other sailors and mercenaries around the fire didn't know the special message the elf relayed to their companion. Aburis was the largest moon and the most prominent at that time in the night sky, Nirahha was the second largest but commanded the tides during the coming summer months. It sounded like casual conversation, but the redhead took special note of the significance of the second moon replacing the first.

Orthymbar smiled in reply and gestured with his pipe, "Will you men excuse us? I have something private I wish to discuss with our business associate. Take the bottle with you if it will make you happy."

The other men eagerly took the bottle and stumbled away. Orthymbar puffed on his pipe and made sure no one lingered within hearing range. "So, tonight then?"

Revwar nodded, "The captain lies ill. The abbess has done her job well. He has just now summoned her to his side to ease his discomfort. She will finish the job while appearing to tend his ailments. I should congratulate you, the new captain of the *Silver Trident*."

129

The red-haired saber wielder smiled. The deal was complete. "I thank you. It has been a pleasure doing business with you."

Revwar responded, "Nay, the pleasure is all mine. You were there when we needed you. The price was right; all you required was an assassination. You even arranged to have the ship moved on short notice to pick us up away from the prying eyes of the town."

Orthymbar asked, "What about those two prisoners you have? Are they not to be included in any deal? I would like the blood of the man that hit me from behind last night. As far as that wealthy wench, she could be a fine ransom prize, or for other male interests."

Revwar shook his head, "Savannah sets her mind to something and she sees it through. If you want to force that woman to bed, you face the abbess' wrath. I don't know why she can be so cold about murders and yet intolerant of molestation. However, we can't allow either of those prisoners to live. I was surprised to learn the person who tracked us turned out to be a village boy that would foolishly ambush us alone in the night."

Orthymbar stated, "You doubt that he was alone."

Revwar nodded, "By himself he could not have afforded those clothes, that weapon, and this good weed from Pluetlo's Island."

Revwar pointed to indicate the pipe weed the red-haired man was smoking. Orthymbar replied, "And a good brand it is too! Fine smoking."

The elf wizard looked around the campsite at the surrounding trees. "Someone else was with him. I suspect that the half-elf that tailed us to Troutbrook was somehow involved. In either case, we hold those two as long as they might have a use to us."

The impending captain of the *Silver Trident* looked towards the tent confining the prisoners. A few mercenaries stood nearby in case the pair tried to escape. "So, when the old captain is given his funeral and the ship made ready to sail in the morning...?" Orthymbar left the question hanging.

Revwar replied coldly, "Then we are done with them, and they are useless. You can have your fun and kill the rainbow-colored hero that charged our little army. The prudish wench will need to lose her head as well. If by some reason we are attacked by anyone else, the hostages are nay use to us; therefore, silence them immediately."

The elf stood and prepared to walk away, but spoke again. "Oh, one more detail."

Orthymbar looked up to the elf, and Revwar added, "In the morning when Savannah is back on board the ship, and out of earshot of any muffled screams that might arise up here...who cares what else you do to the wench? But she must die, in order to hold her tongue."

The elf turned and walked away as Orthymbar smiled. He cast an evil smile towards the tent holding the lady captive. He looked forward to some entertainment the next morning.

*   *   *   *   *

The evening found the companions sleeping fitfully in the ravine near the bluff. They feared a delay in acting, but Cat had talked them into some measure of caution. Despite the arrival of the ship, and maybe even because of it, she gambled nothing would happen that day to change things worse than what they were. Cat did not expect that their quarry would depart yet due to the way they moved supplies to and from shore. The half-elf also guessed that the camp would be very alert, and any chance to run in and attack would be better saved for the night or early morning. Despite their fears and desires they attempted to get some rest before sneaking up to the camp under cover of darkness. For all but Mel, it was a lost effort. Cat, Trestan and Salgor turned and fretted in their attempts to get some rest, while Mel snored and talked in his sleep about running from big rats.

Eventually, Trestan sat up and walked to the center of their camp. There was no campfire; instead, the center of camp simply consisted of packs and supplies piled in a heap. Trestan sat and stared at the shapes in the twilight. The passage of time left too many opportunities to get mired in the thoughts of how hopeless their struggle might be. The young man had a lot of nervous energy waiting for some kind of release, yet there was nothing to do but wait and brood on the capture of his friend. The rising moons slowly banished the sunlight. Cat walked down and joined the young human. She looked at him with uncertainty, before finally deciding to put one arm around his shoulders. He could guess easily enough at the reasons for her hesitation. After such good times and close moments together, the actions of the previous night hurt their relationship. He remained upset, but she was also the closest friend he had nearby. He put a reassuring hand on her knee, and so they sat in silence for some time. Trestan finally felt the need to get up and move again.

"Cat?"

"Yes, Trestan?"

The young man stood and helped her to her feet. "I can't put my mind at ease, and my muscles are all tense. Could you show me those exercises you do in the morning to loosen up?"

The half-elf nodded and began stretching with Trestan. They removed enough of their clothes to keep flexible yet modest, and Cat showed him routine after routine to stretch his muscles. They went through breathing exercises, flexibility moves, and mental discipline. Trestan couldn't manage all of the moves though he felt a burn in his muscles from the attempts. Salgor watched but did not join in. Mel seemed to sleep the whole time. The routine relaxed the young man, working the knots out of his muscles. It set his mind at ease, focusing on every movement and word that was taught.

Afterward, Cat, Salgor and Trestan shared a drink around the pile of packs. Salgor took out a vintage he described as mellow to a dwarf, yet still had kick for a human. They handed the bottle around long enough for Mel to wake and join them.

Trestan asked them about their early adventuring careers. He asked them how they had reacted to fights when they were new to battle. Mel happily talked first, "It was actually quite embarrassing. The first thing I killed was when I accidentally blasted that rat tormenting my sister. That wasn't a real battle, though it was a great surprise for me and the rat. I remember the first time I ended up in combat against an enemy ready to kill me. I was walking through the woods with some friends when suddenly a hail of goblin arrows flew at us. I remember getting off my Rat Blaster spell on one of them. He was only wounded, and a second or two later I blacked out in pain as an arrow hit me. I woke up maybe a few moments later with our cleric friend kneeling over me. She removed the arrow and healed the damage. The battle still raged around us on the forest path. I got up and fired my crossbow at another goblin and missed. Then the same goblin that had originally shot me ran up and clubbed me in the head. I blacked out again. I'm glad my friends won because that's all I remember from it."

Salgor chuckled, "Heh, I can't remember my first but I sure remember one similar to Mel's. Several friends and I ended up in this fight against a wizard and his followers. I figured I had to take out the wizard so I charged right up to him. He used protective spells but I managed to hurt him. That cowardly guy couldn't stand muscle to muscle with a dwarf warrior. He hit me with spells until I dropped. Then our healer came along and cast his miracles, and I got back on my feet. Charged him again! Then I went down, then back up, then I went down, again and again back up. That dang wizard and healer seemed to have nay end to their spells. Anyway, I've hated wizards ever since. We didn't kill that one that day, but we hunted him down a couple months later and finished what we started."

Trestan spoke, "I guess I already passed my first fight back with those goblins. I don't know if you all noticed, but I shivered after the battle. I had gotten so worked up and excited quickly, but then I couldn't calm down when things were over. Things kept going through my mind afterwards, and my hands shook from the excitement and terror of it. I guess there was also the battle on Troutbrook's street, but I didn't really get to play a part in it."

Cat noted, "I hope your hands are steady in the morning, Trestan. We will need to fight perfectly to handle whatever comes up. If lucky, we'll catch many of them with their pants down." The half-elf wrung her hands. "If we can do nay else, we should get the noble to my horse and let them escape. I'll accept that as a win."

They sat in silence in the darkness. Only the moons lit their faces, revealing grim expressions. Trestan recalled something, and he asked about it. "There is this tune I have heard, played in the inn by adventurers that wander through town."

The half-elf looked to him in the moonlight, "What kind of song?"

The smith thought it over a bit. "It's kind of sad. It has a slow, melancholy tune to it. I've heard musicians play it with a solemn reverence. It has words…though I can't remember them."

Salgor prodded the young man, "Hum a few bars lad, perhaps I have heard this tune as well."

Trestan hummed the tune as best he could remember. Even as he did, some of the words came back to him. Cat recognized it, "I know that song. Sir Carlund's Lament."

Salgor hummed a few bars along with Trestan. "Aye, I know this tune too, though the words change a bit depending on who performs it. Every adventurer knows this one."

Trestan asked, "Tell me about it. I know something of the song, but not the whole story. I know it's a sad song that many adventurers sing when faced with a battle."

Cat clarified it for him, "When faced with a losing battle, or toasting a lost friend. It's a sad song, fit for the adventurer who faces death away from home. The original tune was a funeral dirge originating in lands to the east. Sir Carlund, a native of Tuskora, wrote the words. He was a knight of a holy order and a man of good standing. From what little I

132

know of his life, he was very popular before some internal strife exiled him from his country. His enemies caught up with him on the Island of Lar. On the eve of that battle, he sat down and put words to an old funeral dirge. He knew he would not survive the coming fight, and so he expressed his feelings through that song. He died bravely. After his death, his friends back home were able to justify his actions to the officials of the law. The man's body was returned home to a hero's welcome, and the tune he wrote became popular."

Trestan thought over the story. "Fitting if we could sing it tonight, I suppose? I don't mean to imply the worst will happen, yet I am afraid of how tomorrow will turn out. I don't know all the words but if one of you does, I would love to hear it."

Cat looked to him, "I know the words, I'll start and you can join in when you can."

The half-elf started singing, her voice sounding almost enchanted as she recalled the tragic verse. Trestan sang when he could. Mel would have joined in, but he did not know the song at all. The gnome sat and smoked a pipe as the others voiced the lyrics. Salgor knew much of the song as well, and his voice added a deep quality to it. Together, they sang…

Look not for me, to return to my home;
I will die here, in strange lands I have roamed.

I now wear my finest, clothes worn through hard days;
Fitting to die with them, and ever so clothed I'll lay.
My boots long stained, with the mud of long roads;
Long ways from my kin, how far did I go?

Look not for me, to return to my home;
I will die here, in strange lands I have roamed.

Wrinkles on my brow, the sun burns on my face;
Long have I endured, the passing of age.
I left as a young man, years of wisdom I passed;
Leaving far behind, many a lonely young lass.

Look not for me, to return to my home;
I will die here, in strange lands I have roamed.

Give me my sword, as honor is my right;
I shall not die, until one last fight.
Though many come, I fear not their blades;
They can't destroy the worth of my days.

Look not for me, to return to my home;
I will die here, in strange lands I have roamed.

Remember my courage, remember my stand;
In this way, learn the measure of man.
Now some may grieve, and some never know;
But this was the path I chose to go.

Look not for me, to return to my home;
I will die here, in strange lands I have roamed.

They ended the song with Trestan in tears. Through his sadness he offered his new friends a smile and thanked them. "My gratitude for remembering that song with me this day. Thank you also for joining me on this quest, regardless of your reasons. I'll try to get some rest now, for I foresee a terrible fight in the morning."

CHAPTER 11

The eastern sky brightened as Liijay sank into the western hills. The woods around the camp remained dark as a handful of guards stirred life back into the cook fires for breakfast. Voices drifted from the anchored ship. The early risers of the camp were given jobs of cooking, tearing down empty tents, or preparing the rowboats. They moved solemnly, many recovering from a drunken stupor. Last night the sailors committed their old captain to a funeral at sea. A new captain took his position in stride. Little did they know, eyes watched from the trees.

Trestan had sat in one place too long; he stretched some muscles while staying as quiet as possible. During the night Cat had led them, one by one, to their spots around the camp. With her help, they snuck close without thus far being discovered. She hadn't agreed with Trestan's chosen spot, but she respected his decision. The smith sat where he and Cat had spied on the camp the previous night. This put him at the opposite side of the camp as the tent with the prisoners, where Salgor was poised. Trestan chose the risky task of starting a diversion while Salgor charged to rescue the others. Cat and Mel positioned somewhere between, directly west of the camp and facing out towards the bluff and the shoreline beyond. When things started happening, hopefully their crossbows could assist either end with well-placed shots. Cat had wanted Trestan to stay back, or even try the rescue while Salgor made a diversion. Trestan wouldn't accept it, arguing that he trusted Salgor with the tougher job of saving and protecting two people at once. So now the young man sat, quarterstaff in hand and armor donned.

Some of the trees and tents blocked his view. It was easy to tell which tent held the prisoners due to two guards placed directly outside it. At least two other tents were being dismantled and packed away for transport. If the companions had delayed much longer, the group on the bluff would be sailing away. A line of men hauled equipment back and forth between camp and rowboats. The busy haulers meant there were less guarding the camp than what they might have had. On the other hand, there were still a lot of them around the bluff. The smith recognized only one familiar face. The redheaded man warmed his hands over a fire, garbed in a new coat and hat, wearing them like a badge of office. Other men followed his orders when he barked commands. There was no sign of the four who had fought against his friends on the streets of Troutbrook.

Trestan remained nervous about everything. Although the camp area was relatively quiet, the sounds of coughing and throat-clearing were prevalent. The young man heard noises in the woods as well as the camp, and he could have sworn that not too long ago someone's footsteps had passed near him. He studied everyone in the camp: their weapons, their lack of armor and the general way each of them moved. He gripped his quarterstaff with nervous hands as he considered his combat training and how it would be put to a severe test any moment. The elvish sword was safely slung over his back, ready for use the moment things started happening.

A songbird broke the silence of the morning. The men in the camp mostly ignored it, though some looked to the woods. Trestan heard Cat's call and had almost been dreading it. It was his signal to begin anytime. Any later and the sun would rise over the eastern horizon, leaving Cat and Mel attempting to fire at targets backlit by sunlight. Trestan looked over the closest men and planned his steps in his mind. He singled out a man dismantling a tent, not far from his hiding spot. The man left his scimitar lying to the side as he worked. That mercenary would be a tempting target if he could sneak up and hit before the man could react. Trestan Karok half-rose and prepared to move.

Footsteps crunched behind him. Still hidden from camp, and his back against a tree, Trestan froze as he considered the sound. The pace didn't indicate that the person was trying to sneak around or charge. The steps approached closer, as someone walked out of the woods towards the camp. At that moment the young smith wasn't sure he could even swallow, but he had to chance a look back to see who was there. Turning his head and peering out from behind the tree, he slowly looked around the woods behind him.

The footsteps belonged to the dark abbess of DeLaris, Savannah! She approached out of the deeper woods wearing her skull helm and armor, buckling her belt together without looking ahead. Apparently, Trestan hadn't imagined the footsteps in the woods earlier, as the abbess had gone off to relieve herself in privacy. She walked a path that would bring her right next to the hidden smith. It would be the perfect opportunity to take out a tough opponent at the very start of the fight, if she didn't see him first and stop him with a single miraculous touch. Just the prospect of facing her made the young man's knees shake. Trestan ducked behind the tree. He considered the sword slung across his back, but it was too late to draw it forth without warning her. The quarterstaff was in his hands, so that would have to suffice. The young man made sure he had room to make a swing without any branches blocking the strike. He listened and waited.

Nervously, he mouthed a prayer to Abriana. He dared not even speak it in a whisper, for fear of warning the dark cleric somehow. "Dear Abriana, blessed mentor of my mentor. Guide me with strength and courage. Guide me not out of vengeance or the desire to take a life. Guide me for the desire to free my friends whom I love and thus save their lives. Take my own life in return if it must be done, but give me the chance to free them. Thank you."

Footsteps drew nearer. Out of the corner of his eye Trestan watched the open area the cleric would walk through when she passed. Strong arms, used to long hours swinging a smithy hammer and pounding metal, tightened around the shaft of the staff. Everything Trestan hoped for might depend solely on this first swing against a terrifying opponent. Footfalls crunched next to him, bringing the first boot into his field of vision. Trestan set his weight and swung. Savannah's face lingered on the ground ahead of her in a daze, not paying full attention. The cold, blue-eyed villain, who had so casually bent over him and pronounced her mastery over whether he lived or died, passed alongside without any awareness of his presence. Trestan directed his attack at that cruel visage, noting an opening at the base of the visor that didn't totally protect the mouth or jaw. Anyone watching the staff follow its course could have sworn it bent with the force of that swing.

Savannah's eyes widened in surprise as she saw the threat coming.

CRACK!

Trestan almost lost his balance, but his first impression was that he landed a powerful blow. The skull helm tumbled backwards across rocks and into the bushes, as the

136

helmetless cleric fell like a rag doll. Even though the blonde woman went down quickly, fear drove the young man to swing a second strike. As he twirled the staff he realized something wasn't right. The second swing missed because the staff was missing a third of its length. Trestan looked at his broken staff in amazement.

A brief wave of panic hit as he considered his broken weapon. He looked down at the cleric, lying motionless in a sprawled out position. Blood oozed from her mouth and nose. His one swing might have been a fatal blow, but he didn't spend much time contemplating her condition. The nearby camp awoke with noises and shouts.

Trestan turned towards the tents and saw that the closest man had been alerted. The mercenary grabbed his scimitar and moved to attack. He looked to be close to Trestan's father's age. A patch covered one eye, giving him a tough appearance. Trestan had to reach for his other weapon, though he had never hoped to actually have a need for it when it became his to wield.

He drew the Sword of the Spirit from its scabbard, holding the elvish blade of Sir Wilhelm before him in both hands. The bastard sword gleamed in the morning light, though the sun had yet to rise. The hilt accommodated both hands easily. The other man weaved his scimitar back and forth as they faced each other. Trestan accepted the challenge with a bit of fear, but fully accepting of whatever destiny chose. It was time to find out what kind of a swordsman he really was.

*   *   *   *   *

CRACK!

The sound of the breaking staff echoed across the top of the bluff, followed by the lesser noise of a metal skull helm rolling and bouncing over some rocks. Cat and Mel lay nestled in the bushes only a few feet apart. Their deadly crossbows aimed at their prime targets within the camp. Upon hearing the echoing sound, the half-elf concluded that Trestan had launched his diversion. Men around the tents and fires also looked that way, wondering what caused the noise.

The gnome whispered to his taller companion with raised eyebrows, "Now?"

"Now!" She hissed, and both crossbows clicked as they fired.

The bolts flew from their hiding spot. Both guards in front of the prisoner tent reeled as shafts of wood sprung from their chests. They went down quickly, bleeding their life away on the ground.

In the bushes, the half-elf started to reload even as Mel hesitated. "Shouldn't I ready a spell?"

Cat replied, "Have that crossbow ready. We may need to pick some specific targets, and they might not line up nicely for a big explosion."

Mel reloaded his small crossbow.

*   *   *   *   *

CRACK!

Salgor already felt wound up as tight as he could bear waiting for any kind of action to start. He had almost charged when he heard Cat whistle, but the sound of the staff across the camp made him jump up at a run. He charged right towards the prisoner tent, wielding axe in one hand and holding up his shield with another. One guard stood near the woods, but the man's gaze was turned towards the sound of the breaking staff. Salgor didn't waste time trying to kill the man. A shield punch knocked the human to the ground.

"Daerkfyre sends his messenger!" Salgor yelled, despite the small voice in his head that warned him it was better to get to the tent without drawing attention. The dwarf's rage ran through his blood, and his axe would only be satisfied with direct and open violence.

Two men rose from the fire Petrow had attacked the previous night. They grabbed petty blades in a quick attempt to defend themselves from the squat figure running at them. Salgor slowed and spun his axe in anger. Battle cries and screams rang out as the dwarf dove into the attack. The volume of noise from the dwarf overshadowed any distraction Trestan had attained.

*   *   *   *   *

Trestan and the scimitar wielder moved cautiously, testing each other. A few tentative swings brought forth the ring of steel but never got close to hurting either man. The young smith looked at his opponent carefully. He sought a weakness, limp, or any shortcomings aside from the obvious eye injury. The man's patch covered his left eye, leaving him limited ability to see anything that Trestan swung from the right side. At least the smith's opponent seemed as scared as him, judging by the wide eye and skittish strikes.

Weapons clashed again as they moved closer to each other. While both felt each other out, it was apparent that time favored the older mercenary. Other men in the camp were screaming and taking up arms, so Trestan had to risk a determined attack or face numerous blades at once. The tempo of blades stepped up as each man made vicious swings.

The young devotee of Abriana attempted a trick. The elvish blade rose high and dropped towards the mercenary's head. Scimitar rose quick enough to block the overhead attack. Then Trestan spun the sword fast, wrist-over-wrist, even as he dropped to one knee. The low cut connected with something soft and the other man dropped to the ground. Still on one knee, Trestan brought the sword back into a guard position and prepared to parry any response.

The sight before him stunned him about as much as it stunned his opponent. The one-eyed man sat on the ground, a dazed look upon his face, as he discovered one leg ended at a bloody stump. The magic of the keen elvish blade severed the man's calf as easily as if Trestan cut through fruit. The young man recalled the sword's cutting edge during Jareth's fight with the minotaur. The elvish magic had made the blade a truly deadly weapon.

Trestan's hesitation became deadly. As the young man stared at the stump, the wounded man tried a desperate swing. The scimitar arced overhead and came down at the young man's temple. Trestan raised the elvish blade but was too late to block. Scimitar

138

came down and struck Trestan on the head, though the helmet worn by the young man deflected most of the blow. He felt the sting as the tip of the blade flashed by his face. The low visor over his chin deflected part of the blade from slicing through the young man's jaw.

Trestan wasn't sure if he even had both eyes left, but he reacted. He turned the elvish blade straight out and thrust it into the torso of the other man. A scream erupted from the lips of the mercenary. Scimitar fell against the ground as the other man ceased to fight.

Trestan scrambled to his feet and looked down at the dying man. The young smith raised his left hand to feel his face. A fresh cut grazed one eyebrow. He felt a second cut around one nostril, with only a small amount of blood staining the area. Trestan's helm spared him the need to wear an eye patch the rest of his life.

His ears picked up a noise from behind. A guttural voice spewed forth something unintelligible, and the rustle of leaves indicated movement. Trestan spun to deal with the forgotten abbess.

*   *   *   *   *

The newly designated Captain Orthymbar of the *Silver Trident* stood and witnessed the confusion in the camp. The redheaded saber-wielder also shouted in alarm and called for his men to grab weapons. He drew forth his own stolen saber, shaking it in the air to accentuate every command. The two men closest to him he kept by his side as bodyguards.

So far he could only see two attackers: a young man with the exceptionally nice sword, and a tough dwarf who was currently hacking a couple of his men apart with an axe. He recalled hearing the sound of a bolt or arrow whizzing through the air, and it didn't take long before he spotted the fallen guards by the prisoner tent. It wasn't hard to guess where the dwarf was headed at that moment. Orthymbar wasn't about to let the prisoners get away. Revwar said if the camp was attacked then the pair would have to be executed. Aside from the orders given by the elf wizard, the new captain wasn't about to let the young man get away after the axe attack the previous night.

"They're trying to free the prisoners! Execute them! We can't let them talk! You two come with me."

Orthymbar motioned to the closest two men and they fell in by his side. Together they started to head to the prisoner tent. Just then, Cat's bolt sailed from the trees directly at the red-haired man. Orthymbar jumped in surprise as the man next to him lurched from the hit meant for him. The barbed point of the crossbow peeked out at its intended target before the stricken bodyguard dropped dead.

In the bushes, Cat's pulse raced as she saw the redhead and the other man run for the prisoner tent. She pointed at Red-hair and practically shouted at Mel. "Kill that one now! He's going to murder Petrow."

Mel had his smaller crossbow ready. He sighted carefully and let fly the deadly missile. The bolt sailed and landed in a vital part of the back. Mel shouted, "I got him!"

Cat tried to reload, though her eyes were on the man that was still up and running. "I meant the redhead Mel, you hit the wrong guy."

Orthymbar didn't care that his other bodyguard was dead. He would charge in and finish the prisoners before dealing with the rescuers. Now the only one that could get between him and the prisoner tent was Salgor.

*　　　*　　　*　　　*　　　*

The dwarven waraxe, blessed by a cleric of Daerkfyre, dripped blood as the dwarf left the corpses of the two men by the fire. Behind him, the sentry he had shield punched staggered after the dwarf, huffing from a lack of breath. Salgor wasn't far from the prisoner tent, and he pumped his short legs to get there before Red-hair could. There were other men standing around, though none desired to be the first to intercept the maddened dwarf. Salgor ran past a tent flap when a figure flew out towards him.

Loung Chao had been waiting in the tent across from the prisoners for an enemy to show himself. Although Loung could catch bolts and arrows, he wasn't about to stick his head out into the open earlier than needed. When the dwarf ran up, he had prepared his mind and body for a very powerful kick. If done right, it could break the thick wood of a barred door.

The Tariykan marshaled his will and surged forward. He took two quick steps from the tent and then sprang upward. One foot folded under him while the other thrust out. Salgor ran right into it. The Tariykan warrior's lead foot smacked hard against the dwarf's temple. Loung landed gracefully in a fighting stance. His foot stung from the hit.

From Salgor's perspective, the world disintegrated into a pattern of different lights and colors. He felt like he floated in spinning lights. His vision cleared to where he could see shapes, and he focused on the human standing in front of him. Loung looked at him through wide eyes. The dwarf suspected that most targets couldn't stay on their feet when a martial artist hit them like that. Even Salgor had to admit there weren't too many enemies that had similarly shaken his senses. His head swam and throbbed.

Salgor Bandago put on his usual bravado smile, narrowed his eyes at Loung, and spoke, "That was almost nice enough to tickle me. Got anything tougher than that?"

Loung didn't answer; instead the man drew out his sickle bladed weapon. Other men crowded around Salgor now that the Tariykan had slowed him down. Salgor looked over the men on all sides. His most worrisome sight was the redheaded saber-wielder running into the prisoner tent with his drawn weapon. Petrow and Lady Shauntay would be dead in seconds if no one stopped him, and it looked like no one could. Salgor bellowed a war cry and charged. Loung whipped the chain end towards the dwarf but stepped back to let the other mercenaries pile on to the short warrior. A scream from inside the prisoner tent rose above all other battle noise.

*　　　*　　　*　　　*　　　*

CRACK!

When the strange sounds first erupted from outside, Lady Shauntay was struggling to untie Petrow from his ropes. She was only free because Petrow had lost patience and forced up against her back. Although freed, she stalled much of the night through complaints and disinterest. The morning light against the tent had let him know time was short. It was frustrating that this nobly bred girl couldn't give for others as much as they gave for her. Shauntay had loosened his elbows, and he was close to having his arms free. His legs were still joined by a foot-and-a-half length of rope.

She stopped again as she heard the cracking sound. They both paused to listen. The noble's daughter said, "Listen. Something is happening!"

Petrow heard the noise and assumed it was his friends. He could hear the ring of steel on steel and the grunts of pain from right outside the tent. He stood upright, but he stepped closer to Lady Shauntay and turned to keep his bonds facing her. He thought his angry glare would finally force her to act with more haste as he spoke firmly, "We have nay time, get me loose now."

The noble turned to him, talking to him but not listening to his words, "My guards are here! My father himself must have ridden out to rescue me! He'll step in here any moment and take me home."

Petrow shook his head, "Your guards rode away to the south of Barkan's. My friends are probably out there now trying to buy us time to flee. You have to untie me now so we can run!"

Lady Shauntay looked to him in puzzlement. Surely the man could see they were being rescued? He should be as relieved as she was that this was all over. She had dreamed of this moment every painful step taken since that fateful night of her capture.

Petrow saw her confused expression, even finding it pitiful that she was actually smiling and convinced of a storybook rescue. "Get me loose now! Look through this junk in here. Find something sharp."

Light reflected in the tent from the opening, and the cool morning air wafted in. Lady Shauntay looked to the entrance; her expression changed from relief to horror. She shrank away. Petrow knew their time was up. The young handyman turned to the front of the tent and saw the red-haired man he had wounded previously. He had learned the man's name was Orthymbar. He held the naked steel blade of the captain's saber.

Orthymbar waved the point of the deadly blade casually between Petrow and Lady Shauntay. The man promised murder in his eyes. "I wish I could have enjoyed the lady, but at least I'll have the blood of both of you. Now, who do I kill first?"

Petrow acted the most responsible way he could, despite his distaste for the woman they had come to rescue. He elbowed her towards the back of the tent. The young handyman traded stare for stare with his would-be murderer.

Orthymbar found the gesture amusing, chuckling over it. "You first then. I'm going to enjoy this."

Petrow stood steady, as scared as he had ever been in his life. He stood in the best clothes he had ever worn, with the comforting thought that his friends outside had tried to save him. His hands were still bound and his feet tied a short distance apart. There was little he could do to stop the saber as it moved to strike him.

Lady Shauntay screamed.

*   *   *   *   *

Trestan held his sword out to block any attack from the abbess of the Death Goddess. He turned to discover she wasn't a threat. The noises came from her involuntary muscle twitches. Savannah's voice let loose a gurgling noise as she tried to breathe. Her broken nose and mouth oozed blood. The cleric's jaw sat at an odd angle from the rest of her face. As she lay there with closed eyes, she seemed oblivious to anything going on around her.

Trestan felt a small urge at that moment borne out of fear. He could end the cleric's life easily, thus ridding himself of a very powerful enemy. It was a small thought, and he dismissed it, scared that he had even considered the notion. As he looked upon her helpless figure, he reflected how ironic it would be to take her life when she had spared his. Trestan honored a goddess devoted to love and healing, while the cleric represented the deity that claimed control over death. Trestan could not bring himself to end her life and yet retain his faith of heart.

The young man turned to face the camp. He saw fighting on the other side of camp; heard shouts to honor a dwarven god. Trestan ran forward a bit but slowed when he saw several men approaching. Four armed men charged his direction. A big one with a mallet yelled curses at the other three to attack. Trestan watched them approach with the set determination that he might die. He was not about to back down, and the memory of his brave mentor stirred him on.

"Abriana!"

Trestan did not charge, anticipating that he would have to somehow try to single each man out if he was to stretch the fight as long as possible. The first one ran up to him with a short sword ready to strike. A bolt from the trees zipped in and punched out the man's throat despite the fast run. The sailor dropped and rolled in his death throes.

Three armed men were better odds than four. Trestan put his sword into motion as the others charged in. He told himself to remember the three trees by Abriana's shrine. The first weapon arced in and was deflected by the elvish blade.

*   *   *   *   *

Cat pulled back the string on her crossbow with her belt claw. Her shot claimed one of Trestan's attackers, but the rest would still be more than the young man could handle. She spoke to Mel as she tried to reload. "Trestan is in trouble."

Mel aimed his crossbow. He spoke out of the corner of his mouth as he concentrated on his target. "I think Salgor is in worse trouble. He's surrounded!"

Cat looked towards the other side of camp. Salgor fought off a crowd of men. The mercenaries and sailors surged forth from all sides, as Loung stood safely back. The Tariykan whipped his chain at the dwarf from a distance as the others closed in. Mel's shot took out one of the men in that group. Cat looked towards the prisoner tent and cursed at the sounds of screaming from within. Even worse, she saw several men with their own crossbows getting ready to fire at her and Mel.

142

*   *   *   *   *

Salgor swept his axe in a circle. Men jumped back to avoid it, though some weren't fast enough.

"All of you, tackle him now! Hold him down!" Loung yelled.

The dwarf warrior threw his shield over his head as bodies surged at him from all directions. The middle of the pile became a flurry of punching and biting. It was so chaotic and dark under the pile that mercenaries injured each other thinking they were hitting the dwarf. Salgor got in his own fair share of biting and head-butts. Eventually, the dwarf pulled a flask from his belt to his lips using his right arm. He took big swig of it into his mouth, and then worked his thumb and forefinger to use a small gadget on the lip of the bottle. The tiny flint gadget sparked a flame on a soaked piece of cloth. Salgor turned his head from under his shield and belched fluid through the flame to create a small fireball.

A puff of flames and smoke came from the pile of men. They scrambled to get away, several screaming from small burns. Salgor thrust his shield upwards and threw off the remaining men. He turned and shook the bottle out across a wide arc. The rest of the potent alcohol ignited as it emptied and spread more flames. Most men scrambled to get away, others actually took swings at the dwarf. Salgor used his left hand to shield-punch one that got too close. He slammed Loung to the ground.

The short warrior yelled his triumph, "Dwarven whiskey! Puts a fire in your belly!"

Salgor discarded the bottle and picked up his battleaxe. He attacked viciously to gain some ground on the prisoners' tent, but too many armed men still blocked his way.

*   *   *   *   *

Orthymbar's saber sliced at Petrow. The young man stepped to one side, just enough that the tent's center support pole blocked the blade. The redhead growled and pulled his saber free. Petrow tensed his body and sprang. The handyman used his whole body and launched his shoulder into his attacker. Both men tumbled in a tangled heap.

Curses streamed from the new captain's lips. Both men rolled about and tried to get to their feet. Eventually, Petrow just tried to use his leg and kick at the redhead. Orthymbar got to his knees and turned the table on the young man. He bare-handed punched Petrow time and again; the young man unable to defend himself.

Petrow nearly swooned as he squirmed to avoid harm. He tasted blood. His breathing became difficult with the pain in his sides. During that whole time the noble cowered in the back of the tent, missing her chance to run for freedom. As Petrow struggled to breathe, Orthymbar retrieved his saber. The man paid little attention to the bound prisoner writhing on the floor; he turned his eyes on the noble and went to make his kill.

*   *   *   *   *

Trestan recalled his mock fights against the three trees outside of his home village. While the tactics were helpful, those trees had never actually moved to kill him.

The big man with the mallet swore, "Damn it, Julel, get around him. Why can't you all surround him like I asked? We….err…argh! Darrek you let him slip away again!"

Trestan wasn't aggressively fighting as much as he was evading the three men trying to surround him. Weapons slashed and thrust as the young man parried several attempts to lame him. He kept the sword spinning in a defensive circle, changing it every now and then to force a man back or slip through an opening. He had practiced this style against several imaginary attackers in those quiet woods. The young man moved and dodged so that not all three could get around him at any time. Many times one enemy couldn't attack due to Trestan dodging behind another man. When that happened the young smith only had to worry about one or two blades, while the other men were forced to chase. They turned and bolted in such crazy circles that they inadvertently moved close to a sharp edge of the bluff. A steep drop fell away twice a man's height to the shoreline.

Trestan stumbled behind a tree even as the big mallet connected with it. More curses from the big man followed as one of the other men blocked his attack angle. The elvish sword parried the short sword of this new attacker and spun in an offensive arc. The man referred to as "Darrek" stumbled away from it even as "Julel" ran around the other side of the tree. The young smith from Troutbrook switched direction so fast that he and Julel crashed into each other. The men went sprawling in the dirt.

Trestan rolled away and hopped to his knees moments before a mallet smacked the ground where he had been. Julel tried avoiding the bigger man, but rolled into his legs instead. The big man stopped to kick the prone sailor out of anger.

Trestan prayed for a bolt from Cat and Mel would help him out, but he didn't know they were trading shots with other men closer to their position. The area where Cat and Mel hid had bolts and arrows sticking out of the nearby trees. Meanwhile, they were trying to load fast and have every shot count. If Mel and Cat were unloaded at the same time, they risked their attackers rushing forward as a mob.

From the bluff's edge, Trestan glimpsed a number of sailors running from the shoreline to join in the battle. They had been loading a rowboat on the shore when the excitement erupted up top. Most of the friends didn't know it, but several reinforcements had just arrived to fight them.

With the other two attackers momentarily distracted, Trestan dueled with Darrek while trying to get some distance between himself and the others. Both men whirled their swords at each other without injury. Trestan took the opening to turn and run a few steps. The young man hadn't gone far when he realized he was making a bigger mistake. Trestan's foot extended over nothing but open air as the steep edge of the slope opened ahead of him. He caught a tree branch and swung around the trunk, narrowly avoiding a fall to the shoreline below.

Darrek, a step behind Trestan, had been focused only on the young man. The mercenary also saw the edge of the bluff rather late and tried to stop his momentum. He stood for a moment teetering on the edge. The elvish sword slapped the mercenary hard on the back. It wasn't a very clean swing, hitting the target with mostly the flat part of the blade. It was enough that Darrek lost his balance and fell down the steep slope.

Trestan had little time to gain a good stance. The warrior with the mallet and the other swordsman had him trapped against the edge. Cornered, breathing heavily from running around in the metal armor, Trestan couldn't evade fighting two at once.

*   *   *   *   *

Salgor cleaved one man. From out to the side a chain whipped into his face and stung him. The dwarf used his shield to knock down another man, but Loung's kick hammered his abdomen. No more missiles from Mel arrived to take out any more of his attackers. Salgor was truly alone and could not seem to move through the waves of men. For every one he dropped, Loung Chao stepped in to deliver a hit from another direction. The dwarf head-butted a mercenary with a spear, only to feel a fist hit him in the back.

Enraged, Salgor spun around in a swipe that cut low another man. But Loung was in the air, hitting the dwarf with a jumping kick. The dwarf thrust his shield out to shove back another attacker, only to see the length of chain from Loung's weapon whip around his shield arm. A jerk of the chain stripped the crested shield from the dwarf's grip.

Of those humans still near the dwarf, most viewed the damage he had caused to their fellows and stayed back out of fear. Dead men and their body parts ringed the worshipper of Daerkfyre. The blessed axe dripped red. The dwarf had already shrugged off several hits that would have downed most men regardless of armor. Only Loung stood within an unhealthy distance from the dwarf.

Salgor fixed his stare on the Tariykan. "Time for you to go down."

Salgor raced at the martial artist and launched several swings. His axe cut the air around the man, but Loung moved with grace unlike any other. A punch and a kick hit the dwarf and went unanswered. The sickle blade of Loung's weapon stung the dwarf's side, but didn't penetrate past the armor. Salgor finally hit the human with a fist, though it wasn't a very solid connection. Blow for blow, Salgor slowed.

A kick from the Tariykan knocked the helmet off Salgor's head. The blade of the dwarf's axe lowered until it touched the dirt. The strong bouncer sagged heavily from the punishment of the Tariykan's hits. The dwarven muscles had lost their steam.

Loung and the other men closed in around Salgor. The martial artist stopped to bow to the dwarf before resuming a fighting stance again. He spoke to the men, "When I say, move as one. Impale him from everywhere at once."

*   *   *   *   *

Orthymbar stepped over Petrow to murder Lady Shauntay. Petrow breathed through painful gasps. The young man's arms were still tied and trapped underneath his body. He looked down at his legs and saw the redheaded man stepping between them to get to the noble. Out of desperation, Petrow brought up his legs and kicked at the man's knee. The handyman's legs and ankle rope trapped Orthymbar's one leg. The knee buckled

145

a bit, but Orthymbar barely managed to keep his balance amidst the thrashing. He raised the saber to slice Petrow's legs off.

Petrow fought dirty. He kicked out with one leg and nailed the redhead right in the fatherly jewels. A whoosh of air went out of their attacker as he dropped. Petrow scrambled to his knees, then hopped back up to a standing position. In that time the saber wielder slowly regained his feet, one hand covering the tender area.

Petrow had nothing to gain by standing still or trying to retreat deeper into the tent. The handyman hobbled forward and used his body to push Orthymbar. The new captain hit Petrow with the hilt of the saber. Petrow almost had him cornered, but the handyman felt the tip of the saber poke against his upper abdomen. Orthymbar was ready to push the blade through some very vital organs.

Unable to punch, Petrow literally used his head. His forehead shot forward and shattered Orthymbar's nose. The saber still thrust forward, sliding across the skin of Petrow's chest in a shallow cut instead of a deadly thrust. It stung, but Petrow continued with desperate abandon. More head butts followed; blood spilled from Orthymbar's nose.

The redhead finally got a hand on Petrow's shirt and shoved. A moment later, the hilt of the saber rushed up and slammed against the young man's face. He fought a wave of dizziness, only to realize he was again on his back with his arms trapped underneath him. The saber poised to deliver the fatal blow. Petrow closed his eyes to avoid seeing his own death.

CLANG!

The young man was puzzled at the sound, but even more so by the sound of splashing water accompanying it. Petrow popped one eye open. Lady Shauntay stood scared at the edge of his vision, holding a slightly dented chamber pot.

Orthymbar stood with a shocked but conscious visage. The man was bruised and bleeding; a chamber pot and its contents colliding with his head hadn't been in his plans for that day. The captain's coat was going to need a good wash.

His eyes pierced Lady Shauntay with a deadly glare. She dropped the pot and started to back up. His fist launched out and hit the noble hard. Right hand still poised with the saber, his left hand grabbed the noble roughly by part of her low-cut bodice. He threw Shauntay down, her landing slightly softened by the fact that she dropped onto Petrow. Petrow was trapped as she pleaded for her life. She made no move to defend herself, and the saber raised for the kill.

*   *   *   *   *

Trestan didn't have much fight left in him. The constant running battle, in armor, had drained the young man's energy. As he faced the two men, he honestly considered the idea of simply leaping over the bluff and taking his chances in the fall. His friends were in trouble though, and he would give them every chance. In his worship of Abriana, he believed that giving his life for someone he loved was very noble.

The two opponents moved in, the man with the mallet showed the most initiative. Trestan assumed he was a man of rank or simply a reputable fighter. The other man

146

followed his every command. Trestan considered the powerful edge of his enchanted weapon. It was time to try another tactic and hope out of desperation that it would work.

The mallet whirled around at the young man, and the elvish blade swept up to meet it. Instead of a parry, the young smith slashed with all his strength. The mallet came close to the young man's head when the elvish blade collided with it. The metal head of the mallet swished past and over the edge of the bluff to the beach below.

The big man stared blankly at the useless handle of his severed weapon. A relatively clean cut marked where the magical blade sheared off the head.

Hand over hand the young man spun the elvish blade in an arc to finish the move. The swordsman Julel watched as the sword beheaded the big man in his moment of stunned stupor. Trestan watched the body fall with an amazed look on his own face. The young smith from Troutbrook paused at the sight of the headless corpse. He wouldn't have killed the man if he had been given a choice, but his friends needed him.

Trestan looked up at Julel and tried his best threatening face. The blood on Trestan's brow, nose and sword lent weight to the intimidation. Trestan even took a few steps, scaring Julel into running for his life. For a moment, no other enemies were close enough to threaten the young man.

A breathless Trestan turned and the color drained from his face. A figure rode upon the winds from the sea. Cloth flapped in the morning air as the wing-like cloak provided flight to its owner. Yellow eyes looked over the camp battle from above, fixing on the lone attacker closest to him.

Revwar joined the battle, and the elvish wizard flew well out of range of Trestan's sword.

*   *   *   *   *

Cat and Mel ducked several bolts that flew through the air. Mel lamented the loss of his water sack, which lay pierced by a shot from the camp. Cat had used up all the ammunition in one quiver.

As she reloaded, she glanced at the danger facing the rest of the companions. She saw Salgor in a losing battle against the Tariykan and several armed men. No screams were heard from the prisoner tent. The redheaded man had been given plenty of time to finish his task, though he had not exited. Trestan stood staring up at the wizard Revwar. The elf certainly had a host of deadly spells to command, and Trestan couldn't threaten him. The companions' situation seemed hopeless.

Mel shouted, "Cat! I think they are getting ready for something!"

Cat finished loading and took a shot at their enemies. The bolt dropped another attacker, but his friends were all holding loaded crossbows or readied bows aimed at her and Mel.

A voice was heard from the edge of camp. "Fire!"

Cat and Mel dropped low as a host of deadly missiles descended. One skidded off Cat's helm, while another impaled her crossbow and rendered it useless. The half-elf did

147

not know if anything hit Mel, but she heard him whispering in his small voice. Mel prayed to Daerkfyre for strength and courage. At least the gnome hadn't been hurt badly, if at all.

When Cat looked up, war cries revealed their tactic even if her eyesight failed her. Around eight or more mercenaries, melee weapons in hand, charged in for the kill. Even if she had a working crossbow, she would not be given the time to reload it. Mel also looked at the rushing men and dropped his mouth open in surprise.

Cat jumped in front of Mel and drew her rapier. Silver gleamed from blade to cat's head pommel. The half-elf brought it level with the heart of the closest warrior. As the morning breeze fluttered her long, raven hair, her emerald green eyes glared at their enemies. She uttered a plea, "I hope you have a good spell ready. I'd rather not die today and have it all be for nothing."

CHAPTER 12

Cat stared down her charging attackers as she stood her ground. The last thing she expected was a small hand to reach up and pull her back. Mel tugged at her belt and put himself in front, directly in the path of harm. She started to argue, but noticed his wand pointed at the gathered horde of men. Mel spoke a single word. Suddenly, Cat's eyes flinched against a bright flash. A resounding boom, like the roll of thunder, assailed her ears.

The first magical bolt crackled like lightening but surged forward in a straight line. The closest men were blackened as the energy burned them. The beam of magical destruction didn't stop there. It continued in a straight line through a tent, over the bluff, and finally fading into a harmless tendril of smoke over the sea. The wave of attackers stumbled about in shocked confusion. Some held their ears from the roar of noise; others stared dumbly at their stricken companions.

Mel fired the wand again.

Cat stood back and squinted through the bright flashes in awe. She covered her sensitive elf ears from the thunderous booms, each one vibrating the air. The mass of men that had threatened them became separated and consumed in successive blasts from the powerful wand. Battle cries turned to screams of pain and terror. Wherever men stood together in a clump, the gnomish sorcerer would send one of his burning bolts. Living men were instantly charred or thrown to the ground. Some men threw down their weapons to turn and run for their lives. Cat stood in silent, open-mouthed surprise as she watched the carnage erupting from the small gnome sorcerer. Through it all one horrifying sight frightened the half elf more than anything else.

Mel's first blast leveled the prisoners' tent.

*   *   *   *   *

Petrow saw the saber coming down out of the corner of his eye. Suddenly the world exploded in a flash of light and a roar of noise.

The young man felt he was floating soundlessly in space. Dark and light colors danced before his vision. He continued to feel trapped, unable to move. Petrow could remember who he was, but he had no idea where he had gone. Was this the afterlife?

Lights and sounds slowly returned. He heard a mix of shouts and screams, though the noises sounded muffled. His vision fixed on a light in front of him. The handyman saw a blue sky, through the blackened outlines of a torn tent that partially covered him.

If he was dead, why were his arms still tied behind his back? For that matter, why was Lady Shauntay still on top of him?

Looking around, the young man realized he was far from dead. Lady Shauntay was lying on him with her eyes closed. She sobbed and cried; therefore she was also very much alive. The tent supports were burned short, burning scraps littered the ground, smoke rose from tattered, blackened cloth. Whatever hit them had reduced the tent to a smoldering pile of rubble.

149

Then Petrow saw the blackened saber lying next to him. Beyond the weapon was a charred figure missing his right arm. From what Petrow could make out, the person near him wore the remains of a captain's coat. Moans arose from the individual as the man struggled to move. Orthymbar had been burned and lost an arm, but he wasn't dead yet.

Petrow wasn't about to watch his attacker recover. He was upset that Lady Shauntay had him pinned by her helplessness while sounds of fighting still raged. The handyman tried to shake the noble off of his body. "Get off! Get off! We have to get up!"

*   *   *   *   *

Salgor stood worn and beaten. He was surrounded and knew they would charge in to finish him in moments. Loung stared at the bearded warrior with malice and the dwarf found himself looking away to see if he had any other options.

The worshipper of Daerkfyre noticed a familiar broken axe, lying in a discarded pile next to the cook fire. Salgor remembered teaching Petrow how to use it and fight with it. The young man had shown some talent; Salgor had been pleased to pass on some of his knowledge. Helping the young lad become a better warrior had been the most pleasant part of this trip. That same youthful lad who had been willing to learn the axe likely just died only a few feet away because he'd been too slow. Salgor felt a deep anger welling up from inside his heart. From childhood every dwarf learns stories about the strong heroes that carved out their nations. Tales pictured dwarves that could sunder pillars of old stone, or lay low the mightiest giants with one punch. One particular line from those stories came to mind: "The strongest muscle any dwarf warrior has, is his heart."

Salgor got a firm grip on his axe. His heart beat faster, as his breathing quickened. He had fire in his eyes as he raised his head. He stared at Loung with a menacing intensity the Tariykan found hard to match. "You shouldn't have broken his axe. And you really shouldn't have hurt that boy."

Despite the line of naked steel in front of him, the dwarf actually jumped towards the Tariykan. Loung reacted as the dwarf sprang forward, "Now! Kill him!"

Swords and daggers shot forwards from all sides. All the men followed the forward movement of the dwarf and aimed their weapons for him. Loung had his weapon ready, but he backed up to stay out of harm's way.

As the rest committed to their actions, Salgor dropped to the ground and rolled backward, reversing direction so fast that it was hard to react in time. The men in front of him had only air to hit. The men behind him were springing forward, trying to reach the dwarf as he charged Loung. The dwarf rolled into the legs of the men eager to hit him from behind. They tripped and fell amongst their companions who had surged in from the other sides. Screams were heard as weapons found flesh. Loung watched the pile intently, losing track of his opponent.

The first bolt of magical lightening from Mel's wand flew through the camp, followed closely by a second. Loung ducked behind a tent but watched the pile of men to see what happened to the axe wielder. Salgor Bandago, worshipper of Daerkfyre, jumped up from behind the other side of the pile. Several other mercenaries and sailors remained uninvolved in the tangle, and they stood in a position that still separated the two warriors.

The dwarf roared at the Tariykan with anger in his eyes, "You are going to wish you hadn't been born!"

Loung smirked a reply. The Tariykan already knew he was a better fighter than the dwarf. There were also several men between him and the short warrior. "Try to reach me before I teach you a lesson in humility, dwarf."

Another magical bolt of energy from Mel arrived to help his friend out. A blinding flash of lightening erupted between the Tariykan and the dwarf, throwing apart the pile of men in a blast of energy. The group of mercenaries, blasted and burned, either ran for cover or rolled about dazed. There was now a clear path between the two antagonists.

"Gladly," replied Salgor as he charged.

*   *   *   *   *

Revwar looked down upon the smith with the elvish blade. He smiled in amusement at the sight. The elf made a few quick gestures to rid himself of this nuisance. Trestan couldn't hit the elf, and he didn't dare try something as desperate as throwing the sword. Instead, he got ready to dodge whatever spell was thrown his way. The young human spun the Sword of the Spirit in front to parry any attack.

Three flaming swords appeared in front of the elf wizard and flew forward. Trestan saw that spell used on Sir Wilhelm. One magical blade was high and to the left, another high and to the right, and the last one was low and centered towards Trestan's legs. The young smith leaped forward and slid into the ground feet-first. Two blades sailed high, but the last flew straight for him. All the young man's concentration focused on that last sword. The elvish blade whipped across and parried the flaming missile. As before, every missile disappeared into thin air regardless of whether it hit or missed. Trestan scrambled to his feet again.

Revwar hadn't paid much thought to the young man after releasing his spell. The elf wizard flew closer to the camp to survey the battle. He saw the mercenaries being routed by Mel's magic, as well as several bodies on the ground and several flattened, burning tents. The elf noted Salgor and Loung fighting, and he saw that the other humans weren't offering much help to the Tariykan. He scowled at how badly their men were losing to a handful of young attackers. His vision caught someone else familiar who looked to need his help.

The elf wizard drifted to the ground on the north side of the camp. Lying there under some trees was the cleric Savannah. She was still alive, though she had not regained consciousness yet. Trestan wasn't very far from the two of them. The young smith worried that if Revwar could get Savannah back into the battle, then all was lost for sure. Trestan was about to shout to Mel and point out the elf's position, but Revwar cast a spell.

A misty field shimmered in the air between Revwar and Mel. The young smith guessed it might be a barrier to keep anyone from harming the elf before he could finish whatever he was doing. Most likely, it protected him from Mel, who was quite noticeable

151

from the steady barrage of magical bolts launching into the camp. The field didn't separate Trestan from the wizard. With sword in hand, Trestan moved to confront the most dangerous opponent visible.

*   *   *   *   *

Blast after blast flew from the wand. The gnomish sorcerer sent a bolt at every pocket of men that stood too close together. Mel shouted between bursts of energy, "That's how we cook rats back home! Mess with my buddies, you get stung! I bet he wished he had a shield. Oh, you still got a spine do you?! Who's next?"

Mercenaries screamed, ran or died. Anyone of them that tried to charge Mel burned without getting close. Others who raised a crossbow were stricken the moment they tried to aim it. Several ran away from the magical barrage, opting to escape in a rowboat. The campsite full of armed men became a graveyard. Small trees burned, grass fires smoldered everywhere, and not a single tent still stood. The exiled son of the Bellringer family, (renowned makers of fine bells, chimes, gongs, and other acoustical instruments), had taken out more enemies than the rest of the companions combined.

Mel looked over the tip of his smoking wand. Not a single enemy threatened to attack him or get close. Aside from his friends in the camp, most of their enemies seemed to be fleeing or they were fighting too close to the dwarf to risk a shot. As Cat looked onward in awestruck shock, holding her unblooded rapier in her hand, Mel jumped up on a rock and raised his arms in triumph.

He proclaimed, "NEVER mess with a gnome sorcerer that worships a dwarven battle god!"

*   *   *   *   *

Loung sidestepped Salgor's first attack. A foot arced in to deliver a solid kick to the dwarf's ribs. The battleaxe came around as Salgor realized the move, slicing a thin line along Loung's bare chest. The Tariykan stepped back as the axe continued to twirl in a deadly dance. Salgor brought down an overhead swing that barely missed. Loung again stepped to the side just in time. A shattered barrel pelted the martial artist with its splinters. For a moment the axe stuck, so Loung delivered a closed fist to Salgor's face. Salgor didn't move to free the axe at first, opting instead to deliver a punch of his own at the human's midsection. Both opponents landed hard hits. Salgor freed his axe as Loung again looked for room to maneuver.

The Tariykan used his sickle weapon in an attempt to trap the axe, but Salgor pulled his weapon back out of reach. Right after it occurred, Salgor changed and stuck his axe too far out again in another swing. This time Loung got the chain wrapped around the axe handle and prepared to disarm his opponent.

Exactly as Salgor predicted he would.

The dwarf had his weight set and pulled the Tariykan with both hands. Loung found himself dragged towards the dwarf's blade. The axe flashed across where Loung's

152

neck should have been, though the human ducked and rolled under the cut as it launched. Salgor's back swing almost caught the rear of his opponent, but Loung Chao preferred to release the grip on his weapon rather than be pulled back into another close call. The Tariykan tumbled away unarmed and then sprang back into a fighting stance.

"An eye for an eye!" Salgor proclaimed, as he brought his axe down on the sickle-bladed weapon. A couple hits later, Loung's weapon was in more pieces than Petrow's waraxe.

A small length of chain dangled from the dwarven battleaxe as Salgor tried to intercept a new attack. The dwarf missed, suffering a hit as the martial artist pounded him hard on the head before leaping beyond his reach. Salgor turned but was forced to react to another mercenary attempting to spear him. He batted the spear aside, but Loung got behind the mercenary to launch some kind of surprise attack of his own. The dwarf leaned in to head butt the other human with the spear, then used the flat side of his axe to knock the mercenary back towards Loung's position.

With little time to react, Loung had to jump over the next swing of the axe. Although it missed him, the axe blade cut deeply into the spear wielder. The mercenary went down for good, as Loung gracefully danced at the edges of Salgor's reach. Salgor changed angles and came in high. The Tariykan ducked under the blow and turned it into an attack of his own. A foot sweep crashed against the legs of the dwarf. Salgor's muscular legs were as thick as some tree trunks. The legs didn't give, and the blade flashed down to deliver another nick on Loung's upper torso.

The dwarf's blade tested every bit of agility the Tariykan possessed. The two of them charged and retreated across parts of the clearing as they went. Another mercenary tried to hit Salgor from behind, only to end up being split in two. At that distraction Loung got in a hard kick against the dwarf's uncovered head.

Salgor couldn't get his blade around, but he reached out with one hand to grab the Tariykan's foot. Loung's limb couldn't escape the iron grip as he teetered on one foot. The axe arced in for an attempt to sever his leg, but Loung dropped onto his back and brought up his other foot to kick against the weapon hand. The impact met with the dwarf's fingers and stopped the axe short of taking Loung's leg. Salgor lost his grip on the axe. Frustrated, he ignored the dropped axe and grabbed Loung with both hands at the ankle. The Tariykan scrambled on his back, trying to kick free. Salgor summoned his strength and started to pull. The worshipper of Daerkfyre didn't even know what was behind him, but he decided to use his grip to toss the Tariykan into a tree or such. With the strength of his dwarf blood pumping through his muscles, he swung the human around in a circle and let him go. The Tariykan went airborne at a low angle, just enough to send him flying over the edge of the bluff.

Salgor hadn't meant to give his opponent an escape, but Loung tumbled down the slope leading to the shoreline. The Tariykan regained his feet and decided he wasn't going to run back to deal with Salgor. He joined the mass of others driven from the battle by Mel's wand. Several sailors and mercenaries pushed the rowboats away from shore. They saw their ship as their last hope of escape.

Salgor grabbed his axe and was ready to charge the whole group of sailors alone. He stopped when he realized he couldn't abandon his friends at the camp. He turned towards the prisoners' tent.

*   *   *   *   *

Petrow roughly jostled and kicked Lady Shauntay off his body. The handyman tried getting to his feet as the noble's daughter rolled to the side. Captain Orthymbar moved slightly, trying to get his intact hand on the grip of his saber. Petrow had to kneel at an awkward angle, but he got his hands on the blackened hilt first. Lady Shauntay was trying to get to her feet after singeing a part of her outfit on a piece of the smoldering tent.

Orthymbar looked up at the young man. Petrow stood staring at their captor in the midst of shouts, flashes of light, and the screams of the dying. His hands were still mostly stuck behind his torso, but now he held the saber and stood triumphantly. As beaten as their attacker looked, Petrow viewed his own torn, bloody, and now sooty clothes. There was the taste of blood in his mouth from the beating he had received moments ago. Petrow looked down at the new captain with a look that promised death.

Orthymbar scowled up at the young man, "I hope you pay for this in pain."

Petrow responded, "I already have."

The handyman set the tip of the blade against Orthymbar's chest. The young man felt little remorse about what he was about to do, overshadowed by the hate and fear he held against this man. All Petrow had to do was lean into the blade. After some initial resistance, the blade sank through his opponent until stopped partway through the dirt below. Orthymbar was too battered to offer resistance. His eyes glazed over in death.

Lady Shauntay watched through tears, in shock from the events of the whole morning. Certainly her fantasies about her father and his troops rescuing her were a far cry from reality. She watched Petrow until he started trying to use the blade to cut through his bonds. The saber was firmly planted in the ground and the other man, so she turned away as his movements shook the blade and made the corpse twitch. She stood in the middle of the battle and looked around at the bodies and devastation as if she wasn't even a part of it.

*   *   *   *   *

Revwar put a hand out to check on the cleric. She trembled but didn't appear conscious. Her eyelids fluttered atop a bloody face. The elf looked to the side and saw the skull helm lying several feet away. Maybe it was the will of her goddess, but the dark cleric was lucky she hadn't died immediately from a broken neck. The wizard decided to fly the cleric out of there, but he stopped as his elf ears picked up a noise.

Across the clearing, Cat saw Trestan trying to sneak up behind the elf while still wearing his metal armor. Unless the elf was deaf, there was no way Trestan would catch him by surprise. "Mel! Over there!"

154

As Cat pointed out the wizard to her gnome companion, she realized the elf was no longer looking down, instead trying to see out of the corner of his eyes. One slender hand reached into a bag of spell items in preparation for some nasty surprise. Trestan would be unlikely to dodge a spell at that close range or stop the wizard in time.

Mel pointed his wand towards the elf, "That was the elf that passed me on the road! I remember him."

Mel spoke, and a bright flash and clap of noise followed. The energy of his wand surged at his target, but the misty field between them stopped it. Whatever the elf had erected was too strong for the wand to penetrate. The blast earned the elf's surprised attention for the briefest of moments.

*   *   *   *   *

Trestan saw his opportunity. The elf's head jerked towards the distant gnome. The lightening couldn't hurt the caster, but it had distracted him. The young smith abandoned silence to rush the last few steps; the Sword of the Spirit lifted high. Revwar was standing, but still facing away. It seemed the elf should have heard the footsteps behind him by now.

Trestan cleaved the sword downward at his enemy. Revwar spun to the side, avoiding the blade by inches. The sword kicked up dirt not far from Savannah's body. Trestan had planned ahead to deliver two swings. Even as the tip bounced off the dirt, he maneuvered it hand over hand in a horizontal slashing attack at the dodging elf.

The blade hit something solid as it went past the elf's midsection.

Both Revwar and Trestan looked down in surprise. The blade never passed through skin, but it did slash through a bag hanging from the wizard's belt. An item fell through the torn bag to roll near Trestan's feet.

The young man looked at the object in disbelief. Seeing it here and now shook his concentration at a critical moment. His mouth open in surprise, he looked up to Revwar as if to ask a question. Revwar's fingers moved for a hasty spell. A word from the elf and a flick of the wrist caught the young smith before he could defend himself.

Trestan tried to stab the elf with his sword. The elf shrank in his vision as he found the air sweeping him up and away. Trestan flew a good distance before crashing against the remains of a tent. The air rushed out of his lungs as he plowed into cloth, crates, and wooden barrels.

*   *   *   *   *

Cat and Mel ran to get around the perimeter of the wizard's protective field. The half-elf slowed when she saw the object knocked from Revwar's belongings. She was screaming a moment later as she realized Trestan wasn't reacting to the next spell. Her heart dropped as she saw the young man flung across half the camp to disappear amidst a collision with debris. Cat started running again to get around the magic field.

Revwar stopped to retrieve the object. The elf looked upset indeed to have his treasure revealed. The item went into another bag and he turned to pick up the cleric. The

155

elf wizard must have had some spell on him to augment his strength, for he easily hoisted the armored cleric and cradled her against his body with one arm. His cloak spread to catch the wind and bear him away from the bluff.

He stopped instead, deciding to leave one last parting shot against those who had caused him so much trouble. The elf spoke words and extended one forefinger toward the biggest target. Mel hadn't gotten around the field, but Cat had outpaced the gnome with her long strides. She followed Revwar's gaze to see where he aimed.

Across the clearing stood three of his enemies in a tight group. Salgor was cutting the last ropes free from Petrow. Lady Shauntay stood mute, staring back at the wizard's offered death with a removed look. The young noble was obviously not straight inside her head, and the circumstances of the past few days had been more than she could handle. All three targets stood within a step of each other as Revwar aimed his spell.

Cat shouted, "Nay!"

The half-elf raised her crossbow, only to realize she stared down a broken weapon. Though she had picked it up on reflex when she moved, it still had a crossbow bolt sticking out of the shattered stock. It was unloaded as well as broken beyond repair.

A beam of magical energy, smaller than Mel's wand blasts but deadly enough along its path, shot from the elf's finger. Salgor and Petrow saw the danger only when it was too late to avoid it. Trestan stumbled into the path of the beam on purpose. He put his sword out to try and deflect it, but was unsuccessful in doing so.

"Trestan!"

"Lad! Get down!"

"Tres!"

The companions watched as the beam sliced into Trestan's abdomen. The young man continued to stand for a moment, though pain convulsed his body. A glimmer of light became visible through the young smith's back as energy burned through him. The fine elvish sword dropped from the weakened hand of the smith. The beam stopped but Trestan had already paid the price to protect his friends.

The young man collapsed. Salgor reached out and grabbed his crested shield. The dwarf held it out in front of himself and the former prisoners, glaring at the wizard. Cat had no missile weapon available, but in anger she tossed her broken crossbow through the air. It fell short of its target. The half-elf screamed like a madwoman and threw daggers, rocks, anything solid she could get her hands on. Mel finally got around the barrier; wand ready to return a shot at the elf.

Revwar realized it was time to make an exit or risk his own life. The cloak caught the wind and operated like wings to lift the elf and the limp cleric away from the ground. The caster flew away from the bluff, soaring out over the sea to aim towards the ship. Mel followed him with a few blasts from his wand, but the magic missed his opponent. Soon Revwar was far enough away from the wand that it could not hit him.

*   *   *   *   *

156

Trestan laid where the wizard's beam struck him down. He believed by Abriana's faith that it was worth it to save his friends, even if he had to offer his own life. The pain wasn't really as bad after the initial agony. At first it had felt like burning from the inside out, but the sensation gave way to a chill that crept into his limbs. He grunted in pain as he picked his head up. His numbed legs were fine, but he saw the damage to his abdomen. His breastplate bore a melted hole. Through the hole he could see a reddish and black glimpse at his burned insides.

He lamented the wizard's escape, though his thoughts remained confused by the item that had rolled out of the elf's bag. He heard shouts as his friends got closer. Petrow got to him first, looking over the wound and recoiling. With some hesitation, Trestan's childhood friend used a scrap cloth to apply pressure to the wound. Petrow didn't look better than the young smith. Bruises, a swollen eye, and torn clothes were evidence of how badly the handyman fared.

Trestan tried to find words. The first ones came out with difficulty. "Did you see what the elf had in his bag? Was I imagining things?"

"Tres," Petrow started, "You shouldn't talk. Save your strength. I didn't see it but I can guess what it was."

Trestan tried to lie back and relax, but he felt he was losing his breath. "They left the holy relic on its pedestal back at the church didn't they? We looked it over before we rode out that night. Yet, I swear, the one Revwar had looked just like it."

Petrow couldn't answer, but Lady Shauntay stood nearby and offered a brief, stiff response. "It was. They replaced it with a duplicate, or something similar."

Trestan looked up at the noble. Her currently ragged condition didn't diminish her beauty. The blonde hair tumbled free about her shoulders and her lovely eyes hovered over him. He saw hurt hidden behind her eyes, and regretted they hadn't gotten to her sooner. "At least we got you back, milady. You should all get out of here before they send more after us. We rescued this lovely lady, an honor, which makes it all worth it."

Trestan succumbed to a fit of coughing, and missed the frown on Petrow's face. Salgor, Cat, and soon Mel rushed to his side. Petrow mumbled loud enough, "This was nay worth it, Tres. We never should have bothered coming."

Lady Shauntay glared at Petrow, but he didn't care about any opinion she had at that moment.

Trestan looked up again to see Cat's face. In this bright light, she seemed as radiantly lovely as the noble lady they had rescued. Her face displayed a grief-stricken frown and tears, but her green eyes and black hair were part of a very wonderful image. It was one thing he would miss when he left this world, the prospect of a future with either of these two lovely…

Bright light?

Trestan looked over his right shoulder towards the bluff's edge. Out to the east, the top of the sun shined across the water on them.

He commented, "I didn't expect to live long enough to see this sunrise."

*   *   *   *   *

The creature cast a long shadow in the light of the sunrise. His axe and one remaining horn silhouetted against part of the deck. Bortun had seen the bolts of energy strike out across the sky, and had stood by helplessly on the ship while a battle raged on the bluff before him. He didn't like what he could guess about the outcome. A group of sailors and mercenaries had run to the beach like they were escaping the wrath of gods. Loung counted among them; even now he rowed out to the ship with the other survivors. As Loung got closer, the minotaur saw lines of blood across the man's body.

The wizard descended to the deck holding someone else under the cover of his billowing cloak. The dark armor identified her long before Bortun saw her short, blonde hair. Revwar landed on the deck, cradling her bloody head and limp body against his robes.

As the minotaur approached, Revwar smirked and informed, "You picked a perfect moment to leave camp and help load the ship."

Bortun waved his axe with one hand at the bluff. "What happened up there? Did they destroy our plans?"

Revwar didn't answer. The elf picked through Savannah's pockets and pouches. He kept her head supported as he emptied bag after bag on the deck. A potion rolled out of a pouch. Revwar recognized it as a healing draught. The elf popped the cork and forced the liquid down what was left of the woman's mouth. As Bortun and several sailors watched, the jaw reformed and melded back into perfect shape.

Savannah's eyes popped open. Revwar helped her to another healing miracle before she started to sit up by herself. Savannah spit blood and felt around her face in wonder at the remaining proof of the seriousness of her injury. Bortun waited anxiously for an answer as she gathered her wits.

The abbess stood up slowly, cautiously, and looked herself over. She had already noticed that her skull helm was missing. "What happened? I don't remember…"

She looked from face to face, and suddenly a memory came back. Her hands flew to her mouth in retrospect. While Savannah recalled her memory of the quarterstaff strike, Revwar looked about at the gathered throng of sailors. "Who is in charge here?"

The men looked at each other in confusion. Their captain had died the previous day due to a rumored illness. Orthymbar had been promoted, but wasn't among those returning to the ship. The second mate had been a big guy that loved to wield a mallet, and he was missing also. The officer ranks of the ship had been decimated.

Revwar listened to the ensuing discussion and nodded. He had expected as much. "I guess that leaves me in charge. Anyone disagree?"

Bortun turned around and lifted his axe with a sneer at the surrounding sailors. The crewmembers fell quiet and none dared argue the point. Revwar continued, "Raise anchor, we set sail at once as planned."

Loung Chao climbed over the railing. Bortun and Savannah both got their first looks at Loung's scars and bruises. Several of the man boarding from the smaller boats suffered from cuts, burns, and missing limbs. The three of them looked to Revwar. Bortun asked again, "What happened up there? We are not going to fight any more?"

158

Revwar scowled in anger. The others were not used to seeing the mage openly angry. "Beaten by novices. Children! The noble yet lives, so does the young man that attacked us in camp."

Loung looked towards the distant bluff. "Then they will talk. They know too much."

Revwar shook his head. "It matters little now. They will find out what we tried to cover up, but they can't catch us or find us once we sail out of sight. We are out of their reach. For all the trouble this caused us since landing at Barkan's, this whole situation has only delayed us a little."

Revwar reached into a bag and took out a green stone with strange markings. Any resident of Troutbrook who saw the item would swear it was the sacred stone set outside the Church of the Sacred Harvest. The sight of it had shocked Trestan, especially since he remembered seeing it safe on its pedestal back at the village when they had departed. Revwar held the stone between his three companions and spoke, "They may have won a small victory, but they lost the war to come. The holy relic that was once stolen has now been returned to its rightful owner."

The cleric of DeLaris said nothing, but there was the hint of a smile in her eyes as Revwar handed her the stone.

CHAPTER 13

Petrow tried staunching the blood flowing from Trestan's wound. He felt that he was only delaying the inevitable. Lady Shauntay just stood by quietly, with not even a word of thanks to her dying rescuer. Not that one might be expected, for the noble seemed to be in a state of shock. Salgor and Mel looked on quietly, but there was nothing either could do. Mel was eager to ask about the item from Revwar's pouch but he kept his tongue respectfully silent.

In contrast to those who were silent and in shock, Cat was a flurry of activity. She tore through one of her packs. Dry food, some metal lock picks, and the container of jelly from Troutbrook's inn were tossed aside in her frenzy. "I can't believe I would let something like this sink to the bottom of my pack!"

Finally, the half-elf pulled out a vial of liquid. Trestan recognized the significance of it. There was a holy symbol on it just like the vial Cat had shown him on the streets of Troutbrook. He struggled to reach it as she brought it to his lips. The young smith almost felt like retching, but he forced the liquid down his throat. Warmth and calmness flowed through him. Petrow, Mel, Salgor and Lady Shauntay looked on with amazement as the wound started to close. The melted metal hole in Trestan's breastplate remained unchanged, but the open wound dwindled to a puckered scar. The scratches on his brow and nose left by the scimitar strike melted away to smooth skin. The last drop went down his throat and the abdomen wound stopped regenerating. Trestan's expression softened. Although something remained of the wound in his abdomen, it did not seem as life-threatening as it had moments before.

Cat tossed aside the empty healing potion, but Trestan pointed accusingly to the discarded vial. "You told me, beside that lamed horse in Troutbrook, you didn't have any healing potions left."

Cat blushed, but just as quickly her look hardened and she spoke sternly. "I save my potions for emergencies like this. They are not for animals or enemies. My healing supplies are reserved so that I don't have to watch helplessly as a friend dies."

Trestan looked into her green eyes. "I would have saved the horse. But if it was a choice between it and me then I'm grateful. Thanks Cat, for saving that."

Salgor looked to the ship, expecting more people to come back and finish the group. He leaned forward and spit out a gob of blood. Behind him, Mel tried to imitate the move but only managed to create a gob of saliva on his goatee. The dwarf noticed activity on the deck. "Looks like they've had a bellyful too and are giving up! By their actions I think they might be setting sail."

Cat nodded in agreement, "I see men pulling up the anchor and raising the sails."

Trestan winced as he sat up. Petrow lent Trestan a hand, helping his friend stand. The handyman then offered his own comment, "I think they're getting away with the village's holy relic. Or, perhaps a stone that happens to look just like it. Seems we were lucky but their true objective got away from us."

Trestan struggled to get his balance without Petrow's help. He walked slowly, testing his legs, to where Lady Shauntay stood. She had paid little attention to the group,

160

staring off into her own world. Trestan spoke as he reached for her hand, "It was worth it to rescue the jewel of our village! 'Twas my pleasure to be of service milady…"

The moment Trestan's hand touched hers she recoiled. Her hand jerked back out of reach. "Don't touch me!"

The young smith frowned and let his hand drop. He stood uncertainly, awkwardly by her side. Trestan's imaginative mind had visualized this moment of rescue many times during the journey, but reality moved in an entirely different direction. Lady Shauntay gazed across him and the entire group. There was fright in her eyes, and through that window to the soul a fleeting glimpse of the nightmare she endured since her capture. "Don't bother me right now. Leave me alone."

The noble tried to shake her head as if trying to dismiss thoughts in her mind. She turned to leave but promptly tripped over a body. She recoiled and scrambled away from it. As the party watched, she sidestepped a few more bodies, before resigning herself to sit on a crate. She turned her face away from them, leaving only shaking shoulders to hint at her crying.

Petrow moved in front of Trestan, "Are you sure you're well, Tres? That was a wicked spell."

Trestan reached up and reassuringly patted Petrow's shoulder. "Well enough, for now. I can be ready to move if we need."

The party took in the scene around the camp. There were bodies lying everywhere, most of them in scorched groups lined in the path of Mel's wand. Smoke rose from tents and supplies that had been left burning by the magical assault. Bolts stood out from other corpses, silent proof of Cat and Mel's accuracy. Severed limbs and parts of men littered the area of the camp where Salgor fought. When Trestan looked back to where he had been fighting, he knew he would no longer see the cleric lying there. He spotted the two bodies he expected to find: the headless mallet wielder by the bluff edge, and the scimitar wielder who had worn the eye patch.

The latter still moved.

Trestan started to run towards the man but slowed, nearly doubling over in pain. "One is still alive."

The rest of the party, except for the reclusive noble, went with Trestan to check on the man. The mercenary with the eye patch held a vest against the wound in his torso. His other hand applied tension to a piece of leather wrapped around his severed leg. A large amount of blood had already pooled around him. The scimitar lay unattended beside him. The man looked up as he heard the others approach. He made no move for his scimitar, and likely lacked the strength to wield it.

The party ringed the enemy. Cat held her rapier in a ready position, suggesting that any attack would be his last action. Petrow kicked the scimitar aside and held the blackened saber ready. Trestan kneeled close and judged the man's intent. The mercenary didn't raise his hands in surrender, but both hands were occupied trying to stem the flow of blood from his wounds. The mercenary offered no threats or resistance. Trestan actually felt a bit of guilt. This man had tried to kill him, but was no longer a serious threat.

The mercenary spoke, "I can't stop the bleeding. I'm a dead man in a few minutes nay matter what else happens."

To the surprise of everyone in the group, Trestan practically jumped forwards to help apply pressure to the man's torso wound. Cat nervously looked between the two. Trestan had no weapon. The young man had left the bloody elvish blade back where he had fallen. The mercenary also seemed to have no weapon but at least the scimitar was out of reach. A couple of the party called for Trestan to move away, but the young man tried to control the bleeding.

Salgor moved closer with his own bloody axe in hand, "Forget it boy. He won't live to see a prison. You might as well do the right thing and end his misery quick. He tried to kill you earlier, did he not?"

Trestan answered, "Abriana is not a violent deity. She offers love and healing. This man is nay longer trying to kill me, and I won't let a human soul die needlessly."

"Bah!" Salgor scoffed, but held his ground. The axe was ready to drop if the man made any sudden move.

Trestan looked to Cat. The half-elf seemed puzzled by his actions, but she held the rapier less threateningly. The adventuress stared back at the young smith and spoke her mind, "You should not feel guilt, Trestan. This man is harmless now, but he stood and defended the wrong things. He will die, don't blame yourself. We couldn't have saved the noble without bloodshed. How do we know he didn't mistreat the noble like red-hair did?"

The young smith tried his best to hold the cloth of the man's vest against the blood pooling around it. The man weakened enough that he lost his hold on the leather strap wrapped around his leg, releasing more blood. Trestan got his other hand on the leather strap and tightened it as well.

Trestan looked to Cat again, "I will not worry as much about this man's past as I fear for his future. Tell me the truth now. Do you have any more healing potions? Please don't lie to me Cat!"

The half-elf replied, "I have nay more left. I swear to you that is the truth! I lied in Troutbrook and it saved your life today. I do not like to waste healing miracles on enemies, but that seems a moot point right now. I have nothing to save him."

Mel spoke, "I don't even have any poultice remaining. It wouldn't work fast enough to cure wounds such as these anyway."

The man occasionally looked about the others like he expected them to kill him at any moment. He turned his one good eye upon Trestan. No hatred could be found there, only sorrow.

Trestan could do little to help the man. The young smith's hands quivered. "This is not just about my conscience, Cat. I do this because I worship a kind and forgiving goddess. I am expected to defend what I love…but afterwards if I murder a helpless person I would be throwing my morals in the face of my religion. There might be healing potions in the supplies, someone should look."

The one-eyed man shook his head, "We carried nay such supplies to shore. Any healing we had would have been stored on the boat, except for the lady cleric."

162

Petrow stepped closer to him, raising his saber threateningly. "You better talk! Where were they headed with the village stone? Why did they have one that looked similar? You'll answer or I will find a way to extend your misery."

Trestan frowned but looked down at the wounded mercenary. The man looked to Trestan and replied, "I don't know of the stone he speaks. I knew we were to carry them to Barkan's Crossing, wait for them, and carry them again to another location. I don't mind telling you, young sir. At least you have compassion for a dying man who made his living the way he pleased. From here, we were to sail them to an island among some reefs, almost two days sailing straight east. The sea is shallow in that area, and some castle from long ago stands there. I suppose it doesn't hurt to tell you that. There seems to be nay opportunity for you to follow them, even if they left a rowboat behind."

At the mention of a rowboat, Mel used his little legs to run towards the edge of the bluff and see what was left. Lady Shauntay, standing away from the party, looked upon the wounded man with as much scorn as Salgor did. The noble confirmed part of the story. "I did hear something about a castle to the east, over the water."

The wounded man coughed while Trestan focused his attention on trying to keep pressure on the wounds. The rest of the party noticed Mel looking back from the bluff edge. The gnome sorcerer shook his head. Apparently there were no more boats left.

Cat no longer held her rapier poised to skewer the man. She wasn't sure she understood why Trestan was so willing to save the man's life. She respected the young man for his opinions, but she knew that the mercenary was dying anyway. Salgor had also ceased to pay attention to the spectacle. The dwarf openly searched for loot and took the bags of money off the men he had killed.

The wounded man wasn't stirring much. His labored breathing slowed. His eye sank half closed when he began to sing a few lines, "Remember my courage, remember my stand…in this way, learn the measure of man. Now some may grieve, and some never know…but this…was the path…I chose to go."

Tears fell from Trestan's face. The young smith's shoulders shook as he mourned for the man that had almost taken his own eye. A few last words escaped the sailor's lips. "Boys, I see the lights of the port…if you don't mind, I'm going to visit my lady before we share drinks tonight."

*   *   *   *   *

The events immediately following the battle would echo in the minds of three of them as dull images, distant impressions of a place where they barely took notice of the passage of time. Lady Shauntay dwelled by herself off to the side. Mostly all she could remember was some fresh water she found to satisfy her dry throat. Besides that, the rest of the time spent after the battle was merely a dark image of death and horror that her brain would not relive later on.

Petrow wasn't sure what all he had done during the aftermath of the fight. The young handyman recalled finding his old wood axe, and he remembered taking the coins and pipe weed off the dead, red-haired man.

163

Trestan had one visual image of that period that would come back to haunt his dreams. He remembered tracing his steps back to where he had dropped the Sword of the Spirit. The blade had a mysterious shine, blemished by blood and soot. When Trestan first reached for the discarded sword, he was also aware of the red blood coating his own hands. He went down to the shore and scrubbed at his hands for a long time. With an oily rag, he also cleaned the sword until it shined like new again.

The *Silver Trident* sailed off into the distance. Sails harnessed the wind to bear the craft eastward. It faded into the vast horizon of the sea during the time the companions remained at the battlefield.

Katressa, Mel and Salgor saw the aftermath from a different perspective. Salgor never cared to see the dead bodies of his enemies as much more than objects to search for treasure. The dwarf would not mourn for those who would kidnap a person and do business with murderers. Salgor looted coins, though he also liberated several full liquor bottles and other equipment. Mel also went searching for valuables. The gnome was distracted often from his search, noting with awe the damage done by his wand. The magical item had created more destruction than he had foreseen.

At one point Salgor looked to Mel and asked, "You know I don't like magic. That being said, your wand is one good weapon. Why didn't you pull that thing out earlier and use it?"

Mel pointed at Cat, replying, "She wanted me to use the crossbow!"

Cat gaped and replied, "Sorry! Next time I'll know better."

Cat looked over the battlefield, finding no other survivors among the mercenaries. She salvaged a few items of value and supplies for the trip back to Troutbrook. The adventuress found a new crossbow to replace her broken one. The half-elf took the bags of money off of Trestan's two victims and carried the pouches to him on the shoreline. She found him in a somber mood.

"I didn't expect you to be jumping for joy," Cat told him, "But you seem very quiet and reserved. We won the battle." She paused for a moment, glancing over her shoulder. "We rescued your princess."

Trestan's voice shook when he replied. He would not meet Cat's eyes. "Oh, I'm glad; not exactly happy, but I guess proud of myself."

Cat detected something in his voice, and noticed twitches in his hands. "Are you crying?"

Trestan nodded. Cat didn't immediately respond, waiting for the young man to speak his mind. The young human found his voice again a moment later. "I'm proud, and a part of me feels like I triumphed over some big obstacle. And yet, my hands keep shaking and I'm crying. My head seems a jumble of emotions. I keep seeing the battle in my mind. One part of me feels weary, yet another part hasn't calmed down yet."

Katressa Bilil put an arm over his shoulder. "You did your best and came out of it alive. You can't go back and change the past, but all in all we came out of that battle better than we should have expected. I think I was a nervous jumble of emotions after my first big battle too. It was like a rush of energy, and when the fight is over it takes your nerves a long time to calm down."

164

No response came at first from the young man, so Cat continued, "Don't cry or feel too much sorrow for those you killed today."

Trestan replied, "I try to tell myself that. I haven't convinced my heart yet. That man with the eye patch was so scary when he charged me. I killed him, yet he had a life and a loved one somewhere."

Cat nodded, though he could not see the gesture, "You have a life too, more honorable than his. He befriended killers and thieves, who would have slain us without mourning afterward. You are better than them because you care. You'll spend a long time thinking on this morning, Trestan. For now though, you need to gather yourself together and be ready to travel. It serves nay purpose to linger here much longer. We have to get the noble back to her family."

Cat tried to give the money pouches to Trestan, but the young man balked at taking them. The half-elf spent more time soothing Trestan's uneasy thoughts before pushing the money into his hand. He accepted the bounty, though reluctantly.

As Trestan tucked the coins away, he softly stated, "I didn't do this for money."

Cat answered, "I know, but they did. Everything we suffered on this trip, they put on us for a few coins. Well, I don't know what the other band was up to, but these people sold their souls for money. I bet you'll put it to better use. Your father wouldn't mind seeing some income, since his son has not been there to help him at the smithy." Cat put an arm around Trestan and guided him back up the bluff. "You did this because you followed your heart, Trestan. That is a noble thing."

*   *   *   *   *

West and northwest, right foot then left foot, the companions journeyed across the countryside. They traversed wild terrain, claimed by the Kashmer Protectorate on maps but unpopulated by humans. Since they had traveled so far north from Barkan's Crossing to arrive at the bluff, they decided to get the noble back home by the quickest route. They left the town of crafters behind and set their eyes toward Troutbrook. Their path took them through untamed land and small woods. Mel knew some of the surrounding land, reminding that gnomes and goblins both had communities here. The party was on a constant watch for the latter. Through rolling terrain and areas of high grass they marched along. Salgor took the lead, his blocky frame crushing tall grass and his axe clearing some growth that hampered their walk. Cat led her horse, using it only to carry salvaged supplies from the enemy camp.

Troutbrook still seemed a long way off, and no one could guess when they might finally break through the wilder part and come upon the road. Stirring up the grass sometimes brought forth swarms of insects, and occasionally they had to avoid patches of briars. At one point Salgor even guided them around a carnivorous plant. He pointed it out and told them it mostly hunted small game, but wouldn't mind if a larger creature stepped into its tendrils. Petrow and Trestan noted the plant with alarm, thinking that such things had been a myth. Though they walked well away from it, the young men kept their hands on their weapons.

As the day passed Trestan trudged on with more weariness. It became apparent to the others that he still suffered some hurt from his wound. The young man kept a positive facade, avoiding any comments on his health. Trestan talked and laughed with others, but Cat and Petrow could tell he lacked the endurance shown on their earlier marches.

One other person really slowed the party more so than the terrain. Lady Shauntay's feet had been in horrible condition from her tiring journey south. Walking pained her to the point where she ambled and stopped often. Mel wished he had brought more healing poultice to apply to her feet. Trestan trudged on without complaint, yet the noble slowed the pace considerably. Several times the lady stopped regardless of what the party said. She kept complaining that she wanted to soak or rub her feet. Lady Shauntay tried demanding the use of the horse, which was now loaded with burdensome supplies and loot. When they began moving again, Cat tried to walk the horse behind the noble. The bulk of the horse, coupled with Cat's urging was supposed to keep Lady Shauntay pressing forward. The young daughter of the Tessald house refused to be rushed.

Most of the party disliked the noble and didn't care for her pains. Mel was an exception, as the gnome easily got along with everyone. He talked easily most of the journey, but occasionally his subject matter included the blisters and sores on Trestan's and Petrow's feet during their walk south. Such tales of the trials of her rescuers didn't distract the haughty girl from her own discomfort.

Petrow worried over Trestan's injury during the entire march. Since the smith offered no complaint, the handyman began to worry about something else. Petrow observed Trestan give the noble a lot of attention. The smith fawned over her, as if Trestan tried to live up to his ideal dream of enjoying a happy ending with the noble lady he'd rescued. Trestan could not comfort the noble despite his attempts at doing so, but before long she seemed to take advantage of the situation. Petrow watched and silently fumed as his friend fell into the same trap he had back in Troutbrook. Lady Shauntay used him, even though Trestan deserved at least as much care and comfort as she did. The young smith waved off any of his own hurts in favor of pleasing the noble. When the lady would stubbornly sit on a rock to rest her feet, she would call out to Trestan that she was tired and needed a rest. Despite the party trying to move on, the young man would stop and see to her needs. The young handyman was hoping to talk some sense into his friend soon.

Cat had her attention on Trestan as well, and could not miss the exchange. She always marveled at how men could lose their heads over a pretty figure. Lady Shauntay exemplified a lovely image painted over a manipulative mind. It saddened Cat to watch Trestan give so much undeserved attention to the other woman. Cat had grown attached to both Petrow and Trestan, though more so the young smith. She had laughed and enjoyed so many moments of their short journey, and now she was ignored except when Trestan asked her not to bump the noble with her horse.

Cat also worried about Trestan's wound. Salgor had gotten hit and seemed to be no more the worse for it. Petrow's injuries must be bothering him, though he seemed to be moving ok. Mel and Cat had gotten through the whole battle without injury. Trestan, however, almost had a wide hole blasted through him. One simple healing miracle shouldn't be enough to treat the whole injury, even though it closed the wound. She could

166

tell by the way he moved, though he tried to hide it, that something serious still lingered. Cat wanted to get Trestan to a cleric for more healing as quickly as possible.

They slogged on through the daylight. The natural beauty of the land was lost on most of them as they journeyed. The noble looked forward or downward, her mind on places ahead and behind her. Trestan had eyes on the young Tessald noble, eyes clouded by his own dreams. Cat and Petrow had their concerned eyes on Trestan. Mel looked about the countryside but blathered stories about anything and everything. Salgor kept eyes mostly forward, holding onto a single-minded determination to set the course and try to keep up a good pace despite all.

*   *   *   *   *

Lady Shauntay sat down with a determined huff. "I said I'm tired! I won't walk any more today when we can rest here. If you truly are concerned for my welfare you will help me tend to my feet before they fall off."

Salgor let loose a bellow from up front as he heard the whining behind him. The dwarf let loose a blow with his axe that toppled a small tree. The sapling hadn't even been blocking their path. The companions stopped in their tracks as they had been doing several times that day. Cat glared at the young woman; considered trying to force the horse to brush into her again and dislodge her from her seat. Trestan anticipated Cat's feelings and threw an imploring look her direction.

It disturbed the half-elf to see the young smith so quick to give in to the noble's wishes. Cat spoke with disdain, "We have plenty of time left until it gets too dark and a long way to go. Don't underestimate the dangers of lingering in this wilderness."

"I know," Trestan agreed, "but she has had a hard time. She isn't used to these conditions. There is nay real hurry as long as we get her back safely."

Salgor walked back to join them. The dwarf had not taken his oversized pack off since the morning battle, refusing to give in to a full rest. Petrow and Mel just stepped off to the side and shared some water. The dwarf spoke up in his normal, boisterous tone, "We dwarves don't leave wounded behind. We pick them up and run with them. If they had an arm chopped off, they can run fine on their own! I can carry her to Troutbrook and that will save her feet further punishment."

From her perch on a fallen, moss-covered tree, the noble shrieked out a response, "I will not be carried by another smelly creature against my will!"

Salgor gripped his axe tighter and scowled at the young woman. She pointedly turned away from him to massage her feet. Trestan felt the need to smooth things over and explain to Salgor. "You see, that first night the minotaur carried her off…"

"So now I am being compared to the smell o' a minotaur, aye?"

The companionship of the party dissolved into bickering and snide comments. Despite the early hour, the group finally broke out the blankets and cooking utensils to make camp. Mel smoked a pipe and single-handedly carried on a smooth flow of conversation. Many of his comments were the only uplifting statements for the group that evening. Salgor finally dropped his pack and broke out some drinks for the others. Trestan hoped to smooth things over with Cat, but he found himself being asked to do little favors for the young noble. Lady Shauntay knew whom she could count on and she played the helpless role enough to have Trestan serve her. Cat stayed away from the other woman, spending a substantial amount of time simply caring for her horse. Petrow went over and had a silent conversation with Cat. They talked for some time; Trestan didn't miss the looks that Petrow directed towards him and the noble.

Trestan had to do some soul-searching. He silently admitted that he couldn't say nay to Lady Shauntay. She was beautiful, curvaceous, rich and she possessed one of the brightest smiles as well as imploring eyes. The young woman had a particular charm, and even when she whined men moved to jump and fix things for her. Trestan considered the journey so far. He had fulfilled the dream that drove him from home. He rescued the noble from her captors. He faced his most feared enemies and even knocked the cleric of DeLaris senseless during the battle. Lady Shauntay hadn't actually thanked him, though she had given small compliments in his direction. He had caught her eye and did something for her that demanded notice and respect. The young smith finally felt he was getting the recognition he desired from her.

At least, he thought he was. The noble used flowery words to appease him, and those were usually followed by simple requests and sacrifices on his part. The young smith had surrendered to her his homemade utensils, even loaned her his blanket, (despite Petrow pointing out they had extra from the mercenary camp). Indeed, after the smith loaned them he borrowed from their looted supplies so that he covered his own needs. That was what finally started to get to him. He didn't seem to be any romantic interest to the woman. She praised him then asked him for more. Trestan had been nice and courteous to her beyond expectations. At the camp that evening the young smith heated a bowl of water, then cooled it, then heated it. All of that effort to get it the proper temperature so that Lady Shauntay could soak her feet. He cared for her ailments despite the discomfort he felt inside from his own wound.

Trestan felt he was being supportive and helpful, but every action the noble took reminded him that his fancy copper hairpieces had only been good enough for her horse.

CHAPTER 14

Trestan finally had a chance to separate from the noblewoman as she soaked her feet. He wandered away until a sharp pain almost doubled him over. The smith folded his arms tight over his stomach, hoping some pressure might ease the pain a little. He only stayed upright by leaning on a nearby tree. Trestan winced as the pain slowly subsided.

Petrow stood there watching him.

Trestan pretended he was just shivering a bit from a cool breeze. He rubbed his arms and straightened with a smile. The young smith tried masking his discomfort, but Petrow's visage showed the handyman's concern. Trestan decided he might try to distract his friend before Petrow could ask about his injuries.

Trestan spoke, "You looked pretty good traveling today, Petrow. I was worried with your bruises and such. I hope you're doing alright."

Petrow nodded, "Aye, I'm feeling good. But it's you we need to worry about. Not only am I worried over your injury, but also your feelings for that noblewoman. I told you she uses people. Now don't tell me that you can't see that now."

Trestan sighed. He glanced back at the woman as she soaked her feet. "She's just not made out of the strong stuff that you and I are forged. I want to be there to help her, but I'm getting tired of it. I don't think she'll see me as anything more than a good servant."

Petrow set his hands on his hips. "Tres, I spent the night in a tent with her. She always looked down at me, she wouldn't listen to reason, and she never cared one wit about anything I had to say. That woman is very spoiled. She feels superior to everyone else."

"So in other words," Trestan grinned, "You don't like her too much."

Petrow nodded, "Oh aye! We could leave her behind, come home as the conquering heroes bearing that extra gold in our pockets, and I'd consider it a victory. I hate her, Tres. I really worry about how her father is going to marry her off and what will be the future of the village if he doesn't find a good man for her."

Trestan didn't have an answer to that, as he was lost in his own thoughts. Petrow continued, "It disturbs me that we didn't stop the true goal of that bunch of riffraff. We rescued their distraction and it wasn't much of a prize at all. Now I'm left wondering what they intended with the relic. Did they replace it with a fake? Did they simply need something from it for their own stone? Will this come back to haunt the village?"

As he talked, Petrow still had Trestan's health foremost in his mind. He saw the young smith frown and wince. The handyman wanted to get his friend away from that noble. Trestan had spent too long worrying about someone who wouldn't return the favor. Maybe Cat could offer the young smith help of some kind.

Trestan provided an opening. "My mind's a jumble right now. I just had to get some distance from that woman for a while, for my own good. My stomach hurts, but it's nothing to worry about."

Petrow saw his opening, "Cat went down through those trees a short while ago. She told me there's a stream. You should head over and have her look at that wound."

Trestan started to protest, "I'm fine, really. What if Shauntay needs something…"

"Then I'll get it for her. I might even be polite about it. You rest yourself a bit. Remember, Cat has been the one leading us this whole time, and I count very heavily on her opinion. Maybe if you let her know it hurts a bit she might come up with some small remedy." Trestan nodded, but didn't move. Petrow encouraged him. "You better go while you can and have a talk with her. Then maybe you can get some rest as well."

*   *   *   *   *

Cat was lucky to have found a waterfall among some rocks. Her sensitive ears had picked up the soft splashing noises before seeing the water. It was small, only a stream feeding it, but it offered some filtered, clear water to wash up. Cat stripped down to her normal underclothes and washed her head and hands. She was combing her wet hair by the time she heard footsteps approach from the camp. Stroking the brush through her long strands, she turned a bit to see Trestan walking down towards her. The setting sunlight illuminated him as he approached. She had been fuming about him, but that changed when she saw him draw near. Knowing he might be self-conscious about her state of dress, she quickly donned her tunic. The half-elf smiled in welcome. Trestan smiled back, though it seemed a little forced. She noted his short, labored stride.

Her smile faded a bit, letting Trestan know he hadn't quite hidden his discomfort. It alleviated his mood to see she was very concerned for him. It was a refreshing difference compared to how Lady Shauntay would seem mildly irritated when Trestan moved too slowly. The young smith plopped down next to the half-elf with a pained grunt.

Cat put a hand on his shoulder and spoke to him. "I'm glad you came down to see me. I…" Cat stopped. She wanted to say something else, but she changed to a different subject. "I'm worried for you. That wound…you shouldn't be walking, yet we are miles from a proper healer. I want a cleric to look at you."

Trestan grinned, "I'll be alright. We can only do so much out here in the wilderness."

Cat ventured, "I've even thought about splitting up the group. You could ride my horse, taking me or someone with you to get to a town faster."

Trestan smoothed his immature mustache, "I won't leave. There are other dangers out there. We shouldn't split up the party in the wild. I'm glad you thought of my health, but I'm forged from some tough iron."

Cat found her eyes wandering over the young man. She had to admit, he was muscular and displayed a lot of endurance. Eventually she stared at the melted hole in his armor. Trestan wore a different shirt underneath, hiding the wound. He shifted uncomfortably and she realized she made him nervous. She patted his back and brought her hand back to tend her hair. Her eyes snapped back to his dark brown eyes.

"You should at least ride. It will conserve your strength." She offered.

Trestan shook his head. "It wouldn't help, I fear. Lady Shauntay slows us down more than I do. Her feet have been tortured by the journey. It would be faster if she rode and I walked."

170

Cat frowned. The half-elf brushed a few more strokes through her hair. She wasn't sure what she wanted to say about his behavior around the noble, so she settled for a general comment. "You give too much of yourself for others."

"Humble roots," he replied, "I work the hot forge all day for people. But it's time I helped you out a bit too. You've done so much for us."

Trestan gently reached out to her arm and grabbed the comb. Cat arched an eyebrow, but let him take it from her hands. She turned so as to offer her hair towards him and he started brushing her raven strands. His muscular hands gently slid the comb through her long tresses. They paused only long enough to sit down, Trestan slightly behind the elf's side. The half-elf closed her eyes and allowed her nerves to relax a bit. She listened to the bubbles of the small stream. The setting sun gave warmth against her face. All the while she felt strong arms tend her hair. It was very relaxing for the half-elf, allowing her mind free of some of her concerns. While the other companions might hold some fear of the countryside, the half-elf loved the scenery. In her mind, the waterfall near the edge of the wood was a sylvan glen of paradise. It was comforting to enjoy the surroundings under the attentions of a friend. She traveled alone too much.

At one point while brushing Trestan hit a knot. The young man paused as he considered how to get past it. Cat said, "Just pull down through it. Break it."

The voice came from behind her, "You sure? I don't want to hurt you."

Cat smiled, "I may be built on gracefulness, but I'm made of some tough stuff too. It doesn't hurt me; just pull down and break through it."

Trestan tended her hair more. Cat loved the feeling, but some thoughts surfaced that she had to talk about. "You admired her, didn't you?"

"What?"

"The Lady Shauntay," Cat spoke, "You have or you had feelings for her."

Trestan paused a moment. Cat still had her eyes closed and turned away from him, but she wondered how he would respond. The young man found his voice a moment later and continued combing her hair again as he spoke. "I used to worship every glance. The low-cut shirts, the way she moved, her disarming smile…everything about her makes a man let his guard down."

Cat almost frowned, but she kept her face neutral and her eyes closed. Trestan was not in a position to see her reaction. He continued to answer honestly, "Every young man in that town would bend over backwards for her. Every other woman was measured against her beauty. I was nay different. I crafted something really nice once. She took notice of it and wanted it for herself. I gave it freely, but in the end it meant nothing to her. I'm getting the same treatment now. That woman uses her charms to get what she wants without giving back. I feel, well, disappointed and used."

Trestan was silent for a few moments. "How much do I comb your hair? I don't know if I'm overdoing it or not."

Cat giggled, "If I really was trying to look good I would brush a hundred strokes, but generally I just do enough to get most of the snags out. My hair can get real tangled for what I put it through. On the trail like this, it spends most of its time smothered by a helm anyway."

"Well, I'll give you the full hundred. You deserve it!"

They sat in silence for a bit longer. Cat wanted to ask more, but at the same time she didn't want to break the moment. Eventually, Trestan sighed and spoke. "While we're still traveling, I'll help her because she needs somebody. After all this is done, I'll be glad if I never see her again. It might be better that way. I don't need to be a noble's servant."

"Just make sure that you take care of yourself," Cat rebuked, "I wanted to slap her when she asked for your blanket and yet we had a few extra from that camp."

"I said that every young man in the village compared every woman to her," Trestan started, but then paused to choose his words. "Since then I've come to set a new standard."

Those last words hung in the air, conveying a private meaning for Cat. After the young smith seemed to stumble on words, Cat urged him, "Go on."

Trestan blushed, though the half-elf could not see it. "Well, milady, err, Cat. I've come to judge women by your standard. Not just physical qualities either, but the way you helped us and your sacrifices for others. I feel bad for anything I did that pushed you towards any harm during this quest. You are a better person, in body and spirit, than Lady Shauntay could ever hope to be."

Cat beamed a smile. She hadn't expected to hear such a compliment. "Thank you for your praise! I treasure it! But don't regret anything you may have done on this trip. You set your heart on a goal and worked hard for it. It was rather scary at times, but we came through and achieved our task."

"I achieved as much as I could have dreamed. For a short while, I was something more than a humble smith in patched clothes. I worried many times along the road, unsure of what would happen. I've looked to Sir Wilhelm's deity for faith and support. Somehow I did it. Nay, *we* did it. You are a big reason why we fared as good as we did, Cat. You've done a lot for Petrow and me, and we couldn't have come to anywhere as near a happy ending without you. Even though you lied to me more than once, which made me crazy."

Cat felt hurt that she had wounded the young man with her lies. "The last thing I want is to hurt you, either of you. I lied when I did to accomplish a better good. I never meant to keep anything hidden forever. The healing potion was there for when we truly needed it. As far as the camp that night, we're lucky Petrow didn't meet his end; however, if the dwarf had charged in would the outcome have been far worse?"

Cat took the comb back from Trestan, thanking him in the process. They sat together quietly, side by side. Both stared into the trickle of the waterfall.

The half-elf spoke. "You are so nice, my friend, upholding some high yet strict morals. You care very much, even for those who tried to kill you. I don't know if that's a gift. That attitude can leave you vulnerable to someone exploiting you, like that noble. I worry that anyone who feels as you do will come to a hard fall sooner or later. I respect your stance, but I fear that you care too much."

The young man felt her words and warnings were accurate. He snuck another peek at her. Trestan realized he might be falling for this half-elf more than anything he felt for Lady Shauntay. "I know I run a risk, but I just wouldn't live my life any other way. Maybe that's why I felt drawn to Abriana. I care a lot for everyone, and I'd rather care too much than live a selfish life. Don't be too hurt by what I said earlier. You've been a good friend since the start. I care for you," he paused long enough that Cat could tell he struggled to find the right words, "very much. In fact, I was blessed to meet you."

Cat felt herself blush and wondered where his comments might lead. When he came to the stream to be in her company, was there an underlying reason? When he returned the comb, she noticed he looked a little nervous. Were his fingers trembling? She admitted he was handsome, but how far did his feelings extend? For that matter, how deeply did she feel about him? The woman's ears hung on his every word. Cat watched him discreetly from the corner of her emerald eyes.

"You know, I don't remember if I ever said it," Trestan spoke, "but I'd say you are the most wonderful woman I've ever met. I'm serious about that; you've made a large impact on my life. I'm afraid of when we get back home what may happen after all this adventure is over. You travel, yet my home is there. I don't want to see you just ride off into the wild and not look back." The words dangled vulnerably in the momentary silence.

"What do you propose we do? I travel a lot; though do not think I would forget you." As Cat spoke, she had to admit she felt a little excited. Many men tried to seduce her, but none talked to her as sweetly and humble as this strong youth. She knew she would never stay rooted in one spot. Nevertheless, Trestan's words and mannerism granted a pleasant, tingling anticipation in her nerves.

Trestan spoke, "I want to make sure I at least get in the little things that matter greatly to a person. You may insist on buying the drinks, but this time I also want to treat you to a dance when we get home. Maybe if you don't mind staying a bit, I'll craft something nice for you. I'll give you a keepsake to wear as a reminder that you are always welcome back."

Cat realized that Trestan leaned towards her a little more. It popped into her mind that he might try to kiss her! Cat hoped she wasn't misunderstanding anything. Did she simply suspect it, or was she throwing her own hopes into his actions? If he tried to kiss her, should she turn him away or accept it? He had always looked up to her, and Trestan had a way of making her feel like a nervous young girl again! She could not deny the romantic setting: the bubbling waterfall and the last rays of the sun beaming through the trees. Cat couldn't think rationally at that moment.

His offer dangled unanswered, so she responded as evenly as she could manage. "You don't have to go through the trouble to make me something, but I'd stay to accept any gift you would offer."

Trestan hovered even closer. She wasn't sure what she wanted to say; events were going wherever the young smith meant to take them.

Trestan openly studied her face from less than a foot away. The young man commented, "Emerald eyes, night-black hair; what would complement them nicely enough? Anything I make would not do justice to the beauty of the woman."

Cat closed her eyes; she could feel his breath across her pointed ear. It occurred to her Trestan acted uncharacteristically bold, despite previously maintaining a respectful distance. The half-elf waged a brief inner struggle, but emotions overrose reason. Eyes closed, she turned her head slightly towards the young man. If he was going to kiss her, she left herself open and vulnerable. Cat realized she would have been disappointed if he didn't try.

Cat sensed something suddenly going wrong even with her eyes closed. Trestan didn't lean into her as much as he fell against her. His head bumped her shoulder. He limply rolled down her back to land flat on the ground. Cat opened her eyes with shock, wondering what happened.

Trestan twitched on the ground, his pupils rolled up under his upper eyelids. The young man didn't seem aware of anything around him anymore. Sweat covered his forehead and the exposed part of his arms. His lips quivered, but no words or sound came forth. It hit her: he hadn't simply been nervous or shaky from their conversation, something had been genuinely wrong. She put a hand to him and shook him, calling his name. The young man didn't respond. Cat placed a hand against his forehead, only to find it very warm and wet to the touch. Her gut instinct was to check his abdomen wound. When she placed a hand against it, Trestan shook a bit more. The skin underneath the shirt felt similarly warm. Cat had to get to the wound and look at it, but she couldn't get his armor off without help.

"Petrow! Salgor! I need you down by the stream now!"

The half-elf chipped a nail trying to unfasten the buckles of his scarred breastplate in her hurry. Petrow and axe-wielding Salgor rushed to the stream. The young handyman from Troutbrook looked horrified to see Trestan's condition. The other two pitched in as soon as they realized Cat's intentions. As they worked, Lady Shauntay and Mel broke through the trees but stood to the side with worried looks.

When they removed the shirt, they could feel the heat and see the sweat across Trestan's skin. Fluid leaked from the scarred area, some of it bloody. Red, puffy skin surrounded it. Petrow, Salgor, and Cat quietly surveyed the wound.

Cat shook her head, "I worried the potion wasn't enough. He carried on so well but something festered. Looks infected and he may be bleeding inside. He needs a healer."

Salgor considered the young man and the setting sun. "We shouldn't try to move him in the dark, though time is a concern. Let's get him comfortable tonight; try to cool his fever. We can rig up a stretcher o' some kind and have the horse pull it along."

Petrow spoke, "Let's grab a blanket from the camp and drag him back on top of that. We can grab some pots and fill up with water here."

The companions moved about to take care of the young man's needs. Cat leaned over him and held his hand in her own. Her other hand wiped his brow with a wet cloth. When no one looked, she leaned close to the young man and whispered. "Trestan, you had to feel that coming and you put on a good face. You tried to lift my spirits and maybe felt out-of-sorts enough to sneak in a kiss, weren't you? Always caring for others, but not saving enough for yourself."

Cat kissed Trestan on the forehead. A tear rolled from her cheek to touch his. When she pulled back, she whispered again, "Well, you got your kiss, though not how you wanted it. If you can't pull through this though…I just wanted…"

Cat faltered, then recovered. "You WILL get through this. Just hang on and think of home."

174

*   *   *   *   *

The night passed very slowly. They rotated watch over the camp due to the dangers in the untamed areas, and everyone who took watch tended Trestan as he slept fitfully. Katressa stayed awake the first part of the night. Her eyes and ears divided between guarding the camp and checking on the young man. Cat dabbed his forehead with wet washcloths to cool him. During one part of the night, despite his warmth, he shivered and complained of cold. He was wrapped in a thicker blanket, though the half-elf continued to cool the smith's head as he sweated during the night.

With obvious regret, Cat gave up her watch to Mel near the middle of the night. She had already gone past her normal watch time, but didn't think she could sleep well. Mel took over the duties of sentry. The gnome noticed it was awhile before the half-elf seemed to fall asleep. The Bellringer child smoked his pipe and sometimes talked quietly to Daerkfyre, his deity. Mel had a one-sided conversation with his god involving the battle on top of the bluff. The gnome asked for a blessing for Trestan, due to the young man's courage against those odds.

Trestan stirred and whispered. Mel Bellringer walked over to the young man and leaned close to his face to hear. The gnome grabbed a wet cloth and wiped at Trestan's brow as the young man continued.

"Father, how could I? I miss you."

"What's that?" Mel whispered, "Why are you talking to your father? He's not here."

Trestan looked over at the gnome. The young man fought a heavy burden just to keep his eyes open. Trestan spoke weakly. "I couldn't face him that night. Slipped out the door in the dark. I knew he would talk me out of it, so I avoided him, but it never gave me the chance to say goodbye. He must be worried, wondering what happened to me. I've spent every night looking at the stars at least once and imagining my father waiting for me. I feel so proud of what I have done, but he is the one who bears the burden of our separation. Since I left, how often has he stared into my empty room, that empty bed, and wondered what became of his son?"

Mel wiped some tears from Trestan's face. "You are going to make me feel bad. I'm glad your father loved you and it's important you love him. My father sent me off with a bagful of food and the impression I should never return again. I tried going back once, but was turned back by their fears before any glimpse of my childhood home. I miss my home, much as I'm sure you miss yours."

Trestan looked past the gnome and up to the moons overhead. It occurred to Mel that the young man didn't need to hear his own sad story. The sorcerer decided to try another angle. "You know what compels me?"

The young smith turned his head to regard the gnome. "Compels you? In what way?"

Mel Bellringer responded, "You know what compels me to go on, day after day, when I'm always homesick for a place I never can go back to?" At Trestan's headshake,

Mel continued. "It's the notion that whatever path I choose in life, I'll eventually go back and show my father how far I've come. I'm going to make myself a better person and live life in a special way. I will make something of myself that even my father never dreamed! When enough time has gone past I'm going to go back home, and by then my own village will have heard tales of my adventures. Maybe he still won't approve, but by then I will have carved my own destiny and became something more than he thought I could.

"You have to look ahead along the same principles. Your father hopes the best for you. He worries about you. Some day you have to walk back to your hometown bearing a mantle of victory. Look forward to the day when you can walk up to your father, grown into a man in your own right! A parent's lasting legacy is based on what their children achieve. You have to live for that day when you can return to him as a man that he can be proud to call son."

Trestan nodded, "I think he would be proud of me. I hope I can go back to him with my head held high."

Mel rearranged Trestan's blankets. "Don't just hope for it. Do it. I have a feeling he'd be very proud of you already. You get some rest. Tomorrow you are going to need it to go home."

Trestan drifted into a peaceful slumber afterwards. Mel resumed his guard post. The gnome pulled out a handkerchief and started dabbing his own cheeks. He sniffled at memories of his father and his childhood. "Why did he have to get me thinking about home? Now who is going to cheer me up?"

*   *   *   *   *

The morning found the camp alive with noise, foremost of which included grunts, curses and yells. Axes chopped at wood and strong arms bound pieces together. Petrow and Salgor worked at making a litter to hitch behind Cat's horse. They used spare rope and leather from the mercenary camp. Blankets from that camp also served to make a cushion Trestan could rest on. It didn't look very comfortable, but the group put its collective wisdom together to make it work.

"Why are you untying that? I put a lot of work getting that hitched together," exclaimed Petrow.

Salgor bellowed, "Well if you had listened to me in the first place, you would have tied it in the right spot to begin with!"

The dwarf tore at the knot with his hands, cursing as he went. "The horse can't pull it with that crossbar so far up the frame! Its back legs will keep hitting it until the wood or the leg breaks."

In frustration, Salgor pulled out his axe in order to fix the knot quicker. Petrow stopped him before he hacked at the litter. "Ok, just let me untie it and you can fix it however you like. We don't want to smash up the frame fixing it."

"You know, if you had both followed my advice," added Mel, "You would have drawn a diagram and planned it on paper beforehand. That's how the mechanically inclined

176

gnomes do things. They plan a project for much longer than the time it takes to construct it. Obviously, your mistake was a product of bad planning and oversight…"

Two voices exclaimed, "Shut up, Mel!"

The gnome sulked, walking away to a far portion of the camp. He mumbled complaints as he went. Cat noticed that as Mel talked to himself, he imitated Petrow and Salgor in a mocking manner as he carried on some private argument. Cat shook her head, having decided to tend Trestan rather than provide help to the construction of the litter. The handyman and dwarf were each trying to do it their own way, and neither appreciated anyone else's input. The two worked in opposing directions with their ideas. The litter slowly took form, though in a way that neither one had foreseen.

Lady Shauntay stayed quiet and aloof that morning. The noblewoman often glanced at Trestan's unconscious form. Cat tried to read her eyes. The half-elf bet that any concern the lady felt for Trestan was based on her own selfish needs. The young smith had been the only one who had gone out of his way for her. Now the person she had most depended on to satisfy her needs was unable to help at all. The few times the noble had tried to ask anyone for anything that morning, they had barked an answer for her to provide for herself. The noble's daughter seemed glad to be free of her previous captors, but if she expected royal treatment from her rescuers she was mistaken.

Petrow and Salgor took turns cursing as the makeshift litter took shape. Cat finally spoke up to brighten their spirits, "I think it's coming along just fine. We just need something to carry him to town as quickly as possible, not a master work of art. You've been working since before sunrise and it looks about ready."

Petrow and Salgor looked at each other as well as the half-elf. Petrow continued retying the crossbar lower on the litter. "I, err, we are just trying to get it as best we can to carry him over this uneven terrain. Hopefully the blankets we have should help cushion him as we go."

Salgor looked at the young smith, trying to judge the man's condition. "The elf is right. We need to finish this up and get moving for his sake."

Petrow also paused to watch Trestan as Salgor returned to work on the frame. He watched the chest rise and fall to assure himself that his friend still breathed. The young handyman would have returned to work, except that his attention shifted to Cat. The half-elf, looking beyond them, jumped as if something startled her, then ran towards her horse. The young man looked behind him, but could see nothing out of the ordinary. Meadowlands, as well as sparse trees and hills, colored the landscape. Nothing moved. Petrow could have sworn Cat had been looking that way when she jumped up. When he turned back to regard the half-elf, she had her crossbow off her horse and was loading it. Perhaps he wasn't mistaken about thinking she had seen something.

"Cat? What did you see?"

The half-elf gave a shrug as she slid a bolt into the crossbow. "Something in the air. It didn't look natural."

That statement alarmed the camp and got immediate reactions. Petrow returned his eyes to the sky as Salgor stopped to get a good grip on his axe. Mel pulled out his wand and looked for anything odd. Lady Shauntay decided that ducking behind a fallen tree was the better part of valor. The camp went quiet as eyes swept the horizon. They scanned over the wilderness, focusing on wind-blown branches and small birds that flew nearby. Only the lonesome whistle of the wind came to their listening ears.

Finally, Cat spotted something low to the horizon. It came out from behind a small stand of trees in the distance, flying towards them. She called it out and the rest gawked at it. It was unlike anything they had ever seen.

CHAPTER 15

The shape that flew towards the companions did not have a natural look about it. The front of it took the silhouette of a large bird, but in general it did not look or move like a real bird. It was immediately apparent that this was no animal of any variety flying towards them. Although the object was wider than it was tall, it did not appear to be flapping wings to keep its flight. The companions stayed tense and ready for anything. They crouched behind cover with weapons readied in their hands. The flying spectacle did not appear to be heading straight towards them, though it would pass close to their position.

As it got closer, finer details could be seen. The object resembled an elaborate balcony, complete with an ornate rail along its perimeter. From side to side it was a circular platform, and not very tall from top to bottom. The front portion of the railing featured a figurehead of a dove, carved from wood and serving as decoration. The wings of the dove spread out to help form the leading edge of the guardrail. Just behind the figurehead they could see what appeared to be the head of a man sitting near the front of the craft. The platform was slightly larger than a wagon, and one could assume it could carry a few people easily. The companions knew it had to be magical, for they could see no other reason why it could float so easily up in the air.

The party took in the strange sight with mixed feelings and uncertainty. A flying machine was another chapter out of myth and history. There were once reported to be several flying ships of old that battled during the Godswars, but if any existed today they would be a rare find. Petrow, Mel and Salgor almost stared with open mouths at the wonder of seeing it.

Cat called out to the vessel, calling attention to where the party hid. Her shrill, desperate voice pierced the quiet of the camp. Although they had likely been spotted anyway, the rest of the party hoped the magical craft would pass by peacefully. The half-elf scared her companions when she hailed it.

"Help us! Please stop and lend a hand!"

Salgor turned around and shushed Cat, but the vessel already changed course towards them. A low, humming noise came from some crystals mounted on the bottom of the flying platform. The craft swooped lower, though it did not appear to act in any overly aggressive manner. The helmsman peeked over the edge of the guardrails to survey the scene below. The individual appeared humanoid: a peacock feather sticking out of a plush hat, and long blonde hair flowing in the wind. As he floated above them, the party looked at Cat and each other for any ideas.

Salgor scolded, "Why did you call its attention to us? 'Tis probably a spell caster, and not to be trusted!"

Cat replied, "Because it is just one man and Trestan needs help. He needs to get to a town for healing as soon as possible."

The figure on board the flying vessel called down to them, "Why should I trust landing among a band of unknown people, all of whom seem well-armed?"

Katressa Bilil responded, while Petrow and Mel took up positions on either side of Trestan. "Forgive us our arms, but we are in a rather uncivilized area. As you pointed out, caution is the rule out here. We are in need of assistance if you can provide it. We were returning a lost noble to her home, but one of our friends was severely wounded."

The half-elf pointed out the litter and Trestan's sleeping form. "We seek any curative powers you command, or any healing draughts that you might have on you."

The stranger, whom they could see well enough to know he was an elf, yelled back from his high perch, "I shall land then, and offer what I may. Please keep a respectable distance until I approach. Keep your weapons relaxed and I shall see to your friend."

Cat nodded and the rest of the group put away their weapons, Salgor muttering as he did. The helmsman of the flying vessel floated easily away from them a short distance. The craft came down lightly on an even patch of ground nearby. The companions exchanged a few whispered words; with Cat assuring them they needed help for Trestan's sake. Cautiously, the sole occupant of the mystery contraption approached.

Cat would have pinned the elf's fashions as originating from the Kingdom of Gheras, possibly the city of Orlaun. The multiple layers of his outfit were very much a style from that land. A puffed-sleeve shirt emerged from under a long-tailed overcoat. Many elegant trimmings and jeweled buttons adorned his attire, further advertising his expensive tastes. Flowing elvish embroidery accentuated many pockets. A short cape hung upon his shoulders, though the wind had ruffled it a bit. Inexplicably, the same wind proved unable to shift his plush, feather-adorned hat. The elf strode towards them wearing high-topped boots, ending in a folded over rim. He carried a staff as he walked, a short sword belted at his side.

The party decided to let Cat do the talking, trusting in her charms and elvish blood. Salgor was noticeably tense about the whole meeting, not trusting this stranger amongst them. Cat noticed several details about the elf once they stood close. Touches of silver, due to age, streaked his blonde hair. It would be an error to say there were any wrinkles, yet the years of passing had etched strong lines into the face. This was the first elf Mel or Petrow had seen with facial hair: a rough stubble forming a beard. While humans began to grow facial hair during puberty, elves did not tend to grow any until well into their middle years. Even then most of the fair folk shaved it, or outright used magic to remove it, but this elf wore it openly to display his age and demand respect.

"Salutations," the elf spoke, "I am Korrelothar Balshav. 'The Highwater Conjuror.' At your service." He looked around as if someone might recognize his name or title. The rest of the companions mostly looked at each other in confusion, though Cat furrowed her brow at the mention of the Highwater district of Orlaun. The elf loosed a sigh that his title went unrecognized and left them unimpressed.

Cat introduced their party. As she indicated people the half-elf pointed out the spot where the young noble hid. With a frown, the blushing girl stood with as much dignity as she could muster from behind the cover of the tree. Korrelothar seemed to take special notice of her, and Cat thought she saw him tense his grip on the staff.

The elf spoke, "I have heard her name mentioned in Barkan's Crossing. How is it that she comes to be traveling with you?"

The elf heard the rumors about a noble's kidnapping. For a moment Korrelothar suspected them of being the kidnappers, but Cat talked quickly. The elf trusted her and

180

relaxed visibly as she gave a brief and accurate account of their pursuit of the noble and the battle that followed. Korrelothar saw Lady Shauntay nod her agreement of the half-elf's words, further assuring him that the noble was in no danger. Cat was just beginning to get to their urgency regarding Trestan when the noble made her own pleas.

Lady Shauntay interrupted Cat by presenting herself between the half-elf and the stranger. "I thank whatever gods led you to travel this way, sir. I humbly ask if you could spare room for me in your…flying carriage. Please speed me home and I'm sure my father will reward you justly for your efforts."

Petrow and Cat exchanged rueful looks behind the young noble. Neither could recall the noble expressing an interest in rewarding the companions for their bloody efforts. The elf acknowledged her but his attention focused on the injured young man. "Nay reasons to worry, if I can lend a hand I will. Let's first get a look at this man, shall we?"

The rest of the party closed upon the elf as he examined Trestan. They all watched every movement as Korrelothar Balshav felt around the injured man. They tensed when he began casting some sort of spell, but Mel put up a hand to assure there was no danger. One of the elf's hands lingered over the young man's abdomen. Although blankets covered Trestan, the elf determined where the hurt was and concentrated on the area.

"He does have a serious wound here," the elf spoke. "I sense infection at the site. He needs a proper healer in a hurry."

Petrow's concern was evident as he voiced his question, "Might you have any healing draughts or herbs that we could buy?

Korrelothar shook his head. "Nay. I was traveling to visit a friend. I did not expect problems and so I didn't grab any to take with me."

The companions stared helplessly between Trestan, the litter, and the magical craft. With no healing available they privately considered their options. The strange elf visitor stood and addressed Cat again, "Where are you headed?"

"Troutbrook. It's a small village along the road from Barkan's Crossing to Kashmer. It's Lady Shauntay's home and it also has a temple with healers. We expect that it is still over a day west/northwest across this terrain."

The stylishly dressed elf looked between the young noble and Trestan. He weighed the issue in his mind a moment before speaking. "I would be a hard soul indeed to turn away when I can give a hand. There is room enough for us all on *Dovewing*, and I'm flying that direction anyway. The friend I was meeting lives near the Kashmer area. I can speed you along your path quickly. A day of walking across this type of terrain much is slower compared to the distances I can cover when flying."

Cat smiled, yet she looked at her horse uncertainly. "You all should go, but I won't leave my horse out here. I'll ride and catch up."

"Nay worries, fair Katressa." The elf approached her horse. "I can carry her, though in a different form. Do you have any of your valuables, anything you might require still on the horse?"

Cat shook her head. The party's possessions were in bags and sacks around camp. The companions watched the elf magic-user fed something to Cat's horse. He began speaking strange words. Cat's horse became a mist, which then sucked into the elf's hand.

For a moment, the companions stood in awe as they wondered what happened to the animal. Korrelothar presented his open hand to Cat, as Mel also came forth to witness the magic. The horse had become a small, carved figure resting in the elf's palm. It did not impress Salgor, who mumbled under his breath.

Korrelothar handed Cat the small carving which had moments ago been her horse. The half-elf held it gingerly in her hands, amazement clear upon her face. The elf conjuror instructed her on what to say to call the horse back to its normal form, and assured her that it was safe and resting until she called for it again.

Korrelothar gestured towards his craft, "Now, let's get all your equipment on board *Dovewing* and just hope that none of you are afraid of heights."

*   *   *   *   *

She was made of old oaks, and lined with precious metals. Gold and silver gilded the railing. Gems of high quality formed the eyes of many flying beasts carved into the guardrail supports. These adorned sculptures were the pinnacle of her beauty, taking the form of pegasi, eagles, owls, wyverns and more. *Dovewing* was a masterpiece of craftsmanship, built for luxury as well as reliable service. If the details put into the design and artistic pieces were any indication of the magic involved, then the companions did not doubt that the vessel would perform its duty for centuries if needed. Korrelothar Balshav sat at a comfortable chair at the helm, as he handled a few levers that controlled speed and direction. In front of him, the shape of a dove formed the figurehead. Benches ringed the inside of the side guardrails. The most ornate seating was a plush couch that took up much of the rear portion of the deck. Flanking this couch sat chests for holding valuables. Hatches on the floor of the deck hinted at more storage.

The magical vessel dominated the conversation as they took off from the campsite. The companions compiled their knowledge of divine chariots: mythic flying ships of old used in the Godswars. According to Korrelothar, those first ships were blessed by the gods and used by their champions to further their causes. They flew on faith, with a little help from people who eventually became the clerics of the modern day. During those times, the gods walked among men more often, but after the cataclysms caused by those wars no deity blessed the creation of new ships. The heavenly powers exerted less direct influence on the world as races struggled to recover. The magical ships almost disappeared from existence. Several had been destroyed in great aerial battles during the Godswars, with the losing ship and crew sometimes falling out of the sky from thousands of feet up in the air. Other divine chariots fell into disrepair or were dismantled by scavengers in the dark years of survival. Some flying temples had been kept relatively intact, yet were no longer blessed with the power of flight. At least one was told to be stuck on dry land, with faithful followers erecting a church around it, calling it hallowed ground. A select few served as sea-going vessels after their power of flight had been lost. In fact, only one divine chariot was known to function with the power of flight in this part of the realms. In Orlaun, one such ship was tended by a magic-users' guild.

182

The elf regaled them about that divine chariot as they flew, though the companions looked down at the distant ground with fright and wonder. "The only one that still flies, as far as we know. She is the last of her kind, kept in good shape by the wizards in my order, as well as several clerics. I forgot to mention, I am a member of the Brotherhood of the Circles, one of the two prominent mage guilds in Orlaun. What makes *Dovewing* different from the original is that it was made using arcanum. Clerics of faith are required in order to fly the divine chariot, yet this vessel flies on magical power infused in the crystals underneath the deck. There aren't too many magical vessels like this one, for they are very hard to make. We couldn't begin to build another divine chariot without lots of help, and even then only if the gods blessed the endeavor."

The companions looked over the artistry of the craft and didn't doubt his words. On both sides of the vessel the railing swung out to allow people to board. Those swinging doors displayed exquisite carvings: one was a dragon and the other was a griffon. Each door would have fetched hundreds of gold at an auction just for the carvings and gems alone. The companions fawned over the numerous such statues, featuring flying creatures and decorated with gems, that supported the entire length of the guardrail. Overall, the vessel reflected beauty despite spots that revealed battle damage or inclement weather. Even the plush couch Trestan rested upon showed little wear from the years.

Mel fawned over every detail. "This is lovely. Everything about this speaks of strong magic and lots of craftsmanship. It looks gnomish by nature."

"It is indeed," Korrelothar spoke, "I had a team of gnomes doing most of the woodwork and a good deal of the spellcasting required. Other races helped as well, for the project required a lot of resources. It was my largest endeavor ever."

Mel's head popped up, "You built this? How old is it?"

The elf grinned, "Well, I only supervised. *Dovewing* is close to one-hundred-and-thirty years old. She's every bit as wonderful a creation now as she was back then."

Petrow's jaw dropped as he learned the age of the craft. Like his friend Cat, it was hard to guess age when talking about elves and their creations. Cat didn't spend much time adoring the vessel, her hands focused on helping Trestan keep cool. The young man barely opened his eyes since they carried him on board. Sweat ran down his forehead.

As Petrow looked over his other companions, noticed Salgor leaning over the railing. "Are you alright there, Salgor?

The dwarf responded in a strained voice. He bent far over the rail and clutched it with white knuckles. "I'm very fine, thank you. Don't mind me, I'm just enjoying the view."

Petrow caught something odd in the dwarf's voice. The human shifted in his seat a bit to see more of Salgor's face. With a giggle, the handyman asked, "Wouldn't you see more of the view if you had your eyes open?"

Salgor turned back to face the human. The dwarf sneered, a tinge of green in his pallor. "I hate magic, and I hate wizards. Umm, helpful ones excluded of course."

Korrelothar smiled and nodded back at the dwarf. Salgor then continued to lean over the railing and concentrate on keeping his breakfast down. Petrow hoped the dwarf wouldn't lose control, as the designs ringing the guardrail were much too impressive to be spoiled in such a way.

Mel continued to look over the vessel, but the curious gnome also looked over their host thoroughly. The gnome noted many trinkets, probably magical, that the elf wore. The short sorcerer pointed to Korrelothar's earring. "Is that a magical trinket? I don't think I have seen something like that before."

The elf put a hand to one pointed ear, "Oh this? This isn't magical. It's a spiritbond to reflect my commitment to my loved one."

Mel nodded, but furrowed his brow. Although he didn't want to show it, he had no clue what a spiritbond was. Cat noticed his reaction and answered his unspoken question, "It is the elf form of marriage. It is a promise that binds one soul to another; although some elves believe that a couple's souls are bound before they even meet. It's all pre-ordained in their eyes, and wearing a token just signifies the link that already existed. Not all view it that way but it's an old tradition."

The gnome grinned. "Ah, now I understand then. The earring signifies the loyalty and spiritual link your mate."

Korrelothar caressed the curves of the earring a bit as he spoke. "Aye. There are several forms a spiritbond might take. She favored an earring to signify the link."

Mel had to ask, "Why an earring?"

The elf smiled and gave a humorous, though accurate response, "Because a female always wants to make sure she has her husband's ear."

Dovewing sped over the horizon. Ridges and trees passed by at a much faster rate than even if they had been riding horses down a straight path. They streaked past birds and scared some animals below. Mel asked a few times if he could fly, but the elf politely refused. The gnome did watch as their host showed him how he controlled their flight. Korrelothar would turn and move the levers, and the craft would change directions and height as he did so. This greatly amused Mel, but it made Salgor clench the guardrail and grit his teeth. The gnome excitedly asked how to turn, how to climb, how to speed up, and the elf was more than happy to show him. Then the gnomish sorcerer saw the dwarf's mounting discomfort and decided to repay a few remarks. After all, don't dwarves like pranks as much as gnomes? When Mel asked Korrelothar how to dive, Salgor put on a look of alarm. *Dovewing* descended at a fast pace, coming close enough to a treetop that it clipped some leaves. They all heard a grunt from Salgor erupt into a rather undignified noise as the dwarf's stomach emptied. The elf looked back with distaste at the mess dripping off the designs of the guardrail. Carvings that witnessed many flights in a century of service were now in need of a good cleaning.

Salgor turned to face the elf and the gnome. The growl that escaped his lips drowned the noise of the rumble in his stomach. Various unsightly gobs spattered his fine beard. He patted the handle of his axe with one muscular arm. "Look, we have a sick man on board and a scared noble. Now you have an angry dwarf as well! You better fly this thing slow and steady or I'll find a way to slow it down with my axe!"

The elf frowned but resumed a steady flight.

184

*　　　　*　　　　*　　　　*　　　　*

Lady Shauntay spoke sweetly to the elf as they flew onward. "I must thank you for helping me and my 'escorts'. I am indebted to you, good sir. My feet ache from my travels. I will be so very glad to get home and find some rest after this ordeal."

Korrelothar replied as Petrow and Cat shared a scowl at being called escorts. "You are most welcome milady Shauntay. I'm glad I was there to offer a hand. I wish I could have been there sooner, though it sounds like the ruffians were given quite a beating by your friends."

The noble sat on the bench up front where the elf piloted. Lady Shauntay spoke again, though with a side-glance at the companions. Petrow idly wondered if she intentionally leaned forward to show a little too much cleavage, though her clothes and hair were still in dirty disarray. "Aye, the rescue was well-timed, though I prefer not to talk about that." The noble quickly changed the subject. "I am wondering, what business brought you up north? I hope you do not mind me asking, but I am curious."

The elf shrugged before responding, not giving the human woman or her cleavage any undue attention as he flew. "Nay worry, nothing personal at all about it. I seek a friend who might know more about an item that underwent some unexplained changes in our archives recently. I probably could have just sent him a message, but flying *Dovewing* is a rare enough treat."

Lady Shauntay nodded and seemed ready to say more when Korrelothar continued. "It was nothing really: a green stone of unknown origins but with interesting magical properties. We knew it radiated certain strong magic in the past, and our young researchers often study unknown objects such as that. Recently there was some kind of change; it failed to show as much magic as it once had. In fact, it seems to have lost its magic except for a faint, false signature. I had a friend that did more work on it once, so it was a good excuse to get away and visit him."

Petrow perked up at the mention of a green stone. "Could you describe the stone sir?" Lady Shauntay looked at him crossly, as if he interrupted a private conversation. The handyman persisted, "I would really like to know."

"Well, like I mentioned it had a dark green shade to it, and was generally egg-shaped, though larger than an egg. There were some white markings on it."

As the wizard described the stone, it bore a similarity to the holy relic displayed at the well in Troutbrook. Petrow and Lady Shauntay Tessald both listened with alarm at the likeness of the details. Korrelothar's wizard guild knew little more about the stone than the church of Yestreal did. They knew it had magical properties, but had never been able to fully test it. Korrelothar admitted that it wasn't a very remarkable item, except for the recent change in its magical signature.

Petrow finally exclaimed, "That sounds just like our village's holy relic! That band that kidnapped Lady Shauntay had their hands on that stone before they took her."

The elf pilot looked back at Petrow, "What do you mean they had their hands on it? What did they do with it?"

The young man shook his head, "We don't know. They seemed to leave it behind, but they had another one that looked just like it. The stone had long been kept by our church for more years than anyone knows. The clerics said it had been a gift from their god. It sat openly in the center of town. The band that kidnapped the lady here either stole it and replaced it with a duplicate, or they just used it for something."

"Very odd," Korrelothar mused, "I think it was a mistake that we didn't take a better look at our own stone now. What did your church use it for?"

Lady Shauntay jumped in, "It didn't have much value, though the church knew it had magical properties. The head cleric told people that it somehow helped the crops and fields of the village. I didn't regard it as much more than a decoration, except where village pride was concerned. I caught the other group doing something with it in the middle of the night and tried to stop them. That's when a fight erupted and I was kidnapped."

One slender hand absently stroked the stubble on his chin as Korrelothar mused, "A very strange coincidence indeed. It seems I ran into the right people. I'll have to have a look at your village stone when we get there."

The elf looked over the horizon and pointed at some haze from chimneys in the distance. "Which may not be long at all. Does that look like the place?"

The companions shouted surprise. They had camped a long day's march from the village. It amazed them that this magical vessel could bear them so fast from the wilds to civilization. The members of the party looked eagerly at the village in the distance.

Petrow squinted to make out details. "I don't know. It might be…but…I've just never seen it from this angle before!"

As the handyman smiled amidst the pure joy of flying over his home, Lady Shauntay spoke as well. "Three main streets, a bridge on one end of town…I see my father's manor on the ridge! Oh, take me home first! I'll be glad when this is over so that I can kiss my own pillows again!"

The elf shook his head, "Nay, I can see the village temple even from here. We have to land there first and take care of your wounded friend. Relax young lady, you will be home shortly."

The noble pouted, "I do not want the village to see me like this. I want to get home."

Cat glared a hole in the noble's back, briefly toying with an image in her mind. The half-elf imagined how the young noble would feel to get this close and be pushed over the edge of the guardrail. She tended her wounded friend, turning away from temptation. Cat had one arm around Trestan as they hovered over the village.

"I feel like I have died and gone to paradise." Cat turned at Trestan's words. He was on his back, looking up at Cat and the clouds above. "I feel like I'm floating with you, Cat. Where are we?"

She smiled at him. As she spoke, he turned about to see the strange vessel and his other companions. "Hang on Trestan, you aren't dead yet. We are almost to your home."

"Home," the young man smiled as his eyes closed again, "I love that word."

186

CHAPTER 16

He stood frozen for a long time before snapping out of his daydream. He saw his blackened fingernails and metal hammer before his eyes, yet he hadn't actually been looking at them. His mind wandered a lot recently, digging up memories of the past. Despite his best efforts to work, random thoughts kept distracting his heart. His world hadn't been the same since his boy disappeared.

Mikhael's young voice piped up beside him, "Isn't the fire getting a little cold?"

The young boy had helped more than usual during the past few days. Mikhael had responsibilities to his father's shop as well, but the smithy needed a helping hand. Hebden Karok absently glanced at the coals of the forge. Although his mind registered the truth of the boy's words, his head simply nodded agreement at the boy's observation. The master smith should stoke the fires, but he did nothing until Mikhael interpreted the nod as a cue and went to work on it. Hebden sighed. After being such a hard-working man, he started suffering moments of inactivity; as if a sickness had come over his mind and body lately. He did not care to eat and he could not put his mind to work. The village depended on him, but they would have to allow him his grief.

The smith did not even know what happened to his son after the night of the street fight. The memories from that night, and the following morning, were still fresh in his mind. He assumed it was his son that entered the house and made noises as Hebden waited behind a blocked door. He didn't really know one way or the other who it had been. He assumed Trestan would answer his father's pleas. After the unknown intruder had left the house, the evening stretched on unbearably. He had sat by a small candlelight, listening hard for the night sounds beyond his room for a long time. The morning had risen upon a street of blood. Folk found bodies of humans and animals around the main street. People whispered rumors of dark magic, and described the roars of some horrible creature. The noble's daughter was rumored to have been kidnapped by strangers, and indeed most of the Tessald house guards rode south in pursuit. They left behind the body of the captain of the guard. Sir Wilhelm Jareth, prominent citizen and friend of many, also lay dead.

And what of Hebden Karok's son?

It only added to the mystery when Hebden realized Petrow went missing as well. Different rumors argued about whether people had seen those young men lying dead in the street, or running south that night in the company of a dark lady. No one really knew anything that could be taken as the honest facts, no one admitted to being a witness, and certainly Hebden didn't know how to interpret all the rumors. It was now the sixth day since the fight. Six mornings of unnatural quiet in the Karok home.

Hebden forced his mind to the task at hand. Mikhael had gotten used to the older man working quietly, so the young kid did his best to contribute without getting in the way. Hebden went to work pounding away at another piece of iron. The smith worked hard to hit the metal just right, restraining the urge to pound his frustrations out. He had already ruined enough pieces of bar stock. The smith wasn't mad at his son if he had run off, but questions and uncertainty over his son's fate plagued the smith's thoughts. Hebden pounded away the morning, while he avoided staring too long at the unused leather apron on a nearby hook.

The older smith knew his son liked the life of the hammer and anvil. Trestan showed every intention of following in his father's footsteps. Occasionally when minstrels passed through, he watched silently as his son's eyes sparkled at the adventure-filled songs. Often Hebden wondered if his son might seek a different path. Trestan had trained to use a staff to defend himself, and the notion that he might be studying the sword as well was always present. The smith wanted his boy to be able to defend himself. Hebden couldn't prepare himself for the day that his son might be enticed away by the promise of treasures or heroic stories. Hebden knew that his son's future was not his to dictate, but young men had ways of following unachievable dreams before realizing the traps involved. Where was Trestan now? The father would have given anything to learn some news of his son's whereabouts. Did he run off? Did someone take him? Did he attempt a foolish pursuit of the kidnapped noble? How long would Hebden have to wait before knowing if his son was dead or alive?

The smith of Troutbrook tried to bury his continued barrage of internal questions as he worked hard to finish the projects before him. Too many requests and broken items piled up in his yard, and he had to focus on each job to get the work done.

Some commotion started on the street behind him, distracting him from his work yet again. Several people on the street started yelling. Hebden and Mikhael stopped and looked about. Merchants, farmers, travelers and other various townsfolk spoke and ran about in a confused frenzy. Some seemed generally panicked; even horses hitched by the inn pranced nervously. The smith motioned to Mikhael to stay where he was, then walked a few steps into the street. Hebden still carried a hammer in his hand, nervous that he might need to hang onto it for some unknown reason. He followed the line of several pointing fingers. When he saw the strange object in the air, he barely kept a grip on his hammer, though his jaw dropped in wonder.

Uncertainty and wonder mixed as *Dovewing* hovered over the buildings on the main street. Villagers could see people on board the strange vessel and they weren't sure how to respond. One small humanoid, a gnome by his looks, simply waved down at the people below. The flying vessel slowly circled around the temple area, before gliding closer to the inn and stables. A humming sound emanated from it. Some folk ushered children into buildings for their safety; others waved back to the gnome and walk closer out of curiosity. Hebden did not venture far into the street. Upon hearing Mikhael move closer, Hebden waved him to stay back.

The pilot of the flying vessel spotted an area large enough to land. He smoothly brought it down on an open area adjacent to the inn, often used as a small courtyard or wagon alley. The vessel remained clear of the main street. Villagers stayed a respectful distance as *Dovewing* settled softly on the ground. The humming noise abruptly ceased, while the deck of the small craft bustled with activity. A small crowd mumbled and pointed, though none dared get too close. Hebden thought he heard a voice call a greeting from the craft and assurances that the newcomers meant no harm. The smith's view was partly obstructed by other people, but he was content to keep his distance from the odd sight.

188

The tone of the crowd changed suddenly. Amidst excited words and pointing, a few cheers went up for "Lady Shauntay", raising an eyebrow on the smith. Hebden moved to get a different vantage point. When he first saw Lady Shauntay Tessald, it was hard to recognize her. She looked worn and tired, wore dirty clothes, pain evident in every step. A half-elf woman in dark leathers moved beside the noble, guiding her a few steps away from the strange vessel. Hebden did not recognize her, never having seen her when she was in town the first time. The half-elf motioned for people to step back, and they gave way for the noble and her guardian. She spoke a few words to something in her hand. People stepped back as a mist coalesced before her.

Caution gave way to surprise as a horse appeared out of nowhere! The half-elf leapt into the saddle gracefully, extending a hand to the noble. The crowd, especially several younger men, cheered the return of Shauntay as she put on a smile for those around. With both women on the horse, everyone nearby could see the noble above the heads of their neighbors. Noting that most of the crowd's focus shifted to them instead of the flying craft, the half-elf decided to command a little attention of her own while she could.

Cat yelled to the crowd, and all fell silent to listen to her proclamation. "Your Ladyship Shauntay Tessald returns safely after being rescued from her captors! Give thanks of her safe return to your hometown heroes, Trestan and Petrow! They fought valiantly to keep her safe."

A rowdy cheer went up, though Hebden went over the words in his head. The smith wondered if he had heard correctly. Cat, satisfied she had put recognition where it was due, spared a look towards those on the vessel before riding away. Lady Shauntay seemed eager to go, though she kept a smile in the face of the crowd. With a shake of the reins the horse sped off, parting the crowd of onlookers. The two women rode out of town towards the distant Tessald mansion.

With all the excitement caused by the noble and adventuress, few paid attention as a gnome ran past several people on his way to the temple. Hebden moved closer and a friend in the crowd spotted him. The fellow villager pointed past the rest of the crowd and shouted, but the smith couldn't make out all the words. He saw more figures disembark from the flying platform. A dwarf and a flamboyant human carried another person away from the vessel. An elf followed, but after leaving the craft he turned and sprinkled some dust over *Dovewing*.

Korrelothar proclaimed loudly to all those near, "Let none touch this vessel, under pain of the spell I have cast over it! Any who dare try to board her will suffer harmful consequences! I apologize for the precautions, but this vessel is very important to me."

The elf wizard rejoined the others. Hebden paid him little mind, finally recognizing Petrow. Petrow dressed strangely, in colorful clothes beyond his financial means. The dwarf looked unremarkable, save for his fine mail coat and heavy axe. Hebden Karok looked into the closed eyes of the limp human being carried, and in that startling moment he saw his son. His heart skipped a beat. The strong smith almost went to his knees as he stumbled forward. They carried Trestan Karok to the temple, where a small number of clerics were already exiting the doorway. The gnome pointed at Trestan and chattered excitedly. The entourage stopped at the doorway of the Church of the Sacred Harvest, only a few meters from the well supporting the village's holy relic. Several clerics reached out to help carry Trestan. High Priest Gerlach barked orders to the others as they took charge of Trestan's care.

Hebden was still shouldering his way past people as he went towards the church. The clerics and his son disappeared inside, along with the dwarf, the elf and the gnome. Only Petrow, relieved of his burden, stopped to catch his breath before the doorway. Even as Hebden noted Petrow's expensive attire, the smith saw the bruises and scratches visible on Trestan's friend.

Hebden reached out and grabbed the young man firmly. He forced Petrow to turn around and face him, "What happened? Where have you two been?"

Petrow started to open his mouth, stuttering out a reply, "Umm, you know I was thinking about how I was going to explain all this to you when we arrived."

The young man stumbled over his words. Hebden stood over him with hammer in hand. The older man raised his brows, awaiting an answer. Beyond his muscular frame, several townspeople also stood close by, hoping to learn more as well.

Petrow's mouth worked open and closed a few times before he could reply, "I still have nay clue as far as what to say!"

*   *   *   *   *

Trestan watched the few clerics of the church scurry around him. They poked his wound, made him swallow bitter stew, and prayed over him a lot. The young smith wondered why they had stripped him naked just for some healing miracles. They expressed the need to further check the wound, though their healing miracles reduced it to a smaller scar. Trestan felt better than he had in days.

Despite his expressed wishes to leave, they talked him into lying there longer to ensure all of the infection had been drawn out. The young man wondered where his friends were. He recalled a strange flying craft, the visage of an elf…but few other details of that journey were remembered. The young man itched to get home, despite nervousness about his reunion with his father.

The head priest of the temple entered, catching Trestan by surprise. Priest Gerlach stood framed in the doorway, watching the young man with interest even as Trestan had been examining the room for the umpteenth time. Yestreal's chosen speaker almost filled the doorway with his heavy frame. While the cleric was known as a hard-working man, he was also overly fond of food. Muscles and fat contributed to a bulky appearance. A reddish-gray beard hung from his broad face, giving some length to an otherwise squared head. Normally, Trestan saw the older man in his priestly vestments, but today the cleric wore a casual, less decorative robe. Clearly he hadn't expected visitors to drop out of the sky. The chosen of Yestreal spoke with a deep baritone that resonated from deep inside.

"I see the hero has awakened from his mortal injury." The cleric addressed Trestan, though used a third person perspective. "His worried father will be joyous upon hearing the news."

The high priest walked into the room, as Trestan responded respectfully, "Many thanks to you and your clergy. I can't begin to repay the simple pleasure of being able to see my father again. I've missed him so. I'm hoping I might be free now to go see him."

Priest Gerlach began to speak again, "Oh, you are quite well and able to go, though I had hoped to speak with you a moment…"

He was interrupted by a commotion just outside the door. Petrow had snuck up behind the high cleric to get a peek into the room. Another priest noticed him and tried guiding the handyman back towards the church sanctuary. Petrow refused to go, even demanded to see Trestan. After a few comments back and forth, Priest Gerlach intervened. The elder cleric waved away his inferior and allowed Petrow to enter the room. Petrow looked healed and well.

"Just as well you are here," the older man spoke, "that way I can chat with both of you regarding your little adventure."

The conversation was rather brief. Petrow and Trestan offered a rushed explanation. The two youths avoided a lot of questions, unsure if they were in trouble. The priest often tried evasive questions that might pry further information out of them. The two younger men found they could turn the subject around by talking about the stone. The clergy had a great interest in any information in regards to any tampering with their relic. The young smith often answered rather briefly, hoping he could actually end the meeting as soon as possible and meet his father. High Priest Gerlach knew there must be more of their adventures that they weren't telling him, but he was satisfied with what he got.

"They are starting to make up their own stories and rumors on the street," the older man explained. "The dark-haired elf with you really stirred up the crowd. From what I hear, there will be some drinking and music on the main street tonight in your honor."

Trestan and Petrow traded glances; eyes widened at the news that their fellow villagers would be celebrating their achievement. The young smith spoke, "I'll just be glad to see my father again, though I wonder how upset he will be."

Petrow said, "He went outside for some fresher air, since they wouldn't allow us back here."

The cleric nodded, "Quite right, I have detained you long enough. Your belongings are here, and you are free to go. I have my own appointment to keep with matters of importance."

Priest Gerlach stood and made his way out the door. He gave a final bow to the two young men, "Welcome back young sirs. I know the townspeople are looking forward to tonight."

Petrow assisted Trestan in sorting his belongings. The young smith proceeded to get dressed, and for his reunion he picked out the best clothes he owned.

Trestan threw on a good set of pants, as Petrow chatted. "They are throwing a party for us? I can't believe that this morning we were out in the wilds, with you suffering from a mortal injury. Tonight we will see our friends and neighbors have a celebration over an adventure that nearly got us killed."

Trestan didn't slow down as he responded. "I can't believe we actually did it. Though the noble was a handful of trouble, we went out and rescued her from the clutches of some pretty unsavory people. As you pointed out, we came too close to death and yet here we stand."

Trestan finished putting on his shirt and started to carry the rest of his gear out. Petrow stopped him, "Hold up now! You are going to meet your father like that?"

The young smith looked over his clothes. Finding nothing wrong, he inquired, "What do you mean? These are the best and cleanest clothes I have. Each item of this outfit is worth more than all the clothes I owned before leaving home that night."

Petrow pointed at the pieces of armor his friend carried, "I think you should go for the full effect. Wear your armor when you see him."

Trestan thought about it for a moment, then nodded his agreement.

*   *   *   *   *

Not very long after the cleric Gerlach left the two young men, he went to a private chamber to meet a magic-user from out of town. Korrelothar and the village clergyman gave introductions and talked amiably for some time. They briefly discussed each of their hometowns as Gerlach treated the visiting elf wizard with some desserts rushed over from the bakery. Before long, they found themselves turning to the business at hand.

"My good man," Korrelothar stated, "I could talk about far off places and eat desserts all day, but I'm sure we should talk about our common problem."

"Problem?" noted Gerlach. "Does that mean what I fear it does?"

Korrelothar waved a hand to empathize his feelings. "What I learned about the stone out front confirms something uneasy about a similar stone once held at my guild. The holy relic sitting out at the well seems to be a copy of your original. The stone appears almost identical to the one at my guildhall, with the exception of differences in the markings on the stone itself."

The priest paled slightly, setting down his steaming mug. The elf and human did not know they had caught the attention of others. Two eavesdroppers listened outside the room as priest and wizard chatted.

Gerlach spoke, "But…I checked the stone after your arrival. The very moment I heard that someone may have tampered with it, I went out and examined it. It radiates magic."

The elf's eyes narrowed, "How thoroughly did you check it? Did you stop only when you saw that it radiated magic, or did you thoroughly examine its magical signature?"

Gerlach started to open his mouth, but no response came. The look in the priest's eyes confirmed to the elf that the man had only glanced at the magic of the relic. The head of the church finally spoke, but only to deflect the topic, "Surely it is the same one. Why would they plant a fake? I assume you have never been here before, in order to properly read the relic's signature before its theft came into question."

Gerlach had not meant it in a harsh way. The elf knew that it was only proper that the cleric seek all the facts. Korrelothar decided to lay all the grim news before the head priest.

192

The wizard leaned forward in his chair. His voice loud enough to be overheard outside in the hallway. "The stone kept at my guild is the exact same look and style as the one you have outside. The only minor difference between ours and yours is the white markings on the surface. Now, our item radiated some strong magic, though it was hard to place. I would say that it had ties to the earth elements, and it seemed to have a positive effect on any plants that were near it. There were more mysteries hidden inside, but without knowing more we didn't think that much about it. Eventually, it became a novelty that wizards-in-training studied for research. You could say that we knew its magical signature well, though we never unlocked all its secrets."

The elf cleared his throat before continuing. "A short while ago, one of our researching novices recorded something which we mistook for an errant reading. He insisted his reading had been correct, and so I studied the stone to check for any changes. Lo and behold, the stone had changed. By all appearances it was the same stone, but a new magical signature was in place."

The elf paused while that news sank in. Gerlach soon prompted him to continue. Korrelothar said, "It was a false signature. Though we did not understand it at the time, truthfully, we didn't pay it much attention. All we could be certain of was that the magic had faded and changed. Now, many people had free access to that stone. Anyone could have designed a duplicate if for some reason they had wanted to do so. When they had their duplicate, they placed a magical signature on it to mislead anyone into thinking that it was the same stone, although they couldn't quite match the original pattern. Any cursory examination would indeed show magic, but only a thorough look would reveal the changes."

Gerlach nervously sipped at his mug of tea. "In all the heavens…I would never have believed that another stone existed like ours. That was said to be a gift from Yestreal."

Korrelothar asked, "What do you know of your stone?"

"Admittedly, not much," the cleric acknowledged. "We know it was a gift of Yestreal that came to our village in the dark years following the Godswars, and that it would promote fertility of the fields. It was supposed to help us survive the harsh years of sorrow from those old wars. As far as I know, our village lands have always been blessed with good crops and strong herds. We were told it had a way to protect itself as well. It was partly that belief in its self-defense that we left it displayed openly, under the sun, in full view of the neighboring fields. Nay person has ever touched it with the notion to do harm, and we assumed if someone did that the holy relic would defend itself. What little we have learned was from scrolls we have stored away from the light. I haven't read them in decades."

The elf nodded, "It would do us good to read those scrolls and see what may have been forgotten. So far I described what happened to our relic; I was about to speak of yours. You see, with the unexplained changes coming over our own stone, I flew north from Orlaun to seek a sage whom I know. He is getting along in years now, but he was one of the first ones to explore the stone's properties for my guild. I didn't really think there was a theft involved, until I heard about possible tampering with your stone, and the similarity in appearance of your stone to ours. It seems I ran into the right group of young people on my trip."

The visiting elf rested his head thoughtfully on one arm, recalling his experience examining the village stone. "Anyway, I looked over the magical signature of your stone thoroughly as I could in such a short time. It confirmed something…"

Gerlach leaned forward to hear what the wizard had to say. Outside the door, the two eavesdroppers almost forgot to breathe.

The wizard confided, "Your stone reads not only a false signature, but the same false signature as this stone."

From beneath his robes, Korrelothar Balshav produced a stone that was remarkably similar to the holy relic in front of the church. "This is the fake from my guildhall. As you can plainly see, on the casual outside examination it is an identical style of the stone you have outside. It radiates a minor magical field, designed to fool any casual observer. Even more important, this stone radiates exactly the same false field that surrounds the one currently on display by the well. Whoever created this fake also created the one sitting out there right now."

Gerlach visibly paled, and placed his head in his hands. "We have failed to keep the gift of Yestreal? Why would anyone want our relic? Why didn't it defend itself?"

Korrelothar shook his head. "I have nay clue as to the why of it. I am willing to bet that there is something more important about these stones than what we know. Someone wants these very badly and secretively! They went through extreme efforts to hide the thefts."

The priest let loose a sigh as he considered the effects of losing such a wondrous gift from their god. "I would welcome you to go over the old scrolls with me. Maybe together we can place the pieces of this puzzle. I would like to find out more of this artifact's history."

Both rose, but did not move to leave the room as of yet. Priest Gerlach looked to his study desk, at a carving that represented the God of the Sun and Weather, the deity that promoted harvests and crops. The cleric had another question on his mind, "Does your guild have any clue as to who tampered with your stone?"

"Just one clue," said Korrelothar. "The last person to research the stone before its reported tampering gave a name. He was not a member of our guild, but he paid well to access our studies, which many do. He gave his name as Revwar."

The two pairs of ears outside gasped.

The cleric furrowed his brow, searching his memories for the name, "Revwar? Should I know that name from somewhere?"

The elf wizard nodded, "You should soon enough…he was the one Lady Shauntay saw tampering with your relic before she was kidnapped. By an account given to me by her rescuers, he had a similar stone on him during the fight in which she was freed. I'd say we know who our thief is."

Outside in the hall, Petrow and Trestan backed away from the door. "You hear that Tres? Our relic was indeed stolen and replaced by a fake."

Trestan nodded, "I heard. It's scary to think of what might happen to the fields this year. I can't believe I had it sitting on the ground right in front of me, and yet was unable to take it back."

Petrow stood silent for a moment, brow furrowed, "What do we do now?"

Trestan set his jaw and his resolve, "There is nay that we can do. It is beyond our influence. Right now I have to get ready to face my father. That will be a scary enough task, I fear."

Trestan and Petrow turned and resumed their walk to the church sanctuary.

*   *   *   *   *

Trestan and Petrow saw Hebden the moment they stepped into the main chapel of worship. He had his eyes on the door they arrived through, and Trestan would have guessed he had stared at that archway a long time waiting for his son. Petrow mumbled to excuse himself and quickly shuffled past Trestan and towards the exit. Hebden Karok only had eyes for Trestan. Father and son locked gazes for some time, each not sure what to say.

"I missed you," Hebden offered. "I didn't know whether to look for you or buy a gravestone."

Trestan tried to speak past a lump in his throat. "I missed you too father. I...I'm sorry I didn't say anything. I wouldn't want to hurt you."

The older smith looked into the face of his son, "Why didn't you tell me? You couldn't have left word as to where you were going?"

"I wanted to." The young man could not help but think of his father's inquiring voice behind the closed door that night. "You would have talked me out of it. I regretted leaving as I did, though likely, if I had talked to you, you wouldn't have let me go."

Trestan noticed tears in the older man's eyes, and he too began to get misty vision. Gently and quietly, Hebden reached out his arms to his son. They shared a tight hug, and the stress and sorrow of missing each other rolled down their cheeks.

"You are all I have, son. It was very hard not knowing where you were."

"Father, I prayed up to the stars at night, the same ones that glide over the village. I asked for the gods to spare you sorrow, and to speed me back home to you. I admit there were scary times, but I found something in myself out in the wilds that I'm very proud to have. I'm so glad to be back home with you."

They parted to arm's reach. Hebden thoroughly looked his son up and down. "Look how my boy has grown. Where is your rope belt? Your old trousers?"

Trestan stood as tall as he could as his father scrutinized him. The old rope belt was gone. The dirty tunic, shoes, and all of his old clothes were gone. The younger man wore new clothes made of quality material. He wore the same dark red tunic he had worn to the common room of the Eagle's Nest, during the evening their group had met Salgor. His boots were made of good leather and had seen a bit of walking. Atop the young smith's head sat a helm, slightly notched at the front and on the visor where the scimitar had nicked it. From legs to arms, there was a mixture of armor. Leather and padding provided the largest portion of it, though also supported plates of metal over some parts. Bracers and greaves protected the limbs. A shiny breastplate covered most of the upper torso, with the exception of a hole burned through the lower third of it. On his back hung the Sword of the Spirit, Sir Wilhelm's old elvish blade.

Hebden pointed to the hole in the breastplate. "That must have hurt."

Trestan blushed as he looked at the area. "That one got away, but you should have seen the beating we gave to many of his friends."

Hebden smirked, "You'll have to tell me about it soon as we get inside our home. It put a strain on my heart to see you returned, only to watch you be carried to a healer. I didn't realize you considered that pampered girl to be that much of a prize."

"She isn't!" At that Trestan shared genuine smile, disarming his father at such a quick admission. "I found many prizes on the trail, and she wasn't one of them."

"Such as?"

Trestan spoke honestly, "Well, I found my courage, will and strength when faced with determined foes. I found my own self-respect and self-reliance. I saw a part of the world that was beautiful and dangerous at the same time, and I was glad to go out and see it. I found new friends that gave me different perspectives."

The young man paused, though Hebden could see there was more coming. He waited for his son to finish. "I guess I found my faith. I prayed for guidance to the goddess Abriana, and she was there for me. She helped me through the path and I'm guessing she got me back home safely."

Hebden asked the next question through worried eyes, "So, are you looking to become a paladin then? Like Sir Wilhelm?"

Trestan was taken aback by the question. "I hadn't really thought of anything along those lines. I guess I did let loose the warrior spirit within me, but I was looking forward to coming home and swinging the hammer once again. I did have a taste of another lifestyle, but I wasn't seriously thinking of becoming an adventurer. I just went step by step until my heart was satisfied."

"Well, your life is your own path, don't feel tied down by the hammer." Although Trestan heard Hebden's words, he didn't seriously think his father wanted him anywhere but the smithy. "If you must go I can't stop you. I'm hoping that you don't go. I really wouldn't know how I'd manage without you working and growing up by my side."

Trestan gave his father another hug. "I don't think there will be any more adventures for me soon, unless it's a woman."

Hebden ventured, "Please don't tell me it's that Tessald girl."

Trestan laughed, "Not in a million years! The next time I see her on the street, she will be lucky if I even let her buy horse jewelry from me!"

CHAPTER 17

Dusk descended upon the land, but the residents of Troutbrook seemed to have more illumination out than usual this night. Several fires lit the main street outside the inn. Joyous noises accompanied the light and smoke: slamming tankards, laughter, the chewing of food or the burps that followed, people chatting jovially with their neighbors, and the sounds of music and singing.

Troutbrook enjoyed an impromptu festival!

One merchant, who often sold his candies from a cart down closer to the bridge, had moved his portable stand next to the main intersection of town. Other merchants did not complain, as they indulged his treats during the festive evening. Some partygoers leaned out of the inn's second story windows, whistling and shouting, enticing some young maidens to come up and join them for drinks. Men and women donned outfits designed to attract attention or simply be fashionable for the celebration. All wanted to be part of the revelries surrounding their newfound heroes. Several young couples were sneaking kisses, while older couples brought out chairs and sat around the main street chatting with neighbors. Townsfolk helped set a carnival atmosphere, in which several people entertained. The carpenter's oldest son walked on a pair of something called "stilts", which caused giggles from the smaller kids. Laughter and jokes surfaced often, some being retold to the same person who originally spread them around.

Among one group of young ladies and men, Petrow enjoyed free wine while sharing a tale of his adventures on the road. The wine had already loosened his tongue more than usual, helping him exaggerate certain moments.

"…And there I was, using my brand new waraxe to cut through her ladyship's bonds. She could have kissed me right there if not for the angry minotaur guarding her. I urged her to run, but she stuck around asking me to be her hero and knock the thing down. What could I do? A whole camp of armed men stood nearby, but they were also afraid of the monster! I told myself, 'Petrow, you make a living chopping down trees…just look at those minotaur legs, they can be chopped down too!' So I charged in."

Petrow made motions with his arms as he talked about the fight. He pretended to swing his axe, spilling some of his wine. Those with him weren't sure how much to believe, but they had fun listening to his rendition. Petrow continued on with his exaggerated version of events, "Without any help from my friends, I faced this monster one on one! Axes clashed, and I must admit, it had a strong swing. I got a couple hits on it, but the thing just shrugged its loss of blood and kept coming. I shouted for Lady Shauntay to run, but she stubbornly insisted on staying to watch me win. I swear, I didn't want to continue the fight if I didn't have to, but I had nay choice. Finally some misfortune befell me, as the creature shattered my axe. I still made a good show of it, dodging its axe for several minutes, and some of its swings actually hit several of its comrades. It dropped four of its fellows trying to catch me! Eventually, I found myself surrounded by three men with drawn swords, and I would have still fought…had not another crept up on the young noble and knocked her out…"

Not everyone was interested in hearing of the adventure. Despite the tales of the return of the noble, and the rumors of the hometown heroes, stories of fishing took center stage in many conversations. After all, Troutbrook's local pastime focused on angling. At least one avid fisher brought up his collection of poles to the festivities, where he showed them off to a cousin.

The sky darkened under a canopy of stars as festivities continued. Off to the side of the inn, several people looked over the odd flying contraption. None got too close; for word had spread of the wizard's magical trap. Rumors of the protective spell's deadliness spread and grew in the telling. Townsfolk marveled its beauty from afar. The visiting wizard sat near his machine, sharing a drink with a small gnome.

Mel Bellringer spoke from around the sides of his mouth as he smoked his pipe. "So there are actually about six races of gnomes in the realms, descended from the original tribe many centuries before the cataclysms of the Godswars. Humans and elves saw fit to classify them into only two races, the forest gnomes and the mountain gnomes."

Korrelothar Balshav responded, "My pardon then, I didn't know how gnomes classified the different branches of their race. You are from the forest gnomes are you not? Yet you seem to have a lot of knowledge regarding your mountain brothers."

As the elf sipped some more of the local wine, Mel explained, "I was kicked out of my forest home, sad to say. In looking to expand my magical talent, I found myself staying with some mountain gnomes in the range between here and Orlaun. Mountain gnomes are more technically inclined, whilst forest gnomes tend to prefer wooded hideaways and more natural surroundings. As such, mountain gnomes are also more open to innovative and new ideas, such as magical talent. There are forest gnomes who study magic, but my family would not have it."

"I see," replied Korrelothar. "I would like to hear more of your stay with those gnomes. I bet you could tell lots of stories. It's good to chat with you."

Mel beamed, "I could talk all day about my mountain kin! Thank you for your compliments. Too often I am in chats in which I am the only one holding up my end of the conversation!"

Elf and gnome talked merrily despite distracting, albeit good, music coming from a band in front of the inn. Even small villages have their musicians to boast about, Troutbrook had seven. One played mandolin, the other a fiddle, and both seemed to blend fairly well. One member of the band blew merrily into a flute, while another had a smaller pipe instrument fashioned from a seashell. Two women sang along with the melodies, while a final member of the band banged on a hand drum. Half of the band was actually lay members of the church who often performed religious songs during services. Several people danced out in front of the band. Many of the songs had no words, but gave out a beat for certain dance rhythms. During those times the two women vocalists would lead the town in specific dances, popular in larger cities, that followed the beat of the music. The center street of the village became a whirl of rows and pairs of dancing figures.

Down the street a bit, some men were drinking out in front of the local pub. While the inn was a place for socializing, the pub offered serious drinking and other camaraderie.

198

In front of the pub, several men gathered around a dwarf and a brazier. The owner of the pub placed it outside to provide light, though it was not yet lit.

Salgor had already shared some samples of his own "Bandago's Brew" with the owner. His homebrew was dwarven ale, but the stout warrior had no shortage of drink varieties carried in his large pack. He stood by the brazier with patrons, describing dwarven whiskey. "The trick with dwarven whiskey isn't the taste, as long as you have plenty of alcohol. The true test o' the whiskey is how flammable it can be! You attach a flint for a lighter, swallow a mouthful, then you light it and belch…like so!"

The dwarf took a large mouthful from a flask at his belt. He flipped something at the lip of the container with his thumb, igniting a piece of cloth there. Then he blew the whiskey through the flame, sending a sudden fireball into the dry brazier. People jumped back, and even the band missed a beat at the sudden flame in front of the pub. The tinder in the bowl caught fire fast, starting a blaze. The drinking patrons laughed and cheered at the dwarf.

Salgor Bandago then snuffed the wick on the bottle, and downed the rest of the whiskey. "Now that is dwarven fire! It was used with good results many times when I find myself in a pinch."

The dwarf then hushed a bit, as if sharing a secret, though all around could still hear him well. "But the real trick when you start trying it is to practice well enough or you will suffer the worst mishap imaginable…"

Everyone leaned in close, but Salgor made sure all attention was on him before he let out his next outburst. He let them in on the one thing dwarves fear when learning that trick. "Your beard will catch on fire!"

As the drinkers laughed, Salgor put on a show. He pretended to panic and swat at some imaginary fire on his beard. He ran circles and howled to the delight and entertainment of the onlookers.

Slightly removed from the majority of the night's activities, the smithy sat a short walk from the inn. Much of the revelry remained within sight, but the shop itself sat on the quieter fringes. Trestan and Hebden enjoyed a cozy fire outside, socializing with friends and longtime customers. A stand displayed the young man's sword and armor. He showed it off proudly, though he listened more than spoke. Hebden had learned about most of the details of the trip south, but Trestan said little to others about the incident. He remained unsure how much he wanted to express openly after all the hardships of the road. Many people paid a visit, sharing their relief at seeing Trestan home and healthy. A good number of old neighbors were already very loosened up with liquor, treating Trestan as if he was their best friend as they slurred their conversations. The young smith simply smiled, a little shy about the attention. When Trestan had the opportunity, he asked Petrow and Salgor about Cat's whereabouts during one of their visits. The two responded that she hadn't been seen since riding with Lady Shauntay up to the Tessald mansion.

Petrow had offered a guess, "I'm sure the Lord Verantir has a lot of questions, and he will demand full answers. I'm sure she has a lot to talk about up there, but nothing to worry about. She'll be back as soon as they remember she's a commoner."

With a wink, Petrow departed with Salgor. Trestan wandered closer to the celebration a few times. Every trip earned a free drink from someone, but without having Cat for companionship the young man kept drifting back to his father and home. For some reason, it seemed less of a celebration if he couldn't have fun with the beautiful half-elf.

Meanwhile, the companions moved about the crowd during the evening, yet stayed the center of attention wherever they went. Mel Bellringer found himself surrounded by curious children. At three feet tall, many of the human children stood at eye level. The gnome loved the attention of kids, and soon he entertained them. "Now, watch these surprises, young ones. They won't harm you, but they will make a loud noise!"

Mel ringed a small area with a protective field similar to what Revwar had used during the bluff battle. The barrier did nothing to block the view of things going on behind it. From outside of the misty barrier, children watched as Mel tossed a few small pinches of clay on the ground.

POP! POP!

Using a small version of his "Timed Boomy" spell, he set off little firecrackers that popped and fizzled on the ground. Children screamed, squealed and laughed as the little clay pieces blasted up puffs of dirt.

"Ooh! That was a nice one. How about five at once?" Mel smiled to the kids.

Another series of pops and cracks erupted inside the field, to the delight of several children.

Off in the street, a couple dancers fell down laughing as a complicated dance routine resulted in a soft collision. Korrelothar tried teaching a delicate elven dance. At least one dancer was not graceful enough to follow the course without knocking down his dance partner and a few others. The errant dancer climbed back to his feet with much noise and grunts.

"I'm not so full o' the spirits that I can't dance straight!" Salgor Bandago bellowed as he got up. "It's these prancing elf movements, akin to guiding horses through small tunnels. I've a bit too much girth for them. Give me a real foot-stomping, marching rhythm!"

Trestan had wandered back into the main crowd when he caught sight of one of his friends helping a maiden to her feet due to the dance mishap. Petrow laughed as he helped an auburn-haired young lady stand, then both turned around to help dust off the dwarf. Much giggling and laughing followed, before Salgor went to "refill my throat with the gods' water."

Petrow wore a smile when he turned and saw Trestan giggling at them all. The older youth spoke, "And I suppose you've never lost your footing on the dance floor! Especially when fine vintages have been flowing so freely!"

Trestan nodded, "Of course I have, but it is more entertaining when someone else takes a tumble. I didn't realize two people could flatten a dwarf so easy with a dance step."

The young lady clinging to Petrow's side drew Trestan's attention. The handyman saw the two exchange glances, and suddenly remembered proper manners. "Tres, you remember Inedra here? Milady, this is my friend Trestan, surely you have seen him before."

200

The young woman curtsied as she was introduced, then spoke, "The other hero of the village. I am honored and delighted. Oh my, you two have acquired a lot of well-deserved attention tonight. I'm glad I could get one of you to myself for a few dances." Now the young maiden turned her look meaningfully towards Petrow, "And maybe a few more after I return? I'll be right back for another dance if you'll wait for me."

She looked alluring. Trestan remembered her as a daughter of one of the local farmers. He'd seen Petrow spending time with her for the past few months. Petrow kissed her hand and replied, "I would win through any dark night or adventure for the chance to find myself back in your arms for another dance. Be swift and hurry back to me."

She giggled as she walked away. Her eyes went behind her and she winked back to Petrow as she walked through the crowd. Trestan smiled a knowing smile when Petrow finally took his eyes off her. The older youth blushed, "It seems I have a few lady followers tonight, and several have been asking about you too."

Petrow raised his eyebrows in an inquisitive manner. Trestan kept a smile but fidgeted as he replied, "And a few of them have found me. There have been many interesting discussions over at the forge…"

At that, Trestan frowned for a moment, though he regained a smile. "Anyways, I have had time with my father again. That is all the company that I really needed tonight."

"Aside from Cat, who hasn't returned from the manor yet?" Petrow asked. He saw a reaction in his friend and knew he had hit a nerve. Trestan nodded in agreement, but the handyman thought he read something else in his friend's eyes. "There is something else isn't there? Maybe something discussed at the smithy?"

"Aye, there was." Trestan paused before continuing. "I would be happy if my only conversations over there had been discussions of which village girl I would dance with, or how much total strangers seemed to have missed me during my absence. There has been talk about things rather ominous and dire if they foretell the future of the village."

Before Trestan could say more, Korrelothar appeared out of the crowd and put a hand on each man's shoulders. "Ah, Trestan! Glad to again see you doing so well after how much you worried your friends. I'm glad to have come across you in the wilds. It's very rare indeed that two men of your young years do something so noteworthy and selfless in the face of such a scary foe. Mel has told me much, but I surmise that he tells everyone much!"

Both young men blushed and thanked the elf for his kind words. The wizard asked, "I do hope I wasn't interrupting something. I just wanted the chance to compliment you when I could catch you two together."

Petrow cast an unsure look at Trestan, "Not really anything important I guess. We are once and again ever thankful that you stopped to help us."

The elf nodded gracefully, but assumed he had interrupted something private. Korrelothar started to step away when Trestan held out a hand to stop him. "Wait, good sir. There is something I was about to discuss which you should hear."

Before saying more, Trestan suddenly looked around the crowd. He seemed suddenly rather guarded, as if whatever he was to say next wasn't meant for just any ears.

Petrow and Korrelothar looked around too, but then shrugged, unsure why Trestan acted secretive.

The young smith spoke in a low voice, for their ears alone, "Korrelothar, I admit Petrow and I overheard you talking to the head priest in his chambers earlier, about the theft of the stone."

At the mention of the theft, the elf wizard held up a hand in a motion to hush the young man. The elf said, "Please keep it secret. Almost none know or has a clue yet except those of you that went out to rescue the young lady. Nay need in worrying the populace."

Trestan nodded his understanding. He figured most of the companions wouldn't have mentioned the holy relic in their tales, though one could not be sure what may have been said in accident. "I understand and I haven't mentioned word of it to anyone except for my father. I swore him to secrecy unless someone else already knew and asked him. Anyways, since you have had an interest in studying and searching for more answers about the stone, it might be best if you learn what I've heard in discussions."

The three moved out of the street for some privacy. Though people called out to them, they huddled together to have a private chat.

Trestan continued, "As the head cleric told you, Troutbrook has always been blessed with good crops and healthy herds. It's amazing how one can take that for granted, or attribute it to our own methods or soil. Many farmers and herders pay the stone nay special heed, thinking it nothing more than decorative. Yet I have come to believe that the holy relic did have some helpful influence over this land, and its loss is already being felt."

Petrow interrupted, "So, you heard some bad news?"

As the elf wizard listened with interest, Trestan continued. "Aye. Two things stood out in my mind. Our village is not used to having certain afflictions affect crops. Maybe it was the stone relic, but we generally haven't had any plant disease or bad insect infestations in the crops. Tonight I have heard conversations of both. A few farmers, just a small number really, have had some damage to their early crops from bugs and plant disease. This may be normal elsewhere from conversations I heard in Barkan's Crossing, but it is rather unheard of around this area."

The elf listened with interest, but to Petrow this was a disturbing eye-opener. Trestan continued, "I heard some complaints from a rancher as well. Not once in anyone's memories have we had a disease that affected the herds and cattle. It's rare to have an animal die from illness. From what I heard this evening, there is a contagion sweeping three large ranches on the other side of the river. The herdsmen there are having a hard time trying to get control of it, because they just aren't used to dealing with animal diseases. Several animals have been quarantined, and some died rather suddenly and unexpectedly."

Trestan awaited an answer from the elf, while Petrow frowned at the grim possibilities. The handyman felt a chill in the night air for the first time that evening. The wizard absently stroked the hair stubble on his chin. He seemed lost in his own world, but soon realized that both young men looked to him for an answer or reassurance.

The elf put a hand on each young man's shoulder and whispered, "I thank you for telling me. I hope to see what the cleric has in the histories but from the sounds of it I may spend weeks here trying to research it from old scrolls. You have confirmed some things I

202

had feared. It sounds like your village was protected by this gift of Yestreal. Now that it has been stolen, your village is vulnerable to normal hazards that you haven't faced. It will be a dark time and a hard adjustment for your people. I do worry about why someone would steal the artifact besides the magic powers of which we are aware."

Trestan spoke as the elf seemed ready to turn and walk away, "Wait. What can we do? How can you help us?"

Korrelothar Balshav stopped in his tracks, raising eyebrows at the young smith. "What, indeed, can I do for you? I hope to learn more about these items, and therefore understand them better. Maybe one day we can learn enough of why they were taken, and locate the thieves. But, other than that…"

The elf held his hands out to his sides, helpless to suggest further action. Trestan's strong shoulders sagged as he contemplated there was nothing they could do to repair the damage. The elf took pity on the young men and added, "Do not feel that I will let this issue drop. I take a great interest in helping people, which is how I earned the title 'The Highwater Conjuror.' I will find out what I can and some day we may be able to get both stones back where they belong.

"In the meantime, do not despair after all you have accomplished. Both of you earned the celebration today because you are heroes! Without you, the blood spilled on the street that one fateful night would have been for nothing, and the clergy would not know of the theft. I am proud that two people of such humble roots made a difference against a ship full of mercenaries."

*　　　*　　　*　　　*　　　*

A procession of royalty entered from the north part of town, interrupting the celebration as they passed under the candelabra of bright stars and glided down an aisle of torchlight. Though the small village could not boast such magnificent pageantry as the nobles of more enriched societies, the entrance of Lord Verantir Tessald was noteworthy by any means. The presiding lord rode proudly astride his white stallion. Silvery battle mail adorned his body. A decorative circlet signifying his nobility and title crowned his dark, gray-streaked hair. A scabbard on his mount carried a decorative, gold-filigree, two-handed sword. Aside from fancy dress, and expensive materials, this was still a small-town noble. Nobles from Orlaun or even Kashmer would have scoffed at the lack of extravagance. Nevertheless, to the people of the village Lord Verantir might as well be a king.

He rode alongside two ladies also dressed in formal, eye-catching attire. Lady Shauntay Tessald wore her customary smile alongside a rather conservative coverage of clothing. Her garb hid her cleavage and legs, since her father accompanied her this night. An elegant ball gown, likely custom-tailored in Kashmer, accentuated her curves in a more traditional manner as she rode sidesaddle on her horse. Her hair stood fashionably in an upright bun; her skin had been washed clean of the dirt of the road. Perfume floated about her for those close enough to appreciate it. The wife of Lord Verantir was still out of town, likely still in the dark about her daughter's safe return. Therefore, the other lady riding alongside the noble was someone unknown to most of the village.

Dressed in an extraordinary red gown, with hair also done up in a fashionable form, rode the adventuress Katressa Bilil. She also rode side-saddle, (the gown would not permit otherwise.) Every trace of the road had been washed from her body, followed by perfumes and lotions to further enhance her charismatic qualities. Her horse bore her weapons, while the half-elf seemed to wear no implements of war, (except for those hidden in secret areas of her dress). Among the heavenly bodies shining upon the gathering, Katressa's bore radiance greater than that of the young Tessald woman despite the lack of jewels.

Marching in formation, around the trio of riders, were the majority of those house guards that still remained. They bore the modest blue standards of the village and full armor. Missing were those who had ridden south to search for the returned noble, as well as those who still remained on the mansion grounds for security there. Attendants flocked the horses, serving to assist the riders.

The noble's entourage passed the lines of villagers and torches, headed for the center of the celebrations in front of the inn. The crowd parted for the procession, and then closed behind them once they went past. The companions sought each other out as Lord Verantir approached. Lady Shauntay indicated the party with a nod of her head, and her father changed direction accordingly. The noble drew to a halt a short distance from the companions. They stood together in front of the inn, with the exception of Cat, who asked an attendant to lead her horse to the inn hitch post. Lord Verantir scanned over the company, though he seemed to linger on Korrelothar the longest. The whole group made visible efforts to stand straight and avoid appearing like they were nervous, which indeed they were!

Finally, the lord of the village spoke. "Will the brave rescuers of my daughter come forward and stand before me? I would like to personally thank those who rescued the jewel of my manor."

Cat dismounted and joined the others as they stepped forward. She flashed a bright smile to each, her only indication that her time in the manor must have gone well. Cat's gaze lingered on Trestan, who stood straight and apparently healthy. In a line they waited: Korrelothar, then Salgor Bandago, Petrow, Trestan Karok, Katressa Bilil, and finally Mel Bellringer. Lord Verantir also dismounted, approaching the band on foot to greet most of them eye to eye. Lady Shauntay joined them on foot as well, performing the introductions to each member in turn. Petrow had to keep from letting out a smirk when she glared at him as if she'd rather slap him than introduce him in a friendly manner. The young noble put on an extra smile for Trestan, though it was lost on the blank face he returned. The young noble's father had many pleasant things to ask and say of the adventurers, finding out where they originally came from, and commending them on their actions. As Lord Verantir moved down the line, the companions were amazed that he spent a long time conversing with Korrelothar. He asked about Orlaun and confirmed the elf was a member of a wizard guild there. At one point the noble's eyes drifted towards *Dovewing*, admiring the craft. He used exquisite manners thanking each one in turn. Trestan wasn't sure if he expected a bigger fanfare or some rare and exotic gift, yet at the same time he was glad enough to be the honored guest at such a big celebration. He never expected the lord to thank him for something in the presence of the entire village!

204

"You stand here in my gratitude for the return of my only child," Lord Verantir Tessald addressed them all. "There is nay greater gift that you can give to a parent. You saw a crisis and you did your duty well to serve your lord. I hear you performed quite well against long odds."

With a gesture, several attendants wheeled forward a small cart. He threw aside the covering, revealing a selection of wines. "I was saving these for a special occasion. I can think of nay reason why this occasion isn't most special. Enjoy these with my compliments. Resume your festivities!"

Standing closest to the cart as they were, the companions proceeded to indulge themselves in selecting a vintage. Other villagers tentatively approached, ready to assist in drinking the gift. As they awed at some of the renowned wines present, Petrow glanced at the departing lord and whispered to Trestan.

"Psst. I don't suppose you heard what kind of monetary reward he might give us? I don't mean to be ungrateful, but isn't he supposed to hand us a bag of gold or something?"

Trestan smiled, "I can't complain. This is finer than anything I ever expected to happen to me here, in all my life! But, if it satisfies your curiosity, you can always go over and ask him about the gold reward."

Petrow could feel the sarcastic dare of the last sentence. He shook his head, but his eyes went back to the noble. "Seems that he's cornered our friend there."

Lord Verantir had snagged Korrelothar's attention once his formal thanks were over. They stood ringed by guards, having an amiable conversation. The noble offered a lot of congratulatory words for the visiting elf, and the companions overheard him calling the wizard a "distinguished emissary from Orlaun." At some point a remark was overheard to the effect of, "So few people of your high standing pass this way…"

Trestan picked out an elvish wine, which he handed to Cat. She smiled back at him, "We'll need some proper glasses for this, thank you for picking this one out for me."

The young smith said, "My pleasure indeed. We were worried for you. I was wondering how things were going up there."

Cat giggled, "I'd say it went very well. You should have seen the tearful reunion. All this time I was more worried about you! I'm glad to see you on your feet again."

Cat cradled the elvish wine against her, "In regards to the noble, he was all ears. He wanted to hear everything, though some things he showed far more interest in than others."

Her gaze led them all to look at Korrelothar, who was still the object of the noble's attention. Petrow asked, "The wizard?"

Cat nodded, "I doubt we'll get near so much attention from Lord Verantir again. I was pampered and allowed to wash up, but mainly it was a father-daughter reunion and I was more like a visiting servant. Well, with some special treatment I must admit. He is honestly very thrilled to have his daughter back, but the political side of him wanted to get to know our elf wizard better. I mean, look at *Dovewing*! How many others visit this village showing such wealth and possibly prestige? I think once he settled into the realization that his daughter was safe, he saw the chance to expand his own small circle of influence."

Trestan and Petrow both shook their heads. It seemed that getting out of their adventure alive was the biggest reward they received. Their attention turned to Salgor, who expressed a large interest in the beverage selection.

"Nah, not enough kick. Ooh, here is one!" The dwarf pocketed one bottle rather than share with the villagers. At the look from the two young men, he spoke up. "I like a pile of gold too, but you can't drink it! This here is about as good as it can get for me!"

CHAPTER 18

The companions passed drinks to the villagers, though Mel and Salgor indulged samples of each vintage before surrendering theirs. The tongues of many became quite liberated if they hadn't already been so, followed by conversations going along more wandering courses. Off to the side, the noble and his attendants continued entertaining Korrelothar. Lady Shauntay stood beside the visiting elf for some time, lingering close to her father's side. This kept her away from the other companions, which suited both parties just fine.

Trestan and Cat found a small table to share the elvish wine. The young smith was surprised to learn the elegant gown she wore was actually hers, and not something provided by the noble. Cat mentioned, "He offered, but there would not have been much there that would fit me. I often have a need to dress up on occasion, so I keep this special outfit in a protective case in my pack."

The other members of the party remained nearby, inserting into the conversation. They confirmed to Cat the theft of the holy relic. Trestan and Petrow were treated to a description of the inside of the manor…for neither had even breached the border wall of the estate. No conversation subjects stayed serious for too long in light of the drinking and levity of the night.

When the elf wizard walked away from Lord Verantir's side, Mel pointed it out to his companions. They saw the wizard go straight to *Dovewing*, then cast a spell over the flying craft. Mel watched him and explained it to the others. Aside from placing some kind of magical trap earlier, the elf now had a barrier up that would not allow anyone to even touch the flying machine. When he was done, Korrelothar looked for the companions and approached them.

Petrow's remark greeted him, "It seems you have made a local friend? He is giving you a lot of attention."

The elder elf actually blushed, "I'm embarrassed to say, he is rather taken with me and any stories of Orlaun. You all have done much more a service to him and his family, yet he has singled me out for purely political reasons."

Mel pointed to *Dovewing*, "Why the force field now after not having it all evening?"

"Well," the wizard paused, "I was here earlier to watch over it. Tonight, however, I have been invited to stay in the manor as Lord Verantir's guest." In response, several groans and shaking heads followed as the less fortunate members of the party grumbled. Korrelothar quickly added, "It would have been impolite to have said nay! I feel ashamed that he bestows such an honor on me, while ignoring the true rescuers. I am just concerned that if I attempt to stay for any long term in order to research the temple scrolls, I'll have a lord interrupting me the whole time!"

The companions scoffed, wishing they had such a trivial problem such as a noble waiting on them hand and foot! They soon bid their goodbyes to the person who had hastened their road back to the village. The elf departed with the lord's entourage, though the noble had the decency to say his own brief goodbyes to the companions. They got little more than a bow and a few words. Lady Shauntay hastily bid her goodbyes, yet looked much relieved to be going back to the manor. After the noble and his guards left, the party actually picked up a bit.

Trestan invited Cat to come with him to the smithy and meet his father. The rest of the companions had already been introduced, yet Petrow wouldn't have been surprised if Trestan was just trying to get some private time alone with their attractive companion. Not like the notion bothered Petrow much, as he had plenty of local girls competing for his attention. The young handyman went off to the dance floor with one of them. Salgor and Mel continued to drink and chat by themselves. The two shorter members of the party had grown on each other, at least while the drinks were flowing. Mel told the tale of the dwarf stuck in a tunnel, and how he used a shrink potion to get the poor warrior unstuck. Salgor almost laughed himself off his chair as the gnome described the beating his knees took afterwards.

Cat followed Trestan down the street to the smithy. They passed other villagers who insisted on congratulating and shaking hands with them. Hebden Karok was just saying goodnight to a few friends as he looked over the campfire at the smithy. The older smith held out a hand to Cat when he saw her approach.

"You must be Katressa Bilil! Trestan has told me a lot about you."

"Call me Cat, please. Trestan has told me much about you, and of your home." The half-elf shook hands with Hebden. "I'm sorry I did not get a chance to meet you earlier. It is an honor to finally see you."

Hebden smiled, but then narrowed his eyes mischievously at her and asked, "So, do I have you to thank for stealing my son in the middle of the night, off to some grand adventure?"

Cat blushed, "I only wanted my horse back! We actually recovered her before getting to Barkan's Crossing."

The chuckles from Hebden showed he only jested. Hebden admitted he was truly happy to meet a woman of whom Trestan held the highest praises. Cat continued, "As worried as you must have been for him, you should be proud! He is a brave man, and he follows his heart despite fear. You raised a fine son."

Now it was Trestan's turn to blush and shift uncomfortably as Hebden looked upon him. "Indeed, I hope I did. I only worry sometimes that he found too much influence following the path of a paladin friend of mine."

Trestan searched for words of his own, but Cat spoke first, "His arms have the strength of a smith; his heart the strength of a paladin. Whatever the future holds, I doubt he can go wrong."

"And to think," Hebden said, "it seems only yesterday that I swung a forge hammer with one hand and held a baby in the other."

Trestan grew a deeper shade of red, "Can we switch subjects? I was introducing the both of you, so we should be talking about you two!"

The three of them laughed by the forge. Hebden and Cat seemed to get along well. Hebden hid one fear deep within him as they talked. He admitted Cat seemed to be a wonderful woman, but as Trestan had noted earlier she was an adventurer and a wanderer.

He doubted she would stay in the village for long. Now that Trestan's adventure was complete, would the young man be inclined to follow her when she left? The older smith knew his son would pick his own road to follow someday soon. Generations of the family had worked in the area, becoming smiths and other craftsmen. The father had always expected the son to follow in his footsteps, but he realized that Trestan might choose another path.

*   *   *   *   *

Trestan and Cat walked side-by-side to rejoin the merriment outside the inn. Though many villagers had departed, or were passed-out in the street, the music and the dancing continued. The two of them smiled from the pleasant chat with Hebden, who had retired for the evening.

Cat spoke as they walked, "I don't think I should drink anymore wine tonight. I'm feeling a bit tipsy and my head is bound to ache in the morning."

Trestan nodded with a sly grin. "I've had more alcohol tonight than most nights. I agree with you, we should do something other than imbibing wine right now."

The raven-haired woman turned to take in his measure, as she floated ahead of him in her sweeping gown. "What do you suggest then?"

"Well, my mind seems foggy about some things said back at the little waterfall." As Trestan spoke, Cat remembered when Trestan combed her hair, just before he fell unconscious from his wound. "But I do seem to recall a few things. Such as asking for a dance with you when we got back to the village."

Cat smiled. She stopped and turned a meaningful gaze at the performing band, then back to Trestan. "Are you asking me then?"

The young man, dressed in his finest, took her hand and offered a low bow. "I ask the honor of the next dance with you, Katressa Bilil."

She giggled, and returned the bow with a formal curtsey of her own, "I accept, most graciously. Lead me to the dance floor, as you are my humble host, and this is your village."

Trestan took her arm in his. They walked to the dance area, called out by others as they made their way down the street. Trestan's townsfolk cheered his return to the festivities. The couple attracted stares, smiles, plus more bows and curtseys as people passed. Salgor and Mel waved and raised mugs in toast. The attention failed to unnerve Trestan. He walked tall and proud in garments richer by far than any he had ever owned before, and on his arms a radiant beauty that outshined the local noble girl. This was Trestan's reward.

Trestan stopped by the musicians, separating from Cat only long enough to whisper and put coins in their palms. He took her hand and led her to a good space. The first dance was a popular local jig played at all festivals. It had already been played that night, but Cat had not been around for it. Trestan taught her the moves as they went, spinning in circles and pairs with other villagers. After that, they were treated to "River Reel", a song that divided the couples into lines on both sides of the street. Couples darted amongst the other

209

dancers, sashaying up and down the line several times, while others clapped and hollered to the tune.

The "Dwarven Square" came next. Salgor grabbed a partner, a young girl about his height, and put vigor into his dance. The complex dwarf style featured squares and lines that constantly changed across the street. It involved a lot of foot stomping and clapping to a steady rhythm, and one could see where it had developed from a dwarvish military training exercise. From this they changed tempo considerably into a waltz. Cat showed Trestan a graceful elvish style of dance that blended in perfectly. While Cat had the grace and agility to perform an eye-catching rendition of the elvish dance, Trestan tended to stumble about occasionally. Nevertheless, he kept up as much as he could and both of them laughed. Eventually, he nearly matched Cat with some fancy dance steps. Trestan's focus stayed absorbed on the beautiful half-elf. The backdrop of dancers disappeared behind Cat's every move.

During several dances in which participants moved and switched partners, Trestan and Cat kept running into Petrow and Inedra. The young farmer's daughter had succeeded over the other women in getting the most attention from Petrow. Though other women also tried to steal Trestan away for a dance or two, the young man favored dancing with Cat.

Marches, slow waltzes, and other soft melodies allowed moments where the dancers could talk more than dance. It allowed Trestan and Cat more time to converse about various subjects, ranging from foreign dances and songs to different lands and people. The young smith learned more about Cat's own homeland. As he listened to every tale she had to tell, he felt something stir within him. It must have been wanderlust, for he wanted to see far away mountains, elf villages, and other new lands. He longed to see the morning mist over some quiet bay, or enjoy the sounds of strange songbirds under a jungle canopy. He loved his home, and had been only too glad to get back to it after their adventure succeeded. Now he wondered if he was going to get lonely for the open road again, despite all the dangers it held.

As such feelings passed through his mind, he quenched them firmly just to enjoy the moment. He just wanted the night to last forever. In all, he spent only a small portion of the evening dancing with Katressa; however, it was the one thing that most occupied his memories afterward. Their dances were the best part of the evening, and the most exciting thing he could ask for after his long adventure.

Neither Lord Verantir nor Lady Shauntay could have rewarded him any better.

*   *   *   *   *

The band set aside their instruments for the last time that night. Vendors no longer served the crowd, having either turned to fun pursuits themselves or retired to their beds. Many families were back in their homes. A few villagers assisted some of their fellows in navigating the pall of drunkenness to their doorways. The occasional voice still sang or hummed a few bars of some merry tune. Bursts of laughter sporadically echoed through the open street. In all, the lanes of Troutbrook became quiet. Street lanterns still burned; however, the smoke of doused fires and spent pipes filtered the light.

The companions gathered around a table occupying the courtyard beside the inn. Salgor's hands gripped a mug, but the dwarf's face snored through the table planks. Petrow honored his promise to escort young Inedra home to her family. With torch in hand, he guided the woman away from the buildings and down the road. He had promised to return, and even offered what spare room he had in his little home to any of the companions. Cat and Trestan sat together on the same side of the table. Mel contentedly smoked his pipe across from them, his head bobbing a few times. His conversation weaved more erratically than it normally did. The half-elf and human were quite amused at the gnome's attempts to hold a decent conversation when he looked ready to fall off his bench.

"I don't want this night to end," Trestan mused as Mel mumbled incoherently. "I don't know how I will feel in the morning, or what I will do. I'm sure there will be chores to be done at the forge, yet I may feel out of place when I first don my apron and swing that hammer. I don't know if I will get a long, decent sleep…or find myself lying awake and letting my mind wander in the dark."

Cat slipped a delicate hand behind him, massaging the back of his neck as she spoke. "The night really doesn't have to end. I could stay up 'til the morning light shines, and then I may see about sleeping away the day. I'm sure your father won't mind if you rested through the morning after all you have been through."

Trestan closed his eyes for a bit. He didn't immediately respond, instead letting his mind and body relax a bit to Cat's touch. "I do want the night to go on forever. Yet…"

Cat lost her grin. She tilted her head to see his face better. "Yet what?"

Trestan sighed, allowing himself to relax in the gentle massaging of her fingers. After a moment he turned to look her in the eyes. Mel still mumbled sounds as they spoke, lost in his own world. The young smith took Cat's hand in his own and threw a pleading look her way. "Promise me you will stay long enough for me to craft you a gift. I don't want to wake up tomorrow or the next morning to find you gone."

She was taken aback, "Gone? I have nay need to be anywhere soon. I'll be here tomorrow. Why do you bring this up now?"

Trestan fumbled for words. "As much as I want to be here with my new friends and share tales all night, there is something I've wanted to do since getting back. I just couldn't sleep tonight until I got it out of the way. I just didn't want to go before now, yet the hour is late. When I go to sleep tonight, I guess I just want to know that my friends will all be here in the morning again."

Cat felt confused. She wasn't sure what he had been planning to say or do, and the young man hadn't been direct with an answer. The half-elf was willing to trust that he had something important on his mind. The woman put on an encouraging smile to offer him support. "Do what you have to do, and don't worry about tomorrow. I suspect we will all be here and that life will go on. Have faith in the paths the gods offer you, just as you always have shown."

"Thank you. I've treasured your company. We've only known each other for a few days, but it seems much longer"

Cat smiled, "And I have treasured your company. Be safe and well."

Trestan got up and promptly gave another respectful bow to his friend. Mel cleared his thoughts a bit when the young man stood to leave, though he had missed the words between his taller friends. He waved a good night to the young man in a way that spilled more of the cooling pipe embers. Trestan waved back with a grin before he turned to walk southward along the main street.

Cat watched him go as she puzzled over his intentions. She was interrupted by her thoughts as Mel stood up and stretched. "If you will pardon me, I shall visit the little gnomes' shack again and be right back to pick up our conversation." He stumbled away, leaving her beside the snoring dwarf.

The privateer—infiltrator and scout—didn't hesitate to make use of her chance. Trestan was still visible down the street as Cat moved to follow. Even wearing the elegant evening gown, the woman crept along the shadows of buildings as stealthily as she could. It may not have been respectful of Trestan's privacy, but Cat always liked finding the unknown and uncovering truths. She navigated between alleys and shadows. He walked on the opposite side of the road as the smithy, glancing at his home but not stopping. His footsteps brought him past the well in front of the church and the marble stand that now held the duplicate relic. He continued beyond several more buildings until he was near the southern end of the main street. Trestan stopped at a two-story house near the end of the village. Cat found a hiding place, discreet and distant. When she looked upon the building, she guessed the significance of its meaning to the young man.

The house was one of the largest in the village. The structure had been constructed and furnished better than any of the other private residences within the village borders, save the one belonging to Priest Gerlach. The house seemed to lack whatever warmth it had once owned. New wooden boards barred the doors and first story windows. Shutters on both floors were closed and secured to discourage robbers. No lights burned from within, leaving the interior very dark and cold. Often houses were closed up in such a way when the only residents had passed away, with no one present to claim them.

Katressa recalled a memory from the night of the battle on this street. She recalled seeing two figures running towards the battle from the south end. Trestan had been one of the two; the other had been the paladin and mentor. They had rushed into battle from this house, yet when it was over one of them hadn't lived to see the next dawn. The words from Trestan came back to her memory.

Trestan shook his head, "It's too late for my good friend here. I'm glad he fought bravely and good against such odds. In fact, when he knew death was at hand he actually praised his goddess for the life she had given him. He told me only this morning he hoped he could meet death that way. How rare is that?"

This had once been the home of Sir Wilhelm Jareth, warrior and champion of Abriana. Cat watched Trestan walk up to the house. The young man looked up to the windows of the second story. The half-elf could not know of the room with the hearth, grown cold and silent in the empty house. A window on one side, unremarkable to her, was the same window Jareth had peeked out when the first signs of trouble had disturbed the two men. Trestan kneeled on the steps of the house, placing his hands against the wooden boards barricading it. His head bowed until it rested against the closed oaken doors. While

Cat kept her silence and distance, the young smith let his mind wander across his own memories. Hot tea and sword practice, tales of distant lands and long quests, advice on women and being a man…Trestan dwelled on many of those memories. Cat could only pray to her own gods as Trestan lamented his old friend. Eventually, Trestan stood before the cold wood and ran his hands along the door for the last time before parting. The young man turned away from the house but did not go back to the smithy. Cat watched him take a new course, but when he was out of sight she crept back towards the inn and her other friends.

*   *   *   *   *

It was dark, but Trestan knew the path well. He followed the edges of the brook, climbing away from it a bit towards part of the woods. Constellations of stars traveled the night sky, guiding him where Jareth built the shrine. Sir Wilhelm had taught him star-patterns. Trestan saw a steady, white light marking the shrine. Although there had been torch brackets available at the site, this was something totally different.

He came closer to the shrine until he could see the area clearly. The shrine itself was unchanged. Every flower and rock was as Sir Wilhelm had placed them when he had constructed the religious sanctuary. Near the shrine lay something new; something the young man had been told he would find. A mound of earth ringed by rocks and new plants marked the resting place of his mentor.

Trestan knelt by the grave. The light illuminating the shrine came from two gems enchanted by the local priests of Yestreal. They were a precious gift from other lives the veteran swordsman had touched. The soft light bathed the shrine and the grave, warding the nighttime chill. A temporary marker stood at the head of the grave. Few residents of the village could claim a stone marker after death, but Jareth had left behind enough cash and goodwill that one was being made for him. The talk around the smithy earlier that night informed Trestan they were contacting a stone mason in Barkan's Crossing to craft a proper headstone.

The light from the enchanted gems revealed the temporary inscription marking the grave. The writing on the board read: "Sir Wilhelm Jareth. Champion of Abriana, worthy of being a good friend and a second father to many."

The words brought tears to Trestan's eyes. The old man had touched many lives in the village aside from just his own. He had been a second father to many of the young boys, offering advice and guiding words to those who needed them. Trestan remembered Petrow's story about how the warrior had sat with the young lad under the stars and helped build a roof over his head the next day. When the young smith stopped to think about it, Sir Wilhelm had spent a lot of free time assisting other people in one way or another.

Trestan Karok curled up on a bench at the shrine. His eyes carried out a silent vigil over the grave of his old friend. The young man's thoughts drifted, wondering about the parts of the warrior's life that remained unknown. Trestan had never really met a paladin before, and for many years didn't really equate that term with his mentor. The young man mused on how a person could vow their life to a deity, yet fulfill happiness in their own

213

life. The concept dwelled in his thoughts. The young man found sleep, under a canopy of stars, bathed in the light coming from the silent grave.

*   *   *   *   *

When hands shook him gently, Trestan struggled to wake up from a deep slumber. It took him some time to make out who was shaking him and recall where he was. A slight headache, a result of the alcohol that still lingered, did not help his concentration. The young smith stretched and yawned as much as the bench would allow. Petrow was talking, but the first words were lost in a pall of a half-asleep mind.

It was still night!

Trestan became more alert at that. What reason did his friend have of searching him out and waking him up before morning? He begged Petrow to be silent a moment, as the young smith gathered in his surroundings. Morning couldn't be far away. The grave and shrine looked no different as when he had seen them before falling asleep; however, Petrow was different. The other young man had changed into clothes suitable for travel. The handyman respectfully waited until Trestan was wide-awake.

The young smith spoke, "Alright, why did you come up here already to find me? And why are you in a different outfit?"

Petrow gave in a sly smile, "I'm getting ready to travel and so are the others. I wanted to come up here and get you so that you didn't get left behind, not like we would do that to you."

Trestan wore a confused look. "Travel? Whatever for?"

Petrow still wore a mischievous grin. "The rest of us were talking and we hit on an idea. What if I told you that we have a way of getting back the stolen holy relic if we move now?"

CHAPTER 19

Trestan fought a headache and tired limbs just to stand. Petrow reached over and practically pulled him off the bench. The young smith shook his head to clear the webs in his mind. "What do you mean? I'm still half-asleep, and you are talking about chasing that group again?"

Petrow, already taking a few steps toward the trail, nodded and spoke fast, "Aye, but we must hurry! It is almost first light, so I shall tell you as we run back to the village."

Groaning, Trestan started jogging in order to keep up with Petrow. Some excitement seemed to lend the older youth energy. The light from the grave of Sir Wilhelm disappeared behind them as they ran through the wood. Roots and branches posed a hazard in the dark, but they continued as fast as they reasonably could and even sped up their pace when the path straightened beside the brook.

Petrow shouted over his shoulder to his trailing companion, "Remember what that one-eyed man had said back at the bluff? The one you wounded."

Trestan started to answer, but his foot encountered a tree root in the dark. He steadied himself as he ran. For brevity, he simply asked, "What part do you mean? Can't remember it too well."

"We asked him where they were going," Petrow huffed, having also run from the town before waking Trestan. "He said the ship was supposed to take them to an island, with a castle on it, among shallow waters out on the sea. He said they would be sailing for two days straight to the east in order to get there. Do you remember how long ago that conversation was?"

To Trestan it had seemed like a long time. "Aye, come this morning's sunrise it will have been two days since he told us that."

In the distance, some lights burned down in the village. Petrow explained as they navigated the path, "So, my point is, they have either arrived or will be arriving this morning, correct?"

Trestan understood what Petrow indicated. "Aye, I see your point. However, that still leaves them two days out at sea, from a point of land a couple days' travel from here. That is a mighty long distance considering we don't even have a boat, aside from any small riverboats a shallow fisherman might own and lend. None of those would be safe out in open sea. Also, we don't know how long the other group is staying at that castle."

"In regards to that last part," Petrow spoke as he continued running, "that is partly why time is of the essence. We have to move quickly before they leave for some other destination."

"Granted, but you are still dodging the main question…and please slow up a bit!" Trestan appreciated when Petrow slowed, though both still walked fast down a dark path. Trestan continued, "Tell me clearly, what hope do we have of catching them? Never mind the fact that they are very dangerous. I still don't see how we would even have a hope of getting to them quickly."

Petrow chuckled, "You forget, my friend! We have a flying machine! That vessel flew us over miles of land in a very short time, moving much faster than if a galloping

215

horse had been traveling a straight path beneath us. We can cover a lot of ground quickly, and be able to fly right over the open seas."

The thought astounded Trestan, and he almost stumbled as he considered it. "*Dovewing!* You mean to have Korrelothar fly us out there? What a blessing to have him stumble across our path!"

"Umm," Petrow hesitated in conversation, though he continued to jog along the path, "We haven't really asked him yet. Also, he might say nay. Anyway, time is precious. We were ready to try without him."

Trestan glared at his friend's back as they ran. "Haven't asked him? Are you all crazy? I didn't let Cat steal a couple of horses to chase after the noble, what makes you think I'll stand for you stealing a…a…magical flying thing?"

Petrow answered, "See, that is the funny thing about nuances in the spoken language. 'Stealing' is when you take something for your own good and keep it; meanwhile, 'borrowing' is when you take it for selfless reasons and intend to bring it back."

Trestan shouted, "It's still stealing. How do any of you intend to fly it without the elf?"

As the two young men got close to the village, they saw the eastern sky brightening into new colors. The morning sun would be up within the hour. Village folk would soon rise to begin their chores.

Petrow answered Trestan's question. "On the way over here, the elf showed Mel how to fly the thing. He shared how each of the controls worked. The gnome said he could do it easily."

The young smith continued to be astonished, but perceived holes in the logic of his companions. "You can't take off without Korrelothar helping you! He erected that magical barrier around the vessel before heading out to the Tessald mansion. How do you intend to get around that?"

"Mel already made it disappear somehow. He waved his fingers and spoke a few words, and after a few minutes of attempts he made it go away, just like that. Nay worries."

Trestan still fumbled for reasons, "What about the trap he put on it when you all first carried me off the deck? He announced the fact to the crowd after putting some kind of spell on it." The answer dawned on him even as he spoke, "Mel or Cat took care of the trap, didn't they?"

Petrow let loose several large chuckles. "Not quite. We owe Salgor our gratitude for that one. The poor dwarf triggered it, quite by accident."

"I assume he's ok, as you seem to have gotten a laugh out of it?" Trestan inquired.

Petrow, grinning wildly, gave a reassuring nod back to his friend, "Oh, aye! At least, I think he should be. It surprised and horrified all of us, but it seemed to be a blast of cold air that engulfed him. He just got a little numb and stiff. He was already recovering from it when I left."

Trestan looked up, talking more to the heavens than Petrow. "Abriana, please tell me this is a bad dream, and that I yet sleep by the light of my mentor's grave. To think of Salgor hurt, while my friends scheme to steal a most expensive and rare magical treasure!"

216

If anything, Petrow enjoyed another chuckle over his friend's words, unbothered by Trestan's opinion on the matter. Petrow spoke as they left the brook to cut across a field. "Worry not, my friend. Salgor was incapacitated but not really hurt. Korrelothar is a rather nice person. It seems he just wanted to stun or scare with his trap. Mel says Salgor will be just fine."

Trestan simply rolled his eyes and let any further comments rest.

*   *   *   *   *

The streets remained quiet as they ran toward the inn. The two young men wondered how many of their neighbors would sleep late, recovering from the previous night's party. Trestan's first glance of the magical vessel confirmed the force field had been removed. Cat and Mel looked up with alarm at the new arrivals rushing to them, only to relax upon recognition. Cat once again wore her black leathers; Mel sported his bandolier of potions and mixtures. The half-elf and the gnome resumed shoving their packs into the hatches on *Dovewing's* deck. The hold was large enough to store all their provisions, and more if needed. Cat's horse was likely in the stable, since she could not take it with her. Salgor Bandago lay stretched out on the plush couch at the rear of the craft. The pale dwarf trembled under a blanket as his teeth chattered. White frost clung to the tips of his beard.

Trestan boarded the craft, running to the dwarf first. Salgor groaned, but was otherwise conscious and looking about. The young smith asked, "How do you fare? Should we get a cleric?"

Salgor's angry visage rotated toward the young smith. He either nodded 'no', or perhaps the movement originated with his twitching muscles. "Have I not stated upon many occasions, that I hate wizards? I do, I really do. They can take their dangerous and unpredictable magic and go away to some far away land where they shall nay longer be a menace to decent folk. I felt like he almost froze me alive. I'm starting to get more feeling back into my limbs."

"A nice spell if I might say," commented Mel. "I shall have to ask if I can learn it sometime."

Salgor's thick eyebrows lowered as he narrowed a glare toward the gnome. "I'm ever so glad I could demonstrate it for you. Maybe you could return the favor whenever I want to try out a new weapon?"

Mel frowned and went back to stuffing the last of his food into the hold. The companions welcomed Trestan. Their comments encouraged Trestan to gather whatever gear he needed, and to please hurry quietly so they didn't call attention to themselves.

Trestan hissed, "Have you all gone mad? Have you stopped to consider what you are doing?"

The others paused. Cat tilted her head and replied first, "We thought you would want to get the stone back and help the people of your village."

Trestan sighed and shook his head. "Ideally, I would like to get the stone back. This is just so sudden!" Trestan almost stuttered his next words out. "And it's a bad way to go about it. We know how deadly that group can be! I have a certain respect for the damage they could do to us if caught on their ground. More importantly, you're stealing an expensive and rare magical item. This is Korrelothar's prize creation and most likely worth a lot more than the relic."

Cat responded, "We are just borrowing it, not stealing it." As she spoke, Trestan glared at Petrow over the same choice of words they used to justify themselves. Cat continued, "Plus, it is more likely two stones we are recovering. Have you forgotten the one stolen from the elf's guild? We have a chance to take back the stone stolen from Korrelothar as well as the one that helped your village to prosper. Try not to worry, Mel can fly this thing, and we will have it back relatively soon."

Mel looked up at the mention of his name. "Aye. The elf taught me every control. I watched how to work them. It will be easy!"

The young smith studied the awkward way that the short gnome stretched in order to reach all of the controls from the helmsman's chair. Petrow put a hand on Trestan's shoulder, drawing his friend's attention. "We won't let them get away. We can find them just like before and take back what they stole. If things go bad, we will just beat them up again."

Trestan couldn't bite back his retort. "Beat them up again? Did you forget how that battle actually went? Salgor and Mel won the fight for us, you and I nearly got ourselves killed!"

The look on Petrow's face reflected his admission that Trestan spoke truly. The handyman gritted his teeth. "Regardless, I'm going. We're going. I don't fancy letting that group get away when we have another chance to undo the damage they caused."

Salgor groaned from his position on the couch. "It seems the lad did indeed lose his stomach from that spell. 'Tis nay shame in being nervous Trestan, but the gods have shined luck upon you so far. Certainly you are not afraid to join us? I believe there is some unfinished business here that needs to be addressed. Maybe we are serving some higher purpose. Maybe a god is watching over us. Perhaps we were met with this vessel for a reason; though I personally would have preferred the gods to send the enemy to me, rather than using this infernal wizard creation to give chase."

Trestan shook his head, "It's not fear. I am cautious, but that isn't it. You forget that I've been putting a lot of my own faith forward these past few days. I do believe one goddess has guided and watched over me. She delivered me back home safely, and how do I know what her wishes for my future can be? Nevertheless, I worry about taking off into the night with *Dovewing* without her owner's consent."

"So that is your main concern?" Cat looked into his eyes. "Very well. I suppose we can stay around here while you go up to the noble's house and knock on the door. I don't know how they will receive you. For my part, I was standing within a ring of swords moments after showing up at their door with his daughter. It took them some time to even spare a glance my way long enough to tell the guards they didn't have to skewer me."

Cat put a hand on his shoulder as she pleaded with the young man, "You don't really want to bother with going up there at this hour. We can't wait either, for we don't know how much time we have to catch them. If we fail to gain a reception with the wizard

218

immediately, or if he says nay after we already have lowered his craft's defenses and got past his trap, then I doubt we'll have a second chance."

Trestan lowered his head, "I don't like the way we are doing this, but you are going to go ahead and do it this way with or without me aren't you?"

Petrow put a hand on his friend's shoulder, drawing Trestan's attention to him. "Hey, we didn't stop when we had found Cat's horse outside Barkan's Crossing, and yet it was a far better treasure than that girl!" Trestan lost some of his stern countenance in the form of a chuckle at his friend's humor. The handyman continued, "Now why would we stop now when the livelihood of the village is at stake? You were the one who heard the stories about herd diseases and sick crops, yet it has only been less than a week since the theft. Who knows what other things may happen without the stone's power protecting the welfare of the village?"

Trestan nodded, "Aye. I wouldn't want them to get away either. I felt helpless when we thought we could do no more."

Cat turned his head so that the young smith stared into her eyes again. "You want to come and finish this don't you? This is where your heart is leading you, though you hesitate to give in. Please trust your new friends and follow your heart. The quest is not complete, and we wouldn't want to try without you by our side. You belong on this next small journey."

"My heart is hurting, because I belong in two places." Trestan turned his dark eyes to face the forge by his home. "I've made my choice."

He turned back to them, "I'll grab my armor and sword. It may take a bit for me to get back. You have to wait for me. Allow me to part from here on easier terms."

Petrow glanced at the smithy, his eyes roaming over the equipment left out for the night. It wasn't easy to see, though streetlamps illuminated the area enough to show what hadn't been left out in the open. "What happened to your armor and the stand it was on? Where is your sword?"

Trestan sighed, "Father took them inside because we didn't want to trust either of them outdoors overnight."

Cat and Petrow exchanged glances, then the half-elf spoke. "You have to sneak into your father's house again?"

Trestan shifted the weight from one leg to another, then spoke words that were barely audible. "I didn't say I would sneak in."

Petrow raised his eyebrows at this news, "You don't mean to let your father know what we're doing? Maybe you can grab a weapon from outside, or we can scrounge up some other armor."

"Nay!" Trestan's voice split the quiet of the morning. Alarmed by his own tone, he dropped back to a whisper. "When last we left I snuck off into the night. Every day since then, I missed my father greatly. I regretted leaving without a word. I want to do it properly this time. I will not sneak off in the dark, nor fail in leaving him notice that I may be gone for several days. Not this time."

His companions regarded him with a mix of emotions. Even Mel didn't have an immediate comment to that one, though Mel's experience had been his father kicking him out the door. Dwarves valued family honor, so Salgor respected the young man wanting to set things proper before venturing out. Cat and Petrow worried that Trestan would be talked out of coming along but they felt they had to honor his decision.

Petrow spoke, "Don't tarry. Dawn is not far off and we could be seen out here. Do what you have to do."

Trestan nodded, turning to take his first step off the deck. Cat grabbed him, half-turning him toward her and gave him a big hug. The surprised smith returned it. He looked into her eyes questionably.

"For luck," Cat stated. "My father left me without ever being able to say goodbye, and I always regretted parting so suddenly. Don't let yourselves be angry at one another. You are a man now, and can follow whichever course your heart leads you. He will worry, as any good parent would. Be firm. He'll realize he has to give you the freedom you need to be yourself."

Trestan parted from them, attempting to hide his apprehension behind a smile. Trestan wasn't even sure what he would be able to utter to his father past his dry throat. The young man walked to the smithy, wondering why his knees seemed ready to buckle.

*   *   *   *   *

Trestan entered his home, almost immediately spotting his armor and sword displayed on a stand in the common room. He lit a candle at the table, enough to illuminate the common room well enough for the conversation that was to come. He took a moment to wipe his sweaty palms and try to calm his galloping heart. The young man woke his father. Hebden Karok seemed to have as hard of a time waking and clearing his mind as Trestan had earlier that morning. The older smith was baffled as to why he was being wakened, but he always had ears for his son. They sat down together at their little table and Trestan began to talk.

Trestan did not mention anything about stealing *Dovewing*, just announced his intent to go with his companions on their new journey. Hebden, as could be predicted, voiced opposition to the idea. The smith told his son about how lonely and worried he had been. Words were spoken to warn Trestan about the many dangers of the world. The older man disagreed there was any reason for his son to leave the safety of his home and his trade to go on more wild adventures.

"You would have me wait for some unknown number of days again? I saw each morning as the day a rider may come to tell me my son was dead. Each evening I stayed up late hoping you would still arrive to the comforts of home," Hebden said at one point.

Trestan replied, "Would you have me do the same for my friends? I've regretted never giving you the chance to say goodbye or tell you of my intentions. I felt it at every step! Now my friends will journey forth for the good of Troutbrook, facing hazards again. I'm not blind to the dangers, but it's because of those outcomes I must go. I have the chance to go with them instead of staying behind and wondering about their fate. They need me."

"And after that?" Hebden asked. "Would you simply go back to the life of a smith after you return and they leave again, as they surely will? Would you follow that dwarf to build his own inn? Would you follow Katressa on the road of a privateer in the employ of Kashmer? That is a life of constant danger: fighting pirates, monsters and local highwaymen. You have barely known some of these 'friends' of yours, yet they would lure you into a rough and dangerous road of adventure? I wonder if you may have been influenced more than I suspected by Sir Wilhelm, and that you look at the possibilities of becoming a paladin."

Trestan looked up with a start, "You said that yesterday, back inside the church. I barely know what a paladin is, except by Jareth's lifestyle. I can be very happy as a smith, father, but more than that I can't say. I may have touched the path of a warrior, but I am frightened of the concept paladins follow. Paladins and clerics give their whole lives to the greater good of a deity, sacrificing their own wishes and dreams. I can't fathom that depth of conviction. I have dwelled on what it means, but that doesn't mean I am trying to walk that path."

Hebden sounded unconvinced. "I do not want my son to leave me again for the dangers waiting beyond the civilized lands."

Trestan shook his head. "But I can't let my friends do this alone. They gave as much for me as I tried to give for them. I know enough to be wary of the quest they have taken, and yet I would gladly go with them. It's not for selfish reasons, but for the welfare of others."

And so the conversation went in the dim light of the candle. Trestan often stared at his armor when he wasn't looking at his father. Hebden noticed the way that his son looked at the suit of leather and metal. Father and son expressed their views, and neither would settle for the other's desires. Hebden felt the stubbornness in his son's voice. Neither reason nor logic, even the threat of death, would sway Trestan.

Trestan explained, "Sir Wilhelm met death thanking the gods for the life he lived. That changed my whole perspective on life and death. Certainly I hope to live a long, healthy life. At the same time," the youth struggled for words, "I want to live my life in a way that I can die with pride and few regrets. I have a chance to really help some people, and I plan to seize the opportunity. If I don't, then I may die wondering whatever happened to some of my friends, or toasting the ones that didn't come back, and forever wondering if I could have made a difference."

Hebden threw up his hands and walked the couple steps to the far corner of the room. He went silent for a few moments before speaking. "When you were younger, I asked your grandfather how he had raised me during my times of stubbornness. His response was something to the effect that you could guide your young ones, but you can't control them. All you can do is give them advice on their way, and later on you would get the chance to say, 'I told you so.' Indeed, he said those words to me on numerous occasions. I am afraid that if you go on this journey, I may never get the chance to tell you that. You may never return. You know I love you; you are my only child."

Trestan rose and went to his father. He saw tears in the eyes of the older man. It wounded Trestan to have upset his father in any way. Now the young man knew the conversation he had avoided that night of the battle, when he had run off alone. He had to admit, if the same conversation had come up that night, he would never have left home on his adventure.

Hebden accepted the fact that his son was leaving, with or without his blessings. "If I can't talk you out of it, then I can't help you very much. I pray that if there is a god or goddess guiding you, they guide you back home in one piece, and soon. It would be a terrible god that leads you away from such a wonderful home for nothing, and I would have strong words for that patron if they didn't see to your safety." Hebden put a hand on Trestan's shoulder. "I will help you get packed and ready, and pray for you, but know I will worry for you every day you are gone."

Trying to hide his emotions, he wished his son luck. The older smith helped him don his armor. The father gave the son more helpful advice the whole time, and Trestan politely listened. It was an odd sensation for Hebden to be helping Trestan don his very own armor. If his son was indeed going on his last adventure, Hebden would have it no other way. Every buckle and strap was tightened with the greatest care. The candle's light reflected off the shiny surfaces of the armor. Trestan admitted the armor seemed to fit better than ever before. The youth worried they had spent too much time, but he had faith that his companions would wait for him.

Hebden approached Trestan with the magical elvish sword, the last piece to be added. He first looked at it unsheathed, marveling the play of the light across the runes on the blade. After slinging it across Trestan's back, the father stepped back to admire its look.

The smith pointed to the hole on the breastplate. "We never had the time to get that fixed. Are you sure you can't stay long enough to remedy that?"

Trestan frowned at the open slot in his armor, realizing how tempting such an area would be to an enemy. "There is nay time. It will simply have to do the job as it is now."

An uncomfortable moment passed as they searched for something in each other's eyes. After such a long talk, both found words hard to come by. They faced each other for possibly the last time, man to man.

Hebden reached out and pulled a willing Trestan into a tight hug. "I love you, son. You are the best iron I ever forged. Gods speed the day I might see you ride home and tell me all about your adventure. I want you back by my side to help me work that forge; I just can't put as much of myself in the work without you here."

Trestan had tears in his eyes as he responded, "Amen to returning home speedily when this is all over. I love you too, father. If the gods have any sympathy for a poor boy that dares lay claim to dreams, they will bring me back safely. Until I get back, put your heart in the tasks at hand as much as I am putting my heart into this. I'll be back, and I'm hoping you will have all the work done…just so I can sleep in late!" That comment brought forth a chuckle from Hebden's teary face.

For the second time in a week, Trestan Karok walked out of his home on the road to unknown adventure. This time, his heart buoyed by the peace of mind that came from his father's blessing.

*　　　　*　　　　*　　　　*　　　　*

222

Dovewing rested in the courtyard just as she had been earlier, but there was no sign of her kidnappers. The hour had grown later than Trestan had wanted, for the eastern sky had lit up considerably. Other people were out on the streets, paying no particular attention to him or the flying craft. Villagers up at this early hour generally busied themselves with chores in preparation for a new day.

From the stable, Petrow hissed at him and waved to hurry closer. From out of other hiding places the others appeared. Apparently. they had all tried to keep a low profile one way or another. Petrow noticed a waraxe carried in Trestan's hands. He looked at it questionably, but then a gave surprised grin as Trestan presented it to him.

"A gift from my father. He had this axe sitting in a pile of weapons requisitioned by Lord Verantir last month, yet still not picked up. He figures you will want to use it before such time as when the noble gets around to remembering it."

Petrow took the one-handed axe in his hands and smiled. He turned it over in his hands, admiring the virgin quality. The handyman even gave it a few practice swings to test its balance. Opposite of the blade was a flat hammer-like head for smashing things on the backswing if needed. "Thanks, to you and your father. I really was hoping I would have something in my hands better than that old woodcutter's axe."

The companions once again converged on the vessel to take off. Salgor was the only one still hidden on board the ship, resting under a blanket on the rear couch. As quietly as possible, the rest clambered on board and took their seats. Mel hopped up on a low wooden box at the helmsman's chair, though his gnomish nose barely peeked over the rim of the dove figurehead unless he used another nearby box to stand on.

"Now hold on tightly," Mel spoke, "I won't promise a smooth ride when we start out. I'll need time to get acclimated to the proper lift needed…"

Cat grinned from her position, holding onto a portion of the guardrail. "Don't worry Mel, we have faith in you. Please hurry, before someone raises any kind of alarm."

Trestan and Petrow sat close to Salgor, in case he needed their support. Although the dwarf seemed healthier, they weren't sure if he had all his strength back. All their equipment had been stored for easy access under the deck hold, or strapped to themselves. As their chosen pilot readjusted his seat, the rest of them traded hopeful smiles for this new trip into adventure. Trestan heaved another happy sigh, grateful that his encounter with his father had passed. Cat threw him a playful wink. As much as each of them feared new dangers ahead, they felt their kinship growing, and that kinship emboldened them for what lay ahead. They were eager to be in the air and on their way. Finally, after Mel stretched his arms to loosen up his sleeves, he reached out and touched one of the gems on the control panel.

Nothing happened, even after he pushed it a second time.

The rest of the companions still kept grins on their faces, though eyes betrayed moments of doubt and worry. Mel Bellringer cleared his throat, smacked his lips together once, and then reacted with a new idea. "Of course, silly me!" He then moved his hands over a different part of the control panel. The companions heard him flip some kind of switch.

Nothing happened, even after he flipped it a second time.

By this time, worried glances shot between the companions behind the gnome's back. As the tiny sorcerer pulled at his pointy beard, they heard his other hand drum nervously on the chair. Cat began to throw worrisome glances towards the street, noting other people out and about. Indeed, she was a little concerned that after all this effort, they might have some explaining to do if they were found still sitting on the ground when Korrelothar came back to the village. The dwarf, Salgor, glanced over the side of the magical vessel. His fear of magical devices almost overrode his trust in his new friends at the moment, he started wondering if it wouldn't be better if he just jumped off of the magical contraption while he had the chance and found some other course of action. Trestan leaned towards Mel, about to speak.

SLAM!

The five of them jumped in their seats as a sudden loud noise came from overhead. All eyes looked up to see a figure in the window of a second story inn room. The occupant of the room had thrown the shutters open to breathe in the fresh air of the morning, but lucky for the companions the man hadn't looked down yet. The person performed a strenuous yawn and stretch, and when it was complete he turned away from the window. The five of them fidgeted and cast furtive glances at every noise.

Cat whispered a few encouraging words to Mel, hiding her underlying worry. Mel pretended to be more in control of the situation than he was, and proceeded to speak softly as he stared at the controls in front of him. Trestan finally leaned forward, as the gnome's right hand hovered and drifted over a few gems that seemed to work as buttons. The young smith asked, "Pardon me Mel, but you do seem a bit nervous. I was wondering if the elf had indeed taught you everything."

"Aye, he did," Mel answered, though his brow furrowed in concentration over which button to try next. "He taught me everything, well, almost everything that I needed to know. All but a couple things."

Mel found a control that worked. With the flip of a switch, the crystals on the underside of *Dovewing* began their familiar hum as they came to life. The deck began to vibrate. Mel let out a small cheer, then took a sigh of relief. Between the noise of the magical craft and the gnome's cheer, a few heads on the street turned to find the source of the commotion. Cat felt the inquisitive stares from the few people on the street.

The half-elf ducked lower in her seat, as if that would help hide her, and she told Mel, "We need to get up in the air now. Some people are watching us as we speak."

Mel looked about and saw the truth of Cat's words. He wiggled once more to get situated atop his box-seat better, and then he firmly gripped both levers that controlled how the craft maneuvered. Trestan still had questions on his mind, and they would not rest. The young smith spoke. "I just want to clarify something. You said the elf taught you 'almost' everything? All but a couple things?"

"Um, Aye." Mel looked left and right as he noted the open distance between the stables and the inn. It was a tight fit, but Korrelothar had made it look easy on the way down.

Trestan sensed the gnome was avoiding something. It was obvious Mel hadn't seen everything needed to operate the vessel. The young smith wondered how risky this plan

224

was going to get. "If you don't mind me asking," Trestan paused, but realized there was no subtle way to ask if he wanted a straight answer from the gnome. "What was it that you didn't learn about? What didn't he teach you?"

"Well, uh…" Mel decided there was no harm in letting the rest in on some minor details. "Takeoffs and landings. We didn't really cover that part."

Behind Mel, four pairs of eyes bugged out, and four jaws dropped at about the same time that the gnome yanked back on a control lever. *Dovewing* leapt off of the ground with a jerk. The stomachs of every companion dropped as the magical vessel sprung free from the bonds of gravity. The crystals under the vessel hummed louder, but they were nothing compared to another sound coming from the deck. Salgor, frantically hanging onto his seat, swore his fill of dwarvish curses.

CHAPTER 20

The companions gripped tightly to any portion of *Dovewing* they could as it lifted away from the ground. The ornate railing, along with its many carvings of creatures of flight, suffered through several pale knuckles. Trestan and Petrow reached out to assist the cursing dwarf from sliding around. They hadn't yet cleared the rooftops of the inn or the stable. Mel whooped for joy, until he looked up and saw how close they drifted toward the roof of the inn. The occupant that had thrust open the shutters returned to his window to investigate the noise. Cat could have touched him as they rose past.

"Gods save me!" The man cried out as he fell backward from the window.

"Mel! Watch out!" Petrow called to the gnome as he watched the overhanging roof of the inn loom closer.

Cat rolled off her seat and into the middle of the deck. She fully expected the gnome to clip the inn rooftop. Instead, Mel yanked hard on a lever. The ship tipped, but drifted away from the overhanging roof. As the deck rose, the companions saw the inn was no longer a danger.

Unfortunately, Mel didn't notice how close he maneuvered to the stable after making his correction. Trestan, on that side, instinctively looked that way just in time. Roughly two feet of wooden planks hung past the stable walls to dangle over the courtyard. Trestan pulled his hand from the guardrail only a moment before the rail met the overhanging stable roof. The port guardrail and its ornately carved griffon door raised several planks. *Dovewing* jerked abruptly as the old oaken craft shattered past that portion of the stable roof. Pieces of boards dropped onto the deck or fell to the courtyard below. Trestan squeezed into Salgor on the couch to avoid the mess of wood and dust scattering over that side of the craft.

Several new scratches could be seen on the railing and the ornate carvings along that side. The stable, however, had a gap in that side of the roof. They could hear the panicked whinnies from horses inside the building. Several people on the street witnessed the collision. They pointed and shouted at the flying vessel. Although the companions couldn't hear it, there were frantic prayers in the inn room they had passed by so closely.

The companions, now scattered in disarray on the deck from the scare, shakily got back to their bench seats. They looked at the cracked wooden pieces of roof lying on the deck. Only Trestan was close enough to venture a look over the side rail to see the new scratches marking those carvings.

Mel looked back over his shoulder sheepishly. The gnomish sorcerer ascertained the scratches that he could see, and couldn't help but notice a few glares directed at him from the rest of the companions. "Don't worry! That section already had some past battle-damage on it already. I'm sure he will hardly notice the scratches, if he even sees them at all."

*   *   *   *   *

226

Once settled in for the ride, they truly enjoyed the beauty of the journey. The buildings of Troutbrook shrank below them. The church looked no larger than a wagon, and soon the path of the brook became little more than a blue line running a crooked course across the landscape. Mel planned to fly in the same direction they had come from before, retracing their steps back to the bluff before venturing out across an expanse of open water. Very soon after their flight started, the sun ascended enough to put them in an almost dreamlike world.

Trestan had not been able to enjoy the flight that brought him safely home. Even for the others, the sights that morning were a special treat. The rising sun cast light and shadows across the whole world. As they traveled, flights of birds could be seen around them, and sometimes below them. Somehow the air seemed clearer, as the miles stretched out below. Morning mists rose off of bodies of water, only to play odd tricks with the sunlight that tried to burn through them. The southern mountains loomed in the distance, though from the ground it was a rare day you could see them so well from Troutbrook. Clouds took up some portions of the sky, yet the magical vessel found itself flying high enough to pass through several wispy ones. Indeed, shortly after first taking off, Mel climbed altitude to see the world from a whole new perspective. Even hawks that soared at lofty heights passed below the vessel during the first part of that journey.

Eventually Mel descended to a lower height, so as not to miss any landmarks. They still floated effortlessly over hills, woods, and rivers, though no roads were easily visible between Troutbrook's surroundings and the eastern shoreline. At best, they saw occasional game trails or signs of campfires from whatever races lived and thrived in the wilds. Everyone simply enjoyed the view or chatted quietly. No one admitted to being tired despite the long night. Their surroundings were so visually stunning that they were too excited to rest.

"My, that is a magnificent wonder," Petrow pointed away to the east. "Look over there, below those feathery clouds."

The companions all looked to see what had grabbed the young man's attention. They saw some low clouds over a pasture. A rainbow stretched from some distant place down through those clouds to the valley below them. Never had any of them had such a wonderful and full view of a rainbow from its towering arch down to its base. The expanse of vibrant colors stretched for miles.

Mel said, "Among my people is a saying. A rainbow is actually a full circle, though we only see the upper half of it. The lower half travels underground, for the rainbow is a ring that binds air to earth. This connects the land that we live on to the air we breathe."

Cat recalled a tale from the elvish people. "The elves have spoken of the legends of rainbows. I can't tell you what exactly a rainbow is, but I can tell you what is found there. The elves say that wherever the rainbow touches the land, you will find unicorns at play there."

"Bah," scoffed Salgor.

Cat looked over to the dubious dwarf warrior. Physically, he seemed to have recovered from the cold spell. Certainly, Daerkfyre's follower seemed to have recovered his old manners.

"Really, I'm serious." Cat continued, "There's a song about it. 'After rains surrender to the brightening day, where rainbow touches earth is where unicorns play.'"

The companions looked at the rainbow and the never-ending horizon. Mel thought about what Cat said. He turned to face them and asked, "Why don't we just have a good look for ourselves?"

Salgor protested immediately. "So now we're choosing to take a scenic route?"

Cat remembered how sick Salgor had gotten on the first flight. The dwarf didn't want to be on board the flying machine any more than he had to. The half-elf, intrigued by Mel's suggestion, wanted to take advantage of what might be her only opportunity to see if the elven legend held true.

Cat moved up beside Mel and pointed down to the base of the rainbow. "Let's go down there and see. It doesn't look too far away and it might be worth the detour."

Trestan and Petrow moved closer to the front of *Dovewing* as the gnome changed course. Both young men wanted to get a better look at the beauty of nature that lay before them. Salgor defiantly settled into the couch at the back, putting his arms together in a huff. The angle of the rainbow seemed to shift somewhat, but they could easily make out the valley that seemed to be its hold on the earth. The vessel flew in over some low ridges. When they got close enough, the rainbow itself could not really be seen unless they looked up towards the high arch.

"Well, that's something." Petrow pointed at a pasture below them. "You found a herd of wild horses, but nay unicorns."

Cat could see something that Petrow couldn't. "They often look like ordinary horses at a casual glance, you have to look harder and really open your eyes. They're magical; hiding their true nature. Look with your heart open, and you will see them for what they truly are!"

Mel leaned a bit over the figurehead to get a better look, and the gnome smiled. Being of forest folk like Cat was, the two of them saw what the others did not. Petrow and Trestan stared at every movement of the herd below, searching for anything out of the ordinary. Salgor also came forward to scrutinize the view. The skeptical dwarf examined the scene as intently as the two humans. Mel flew closer, the wild herd ran below them through the flowery meadow. Suddenly, it was as if a curtain had been lifted in the minds of the humans and the dwarf. No longer did they mistake the creatures below for ordinary animals. Once the illusion was pierced, they honestly wondered how they could ever think that such fine creatures were horses.

The run of the unicorn herd was almost mesmerizing, even enthralling. Few sights could have been any more magnificent. The unicorns were trophies of beauty and grace, and the spring flowers and windswept waves of tall grass complemented their run.

Unicorns stood shorter than horses. While a horse often had muscle, a unicorn preferred grace and light-footedness. Both horse and unicorn were built well for speed. While a horse might carry a charging knight, a unicorn was more likely to spring with superb agility to avoid enemies or attack from above. Horses could pack on muscle, but unicorns favored dexterity and grace of movement. Unicorn coats favored bright white, yet they displayed a rainbow variety of colors on their manes and tails. Varying shades of yellow, pink, green, blue, red, and other mixes of colors individually characterized each one. These same manes and tails flowed long and curly, glistening like silk in the sunlight, bouncing and swaying gracefully along the wind as they ran. Each horn also bore its own distinctive mix of colors twisting up the lengths of the shaft. Some horns gave the impression of a rainbow twisted and perched upright on the head of the unicorn. Seeing the colors highlighting the herd, it could only astound one to think that there must be a connection between the animal and rainbow.

The companions crowded the rails, looking in awe and wonder at the running herd below. The pasture rippled as rich and vibrant as the magical creatures themselves. The herd ran smoothly through blooming wildflowers and sweet fragrances. The unicorns raced across the meadow, changing course several times to elude the strange vessel flying overhead. As Mel flew low enough, they could make out distinctive calls between the leaders of the herd. There had been songs composed referring to the language of the unicorns, calling it the "whistle-song". As the companions listened to the calls, it did indeed sound like a variety of whistles set in a musical tone. The noise differed from anything a horse might utter. Unicorns voiced a distinctive variety of singing whistles to communicate. The herd leaders, always matriarchs, used the whistle-song to guide the rest of their followers in evading the path of *Dovewing*. The echoes of the song trilled and reverberated as it guided the direction of a hundred sets of unicorn hooves. The companions had a fine overhead view of the herd as it switched course on the run, flowing one way then striking a new path as the leaders whistled out directions. The movement felt akin to the way flocks of birds and schools of fish changed direction, seemingly on impulse.

Trestan and Petrow were briefly shocked when a sound much like the whistle-song came from beside them. Cat had often heard and imitated the call of the unicorns in the woods. The half-elf tried her best to sing to them, her voice fluctuating to match the qualities of their song. To her pleasant surprise, a few unicorns whistled back. The companions wondered if any sound she made conveyed any message to the unicorns, but if it did, they did not respond in any special way except answer her call. The herd still continued to run and frolic to evade the flying vessel. Petrow decided to try his hand at calling out to the unicorns. He whistled out some notes, though he couldn't quite seem to match the quality of the unicorns. Mel also started whistling, even as he tried to follow the herd on its constantly changing path. Before long, Trestan attempted to whistle a song as well. Sadly, the young smith could not even whistle a note, much less try to mimic the whistle-song of these magical creatures.

Petrow laughed at the attempt, "I can't believe you never got the hang of whistling, Tres. It's really easy!"

The young smith shook his head, "I try pursing the lips and blowing, but I can never make those sounds. Believe me, I wish very much that I could whistle, at least this one time!"

"Would the choir please settle down and quiet themselves? For all you know that blasted racket will just scare them off o' maybe incite them to attack a human settlement o' such." Salgor scowled at the others.

The others scoffed or rolled their eyes at what they perceived as the dwarf's normal irritability with things of a magical nature. They stopped their whistling without understanding their companion's real motivations. Salgor's eyes fixated on these magical creatures in motion, and for some reason their freedom and spirit brought a grin to his usually serious face. The dwarf honestly just tried to listen to the unicorns' whistle-song without distraction.

Still observing the herd, the companions saw how the movement of unicorns differed from their larger and more mundane cousins, the horse. Unicorns simply did not thunder along the ground, as a herd of horses would do. These magical animals substituted the galloping pace with graceful leaps and bounds. They sailed through the air over obstacles more akin to the motions of a gazelle or deer. Cat remembered legends about graceful unicorn mounts carrying elf bowmen into battle. The stories were likely myth, but she remembered how it was told that the graceful jumps of the unicorns had kept the bowmen away from their enemies long enough to defeat their foes. Cat could imagine how elven riders would look on such fine mounts. Unicorns were very free-spirited creatures, however, and it would have been an odd situation for such creatures to even accept riders, much less carry them into battle.

As Cat thought about it long enough, a song came to her head from the elvish home of her younger days. She sang, softly, and her companions listened.

Manes will wave under windswept sky,
Tails flowing behind as they prance on by,
Gold, silver, red, green and lots of blue,
The sun, on each, shines a different hue.

Where the rainbow bonds with the ground,
The unicorns will frolic round and round.
After rains surrender to the brightening day,
Where rainbow touches earth is where the unicorns play!

The unicorn's crown is a rainbow horn,
The blessed birthright of each foal born,
Tall, straight and proud stands the unicorn's lance,
And blessed is he to see it close by chance.

Where rainbow bonds with the earth,
The unicorns will be dancing in their mirth.
After rains surrender to the brightening day,
Where rainbow touches earth is where the unicorns play!

An insult, it is, to compare to a horse,
For these are magical beasts of course,
Hear their whistle-song floating on the breeze,

Soothing melody to put hard hearts at ease.

Where the rainbow bonds with the ground,
The unicorns will frolic round and round.
After rains surrender to the brightening day,
Where rainbow touches earth is where the unicorns play!

Silence descended upon their vessel as the companions let the words of the song linger in their minds. The unicorns ran wild and free below them, still dodging the path of the vessel. Few individuals ever saw a herd of unicorns for so long, and enjoyed the vantage they possessed. They were still in their peaceful contemplations as the herd began to distance themselves from the vessel. *Dovewing* flew a straight course, despite the unicorns latest change in direction.

Eager to swing about and watch the unicorns longer, Trestan called to their pilot. "Mel?"

The gnome responded right next to him. "Aye?"

Mel startled Trestan, since the human expected the gnome to be at the helm. The young smith snapped his head around. The gnome had leaned over to get a better view of the herd, leaving the helmsman's chair empty. Not too far ahead of them, a sloping hill capped with some high trees stood in their path!

His voice almost a hoarse croak, Trestan stared into the gnome's face with wide eyes, "Look out! Trees ahead!"

Mel Bellringer whipped his head around to discover they were on a collision course. With a wild yelp he scrambled back into the chair. Even as he moved, the deck started to slant sideways, slipping a bit towards the uneven terrain below. Mel didn't have time to properly get into the seat before grabbing a control lever and pulling it back hard. Everyone hung on as the front of the craft lifted at a sharp angle to get them over the hill. Trestan held the bench with a death grip, eyes closed tightly as he feared the worst. He expected to feel the craft break apart as it hit something solid. Salgor swore again, but the words were taken by the wind.

The sound of tree limbs and leaves brushing the underside of the craft preceded a cracking noise that jolted them slightly. Everyone held their breath as they expected another impact with a lot more force to it. Then the vessel leveled off, no longer climbing but heading forward again at a steady altitude. They all climbed shakily back to their seats as they looked back at the ridge they had narrowly missed. Trestan and the others could see where one of the tall trees had snapped branches at the top. Leaves shaken loose from the collision floated downwards.

Mel got back on top of his seat and made himself comfortable, though he dared not look behind him at the expressions of his companions. Sheepishly, he said, "I'm sure he won't notice that. We scratched the bottom a bit, but he probably never looks under there anyways. No real mess there."

The gnome barely finished speaking, when suddenly Salgor's stomach rebelled against the continued treatment he'd had to endure flying in this magical contraption. The dwarf heaved a good portion of the previous night's food and drink back up into the light of day.

*　　　*　　　*　　　*　　　*

They turned *Dovewing* to pursue the unicorn herd again, but found themselves soaring over an empty pasture instead. Not a sign could be seen of the magical beasts. There were enough woods and narrow valleys below them to hide a herd of magical creatures. All of them expressed sadness that they could not have enjoyed the moment longer. Even after they flew away, Salgor looked back with some longing at the pasture left behind, though he hid his disappointment from the others.

They raced on to their more urgent destination. The day passed by slowly, while the land slid swiftly beneath them. Although the view was wonderful, the companions made attempts to catch up on the lack of slumber from the previous night. It wasn't easy trying to sleep during the flight, but they were able to nap for small periods. Even Mel rest his eyes, after giving Cat a quick lesson on the basics of steering and keeping a level altitude. The half-elf loved getting a chance at the controls, even if her biggest concern was keeping a steady flight while the gnome slept.

Valley, river, hill and plains went past. Much of the exact terrain would be remembered only as a blur, but it was wonderful to experience at the time. Before the day was half done, they arrived along the shoreline. The continent of Quoros ended, and the Sea of Krakus stretched out before them. They did not fly straight out to sea, instead following the coastline southwards to try to find their way to the bluff where theier enemies had camped. The weather turned cloudy, but that did not hinder their flight. They recognized the bluff as soon as they saw it. The ground bore black scars from the energies of the wand. The abandoned camp stood in the same disarray as it had following the battle. Seeing it brought back memories of their struggle. It also reminded the companions of how desperately close they had come to dying in pursuit of these enemies.

Mel circled the battlefield once, as the others looked on in quiet contemplation. Trestan moved his lips in some silent prayer. Petrow looked often at the area where he had fought the minotaur, as well as the blackened remains of the tent in which he had been held captive. Cat had her eyes closed part of the time, remembering more than observing. Salgor eventually withdrew his axe and began sharpening it again. The battleaxe didn't really need it, but to the dwarf it was something to do as he anticipated his next meeting with Revwar. Mel kept busy flying, though his thoughts strayed to the field below. Mel wore a frown, but then the gnome patted the wand on his belt, and brightened at the thought of how well it served him when he really needed the help. Petrow soon drew out the waraxe Hebden crafted, and gave it a few sharpening strokes as well. As Trestan watched Salgor and Petrow sharpen their axes, he decided to draw out his elvish blade and re-examine it.

They bid their silent goodbyes to the bluff and the ghosts lingering there. Mel turned straight east, using a compass built into the back of the dove figurehead. Though the others on the craft had no idea what a compass was, Mel understood it and had been using it to help direct him. The bluff, and the land, drifted behind them, while the open sea stretched beneath.

Trestan Karok stared at the runes of the blade. He reflected how his life had changed in the last several days. He considered the differences between wielding a smith's hammer and a sword. Hebden's question of his interest in becoming a paladin had sparked thoughts on that subject. Although Trestan could not deny interest, he didn't know if it was a wise decision. A good portion of the young man wanted to go back home when this was done, swing the hammer again, and resume the only life he had known. Another part of him actually craved the excitement and wonder that the open road offered. He prayed to Abriana for guidance often, but felt unsure if he could follow that course from his livelihood and home. He loved everything that Sir Wilhelm and his goddess stood for, but could he love that life enough to abandon his personal freedom?

Dovewing flew out into the unknown, open sea, leaving their homes behind.

*   *   *   *   *

"I hope we spot something soon," Petrow leaned over a front rail, observing the water below. "I don't think any of us wish to be flying over this broad expanse of water after nightfall."

Salgor pointed to some dark clouds ahead, "It's going to get darker sooner than expected. The God of Storms is o' the prowl. We're going to get wet flying through that mess."

The others looked with concern at the storm clouds lurking directly in their path. Behind the flying vessel, the descending sun hid behind more clouds, making it harder to determine the time. Despite what loomed ahead in the sky, a scattering of reefs in the water offered hope. Coral and sand formed breakers in the frothing sea, though as yet they had not seen any sizeable islands.

Trestan reminded them of that fact, "Pray that we are not far away. The sea is shallower here, just as the one-eyed man had said. Keep your eyes on the horizon. If the island and castle are large enough we might see them from some distance."

Mel piloted the craft even higher to get a better look at the surrounding area. This put them uncomfortably far up, but the companions did not protest. They flew along the lowest wisps of the clouds. All eyes searched for some sign of a large body of land, enough to accommodate a castle.

"Down there!" Cat pointed excitedly.

The others had trouble making out what her half-elven eyes had spotted, but they could barely see an area where waves broke against a shoreline. Undoubtedly there was some sizeable landmass down there, surrounded by sharp coral reefs.

A bright light momentarily blinded everyone. A loud clap of thunder reverberated against the deck barely a moment later. With the afterimage of a lightning bolt slowly fading from their eyes, they realized the dark clouds had arrived. More of the same violent lightning and thunder erupted in their path.

"Mel!" Trestan ran forward, ducking beside the helmsman's chair and holding the railing. "Take us down closer to the waterline! We don't want to be flying this close to thunderclouds."

The gnome nodded his head and maneuvered the vessel downwards. Everyone else hunkered close to the deck as they also grabbed handholds. Mel turned the craft to make for the island. From here it looked small, barely visible except through brief flashes of the storm's light. The clouds darkened their world. The first drops of rain splashed the deck as they descended. Storm winds buffeted the vessel, though it held its course well. Fierce winds intensified the rain, sometimes whipping it in from the sides.

Trestan tried to shift his position. Another lightning bolt passed in front of them, another resounding boom echoing over the deck. With the vessel still in a sharp descent, the storm winds caught Trestan at the wrong time. He slipped on the wet deck. He flailed his arms for a handhold, but his body fell against a solid object. Something snapped behind his armored back, accompanying Mel's pained yelp. Trestan steadied himself on the railing. The young human watched as Mel shook his right arm, and then sucked on the first couple fingers of that hand. The gnome seemed mildly hurt, but he reached for the lever on that side again.

However, the control lever protruded from the figurehead at an odd angle. Mel got a hold of it, but as soon as he tried to use it he knew something was wrong. The others looked through the rain-splattered deck in horror as the gnome raised the broken control stick, revealing that the wooden joints had separated from the mechanism inside.

Dovewing continued descending sharply, an empty hole in the console where a control stick should have been connected.

The deck began tilting out of control. Not one of them had ever been so high off the ground, and now they found themselves falling to their deaths. Another lightning stream illuminated breaking waves and sharp coral reefs far below them. Mel acted quickly, muttering a few words for a spell. His fingers on one hand stretched and became more flexible. The gnome slid his elongated fingers into the hole for the disconnected lever. Mel manipulated the stub to which the lever had been attached, though it wasn't easy. Their descent slowed and leveled out. The gnome's fingers still couldn't maneuver the craft as finely as the control stick could. Trestan heard Mel muttering a string of whispered words, talking to himself as he struggled with the craft. Strong winds pushed at them from one side, then the other. The deck still jerked and dropped at irregular intervals as the gnome tried his best to regain some semblance of stability without the lever.

Rain fell to the deck in sheets, driven by fierce winds. Trestan hauled himself closer to Mel's seat as the gnome worked at guiding the wounded vessel. He glanced behind to see the others also holding tightly to the railings. Most of the equipment was safely stored in the hold, but a few loose items slid on the deck. The darkness, rain and jostling movements made visibility very limited.

They had a cold wake-up of how low they were flying when a wave slammed over the deck. A spray of froth mingled with the driving rain. Trestan heard someone coughing up water, but his attention focused on Mel. The gnome furiously worked the one remaining control lever, while still using his fingers through the hole left by the other one. The young

234

smith prayed the second lever wouldn't come loose as well, for that would certainly spell disaster. Trestan chanced a gaze over the rail; the sight frightened him. They still sped at a fast rate only a few feet above the storm-driven waves. He looked for the island they had spotted from above, but between the darkness and the rain he could see very little. In lifting himself up to see, the young man suddenly felt the weight of his attire. The leather and metal plates he wore reminded him that if he happened to go overboard, or if they started to crash and sink, he would likely drown.

Mel said something, his words lost in the roaring crash of another wave. Salty water slammed the deck and the guardrails once again, sweeping loose equipment overboard and drenching the companions. Trestan imagined that the others were also just trying to hold on for dear life. Brine from the sea made the railing a bit slippery to hold. The force of the last wave spun the craft into a slow rotation. The gnome sorcerer found himself trying to control the turn, and to hopefully get the front of the ship facing the direction they were headed. They were soon flying backwards. Trestan looked out the front of the vessel at a large wave they were outrunning.

"Reef!" Cat shouted.

Trestan turned back only in time to witness the collision.

The rear portion of *Dovewing*, including the plush couch and a good section of guardrail, buckled as it collided head-on with a sharp reef. The magically strengthened oak boards of the deck splintered as they broke apart. Trestan's teeth gnashed together upon impact. Wood and water sprayed apart into the air. He saw one body launched upwards from the deck, but did not know who it was. The couch and a portion of the rear guardrail fell away from the rest of the ship. The vast majority of the deck remained intact as the damaged vessel slid over the coral. The sharp reef scraped away several underside crystals, sabotaging *Dovewing's* maneuverability. Trestan had to concentrate on his own handholds when another danger loomed over the moving deck. The wave they had been distancing now surged toward them.

Trestan held his breath as water rushed over his body. Most noise drowned underneath the surface of the wave; much quieter than the crunching boards and screams that had assaulted his ears a moment ago. He hugged the rail for what seemed like several seconds and still he remained underwater. Trestan fought the instinct to let go and swim, knowing he would drown. Finally, a rush of bubbles and froth moved over him before the deck rose above the wave again. He gasped for air.

The magical vessel was battered, but its remaining crystals still offered buoyancy. It continued to fly randomly, skimming several waves. Trestan had water in his ears, but could hear the gnome sputtering and coughing next to him. Sadly, all Mel could do was hang on tightly to his chair. Without anyone controlling the vessel, waves turning and battering it, the deck began to spin in odd ways. Without Mel or Trestan truly being able to see what happened, the vessel angled until it rolled on its sides. The floating, circular craft cartwheeled across the surface of the water like a coin across a floor. Guardrail, woodwork, intricate designs and precious metal highlights ripped off as it went.

Trestan finally lost his hold as the guardrail in front of him shredded like a rotted log. The young man suffered a disorienting fall before rolling across wet sand. *Dovewing* rolled past him on its side up a dark beach. The vessel continued to shred apart, with precious carvings and gem ornaments flying off into a trail of rubble in the sand. The old oaken boards scattered in a trail of fragments along the beach or floated with other debris out in the water.

Trestan got on all fours and gathered the strength to raise his head. Whether by luck or divine guidance, he ended up on the island. The young man swayed on hands and knees as he watched the last large piece of the vessel roll to a stop many meters away. Somehow, he managed to get his shaking body upright. He reached back and confirmed, with considerable relief, that Sword of the Spirit still sat in its scabbard on his back. He took several shaky steps along the trail of rubble, looking for his other friends…or their bodies. The rain pelted him, water drenched his clothes, his muscles ached from gripping the railing, the wet sand slowed his feet and he worried over the fate of his friends. He approached the busted helmsman's chair, hoping to find Mel.

Mel Bellringer sprawled not far from the remains of the chair. His fingers had returned to their normal size. His other hand clutched the formerly unbroken control lever. Trestan looked over him with apprehension. Mel let out a cough before he rose into a sitting position on his own strength. It relieved Trestan to see that at least the sorcerer lived.

Trestan dropped to his knees beside the gnome, "Are you alright? Nothing broken?"

Mel spit sand before he replied, "I've had worse beatings. I don't think I broke any bones."

Trestan sat beside the gnome as they faced the shoreline. Both tried to catch their breath as they looked over the remains of *Dovewing*. Not twenty feet away lie the ornate dragon door from the starboard side, divided into three pieces. All along the beach shattered crystals and decorative gems glittered. A trail of splinters, metal pieces, nails and larger boards marked the path of the craft from where it had first hit the beach, to the position where the core of the deck's hold ended up. Crashing waves carried more floating pieces of debris, but hid those precious metals and gems that sunk offshore. The hundred-year-old creation of Korrelothar was reduced to scattered pieces of junk on some unnamed island out at sea.

Mel drew in a deep breath, frowned, and offered his foremost thought. "Well, now all those other scratches we picked up earlier seem rather paltry by comparison."

CHAPTER 21

Trestan and Mel wandered the beach searching for any sign of their friends. They spotted someone foundering in shallow water. The weakened individual struggled towards shore, but waves buffeted every attempt to stand up. Trestan unbuckled his sword baldric and let it fall to the beach as he ran down to the water. The weight of his own armor was of some concern, but he didn't dare take the time to try undoing the straps. Mel ran alongside but stopped just inside the tides. The tall waves battering the other person would have given Mel trouble as well.

As Trestan got closer, lightning illuminated Salgor's chain mail and beard. Weighed down by his armor and disoriented by the crash, the dwarf had difficulty staggering in the stormy waves. The whitecaps forced Trestan to work at keeping his own balance, but he finally reached the sputtering dwarf. They made slow progress, buffeted by waves on the shifting sand. The wind and waves made it hard to speak. They reached a patch of sand far from the surf and dropped to the ground. The poor dwarf breathed heavily through a beard plastered to his armor. Mel ran back to the broken deck in order to salvage something. Salgor and Trestan just relaxed for the moment and tried to regain their strength. Despite their exertion, they felt chilled from the cold rain and seawater.

Mel ran back to the beach with a coil of rope in his hands. Trestan wondered what the gnome intended to do with it, but didn't spare breath to ask. Worries for their comrades motivated them to go closer to the sea and search. They called out for Cat and Petrow a few times while wandering the shoreline. They were slowly giving up hope that their friends had survived.

At one point, Salgor and Trestan were both calling out when Mel shushed them. The gnome turned one ear towards the water. He stood there listening, hoping it hadn't been his imagination. All three heard someone yelling. Trestan called out again, and then stood silent as they heard Cat's reply drift over the waves. They could not see her, but her voice restored their hopes.

Cat endured turbulent water. The waves pushed her toward shore, but shallow, sharp coral loomed as a danger. The half-elf put all her strength into keeping her head above water as she swam onward.

"Petrow! Still with me?"

From behind her, a voice answered over the tumult of waves. "Aye!"

Cat continued to struggle forward. She felt as tired as ever, but the sound of voices kept her spirits up. She gasped through waves and breaths. "I hear them...up ahead...close."

Because of the storm, Petrow could not define the shoreline in the darkness. As it was, he barely tracked Cat's form as they swam in an endless, violent sea. The blue-eyed man was strong and muscular from his life of hard labor but his lungs had also taken in a lot of seawater.

The shoreline became visible when Cat crested each wave, compliments of her elf heritage. She knew she led Petrow in the right direction. She heard him cough and sputter. Between waves he called out. "Is land close? This is tiresome."

Another wave surged forward, and at its crest Cat could make out their companions on the beach. "Not far! I see them! Please…"

Cat's sentence broke as a smaller wave caught her by surprise. It wasn't the first time she choked on water during the swim. Petrow caught up to her and stayed by her side, riding the rough waves. "Are you well?"

In the distance they heard Trestan's and Salgor's voices. Cat adjusted her direction and kicked forward. "I'll be fine. Stick with me!"

The lighter-shade beach loomed ahead, portions of the broken flying vessel becoming visible to the half-elf. The human barely had time to react when he heard Cat yell. "Shallow!"

The sharp reef raked along Petrow's abdomen and thighs, but the handyman avoided serious injury. Both swimmers struggled while still wearing their leather armor. It was a bit heavy and unyielding, yet at the same time it had already saved them from a few cuts off of similar coral.

They were past the danger, still navigating through the high waves, when Cat screamed. The half-elf started thrashing in place. Petrow swam closer to her, but she held up a hand to stop him. "Stay back! Something is here!"

"Something?"

Cat struggled, she spat words between waves. "Wrapping around my waist! I'm trying…my dagger…cut free."

Petrow felt it too. A thin, tentacle-like appendage started circling his hips. Petrow went to reach for his knife, but remembered he wasn't wearing his utility harness. He had no weapon to use against whatever new threat was grabbing at them.

Something broke the surface of the water between them. Tendrils of seaweed clung to it. Cat and Petrow both looked with wonder at the strange object wriggling between them.

Cat was puzzled. "That's a rope!"

On the beach, Mel stood over a coiled end of rope. The rope wriggled away from him and disappeared into the water, where the distant end encircled his two friends. The gnome had his arms out before him, swaying like a flag in the wind as he reached out his will along the tether. Cat spotted the gnome manipulating the rope without really understanding the strange sorcery involved. His spell buoyed his friends and pulled them to shore. Trestan and Salgor soon helped with the latter part. Arm over arm the smith and the dwarf reeled in the length of rope, while Mel assisted by the use of magical hand gestures. Cat and Petrow still swam, though progress came a lot easier. Mel's power over the rope lent it the strength to keep them afloat. Despite the tossing current, no more waves managed to force salty water down their throats.

Cat and Petrow stumbled several steps away from the water's edge before collapsing. Pieces of old oaken wood littered the spot, but the companions were content to lie where they dropped. Cat's long hair tangled about her head. Bits of sand stubbornly clung to most of the companions. Petrow coughed water out of his lungs until his voice wheezed. For the longest time, they relaxed together as the rain rolled off their faces. The others glanced over to the scattered remnants of *Dovewing*. Flashes of lightning helped

238

illuminate the trail of debris. They shook their heads and tried not to think about how angry Korrelothar might be if they ever lived to see him again.

Though most of them suffered bruises from the rough landing, no one was seriously hurt. Petrow and Cat had scratches on their leather armor from brushes against the coral reefs, but no cuts. Everyone felt less weary after that brief respite, though hearts and minds alike still tried to calm down. They picked around the craft for their supplies. The hold under the deck remained mostly intact, saving most of their equipment. Since it had been in the center of the craft, it was the portion that rolled the farthest from the shore. They had lost a fair amount of food, so the group hoped they weren't stranded on an island with limited resources. They went through the packs, looking for items jostled free during the bad landing.

"About all I can be thankful for is that I left my wood axe here with the rest of our things." Petrow pulled his woodcutter's axe free of the wreckage. "That battleaxe Hebden loaned me washed off the deck at some point."

Trestan chuckled at that. "You seem to have a tendency of losing good axes. Remind me not to have you carry this sword for any length of time."

"I don't know whether to feel lucky or unlucky after that landing," the handyman responded. He brushed wet sand off of the axe, and felt around the blade in case the experience might have taken the sharp edge off of it. "That was some quick-thinking in trying to save us Mel, although I don't think I'll trust any more flying contraptions for a while."

The gnome scoffed through a veil of smoke. Somehow, despite the drenching water, the sorcerer enjoyed a lit pipe. Mel spoke, "Believe me, it really hurts to have brought such a wonderful creation to such an end. I sure hope we found the right island."

Cat looked ragged, but she carried all of her bags and equipment. "On that subject, we really should move off this beach. The sooner we explore the sooner we can find out if this is the right place, and where we might find shelter. I'd like to be able to get under a covering of any kind and warm myself by a fire if we can do so safely."

*   *   *   *   *

The companions moved off the beach under cover of the nighttime rain. There was nothing to do for *Dovewing* except bid goodbye to its scattered pieces. Cold settled about the companions like a mantle. Their breath formed in the air, adding to the foggy visibility before them. Weary, they all longed for the comforts of a warm inn and fire. Mel asked for a fire to be made under some short trees near the beach, but both Salgor and Cat spoke out against it. If they were on the right island, then it might be easy for the wrong kind of eyes to see their fire and investigate. The five of them walked in relative quiet through tall grass interspersed with sand. They made their way past the edges of the island and up onto a raised plateau that supported more plant life. Cat's superior eyes guided them.

Her eyes also spotted the outline of a castle. It nestled on a different part of the shoreline. As they all moved closer, the outlines of the wall and towers appeared during lightning flashes. Two things became apparent as the party approached it from afar. First, there were no torches or lights on or in the castle itself. Second, a light source came from somewhere near the foot of the castle, hidden by a ridge. Flickering illumination reflected against the base of one wall.

The castle wasn't the only thing that caught their eyes. An old watchtower sat on a section of high ground, between them and the castle. It was built far enough away from the beach so that it shouldn't have to worry about high waters, yet its location placed it slightly out of sight of the castle. A ridge with trees blocked the line of sight between the two, though in old days guards atop the tower could likely signal the castle using fire or flags. The watchtower stood guard over parts of the shoreline not directly in view of the castle. The companions worried that occupants of the tower might see their approach.

Petrow, Salgor, Mel and Trestan went into hiding, while Cat left behind her packs and scouted. Salgor would have been eager for them to all charge in at once. Cat reminded him that too much was unknown. It wouldn't be hard for a watchman to alert whomever or whatever tended the fires closer to the castle. The half-elf, trained for scouting and sneaking about, disappeared into the darkness. The others settled into an uneasy silence while they waited. Mel occasionally broke the silence with a few words, mostly commenting on how fun their flight had been, or lamenting the destruction of the fine vessel. The others stayed silent. Mel contented himself with a smoke on his pipe. Ears stayed alert for any noise from the watchtower.

The darkness gave no clues, nor did they hear anything for some time. When a noise arose beside their hiding spot, it caused all of them to jump. Salgor straightened with axe ready and shield held high.

Black against the dark, Cat's hidden voice carried easily to their spot. "The watchtower is abandoned. Nay eyes or ears guard there. It will make a good shelter for us until we know more about what is over the ridge."

Salgor replied, "What did you see o'er the ridge? Did you see that damned wizard?"

Cat, frustrated that the dwarf would continue to pursue the wizard despite normal caution, failed to keep the irritation from her tone. "I didn't explore beyond the watchtower. Once we are settled there, I will scout over the ridge."

The companions once again moved onward. The efforts of getting this far had strained their endurance. All of them were mentally leaning on each other for support as they walked forward through the gloom. Cat led them to the front of the watchtower. Tough stone composed the first level of the structure, but the taller portions were more of a wood framework from which a watchman or signalman could ascend higher to perform their duties. It had the feel of being incomplete whenever it had been abandoned. The outside had seen many years of rough weather. The upper platforms of wood were in bad shape; rot weakened parts and left some planks dangling from worn rope. The party moved past a creaking door into a dark interior. They could hear dripping water from above. Mel stopped to cast a spell, and a small light beamed from his hand. The simple spell illuminated the inside well enough for the others to see easily. Rainwater pooled against the inside of one wall, and lichen grew unchecked over many surfaces inside. The wooden ladder leading to the top of the structure seemed rotted and old. They saw rust-claimed metal brackets for

240

torches, as well as some old weapons similarly beyond use. It reminded Trestan and Petrow of the keep they had seen in disrepair during their trip south to Barkan's Crossing. A lot of tavern tales were told about the ruined structures that predated the Godswars. In all likelihood, the nearby castle was either abandoned or overrun in the dark years of recovery following those wars.

"Someone stocked dry firewood here." Petrow pointed to the treasure he'd found, hiding under an oil tarp.

Salgor and Cat exchanged glances. Salgor ventured, "Had to be recently."

Mel looked up with wide, pleading eyes, "Surely we can spare a small fire?"

Cat frowned, but relented due to their discomfort. "It's dark and the wind favors us. We can tolerate a small fire."

They built a modest fire and proceeded to dry their equipment and clothes. Katressa Bilil was an exception. She set some of her things in close proximity of the warm fire, but kept her dark leathers on as she prepared to head out into the rain again. Trestan watched as she checked her crossbow for any damage in the firelight, then slung it over her back. The young man asked, "How long before we should expect you back?"

"Not long," she answered. "I just hope to see who is camped by the castle, nay more than that. It's not too far, and the weather will aid in obscuring me from watching eyes. I will be back soon to properly enjoy that fire. Hopefully someone will get a meal cooking. I've worked up quite a hunger in the past hour."

She smiled and disappeared.

*   *   *   *   *

The small fire warmed and dried those seeking refuge in the tower. Meat sizzled, bread and cheese exchanged hands. Alcoholic drinks that survived the crash had been poured. Tendrils of smoke escaped out the top, but faded in the dark rain. Raindrops splattered the unfinished upper reaches of the tower, scattering from the impact to spray the ground below. Outside, an overhang offered limited shelter before the aging doorway entry. A lone figure stood sentry underneath despite the continual misty spray of water. He heard laughter and jokes inside the shelter. The smell of cooking meat wafted through the openings in the door, tempting his hungry stomach. Yet alone he stood, for he liked to find quiet time whenever he could to pause and consider his thoughts.

Trestan Karok's muscled and stained hands gave no indication that he was also a thinker. In one hand he held the Sword of the Spirit, in the other a mug that was still near-filled with Bandago's Brew. In the darkness and rain, he did his best to capture some fleeting thoughts. Occasionally he could not help but put on a smile as he overheard some amusing tale from inside, but his mind focused on serious paths.

He still did not know who dwelled near the castle this night, since Cat had not returned. The young man felt with all confidence they were in the right place and there should a ship somewhere near. Before the battle on the bluff, he had gone over all sorts of thoughts about being a hero, or of dying terribly. His mind had conjured up plenty enough images of him riding a sea of blood to rescue the noble. Nevertheless, he also feared what the minotaur or wizard would do if he was at their mercy. He had once feared the cleric even worse, but he felt that some fear dispersed after he had flattened her so well in the opening blow of that battle.

When Trestan had walked out of the watchtower, his first motive was to clear up any thoughts or doubts in his mind before any other battle. This last line of reasoning led him to a totally different set of questions. An issue rose up in his mind that changed his subject of consideration.

Hebden's words stuck in his memory: *"I wonder if you may have been influenced more than I suspected by Sir Wilhelm, and that you look at the possibilities of becoming a paladin."*

It had been sitting in the back of his mind for some time now. He respected and admired everything Sir Wilhelm valued. At the same time, he admitted it had never been a path that he sought or gave much thought. Trestan prayed to Abriana for the qualities and virtues his mentor championed. The young lad could get angry at people on occasion, but even that would only go so far. Part of his restraint rooted in the feeling that you could never truly understand the motivations of another person. Jareth had envisioned bad people as simply misguided, or uninformed, or any of a number of situations that caused them to diverge from a loving, caring lifestyle. Despite this undeserved compassion, and his love for all people, he nevertheless felt that many things were worth defending and fighting. Tales spoke of paladins differing in their views, depending on the gods they championed. This particular viewpoint from Abriana intrigued Trestan. It loved people unquestionably, but didn't blindly forgive unrepentant criminals. Justice was dealt from the perspective of sorrow for those that had chosen an immoral lifestyle.

Trestan admired Abriana's virtues. He felt another life offering itself to him, if only he reached out and seized it. He felt he could brave a life that championed good values, but the cost of serving someone bigger than him scared Trestan. Would he surrender control of his life? What limitations and controls would be placed upon him if he followed the lifestyle demanded by a higher consciousness? It felt good to know that Sir Wilhelm seemed content and happy with his life, but Trestan knew little of his mentor's service before he settled down in Troutbrook. Trestan's life had shaped around the humble footsteps of his father. Smithing appealed to him, and had been the only life Trestan envisioned while growing up. The young man stood in the dark, picturing both lives, balancing the goals and consequences. If he pursued the life of a paladin, he did not know where to start. Did he really crave such a life over the happiness of his home and the pounding of a smith's hammer? It was the first time in his life he seriously considered a future different to his upbringing.

"Sir Wilhelm said the proper way to pray to a god was to thank them and count their blessings first," Trestan spoke softly to his unseen benefactor. He had faith that Abriana heard his prayer, without expecting a response to be forthcoming. "He also said prayers should never demand anything, especially anything specific. He explained that the gods bestowed favors as they deemed, and were more likely to honor humble requests than those self-righteously demanded. In return, gods expect something from mortals as well, whether it is obedience, faith, lifestyle or sacrifices."

242

Trestan paused for a moment to consider his words. His hand shifted its grip on the elvish hilt, mindful that it was the sword of a paladin. "I can't promise anything. I can't commit myself, until I know my own wishes better. My faith tells me you have guided me around harm and lent strength to my courage at every step. I can't have just been that lucky. Someone watched over my shoulder and helped me stand against those who would harm those whom I love. I am in your debt.

"But what price do you ask? Am I given the choice to go home and live the life of a smith when this is done? Will I be bound to another choice, expected to take up the sword forever, and pledge my right arm to your wishes? Somehow, I feel that you would not force it upon me, and I try to look at it as a choice freely offered. But my debt to you scares me. I just can't make a decision. I don't know for sure how I could decide, or whether I am pressed for time to do so. So, I can't make any promises."

Trestan lifted the Sword of the Spirit and stared into the contours of the leather scabbard covering the blade. "I need your help and direction. I pray you will continue to guard me and my friends. We need divine help if we are to triumph. But I just can't promise anything afterwards. I must find my own heart and direction."

Trestan almost turned to go back inside, when a figure appeared through the rain and darkness. Cat's voice whispered, "What were you saying?"

The young man almost jumped, though he had been expecting to see Cat return soon. The surprise caused him to spill some of the dwarf's fiery ale. "I was just praying. I'm glad to see you back."

Cat stepped under the overhang beside Trestan. He looked into her face, though not much could be seen in the dark. Some firelight seeped through a crack in the door to illuminate one soft cheek. She hadn't worn her helm, for fear that any reflection off the metal would give her away to the people she observed. Strings of drenched hair clung to her cheeks and pointed ears.

The half-elf glanced over his soaked form, measuring something in him before speaking. "You're a very spiritual man; I notice you pray often. They say a person has many sides to their personality and you seem to bolster that sentiment."

Trestan shrugged. "I'm nay priest or anything, but it feels good to have someone in which to confide. It's like someone you can't see, but you feel they know you and have endured your dark times with you. Shares one's moments. It helps to believe someone is always there, even when you feel alone."

"You aren't alone," Cat offered.

Trestan nodded, but didn't offer an answer. The half-elf suggested an alternate view, "Helps when you are nervous or afraid also?"

"Aye, there is that too," he confessed. The admission felt like it dropped a burden from his shoulders. "I'm afraid of what we might run into, but not to the point that I would think of abandoning the quest. That doesn't sound right, let me try it another way." Trestan licked his lips as he glanced to the side. "I guess I'm afraid of what that other group could do, even though I know they have their vulnerable times. I think it's called a healthy respect for one's enemies. There was more on my mind, but not something I feel inclined to share at this moment. Talking out loud can be a way to clear one's mind; helps a person listen to their own words."

Cat's eyes studied him as she nodded her head. He could barely see the emerald green highlights. Trestan wondered if Cat ever prayed for anything, and what she thought of him at that moment. Akin to her own words, she proved a person could seem to have a number of sides to their personality. A man could probably know a woman for a long time and never discover all the secrets and hidden places of their heart. Trestan felt like Katressa Bilil's soul wove a more complex tapestry of mysteries than most. Trestan would have given money just to learn what she was thinking that moment as she studied him.

Cat smiled as she broke the silence, "Can I get past you and into the door there? It's cold and wet out here."

Trestan almost jumped out of the way. He balanced the sword and mug well enough to reach back and open the door like a gentleman. He even managed to bow as she walked through, and she turned a smile his way. The young man followed her inside as she proceeded to discard her wet equipment. The half-elf kept a closed mouth even as the others threw questioning looks in her direction, eager for a revelation on anything she might have found. All four men eventually turned their backs to her out of respect. She ditched her wet clothes and put on something dryer for the night. Before long, the five of them sat around the fire sharing strips of hot meat over warm mugs.

Cat shared the news they hoped to hear. The firelight which had thrown its glow upon the castle walls came from a camp of sailors and mercenaries. Sheltered from the storm waves was the same ship they had seen before: *Silver Trident* was anchored in the calm waters of the castle's bay. Cat had even noted a familiar, one-horned minotaur present on the deck of the ship. The others were glad to have found their quarry again, even as they unconsciously tensed their grip on their mugs. As they listened, it sounded like Cat had ventured very close to the camp to get a look. Trestan assumed that the adventuress may have tried to steal the two stones and avoid a big fight. Salgor guessed as much too, and asked her directly. Cat admitted that she might have tried for it, except that she doubted the stones were on the beach. Much of the other band's tents had been left behind on the bluff after that battle. The few tents on the beach looked like they served only as storage, while the few armed men present were sleeping out in the open, under tarps. The castle appeared dark and void of life. The half-elf doubted anyone was currently in the castle, and she proposed that they were probably sleeping in the comforts of cabins on board the boat. Having scouted thoroughly with no real plan of what to attempt next, she had returned to the watchtower.

"So, now what?" Salgor asked. "What's your plan when the sun rises?"

Cat frowned at the dwarf, willing to bet he would not accept any course that didn't involve another straightforward fight. She spoke firmly. "We wait and watch for an opportunity. Stealing the stones won't be enough if we can't get off the island. Fighting may only put us in a quick grave. We'll need the proper timing to carry off a theft and get away with our skins intact. That ship may be our only escape."

244

Salgor shook his head in disagreement. "We should hit them as soon as possible, maybe even go down there right now and beat them up before they get a chance to defend themselves."

Even as he said it, the expressions on the faces of the other companions indicated they were unwilling to try such a gamble. Cat offered another choice. "We might also simply try exploring that castle. Maybe it holds the clues to help figure out what is behind this. It may be that we can set up an ambush inside there."

"Bah!" Salgor spit. "Wake me up when there is some action going on!"

With that, the dwarf laid back and prepared to sleep. The other companions followed his example, rolling themselves into comfortable positions around the fire. Petrow stayed up to guard until the next watch, as they agreed that a sentry should be kept overnight. The inside of the tower quieted, interrupted by the sounds of rain splashing against the outside walls. Sleep claimed them one by one. Trestan Karok had one last thought before he fell asleep. He missed his father. For some reason, the young smith couldn't get his home out of his mind.

"Goodnight father."

*   *   *   *   *

Hebden Karok stirred restlessly, pacing his house as if he could chase down his elusive sleep. He stopped in a doorway, holding a lit candle in one hand and sipping from a mug with the other.

The warm drink had cooled to room temperature, but Hebden paid it no mind. Nor did he pay much heed to the low-burning candle in his other hand. His aged eyes scanned the room with curious intensity. The lone bed's linens had been made up about a week ago and hadn't been slept in since. Even though Trestan had spent that one night back in his hometown, the young man hadn't even enjoyed the comfort of his bed. Off to one corner, a simple cabinet that usually contained Trestan's clothes and personal belongings now stored only his work shirt and pants. The emptiness in the cabinet stretched to envelop the rest of the house. On top of the cabinet sat a candle. Trestan had blown it out that morning after donning his armor and removing all he had cared to take. Left behind were old toys from boyhood. Several bronze game pieces sat abandoned next to a cloth game board. Leaning in the corner was one end of the broken staff which had been brought back from the bluff battle. Trestan kept it for sentimental reasons, but the young man didn't need it on his new adventure.

As much as Hebden's eyes searched, he couldn't find the answers he sought. He worried about what paths his son would walk, or which ones he would never walk again. The older smith could picture a time when Trestan was a baby in his mother's arms. Hebden remembered comforting his boy after a smith's hammer fell on his foot when he played with it. Hebden's look into the past found no clues to see the future. All it confirmed was that his only son had grown into a man and left to make his own choices in the world. In a flash of years, the days of youth had flown away, never to return. As Hebden stared into the vacant room, he wished he could have a few of those years back. Trestan went with his

245

blessings, but it didn't spare Hebden Karok from worrying about his son. The years since the death of Hebden's wife had been alleviated by the presence of that growing boy. Now the young man might not come back…or if he did, he might not stay. Either way, Hebden could not help but feel a mix of loneliness and pride for the man he fathered.

He had no good singing voice, but he whispered the words of a play from older years.

Oh, where has the child strayed?
Years passing until full bloom
Flower of my life, gone away
And I stare into an empty bedroom.

The linen on the bed
Lays flat and evenly spread
Old toys of youth lay discarded nearby
Time here is suspended
From the moment youth ended
How fast have the years gone by?

Oh, where has the child strayed?
Years passing until full bloom
Flower of my life, gone away
And I stare into an empty bedroom.

Some voices I do hear
Though none now are spoken here
All are memories passed down through the years
Quiet darkness rules about
No more cries, screams nor shouts
Just silence, except the sounds of my tears.

Oh, where has the child strayed?
Years passing until full bloom
Flower of my life, gone away
And I stare into an empty bedroom.

I pray blessed you'll be
Though you wander far from me
But know that my heart journeys with you
Over roads that you may roam
And hardships yet unknown
Let a moral compass guide you true.

Oh, where has the child strayed?
Years passing until full bloom
Flower of my life, gone away
And I cry inside an empty bedroom.

Hebden choked over the last words. He steadied himself with a deep breath, then turned to leave the room. He paused and spoke as if his son might hear him from afar. "Goodnight my boy. I hope you someday realize the love between a father and son. Sadly, I don't think anyone truly realizes it until their own son has grown and gone away. Gods watch over you whenever I can't."

CHAPTER 22

The companions nimbly picked their way around rocks and trees to approach the castle from behind. Cat led the way, taking them along the far side of the ridge from the sailor encampment. They hoped to pass into the castle unnoticed. Cat's attempts to keep the party moving stealthily were sabotaged by a battle-hungry dwarf, who stomped and spoke out as they walked. Salgor desired a fight, and would not care if the fight sprung on them as long as he could wet his axe with a wizard's blood. The dwarf had only himself to blame that Cat picked a route even more roundabout than was probably needed. The companions approached the castle under the cover of its own shadow, cast by the morning sun.

The castle looked ancient and foreign. Curves and wave-motifs in the architecture differed from anything seen in Kashmer Protectorate. Vines and greenery climbed every stone buttress and crack. The towers and walls forming the sides seemed to be almost one large building, inside and out. This was not a castle within walls, as much as it was an oversized keep. It loomed four stories high, topped by a ring of battlements and guard emplacements. There were poles at the top to display banners, but any such decoration had been ripped away by the elements. Old shutters creaked and banged in the wind. The foundations of other, smaller buildings patterned the approach. These scattered homes and businesses had been razed long ago. The companions moved among the ruined walls and stone piles furtively, eyeing the battlements for signs of sentries. The husks of the smaller buildings added to the overall gloom and loneliness emanating from the keep. In the realm of Dhea Loral, such ruins were all too common after the Godswars and the dark years that followed.

The companions avoided the southern front gate. Many keeps had smaller doors by which servants could go about as they pleased. This castle was no exception. A rotted servant's door stood ajar on the side closest to them. With no one in sight, it seemed to be their best course to gain entry. Salgor, by his very nature, would have welcomed an enemy guarding the door. The dwarf fighter became even more impatient as the party stopped and quietly observed the door.

"I see nay need for sneaking in a group to yonder door," he said. "We already made more noise than a group of miners running from a cave-in. If there was anyone there, they've seen us."

The shadow of the castle, scattered trees and low foundations together could not give them full cover from any observers. As Salgor spoke, Trestan and Petrow both felt the unnerving sensation that eyes might already be looking down on them. Mel, as always, seemed unbothered by any hint of danger. The gnome looked at the castle in awe of what it must have been like in its glory days.

Salgor spoke again, when his first comment seemed to go unheeded. "We aren't quiet. Either they see us o' they don't, and the longer we stay in the open the more likely someone will see us. It gives them more time to arrange a surprise."

248

An exasperated Cat nodded her head in agreement. "I think you are right. We might as well get across this area and into the keep as fast as we can. Try to make as little noise as possible. Go straight for the door."

The group darted into the exposed terrain, making a line for the open entry. Trestan and Petrow looked at the windows more than the ground in front of them. Their imagination turned every sound and movement into a possible observer. A bird flew out of one window, startling Petrow enough to nearly trip him up. Salgor caught him by the arm and propelled onward.

"Keep your eyes o' your feet and make a straight line for the door, young axe-warrior. Get yourself inside quick and safe."

The group made it to the archway without any obvious signs of being discovered. Cat slipped past the door without having to move it. Trestan had to push at it a bit, old hinges squealed as the door protested. He paused, but Salgor didn't. The dwarf shoved Petrow and Trestan through the opening. A breathless Mel came last, taking some last looks at the scenery before following the others inside. Their eyes had to adjust to the darker interior. The entry room ran straight and narrow like a hallway, ending at another door. They observed torch brackets and coat pegs on the walls. Cat saw several open slits in the stone walls of the room. She looked up and saw holes in the ceiling leading to the room above. The half-elf looked at them curiously.

Cat's eyes widened. She grabbed Trestan's arm firmly. "Into the next room, now!"

Cat pulled Trestan along, quickly followed by the others. They all entered a room that branched in more directions. As they paused again to consider their next move, Trestan had to ask, "What were those openings for? Was that what had you worried?"

"Aye," Cat responded. "Those were murder holes, in case an enemy breached the side door."

Petrow and Trestan stood dumbfounded wondering what murder holes were, but Cat and Salgor proceeded to explore this new room further. Mel understood the expressions on their faces, and as always he was ready to share his knowledge. The gnome went back to the doorway and pointed up at the openings.

"Those are made for castle defense. If someone is besieging the keep, and they break into that side door, those openings allow the castle defenders to turn this room into a death trap. Archers occupy the rooms on either side, firing through those side ports, while men in the room upstairs drop boiling oil or simply stab downwards with spears as the attackers bottle up in this room."

Mel wandered back into the room as he explained. Petrow hissed at him, "Mel, don't stand in there! Get back in here."

Mel chuckled, but walked back to join them. "Nay defenders here or we might be dead by now. Usually attackers have to try bashing down the inner door while arrows and worse things rain down on them. Now imagine adding a wizard to that defense," Mel grinned wickedly. "And then you truly have unholy hell unleashed. That is why those openings are called murder holes."

Petrow and Trestan looked back into the entry room out of morbid curiosity. Both men could only imagine what storming a castle was like from stories, but of course neither had any firsthand experience. The two stared in awe as they imagined what it would look like if a group of attackers poured into the room, only to be held up by a locked door as arrows hit them at close range. Having seen the battle on the bluff, they could imagine men falling in piles as they were assaulted from the walls and above. This room would seem like hell if the defenders were desperate enough to pour burning oil on the heads of those men as well! Trestan could well imagine how Revwar could cause a mass of killings with spells if he had been waiting for them. Imagination painted a vivid picture.

Their attention returned to the inner room and the exits branching off from it. Cat and Salgor had glanced through open doorways while the two young men listened to Mel. The half-elf and dwarf confirmed that it connected to a kitchen and storage. In this way, servants could go out, get supplies, and then walk back into the kitchen area without going through the main gates. The room smelled of old mold and rot. Rat droppings on the floor gave evidence of the current rulers of the castle. The companions appreciated that the door allowed a breeze to carry some of the smell outside.

Salgor could not help but keep his nose to one door that led to a stairway down. A bad smell wafted from below, but behind it was something vaguely familiar. He gave a wide, yellowish smile through his beard as he revealed what caught his interest. "I think this is a wine cellar. That is worth checking out before we leave."

* * * * *

One figure walked up the beach with the thunder of muscles in his every step. Another contrasted the first with his graceful gait. The woman of the group had blonde hair glowing in the sunlight even as her black armor radiated cold. Their wizard, elvish build and yellow eyes, strode with confidence and superiority. Revwar and Savannah walked in front, while Bortun and Loung silently followed.

The four adventurers approached the front door of the castle, leaving the camp of sailors and mercenaries behind. The men from the ship were glad to be able to keep their distance from the imposing castle, whispers told of the haunted structure. The sailors had given up enough blood already, and they weren't about to taunt the unknown ghosts that dwelled in such an ancient ruin. The ship's crew proved content to relax on a beach and watch over the ship until whatever mysterious business they had here was finished. After the disastrous battle on the mainland, they had continued to set sail under the threat of what Revwar and his party would do to them if they didn't. Each hoped they would still have a fat purse and be rid of the bullying minotaur soon. If such was not forthcoming, they would be just as happy to deliver the party wherever it wanted to go and then find their own safe port for drinking in honor of dead friends.

Unconcerned with the worries of the men on the beach, the four relic thieves walked into the open doors of the castle. The giant gates of the main entrance had long ago been ripped aside by unknown intruders. Pieces of rusted metal and rotted beams littered the threshold. The adventurers swept past the portal with no concern for any ghosts from within.

250

"There isn't one left among them who can claim to have a spine," Revwar commented. The elf strode along gracefully and with purpose. He wore a black robe trimmed with red, embroidered with various sigils and magical runes. The elf's long, silvery hair was braided in high fashion. He dressed in his best for today's special occasion. As usual he still wore many magical pouches, a slender dagger, and carried his magic staff. His topic of conversation centered on the crew of the *Silver Trident*. "All their smart ones seem to have been left dead back on the bluff. One disastrous morning, and all their strongest backs and leaders were laid low, breaking their resolve."

Savannah ventured alongside the elf into the foyer of the keep. The high-ceiling room must have been a grand entryway in its living years. Broken busts and statues of forgotten men stared through age-worn, sightless eyes at the intruders who crossed their ancient threshold. Sunlight filtered through tall windows baring remnants of stained glass clutching to the aging frames. The marble floor and stone walls teemed with vines and invading plant life. The faithful servant of DeLaris, Goddess of Death, took in every detail. She had been in this room before, but the beauty and silent secrets of the long-dead castle intrigued her. The cleric's favored garments were the ones she normally wore: black armor etched with the symbols of her goddess and her heavy flail at her hip. The only thing missing was her skull-helmet, abandoned somewhere in a stand of trees back on the mainland. The blonde woman found a visual substitute for her missing helm, inspired by the spirit of her dark religion. Savannah had liberally applied black makeup around her eyes, giving the appearance of sunken orbits, akin to a skeleton. Her blue eyes stood as stark contrast to the dark coloring, accentuating the look. This was a common appearance DeLaris' clerics adopted to pronounce their faith in public.

As the cleric listened to Revwar's words, she voiced a question of her own without so much as a look in his direction. "And if I may ask, how comfortable is the captain's cabin?"

The wizard grinned, "Do I sense a hint of jealousy? Did I not also share the cabin with all of you over a supply of old rum? Forgive me, but with the top officers of the ship dead it was mine for the taking. The crew didn't seem to put up much resistance when I moved in there."

A low voice growled behind them both. "You could have offered the room to someone who needed the space more than you do."

Revwar did not bother to look over his shoulder at the hulking minotaur. "I heard you have nay problems stretching out in your current quarters."

With the ship being a rather small place to pack a bunch of men during potentially long voyages, the minotaur slept on the common deck with the majority of the crew. That deck level was cramped for someone of Bortun's bulk. More than once, the minotaur had bumped his thick skull and horn against the rafters. When it came time to stretch out and sleep, the minotaur easily found all the room he needed. Even without the loss of crew after the last battle, no one was about to sleep too close to the smelly, arrogant creature. The rest of the sailors observed how roughly the minotaur treated anything that impeded his movement. Hammocks had been ripped apart and wooden stools bashed aside whenever they interfered with the ability to stretch his eight-foot frame.

251

The creature snorted, "A small cave is more welcome than the hold of a ship. I should like to be done with sea travel before I start using my axe to make more space."

Bortun's companions realized he spoke frankly.

Continuing onward, the four adventurers passed through several reception chambers before approaching a large chamber at the hub of the castle. They entered the largest room in the entire structure: a court which had been the center of rule in years past. The once-lively throne room opened before them with cold silence. A tall ceiling reached up past the next floor, where a balcony provided a vantage point for spectators in ages past. Chandeliers of large size were suspended by rusty chains. Though no lit candles spilled forth from the chandeliers, the room was still bathed in a glow. Light sprang forth from magically lit stones embedded high on the walls. The thrones stood mutely on a raised dais on one end of the room, barely standing on weathered frames.

All of these items showed their age as being around since the castle's abandonment, but there were traces of recent habitation in the room as well. Magical runes formed patterns around the center of the chamber. New tables sat near one wall. Mixtures of magical chemicals and scrolls of arcane lore perched upon them. Pottery jars and other containers held various secret items necessary for the preparation of the room and the casting of a specific spell. A ceremonial stand sat in a position close to the center of the floor runes, supporting a book with arcane instructions. Next to this stand stood a smaller table which currently held nothing. The old, musky smell of the castle had been disguised by aromatic herbs burning in small bowls around the room. A large campfire sat on the open floor, leaving blackened scorch marks on the stone. This fire was currently just warm embers, but more firewood had been stacked nearby.

Revwar looked about the room proudly. "It looks ready. We should go over the runes and markings again to make sure nothing was smudged or disturbed. Loung, please place the items on the empty table near the book stand. We should start a fire to boil some more materials as well."

Loung wore his traditional silks from Tariyka. As usual, the silks left visible a muscular chest and strong arms. In one hand he held a bamboo fighting staff, but in the other he carried a simple bag. He carried the bag over to where Revwar had indicated. The martial artist voiced a question as he went. "I never asked, but why did you pick this place to start?"

Revwar answered, though his eyes stayed on the decorations the group had added to the old throne room. "This location was picked for us, mainly due to its secluded but defensible nature. We could have done this at any place in the realm, but secrecy is paramount. It needed to be away from prying eyes and interfering parties. Savannah and I were directed that even the theft of the stones had to be done with care, so that we could delay anyone realizing they had been stolen."

The wizard paused, "Well, the one I procured years ago wasn't subtle, but it shouldn't have led anyone into thinking I was after that specific stone. Mostly, this place offers a secluded location by which a new empire can be launched in secret. The forces we muster will have time to get fortified and settled in before others become aware of the danger."

252

Loung set the bag, with its unseen contents, on the stand near the center of the room. The Tariykan considered the words. He asked, "Who are we keeping this secret from?"

Revwar flashed a dangerous glare at the human. "From a god."

Loung's eyes opened wide at that statement. "A god? One who could simply strike us down without warning at any time?"

The elf shook his head, "That would be a breach of the Covenant, wouldn't it? Gods nay longer may strike mortals or walk the realms with us. Gods are bound by the Covenant, and they simply can't interfere with the mortal realms in such an open manner. Since the devastation of the Godswars, the deities have forbidden themselves from directly interfering in mortal affairs ever again. However, if this god is alerted to what we are doing, and I dare not mention a name which might attract his attention, he could send a message to his followers to intercept us. Though a god could not strike us down, they have followers they can use. We may find ourselves dealing with a small army of paladins and clerics trying to knock down our door before we even get started. Therefore, we needed secrecy. I seriously doubt any chosen champion has been sent. Our tracks were covered well despite the revelation of the stolen stone to that young scrapper and that foolish noblewoman. Once we complete this ceremony, I think we will have already gained enough of a head start to leave nations unaware and vulnerable for what will spawn forth here.

"Besides, we are agents working on behalf of two goddesses who seek to settle an old score. If successful, a new empire will sweep across Dhea Loral. Until then, we will get all the support we need from DeLaris, as well as…"

A creaking noise, followed by a loud curse, interrupted the elf. Savannah had been working at building up the fire off to one side, when her path took her over a loose grate in the floor. The rusty grate served as a hatch for gathering or lowering items from storerooms below, and from previous experience the adventurers knew it was barely held closed due to the wear of time. A little pressure might cause the hatch to fall open, spilling a person into the room below. The cleric froze at realizing where her careless steps had taken her. Slowly, she stepped off to the side, getting her weight off of the dangerous bars. Once out of danger, she gave a quick prayer to her patron deity.

"You must really be careful," Revwar spoke. "I don't know what held that grate up for all these years, but it's not exactly a safe place to walk."

Savannah glared at the degraded bars that were questionable protection from falling into the room below. "You'd think I'd remember the first time I stepped there and it shifted. That thing is liable to fall through the floor at any time. I don't want to be the one to ride it down into the cellar. I serve DeLaris faithfully in her control over death, and I'd rather not be standing before her because my footsteps were careless."

Revwar chuckled, one of the rare times he did so. The elf turned back to his study of the magic symbols. Savannah looked to him and asked, "You seem to be in a good mood. You are really looking forward to this, aren't you?"

"Of course!" He answered. "It's not every day you get to summon forth a powerful demon, let alone one that is such a strong ally."

*   *   *   *   *

The party from Troutbrook navigated long-abandoned passages, their footfalls avoiding animal refuse littering the halls, while venturing toward the front of the castle. Unfortunately, the current passage dead-ended in a rather odd room. It seemed devoid of purpose, except for a circular metal platform in the middle of that room. Around the perimeter of the metal plate they observed stamped words in a language other than the human tongue. Oddly, the ceiling directly above the area opened into a vertical shaft leading straight up. The shaft spanned a meter, large enough that a person could easily climb through it with the proper climbing equipment. Cat and Salgor, in the lead, exchanged questioning glances as they guessed how this room had been used. Neither approached close enough to look up the shaft, fearing what tricks the room might hold.

From the back of the group, Mel grew curious. He couldn't see past the wall of tall people. "What do you see up there? Anything interesting?"

Salgor irritably grunted. "Nay. The room contains nothing other than a metal disk and a hole in the ceiling. You could get more excitement watching a dead orc lie on the ground."

Mel's ears perked up at the description and he promptly asked, "Does it look magical?"

Cat and Salgor both shrugged. Mel saw the motions from their backs, but wished for a closer look. Gnomes liked puzzles and odd rooms, yet he could see nothing from his position in the back. Cat added, "It might be magical. The metal plate is shiny and polished as if new."

"Ooh!" A thought struck Mel. "Tell me, are there small pebbles scattered around the plate, and is it about three feet in diameter?"

The half-elf looked about the area and saw several small stones near the platform, though none stood on top of it. "Aye, it looks like you say. It is three feet across and several small stones near it. Let's get you up front so that you can see this thing."

The group parted for the gnome sorcerer. As soon as he saw the metal disk on the small platform, he let out a squeal of delight. Mel smiled and eagerly rubbed his hands together. He had no qualms about walking closer to the platform than Cat or Salgor dared. Mel grabbed one of the small stones on the floor, and he tossed it towards the magical disk. Moments before the pebble would have landed on the plate, it stopped in midair. Suddenly, an unseen force hurled the rock straight up the vertical shaft. A moment later, it fell back down. This time it did not stop in midair just above the platform. It landed on top of the metal piece with a ting and bounced off to the side.

Mel giggled, "Hee, hee. I'm glad I tested it before stepping there. Nobody say a word please, it could be dangerous." Turning back to the plate, he whispered, "Zero."

He stood on top of the metal disk and looked up. The companions traded befuddled glances while the gnome looked up the vertical shaft. The gnome arched his head all the way back, and he even spun in place a bit as he looked up the shaft from slightly different angles. Finally he stepped off the platform, displaying an infectious smile. The others found themselves smiling back at the gnome, with no clue as to why. One exception was Salgor,

254

who already deduced the metal plate was magical, and therefore something to be hated and feared.

Mel looked back and forth between the metal plate and the rest of the party. "I always wanted one of these in my home, if I live in one that has a few floors. It's a Vertically Mounted Magical Elevation/Lifting/Descending Assistant. They are quite nice to have, but expensive and sometimes used as more of a status symbol. I didn't realize the mountain gnomes have been making them since back during the Godswars era. The bigger races tend to call it by a shorter name. They call it a 'lift'. I'm surprised to see one here."

"Another gnomish magical device?" Salgor shook his head. "Didn't we learn something from the breakable flying machine? I won't have anything to do with it. Let's turn around this minute!"

Intrigue showed plainly upon Petrow's face. "Mel, what is it and what do people do with it?"

Mel looked at him, "You haven't guessed? Gnomes name many devices after their basic use. If this was on its side it would be a Horizontally Mounted Magical Pushing/Moving Assistant."

Only puzzled stares greeted his explanation. Mel continued, "Anyway, the point is that you use these to transfer people or objects to different levels within a tall structure. A person calls out…well, I'll just show you."

The gnome started to step near the device, but stopped in mid-stride rather abruptly. "Whew, that was close." He looked back to his companions. "I forgot to clear the last command. That's why you saw that pebble launch upwards the first time. The 'lift', as you all would call it, had never been cleared after it heard the last command."

"Cleared?" Trestan had a hand on his head as if already suffering a headache from figuring out strange gnomish devices. "Gnomes seem to come up with some odd ideas. Forgive me for saying it."

"Odd?" Mel felt insulted. "This is the most useful device since someone invented the sail, which helped advance boat travel! Anyways, let me clear it of the last digit spoken. After that, I'll call for which floor I want. Don't anyone speak a word, until I've told you how this works."

Mel approached the metal platform again, and as before he spoke the numeral "zero" before stepping onto the device. He then planted both feet firmly on the metal disk. The companions looked at him as if he might explode or suffer some other nasty fate. Mel then spoke the numeral "four", waving back to the others as he did so.

To their astonishment, Mel's body shot straight up into the vertical shaft. The metal plate never moved, and there was no impressive magical display, simply the sight of the gnome shooting skyward until the edge of the ceiling hid the rest of his ascent. Unlike the pebble which had fallen back down the first time, Mel didn't drop back down. Several seconds passed quietly, with no sign that the gnome was returning for a hard landing.

A voice called out from somewhere up the shaft. "How is that for luxury travel, eh? Nay need to climb ladders. Nay need to lug a heavy package up several flights of steps. Just say the number of floors you want to ascend and the magic pushes you up! I'll be right back down. It's as easy as going up. Zero!"

A moment later, the gnome dropped out of the shaft as fast as a normal person falls. The companions had a brief flash of panic when it had appeared that the gnome was falling to his death. Before reaching the ground, he slowed abruptly in midair, and then settled softly on the metal platform. The group remembered to breathe again after he landed safely. Mel exited the platform with a small flourish. "And that's how it works! Let's all go up and check out the upper levels."

Salgor's eyes widened with alarm. "Nay! We all turn around right now, quickly walk away, and then lock any door we find that could ever again lead back to this room!"

Mel threw up his hands, "When am I going to get more respect from you, Salgor? My mountain brothers come up with some pretty decent inventions. You may not have liked *Dovewing*, but surely you could see the uses of such a wonderful craft! This lift may be the quickest way we can use to get to the upper floors of this place and search up there."

Cat walked over to where the metal platform rested on the floor. The half-elf tried to get a look up into the vertical shaft. Mel noticed her movements and was quick to warn her. "I wouldn't do that, not unless you clear the lift first. Anything that hovers over it, in the vicinity of its magical pulse, will be lifted to their requested destination. You don't have to step on the device to make it work; leaning over it will send you upwards as well."

Cat wisely stopped short of the strange device. "How do I clear it? What does that mean anyway?"

Mel went into his lecturing mode. "Well, when was the last time someone here said 'to', 'forehead', 'won', 'tent', or even 'sex'?"

The group exchanged puzzling glances behind Mel as he continued. "Each of those words can be mistaken for a numeral command. I believe someone said the word 'to', just before you approached that platform. The elevation device can't differentiate when certain words sound just like numbers. It would respond to the word 'to' the same way as it would respond to someone asking it if they could go upwards 'two' floors. 'Forehead' would send you upwards four floors before you realized you said the wrong thing. That's why I kept asking for quiet when I was trying out the device. That's also why I first approached it after throwing one of these many pebbles on top of it, to see if it had a command that had not yet been carried out. Once it delivers a person or item to the requested floor, or if someone asks for floor 'zero', the device will not send you upwards. In fact, requesting 'zero' is how you return safely to the ground floor if you jump into the shaft from one of the floors above. The device cushions and stops your fall right on top of it. I should also add that when you request a floor, it doesn't just throw you up in the air and let you fall again. It throws you up to the right floor on top of a magical cushion, which lasts for about a second, before you drop. This gives you a chance to float for a moment at the right height, and grab the bars on the sides of the doors up there. If you were just sending up a package, someone on an upper floor would have time to extend a plank underneath the floating package, then retract the plank after catching the package."

Petrow and Trestan traded glances, thinking that gnome devices certainly had weird oddities. Mel continued, "Another nice thing: this is portable. See those notches in the stone foundation, under the sides? The whole thing is just a flat disk. You can carry it to another location and use it."

256

Cat softly spoke the numeral 'zero', then approached the device. With a nervous smile, she lightly stepped one foot onto the metal platform. Then the other. She turned to the others and put a hand over her chest as if trying to still her rapid heartbeat. From where she now stood, Cat looked upward into the shaft. As soon as she had taken a good look, she stepped off the metal plate. Cat made sure she was well away from the device when she spoke again.

"There seems to be four floors to the keep."

It was Mel's turn to look puzzled. "I only saw three!"

Cat turned to regard him, "Three doors up the shaft, four floors total, including this one."

Mel suddenly slapped himself in the head. "Pardon me, I forgot. You go by the backwards human terms of measuring floors."

Just when Cat, Petrow, Trestan and Salgor thought they were as confused as they could get, Mel surprised them with another fact of gnome life. "Gnomes count floors differently than humans do. To you, this is the first floor; to us it is either the ground floor or ground zero. If you go one floor up, you call it the second floor; however, we call it the first floor. That is an abbreviated meaning: the first floor *up from the ground.* Your third floor is our second floor *up from the ground.* And so on."

Trestan nodded his head, even as he held back laughter at this dose of gnomish logic, "Ok, I get it. So, to get to the third floor in human terms, I would ask the device for floor number two. This would propel me two gnome floors up from the ground floor, landing me on the human's third floor."

"Wrong. Something is wrong with your logic." Mel looked at Trestan with raised eyebrows.

Trestan now stood more confused than ever. "What floor should I ask for? I thought that you just said that third floor to a human is second floor *up* in a gnome's view of things?"

"Oh, you forgot to convert for size." Mel explained, "These devices are built for gnome floors, not human floors. Humans are twice our height! Two gnome floors equal one human floor. I'm sure that whoever bought this was reminded that they had to ask for the proper floor in terms of not only gnome floors, but the size between gnome floors. You have to go up two gnomish floors for every human floor."

About this time, Petrow, Trestan and Cat wished they had started writing all this down to keep track of things. Salgor just rolled his eyes and shook his head as Mel went on. "So, to go up one human floor, you ask the device for 'two'. If I asked it for three gnomish floors up, I would find myself stopping between human-sized floors, specifically floors two and three in human terms, before I would find myself falling again because there was nay door there with bars to grab. If you want to go to the third floor…pardon me, the fourth floor in human terms…you ask for 'six'. Cut the number six in half, and you see that this propels you upwards three floors—to human level four. Am I clear on that point?"

The whole explanation proved ridiculous enough that Petrow burst out laughing. Trestan quickly followed suit. While the two young men found this all amusing, Salgor was quick to realize a flaw in the gnomish design.

257

The dwarf motioned to the device and asked, behind a devilish grin, "So all these things are built the same, with nay concept of whether they are in a human-sized building or a gnomish cave?"

"Aye," Mel replied. "It is the same concept either way. Objects all weigh a certain amount. The device is given a floor to shoot for, it is smart enough to be able to weigh the person or object it is lifting, and then provides sufficient force to propel them up to the right level. So whether the object is five pounds, or a two hundred pound man, the device senses the weight and tosses them up to the requested floor."

"But my question is," Salgor leaned forward, squinting at Mel. "The device doesn't know how many floors are above it, does it? What happens if you ask for a floor higher than what exists?"

Mel gulped, "Well, mind you, riding lifts are still considered safer than riding horses. All lifts should have a number posted which will inform you the safest height you can be lifted to without hitting the ceiling. Also, if you ever do find that you weren't able to get a hold of the floor you wanted, remember to say 'zero' again before you hit the bottom. Then the device can catch you and set you down easy. But generally, the device isn't smart enough to know how high you can actually go, since it is designed to be portable and re-used elsewhere. Gnome lifts are always set to a maximum height of fifteen levels."

Salgor spoke again, "My question remains. What happens if you ask for a floor higher than the ceiling? Let's say I moved the device over here where there is a low ceiling and asked to go to fifteen?"

Mel winced, "Well, gnomish engineers expect people to use their devices properly, and at their own responsibility. The machine would weigh you and would provide sufficient force to throw you upwards fifteen gnomish levels. Needless to say, you would hit that ceiling rather hard."

Trestan and Petrow stopped laughing.

After Mel's instructions regarding the lift, the party had a discussion on where to go next. The talk degenerated into an argument lasting over half an hour. Mel wanted to use the lift and explore the upper levels quicker. Cat expressed caution over its use, but also favored searching the higher levels. The more Petrow dwelled on the lift, the more he realized how valuable it must be. Whether or not they used it, he felt that if they survived their adventure they should take it with them to see what kind of cash they could get for it. The mere idea of taking the dangerous item caused several protests from the others.

Mel offered the most caution, "Be warned that unless you have a special magical cover over that disk, it can hear everything people say. If someone says a number or a word that could be interpreted as a number, the device will react to that and launch whatever is in front of it."

Petrow quieted, so Mel felt that his point had gotten across. Nevertheless, the young handyman kept stealing glances at the item, appraising its value. Salgor refused to have anything to do with the magical lift. The dwarf reacted with typical stubbornness, vowing to not move one step closer to the device. Trestan voiced his willingness to go along if the others did, but he preferred to finish exploring the ground floor first. In the end,

258

Cat decided to do things her way. Though she was more scared than she would admit, she approached the device. Remembering to clear it by saying "zero", she stood upon the lift.

"Two," she said, ever so softly that for a moment they doubted the device heard the request.

With a scream, she suddenly launched into the shaft. The others could not see from their vantage point, but Cat rose two standard gnomish levels, (or one level in human terms), and quickly grabbed the handles at that portal. Once she safely swung herself inside the doorway on the second floor, the screaming noise turned to whooping and hollering of pure excitement over the thrilling ride. The others listened as Cat let out her excitement.

"Who's next to join me?" Cat's voice called down to them. "It's fun! I only went up to the next level. It's really not that bad when you experience it yourself."

Mel stepped closer to the metal plate. "I'll go last. I will stay behind and make sure that everyone gets up safely. I'll make sure the device is cleared before any approach, and I'll call out 'zero' if I see you falling because you weren't ready to grab the handles."

Salgor was quick to protest. "We need to keep together! I will not use that infernal magical contraption."

Petrow chided the dwarf, "You are going to let a little gnomish toy block you from getting your axe on that wizard?"

Salgor glared at the blue-eyed man, "You're trying to tempt me. I don't need that gnomish catapult to get my hands on him."

Trestan mustered up the courage to approach the platform next. He called up to Cat that he was coming up. Mel cleared the disk before the young smith stepped onto the plate. Trestan hesitated, taking in a deep breath to steady his nerves. Without being asked, Mel took the initiative and called out 'two'. Trestan's eyes went wide, and he half-turned to argue that he wasn't ready. There was no time to speak before he was tossed up the shaft by the power of the device. Mel watched from below, but all Petrow and Salgor could observe was a scream coming from up in the shaft. The scream started to get louder and closer. Mel shouted out "zero", a bare second before Trestan dropped back into view. Although the shaft was rather narrow, the young man splayed out with arms and legs as far as he could stretch to catch the walls as he fell. The armor coverings over his knees and elbows scraped metal on stone as he slid back down. The fall was stopped abruptly but easily, and Trestan drifted down the last two feet to rest easily on the platform. With a bit of heavy breathing, and panic in his brown eyes, he unsteadily got back to his feet. Trestan looked up the shaft. Cat peered down at him as she waited. He smoothed his mustache, as if the close call had somehow messed up the long whiskers.

"Not bad," Mel spoke, being careful about what words he used. "Try again. Two!"

Trestan tried to hold up a hand to stop the gnome, but again he catapulted upward. This time, he succeeded in grabbing the bars by the sides of the doorway. Cat reached out a hand to haul him over. He easily got past the doorway and into the hallway on the second level. He breathed rapidly and looked pale, eliciting a smile from Cat. Before long, the young man also gave in to laughter. A glance around the new floor revealed a hallway which branched to several doors.

There was some time before the next person could be convinced to ascend the open shaft. Petrow insisted he was willing and able to go, but he wanted to be the last one up. Mel Bellringer wanted to stay behind as much as possible to help the others. Salgor Bandago refused to use the magical device at all. Finally, the dwarf was convinced to follow the rest of the party, but he did it his own way. The dwarf cleared the magical device with his bellowing voice, then got his fingers into the holes around the sides of the plate. As Mel had stated, the lift was a thin, metal disk. The dwarf dragged it away from the shaft, setting it in a corner of the room. The stout axe-warrior produced a length of rope and a grappling hook. He threw up the hook, Cat and Trestan secured it. The dwarf planned to go up the shaft the old-fashioned way, and he didn't want the magical device under him when he did so. In stubborn defiance, the dwarf warrior climbed hand over hand up the shaft under his own power. Mel stood underneath, shaking his head at the dwarf's mistrust for handy magical items.

Once Salgor was safely up, Mel prepared to go next. The gnome dragged the metal plate back to its proper spot. "Are you sure Petrow? I should go last to make sure you get up safely."

Petrow put on a disarming grin. "I'll be fine. If I fall, I call out 'zero'. Besides I have something in mind."

The gnome shrugged and used the lift to get up to the second floor. Once up, he stood near the entryway in case Petrow had any troubles. Cat, Trestan and Salgor were already scouting out the hallway. When Petrow appeared in the doorway, Mel noticed a rope tied to his belt, stretching back down the shaft.

The gnome tilted his head and tugged at his beard. "What is that rope doing there?"

Petrow gave a sheepish grin, "Well, I just can't leave this behind. I'm going to find what I can get for it."

The young man turned around and started pulling on the rope. Before long, over Mel's stream of protests, the other end of the rope appeared. Petrow had tied it around the magical metal disk. The young handyman undid his knot, but started to strap the disk to his backpack.

Trestan, Cat and Salgor, all scattered along the length of the hallway, started to talk Petrow out of it. Salgor actually opened up a rotted door, using it as an extra shield in case the magical device sent anything flying at him.

Finally, Trestan said the wrong word, "Petrow! Just put it down. We have other things to worry about!"

The gnomish device could not discern the difference between "to" and the number two. Propped on its side, and strapped to Petrow's back, it attempted to launch him parallel to the floor. Both backpack and disk ripped away in one direction, while Petrow catapulted across the floor in the other direction. The young man flew several meters before hitting the ground and sliding to a halt. He had been lucky that he wasn't facing a wall when the wrong word had been spoken, or he would have had more bruises to show for it.

Petrow groaned, "I see your point. I'll leave it."

Trestan ended up being the closest to where the device landed. He shushed everyone, spoke "Zero", and carried the disk into one of the rooms. A short distance inside

260

the door there stood a stone bench which butted up against one wall. Trestan propped the device on its side, putting one edge on the bench and leaning it against the wall. He belatedly saw the humor in his positioning. By setting it on its side, he had now turned it into a Horizontally Mounted Pushing thingamajig, instead of a Vertically Mounted Elevation whatchamacallit—as Mel had referenced earlier. Once done, he turned his back on the device and left the room.

No sooner had he returned when everyone reacted to a fearful sound. Mel yelled out for help, but the sound faded away for some reason. Trestan and the others glanced frantically around the hallway, but no immediate sign of the gnome was to be found.

Cat pointed to a small opening in the stonework, set against the wall near the floor. "Last I saw he was ducking for cover in there when Petrow was thrown across the floor."

Trestan and Cat rushed to the small opening. A rusted grate once covered the hole, but it sat against the wall nearby as it had for maybe a thousand years. The opening itself seemed to be either for ventilation, drainage of chamber pots, or maybe some other type of disposal used by occupants in times long gone. As soon as the two companions checked the opening, they saw an interior slick with grime, sloping down. They could hear Mel's voice echoing for help from the depths of this new shaft.

"This is too narrow for everyone but me," Cat lamented. "Oh, where did he end up?"

*   *   *   *   *

Mel slid down a slick, grime-coated ramp into darkness. He yelled until his tiny lungs emptied, took a sharp breath, and screamed again. A light became visible, and he reached out for it. His body jolted as he caught the edge of a portal. He hung there for a moment, wondering where he was. There was a good light source coming from the room past the rusty grate, although he could not see much of it. Fearing the dark depths of the tunnel more than the lit room, he prepared a means to open the grate. He utilized a small cubby space between the grate and the slick ramp. His small stature barely fit.

He reached into one of his many pouches and retrieved a small bottle. Careful not to get any of the substance on himself, he uncorked it and then poured the potion on every corner and edge he could cover. He used up the whole supply as he worked. Smoke wisps curled up from the hissing bars. The bars took on an icy appearance and changed color. Soon the edges were brittle, and a shove from Mel knocked the barrier away. The gnome crawled through and got to his feet.

He was in a large room, an upper balcony looked down from the floor above. A great part of the floor had been marked by magical writing, which grabbed Mel's attention despite other important aspects of the room. Curiosity caused him to thoroughly examine the runes. It wasn't every day that one saw these exact markings, and the presence of them here was quite alarming. The rest of the room was laid out properly for the ceremony, and someone had gone through a lot of trouble to have everything prepared and on hand.

That someone patiently watched him with cold, yellow eyes. Revwar held staff in hand, his fingers wrapped around certain sigils along its length. The elf did not make a threatening move. He simply stared back at the small, unexpected intruder. There was the impression of amusement on the wizard's lips, probably the result of watching the gnome wriggle through that small passage after screaming his head off. However, the eyes betrayed the true menace building within the elf.

The others stood nearby, and all had been paying attention to the source of the noise. Bortun had a stance akin to an animal, muscles taught and tensed to spring. Loung Chao stood calmly, arms folded in front of him. Savannah positioned further away than the others, but due to the miracles granted by her goddess, that was scant comfort.

Since Mel was offered time to speak, he did what came naturally. He put on an easygoing grin and started a conversation. "Pardon me for dropping in like that, it was quite accidental."

Four pairs of stern eyes stared back at him. Since Mel wasn't going to get anywhere that way, he thought he'd try another tactic. "Sure you've got all those symbols done right? It can be very bad if you summon in that tough of a demon and you don't have all the proper protection in place. Hope you've studied up on it a lot."

"I have a good memory, gnome," Revwar spoke. His voice never raised above the level of normal conversation, yet he spoke with enough clarity that he could be understood at a distance. "I had almost forgotten you from when we rode by your little wayside camp. We could have killed you there to silence your tongue, but a dead witness is sometimes more proof of passage than a live one. In return, you sided with that band of troublemakers attacking our camp. You have an annoying habit of sticking your nose into our business. I'm afraid I didn't catch your name, and I'm curious to know."

Mel was only too happy to introduce himself. "My name is Mel Bellringer. I am from the Bellringer family: makers of fine bells, chimes, gongs, and other acoustical instruments. I also dabble in magic, and am a devoted follower of Daerkfyre."

The gnome sorcerer showed no nervousness, but he knew he was in big trouble unless his friends found him fast. The other band looked as if they would injure or kill him at any moment, so during his introduction he slipped one hand down by his belt. As he got a good grip, he pulled out the lightning wand and brought it to bear against his enemies.

"And I'd like to introduce my little friend, the zap-wand!" Mel spoke the command to fire the wand as the other band exploded into motion.

CHAPTER 23

Intense light burst from the tiny wand the gnome held. Thunder echoed through the large chamber and resonated up the shaft to reach the ears of the gnome's companions. The wand's magical blast surged directly at Revwar. The elf had prepared for such a tactic when his group first heard the ruckus in the shaft. Scowling, Revwar raised his forearm. When the blast hit the arm an outline resembling a shield flashed into visibility. Streamers of the wand's energy reflected in jagged patterns throughout the room, putting black spots on the walls. Revwar's group kept low in the face of the deflecting energies, but no harm touched them.

"Uh oh, not good," lamented Mel, as the others began their attack.

Loung sprang to a table and produced a knife. The Tariykan moved forward gracefully on the balls of his feet as he held the knife up for a throw. Bortun gave an animal roar of rage as he charged forward with his large axe. The minotaur covered the room in long strides. Revwar dropped his left arm slightly as he brought forth the hand carrying his staff. His fingers worked deftly on its symbols as he prepared a spell of his own. Savannah took cover behind a doorframe, but Mel could hear the dark cleric chanting to her deity.

Mel kept the wand pointed with his right hand, but his left dug an item out of a pouch on his bandolier. The gnome poured his concentration into that hand's deft movements: hooking a finger one way, twirling another finger, all the time murmuring an arcane phrase. This was a true test of a sorcerer, as well as a worthy challenge for a worshipper of the dwarven god Daerkfyre. With deadly enemies charging and distractions in every direction, he had to hold together the courage and concentration to cast a spell. The magic flowed from his tongue and hand as a mist took form in front of the gnome. Two attacks already sliced the air towards him. Loung's knife spun through the air alongside a deadly beam of magic from the elf wizard.

The mist coalesced into something tangible before the gnome's eyes. The knife deflected inches from Mel's chest. A section of the misty wall lit up different colors as the beam tried ineffectively to burn through it. The gnome smiled in relief as his magic barrier solidified. Revwar realized it was similar to the barrier he used at the bluff battle. The inventive gnome had added a few features to his own version of the wall. The barrier varied in height along its length, much like castle battlements. In places it was tall enough that a human would have to jump over it, and in others it was only as high as Mel's waist. The translucent barrier was solid enough to block many different kinds of attacks. It stretched across most of one side of the room, but was not impassible to anyone that could jump over it or go around it.

Mel leaned across in order to aim his wand through one of the openings. Revwar cursed, seeking a new strategy by which he could directly attack the small caster. Savannah reappeared from behind the doorframe, visible energies wrapped protectively around her form. Mel also noticed that the spiked iron ball of her flail crackled with a dark power. At this point, the gnomish sorcerer's worst threat was the minotaur charging at him. The wand pointed at this new target and prepared to let loose its burst of power. Bortun had almost gotten to the barrier when Mel took aim. The minotaur couldn't dodge the blast, nor did he intend to try his luck at seeing if he could survive the effects. He brought up the head of his massive axe. Mel fired from only a few feet away as the minotaur kept his axe up in preparation for the attack.

"Daerkfyre, witness my courage!"

Another blast thundered across the room as Bortun's frame silhouetted in the eyes of the rest of his band. The blast slammed the minotaur backward in a burst of white light. Arms, hooves, and his lone remaining horn twisted about in the air as he reeled from the energy. The creature landed in a heap on the fringes of the floor sigils. Wisps of smoke rose into the air.

*   *   *   *   *

"Can you all hear that?" Cat asked, as she leaned down against the opening.

The companions gathered around the small, open shaft. From the dark maw of the hole, they heard battle screams and the explosions of spells. Salgor heard one name screamed above others, and it caused him to jump up and raise his axe.

The dwarf gritted his teeth. "He's calling out to my dwarven god even as he's blasting the wits out o' them overgrown goblins! That brave little blasphemer!" The dwarf hopped about as he looked for an exit from the hall. "We have to get to him! We have to find him and help out now!"

The others scrambled to their feet in a rush. Cat, Petrow, Trestan and Salgor took off running, with no clear direction in which to go.

*   *   *   *   *

Mel wore a big smile on his face when he watched the minotaur tumble down. Afterimages of the bright light danced in his vision. His smile faded as Bortun started to move again. The minotaur grunted as it braced itself on an arm. The creature sat up, holding its axe before it…a blackened, scorched axe which was mostly intact and still sharp. Bortun's chest bore burn marks, but the massive axe had absorbed the greater effect of the wand's power. The creature howled in anger as it staggered back to its feet.

Mel ducked behind the barrier again as a spell from Revwar tried to bypass it with a wave of fire. Flames curled around the misty wall, toasting Mel considerably. He sprinted to another part of the wall and aimed his wand again. This time he picked Loung Chao. The gnome was prepared that the Tariykan would dodge, so the gnome tried to lead his shot. Mel aimed intentionally a bit to one side, waited for the warrior to dodge the other direction, then swung the wand across to fire. Loung stepped where Mel hoped he would; the gnome commanded the wand's energy forth.

Or at least, he tried to.

The wand didn't respond. Mel screamed the command again, this time more than a little worried. No lightning came forth, nor thunderous noise, nor blinding beam. Mel realized the energy of the wand had been used up. Many arcane items such as the wand

264

and even *Dovewing* had to be refilled with magical energy from time to time. Mel was just beginning to get really worried when another danger struck.

Savannah sprinted up to the misty wall on the other end from where Mel stood. She uttered a quick prayer before swinging her crackling weapon. The dark flail connected with the barrier and sent a shudder along its entire length. The formerly solid surface rippled outward from the point of impact. A moment later, the misty wall shattered into many pieces. Translucent shards dissimilated into a gaseous form again, robbing Mel of his greatest defense.

The gnome tried not to give in to panic. He just needed something to buy time so he could dive back into the open shaft and hopefully end up somewhere better than here. Mel carried a crossbow but it was unloaded. The trusty mace hung from his belt, useless against any of these opponents. He tossed the drained wand aside as he dug into another pouch. He concentrated on the spell despite the distracting dangers. Loung, Bortun, and Savannah charged in from three sides, while Revwar stood safely in the back with his staff ready.

Mel's attention stayed focused as he pulled out a piece of material from an old leather pouch. His fingers went through the intricate motions, unconcerned with the thought of the approaching danger. All fear and uncertainty had to be pushed aside for the spell to succeed. Arcane words flowed from his tongue has he concentrated on the incantation.

He was still concentrating by the time Loung leapt into the air and landed a powerful kick to the gnome's head.

*   *   *   *   *

The companions took a long time trying to find their way around the castle. The structure was a maze of chambers and passages. They ran from one door to the next, some doorways hung as empty frames, others were blocked by the warping of time. Salgor would not let a stuck door slow him down. Swift and heavy were the blows from his axe as he sought any passage to the first level. Sometimes part of the group started to run one way, while the rest almost went another. The dwarf felt he followed his nose to the right place, so everyone learned to follow Salgor or be left on their own. He led the way, shattering more doors as he went. They found more bedrooms, servant quarters, some studies and another kitchen. More hallways and servant passages branched off in sometimes random directions. As the halls twisted about, they soon lost track of which directions they had been running.

Salgor grumbled as he went. "Should have all listened to me and the smith, but you had to do it your way!"

Another axe blow spun a warped door off of dusty hinges, revealing another dead end room. The dwarf growled and moved onward. "We should have finished exploring the first floor, o' we could o' charged the sailor camp...*anything* but trying to use a risky magical device to get to the wrong level."

265

Trestan, sweating in his armor, huffed, "Let's just keep going and find a way down."

Cat shook her head sadly. All her hopes of sneaking in and out with the relics had gone down the shaft with Mel. There was no turning back now, and yet she felt they were charging into a hopeless fight. "Be careful of what we might run into. If you see an enemy, strike hard and fast."

A double door reinforced with rusted bands barred their path. Salgor was ready to put his full weight at it. Before the dwarf warrior reached it, a slender, long blade swung overhead. The elvish sword sliced through the reinforced doors as easily as Salgor's axe had handled the weaker ones. The dwarf looked in wonder at the sundered doors, then glanced at the young smith. Trestan re-sheathed the magical elvish blade with a smirk, having some amusement at beating the dwarf at his own game.

Salgor pointed at him, "We need to get you a proper axe to match your strong swing."

Trestan offered a partial grin, even though his mind worried about what might be happening to poor Mel. It might have been a few minutes already, but there were no more sounds of battle from below. They were all anxious that whatever challenge Mel faced was now ended one way or the other. They were still in shock that the small sorcerer might have met his death while they had been helpless to stop it. At the same time, all of them were ready to pay back anyone who dared lay a finger on their small companion.

At last, they found a wide stairway winding downward and around a corner to the ground floor. The stairs suited design more than expediency. The walls to either side had been done decoratively, and sunlight streamed in through some tall, broken windows. The companions hardly glanced at the lavishness as they rushed to get to the first floor. By the time they hit the ground level and looked about, the two humans gasped for breath. Salgor paused indecisive for just a moment, as he looked up and down this newest hall for a clue on which way that he should charge next.

Cat spoke, "Quiet! I thought I just heard something."

The others became as still as statues. None dared move, and all ached to try hearing past their own breathing. Cat wondered what they would think if they knew that she had just told another lie to help out the party. She did take the opportunity to listen intently down both sides of the hall, but her true motives were to slow down the dwarf and let the two young men catch their breath. She felt that the dwarf's haste would have them blunder into a trap.

Her green eyes swept over the party. "Now listen to me. I nay longer hear anything. Nay battle, nay screams, nay anything."

Salgor started to move, but she held a hand up in front of him. He looked up at her. Cat whispered, just loudly enough that they all had to be quiet in order to hear her. "Whatever happened has happened and finished. Much as I am worried about our friend, we won't help him by rushing into the same thing he did without a little more caution."

Salgor glared at her, "I think you are still just afraid."

Cat returned the glare with as much steel in her eyes as Trestan and Petrow had ever seen. She stepped right up to the dwarf, reached down, and grabbed a fistful of his beard. Trestan and Petrow watched with gaping eyes, for dwarves were known to get extremely insulted at anyone who messed with their beards. Salgor didn't move, just stared straight at Cat as she leaned over and brought her eyes up close to his. The two young humans looked between their friends and wondered if even a medusa would survive those glares.

"Get this straight dwarf, I am not afraid!" Cat's tone sounded unyielding as she spoke. "Mel is my friend too! I love that little guy so much. I wish he were here right now to talk my ears off." Cat's eyes got wet as she frowned at Salgor. "I will do whatever I can for him, for you, for any of us! That does not include running in and getting killed because I am too tired to move my legs once I get there. If he is dead, we can't change that fate; if he is alive, it is because they don't want him dead. We won't be doing him any favors if we rush in and get captured by the same people that may have hurt him. If we can get to these people, we want to be smart enough to win. I only fear dying alongside Mel for nay gain."

Salgor returned the hard stare, but raised one hand up to encircle Cat's tense fist. He firmly pulled her fingers away from his beard, and she willingly let go as she continued to stare him down. The dwarf warrior nodded his head and started to grin. "While we are at it, we'll need an axe for you too. You seem strong enough to wield one."

The tension evaporated as Cat and Salgor separated. The dwarf had to add one more thing, brandishing his axe as he did to emphasize the point. "When I get a shot at that wizard, I will charge. Best way to deal with a wizard is to cut him in two before he can react."

Cat nodded, wiping at her eyes a bit, "I understand, but for now it's time we went back to some attempt at stealth. Hear them before they hear us."

*　　　　*　　　　*　　　　*　　　　*

Cat, Salgor, Trestan and Petrow moved quietly along passage after passage. The pace slowed considerably, but Cat went about things her way. Even her companions could not hear her footsteps despite shadowing her. Half-elven ears guided them when their own ears heard nothing. Salgor held his axe ready at all times, tensing and relaxing his grip with every corner turned. The foreign architecture left them guessing what kind of rooms and halls this had once been, and where they might need to go. They moved through the cold gloom of the keep with the fear that any doorway might bring them face to face with an enemy. Cat found a new path that appealed to her, down a wider corridor with many side passages. Four sets of eyes looked about warily as they crossed into this open section. The half-elf guessed this area might lead to the core of the structure.

She turned her head to better listen to some perceived noise, unheard by the others. Though no one spoke, she glanced back and put a finger to her lips. Trestan tried to listen for any noise when he saw Petrow made a strange motion. The handyman pointed at his own nose and made a sniffing gesture. Trestan inhaled deeply, detecting the scent of burning wood.

They ventured further to investigate. Step after cautious step, they crept along the ancient hallway. Clues indicated the presence of others nearby. A light source reflected through a large entrance to a chamber. Voices echoed down the hall from the same general area. It seemed that at long last they might find some of their elusive hosts. They hoped they were dealing with a small number of people. It did not sound like the entire boatload of mercenaries and sailors were hiding around the corner, but the party from Troutbrook knew that they might still be outnumbered.

Salgor's caution faded. He took strides that almost put him beyond Cat in the lead. A few hurried steps and the dwarf would be in full view of anyone that might be inside the room. The half-elf blocked his passage. Warrior and scout traded silent stares for a moment before Cat started gesturing with her hands. Trestan and Petrow glanced to a side passage that Cat pointed out. The passage was a set of stairs ascending to the next floor. The companions could see a balcony half-wall beyond the top of the stairs, likely overlooking the same room that was around the corner. Voices carried through the stairwell. Cat motioned for silence. Using hand signals, she indicated her intent to peek over the railing at the top of those stairs. Salgor scowled, but he held his tongue and relaxed his posture.

The agile adventuress crept up the stairs with no more sound than a mouse's breath. It amazed Trestan and Petrow that she could be so silent wearing armor and weapons. Even her crossbow and rapier were strapped in a way that neither swung carelessly. The two young men were so intent on Cat's silence that they found themselves holding their breath. Foreign words emanated from the next room, flowing like a chant. A male voice, clear and distinct, sounded like Revwar. A female voice, assumed to be the dark abbess, joined the first. Although they could not understand the words, the tone gave them shivers. Cat stole her first glance over the balcony railing. She looked down into the next room for several heartbeats before ducking back into the stairwell. Cat frowned as she crept back down the stairs.

Her emerald eyes swept over the party. "Well, the one good thing is that the crew of the sailing ship isn't here. On the other hand, the four adventurers are there, performing some ritual."

"The wizard is in there?" Salgor hefted his axe.

Cat narrowed her eyes at the eager dwarf. She anticipated he was about to do something rash. "Revwar is standing at a podium, reciting a chant. Savannah stands next to him, and her body is surrounded by some protective miracle. I can see it swirling about her form. The minotaur and Loung are standing off to either side, holding candles. I could see nay sign of Mel. He doesn't seem to be in the room unless he was under the balcony."

Before Trestan or Petrow could say anything, Salgor responded, "So all our enemies are in one spot, and none of them have a weapon to Mel's throat? It's settled! We charge in fast and kill the casters first."

The half-elf shook her head, desperate to change the dwarf's mind. "We don't even know…"

"We know enough!" Salgor declared. He readjusted the grip on his shield. The dim light shined on his crest: a dwarven temple, supporting the weight of a large ale cask, with a hammer ready to tap the keg. "We can still surprise them and sweep through their defenses! You get your crossbow on that balcony and cover us as we charge."

Cat tried to stutter a response through Salgor's words, but she could not get her message across. Trestan and Petrow nervously had hands on their weapons, but they looked between their arguing friends with alarm.

Raising his axe, the dwarf roared a challenge that easily carried to the occupants in the next chamber. "Daerkfyre grant me strength as I cleave my enemies, and tear down their dark arts!"

Salgor Bandago turned and charged towards the entryway. Fire lit in his eyes as he moved to kill the wizard that had caused so much indignity to him in Barkan's Crossing, back during a time before the group had even arrived in Troutbrook.

Petrow and Trestan watched him charge with unbelieving eyes. Petrow thought that this course was foolish, but at the same time he wasn't about to let Salgor charge in alone. He did not hesitate long before raising his axe and following the bold dwarf. The young handyman searched for his own war cry as he charged. He yelled out the first thing that inspired his sense of home and duty. "Troutbrook!" A moment after he shouted it, he regretted it wasn't the kind of war cry that inspired fear.

Trestan and Cat locked wide-eyed glances at each other over the stupidity of their fellows. Cat finished the sentence she had been trying to get across to Salgor. "We don't even know if they have the relics in there, or if this is for nothing."

Trestan shook his head, but the young man did not hesitate long. Battle had initiated, for good or for bad. The young smith gave Cat a goodbye salute even as he turned to follow Petrow and Salgor. The half-elf ran up the stairs to the balcony. She skipped every other step as she bolted. Cat planned to cover the others with her deadly missiles just as the dwarf suggested, though she would have preferred a surprise shot. She wanted to curse all stubborn, inflexible dwarves at that moment. Katressa Bilil reached behind her back to undo the strap holding her crossbow in place. The weapon came free, as she used her other hand to grab a bolt. She could not see the reaction of their foes inside the room, but she could hear the battle cries of her friends as they charged.

Trestan's long stride carried him to Petrow easily. His lifelong friend jogged slow enough to keep Salgor in the lead. The smith wished he could turn back the sands of time and been more vocal about caution. He noticed Petrow wore a hint of worry behind his eyes. The smith seriously considered every armed fight he had been involved in up to this moment. This same group had paralyzed him easily the first night, in the streets of his hometown. He had fallen during the goblin fight over such a small thing as stepping on a stone with his bare feet. Although he was proud to have done so well in the bluff battle, it had ended with him mortally wounded. He told himself to feel proud, if nothing else, that he stood up for his hometown against such fearsome opponents. Mel might still be alive, depending on them to save him. Trestan bolstered his will with the thought that a relic which had prevented many hard times for his village was now being used to further some dark purpose. The young man strengthened his courage with the image of Sir Wilhelm charging into battle, and he found the voice to proclaim his own war cry.

"For the love of friends and all good men! Abriana guide me!"

His right hand reached for the handle of the elvish blade. In the past he had always considered it Jareth's sword, not wanting to claim it. Now the Sword of the Spirit whisked free of its scabbard as Trestan drew it forth. The young man placed both hands on the hilt. Although the sword had belonged to a paladin, it felt right and whole in his hands like it never had before. Light from the chamber ahead danced across the runes of the magical blade as Trestan Karok beheld it. The bastard sword was ready for a fight, with a keen magical edge to cleave through any obstacle. His hands fit it well, balancing the blade as an extension of his own body.

In that moment, as he and his friends charged at the enemies they had pursued over many miles, he truly felt it was now *his* sword.

CHAPTER 24

The battle cries echoed into the throne room. It was not unexpected, though the timing was unforeseen. It had been so long since the battle with the gnome, that Revwar and Savannah had started the ritual as planned. At the sounds of enemies, the elf and cleric were forced to abandon the spell to deal with the new threat. Revwar stepped from the ceremonial stand and the book bearing the words. Savannah also gave up her chant, as she looked around for the approach of the attackers. Bortun and Loung dropped their candles, which had been more for potency rather than actual necessity, and grabbed weapons. The minotaur hefted his treasured waraxe, while Loung lazily spun a bamboo quarterstaff in complex patterns. They looked about for their enemies, for there were many passages from which someone could approach. The throne room had its balcony, but it also had doorways leading from every wall.

Three figures swept around a doorway, anger burning from their eyes. Individually, recognition and hatred flowed between them. Loung scowled at the dwarf, but Salgor's glare went to Revwar. Yellow elf eyes returned the glare at the dwarf and the breastplate-damaged human, reflecting the annoyance of being chased so determinedly. Trestan's eyes went from the one-horned minotaur that Jareth failed to kill, to the death abbess he hadn't been willing to finish at the bluff. Savannah likewise scowled upon the youth she had once spared; as well as Petrow, whose screams she had come to know almost intimately through Bortun's torture. Petrow shuddered from fear at seeing the cleric and minotaur once again, but tried to find strength in his reliable old woodaxe. Bortun snorted at all three, though looked at Salgor in a sporting way. Minotaurs did not like dwarves, and more than one ferocious battle had raged in caves and mines as the two races clashed.

Above the deadly glares traded across the ancient throne room, Cat calmly rose from a crouch behind the second-floor balcony. A short stone wall bordered the balcony, giving her ample cover from the eyes below. The butt of the crossbow came up to her shoulder as she held it ready. With all the shouting and confusion below, she hoped that she could get off one good shot unnoticed. One shot might separate disaster from triumph.

Salgor hit a burst of speed in his charge, going single-mindedly for the wizard before the elf could attempt a spell. Revwar saw the approach and put one hand inside a pouch, hurrying to get his own magical attack underway. The dwarf raised his axe and seemed ready to throw it across the remaining distance to stop the wizard in time. He still had a large mace hanging from his belt as a backup. Revwar slid into his concentration and prepared the spell.

Bortun charged into Salgor's path. The minotaur had his great axe cocked for a swing, and he let loose with all his strength. Salgor raised his shield but did not slow. The large waraxe cleaved across at the dwarf's chest level.

Clang!

The minotaur's waraxe jolted the reinforced shield. The dwarf's waraxe went up into the air, not on purpose, and fell without harm to anyone. The tremendous blow sent the minotaur off-balance. Salgor's limp body slid across the floor; the shield dragged along by the stubborn grip of his left arm. When the dwarf finally slid to a halt, there was no sign of movement. The shield lay on his arm, but the weapon hand lay open and empty.

*　　　*　　　*　　　*　　　*

Trestan yelled a warning for Salgor when the minotaur approached. The two young men assumed the seasoned warrior of Daerkfyre would handle Bortun. Needless to say, it surprised them when suddenly their strongest warrior was apparently knocked out cold by one swing from the creature.

The charge of the two young men diverted to avoid any direct line at the huge creature. Even in this disheartening moment they couldn't turn back. They were committed to the attack. Whatever happened next, they would fight or die.

The abbess, Savannah, stood close enough to be a tempting target. Miraculous, goddess-blessed energies spun protectively around her body. The cleric started speaking, offering some prayer to her goddess.

Trestan and Petrow hesitated in their attack, waiting to see what would happen. Savannah completed her prayer. She stepped forward, disappearing as she stepped into nothing. Petrow froze with fear, unsure what to do next.

Trestan had seen that same trick performed on the streets of his home. He realized one of them was about to get a paralyzing touch from behind. Even as Petrow stood frozen with indecision, Trestan shifted his weight and reversed the direction of his blade. He expected to find the cleric standing within deadly inches behind them.

Savannah stood as he predicted, uttering the first words of her prayer. Her cold, blue eyes fixed on Trestan, even as one hand reached for him. "DeLaris, please stop this soul from…"

The Sword of the Spirit came at an arc which would separate her head from her shoulders. Since the magical blade had cut through many things with no effort at all, it surprised Trestan when he felt it bounce against something solid. A tingling numbness momentarily went through the young man's fingers at the shock. The surprised cleric stepped back, as her mystical protection wavered and disappeared. The impact interrupted her divine prayer. The cleric registered shock that her protective field was smashed, and concern as she suddenly found herself on the defense.

Petrow turned around and brought his axe to bear on the cleric. Trestan shook one hand of the numbness now plaguing it before concentrating on his opponent. The young smith focused single-minded determination to deal with this one foe despite the dangers around him. Savannah did not hesitate for long. The dark cleric pulled out her flail; the spiked ball emitting a dark glow. Petrow and Trestan separated as they approached, coming at the cleric from different sides. Savannah faced them directly with her enchanted weapon.

*　　　*　　　*　　　*　　　*

Bortun approached the dwarf's unmoving body with long strides. Salgor showed no response. The dwarf's fingers still extended loosely through the straps of his shield,

272

while the other hand lay unmoving next to the mace on his belt. The axe from the short warrior lie discarded several steps behind the minotaur. Bortun snorted unpleasantly at the smell of the dwarf.

Bortun smiled as he raised his axe for a killing blow. His eight-foot frame tensed as he readied to chop the dwarf in half.

Salgor exploded into motion. The dwarf warrior rolled over and punched out with his shield at the minotaur's leg. The crest of the shield smacked hard enough against the minotaur's knee to leave an imprint. Bortun howled in pain as he doubled over. The large axe blade whooshed down to chip the stone floor. While Bortun hunched over, Salgor's mace whipped up and slammed the creature on the side of the head.

The muscular minotaur lost his balance and went down. Bortun's head reeled, dizzy from the painful sting of the mace. He tasted blood deep in his throat. Any second the creature expected the dwarf to fall on him with a series of blows, but it was mistaken.

Salgor hopped up to his feet, but only to face Revwar, standing easily next to Loung. The elf had canceled the completion of his earlier spell when the minotaur had intercepted Salgor. Hatred for the wizard as well as fear of his spells stirred the follower of Daerkfyre to attack the elf. Salgor started pumping his short legs into a charge. Bortun reached out with one hand to grab at Salgor, but the stunned minotaur missed.

Loung was ready to intercept the dwarf, but Revwar held out a restraining hand. The elf then chanted more arcane syllables as he motioned with his other hand. His staff merely leaned against his body as his hands went about magical gestures. Salgor charged onward, determined to strike the wizard before he could complete the spell. Salgor knew that if he landed a hit from his mace on Revwar, the elf wizard would not be getting back up from it.

*   *   *   *   *

Cat lined up her crossbow sights. In the room below, the elf stood in the throes of his casting, unaware of the deadly bolt pointed at his heart. She put the minotaur and the charging dwarf out of her mind. Her sharp ears put aside the sounds of the cleric fighting her two human friends. All of her world focused on that first surprise shot. Like the hunting cat displayed on her rapier pommel, her green eyes narrowed on her prey.

She fired her shot. The bolt stopped in midair inches from Revwar's chest, caught by the hand of a martial artist.

Cat remembered that unpleasant battle on the streets of Troutbrook, when Loung had caught every bolt fired at him. Loung smiled up at her, snapping the bolt with one hand. He stood calmly, staff held in one hand, no armor other than silk fabric. The Tariykan warrior had been there to protect the wizard from the known, but hidden, crossbow wielder. Revwar's spell continued, and the dwarf still charged, but Cat had used up her surprise shot.

The frustrated half-elf went back to reloading her crossbow, aware that Loung would wait for anything else she might launch at the wizard. Cat's best asset was her precision with a crossbow, yet that meant nothing if someone prevented her from hitting

273

her target. She could only hope the two young boys from Troutbrook could stand toe-to-toe with an abbess of the Death Goddess.

*   *   *   *   *

Petrow's first excited swing actually made Trestan evade to one side. It also backed up the deadly cleric, but she came at Trestan with her infused weapon. The young man got his sword up to block, and shards of light burst from the impact of the weapons. Trestan stood ready for another blow, but the cleric switched direction. It was akin to some of the strategy that the young smith had used when playing around the three trees back home. She backed up one opponent only to attack the other. Petrow was surprised, but the spiked ball of the flail did nothing more than glance off of his raised axe.

Trestan responded quickly. He went at the abbess with numerous swings of his own. He hoped Petrow would do the same. His sheer ferocity forced her to give ground, though he failed to strike her with his blade. Petrow shifted his position as the abbess backpedaled from the assault. A couple of times the elvish blade and the imbued flail met with a shower of sparks.

The abbess possessed more skill with a weapon than she appeared, though the flanking men kept her fighting defensively. A couple times she gained more room by feinting towards Petrow. He flinched more than Trestan whenever an attack came at him. As they moved across the throne room with their sparring dance, Savannah took every opportunity to try separating her attackers.

Petrow stepped in a few times with his simple woodcutter's axe. He tried to catch the cleric between his blade and Trestan's. At one point his axe scratched a trail across the side of her dark armor. Meanwhile Trestan continued to swing his sword with two hands. Wrist over wrist, in Jareth's style, he kept his sword spinning. It was a display that demanded Savannah's attention. She knew the enchanted sword and its wielder would be the larger threat.

The fight staggered to one side of the throne room. One of many exits from the chamber loomed behind Savannah, with many side passages beyond. The cleric could not earn any easy advantage, though she decided it was time to make one. One of her hands reached into a pouch, while the other renewed greater fighting tempo with the flail. She had to buy time for a miracle, and the two young men weren't about to give her the opportunity to cast anything.

Trestan wanted to push closer, but several of her swings came close enough to create a real danger. Trestan saw her take an item out of a pouch. The elvish blade pushed the attack with new vigor, desperation giving it more ferocity. Trestan backed the cleric up faster than Petrow could adjust. Savannah was forced to leap back a step, but she used Trestan's charge to her advantage. Crouching low, under the latest swing of his sword, she brought her flail against his knee. The blow connected, and Trestan's balance faltered. His knee stung from the hit, though a metal guard plate absorbed most of the damage. Savannah followed up the attack by throwing out her other arm towards Petrow. He recoiled as he feared the magical reagent in that hand.

Her fake throwing motion succeeded in backing Petrow away even as Trestan stumbled. The abbess retained the item in her grip so she could prepare her miracle. Stepping backward, into the archway exiting the room, she uttered a quick prayer. "DeLaris, hear me! Shadows that once existed, faces loved, obscure the vision of those here!"

A red mist expanded out of her hand so fast that Trestan and Petrow were enveloped before they could react. The mist spread to include much of that side of the throne room. The young men stumbled in a dark haze, unable to see more than a foot in front of their faces. They shouted to each other; neither located the dark cleric in the mist, nor could they see each other.

Shortly after the red cloud rose about the two men, Trestan saw a shadowy figure walk toward him. He poised his sword for a strike, but dared not attack blindly. He perceived a female form and assumed it to be the abbess. He let out another war cry…

…but a moment later his voice faltered. The shadowy figure was that of his long dead mother.

*   *   *   *   *

Salgor never had a chance of getting to Revwar in time, but the dwarf covered much of the distance before the elf's spell finished. The bearded warrior raised shield before him, expecting a deadly energy blast or a blaze of fire. A point of light did spring forth from the mage's hand, landing on the ground in front of the dwarf. Salgor was mindful enough to worry about the possible threat, so he changed direction.

The spell mutated into something bigger. Light faded into a blooming mass of fur and hide, forming a creature. Salgor glowered at it as he saw claws and fangs form. The dwarf put his head forward, raised his mace, and roared in fury. He did not fear summoned creatures, and committed to destroying it before it could react.

The monster grew larger than most dogs, resembling one despite some differences. Its muscles and legs tended to move more like the grace of a cat, but the snarling visage was definitely dog-like. Saliva dripped from fangs as claws stretched forth from its paws. Black eyes looked upon the charging dwarf. The tail proved to be the oddest sight: a crab-like claw appendage poised and curled forward scorpion-like over the creatures back. It was ready to attack the dwarf even as Salgor barged into it.

"Damn wizard abominations!"

Salgor slammed into it with his shield, though the monster side-stepped most of the blow. A canine jaw snuck around the side and snapped at the dwarf's legs. Salgor could feel sharp teeth squeezing the chain armor, and he responded with a heavy hit from his mace. The creature let out a yip and released him. Salgor roared in rage as he tried more hits to the creature. Slinking with cat-like grace, it kept its distance for some time, sizing up the reach of its opponent. Finally the creature pounced straight at the dwarf.

The heavy creature knocked Salgor down. The dwarf kept his shield held high, and now the wizard pet tried to claw the shield's surface to get at him. The dwarf rolled about the floor and moved his shield around to keep the thing from getting a good bite out of him.

Salgor swung his mace, but it wasn't easy to get in a good hit. The creature started snapping at the dwarf's face. Spit and bad breath assaulted the warrior of Daerkfyre. The dwarf raised his shield too high, so the creature shifted to bite his legs again. A strong kick snapped the canine maw shut. Salgor got to his feet as the monster reeled from the metal-tipped boot. He held his mace ready for another strike as he and the creature circled each other warily.

In a sudden surprise, both combatants were attacked by other enemies. Cat's bolt sunk into the back of the summoned creature, sending it into a brief panic. The jaws reached around and pulled the offending bolt from its hide. Blood matted the creature's fur, but did not seem to slow it enough.

Meanwhile, Salgor heard Revwar chant another spell, aimed at the warrior's back. Salgor turned to face the elf as a magical bolt surged forth. Crested shield rose to meet and deflect the blast, though it still knocked Salgor back a bit. The dwarf scowled over the rim of his blackened shield.

"I'll deal with you soon enough! Just sit back and grab an ale 'til I get there, 'cause it will be yer last!"

The creature rushed Salgor again. This time it went in low, trying to bite under his shield. Salgor got the shield down low, and tried attacking over it with his mace. He brought the weapon overhead, but a sudden jerk halted its path. The tail crab-claw of the creature had snapped up and grabbed the shaft of the mace. Salgor cursed as he tried to pull his weapon back. The monster was well-rehearsed on this move, as its tail was meant to disarm opponents as well as for rear defense. The muscular tail pulled back, and the front portion of the creature lifted up to push away the dwarf. It shoved Salgor backward, while his mace ended up firmly in the grip of the claw. The monster threw the mace away without a second thought. It readied another leap at Salgor.

The dwarf kept his shield up while looking about for another weapon. His axe lay some distance behind him, if he could just get to it in time.

*   *   *   *   *

Cat put another bolt in place, wanting to send it through the wizard's heart more than anyone else. She had helped the dwarf, but it was the wizard that needed to be brought down. Loung still stood protectively next to him, so Cat had to think of another way. The half-elf crept further down the balcony, hidden behind the stone guardrail. She picked another angle by which she might shoot at Revwar before Loung could react.

Cat held her crossbow ready and raised her body enough to see the room below. Revwar finished another spell, and the result dashed her hopes for any kind of shot. The misty barrier appeared in a half-circle around the wizard, blocking any angle from Cat's side of the room. Loung still stood near to the mage, but was no longer needed unless Cat ran to the other side of the room. She could not see the abbess or the two young men through the dense, red cloud covering that end of the throne room.

She picked a new target. Bortun stood on his feet, threatening Salgor from behind. The dwarf was already in trouble from the summoned creature, and Bortun could charge

276

him at any moment. She let fly her shot at the minotaur, which also alerted Loung to her new position.

The bolt hit Bortun in the back, sending a roar of pain from the minotaur. He turned around and yanked the bolt from his thick hide. Bortun saw the half-elf but could not reach her. Loung pointed her out to Revwar, and the wizard turned to face the only companion that hadn't been directly attacked. Cat knew she would have to dodge a spell very soon.

    *   *   *   *   *

Petrow saw images through the dark red cloud. His parents were there, just as he remembered from his youth. They hadn't changed despite the years. They called to him, motioning to follow. He vaguely heard Trestan calling out to his mother, even as Petrow watched his own parents in confusion. There was no way they could be here, much as his heart had ached to see them again.

The young man remembered the words uttered by the cleric, "Shadows that once existed, faces loved…"

He viewed some type of illusion. Somehow the abbess of the Death Goddess could create images of those long dead that were dear to him. As much as he ached to see his parents again, these images were just phantoms of his own imagination, concealing the cleric somewhere in the cloud.

From nearby, he heard Trestan, "Sir Wilhelm! I thought you were dead?"

"Don't believe what you see, Tres!" Petrow shouted, "This is an illusion spawned by the cleric! We have to find her before she casts a deadlier miracle."

Petrow brought his axe across the images of his parents. The blade sliced through the mist, and the forms melted into the insubstantial cloud. Believing that the tricks on his mind had been trying to turn him away from the cleric, he turned and went the other direction. Other images soon called to him, begging him to return to his original course. One such face was that of a childhood friend, killed in an accident years ago. Every image caused him to hesitate as he looked to see if it was the cleric. Petrow turned away from them all, listening through the red fog for any sounds of footsteps.

"Ghosts begone!" He heard Trestan yell.

He heard a set of boots, but decided that it belonged to Trestan. From the same direction came a grunt, as the young smith swung his sword at something in the cloud. Petrow at first thought it was the cleric, but then he heard a lighter set of footsteps from another direction. He was glad that Trestan rejected the illusions.

Petrow bumped into a stone wall. He hadn't seen it until it was only a few inches from his face. Pausing to consider his next move, he again detected the sound of a lighter pair of boots moving off to one side. Petrow readjusted his axe grip and followed the wall in that direction. Sooner or later he would find where that woman hid.

    *   *   *   *   *

Cat ducked low as she moved to a new position on the balcony. She hastened due to the ongoing sounds of the struggle. Twenty paces or more down the balcony, a new bolt was ready and she decided to try another shot.

Bortun and Loung scanned the balcony for her, looking the wrong way. Neither opponent had much chance at actually getting at her. She could see Revwar was still protected by a magical field. Cat almost targeted Bortun, but she saw Salgor backpedaling from the claw-tailed creature. It snapped time and again at the dwarf, but Salgor kept his shield in the way of its bite. Salgor's axe lie near if he could get an opening to grab it. Cat turned her crossbow upon the monster.

The monster yipped in surprise and spun around as the crossbow bolt tagged its flank. The creature ran a quick circle as it looked for an attacker that wasn't to be found. The thing snapped its maw on the bolt and pulled it free. The distraction was long enough for Salgor. The dwarf rolled over the axe and jumped to his feet with it ready. Now the bearded warrior advanced on his attacker.

Cat's efforts had not gone unnoticed from below. Revwar moved to the table alongside the podium stand. He reached one hand into a bag, and pulled forth one of the stolen holy relics. The stone reflected light off of its green surface as the elf held it towards Cat's perch. The half-elf prepared to dive right or left to dodge whatever might follow. Revwar chanted a few words into the magical stone. A pale green light flashed towards the balcony. Cat ducked behind the stone railing. Though she saw the light spread over her, she felt no effect.

Snapping and splitting noises assaulted her ears. She watched in amazement as cracks spread on the balcony and the stone railing. Green light still bathed the area, but the effect was not meant directly for her. The balcony crumbled under the strange magical assault. Stone chunks broke apart and fell away. Cat tried to get to her feet and move, but the floor underneath her became very unstable. How would the residents of Troutbrook react if they discovered their holy relic had the power to sunder stone? A rending tear signified a large section of the balcony coming free of the wall. Cat's perch broke apart in a rain of boulders and dust, cascading down into the floor of the throne room. She tumbled along with a shower of loose rock. The black-clad infiltrator bounced along with several fragments, dropping into the throne room in a sprawl.

The Tariykan ran to finish off the woman. From a different part of the room, the minotaur ignored the dwarf in favor of repaying Cat's harmful bolts. Both enemies charged after the prone half-elf with deadly intent.

*   *   *   *   *

Trestan, lost in a fog of darkness and false loved ones, no longer knew where Petrow or the abbess might be. He stumbled blindly and ignored the distracting visions. Ahead, the mist seemed to thin. He heard sounds of battle more clearly, and above all was the sound of cracking, tumbling stone. Moving past a few pleading friends and relatives, all long dead, he broke away into the light.

278

Immediately Trestan saw the source of the noise. Through a pall of dust, he saw the remains of a portion of the balcony dashed to the room's floor. He spotted someone moving in the rubble of stone. Katressa, bruised and hurt among the cascade of rocks, groaned as she attempted to get back to her feet. White powder coated her black leathers. Trestan's concern and alarm mounted when he realized two foes converged on her.

Trestan gave little thought to what he did next, he simply reacted. Jareth had always said that a warrior of Abriana is there to protect his friends and all else that he loves. The young smith from Troutbrook put on a burst of speed, coming at his closest opponent from the side. It didn't unnerve Trestan that he charged a minotaur, but he wasn't really stopping to consider his actions. Bortun was less imposing when you charged him from ambush.

The young man launched himself at the creature, though Bortun realized the threat at the last moment. The minotaur tried to evade, but Trestan dove across his legs. The move by the minotaur probably saved the limb from being gravely injured, but the elvish blade succeeded in drawing a line of blood across his calf.

Trestan rolled past his opponent and sprang back to his feet. He held the magic blade ready over his head. Bortun glared and flexed his axe arm. Blood trickling down his leg, he roared in rage. Trestan's fear showed plainly, as he had just put himself face to face with the eight foot, half ton monster.

The axe swept across at Trestan, the young man dodged. A second later the smith tried to attack, but he was forced away again as the minotaur swung the axe with its long reach. Trestan tried moving to attack from one side and then the other, but the minotaur's stride cut off such flanking maneuvers easily. Bortun limped a bit from his injured leg, but did not seem to surrender any major advantage. Trestan couldn't reach the minotaur, so he tried to attack the axe in the same way he had cleaved the enemy's hammer during the bluff battle. The axe, magically forged and strengthened, sent shock waves up Trestan's arms upon impact.

Jareth once complimented Trestan that he was probably the best swordsman in the village, aside from himself and Sahbin. Coincidently, the two villagers that were supposed to be better than Trestan had fought this same minotaur. Both were dead from their encounters, Sahbin because of the same problem Trestan now faced: the long reach of the monster.

These thoughts flitted in the back of his mind. He dodged swings in the hope of strikes of his own, but many times he fell short, and then evaded the axe again. Trestan needed an opening to get close, but at the time he was too busy trying to avoid getting hit.

Then Trestan backed into a wall.

Bortun went for a savage blow that should have caught Trestan between axe and wall, but the young man used one of his evasive moves once practiced in the woods during his imaginary swordplay. The smith dropped and dove to one side, rolling away from the tight spot. The minotaur's axe chipped the ancient stone wall. Trestan stumbled to his feet, using a doorframe for support. He turned to face Bortun again, only to find the creature coming at him as before.

Trestan went through the open exit to avoid another impressive blow from the axe. The swing collided with the edges of the open arch, sending more stone chips flying to the

279

dusty floor. The young man didn't want to be pulled away from the throne room and the rest of the fight, but once forced through the opening, the minotaur's bulk blocked any path back. Bortun would not let up in his attack, and Trestan could do nothing but retreat in the face of the creature's relentless assault.

Before he even had time to consider any further tactics, Trestan turned and ran. Bortun stayed on his heels.

*　　　　*　　　　*　　　　*　　　　*

The summoned monster sprang at the dwarf warrior. Salgor raised his shield to block the brunt of it. The leaping body knocked the dwarf to the ground, but now Salgor had his axe in hand and readied. Even as his left arm held the shield high, his right hand swung the axe underhanded, passing below the shield. The pouncing monster found its vulnerable belly sliced open. It hopped ungracefully off the dwarf.

Salgor sprang to his feet and launched his own attack. He punched outward with his shield, slamming the four-legged monster to the ground. Even as it scrambled to get to its feet, the dwarf dropped the shield in favor of grabbing the creature by its clawed tail. Dwarven muscles flexed as the claw repeatedly snapped shut near the end of his beard. The creature's nails skittered against the floor of the room as it sought to be free of the iron hold of his left arm. Salgor's right arm raised his axe high.

The deity-blessed weapon came down hard, severing the claw-tail from the hindquarters. The summons made a pitiful scream as it flopped on to the floor. Salgor wasn't about grant pity. The monster made a move to leap away, but Salgor wrapped his left arm around the creature and held on. It succeeded in a short leap, but as it landed Salgor's axe came slicing down at it again.

And again.

And again.

Salgor blew out a tired breath as he jerked his axe blade free of the carcass. The pieces of the creature became mist as it returned to the energies which spawned it. The chunks of bone and blood that spattered the dwarf also turned to vapor. He didn't have time to revel at this victory, for his opponents still controlled the room. The dwarf turned a glare at the elf wizard.

"That effort was all for nothing, mage!" Salgor bellowed, "I've eaten bigger and tougher things just for dessert!"

Salgor advanced, but Revwar still had a trick at his disposal. Though the wizard had no more bodyguards nearby, he had the power to create more. The elf wizard once again held up Troutbrook's holy relic, this time facing the dwarf. Salgor worried that Revwar was going to cause damage to the stone floor. The effect of his next casting revealed another unknown power of the green stone relic.

Several green rays shot forth from the stone, striking harmlessly at several points on the floor around the dwarf. Salgor hesitated for a brief moment, expecting some great magical effect. When nothing immediately happened, the dwarf grinned and stepped forward.

The ground opened up around him. Forms arose from the floor: gaunt, skeletal, and hungry. The skeletons and cadavers of people long-dead climbed up from the stone floor around Salgor. Eyeless sockets stared forth as fleshless arms reached out for him. A stench clung about them: the results of years of moldy decay and the rot of death. Some wore rusty armaments from a bygone age, others were not even whole skeletons. They all advanced upon the dwarf. Each form was infused with a malevolent spirit given shape for only one purpose: to kill the enemies of their master. The souls had fled the corpses ages ago, but the bodies themselves could be made into vessels the spirits could use.

Salgor rolled to one side, going for his discarded mace. An undead creature reached for him, only to be hit by both weapons at once. Though the dwarf had been on the ground, he severed its legs with his axe even as his mace slammed the undead monster in the pelvis. The cadaver went down, only to start crawling towards the dwarf. Salgor got to his feet quickly. He held the axe ready in his right hand, while his left carried his heavy mace.

"Daerkfyre!" He yelled, even as he used his mace to slam another monster's fleshless skull down into its open ribcage. Several more undead surrounded him.

*   *   *   *   **

Petrow tried following the sounds of footsteps, even though more noise came from the room behind him. He closed his mind to the other haunting images inside the mist. He felt very alone as he traced his way along the wall. He heard Trestan shout somewhere behind him, but it felt far away. The faces of those long dead called to him, but the illusion did nothing except make him feel the losses and loneliness more acutely. The owner of the footsteps he followed stopped somewhere just ahead. The mist itself seemed thinner, so Petrow assumed he was about to step past the edge.

Petrow leaped forward, swinging his axe blindly. It connected solidly with a magically charged flail.

His lunge took him beyond the edge of the reddish cloud, which spread across the hall to block the passage behind him. Ahead were a series of branching halls and chambers leading away from the throne room. The abbess of the Death Goddess, discolored by the dark shading around her eyes, stared back at him. Her gaze promised death.

She gave a few vicious swings which almost forced him back into the mist. The dark flail seemed to take on a deadly life of its own as it danced through the air. Petrow could feel the red cloud at his back. The handyman stubbornly refused to be forced back. He moved to one side and tried a few strong swings of his own. Neither combatant connected with any solid blows, but the young man distanced himself from the red cloud. They twirled and dodged as the fight carried them further away from the throne room.

Petrow felt more vulnerable without Trestan at his side. The young handyman doubted he was up to the task of facing the abbess by himself, but there seemed little choice unless he dove back into the dark mist. He hoped Trestan fared better.

Petrow put random thoughts away as he focused solely on the dark cleric. Memories of his encounter with her during his failed rescue haunted his background thoughts. This was the same person who had healed him several times only to let the minotaur beat him again, to the amusement of the sailors and mercenaries. If he got the chance, Petrow would kill her.

*　　　　*　　　　*　　　　*　　　　*

Cat struggled to her feet in a daze, aware of her vulnerability. Her vision spun from the fall, but she had to focus. She wasn't even aware of Trestan launching himself at the minotaur only a few feet away. Her first and foremost efforts drew in a few good breaths despite a choking pall of dust.

Loung came into the edge of her vision, and that fact startled her into recovery. She didn't know where her crossbow lie. Cat drew out the silver rapier. She fought for balance between her foothold on top of some rocks and her own disorientation.

Loung's first strike was straightforward and easy, but Cat almost didn't parry it due to her stance. The rapier turned the staff aside, and Cat tried to move to flat ground. Loung jumped into a routine of kicks and staff swings that would have impressed any onlooker. Cat stumbled on the defensive as she attempted to get away. The momentum was fully in Loung's favor and some of his kicks touched her. As agile as Cat was, she had trained to roll with blows to lessen their impact.

The half-elf lost track of everything else, focusing on Loung's attacks. The woman started feeling trapped, as he backed her towards a wall. Debris littered the floor, threatening to trip either of them. In the midst of this, Cat tried to find room to gain any advantage. Her foot almost stumbled over a small rock, but she got her stance set in time to block another quarterstaff attack with her rapier. She snuck her toes under the edge of the rock, even as her left arm blocked a kick. Loung stepped back slightly after that last attack, and it gave Cat the opening she wanted. Her foot kicked out, hurtling the rock up at Loung. The projectile sailed up and smacked him just below the beltline, barely missing a more vulnerable male area.

Though it failed to give Cat the full effect she sought, it caused him to flinch and step back. Now Cat had full control of her senses, and she started pushing Loung back with thrusts from her weapon. Loung used his staff in a similar fashion, attempting to jab at Cat or sweep aside her thrusts. Cat even tried a few kicks of her own, her grace a close match for Loung's.

Loung did not appear worried. He bided time measuring up his opponent. As the two of them fought, they came close to an archway leading out of the throne room. Cat remained aware that Revwar could launch a spell at her back at any moment, and she decided to take the fight away from that open room. She heard Salgor yelling challenges at the wizard, and she could only hope that the dwarf might get lucky. She held no illusions about Salgor's chances or her own. Salgor had been helpless to fight the wizard during their first encounter in Barkan's Crossing, before she had followed them to Troutbrook, and Cat doubted that now would be much different. Despite her best moves in Troutbrook, Loung had already been close to beating her to death on the rooftop. He would have killed her if not distracted at a critical moment.

Cat fled through the archway and into a side chamber, and Loung followed.

Thus the battle of the keep unfolded, with events going as Cat had feared utilizing such a straightforward attack. Salgor and Revwar were the only living combatants still in the throne room. The dwarf fought a seemingly endless struggle against summoned creatures, unable to get close to the wizard. Cat faced an enemy that had stripped her of all her weapons in a previous fight. She baited him away from his wizard companion, but the Tariykan could probably beat Cat well enough on his own. Petrow, the former handyman of the village of Troutbrook, dueled alone against the cleric representing the Goddess of Death. Savannah continued to lash out at him with her enchanted flail, as they also moved further and further into the maze of hallways making up the keep. Trestan had to deal with Bortun the minotaur. The young smith did not even fight so much as he ran for his life from the eight foot monster.

And not one of the companions knew the whereabouts and fate of Mel Bellringer.

CHAPTER 25

Mace and axe worked in furious tandem. Every second proved critical. Grunts of exertion interrupted the sounds of crunching bones. One opening offered itself and Salgor went for it. Before he could get through, several other skeletal arms reached into his path to grab at his legs, arms, and beard. The chilled, grave-like quality in their bones numbed some of the areas they touched.

Salgor became enraged. "Nay touching the beard!"

The path which should have carried him out of the circle of undead closed before he could make use of it. The bearded warrior spun about with axe and mace, driving back the smelly cadavers. He shouted the names of ancestors as he drove his weapons through their ranks. Some of the more distant creatures were pelted with pieces of bone as the front rank met the swings of the dwarf. The floor became coated in masses of dried skin and decayed body parts. Some partially-dismembered corpses crawled onward; clawing, clacking across stone with malicious intent.

One such corpse clawed at the dwarf's boot. Salgor reacted with a chop of his axe. Though the dwarf severed the grabbing arm, such a blow didn't finish the undead creature. It still had one good arm, and that limb moved forwards to latch on. As soon as Salgor could spare the time to do it properly, he followed up the first blow with a skull-shattering hit from his mace. As the head and residual brain matter were crushed, the malevolent spirit emptied out of the corpse to trouble Salgor no more. It often took direct hits to the head, brain or spine area to drive the spirits from a corpse, even if the corpse was nothing more than dried bones.

Salgor worked to create a hole by which he could escape when he stumbled upon another piece of his equipment. His foot touched his discarded shield. He gave it a kick. It careened across the floor to strike the legs of several undead. The dwarf barged through the path it made.

He charged in behind it spinning a tornado of dual weapons. The possessed dead were slammed aside or cleaved in two as they tried to fight back. Body parts flew as Salgor even went so far as to head butt one skeleton, then trample it as he ran past. Finally the wall of undead broke.

Salgor looked up and could see the wall of red mist before him, though the ominous cloud was finally thinning out. He had lost track of direction during his most recent fighting. The dwarf turned to get his bearings only to see that he had broken through in the wrong place. Revwar was on the far side of the rows of undead. Salgor charged back into the ranks of walking cadavers in order to reach his true opponent.

*   *   *   *   *

Petrow let loose another wild swing which forced Savannah to duck. She returned the favor with a backswing from her weapon, narrowly missing Petrow's back. Though the young man still wore leather protection, he imagined it would be defenseless against the imbued flail.

284

He turned and faced the cleric, holding his axe across his body defensively. Savannah lazily swung her flail as she slowly stepped towards him. She feinted in one direction, and then swept it overhead instead. Petrow brought his axe up in time to block. The impact shocked his hands. A burnt, black mark was left on the handle from the flail. Petrow believed the blow came close to breaking the handle, and decided not to try such a block again.

As they exchanged a few more swings, they came to a dim and cluttered section of hallway. The floor slowly ramped down to the next level below. Several doors lined the ramp, and outside of them were crates of materials. Long ago someone had been either packing or unpacking items from these storage rooms when they had been interrupted. Barrels sat with a layer of dust and mold on them. A couple barrels had burst open after their rusty metal bands snapped over the years. A rotted smell wafted from them, even as grimy substances coated the floor around them. Pottery pieces had scattered about in crates or stacked in places on the floor.

Petrow and Savannah maneuvered using the cluttered terrain to their own advantages. More than once an errant swing would smack into a barrel or crate instead of an opponent. At one point Petrow's axe missed the cleric, only to slam down on top of one such barrel. The axe stuck. Petrow's eyes grew wide even as he saw the cleric taking advantage of his predicament. She went in for an easy hit, but he ducked her swing. He released his hold on the axe handle long enough to land a punch on her face. The quick move staggered her back. Petrow wasted no time in grabbing the axe and jerking it off of the barrel before the flail came at him again. The same barrel split in pieces from the abbess' blessed weapon.

In the midst of their next attacks, the weapons tangled. The chain and ball of the flail wrapped around the axe just below the blade. Savannah's first move was to pull back and try to jerk the weapon out of his hands. In that quick moment Petrow used a trick tactic Salgor had taught him after the group left Barkan's Crossing. He kept his grip on the axe and pushed forward. The top of the axe slammed solidly against Savannah's dark breastplate. Both her momentum and the shove of the axe combined to send her tumbling backwards. Petrow was surprised to find *he* had disarmed *her*. The chain of the flail remained wrapped around his axe though she was knocked away.

The young man shook the entangled cleric's weapon off of his own. It flew back up the hallway a bit, well out of easy reach. The dark glow of the flail faded. Petrow returned his attention back to the abbess, sitting on her rear on the side of the passageway. He raised his axe and moved to finish her.

Savannah made a quick gesture with her hands as she let out a sudden prayer, "DeLaris, move him away from me!"

She finished the prayer with both hands in the motion of pushing towards Petrow. Adding to that gesture, the cleric also blew as if blowing out a candle. Petrow's axe fell short as a divine wind lifted him. The young man landed in a sitting position on top of a crate, though the old wood buckled under his weight. He lost his grip on his axe. He couldn't see it, but the weapon slipped down between some containers and the wall.

285

Both combatants struggled to get to their feet. Savannah stood up and began fishing for something from a pouch, while Petrow pushed up from the broken splinters of the crate. The young man was not about to let the cleric cast another miracle if he could reach her. Petrow charged into the abbess as she withdrew her hand from her pouch. He slapped away the object; it went flying to the side. Savannah followed up by landing a punch on his cheek, then trying to step away from him.

Petrow would not let her slip away. He got both hands around her and bore her to the ground. A wild frenzy followed as both punched, clawed, and bit at each other. They rolled around between crates and barrels, grunting and screaming as they went. At one point Petrow remembered getting in a solid punch to her cheek, only to have her nails digging into his face a moment later. He pulled her hand away but felt a bite on his own hand, to which he responded by head butting her. Petrow's left fist slammed into her side once, hurting himself on her armor. Arms flailed wildly as both sought to punch, strangle, or slap at each other.

Despite the fighting spirit of the abbess, the bigger, stronger handyman started tiring her. Petrow got each of his hands on each of hers, and started pinning her to the ground. Savannah returned to more rational thoughts in that moment, realizing she still had some divine tricks.

Petrow was so busy trying to restrain her that he didn't hear the first words out of her mouth. He realized she was casting a miracle, but both of his hands were busy trying to pin hers.

She stared straight into his eyes as she spoke. "DeLaris, please stop this soul from moving. Relax his limbs like the coldness of death."

She was already touching his hands as he held her down. Petrow limply dropped, partially covering Savannah. The young man wasn't sure what was happening, but he could not move his limbs. Savannah did not move either; however, the abbess was just trying to catch her breath. Petrow could feel: the cold stone floor, the body of the abbess beside him, his own legs and arms…but he could not move.

Finally, Savannah sat up. She regarded Petrow silently from beyond her dark eye make-up. Petrow helplessly rolled to his back as she pushed his body away. The cleric got to her knees, but did not stand yet. She brought her face down to Petrow's eyes, hovering just over him.

Savannah pronounced Petrow's fate, confidant that she was in full control of the moment. "I act in accordance of the tradition of my goddess; who brings death or spares it, escorts lost souls to their judgment, and ultimately decides the fate of many by her power. You must respect and acknowledge the control she has over your fate."

Petrow could do nothing but watch her eyes as she spoke. No matter how hard he tried, he couldn't raise a finger to defend himself. She continued, "On this day Petrow, your life is claimed, and shall be extinguished by the will of my patron deity. May the *Karet-Atriul* speed you swiftly to your judgment."

Petrow's eyes went wide with fear. A *Karet-Atriul* was a Death Angel: demons that carry the souls of the recently deceased to their judgment in the afterlife. The young man never knew if they really existed or were just a tale to frighten children, but he did not

286

want to find out. It seemed as if he had little hope of stopping Savannah. It took all of his effort just to twitch his head, which didn't move very much. The cleric shifted her position, and Petrow tried to glance out of the corner of his eyes at the floor nearby. The woman's flail rested a few steps away. Petrow couldn't see his axe.

The abbess of the Death Goddess did not move towards her weapon, but instead she straddled Petrow's form with her legs. Resting both of her hands on his shoulders, she leaned in close and examined his neck. Petrow was helpless as he felt her hands slide up to his throat.

"Some may think of me and other followers of DeLaris as evil, but we simply follow a different standard than most people." Savannah irritably brushed a loose strand of hair from her eyes, then resumed probing Petrow's neck with her hands. "We follow a goddess that exists above mankind's rules and restrictions. If an envoy of the Death Goddess kills a man, is it really murder? Or is it the fair decree of the goddess who controls such fates? I know that I follow she whom I hold above all others. In return, she grants me that intoxicating power to grant or take a life."

Her hands constricted in a stranglehold around his neck. "Goodbye, Petrow. DeLaris claims your soul this day."

Savannah, and other clerics of the Dark Goddess, probably preferred killing by this method: their bare hands. Savannah hovered over Petrow, inquisitive eyes locked on his frightful look as he fought for air. Under the paralyzing spell, he could not force a deep breath. Try as he might, Petrow could not raise his hands to stop her. Her hands clamped like a vise on his airway, allowing him no air to breathe. Her breath could be felt upon his cheeks. Two of her fingers pushed against the major arteries in his neck, slowing the blood flow to his brain as well. The abbess grinned. The power and control fueled her emotions and stimulated her desires. Darkness crept into the sides of Petrow's vision, outlining the blue eyes that would witness his death.

*   *   *   *   *

Katressa Bilil dodged as the bamboo quarterstaff smacked the wall beside her, taking away an escape route. Her rapier snaked out to threaten Loung, but he parried. She backed down a new hallway as he became more aggressive with his strikes. Her blade strained to find an opening. She would feint and try from another direction, but even quick thrust attempts after parrying the staff did not get her any closer to wounding the man. Cat could strike and move very fast, but he moved faster.

Cat finally got some distance from the man, using a door that was ajar into the hall. She kicked it further open, into his path. The door didn't hurt Loung, but it did back him up. Instead of pursuing the initiative further, Cat started running down this new hallway.

Loung gave chase. The hall became a descending ramp, leading down to the basement level. Cat saw an area ahead that promised a new strategy, as there were obstacles of all kinds that might offer her an advantage. Crates and barrels lined the sloping hallway as she ran past.

Then Cat saw another danger. Savannah sat astride Petrow, choking the life from him. The half-elf worried that the limp handyman was already dead, but she saw his eyes roll towards her in a silent plea for help.

Silver rapier rose for a thrust, but even before Cat got to the woman she remembered the threat from behind. The half-elf grabbed the tops of two barrels as she ran by, spilling them behind her. Knowing that might not be enough to slow Loung down, the tip of her rapier snagged the handle of a pottery jar sitting on a crate. She flipped the jar over her shoulder.

Loung started to leap the barrels when the jar appeared near his face. The distraction proved sufficient in stopping him from clearing both barrels. Tariykan and staff tumbled to the floor in a heap. The antique jar shattered nearby. The martial artist almost landed on top of the discarded flail.

Savannah barely had time to look for the noise when the rapier stabbed her. Cat thrust her blade into the cleric's side, through an opening under one outstretched arm. Savannah screamed in pain even as the Cat collided into her. The impact drove Savannah off Petrow, sending both women rolling down the slope of the ramp. The hallway curved as it descended, and Savannah's roll brought her to a stop within a doorway. An open, reinforced door hung on rusty hinges next to her. Cat landed in a controlled roll which quickly brought her into a crouched position.

Cat was not about to face two opponents at once, certainly not with the skill possessed by the Tariykan. Cat had to react quickly. The half-elf jumped and landed a kick on the wounded cleric that knocked her through the open doorway. Savannah tumbled into a darkened room, blood flowing from beneath her arm. The half-elf grabbed the reinforced door and pushed against the aging hinges to close it tightly. The door closed with the abbess inside, but it had no external lock.

Cat needed to secure the door shut, but she was out of time. Loung was on his feet and charging at her. He had momentum built up to shove her away from the doorway, but Cat thought she might use that to her advantage. She spread her feet and prepared to dodge the staff. She avoided the outright thrust of the staff, but still got smacked by it as Loung readjusted quickly. Cat accepted the blow for what she needed to do. The hand without the rapier locked on to the staff, tucking it under her arm. Cat dropped backwards along the line of Loung's charge, and kicked up with her foot. As Loung's upper body pulled forward and down by the held staff, the half-elf's foot connected with his hip enough to lift his legs. The Tariykan warrior catapulted over Cat as she rolled onto her back. Loung Chao rolled down the slope of the hall before he could bring his momentum to a stop. Even when the warrior got up, he saw a thin line of blood drawn across his leg where the half-elf managed a minor slice with her rapier.

By then, Cat pulled out a small wedge from a pocket and seated it under the door. The half-elf had no time to hammer it in before Loung came at her again. Cat flopped on her back fast enough to avoid the swinging staff. It smacked into the reinforced door at the level her head had occupied. Though she wore her helm, she knew that blow would have likely knocked her cold. For a brief moment, she seemed just as vulnerable laying on the

288

floor at Loung's feet. By the time that staff descended to strike her again, Cat had kicked away from the door. The same kick hammered the wedge tightly under the door.

Cat rolled around as Loung made swing after swing. The bamboo rod smashed the rotted wood of the crates and knocked over a tall candelabrum on its path of destruction. The half-elf stayed one step ahead of getting hit, but only barely. The woman lashed out once and scored another nick on the foreign warrior with her rapier. Loung's response sent her tumbling backwards from a solid kick.

The half-elf's tumble turned into a graceful cartwheel, as she descended to where the hallway finally leveled out on the basement floor. Loung gave chase, confidant the woman had been hurt more than he, and enjoying the longer reach of his staff.

Behind them, up the ramp, lay Petrow. The cleric had failed to kill him, but only for the moment. The young man's strength only allowed him a twitch of his muscles and a slight turn of the head. For the most part, he was still paralyzed, alone and helpless. He was an easy target for any enemy that happened to come along.

*   *   *   *   *

Trestan ran three steps ahead of getting chopped in half. The minotaur gained quickly. The young man jumped over an abandoned trunk left in a hallway. As he went over, he grabbed the lid and lifted it to a raised position. Trestan kept running as he heard the minotaur trip over the chest and land in a sprawl. Part of the creature bumped the young man as it went down, doing no damage but reaffirming how close Trestan had come to getting an axe in the head. If Trestan had kept his mind about him better, he might have used that moment to strike. Fear spurred him onward, and he did not stop to wait for Bortun.

The young man turned through several openings, looking for anything that might give him the upper hand. Behind him, the minotaur got up as it cursed the human. As Trestan came to one chamber, he noticed a stairwell but decided to stay on the main floor. He turned through another doorway, but just as suddenly skidded to a halt.

The newest room had no other exits other than the door he had just come through. It was a deathtrap. As soon as he realized it, he turned to sprint back out of the room. Bortun arrived just as Trestan ran out. The great axe came up for a swing. Trestan dove right at the minotaur's legs. They collided with enough force to knock Trestan's helmet off. The minotaur roared as Trestan impacted against his leg wound. The young man rolled away with new bruises, while Bortun stumbled several unbalanced steps into the room. A moment later, Trestan heard a crash as both minotaur and axe hit the floor again.

Trestan shook himself into action, despite a sore shoulder from the collision and a continuing throb in his knee from the cleric's blow. The young man took the closest exit available, which happened to be the wide staircase leading up. He jumped them two at a time in his initial efforts to outdistance the creature. Bortun ran out of the dead-end room in pursuit. Bortun jumped up steps three at a time.

Trestan saw the top of the stairs, but realized he would never make it in time. The smelly, raging beast pounded its hooves closer to his vulnerable back. The young man wanted to slay the monster, but victory seemed hopeless. Facing a wizard was one thing, because if you got close the wizard would be vulnerable. Bortun was a different matter, being such a larger-than-life opponent that shrugged tough hits and dealt tremendous damage in one swing. Trestan had no idea how he would defeat this creature.

The elvish sword gave him some small comfort, since it could surely hurt this monster. Trestan had to come up with a plan in a hurry, for the creature was once again almost upon him. The young man could detect its musky stench.

When Trestan determined the minotaur was close enough, he acted. He reversed his momentum. The young man planted his feet against the steps, crouched, and brought up the sword up to strike. He stabbed the elvish blade back over his shoulder, without even really seeing the target behind him.

Bortun howled in pain, as Trestan felt the blade slice into flesh. In turn, Trestan was clubbed by the blunt axe handle. The axe blade missed hitting him squarely, though it took a chunk out of the stone steps.

Trestan followed up his first weapon thrust, Bortun still at his back. The smith pulled the sword free of the minotaur's flesh, noting blood on the sword as he did so. Trestan sprang from his crouching position and spun simultaneously during his leap. The magical sword rose and fell in an overhead slash aimed at Bortun's head. The minotaur fell backwards as the blade descended. Trestan flinched as he struck the blow, although he felt a solid impact from the strike.

Trestan fell back to the stairs in a heap. He scrambled back to his feet. The minotaur tumbled down the steps, head over hooves, somehow still holding its axe. The monster stopped at the bottom, and Trestan dared hope he had struck the creature a mighty blow. It uttered a grumbling noise, turning slowly into a low growl. Bortun staggered back to his feet, breathing hard, looking more mad than hurt. Trestan assessed the result. The initial strike over Trestan's shoulder did little more than leave a wound on one side of the creature's abdomen. Combined with the gash in the calf, the small puncture from one of Cat's bolts earlier, and the hit to the side of the head from the dwarf, it seemed that little would slow this creature down. Trestan sought where his last overhead blow had struck, and he could see something very obviously different about the creature.

Jareth had sliced off one horn during the battle in Troutbrook; Trestan had just sliced off the other.

The severed horn lay a few steps down from Trestan. Bortun saw it and put a hand up to confirm the loss. The young man watched as a reddish haze came over the minotaur's eyes. Bortun flexed its oversized muscles as it glared a promise of death at the young smith. The creature roared out its rage. Its bellow thundered up the walls and kicked up dust. Bortun charged up, four steps at a time. It even used its free hand and axe to push past the side walls, sending cracks through the faded reliefs upon them.

Trestan, more terrified than ever, turned to flee again.

*   *   *   *   *

"This is for the stink of goblin breath!"

The axe swept across, slicing through the torso of one undead creature. Old leather armor once protected the body, though now it hung in tattered, dry strips much akin to the monster's own flesh. The undead creature fell in halves to the ground.

"This one is in honor of my dead grandpa, to rest in peace and never have his body raised by dark magic!"

The mace came down heavily on a skeleton, shattering bones like dry twigs.

"This is in return for all the full-bearded women who never wanted to settle down with me!"

Salgor went in head first, using his helmet to smash a skeletal face. The monster held a rusty sword, but the dwarf's attack slowed it. Salgor followed up with a cleave of his axe.

"This one is because I'm out of whiskey!"

His leg kicked out to trip a zombie. The monster fell to the floor, then never got up again as a mace crushed its head.

Salgor Bandago whirled around to find the next target. His gaze swept across a room full of broken bones, body pieces, and rusted weapons. He wanted to smash more creatures, having barely touched on his list of hateful things. Not a corpse moved. The bodies covering the floor gave every appearance of being lifeless once again. Salgor stood alone.

The voice came from behind. "And this is because you make far too much noise."

Salgor turned to face Revwar, standing alone across the room. The elf made a pulling motion from the very air. Salgor heard a noise approaching behind him, and he turned to look. It was a spell the wizard had used in the battle in Troutbrook, though Salgor had not witnessed it before. The wizard's magic pulled an invisible chain across the floor. The effects were easy to see. Pieces of cadavers and scattered bones were moved or thrown into the air as the magic force traveled along the ground. Salgor saw it with barely enough time to react.

The dwarf brought his axe down on the invisible force, but the magic could not be 'cut' so easily. Moments later the mystical energy swept his legs from under him. The dwarf rolled about on the floor for a moment before he could scramble back to his feet. The noises caused by the dragged bones diminished. Salgor once again faced the wizard, muttering curses. Some of the body pieces and skeletal remains were still rocking to a stop when the next spell blasted the area.

Revwar no longer pulled on the invisible chain. A wind roared through the chamber as he formed new magical energies. The elf's black robe, trimmed with red, whipped around his body as he lost himself in the throes of another spell. Salgor took a couple steps forward before the spell took form. Several loose objects in the room, many of which were the remains of the undead creatures, launched forth from wherever they rested. The objects all hurtled towards the bearded warrior. Salgor felt a clay cup shatter against his helmet. A skeleton's pelvic bone bounced low and clipped his leg. The dwarf leaned forward as a storm of flying debris slammed into him. As the small warrior stood strong, a piece of stone from the shattered balcony drew blood as it struck. He dropped to his knees as more objects pummeled his short frame. Debris hammered down until a pile of cluttered objects made a mound where the dwarf had once stood.

Revwar let his spell expire on its own. Loose objects finally settled around the mound even as a cloud of dust obscured the far corners of the room. Silence reigned in the ancient throne hall. The elf watched and listened, silently leaning on his staff. He began to feel the toll of all the magical energy he had expended. For the first time in long minutes, no more sounds of battle issued forth from the chamber. Revwar stood alone next to the podium and the undisturbed pattern created for summoning the demon.

As Revwar looked over the room, he heard a grunt from the pile. One muscled hand broke through the top of the debris, holding an axe. Soon another hand raised a mace, partially draped by a skeletal limb. The stubborn dwarf lifted his entire body from the pile. He shook vigorously, trying to dislodge all the bits and pieces hanging from his armor and beard. Revwar normally kept a calm front despite any circumstance, but his jaw dropped at seeing his opponent still standing. As Salgor stepped out from the mound, the elf wizard's mind cycled through his remaining spell tricks.

Salgor used his dirty sleeve to wipe some blood off of his lip. The dwarf spread his arms out wide in an open challenge. He reveled in the worry dawning on the wizard's face. Salgor called forth, "Running low o' the tricks elf? I'm still coming for you!"

Salgor started to walk forward, slow and deliberate. Revwar did indeed back up a step, then another, frustration on his face. Salgor actually started laughing.

"Run out o' monsters have you? Nay more undead left in your pockets?" Salgor noticed one fleck of pottery on his beard, and he casually flicked it off as he spoke. "All the bits and pieces you can throw at me won't do you much good. You might as well try to get the walls and floor o' the keep to try to stop me!"

Revwar's face changed; an evil grin spread across his face. "Dwarf, you offer me an idea!"

Salgor Bandago stopped laughing as the wizard moved to lay his hands on the relic stone. The dwarf broke into a charge. Revwar spoke more words to the holy relic as he held it before him.

The holy relic set loose another of its many hidden powers. The floor seemed to melt upwards in two different places ahead of the dwarf's charge. Stones and dirt bent up from the ground to form into two humanoid creatures of rock. The surface of the floor unattached from the two creatures, resuming its normal shape. The monsters were elemental spirits, locked in bodies created of earth. In many ways, they were much like the possessed undead bodies Salgor had just defeated, but were much harder to kill.

They advanced upon Salgor, moving on legs of stone and rock banded together.

*   *   *   *   *

Petrow grunted with exertion and won a small victory. He used his trembling arms and legs to flip onto his belly. His skin tingled. He'd had similar experiences when waking up at nights to find one limb still asleep. It was the same effect now, though over his entire body. He moved his arms and legs, but could not manage much of a crawl.

292

He could look about, though his head felt much heavier than normal. He had a scare only a few moments earlier when a noise came from the door just down the hall. Savannah had weakly attempted to open the wedged door, lacking success. It left Petrow wondering how badly Cat's rapier attack had left the woman. If the cleric escaped the room he would still be very vulnerable.

Inch by inch he made his own struggle for a nearby doorway, seeking shelter. He would have appreciated having his axe somewhere close, but he did not know where it landed, nor did he possess the strength. He had a hard time getting to the side of one crate. After that, he struggled to slither past a barrel. All the time, his worries screamed about being discovered before he could get out of plain sight. Petrow breathed hard as he moved towards a doorframe. His own noise kept him on edge. His outstretched fingers could finally touch it. It wasn't enough of a hold to pull him forward, so kept using his legs.

Petrow's shoulders got through the doorway. Hand and foot, he crawled into the room and past the open door. More sensation began returning to his body. Petrow brought his feet past the doorway, only to hesitate on how to proceed. His best option seemed to be closing the door. He pushed at it, and at first it seemed the door had weathered the years enough to close smoothly. Unfortunately, it got to within a few inches when it suddenly stuck. Petrow wasn't sure if it was a hinge, or any other object, but for whatever reason the door wouldn't easily relent. The young man did not try to force it, suspecting the noise might invite more danger than an open doorway.

He appreciated getting past the doorway when his senses recovered enough awareness to reveal a new sensation. He felt something that might be blood in his pants. Looking down, he realized his crotch was wet. A particular smell came to his nostrils: he had wet himself!

Petrow was aghast that he had lost control. The more he gave thought to it, the more he realized that he hadn't. Trestan had been right after all! The paralyzing miracle apparently relaxed more muscles than one realized. Petrow would have been red-faced if any of his friends had seen how he looked now.

He had little time to ponder it, as he heard sounds coming from where Savannah had been trapped.

*   *   *   *   *

They tangled close for a moment, twirling in a flexible but deadly dance. When Cat and Loung broke apart, she had a new bruise from his staff and he wore another nick from her sword. Loung expected another assault, but the half-elf turned and evaded him once again. She ducked through another entry into a darker room.

Cat heard the Tariykan follow her. She hoped the dim light would grant her an advantage. From what she could see, it had been another storeroom. Unlit torch brackets jutted from walls, racks holding old wine bottles lined one side, weapons racks stood present but empty, and all sorts of rotting containers stood in unstable stacks. The darkness and clutter of the room would favor Cat, or so she hoped. One shaft of light entered the room from a rusted grate in the ceiling. Distant sounds of fighting could be heard from above. The light illuminated an area in the center of the otherwise dark cellar.

Cat ducked off to one side as she entered. She crouched and slowed, becoming a hunter. The half-elf slinked past a few piles of debris to get a better ambush position for her adversary.

Loung ran into the room but slowed immediately. His eyes searched the room, ascertaining the danger. His staff came up before him in a defensive stance. He moved forwards slowly, gracefully, retaining his balance at every moment. The martial artist went into a trance. He pushed the world away, refocusing his senses in another way. His mind looked for things unseen, and listened for things silent. The meditation allowed feeling the world from a different enlightenment.

Movement and noise came from one side. The Tariykan twitched, realizing a bit late that it belonged to a rat. Nevertheless, the distraction almost hid the real threat from his other side. Cat took the opportunity to lunge at his unprotected back. The inner senses of the Tariykan warrior moved more on reflex than actual thought. Even so, the tip of the rapier stabbed into a portion of his back before his twisting body rolled with the strike. Staff whipped around as he spun, lashing out at the figure behind him. His blow hit, though the whole twisting motion brought further pain to the injury.

Cat fell back with a numb hand; rapier sailed through the air. Its silvery blade glinted in the grate's light shaft as it flew out of sight.

Disarmed, Cat jumped over a crate and rounded a stack of barrels. Loung sprung over obstacles in his race to get at her before she hid. He rounded one corner as her foot lashed out in a sweeping kick. He fell to the floor hard. Loung reacted quickly, rolling to his back as she sprang on him. He kicked outward, pushing her over a barrel with the blow. He got to his feet in time to get hit over the head by a pottery lid. The darkness gave Cat enough advantage that Loung's staff thrust split a crate. She wasn't feeling so confident seconds later, when a kick from the man connected solidly into her abdomen.

Cat and Loung whirled around debris piles and vaulted obstacles during their chase. The darkness slowed Loung, but his reflexes compensated for his lack of vision. Loung's bamboo staff also gave him an advantage. The fight slowly went against Cat. As much as she might have tried to match Loung in agility, he had superior strength and a weapon. Cat had a hidden dagger in her boot, best saved for when she had the surprise and opportunity to use it. As the fight wore on, she lost her opportunities. For every hit she landed, she suffered worse. A punch to Loung's face resulted in a staggering blow to the head. The staff knocked her helmet away. Cat stumbled yet managed a weak kick. Loung accepted the hit. As he did so, the human spun into a roundhouse kick. The half-elf went to her knees after her jaw shook from the blow.

Cat retained the state of mind to get back to her feet, but her opponent's moves came as a blur. She doubled over as his staff slammed into her gut. The human warrior put his staff between her legs and slid under her bent-over frame. With a practiced move, he flipped her over one side. Cat flailed airborne for a moment, sailing over another crate to land heavily on the cold stone.

294

She lay hurt and bleeding, staring through blurry eyes as Loung casually walked closer. It reminded her of that moment on the roof in Troutbrook. She felt helpless at his feet. Back in Troutbrook she had been saved by a timely distraction, but such an event was unlikely here. Cat felt angry and sad at the same time. Loung could kill her, and somewhere up the hallway Petrow lay helpless. She had been one of the most experienced adventurers of the group, and she felt she let the rest down.

CHAPTER 26

Trestan couldn't see much from his hiding spot. A few cracks between weathered boards offered a restricted view of the outside room. Out in the halls, he could hear the stomps of the minotaur, alongside monstrous roars of frustration. The young man had yet to regain his breath. Every gulp of air sounded loud in his ears. The prey may have gone to ground, but the hunter remained near, searching.

When Trestan had reached the top of the stairs, he found another maze of corridors and side rooms. He dodged through several trying to lose the minotaur. When short of breath and his muscles ached, he opted for a new tactic. Trestan hid in an old wardrobe closet, standing against a wall of a bedroom. Although scared to remain in any one place for long, further running would have been fruitless. The monster had run past this same room and looked inside. Trestan had been an absolute statue inside the closet, with no movement or breathing at that time. Trestan felt relief when Bortun rushed past, continuing his chase elsewhere.

Trestan's heart prompted some kind of action, or some attempt at returning to the throne room. He felt the despair of letting his friends down. Darker thoughts whispered that all his other friends might already be dead. Such thoughts were reinforced by the distant roars of the minotaur. Trestan even heard the minotaur chopping something apart with his axe out of frustration.

He tried to bolster his courage. No matter what he feared, he had to make a stand beside his friends! Abriana's whole philosophy involved struggle for that which you loved. As with Jareth, Trestan should not worry about dying if he fought for the right things. He may not be a paladin, but Trestan vowed to find his courage and make his stand with the others.

A new noise came to his ears. Bortun was making noises with his bullish snout, not far away! The creature snorted several times.

Trestan suppressed a new wave of panic. The young man peered through the cracks of the wardrobe doors to get a better look at the entry to the room. He saw the edges of Bortun's outline standing very close to his hiding spot. The minotaur turned its head about, making more sniffing noises. It snorted a blast of air directly at the wardrobe, and then its axe went up for a swing. Trestan's eyes went wide.

Bortun roared as he slashed with the axe. The massive blade cleaved through the double doors of the wardrobe. Old wood splintered, flying about the room in a shower of debris. As wooden pieces scattered about, a crouched human bolted from his hiding place. Trestan ducked underneath the minotaur's swing; pieces of wood sprinkled his head and armor.

Trestan stopped abruptly and turned, attacking while he had the chance. It almost caught Bortun by surprise, but the minotaur got his axe into position in time. The elvish blade sent sparks flying from the massive axe head. The minotaur pressed forth. Trestan wanted to try another attack, but unless he moved quickly the minotaur would block the only exit to the room.

The young smith rolled toward doorway. A swing from the axe just missed him as Trestan tumbled his body into the hall. Bortun followed closely, but was still not beyond the doorway when the young man got to his feet. Trestan tried to bottle Bortun's great bulk into that doorframe. Trestan went into a flurry of two-handed sword swings. The spinning elvish blade wove a deadly dance in front of the minotaur. Bortun let loose another roar while shoving his axe forwards.

The axe head pushed Trestan aside, and the minotaur's large frame squeezed into the hallway. Now, it had room to swing again.

*   *   *   *   *

Her side felt warm and wet. The only sliver of light came from the crack under a closed door: her only escape. Savannah shoved the door with the shoulder on her good side, but something blocked it shut. The cleric almost swooned from the pain of the attempt. The agony forced her to rest until it subsided. Savannah turned her mind to her injury. Her lungs felt labored and she tasted blood.

The abbess of DeLaris forced herself to regain her concentration. She was a healer, after all, she needed to get rid of the wound and return to the fight. In that darkness, she prayed. Chanting a mantra of praise and healing to her goddess, her fingers traced symbols in the air. She raised her weakened arm, wincing, and touched her other hand to the wound beneath. Miraculous healing energies filled the puncture left by the rapier.

Skin and tissue knitted together seamlessly. The wound expelled dry blood. The body's normal process of forming scar tissue was bypassed as the edges of the skin stretched together and reattached like nothing had happened. Her lungs took a deep breath of air without any pain. Savannah's clerical powers healed the wound completely, leaving her with a clear mind.

The abbess stood upright, though still in darkness. The room housed an awful stench. It was probably for the better that she did not see whatever caused the foul smell. The human woman reached out and touched the stuck door holding her prisoner. The walls, made of solid stone, were beyond her power. The door was a different matter entirely, despite being wedged shut. Her faith allowed the abbess control over the bodies of any living, or once-living, beings. The door, mostly composed of wood, was akin to the skeletal remains of a once-living creature.

Savannah prayed for rot and decomposition to hasten, commanding the wood of the door to yield to the effects of time. The wood lost its strength. Nails and bolts fell out; planks came off of their hinges as the door came apart. The commands of the devoted follower of the Goddess of Death turned the wooden portions of the door into a pile of dust.

Savannah stepped over the metal and ash on the floor of the entry. She gave no more than a glance to a wooden wedge resting on the floor. Savannah looked about the hallway for any signs of others. The half-elf and the Tariykan were missing, as well as the young man she attempted to strangle. Truthfully, the cleric didn't give Petrow much thought. It disturbed her to think he might still be alive after she claimed his life for DeLaris, but she doubted he could escape the island alive. She walked back up the hall to retrieve her weapon. Savannah remained unaware that Petrow held his breath behind a nearby door. It relieved Petrow when the woman continued walking up the hall, making her way back to the throne room.

The dark cleric had to look around a bit to get her orientation back. Savannah approached the throne room cautiously, unsure what to expect. Oddly, two distinct sounds came from the room. There was a sound akin to rocks shifting, as well as a noise like someone setting up a dinner table. Her brow furrowed as she tried to guess at the source.

Savannah entered the doorway to the throne room, and gazed over the effects of the battle. Piles of stone and rock occupied two different places of the room. One pile settled beneath a shattered portion of the second floor walkway. The cleric had not been able to witness the half-elf's plunge as the balcony broke apart. The abbess could not help but notice the remains of several undead corpses around the room. Limbs and rusted pieces of armor left few areas uncluttered by the fight. An exception to this was the floor on which the symbols of the summoning had been inscribed. Someone had used magic to clear the area for its proper use. The elf mage, Revwar, set items back in their proper places on tables. The spell caster worked calmly, undisturbed by enemies. The cleric watched as he unhurriedly put back jars, relit candles, and practiced reciting phrases.

Savannah looked into the far corners of the room, still expecting trouble. He must have heard her approach, since her metal armor made enough noise. Even if he did, however, he continued to work at restoring summoning components until she spoke to him. "All is so unnaturally quiet. Where are the others?"

Revwar faced her, but gestured to the many doors and arches exiting the chamber. "Somewhere about, scattered here and there. I shouldn't worry much. The half-elf was much bruised, and Bortun can handle a boy with a sword. I assume your opponent met your goddess?"

Revwar turned away, anticipating the answer. Savannah shocked him a bit with her reply. "Actually, he yet lives as far as I know."

Savannah preferred not to dwell on the repercussions. When a cleric of DeLaris claims a soul, they displayed the goddess' control of death by following through with the kill. By arrogantly proclaiming her control, and then not being able to carry out that death, it became an insult to her goddess. DeLaris expected a certain respect and fear from mortals, due to the finality of their days always tugging at the corner of their minds. To be free of such a fate emboldened individuals. It was imperative that Savannah or one of her companions carry out the decree of death soon.

When Revwar turned questioning eyes toward the cleric, she responded, "I also ran into that half-elf. She was fighting Loung, with a lot of spirit still in her."

Revwar nodded, but returned to his work. The abbess asked, "What about the dwarf?"

The elf offered a rare smile. He waved a hand towards one of the two rock piles in the room. The first had been easily identified as being the remnants of the upper balcony. The grating noise of rocks came from the second pile. The rock pile looked odd, as it slowly moved about itself and stacked more vertical than what would normally be allowed in respect to natural balance and gravity.

298

Revwar proclaimed, "He is underneath that pile, though still alive it would seem. He is trapped and slowly suffocating under two earth-bonded spirits…elementals."

The blue-eyed woman nodded. Her gaze swept across the piles of undead in the room. "You have been harnessing the powers of the relics. You brought forth their guardians to aid you."

Revwar nodded. "I had to use many spells, both for offense as well as spells to cloak me in safety. After a time, it was best to use those other available powers. Should the dwarf break free, he'll find I've had the time to prepare myself better. Though I believe I have little to fear now. You are here with me, and we can complete the summoning."

The abbess was a bit surprised. "Without knowing about the others? We still have enemies somewhere near."

The elf caster shrugged. "I think it will matter little. I've heard occasional sounds, from items being smashed to Bortun's roars, though each seems far away. These enemies are young and disorganized, and little threat. Besides, the summoning is the reason we are here. Once the gateway is opened and the demon comes through, we will have achieved our goal. Let them try to do anything to us with it present, I'm sure we would find the result entertaining."

Revwar turned back to preparing several items that had been left abandoned when the fight erupted. "Do me a favor," he pointed at the fire they had constructed off to one side, "Make sure the kettle is boiling and bring that back over here. Don't let it touch your skin if you can help it, the mixture is quite corrosive."

*　　　　*　　　　*　　　　*　　　　*

Cat struggled to rise from her prone position. Loung stood threateningly close, his quarterstaff in hand. He spoke casually, "Did you ever hear of the Philosophies of Torichi?"

Cat got to her hands and knees, listening only distantly to the Tariykan's words. She had to come up with a plan to defeat him, or a distraction by which she might plunge her hidden dagger into a critical spot. He stood just out of easy range for any physical attack, but well within range to deal a good hit from his staff.

Loung continued speaking, "Among his many teachings, the wise man talked about fate. In his opinion, fate and destiny could be avoided by chance once or twice. Despite the initial avoidance of these two powerful paths, all of us are drawn into the way of our calling sooner or later."

The hard bamboo staff slammed across her back, stealing her breath. Cat grit her teeth. Anger filled her thoughts. Her muscles shook from the strain of the fight, but also with nervous energy to fight or flee.

The martial artist chatted calmly, pacing around the woman at a safe distance. His once-loose silk outfit clung, wet from sweat and spots of blood. "I believe you had more chances than life usually allows. You should have died on that village rooftop, or by the hands of mercenaries at that camp. You persistently taunt fate. In the end, the result is the same. Fate will take your life, and those of the children you foolishly led here."

299

Cat struggled back to her hands and knees. Her green eyes glared through loose, sweaty strands of her dark hair. Directly in front of her, the male warrior stopped with the end of his quarterstaff pointed at her face. Loung proclaimed his words fearlessly, as he stared down into her eyes. "*I* will take your life. Then I kill the two boys if the others haven't already done so. You've avoided that long enough."

Cat wanted to pounce, but her thoughts wandered irrational paths. Her eyes focused on the end of that bamboo. She surprised herself with her first gut reaction. Cat gave a short jump forwards, landing on all fours. Her teeth snapped over the end of the quarterstaff before Loung could move it away. The Tariykan seemed just as surprised as the half-elf. Before Loung could withdraw it, her left hand fastened hard on the staff. Katressa Bilil swept a foot into Loung's knee.

The Tariykan warrior went down; the staff now in Cat's hands. She adjusted her grip as she bounced to her feet. Loung rolled and sprang into a combat stance as the agile woman attacked. Both slender female hands twirled the man's own staff against him. Cat thrust and spun around in slashing motions. Loung Chao backed up as a frantic flurry of strikes began. The martial artist proved his mastery of such fighting, as he avoided each of the first few attacks. The bamboo smacked across planks and even toppled an aged weapons rack. The half-elf let her fury show. She put a lot of energy into each swing in a desperate attempt to get in one decisive hit.

Loung was still handicapped in the darkness. His feet tripped against some object, which encouraged Cat to attack harder than before. The staff left a red welt on Loung's shoulder. Moments later she rapped him on the side of the head with another blow.

Loung Chao turned and started to run. Cat was quick to pursue, but it almost cost her dearly. The Tariykan hooked one hand on a wine rack and jerked it off balance. The bottles crashed down, which forced Cat to avoid the flying glass. She went around the mess only to find that the human had simply retreated to better ground. He stood within the light coming from the grate above.

He stood in a sort of trance, going through exercises and motions that seemed out of place considering the threat of combat. Cat went cautiously closer, holding the quarterstaff ready to execute a fast strike. She expected him to attack her, but his eyes were fully squinted shut. Foreign words rolled out of his mouth, droning a fighting mantra from his homeland. Seeing no obvious threat, and wanting to end this while she still had strength, Cat thrust the end of the staff at his face. The man's reaction was skilled and swift. Both hands crossed under the staff to deflect it high. He then grabbed the staff and pulled it down. At the same time, he let out his breath forcefully as his foot snapped upwards. As strong as the bamboo had been, his kick sent splinters flying. The staff snapped in two, smaller bits showering the two opponents.

Cat dropped her half even as the Tariykan dropped his. Breathing heavily, the half-elf attacked in a frenzy, using her hands like claws. She raked scars across one side of his face as he retaliated by lifting his knee into her stomach. She had no time to react to the wind being knocked out of her as he slammed a fist into her leather vest, painfully bruising one breast. Cat still tried pushing her attack forward, but all she accomplished was to fall against the force of his punches.

300

She went down hard, wracked by a coughing fit. New pains and bruises throbbed. Before her vision cleared, she felt something cold and wiry underneath her right arm. Cat glanced over, pleasantly surprised to see that her hand had fallen against the hilt of her missing rapier. Loung was about to close in for a deadly strike, when he also noticed that the half-elf had another weapon at hand. He stayed back and awaited her first move.

But Cat despaired anew. As much as having her weapon in hand should have brought back hope, it only reminded her of her ineffectiveness in using it against this man. Every weapon she wielded had been knocked from her grasp. Despite her rapier, she knew Loung had too many tricks up his sleeve to allow her to get in a hit. Even worse, she was on her back, out of breath, while he poised upright in a combat stance. Despite the silver-edged weapon, Cat suffered a disadvantage.

Unless…

From where she lay, Cat saw something above Loung's head. A rusted metal grate, which allowed in some light, looked old and worn by time. A chain, running through a ceiling loophole and down a beam next to Cat, seemed to be the only thing holding it in place. If the chain released, then the heavy, wide grate would swing down and possibly crush Loung. The half-elf could not cut the chain with her rapier, but she looked to where it connected. The chain wrapped around a peg extending through the narrow pillar. The peg fit rather loose, but tension on the chain kept it in place. In a pinch, someone could knock the peg free of the pillar, thus dropping the metal grate.

Loung looked up briefly, to see what had drawn her attention. Cat rolled over with her rapier. The half-elf punched out with the basket hilt of the weapon, slamming the peg loose from the wooden pillar. The chain went slack, allowing the grate to drop. The rust around its edges stubbornly held it in place despite the loss of its support chain.

Loung saw he was in no real danger. Cat's ploy had failed, and the man reveled his moment of victory. But he turned away before seeing something which drew Cat's attention back to the grate. In the room above, someone's boot stepped out onto the grate.

*   *   *   *   *

Savannah's heart leaped again as she realized that she stepped on the same loose grate as before. It was the last thing she wanted to do while carrying a corrosive mix of hot liquid for Revwar's needs. The abbess had stepped on the same loose grate no less than four times since they occupied the castle, and not once had it ever given away. Something kept the grate from dropping her into the room below.

What she could not know, was the 'something' had been a chain wrapped around a peg…which Cat just knocked loose in an attempt to get the grate to drop on Loung.

The weight of the abbess was more than the rusty grate could bear. Savannah felt it drop and screamed as she fell through the floor. One thought stabbed through her brain: get rid of the boiling liquid in her hands. As she fell, Savannah threw the pot away from her body. She landed hard on the cold stone floor. The abbess heard the splashing fluid, followed by a wail of pain.

Savannah struggled to her feet with a pained groan. She was glad to have avoided the splashing mixture, but in the dim light of the cellar, she saw Loung writhing. The descending grate had smacked him hard, but the liquid splashed a burnt path across a good part of his torso. The corrosive fluid melted parts of his flesh.

Even as Savannah gasped at the sight, a rapier-wielding figure took shape in the darkness. The abbess of the Death Goddess did not question her appearance, nor hesitate in how to act. The cleric went into a rage. She chanted a quick prayer, motioning her hands to throw the effects of the spell outward. A fan of electrical charges crackled through the air. Black tendrils tinged with a golden flame covered the distance between the two women. Cat tried to dodge behind another wine rack, but was not quick enough. Painful bolts shocked her right arm, causing it to twitch and spasm. Her arm quickly went numb. She heard the metallic clang of her rapier hitting the floor. A black orb flew from the hands of the abbess. Cat dove behind some crates as the energies of the orb exploded before her. Interposing crates and barrels shielded her, but obvious effect put fear into the half-elf. The miracle withered the once-living things it touched. The wood of the crates and barrels decomposed within a few seconds.

Cat wasn't about to see what other tricks the cleric held. She glanced at her rapier, several feet away, but her arm remained numb and useless. Looking ahead, she saw an outline of an exit. Cat sprang to the doorway and ran from the cellar storeroom.

Savannah did not chase the half-elf. The abbess looked over Loung Chao, squirming in agony on the hard floor. Savannah examined his reddish-black marks and minor rapier wounds with a cool expression. Her anger faded as she focused on matters more familiar to her. She extended her hands over Loung's form, chanting prayers of healing to her goddess. It was time to get Loung back on his feet.

*　　　*　　　*　　　*　　　*

The great axe chipped away at the stone wall, a half-second behind Trestan as he dove into the next room. The young man scrambled to get back to his feet as the minotaur emerged from the entry. A few hearths lined one wall, rows of counters and tables crossed the room's interior. Some of the furnishings had collapsed from old age. Various cooking implements hung from hooks, or lay cluttered on the floor. Pottery items were in abundance, many broken.

Trestan had little time to appraise the qualities of the room. Bortun came through the door swinging, the axe dislodging several items hanging from the ceiling. Corroded metal pots clanged to the ground. The young man tried a few thrusts of his sword, but once again he was afraid to step too close to the minotaur. Debris in Trestan's aisle blocked any easy retreat. Bortun had just enough headroom that he readied a swing over his shoulder. Trestan saw the danger and evaded in the only way available. The young smith rolled his body over the top of a table. The axe swept down, hacking into some of the debris. Bortun followed with a horizontal cut. Even as Trestan rolled over the edge of the table, he heard the passage of the axe blade cut the air behind him.

302

The youth ran at a crouch to the end of the aisle. When he dared look up, Bortun was not far behind. Bortun let out a roar and slashed with his axe again. The deadly blade shattered a collection of old pottery jars, showering Trestan in a hail of clay pieces.

Trestan ran down another open row between tables. Bortun charged after him, but in the next row over. The minotaur grabbed an old pan as it ran. Trestan looked back to see the beast hurtling it through the air. Elvish blade sliced across, separating the handle from the rest of the pan. Bortun came within a couple steps, so Trestan tried another strategy. The young man rolled under a table, heading towards the minotaur's aisle. He had no sooner gotten to his knees when he hacked away with all his fury. The attack failed as Bortun got his axe head down to deflect the blows.

The minotaur towered over Trestan's kneeling form. The young man rolled once more, continuing his momentum under another table. The minotaur brought his axe down hard where he expected the young man to be. The table shattered. Trestan was caught in another storm of falling debris as he moved.

Trestan did not stop rolling until several rows over. By the time he stood up, he figured he would have a few precious moments to come up with a new plan of attack. Bortun spotted his head as Trestan popped up and the minotaur charged. It no longer mattered to the muscular beast that several hanging pots and numerous tables separated the two combatants. Bortun charged through it all, axe swinging continuously to bust apart obstacles and overturn furniture. Wood splinters cascaded into the far corners of the room, along with bits of clay and at least one rat unfortunate enough to be hiding in a drawer. The minotaur's horn stubs knocked loose several hanging utensils, although one metal whisk fell, only to dangle precariously from one broken horn during the charge. Muscle and bulk carried the beast through a storm of broken obstacles.

Trestan gawked wide-eyed with fright before defending himself. The human stabbed forward with his blade, but the minotaur did not charge blindly into that. Bortun, an experienced fighter, stepped aside and brought his axe down hard. The heavy axe came down on the tip of the elvish blade. A table edge acted as the fulcrum which popped the sword from Trestan's fingers. The magical elvish blade, Trestan's only real hope of harming the creature, flipped end over end somewhere into the rows of debris.

Trestan almost froze, still reaching for the sword, as if sheer willpower would bring it back to his hands. He barely ducked the swinging axe once more. The young man winced as he heard more objects shatter.

Trestan resorted to running again, though it meant abandoning the sword for now. His lungs burned as he aimed for the exit to the room. The thunderous steps chased right behind him. The frame of the doorway loomed ahead as a temporary shot at safety. Trestan barely passed the doorway when the minotaur caught up to him.

Trestan's body jerked to a halt as Bortun's muscular arm grabbed his neck.

*   *   *   *   *

As much as the dwarf tried to inhale fresh air, very little could be earned. He had lost track of how long he had been slowly smothered under the earth elementals. Both of his hands still tightly gripped the axe and mace, but the rocks kept his arms pinned to his sides. The dwarf growled and grunted as he fought against his entrapment, but the rocks adjusted to put pressure wherever he tried to gain freedom. Sweat dripped from his brow.

The rocks shifted to reveal a soft green glow hovering inches in front of Salgor's eyes. Salgor watched, awed, as he realized that the softly shining stone resembled the holy relic. The dwarf figured this was the magical heart of the creatures, since they had been created by the relic's magic. It was likely the weakest spot in a creation composed of rocks and sand. If Salgor had been able to attempt it, he would have tried to destroy the thing with his weapons.

As it was, his arms remained pinned to his sides. The dwarf slowly suffocated.

*   *   *   *   *

Petrow sat in silence for some time after the abbess walked past his room, awaiting all effects to wear off. Magical lights in the hallway and a thin archer-slit window provided scant lighting. Once recovered, he still took refuge in the silent near-darkness. Physically, he had recovered, but emotionally he feared to continue. He couldn't erase the memories from that night on the bluff when the minotaur and abbess participated in his torture. When Savannah had made him helpless out in the hall, the memories and feelings from that bitter night rushed back. Petrow grew up with a high opinion of himself. He'd walked confidently through his teen years. The humiliation and pain faced during this adventure brought him fears he had never known.

Eventually, Petrow forced away his bad thoughts. He feared to go out there, but he knew he couldn't stay here. The hallway remained quiet as he got up. He decided to explore the room. He spotted crates, barrels, and stands of rusty weapons in the dim light. One particular wooden box caught his eye.

Despite the age, it still seemed to keep an effective seal in protecting whatever was inside. Petrow worked at the box, breaking the seal and opening the top lid. He noted several items kept inside, but one set in particular grabbed his attention. There were several candles, as well as the resources to light them. Soon Petrow had two of them lit. It wasn't enough to adequately bathe the room in light, but it illuminated another special object.

Several stands of armor stood against one wall. Much of the collection deteriorated over the passage of time. Amidst all the worn pieces stood one set of armor that sparkled as if fresh from the crafter. It was mostly made out of leather, but it included a metal breastplate and other metal pieces at the shoulders and thighs. The suit had obviously been touched by magic or a cleric's blessing. When Petrow looked down at his own battered leather outfit, he decided that a new, magical set of armor would do a lot to bolster his confidence.

Petrow changed armor quickly. He would have preferred a clean, dry set of leggings as well, but that would have been too much to ask of the gods. He admired the outfit in the candlelight. The suit felt every bit as light as the armor Petrow just abandoned. The new look distracted his mind from the dangers of his current location.

He heard footsteps in the hall.

304

Petrow shuffled over to the door, peeking around the edges. The door had been left cracked open, offering a limited view of the hall. Savannah came into the view, walking up from the basement. It brought a chill to Petrow to observe her again. He was puzzled that she came from the basement after he had heard her walk upstairs, but he didn't dwell on it. He noted her flail was missing; an empty pot occupied her hands. As Petrow watched, he recalled the candlelight burning in this storeroom. If he tried to shut the door, she would probably notice; yet if he left it open, she might see the flickering light.

Petrow had to gather up the courage to act. Despite also being unarmed, he had a chance to surprise her. As the abbess walked closer to the door, her gaze drifted to a line of light emanating from the crack. As her eyes narrowed on that oddity, the door flung open. Petrow leaped out and landed a firm punch on the side of her face.

Savannah reacted blindly, swinging the pot against Petrow's head. The young man latched one hand around the right wrist of the abbess. His other hand grabbed a fistful of hair. She struggled to no avail against his muscles as he pulled her into the room and kicked the door shut behind them. He twisted her arm enough to make her drop the pot. Savannah responded with a swift kick between the legs.

Petrow appreciated the metal, cup-shaped groin piece on the new armor. The two of them continued their struggle in the candlelight. Petrow clamped his other hand down on her free arm. With his physique, he proved more than a match for her strength. He backed her up against some crates.

It should have been easy to find a way to put her out of the action, but Petrow forgot the nature of his foe. Her lips parted as she started in prayer, "DeLaris..."

Petrow realized he had entered the same situation as before. It didn't matter that he had her arms restrained; her prayers had the power to immobilize him. His new armor would be useless. The young man foresaw her hands wrapped around his throat.

If Petrow didn't stop her, he would soon be dead.

*   *   *   *   *

Cat stumbled through a maze of passages in the cellars, musing that it was the perfect place to be ambushed by a minotaur. The feeling came back to her right arm, but it was a small victory. She could taste blood, and the rest of Cat's body felt stampeded by a herd of animals. She passed room after room, looking in each as she went. The half-elf wondered how she might get back up to the main floor without crossing the storeroom where she fought Loung. Petrow's fate weighed on her mind also. Cat remembered getting the cleric off of him and trapping her in a room, yet the same cleric had just attacked her.

Cat shook her head. The odds of their survival looked so bad, victory didn't even seem to be a consideration. She wondered how many of them still lived. These thoughts swam through her head as she searched room after room in the cellar.

She glanced into a dark room, lit by a barred window. A shaft of light illuminated the small body of a gnome lying against one wall. Cat's breathing halted when she saw him. Mel neither moved nor made noise. Cat noticed chains in the wall attached to the gnome's wrists. If Mel was dead, they would have no reason to chain him.

Cat stepped over to the small body, looking warily for traps. She saw a shelf above him, but that was empty. His pack and weapons sat nearby, hiding out of reach behind a corner. Cat exercised caution. She wanted to have a weapon handy. The half-elf grabbed his pack and crossbow, then knelt next to him with both. She rummaged through his belongings until she found a bolt. She set the loaded crossbow on the empty shelf, within easy reach if necessary.

Katressa reached out a hand to touch him. Suddenly, the gnome jerked upright to the limit of the chains. Mel's eyes looked about, locking on Cat but not recognizing her at first. One eye was swollen and bruised from Loung's kick. His gaze softened, although it was hard to read his expression. A gag prohibited him from spells or saying hello.

Mel began to cry and Cat gave in as well. They tried to hug each other, but Mel's arms were chained behind his back. Tears ran from his eyes down Cat's leather, making trails through the powdery dust left over from the shattered balcony. His three-foot-tall body pressed against hers tightly. A pitiful noise came from his mouth, muffled by the gag. She told him everything would be fine, over and over again. Cat undid the gag from his mouth, tossing it away like a thing possessed. Mel started to mumble apologies, but Cat told him not to worry. Simply finding Mel alive rekindled hope in her heart.

Cat looked over his restraints. "Let's get these chains off of your arms. Then we can get out of here and find the others."

Mel leaned to one side, allowing the kneeling woman access to his bindings. Cat withdrew some metal implements from a pouch and set to work. Mel spoke past a dry mouth. "I hope you all stopped them in time. They planned to use me as entertainment for the demon."

"Demon?" Cat asked, "What are you talking about?"

Mel continued to hold still as she worked on the lock. "Did you see the throne room? All those markings on the floor? For whatever reason, they were about to summon a powerful demon."

Cat paused in her efforts. She remembered seeing the etchings and symbols around the floor of the throne room. "Are you sure, Mel?"

The gnome nodded. "I've seen such spells before, though mostly for teaching."

Cat finally worked loose the catch on one manacle. It slid free of Mel's arm. The half-elf wondered if they would ever get any good news. Every turn in this adventure attracted more enemies than they ever expected. Now an otherworldly creature!?

The gnome flexed his freed wrist. His other wrist remained trapped. Cat hunched down over the gnome, about to work on the second lock, when she spoke again. "Aren't we ever going to get a break?"

A voice came from behind her, "Just the one on your necks."

Cat almost dropped her tools. She slowly turned one look over her shoulder. Loung Chao blocked the doorway. His silks showed damage, but Savannah's prayers had left his skin unblemished and whole. The Tariykan warrior looked as strong as ever!

Cat turned back to Mel with a defeated look in her eyes. The pain from her bruises still throbbed. She felt weary to her core. Mel's expression betrayed his worries. He no longer had his wand. A wall-chain still secured one arm behind him.

306

The small, loaded crossbow sat on the shelf above his head. Cat's body blocked Loung's view of it, but that brought no comfort. So far, the Tariykan had easily caught every missile she had fired at him. The half-elf doubted her dagger would make any difference. Even worse than death, he might let one or both of them live to be gruesome entertainment for a demon.

They needed a miracle, or Cat and Mel would soon be dead.

*   *   *   *   *

Bortun's bulk filled the hallway as Trestan struggled for freedom. The minotaur's nails dug into the human's tender neck. Even worse, the minotaur raised his axe for a one-handed slash. Trestan poked outward with two fingers from his left hand. Bortun yelled and moved to cover the pained eye with a hand. Trestan hoped that would have broken the grip, but it was the axe the minotaur dropped in order to protect his vision. At least the large axe was no longer in the creature's hands.

Upset over Trestan's persistent struggles, Bortun used his free hand to punch just underneath the human's breastplate. Trestan nearly expelled his last meal. His struggling abruptly ceased. Bortun delivered another punch, hitting Trestan's head hard enough to send his vision spinning. The young man had never been hit so hard in his life. Stunned as he was, the smith didn't have the presence to kick loose when Bortun shifted the way he was held. Bortun slammed the human against the ceiling, then let go. As Trestan fell, the minotaur used a short hop to head-butt the man. The stubs of the broken horns blasted the air from his lungs.

Trestan dropped in a heap. He tried to get up again, but a solid kick from the minotaur sent Abriana's worshipper tumbling across the hall. Trestan barely staggered to his feet after that punishment when he saw a new danger.

The minotaur charged low, leading with his stunted horns. The young man threw himself to one side, rather than get pinned between the charging beast and the stone wall. As it was, a glancing hit from Bortun's shoulder knocked Trestan flat.

Trestan gasped for air. The minotaur finally let up, but only to pick Trestan up and stand him on wobbly legs. A solid punch belted Trestan enough to lift his feet off the ground. Trestan felt like he was dying on his feet. He wouldn't have been able to keep upright on his own.

The young man felt himself picked up, unable to see through teary eyes. He winced at the thought of being slammed against the ceiling again, but Bortun had a different plan. The minotaur flung Trestan outward. The young man tumbled in flight, glimpsing a closed door ahead. He idly wondered how rotted the door must be, in the hopes that it wouldn't hurt too much.

Trestan collided with the door in a jarring hit, blasting through in a shower of planks. He fell limply to the stone floor inside the new room. He lay mostly on his stomach, but other than that he wasn't sure how his limbs were arrayed.

The minotaur didn't immediately pounce on him. It would have been so easy for Trestan to give in to unconsciousness, but he promised himself he would do what he could

307

to help his friends. Even if all he could do was prolong his torture before death, it would help give them time. Trestan set his hands on the floor, noticing how much they shook. He lifted his head with much effort. He watched drops of his own blood drip from his face onto the pale stone. The young man tried to banish his panic. He determined to do his best to keep Revwar from reclaiming his fine blade. Somewhere to the west, his father worried for his return, and he didn't want to disappoint his father either. Even if the worst happened, he recalled how Jareth smiled a thank you to his goddess in his final moments. Trestan could do no less.

A sound came to his ears. The minotaur stooped to retrieve its axe from across the hall. Trestan trembled as the metal blade scraped across stone, hooves stomped closer to where he lay. The smith had risen to his knees by the time the minotaur appeared at the broken door of the room. A few casual swings with the axe left nothing remaining of the door to hinder the large creature's entry. Trestan lacked the strength to stand. His own body betrayed him with tremors.

Bortun paced partway around the young human. The monster raised its axe, snorting as it glared down the length of its inhuman snout. "This is the end, little man."

CHAPTER 27

Salgor's slow death reflected a nightmare of all dwarves, crushed and suffocating under a collapse of rock. For any dwarf, it was better to go out swinging a weapon, laying low several enemies before dying honorably. Occasionally, he heard Revwar's or Savannah's unconcerned voices, but mostly he only heard the grinding of rocks. The vulnerable center of one elemental spirit hovered just in front of Salgor's vision, shaped in the form of the holy relic. Its green glow illuminated the otherwise dark space. It taunted him, whether intentional or not. All attempts to raise his strong arms against the smothering rock creature proved futile. It was hopeless, or like the humans say, like banging your head against stone.

Why didn't he think of that before?

Salgor did not have much room, but he tilted his head back. Mustering one last breath of stale air, he proclaimed, "Daerkfyre!"

The dwarf slammed his head forward. His helmet smashed against the relic's replica. The stone creature stopped shifting but it did not free its grip. Salgor tilted his head back for another try. Once more he slammed his head into the glowing stone.

The stone-bound spirit recoiled. It tried to withdraw its 'heart' away from the dangerous dwarf. Other rocks shifted in an attempt to cover up the vulnerable one. Salgor smashed his head a third time, once again hitting the glowing target. As the first earth spirit recoiled, several rocks loosened their grip on the dwarven warrior. The second creature tried to compensate. Salgor finally got an arm free. His axe arm plowed through the moving rocks. The cleric-blessed weapon impacted the green relic's duplicate hard enough to crack its entire length. The creature's heart split, then disappeared as control of the spirit broke.

The first elemental became nothing more than a shower of ordinary rocks raining upon the floor. Salgor sucked in a deep breath of fresh air. The second creature retained its grip on one of his legs, but otherwise lost its hold on the warrior. Salgor no longer felt threatened by this manifestation of magic. Axe and mace chipped away the rocks of the creature's body. Another glowing green stone came into view, Salgor was quick to crack it with his mace. The second earth spirit fell in pieces to the floor.

Salgor stared across the chamber at his nemesis. The elf wizard watched, wide-eyed, at the destruction of his latest creations. Salgor raised his axe in a mocking salute. "Hope you enjoyed good ale while I was napping in there, like I told you!"

Salgor Bandago pumped his legs as he charged the troublesome foe. The dwarf wondered if Revwar had any more creatures to summon. Revwar rushed a few hurried steps to retrieve his staff. He seemed to be out of conjured monsters. Salgor knocked aside the podium and book during his charge. The blessed axe slashed overhead. Revwar had only his wizard's staff.

Salgor wasn't worried. Once a dwarven warrior got within reach of a wizard, the wizard was as good as dead.

*   *   *   *   *

Petrow felt panic building as Savannah continued her prayer. "…please stop this soul from…"

Petrow couldn't allow himself to be paralyzed or he would never live to see his friends again. The handyman pulled her forward by her wrists, blasting out her breath with a knee to her gut. The prayer faltered. He released one of her arms to deliver a punch. Petrow had no idea how he could kill her with his bare hands before she could simply intone another prayer.

He barged into her with all his weight, pinning Savannah into the corner and trapping her left hand behind her. The young man retained his firm grip on her right arm.

"DeLaris, please stop…"

Petrow slammed the heel of his free hand against the bottom of her jaw, shutting her mouth. He had her trapped. The heel of his hand pressed hard against her jaw, forcing her mouth shut and her head back. She was under his control at the moment, but he knew that might prove fleeting. Savannah grunted as she wiggled, kicked, and otherwise tried to free her left arm. Petrow kept pressing against her, even trying a few kicks of his own but mostly trying hard to keep his balance. She fought savagely.

Without warning, she stopped. She relaxed her muscles and stared at him with those cold, blue eyes. He looked upon her hateful glare, fully remembering how heartless and cruel she could be. Petrow couldn't help but think of her strangling him, or the night she let the minotaur torture him. Now she was trapped and he was in charge. Petrow knew it to be an illusionary situation, since he could not hold her forever, and all she needed was to be free for a few seconds and she would have him. As Petrow stared past the hand that held her jaw shut, he noticed her nostrils flare. Her breath fanned over his fingers as she awaited her opportunity.

An idea came to Petrow. With the heel of his hand firmly pressed against her jaw, Petrow's middle and ring finger pinched over the abbess' nose. Her eyes shot wide with fear, signaling a scream she could not release. The young man no longer felt air passing over his hand.

The last thing Petrow wanted was to suffocate a woman with his bare hands, but she had already proved no qualms about doing the same to him. He covered his own misgivings with false bravado.

"You claim my life for your goddess, do you?" Petrow shouted in her face. "Well what if I claimed your life instead? Why don't I claim you for any god I choose?"

Savannah squirmed and thrashed in desperation underneath his weight. His right hand clamped down on her jaw and face harder than before. He pushed her head back so far that he thought her spine might snap. Petrow would have liked to step away from his body at that moment, to do what needed to be done and then walk away to find his friends. He had never heard of heroes winning like this. Every muffled noise of despair from her throat came to his ears. Her wrist felt so small and frail in his hands, yet he continued to twist it to keep her under control. He hated himself for this nightmare of his own choosing, but he could not let her kill his friends.

310

Petrow saw tears run from the abbess' shaded eyes. The young man cried as well, though he would not ease his grip. He yelled at her, wanting it all to end. "Why can't you just die?"

His voice cracked, and he closed his eyes. Petrow no longer looked at her, though he could not shut away the sounds she made. Her limbs struggled…then twitched…and then finally went limp.

He held her for a few seconds longer, unsure if she attempted deception. Her entire body felt limp. Opening his eyes, Petrow stepped back. The woman who served the Death Goddess collapsed and lay still. The handyman from the small village of Troutbrook trembled as his own emotions tried to recover.

He heard Savannah gasp in a breath. Petrow wasn't sure what to feel. He nervously drifted between feelings of whether he should run or strangle her again. Savannah showed no signs of consciousness. Just the sound of her breathing caused his knees to shake.

As evil as he viewed the woman, he didn't want to live with the memory of ending someone's life that way. Petrow felt he had to find a way to remove her as a threat without suffocating her again. He set about removing any items from her that might be used against him or his friends. Petrow scrounged until he had come up with several lengths of leather and cloth: some from her and the rest from storage in the room.

Petrow tied her arms and legs then gagged her mouth. By the time Petrow finished, Savannah remained unconscious. Petrow hoped he wasn't making a mistake by allowing her to live. He blew out the candles in the room and shut the door behind him. In such a large keep, Savannah lay captive behind one of many doors. Her friends would have a hard time searching her out. From Petrow's belt hung Savannah's gold pouch. He figured that somehow she owed him that much. Petrow retrieved his woodcutter's axe in the hallway and went off to find his friends.

*   *   *   *   *

The Tariykan faced Cat's back as she turned her head away from him. He saw her shoulders sag. Loung stood easily within the doorway, expecting some last ditch trick. His confidence and patience allowed him to stand in meditation at the door. Let them try another trick, then he would finish both. By all appearances, the gnome was still chained helplessly to the wall. A few seconds passed as the Tariykan detected whispers between Cat and Mel. He watched the muscles tense in her shoulders…her subtle shift of balance…a slow, methodical movement from one arm almost hidden from his view.

Loung released his muscles to a relaxed state that would react by instinct more than rational thought. Cat spun around fast enough that Loung had to admire the attempt. Despite all her bruises, the woman remained as agile and swift as ever. Cat held Mel's tiny crossbow. As she aimed, Loung could look directly down the sights and into her green eyes.

Cat fired. Less than ten feet separated them, which gave little time to react. Loung Chao's physical body and mental focus reacted like the masters of his homeland. The next moment became a blur in the eyes of Mel and Cat, as the Tariykan twisted around.

311

Loung faced them once more, smiling his victory around the bolt caught in his teeth. As he looked at the two adventurers, he noticed something odd about their reactions.

Cat and Mel smiled back.

If Loung had a good look at the bolt clenched in his teeth, he would have noticed a ball of clay on the end of the tip—a tip hovering inside his mouth. That clay was a special spell of Mel's design. The gnome had bragged that he could set the time to detonation when he threw it, or that he could leave it ticking away a countdown…and did he mention that he is usually quite accurate with it? Even if Loung had examined the clay ball, he still might not have guessed the terrible explosive force it unleashed against two goblins just south of Troutbrook.

A blast of heated air, followed by a roar of buffeting wind erupted from the entryway of the room. Cat turned to protect Mel from the deafening blast, but the force of it knocked her into a roll. Dust and debris were forcefully relocated to other areas in a pelting storm. Objects clattered down like a hailstorm. Although the initial blast died quickly, the resulting cloud took time to settle. Cat felt her way through darkness for Mel. The sorcerer coughed up dust. The half-elf and the gnome found each other covered in dark soot. The two of them looked toward the entry of the room, searching for any sign of the Tariykan warrior.

They spotted most of his body. Loosely draped in shredded silks from far off lands, the man's headless corpse rest in the doorway of the room. Loung Chao had finally fallen victim to a projectile, only because he preferred to catch them instead of avoid them.

Cat and Mel smiled, bright teeth gleaming through soot-stained faces. As one, they gleefully shouted the name of Mel's prize spell.

"Timed Boomy!"

To complete their jubilation, Cat finished unlocking Mel from his bonds. The two of them then proceeded to find a route upstairs.

*   *   *   *   *

Trestan knew he couldn't escape the minotaur. Every breath brought more pain than air. Bortun spit on his massive hands, adjusting his grip on the handle of his weapon. The minotaur lifted his axe for a finishing blow. The young smith from Troutbrook took a final look around the room, scanning the walls from his kneeling position. He wondered if anything could turn the course of fate. Suddenly, the young man found an idea.

Trestan looked up into the dark eyes of the minotaur. "Sorry about the horn. I shouldn't embarrass you like that, making you go through life as the hornless minotaur."

Bortun's eyes widened in surprise at the doomed man's insult. He snorted his displeasure as he spoke. "I think you should be begging for mercy, boy."

"Not at all," Trestan shook his head. As he continued to speak, his voice took on a daring tone. He chose his words carefully. "It would be an honor that you end the suffering I now face of smelling your ugly hide! It's embarrassing that I lost a fight against a worthless…hornless…abomination. You aren't even half as tough as a dwarf!"

312

Bortun roared in rage. No one ever dared insult him in the face of his mighty axe. The creature backed up one step, then two. He snorted his anger with blood-shot eyes. Trestan recalled stories of minotaurs so enraged that their eyes sparkled a promise of blood. The creature's two hooves pawed the ground like a bull ready to charge. Bortun jumped forward in a great overhead swing, throwing more than enough momentum to split a human in half.

Trestan dove flat, shouting one last, desperate word. "Fifteen!"

Bortun didn't have time to puzzle over an object propped on a stone bench behind the young man. The metallic disk, three feet across, leaned casually against the wall. In such an upright position, the gnomes would name it a Horizontally Mounted Magical Pushing/Moving Assistant. The magic of the device responded to Trestan's command as the young man lie flattened below its area of effect.

The magical device quickly halted Bortun's 'descent' towards its surface. It weighed the half-ton minotaur, including the great axe and the momentum of his charge. The magical mind of the device calculated the force required to launch the minotaur fifteen gnomish equivalent levels. Of course, the device was not expected to realize it sat within the confines of a small room, since gnomes expected buyers to use their trinkets respectably and carefully.

Bortun shot backward in a blur. Trestan stayed flat, covering his head, when he felt the impact of the creature striking the opposite wall. He heard the cracking of bones mixed with the noises of stones tumbling free of the age-old mortar. Trestan waited for more sounds, but eventually the noise died after the last few chips of stone tumbled to the floor.

Trestan peeked from under his arms. He saw a portion of the minotaur's body, lying in blood. The young man pushed himself to his knees. Parts of the creature had popped like a ripe fruit when it hit the far wall. Some portions of the creature blasted through the wall and into the next room. Trestan peered through a sizeable hole in the thin, stone wall of the chamber, spotting the axe. Its magical edge and great weight left it firmly embedded two walls over, between the halves of Bortun's head.

For a moment, Trestan stared speechless with disbelief. The young man almost expected some portion of the creature to rise up against him as an undead ghost, claiming revenge for the killing. The great bulk of the minotaur stayed splattered amidst two separate rooms. The facts sank in, elating Trestan. He had passed his test of courage.

"Huzzah!" He threw up his hands in victory. "I had faith, Abriana! I actually won!"

Trestan forgot to guard his words while kneeling in front of the magical gnomish lift. The device misinterpreted the word 'won' as a request for 'one' standard gnomish level. Trestan found himself tossed head-over-feet towards the other side of the room. He came to rest almost upside down against the pile of stones and minotaur body parts. The young man viewed the gnomish device from an upside-down perspective.

Trestan kept his next words as silent thoughts in his head. "If I live to have grandchildren, and I retell the tale of how I defeated the minotaur, I'm leaving out any word about this last little mistake."

*   *   *   *   *

Salgor roared as his axe came down at Revwar. The dwarf's axe bounced harmlessly off the wizard's staff. Revwar had not even been moved by the blow. Salgor cursed all magic! Revwar possessed enchantments that gave him a warrior's fighting chance at survival. The elf withdrew his staff just enough to coil his muscles for a strike. Ignoring the big stick, Salgor readied his axe for a swing. The end of the staff rammed outward, slamming into Salgor's armored chest. To his surprise, the hit knocked him flat.

Salgor stared back at the standing wizard. He recalled a scene during the bluff battle when the elf picked up Savannah's armored body and carried her like a toy. The dwarf thought it a tragedy that one who studied books could magically achieve the muscles of a battle-hardened warrior. Even the wooden staff showed more resilience than it appeared. Salgor resigned himself to fighting another strong opponent.

Salgor rolled aside as Revwar brought the staff crashing down on the floor. The dwarf barely gained one knee when Revwar swung the staff like a club. Salgor started to block with his mace, but the ensorcelled staff sent him flying. Salgor landed with a crash, but sprang to his feet before Revwar could approach. Yellow eyes stared at the bearded warrior with open hatred. Salgor realized he had lost his mace. He didn't bother to look for it. The dwarf put a firm, two-handed grip on his treasured axe. His victory would be that much sweeter when Revwar finally did go down.

Daerkfyre's warrior raised his axe, ready to face whatever other tricks the wizard had in store. "Throw it all at me! I'll take your worst and keep coming!"

Salgor launched at the wizard with fury. Revwar met him halfway. Magic lent the wizard strength and sped his movements. Aside from those qualities, the mage lacked actual combat knowledge. The wizard fell for easy feints, but usually his enhanced reactions recovered in time to defend against Salgor's real attacks. Salgor did succeed in getting past his weapon a few times, ripping tears across Revwar's black robe. The blessed axe drew blood: hits which would have downed most of the dwarf's normal opponents. Revwar's magical reserves handled the physical threat, and those energies kept him fighting where others would already be dead.

The wizard also hurt Salgor. The staff spun with bruising force, knocking the dwarf away time and again. Revwar hit as hard as a heavily muscled dwarf. The elf managed to bring a heavy blow to Salgor's forearms. The move almost knocked the axe from numb hands, but the dwarf held tight. Revwar hit the dwarf with his best shots, but the veteran warrior held the advantage.

Beaten but not down, Revwar made one last rain of blows on the dwarf before leaping away from his opponent. Salgor accepted a few brutal hits, but when the elf tried to withdraw, the axe succeeded in slicing another cut across the mage's back. The elf made a strong jump, enhanced by the spell powering his muscles. He landed next to the holy relic he had used earlier. The elf grabbed it as Salgor charged. The dwarf was determined to stop the wizard before he let loose any more surprises.

Revwar's cloak opened like a pair of wings. Just like his arrival at the bluff battle, Revwar's cloak empowered him with flight. The wizard soared over the slash of Salgor's

314

axe. The dwarf could only watch helplessly as Revwar alighted on the second story balcony.

Revwar stood upon a section of the suspended walkway that still remained whole. The wizard glared down at the dwarf. Salgor held tight to his axe with both hands, scowling up at his distant opponent. The dwarf stomped angrily, unsure how he could reach his adversary. He dared not throw his axe, knowing the attack would be foolish. He glanced around, noting the distance to the different exits to the room, looking for objects he could throw, and watching out for any other enemies that might have reappeared. He spotted the mace well away to one side, though it would be useless now.

Revwar looked down at the dwarf. His quiet tone carried to Salgor's ears. "Curse the stubbornness of dwarves. Your ragged entourage interfered in something much bigger than yourselves, something you cannot understand. The end result will be the same." Revwar paused, and then added, "I do thank you, however."

Those last words puzzled Salgor. The dwarf decided to keep the elf talking to learn what he could. If the elf wizard was going to try another escape, Salgor wanted every advantage in finding him again. "I have gladly tracked you down for many miles, and beaten many o' your henchmen. You will have your death by my hands someday, as sure as every bad ore eventually breaks under pressure. But, why would you thank me?"

Revwar leaned forward, holding aloft the holy relic. "For standing on an unmarked section of the floor."

Salgor reflexively glanced at the magically-inscribed patterns on the throne room floor. Apparently, Revwar still planned to use those symbols for some purpose. Whatever Revwar planned to do next, however, would probably result in the destruction of the floor where Salgor stood.

Salgor raced forward, trying to run under the balcony and out of Revwar's sight. Words from the elf wizard flowed into the relic, causing it to sparkle in greenish lights once again. The light bathed Salgor in its glow. The dwarf was not affected, but the floor underneath him started to buckle and crack. Salgor threw his arms and his axe forward, straining to get to the edge of the spell's effect. The floor tumbled away into the cellar much the same way as part of the balcony collapsed earlier. Salgor leaped to the edge of the open expanse, barely catching a hold on the side of the open pit. His axe slid several feet ahead, thrown to the safety of firm footing. The dwarf dangled at the edge of the open hole, listening to the crumbling floor smash into the cellar room below.

Revwar noted the dwarf's predicament, so the wizard refocused the energies of the relic. The green rays of the stone stretched up to touch the roof of the throne room. Stone and rock shifted again, buckling as the magic of the stone ripped into the structure. The section of the roof above the dwarf came down in an avalanche of rock and dust. Revwar had to step back to avoid falling debris. The elf lost sight of the dwarf, but witnessed the cascade of stone coming down past the balcony. Several large pieces clipped the second floor walkway, taking that stone guardrail into the cellar as well. The dwarf yelled out in pain once. The fall of stone and marble brought a crescendo of crashing noises to assault the sensitive ears of the elf caster.

The downfall of debris soon ended. A cloudy pall of dust hung about the throne room. A shaft of sunlight pierced the damaged ceiling. Revwar peered over the damaged balcony. The cloud of dust limited visibility, but he could see what he expected to see. The edges of the hole had been widened when the stones rained down. Several broken pieces decorated the perimeter of the damaged floor. The dwarf's axe rested a few feet away from the edge. Of the dwarf himself, Revwar saw no sign. That section had been slammed into the cellar. Piles of stone and marble were visible in the cellar storeroom, unmoving now that the rocks had settled. For the longest time Revwar stared into the depths of the hole.

"That is some of my worst and I'm waiting for you to keep coming," the elf wizard spoke in a mocking tone. Silence was the only reply. Revwar shook his head. "I didn't think I would get a reply; it seems I won't be disappointed."

*   *   *   *   *

Trestan made his way through the confusing passageways of the keep. He didn't attempt to backtrack to the stairway that brought him to this level. Instead, he tried to find a different way back towards the center. The young smith remembered the second floor balcony that ran along the throne room and thought it would be a good destination.

He'd suffered numerous hard hits, resulting in a good deal of pain. Even breathing brought a stabbing sting, but the young man would not relent. His love for his friends and his determination to finish the quest fueled his weary muscles. His helmet remained on the first floor. The young man's armor displayed the dents from the minotaur scuffle. The Sword of the Spirit, retrieved from the demolished kitchen, led his path. In the other hand he carried a different magical item. Trestan wasn't even sure that he should carry the magical gnomish lift, but the young man figured he might put it to more good use. As long as he wasn't speaking, and there was no one else with whom to talk, the device should be safe.

The hall shook from the avalanche of stone somewhere ahead. The young man thought the sound was similar to when the balcony crashed down with Cat. The proximity of the rumblings suggested that he was closing in on the battle. Trestan flexed the fingers of his sword hand a bit, shifting his grip. Any action he took would have to be quick and decisive.

Trestan Karok rounded a corner amidst air swirling with dust. He faced a short hallway, ending in an open arch to a larger room beyond. The second floor balcony was hardly recognizable, missing the guardrail. The dust in the air suggested the collapse had come from this area.

The elf wizard, Revwar, overlooked the room below. His torn robe whipped around his lean frame. At Trestan's approach, the keen senses of the elf alerted him to danger. Revwar turned, holding aloft the staff in one hand and the relic in the other. Trestan had the chance to act before the wizard could incant a spell. Trestan charged, but several steps separated them. In order to gain a surprise advantage, Trestan made a rash move. He tossed the magical gnomish lift at the wizard.

There was no time to dwell on whether this was the wisest action he could take in light of its magic. The metal disk spun through the air. The act and the strange item surprised Revwar, leaving him no time to dodge. The flying disk clipped the hand bearing the holy relic. Both the gnomish lift and the mysterious stone from Troutbrook sailed over the edge of the balcony, out of reach.

To Trestan, it seemed to work to his advantage. The young man had both hands on his sword as he closed the distance. The young smith charged through the opening, meeting Revwar on that narrow stretch of damaged balcony. The wizard's spells aided his reflexes. The wizard's staff blocked the swing, suffering only a scratch in the process. Trestan went wide-eyed, but spun the blade in another attack.

The second hit never landed. Revwar's staff spun around and hit Trestan with jarring force. It flung the human's body from the entryway, leaving him to fear a fall into the throne room below. By luck or fortune, Trestan landed on a section of the balcony that still retained a guardrail.

Trestan immediately tried getting back to his feet. The elvish sword lay several feet away, in the direction of the elf wizard. Trestan succeeded in getting as far as a sitting position, his back against the chamber walls, as Revwar launched another surprise. The elf traced a pattern in the air until a gooey, bubbly object appeared, floating around his hand. The wizard finished his spell with a shout, and the object flew like an arrow. Trestan yelled something unintelligible. The object struck him with a wet splatter, as if someone had hit him with a thrown tomato. The substance spread of its own accord over his body. Trestan tried brushing it off, but the spell somehow coated his chest and arms.

He felt the effects right away. A tingling sensation enveloped his limbs. Soon, Trestan's arms and legs felt heavy. Any movement required every ounce of strength he could muster. The smith couldn't get to his feet. He doubted he could grip his sword, which lay beyond his reach.

Revwar sagged against the nearby entryway, drained from the effort put into casting this newest attack. The fighting had taxed him well into the last reserves of mental energy available for spells. The elf's moment of weakness passed, while Trestan remained a prisoner of sabotaged muscles. Revwar took a step towards Trestan, eyes promising death.

Revwar looked beyond Trestan in surprise, spotting Cat and Mel charging at him from that end of the walkway. The two combatants looked dirty and hurt, but they retained an appetite for battle. Trestan's heart soared at the sight. Mel wielded some item in his hand as he ran. The gnome slowed, but only to begin casting a spell aimed at Revwar. Cat, who did not appear to be armed, dropped her pace to stay well behind the sorcerer's spell. To Trestan's surprise, the exhausted wizard tried to flee down a side hall to escape the sorcerer's sight.

Petrow ran out of the same hallway Revwar sought safety. It boosted the companions' morale, seeing so many of their friends survived and reunited at a critical moment. Revwar and Petrow skidded to a halt right on top of each other.

Petrow stepped back as he readied his axe for a swing. Revwar moved quicker, aided by magical means. The elf delivered a punch to the face. Bolstered by his enhanced strength, Petrow almost fell to the ground. Revwar dropped his staff as he grabbed the human with both hands. With Mel's spell nearing completion, the elf turned his attacks in a new direction. The empowered wizard picked up Petrow and tossed him down the balcony at his friends. It looked odd that a slim being could launch a man that impressively, but such was the potency of the elf's spells.

Mel finally completed his rather difficult spell, hurling all its energy at the elf wizard. Multi-colored bands of light and magic unraveled from the elf's form. Trestan had his eyes on Revwar, hoping the spell would finish off their opponent. Instead, Revwar seemed unhurt, though some worry dawned in those yellow eyes.

Mel remembered well when his first wand blast had reflected harmlessly off an arcane shield during the opening shot of the battle. Instead of trying to harm the wizard, the layers of supportive enchantments woven around Revwar were stripped away in a single, powerful magic attack. The elf lost his strength, his speed, the ability to fly, and other spells which made him more resilient to physical damage. It left him very vulnerable.

Sadly, Mel could not follow up with another spell. Trestan looked over to see Petrow and Mel lying in a heap on the balcony. The young handyman from Troutbrook seemed dizzy and disoriented. Partly trapped under him was a now unconscious Mel Bellringer.

Trestan struggled to stand, but his muscles could not get past his sitting position. Looking back at the pile of Mel and Petrow, Trestan saw Cat make her attack. She seemed to be their last hope of stopping Revwar. The half-elf pulled free her hidden dagger as she charged, one well-balanced for throwing as well as melee combat. The dagger was Cat's last weapon, but too much distance separated her from the elf wizard, and a thrown dagger could take him out.

Trestan called out, "Use my sword if you can get to it!"

Cat hopped over the tangled bodies of Petrow and Mel as she ran. Her arm came up and flipped the dagger at her opponent. Trestan turned to follow its tumbling flight. Trestan also saw Revwar's beam of deadly energy cut through the air, the same beam that injured Trestan on the bluff and killed Sir Wilhelm. Revwar was still firing away with his deadly beam when the dagger pierced him. The blade sunk into one shoulder, ending the elf's spell and drawing blood.

Trestan felt the impact as Cat fell face-down across his lower limbs. The strength-draining spell left Trestan helpless as he looked over Cat, lying stricken across his legs. Her long, dark hair obscured his view, but the half-elf's hands reached for a spot somewhere between her face and her upper chest. The young smith watched, horrified, as her blood proceeded to run down his legs.

Only moments ago, everything seemed to be coming together miraculously for the group, but now everyone was down. Petrow still knelt, shaking his head to clear the jarring effects of his landing. Mel sprawled unconscious. Trestan's muscles wouldn't cooperate. Cat suffered from a serious injury. There was no sign of the dwarf.

Revwar, breathing heavily, reached up and pulled the dagger from his shoulder, wincing at the motion. The fight had loosened some of his silvery hair from its braids, his torn black robe was stained with blood, and his stamina had been taxed by the casting of so many spells. He worried over the absence of so many of his comrades in arms. Savannah was not around to heal his injuries. The two fighters were not there to provide him with a wall of muscle. Without his protective incantations in place, even a nonmagical dagger could threaten him. The elf wizard still retained the upper hand, and he wasn't about to give the others the opportunity to harm him again. He took a deep breath to steady his shaking hands. Leaning against the shattered balcony railing, he began uttering magic words. Flames danced at the edges of his fingertips, promising an end to them all.

Trestan wanted to deny what he saw, after all they endured. Every step of the way they had stood their ground through some tough spots. Only one opponent still stood in their way, and yet he was about to put a final end to them all. One of the smith's hands stroked Cat's quivering shoulder, and that simple touch brought some peace to his heart. The half-elf did not see the flames forming, too occupied in stemming the flow of blood. Trestan wished they had more time: sharing a drink with the dwarf, listening to Mel's stories, joking with Petrow, and telling Cat she was the most beautiful thing that ever happened to him.

Trestan remembered Sir Wilhelm's parting words. He whispered, "Thank you, goddess, for the life you have given me."

As Revwar's spell approached a crescendo, another voice boomed with the ferocity of a follower of Daerkfyre.

"Six!"

The gnomish contraption, lost to the cellar, launched its most tenacious critic.

'Two' would have been enough to lift Salgor to his abandoned weapons on the throne room floor, but wouldn't have saved his friends on the balcony. Fortunately, the dwarf found a silver rapier, a hunting cat sculpted on its pommel, among the cellar debris.

'Four' would have been sufficient to bring the dwarf level with the balcony with the broken guardrail. Revwar, deep in concentration, lost his focus as the rapier punched through his abdomen and burst forth from his back. Thus skewered by the catapulted dwarf, the spell flames died away in a puff of smoke. Revwar grunted in pain as the impact of the dwarf and rapier spirited him upwards.

'Six' left enough momentum even after the collision to send both combatants soaring even higher. With all the force behind the dwarf's launch, the elf wizard was crushed between the immobile ceiling and the flying dwarf.

Both fell back to the balcony. This time Salgor landed on the bottom. Revwar, impaled on the blade of the rapier, lay draped over the dwarf's back. Salgor rose up with a roar of anger. He used his arm muscles to throw the elf up and away from him. Revwar slid off the end of the piercing blade, trailing a stream of blood as his body flew over the edge of the balcony. The elf crashed into the cellar, two floors down.

Salgor limped to the edge of the balcony. He observed the wizard's body sprawled atop a pile of broken stone. The dwarf worked up a wad of bloody spit and let it fly at the unmoving elf.

He bellowed with his gruff attitude, "You should have brought a few dwarves with you instead o' a minotaur! I would have enjoyed having more o' a challenge!"

CHAPTER 28

A moment of silence followed the dwarf's bellow. A moment mixed with indecision and uncertainty, and of victory tainted with pain. Mel moved his hands and groaned as he raised his head. Petrow shakily got back to his feet. Salgor stretched out his sore muscles, popping joints and cracking knuckles. The dwarf picked up the elvish blade as he approached. Trestan felt Revwar's gooey spell flake away, allowing strength to return to his limbs.

He worried for Cat, still draped over his legs. Trestan used his reinvigorated strength to help Cat roll over. Her condition struck a blow to his heart. Katressa held her hands to a wound near the base of her throat. The wizard's ray left a smoking gash that marred the half-elf's soft skin. Blood soaked through her fingers despite her best attempts to hold it back. Her lips moved as she struggled to get a message into words, but no sound other than a strained wheeze came from her mouth. They stared eye to eye. Trestan saw the depth of seriousness behind her glance that told him how precariously her life hung in the balance. He saw many emotions go through those tearful emerald eyes: fear, regret and despair.

Petrow helped rouse Mel from slumber. The human profusely apologized to the bewildered gnome. Both heard the young smith's urgency as he questioned Cat. "Can you breathe at all? Can you say anything?"

Those few words got everyone's attention on their companion's plight. All of them saw Cat's response as she shook her head, wincing in pain. Another feeble wheeze escaped through her injury. A moment of shock passed through all of her comrades.

The half-elf continued applying pressure over her wound. Trestan held Cat and tried to comfort her, but his eyes darted about wildly as he tried to think of anything that would help them. "Healing draughts! Anyone have a healing draught on them?"

The question met a chorus of shaking heads. Their group had been in Troutbrook long enough to enjoy a party, but left when the group spontaneously decided to use *Dovewing* to pursue the relic thieves. No one had taken the time to secure healing supplies of any kind. Trestan's hopes and Cat's chances of survival diminished. The young smith jumped to the next logical course of action. "Well, find some! There has to be some around here somewhere! Check those tables and containers they have set up down there."

Petrow ran back to the passage from which he had entered earlier. He knew a stairway that would take him down to the throne room. Salgor took a more direct course. He dropped both rapier and elvish blade beside Trestan and Cat. The bruised dwarf brazenly jumped off of the balcony, landing in a roll on the ground floor. Mel frantically searched through his bandolier of pouches. The gnome sorcerer tried to find anything helpful, but his frown revealed his lack of progress.

Trestan Karok wanted to find a remedy for Cat as well, yet at the same time she needed someone close to her. He placed one hand to cover hers, both trying to slow the bleeding at her throat. His other arm supported her back, and Cat lay her head against him. He cradled her close, their eyes intimately near as they tried to get control of her loss of blood. Their attempts seemed futile in the face of the greater problem. She continued to

320

struggle for air, drawing in meager amounts. When their pressure on her wound tightened, she couldn't breathe, but when loosened, she bled more. Trestan saw the hurt in her eyes as she tried to draw breath. The wheezing noises indicated she could not get enough. The young man whispered soft words of encouragement into her ears. Cat closed her eyes and leaned into him. The hand against her back moved in comforting ways as he caressed her long hair during that sad embrace. For the short time he had known Cat, he had always admired her inner strength. Now she seemed so small and weak as she leaned to him for support.

Petrow and Salgor searched for a vial containing any healing miracle. Jars were read and then thrown aside, bags emptied out on the floor and tables cleared from end to end. Useless objects were cast away. Petrow and Salgor searched as fast as they could despite many containers of powders and herbs.

Mel Bellringer had given up looking for anything useful in his pouches. The sorcerer crawled closer to Cat and patted her leg to offer up whatever comfort he could. Only minutes ago, Cat rescued him from chains. The gnome wished he could save her in return.

Trestan looked to the gnome, "Mel, what do you know about our other enemies? Are any of them dead or still running around?"

Mel looked up and replied, "We took care of that Tariykan. Loung Chao? I think that was his name. Cat and I helped him lose his head! How did you fare?"

Mel patted Cat's legs as he spoke. She reached out to give his hand a firm squeeze in return, managing a brief smile. Trestan answered the gnome, "It didn't look like I would make it, but maybe Abriana looked over my shoulder. I found a way to kill Bortun. How about Savannah?"

Mel shrugged. The gnome peeked over the balcony rail to yell at the two friends searching the room below. "Do either of you know what happened to Savannah?"

"She isn't a threat for now," Petrow yelled back. "She's in a room in the lower level; tied and wrapped up in so much leather that she might get mistaken for a cow!"

That brought another fleeting smile to Cat's face. Despite the brief levity, her condition worsened. Cat squirmed a bit, trying to force more air through her injured throat. Her other hand tried ineffectively to pull at her tunic's neckline. She seemed much weaker. Even as Trestan watched, the half-elf lost the strength to keep her arms up. Trestan, alone, held pressure to her wound. Cat looked up into Trestan's eyes once more as she pressed against him.

"Hurry, please, find something!" Trestan yelled.

Cat tried to lay a comforting hand on Trestan. Tears streamed down her face. It hurt Trestan to see her suffer like this. The woman put forth every effort to retain her grip on life, but it was inexorably slipping away.

Trestan leaned very close to Cat. The arm draped around her shoulder squeezed her reassuringly, while he delivered a gentle kiss to her forehead. With their heads together, Trestan whispered into her ear. "Hang on as long as you can. Don't leave us yet. I…I love you too much to let you go like this."

Despite Trestan knowing Cat for only a short time, he spoke from the heart. The adventures they shared on this trip had put her in the forefront of his mind many times. The memories of her morning stretch routine, the generosity of her purse, as well as her outline silhouetted in the moonlight back at Barkan's Crossing, were etched into his mind. Her smiles warmed his days. Now the woman he admired and loved struggled for life in his arms. What could he do? Trestan had put his faith in the Goddess of Love and Healing, yet was this the cruel price? How could they have achieved so much, only to be helpless as lovely Cat died of her wounds?

A memory rose unbidden into his mind, from the night of the battle in Troutbrook, centered on Savannah.

The elf wizard bleeding to death near her required the most obvious need for her talents. She held up her holy symbol and mouthed a few words of prayer to her goddess. Kneeling by Revwar, she grabbed the bolt and pulled it out with a quick jerk. The elf writhed and screamed, but her prayers continued. Unseen beneath his robes, the wound closed and mended. The effect became plain to see: he took in a deep breath and pulled himself back to his feet. Drying blood still soaked a portion of his robes, but the wound miraculously vanished.

Trestan considered the memory, even as another one surfaced. This was during the same battle, after Jareth had been brought down by the same wizard's beam.

He caught movement from Sir Wilhelm. The warrior brought one of his hands close to his side and uttered prayers. Trestan couldn't hear what was said. The warrior spoke softly, his eyes closed in reverence...

Trestan looked between Revwar and Sir Wilhelm as events hastened. The old warrior's prayers to his goddess somehow healed some of his wounds.

The goddess Abriana could give the power to heal, as many gods could, but why couldn't she save Cat? Trestan believed Abriana guided him up to this point in their adventure, yet this ending questioned his faith. Trestan wished that he could call on those healing powers to save the woman who guided them through so many dangerous moments. The young smith looked down. Cat did not move at all, she simply lay still while gasping for air. Her face turned pale, and blue tinted her lips.

As Trestan held Cat close, they could hear the frustrated sadness in Petrow's voice as he shouted up to the balcony. "There is nay potions down here! I can't find any healing draughts! I'm sorry Cat! I'm so sorry, I tried my best!"

While Petrow gave in to tears and apologies, Salgor's search became decidedly more violent. The dwarf's axe began searching by means of destroying tables and containers. The warrior of Daerkfyre roared his rage as he destroyed everything that might hide a potion.

As Trestan held Cat's dying body close, a revelation struck him. All the faith in the world could not help channel the healing miracles of the gods unless bolstered by commitment as well. A person had to be an extension of that god's will, bridging the gap between the heavens and the world. This required the ultimate dedication to that god's cause and beliefs.

322

Those words from his father came back to haunt him: *"I wonder if you may have been influenced more than I suspected by Sir Wilhelm, and that you look at the possibilities of becoming a paladin."*

He debated those thoughts the previous evening, but it was a step he feared to take. The young man would be forever stepping away from his old life. How could a person give up everything they wanted and aspired, pledging everything to serve something so far above them? How could one give up their life that way?

Another voice spoke inside his head, adopting Sir Wilhelm's tone. He could hear his mentor speak as if they debated philosophies near that shrine in the woods. "Serving a goddess like Abriana is not about giving up your aspirations or plans. Instead, you become a champion for all that you already love and hope to achieve. Walking beside Abriana's grace also allows you to satisfy the wants of others that you love. It's a common interest. You are not required to give up anything outside the boundaries of your beliefs and character. Instead, you are merely committing yourself to be more outspoken in your ideals and uphold your beliefs. Ideals you share with her already."

A question still concerned him. Through his thoughts, he addressed the voice which just provided such insight. "The thought still scares me. How brave will I have to be? What sacrifices will I have to endure to follow the path?"

Sir Wilhelm's phantom responded to his doubts. "You have already faced perils for your own beliefs. Being champion to a goddess is less risky than attacking a minotaur, or of risking a beloved father's anger. The commitment itself is safer than facing three or four armed men all alone. In the course of adventure, you have already risked all of this, as well as the wrath of wizards and an enemy cleric who championed her own goddess. You were willing to jump in the way of a magical spell to spare the lives of your friends, and you would have done the same selfless heroic deed if you had the power a moment ago when Revwar cast his fiery spell. You argued true to your convictions at every turn: refusing to steal horses after the battle in Troutbrook, and voicing your displeasure at stealing *Dovewing* to continue the pursuit. In the end, you journeyed with your friends to protect them and face every danger beside them. Committing yourself to a goddess is nay more risky, and only signifies the path you have already chosen."

Trestan considered the reasoning. He possessed the spirit, love, and courage. It did seem a silly thing to resist the call, when in truth it supported his own beliefs.

Trestan looked down at the beautiful woman, mortally stricken, awaiting her inevitable death in his arms. Cat was no longer conscious. Those once-sparkling emerald eyes were closed and hidden away. Her limp body strained for air. Trestan noticed Mel, cupping one of her hands, but crying against her leg. Petrow still wailed apologies from below as he and Salgor gave in to the realization there were no sources of healing available.

Cat only had one chance, and Trestan wasn't sure how to go about it, or if he possessed the ability. The young man brought his thoughts back to Savannah and Sir Wilhelm Jareth. Every miracle came from prayers. Trestan would have to pray also, in a way he never had before. All his beliefs and commitment would be brought to the test if he was to leap this barrier. Trestan focused his concentration into his bloody hand covering Cat's throat.

"Abriana, please heed the call of your faithful. Heal this person whom I love."

Trestan felt a change in his hand, mind and body. A rush of energy poured from his soul and flowed to his limbs. It surprised his senses. Even as he called upon it, the energy asked for a release. Trestan tried to focus on Cat and Abriana, trying to will the power onward.

Something still blocked the energy. Abriana heard his prayer and responded. Somehow the power would not flow into Cat. He tried to figure how the miracle could be begging for release and yet stay trapped within him. It had to be his commitment. For the miracle to work, he had to dedicate himself to his goddess and allow her to work through his human frame.

Trestan threw back his head and declared his devotion. His words rang across the throne room. "Abriana! I declare myself thy champion! I live to serve you in our common beliefs! Take my body as a vessel for your influence in this world. Heed my call and heal my friend."

Trestan gave himself to the power stored up inside of him. Abriana reached through her champion, passing her healing energies across his limbs and into his touch. The smith from Troutbrook became a part of the love and healing. There was no more doubt and worry about losing himself and his dreams, for the power granted to him flowed forth to accomplish his own goals. His will and commitment opened the gate. Trestan became a paladin of Abriana, the Goddess of Love and Healing.

Mel didn't expect that Trestan's shouts would have any effect. He believed Trestan was just as grief-struck and helpless as the rest of them. The gnome cradled Cat's limp hand between his own. When a small light sprang forth from Trestan's hand, the gnome assumed it was just a trick of the light. Mel wondered if his teary eyes played a trick when he saw Cat's spilled blood dry up and blow away in the midst of an unexplainable wind. The sorcerer peered closer as the edges of her wound stitched together into unblemished skin.

Mel nearly jumped when Cat's hand found its strength and instinctively gripped the sorcerer's. "Aagh!"

The amazed gnome observed Cat's chest rise with a deep breath of fresh air. Her eyes sprung open, viewing the world once again. She blinked at Mel a few times in bewilderment. Each breath came easily to her now. She felt warm healing energies flow through Trestan's hand and into her restored throat. Cat looked with wonder at Trestan, seeing something more than the young man she had known before. His eyes reflected the power and love of his goddess. His embrace sheltered and comforted her like nothing before. His miraculous touch caused health and wholeness to flood throughout her body. The experience also brought forth a peace and contentment of the mind she'd never felt before. It reminded her of the day beside the small waterfall, thinking that Trestan would lean close and kiss her.

Trestan offered as much as he could without any formalized training. The flow of energy trickled and stopped, leaving Trestan even wearier than before. The man's heart felt oddly replenished and buoyed, but his mind and muscles needed rest. It gave him an appreciation of the physical and mental drain of utilizing divine energy.

Trestan and Cat locked eyes once again, keeping their thoughts private. He rested his head against her, and she leaned closer to his chest. They embraced for companionship and support. It was a tender moment, broken only by the sounds of both regaining their breath.

Salgor called up from below, "What is happening up there?"

Mel could barely contain his excitement. The gnome rushed over to the balcony railing and peeked his eyes and nose over the edge to respond, "Trestan healed Cat! She looks like she will be well!"

Salgor stood among a pile of broken tables and scattered pieces of glass and pottery. The dwarf threw his hands up and said, "If he was able to do that all along, then what are we doing down here tearing up this room?"

*   *   *   *   *

With the immediate threats no longer hanging over their heads, the companions relaxed and talked about their experiences. They shared the tales of the destruction of the minotaur, the beheading of Loung Chao, and the imprisonment of Savannah. Salgor talked about the tricks the wizard pulled from the relic stone, which brought awe and disbelief to Petrow and Trestan. The two young men could not believe that such a weapon had always sat on display in the middle of their village.

Cat and Trestan retrieved their weapons from the balcony. Cat cleaned her rapier before returning it to its scabbard. Trestan also wiped his blade, though he wasn't ready to put it away so soon after the action. The gnome was still injured and weary from his fighting.

Mel looked up at Trestan, "I don't suppose I could borrow a little of that healing magic you seem to have acquired."

Trestan felt ashamed that he had not offered to try healing the poor gnome. At the same time, he felt so taxed that he wasn't sure if he had anything left in him. Nevertheless, Trestan placed his free hand against Mel's shoulder and prayed for the healing energies once again.

At first, nothing happened. Trestan felt the energy but was too weary to let it flow through his body. The young man realized it would take time and training to be more efficient at his new ability. In his state, he could not enact the healing powers of his goddess.

But something unexpected did happen as Trestan struggled to reach that miracle. Some foreign energy channeled through Trestan's arm into the gnome. Mel started to feel re-invigorated. The bruise around his eye lost its swelling and discoloration, becoming healthy again. To Trestan, the feeling was vastly different then when he had prayed earlier. There was no feeling of Abriana reaching through his body, or of his heart buoyed by love. Instead, pain and suffering wracked Trestan's body. Cat and Mel watched as the same bruise appeared near Trestan's eye, before he doubled over from pain.

Trestan wanted stop the flow, but he had to figure out what was different. He looked within and traced the source of the energy. His will to heal another had sent a message into the elvish blade in his hand, and somehow the sword's magic responded. The Sword of the Spirit borrowed health and energy from Trestan's body and sent it to Mel. This new flow of power had nothing to do with his faith; this was simply a power of the magical blade previously unknown. With the connection discovered, Trestan severed the willingness to heal. The sword obeyed, shutting off the damage to his body and bringing Mel's healing process to a stop.

Cat and Mel tried to catch Trestan as the young man tipped over. They both worried over his bruised expression.

"I'm fine, I just need a moment." Trestan replied, although by that time he was kneeling on the ground.

Mel spoke out in apology, "I'm sorry, I didn't realize your healing magic hurt you like that!"

Cat's concern reflected in her eyes. Trestan read her glance and realized she was wondering what price Trestan had paid for her healing. The young man quickly explained, "That wasn't my goddess using her healing miracle that time. When I healed you, I channeled Abriana's energies. It alleviated me even as it healed you. This time, I was too tired to tap into that source, and another one opened up." Trestan held forth the elvish blade. "This sword has the power to heal, but at the expense of another's health. We never knew it before, because I don't think anyone ever touched the sword when using healing magic. I didn't have it when I called on my goddess to heal Cat. That's interesting…we had a source of healing with us all along, as long as someone sacrificed a portion of their own vitality for the wounded person."

Mel found this to be very curious. The gnome studied the runes of the blade intently. Cat, watching Trestan, noticed a pall come over his expression. Trestan's eyes were introspective, seeing something from his past that did not seem to be a pleasant memory.

Cat laid her gentle touch upon his cheek, turning his head to face her directly. "Trestan, what is it?"

Trestan replied, "I could have saved that one-eyed man back at the bluff. We had nay other healing, but the sword was there."

Cat hugged Trestan close, and whispered in his ear, "You were hurt as well, and if you had given up any of your health at that time you wouldn't have lived to see Troutbrook and your father again. Let go of that memory."

Trestan took comfort in Cat's embrace and let go of any guilt he still felt for that man who had tried to take his life.

Salgor's voice yelled up from the room below. "Now that we accomplished what we wanted to do, it's time to take what we can and secure ourselves some travel off of this island."

His words reminded the other companions of their remaining plight. Petrow voiced his thoughts, "You think we can somehow do anything in regards to that ship that brought them here? I don't see how we could steal it."

"Steal it?" Salgor questioned, "Do you know how to steer it o' work the sails?"

Cat, Trestan and Mel got to their feet and looked down at their two companions below as the conversation continued. Trestan called down to the dwarf, "None of us here really know how to operate a ship do we? Certainly it is too big for us to even try. What else could we do?"

Salgor grinned and hefted his axe. "Well now, help out an aging dwarf with his memory." From beneath the beard came a toothy smile, minus one tooth. "Isn't this the same ship o' mercenaries and sailors that we already beat up once? How many o' those men did we leave lying behind o' that bluff? Didn't we just kill o' capture all of their big, bad bosses today?"

Trestan and Cat nodded, already seeing the dwarf's reasoning. Salgor continued, "So we just walk down there like we own the place, and make whatever demands we want. I'll walk in there with my axe; Mel can take his wand…"

"The wand ran out of power. It's nay good anymore."

Salgor looked to Mel for a moment before replying, "Well, *they* don't know, do they? Just walk around with a stick and wave it at people occasionally, they'll jump to obey you. Hmm, it would help if we could offer a bribe as a reserve plan."

Petrow continued rummaging through a bag when he responded, "Savannah had a good amount of coins and jewels on her. She won't protest while we keep her tied up."

Trestan spoke as well, "I admit, I took Bortun's gold pouch as well. I had nay qualms about that one. Felt heavy but I didn't count it yet."

Mel and Cat shared a smile. Cat said, "Loung Chao carried a fair amount of wealth as well. I guess none of them trusted their goods to those sailors while stepping onto an island."

Salgor chuckled, "Am I the only one that hasn't looted my opponent yet? Anyways, I believe we have all we need to bully o' buy our transport back to the mainland."

"Whoa!" Exclaimed Petrow.

Everyone looked at him. The young handyman stared wide-eyed into a large bag. Petrow looked up at the sets of eyes staring at him, and he offered a cocky smile back at them.

"I have a question," he began to ask. "How many stones did we set out to retrieve?"

All of his companions held up two fingers, though it was Cat who verbalized, "Two. One stolen from Troutbrook, the other stolen from the mage guild in Orlaun."

Petrow pointed across the floor at the relic stone that had been knocked out of Revwar's hands when Trestan threw the disk. It rested intact and unbroken on the throne room floor.

"That's one," Petrow said.

He then reached into the bag and pulled out another greenish stone. White markings adorned its surface, appearing much like the first one although slightly different.

"Two."

Petrow set the latest stone aside, and reached into the bag once more. As he pulled something forth, he upended the bag to show that nothing else remained hidden inside. Yet there in Petrow's hand was something similar yet different from the original two.

"Three!"

Petrow held the third relic stone, wrapped in some kind of leathery material. It seemed to be a leather scroll, scratched with Elvish lettering.

While the others stared in awe, Cat put forth a suggestion, "One of those could be a fake. They had used fakes to replace the real stones at Orlaun and your village."

Petrow shook his head, "This one with the strange wrapping did not come from our village, and Korrelothar did not mention anything in regards to their stone having a covering with writing."

The blue-eyed youth looked to the sigils and inscriptions marked into the floor. Mel had shared with the others that the wizard intended to summon some kind of demon. The companions went silent as they considered the third stone as well as any motives that might explain a demon's involvement. It seemed they had not solved all the mysteries regarding the theft.

*　　　　*　　　　*　　　　*　　　　*

The river opened up, giving him a view of a large lake at the base of some steep cliffs. The evening sunlight shone with a red hue across the lines of the ship, giving it the appearance of red sails. Trestan looked over the edge of the bow, watching the keel of the *Silver Trident* as it sliced through the calm waters.

Soft footfalls approached from behind. He turned, pleasantly surprised to see Cat. She put on a smile for him, "You were maybe expecting one of the crew to put a knife in your back?"

"Nay, they won't try that here. If they planned to try anything against us, they would have done it by now. As it is, I think they were happy to be rid of the other band. Once we dock at Barkan's Crossing we will leave them, and they will be in a good place to pick up a profitable cargo to take anywhere. Besides, despite their earlier anger and resentment toward us, they liked the gold we offered and the pipe weed Mel shared."

Trestan looked beyond Cat to the deck of the ship. The crewmates made ready to drop anchor in the nearby port. Salgor oversaw them and shouted a few words as they went about their tasks. The dwarf had shared drinks and tales with the sailors, but he made it clear he was in charge right from the start. Given the fighting ferocity of the dwarf they witnessed during the bluff battle, none of the sailors argued the point. Next to the dwarf, Mel smoked contentedly on his pipe.

Trestan looked back at Cat, extending an arm around her waist. The half-elf allowed him to pull her close, and together they stood on the bow of the ship. Trestan and Cat spent a lot of the sea voyage in private conversations, as a romantic bond began forging them together.

As they looked over the lake, Cat asked Trestan, "I still worry about the outcome of that fight. I'm troubled that this isn't over yet."

Trestan nodded in agreement. "Aye. I'm worried as well that they seemed to disappear on us."

Trestan and Cat relived the memories of when they left the keep behind them.

328

Petrow looked through the hole in the floor, searching for something in the cellar below. "Did Revwar look dead when he fell down here?"

The others rushed up behind him. Mel, Salgor, Cat and Trestan stood together as they stared down. They could see the dark red stains of blood on the pile of stone, but the elf wizard no longer lay there.

Salgor looked ready to leap into the cellar. "He isn't getting away! I'm going to kill him twice over if I have to!"

"Wait," Cat held out a hand to stop the dwarf from plunging into the hole. "We barely survived the fight, and our escape plan is based on intimidating the crew of that ship to accommodate us. Let's find that cleric and take her with us if we can, but now that we have the relics I'm not about to have us risk our necks again!"

Salgor's argument was pushed aside as the companions raced into the cellar behind Petrow's lead. The young handyman brought them to the where he had tied up the cleric...but the door to that room stood wide open. There was no evidence of the leather bonds or cloth gag which had kept her prisoner. Just like wood, leather and cloth were also pieces of a once-living creature, and well within her goddess' influence. Either the cleric freed herself with the decay of her bonds or the wizard somehow helped her.

Salgor desired to hunt them down and spill more blood, but Cat would not let him lead them into another fight. The half-elf spoke logically to all of them. "It is more important that we get the stones and ourselves to the ship and away from this island. Let Revwar and Savannah worry about how they will get off of an island in the middle of nowhere. As for us, we did what we could, and we took back what they stole. I doubt even Savannah could restore Loung Chao or Bortun to life, and I sincerely doubt they have another way off the island since they needed the boat in the first place."

Trestan and Cat let those memories run through their minds again, anxious about the implications if Savannah and Revwar ever got off that island. There had been no sign of the two troublemakers during the companions' escape to the shore or at the 'negotiations' with the sailors for passage back to the mainland.

Cat sighed, "Well, things went better than expected, considering everything that went wrong."

Trestan hugged her close, "We survived this far. That's important. I didn't expect any of us to come out of this unscathed. I'm looking forward to going home again, and seeing what else the future holds for me."

"If we have a future."

Trestan raised his eyebrows, and she continued. "Well, there is the small matter of explaining to Korrelothar why his rare flying machine left with us and why we're walking back."

Trestan rolled his eyes and groaned. "I don't look forward to that meeting."

Together they lingered, looking across the lake. Standing together with arms entwined around waists, they were comforted by the affinity they found for each other. The two of them looked forward to the chance of getting a warm bath in one of the inns in Barkan's Crossing. Even so, Trestan admired a slight scent of perfume coming from Cat's hair, and he found himself stroking his fingers through her raven strands. The overland journey from here to Troutbrook promised to be an easy one compared to the walking and fighting they'd experienced so far. The young man looked forward to one last road before arriving home again.

Cat interrupted his thoughts. "What do you plan to do now? You pledged service to Abriana, and I assume you aren't going to turn back on that vow?"

Trestan pondered a hidden motive behind her question. It was a thought that had been on his mind throughout the boat trip. "I won't turn back on that vow, I can't."

Trestan turned to look directly at Cat. "I realized this vow doesn't bind me to anything that I don't wish…that revelation came to me even as you seemed to be dying in my arms. Through Abriana, I can help make my own hopes and dreams come true. Even more than that, I can work to help others achieve what they love. I don't know what path lies before me in her service, nor do I know where to start, but I am committed to traveling wherever she guides me. I will have to study and train, and that could take some time. Maybe even a few years."

Cat did not reveal any emotion behind her eyes. The woman turned to look once again at the distant shoreline. "There is a seminary in Kashmer devoted to her. I've seen it many times when I traveled through there."

Trestan nodded, "Then that would be a good place to start."

He looked across the water, as Cat spoke again. "How soon will you go there?"

Trestan shrugged. The new turn that his life was taking left him unsure about many things in regards to his future. He found that he looked forward to this new change to his life, yet at the same time he was delving into the unknown.

"I won't be leaving right away, I know that," Trestan said. "I plan on spending some time in Troutbrook with my father. He will likely be behind on chores and work, so I should help him around the smithy. I don't know what ramifications we will face for stealing and losing *Dovewing*, so I don't know what punishment we will face for that. I also…"

Trestan hesitated a bit before speaking again, "Please tell me you will stick around for a bit before you do any more traveling."

The arm wrapped around his waist gave him a reassuring squeeze. "I don't have any reason to move on anytime too soon. I'm in nay hurry."

"Good," Trestan shifted his feet, uncomfortable that his next words might not come out right. "I still plan on making you a little gift. I also…want to spend more time with you."

They held each other close, standing on the bow of the ship as it sailed closer to the lower harbor of Barkan's Crossing. Trestan and Cat enjoyed the vista presented before them. Rising above them, almost blocking out the setting sun, the silhouette of the town settled around the top of the ridge. The river from the mountains spilled over the ridge as it had for centuries, cascading down the rock face into the far end of the lake. The few clouds in the sky revealed pink highlights. The red rays of the sun sent colored sparkles through the spray of the waterfall. The water seemed to be mixed with sparks as it thundered down. As the water moved across the lake and out towards the sea, it reflected the colored sky as the bow of the *Silver Trident* sliced a pathway along its surface.

Cat glanced at Trestan out of the corner of her eyes. The young man was no longer the same village boy that once offered to treat her to drinks. The young, scraggly mustache did not seem any different, and Trestan still had a few black flecks of soot from the smithy embedded in his fingers. Despite these similarities, this young man had grown and changed. Gone were the rope belt and patched trousers, the uncertainty, and some of his youthful innocence. In many ways he remained a simple man, straightforward, true and honest even after the dangers of the road. Now Trestan stood straighter, ready to take the destiny of a paladin. He bore scarred and dented armor, and his countenance revealed a new reservoir of strength that was hard to scour in the face of danger. The fine elvish blade on his back perched ready to defend any friend, and yet the man had grieved for at least one of those enemies taken by that blade. His gaze looked at the waterfall before them with a mixture of that youthful yearning coupled with the beginnings of new wisdom. Trestan had become something more than the young, poor man she had first known.

Cat leaned in close to him as he turned his remarks towards the scene before them. "It's a beautiful sight."

Cat couldn't help but be inspired to borrow and modify one of Trestan's own phrases, spoken right after the battle on the bluff. "I didn't expect to live long enough to see this sunset."

CHAPTER 29

The crew of the *Silver Trident* did not attempt any violence upon the party before docking at Barkan's Crossing, though many unfriendly comments were muttered. The band of friends left the ship without incident. The crew did not intend to return to the island, thinking Revwar and his accomplices had perished, leaving the rest of them better off. Although Revwar had flashed gold to the original captain of the ship, the real payment had been the quiet assassination of the same captain for the benefit of the first mate. This left the ship's coffers low on funds. The crew of the ship proved eager to leave the whole affair behind them and pick up trade goods again, now that they were in a good port.

The companions ventured with good spirits through Barkan's Crossing. The long adventure finally seemed over; the weight of any concerns lifted from their shoulders. The group once again took up rooms at the Eagle's Nest to enjoy the scenic waterfall. Salgor proved good to his word in paying off the damage he had done to the inn's table. The dwarf did not plan on staying to take up the job of bouncer again. Salgor Bandago traveled a lot as a habit, but his reason this time involved a sense of responsibility.

"Nay darned elf wizard is going to give my friends grief about losing his dangerous flying toy," Salgor proclaimed. "If he gives you trouble, I'll be there to keep him in line."

The companions celebrated their night in Barkin's Crossing. They had gold from the pouches of fallen enemies, coupled with the joy of being alive after all their trials. Petrow's speech became slurred as he chatted with Salgor more about dwarves in general. Trestan and Cat found the opportunity to dance to a minstrel's lute, though an expensive elven wine made the graceful woman tipsy. Meanwhile, Mel added to the smoky atmosphere of the room with fresh pipe weed. Several locals watched these adventurers with interest. Local residents knew that adventuring types were often loose with their gold and their tongues, telling many stories of the world. Trestan found himself entertaining a group of boys not much younger than his age. They sat around him in patched clothes and dirty faces, listening with wonder as he described the flight over the unicorn herd. Later Trestan realized that it hadn't been so long ago that the situation had been reversed, and he had been one of them.

Although the companions still bore bruises and scars from the fight on the island, they slept well that night. In the morning, they sought out a temple and healing services to ease their aches and pains. The long quest seemed over, but they still decided to purchase healing draughts…just in case.

The five of them began traveling up the north road towards Troutbrook. Once again they traveled by foot, but it was a pleasant journey. The planting season touched the land, creating a flowery landscape. They shared the road with the many early-year merchant caravans traveling from village to village around Kashmer's Protectorate. Through all the sights and pleasantry of the scenery they shared nice conversations. They had only known each other for a relatively short time, so they still discovered many interesting subjects such as their different cultures and distant lands.

They passed a section of road in which Mel seemed distracted. The gnome did not contribute much to the conversations—an odd sign upon itself. When Cat brought it up to him, he explained the reason for his preoccupation. They walked close to Mel's home village, and the gnome had been giving thought to his family. Mel explained that he wasn't sure about what he wanted to do in regards to his exile from his father. The gnome simply said he was giving it a lot of thought, and he continued walking with the rest of his companions to Troutbrook.

*   *   *   *   *

The five of them entered Troutbrook from the southern bridge, striding over it to face a small crowd gathered near the Church of the Sacred Harvest. Word of the companions' return reached the village before they did. Amongst the crowd stood High Priest Gerlach alongside the elf Korrelothar. The priest and his acolytes wore their formal robes. Korrelothar still dressed in the fashionable clothes of Orlaun, topping the outfit with his plush cap. Those two imposing figures waited impatiently for the companions to approach.

Cat, Petrow and Trestan exchanged nervous looks between themselves, well aware that Korrelothar's first concern would be his missing vessel. Salgor showed no nervousness. The bearded warrior wasn't about to let a wizard treat his friends harshly. Mel was, as always, seeing only the bright side of things. The gnome appeared cheery about arriving at their destination, impressed that they had a welcoming group ready to greet them.

They steadily traveled the street past all the villagers. Only a few of the locals knew about the holy relic's theft. The sight of the heroic band returning from another surprise absence sparked interest with several people. Their approach didn't match the grand spectacle as when they had flown into town aboard *Dovewing*, yet the occasion distracted many on the street. Merchants left their stores and carts in the hands of family or apprentices. A crowd of people lined the street or formed behind the companions as they walked.

In front of the church, right next to the well supporting the false relic, the companions stopped and faced Korrelothar. The wizard from Orlaun and the fatherly cleric both stared at the young group, stern and angry. Trestan, Cat and Petrow prepared to soften their reception right from the start. Each of them held one of the three relics they had discovered. Priest Gerlach and his acolytes gaped at the presence of three such miraculous stones. Korrelothar glanced over their hands, a temporary distraction from his otherwise hard visage. The elf spent an extra moment studying the stone in Petrow's hand, still partially wrapped in that odd leathery material.

The elf wizard remained silent. Priest Gerlach cleared his throat and addressed the companions. "You all were spotted leaving the village with Korrelothar's magical creation. Where have you all been?"

Cat answered for the rest of them, "We apologize for leaving so suddenly, but we had a chance to win back that which was stolen from the village. We dared not try waking the Lord's keep at an early hour when time proved valuable. The holy relic is returned to its rightful owners, and the relic from Orlaun has been found, as well as a third stone."

Trestan, holding the village relic, removed the false relic from the well and replaced it with the rightful stone. This caused a lot of murmurs from the other villagers. Trestan stepped back with his friends, holding the false stone. The young man glanced around and saw Hebden's face in the crowd. His father held a smile, though his eyes also looked wet with tears.

Cat and Petrow offered their relics to Korrelothar. The elf once again glanced down at them, but didn't move to take the relics. His firm gaze took in all of them, "Where is *Dovewing?*"

An uncomfortable silence stretched among the companions before Trestan spoke, "We had an accident."

Korrelothar looked to Trestan. The smith's son drew the eyes of every villager and acolyte in the vicinity. The young man swallowed his pride as he continued. "We're sorry, and we know it was wrong to take her. The needs of our village prompted our journey, but we never wanted any harm to come to such a fantastic vessel. She is, sadly and regrettably, smashed beyond repair."

The elf scowled at each member in turn, but one of the companions would not be intimidated. Salgor did not believe in flowery apologies, nor would he make excuses when he figured the village's fate was more important than an untrustworthy magical contraption. The dwarf's deep voice commanded attention. "For those that weren't aware, let me enlighten you. The holy relic displayed here contains destructive power. We witnessed its danger as it summoned forth undead minions, shattered the solid stone of a keep, and created other earth-borne monsters to fight for those who stole it. In its absence, Troutbrook's crops withered. Herd animals became diseased. This group did steal that flying vessel, but we did so to take away the relics from those who would abuse them. We come back victorious in our quest, though the gnomish contraption paid the price. That's all I have to say."

The other villagers whispered excitedly at the dwarf's revelations. Korrelothar hid his feelings well, but the dwarf's mention of the relic's powers grabbed his interest. The elf simply held out his hands to accept the other two relics. Petrow and Cat handed their stones over, and the elf examined each in turn with renewed interest.

The wizard held up the one wrapped by the leathery scroll. "A third stone? What is this on it?"

Cat replied. "We don't know its origin. The lettering is Elvish, but it's scrambled in some sort of code."

Korrelothar drew himself up to full height. He looked down upon each companion, but they kept a respectful silence. He finally spoke again, "I wasn't expecting that I might see any of you back, but your small victory is some good news. I am very distraught over the loss of a very important and useful possession. I suppose I will hear your story out, before I give in to any temptations such as…turning you all into big, fat fish and releasing you beside the fishermen on the river."

The wizard's threat, whether sincere or not, succeeded in making the companions more nervous. Salgor only glared back, as if daring the wizard to try it. The nearby villagers murmured discontent.

334

Korrelothar held up a hand. "Like I said, just a temptation. Wizards have done far worse to people who steal their finest magical items. Yet you all seem to have done so for a noble and worthy purpose." The elf spoke chidingly, but this last sentence had seemed an honest compliment. He continued, "In truth, I would rather we take the rest of this conversation inside the church, so that we may discuss everything in its entirety."

"Indeed," Priest Gerlach agreed. "We shall take this into the sanctuary, to a private meeting, and have all our questions answered there."

Salgor stood his ground, even though the others made their way to the church steps. As the priest and wizard looked back at him questionably, he sneered as he voiced a question at them, "And then are we to be *punished*?"

His expression showed his contempt for that idea. Korrelothar answered, "Not punished perhaps, but we might say 'repayment' for the loss of my most prized possession."

*   *   *   *   *

A church scribe recorded the tale told in the private chambers, despite her own expression gaping and giving pause during portions. Korrelothar remained upset by the loss of *Dovewing*, though he never spoke out angrily at the companions. The companions could feel his bitter mood in his actions. Both priest and wizard showed plenty of interest in the news of the stones' apparent powers. Korrelothar admitted that the members of his wizard guild never suspected the relic held so much power. Before the sky turned dark, Gerlach and Korrelothar placed protective enchantments around the well relic, guarding it heavily against further theft. It had briefly been debated whether to bring it inside the church, but Yestreal was a nature god. Important relics of such a deity belonged out in the open air. They determined that the other two relics would go to Korrelothar for further study. One belonged to his guild anyway, and the coded writing adorning the wrapping of the unknown stone puzzled the clergy. Korrelothar thus volunteered to take the new stone and wrapping back to his guild to research.

As the companions relayed more of their tale, they could feel more respect earned from everyone in attendance. Although Korrelothar gave them a gruff attitude, the elf's eyes and motions revealed that his anger had softened. The acolytes who overheard the tale swore an oath to secrecy…but by day's end the adventure became the village gossip. Several renditions and rumors circulated, painting an even more heroic and epic picture of events than what really happened.

Soon enough, the companions found out what Korrelothar had in mind when he suggested "repayment". During their few days of absence the wizard went ahead as planned in researching church documents and histories regarding the holy relic. However, the search for knowledge became greatly hampered by the attentions and gestures of Lord Verantir. The noble was not about to let such a prestigious visitor linger without attempting a good impression. The lord practically catered to the wealthy wizard, seeking an audience almost daily. Each encounter involved formalities and banquets that took hours. It did not help Korrelothar that Troutbrook was a small town with little else to distract the ruling lord.

The companions were surprised to find out that the same lord, who had rewarded them for rescuing his daughter, offered their heads to Korrelothar for stealing his property. The wizard had asked Lord Verantir not to do anything of the sorts. When the companions heard this, they appreciated running into the wizard first and not the local lord. Korrelothar's revealed troubles involving a serious diplomatic problem with researching at the church while the noble was around. The elf tried his best to make excuses and seclude himself from the noble, but it was a difficult diplomatic stance. The wizard even told the church acolytes to keep anyone from entering, but Lord Verantir ruled the area and would not be dissuaded by minor priests.

Korrelothar intended to continue his examination and translations of the church histories in order to learn more about the powerful relics. The elf wizard believed the companions might help him study in privacy, and he made it clear that they owed him after losing *Dovewing*. After the day of their return to the village, they started work to assist the wizard. At first this seemed a simple request, but Korrelothar had much more in mind.

The companions worked in shifts and found out how far Korrelothar could stretch the term "repayment". Their duties included fetching candles, keeping the room well-lit, bringing food and drink to the wizard, disposing of his trash, washing his robes and the challenge of finding some way to divert the company of a local lord. As days went by, the chores added up. It became obvious that the elf intentionally made them go out of their way for certain chores, yet the wizard had a way of taking advantage of the guilt they felt over losing the magical vessel.

"Katressa, this tea won't do." Korrelothar said to the woman one day, when taking a break from reading a long scroll.

The mage's words halted her just as the half-elf was leaving the room. At the time, she was the only companion assisting the elf mage, and she had just brought a lunch for him. Cat heard him take the smallest sip of the tea the acolytes prepared, and saw the resulting scowl on his face.

She put on her best smile, even though she knew the tea was probably perfectly fine. "Shall I get you another one?"

Korrelothar nodded, "That would be most sweet of you, thank you, but not this kind. That farmer Isodeiah grows the best herbs for tea; I would like some of his ingredients."

Cat held out a hand to accept some coins from the wizard, grateful that he was only sending her on a small errand. The merchant of interest had a cart set up in a farmer's market at the south end of the main street. After handing her the money, the wizard added in a special request, "Oh, and I'd prefer only leaves grown from the portion of his farm that is in the shadier area, near the water."

Cat had almost made it to the door, but now cringed at what she feared he might add. The woman spoke, "All his herbs are mixed together at his cart. I'm sure he won't remember which ones were grown in which part of his fields."

The wizard nodded his agreement, "Quite right, you have a point there. You'll have to go with him, directly to his garden, and have him pick the ones I want. That way we'll know we got the right ones. It's a good thing they are in season."

336

Bewildered, Cat turned to face the smiling wizard, "But...his farm is two miles downstream!"

Korrelothar set aside his lunch for a moment. The wizard fixed his unwavering gaze on Katressa. The half-elf instantly knew she had protested too much, and was about to suffer the consequences.

"Too much sun can damage anything, you know. Whether it is plants, paintings, or even our skin, the sun damages things. That's why the best herbs are grown in slightly shaded areas. You know who taught me that? Grenario the carpenter!"

Cat listened quietly as Korrelothar went on, "Oh, you never met him. He died several years ago, and not a finer artisan has been found since. It was Grenario that carved the two doors on *Dovewing*. The griffon door was his favorite; he actually spent two years coming up with the final design. He made previous doors and threw them out, saying they 'weren't perfect enough' for his tastes. He slaved alone the whole time, insisting on doing all the work himself, trusting nothing to apprentices. After all, flying vessels like divine chariots are one of the rarest things in the world, and he wanted to have everything done to the peak of his abilities. He even became disturbed about the wear of color on things exposed to the sun for too long. He experimented until he came up with a stain that should protect the vessel through centuries of flying around in the sun. It was time-consuming to make, but he always insisted on the best. I hear it took two months for the solution to be boiled, stirred, cooled, mixed anew and redone over and over again in order to come up with the final mixture..."

"Korrelothar?" Cat interrupted, feeling guilty as always when the wizard droned on about the amount of work that had gone into making *Dovewing*. "Much as I'd like to hear more, I'll go get that tea for you now."

The elf wizard smiled, "Have a nice walk."

Cat's experience that day was typical of what all the companions went through at one time or another. Trestan ran into Salgor as the dwarf carried an ink vial to the wizard's study. "He isn't getting any more than this from me!" Salgor declared, "I'm not his page or some acolyte!"

Minutes later, Trestan spotted Salgor hefting a pack and leaving Troutbrook by the southern road. Days later, the dwarf walked back into town carrying a small package. Salgor saw the smith's inquisitive eyes and warned, "Not a word!" At which Trestan wisely decided to go back to his own business.

Korrelothar favored Mel with the most errands. The little gnome was so talkative that he became a worse distraction for the elf mage than the local noble. The wizard soon put Mel's conversation expertise to good use. Most folks couldn't deter Lord Verantir's frequent visits, but Mel somehow cornered the local lord into a three-hour conversation once. At the conclusion, Lord Verantir turned around and went back to the mansion without bothering to see Korrelothar. From then on, the wizard appointed Mel to seek out and intercept the noble every time the lord sought out Korrelothar. The elf wizard enjoyed many days of peace and quiet study as Lord Verantir was subjected to discussions of gnome customs, things found in goblin stewpots, dances from Pluetlo's Island, good fishing spots in other lands, color patterns of gnome clans, the mating habits of centaurs, and so many other subjects of which Mel was an expert.

The month of Florum surrendered to the summer months. The wizard from Orlaun continued his studies, always keeping a watchful eye over the strange relics. The villagers, impressed and awed by the stories of their relic's powers, spent more time around the well marveling at it. Farmers and herders alike made pilgrimages to see the relic and pray for their lands and crops. Protective wards kept anyone from actually removing the relic from its place. During the summer months, the companions catered to the wizard but went about their own lives as well.

Trestan enjoyed being home, in the company of his proud father. Hebden was amazed at the stories he heard and what Trestan shared about the struggle. With some awkwardness, Trestan relayed the part about accepting the calling of Abriana and healing Cat as she lay dying. Hebden wasn't sure how to take the news, though it swelled his pride that his son harnessed a miracle to save his friend. When the father asked how his son would follow his calling, Trestan replied that he wasn't sure. The young man knew he would have to study and train. While Trestan stayed and repaid Korrelothar's debt, he worked that summer as a smith. He thought it might be his last days working the hammer and forge.

The sword which once displayed over Sir Wilhelm's fireplace now decorated the common room of the Karok home. The armor hung on its own stand, after Hebden and Trestan repaired the damage it had taken. Trestan still wore a patched tunic and trousers when he worked at the forge, but when away from it he finally garbed in nice, fashionable clothing. Despite bringing back a hefty amount of gold from the pockets of Bortun and his group, the young man set most of it aside for his eventual schooling. There was much work to be done, and Trestan worked the forge alongside his father to help with the chores.

The long hours at the forge helped out his father and the villagers, but it also gave Hebden time to reflect on the changes. The older smith knew his son yearned to follow his new path, even as he stayed to finish what he could at the smithy. Others noticed odd happenings as well. Trestan worked longer hours into the night on some secret endeavor. Hebden knew the secret, but revealed nothing. To the amazement and rumors of the other companions, Korrelothar made several visits to the blacksmith yard. A few times one of the other companions would approach, only to see Trestan and Hebden hide whatever they were working on. Korrelothar, standing nearby, would give no clue as to the reason for his presence. The wizard and the two smiths would chat about the weather or the crops, but it was obvious that some surprise brewed in the forge.

All the companions sought work or distraction while helping the elf mage with his study. Petrow had coins and was more willing to spread the wealth. The young man began to experiment with different fashions, wearing varieties of bright clothes. Yet Petrow also went back to doing some hard work for the villagers. Once again, he could be counted on to collect firewood, work on the ranches, assist farmers with crops, repair roofs and slaughter chickens as needed. During this last chore Petrow found himself distracted at times. He performed the job with the same woodcutter's axe he had carried as a weapon…the same black-marked woodcutter's axe that never actually drew blood during the adventure.

A new development took up a fair amount of his free time. A farmer's daughter had caught a fancy with the handyman. The maiden Inedra, who had danced with Petrow during the night of revelry in Troutbrook, found herself the subject of his attentions. The young maiden returned his affections, and many days Petrow and Inedra went off by themselves for picnics and long walks.

On the outside, he remained positive and sure of himself. The young man always acted as if the world was something he always understood, and no worries would trouble him. None of the other companions witnessed Petrow's struggles with the nightmares. Visions of a powerful minotaur and a cleric with ice blue eyes would wake him in the depths of the night. Breathing hard and heavy, Petrow would lay awake for a long time after one of those dreams tormented him.

Salgor Bandago was not very useful doing chores for the wizard, but he found another job in Troutbrook that suited him well. He worked for the pub where the hard drinkers of the village congregated. As always, the dwarf felt home in a place devoted to drinking. He even had the chance to brew more of his own drinks, sharing them with the patrons. The pub had no particular need for a bouncer, but Salgor worked cheap and shared a few brewing secrets he had picked up during his journeys. The dwarf continued to demonstrate his method for breathing fireballs out of a swig of dwarven whiskey…though those demonstrations had to be done outside the building. Such spectacles brought in more customers, making the owner of the pub a happy man. Once the new patrons moved inside the building, Salgor found himself as more of a storyteller than a bouncer. The dwarf shared many stories of his travels, and gained much recognition around the local lands.

*   *   *   *   *

The day Trestan secretly dreaded came to pass, when Korrelothar had researched as much as he could. The wizard had poured over long scrolls from the temple archives, and spent a long examination of the scrap of material wrapped around the third relic stone. The writing on that piece was beyond his ability to translate. What he learned of the temple histories didn't help greatly, but it illuminated some history on the village artifact. According to the records, the relic arrived during the confusing dark years just after the signing of the Covenant. A priest of Yestreal, reportedly a high-ranking one, settled along the brook when barely any humans lived in the area. He bore the relic, though the histories did not speak of its whereabouts before settling here. His followers erected the sanctuary near a lonely bridge. People settled around the church along the trade route. The church simply handed down the knowledge that the stone was a gift of Yestreal, and it would bring good health and fortunes to their land and crops. No mention had ever been made of its powers to break stone and create guardians. If anything, the history handed down by the original high cleric of the area was either ignorant, or purposely misleading as to the true nature of the relic.

339

The elf wizard, having nowhere else to turn for information locally, declared it was time to move on. He intended to follow his original plan of visiting his old friend in Kashmer, then returning to Orlaun and his guild there. He hoped divination or spells might reveal more about the stones, or at least of the strange writing accompanying the third relic. Knowing that the relics dated back to the Godswars, the elf grew concerned about their history and original purpose. Also, he worried over the fact that someone had coveted them badly for whatever nefarious reason.

By the time Korrelothar bid his farewell, the companions felt sorry to see him go. Granted, he had caused them to bend over backwards at times to appease his loss of *Dovewing*, yet at the same time he had provided a lot of interesting conversation and guidance about small matters. Considering his loss, the companions felt he acted charitably. The companions, as they thought it was only fair, bought Korrelothar a horse for his travels. The wizard thanked them for their help during the summer months. He commended them for acting on behalf of the village in seeking the stolen relic, and forgave them for losing the magical vessel in the process.

"If you ever visit Orlaun in your travels, just ask for 'The Highwater Conjuror', I'll be happy to receive you as guests." The companions had heard his nickname before, but none thought to ask him about it. Just like that he was gone; up the road to Kashmer to visit his old friend.

After Korrelothar left, nothing remained to hold some of the companions to Troutbrook. It was still a small village that saw little adventure or stories aside from fishing. The village may have been home to two of them, but to the rest it was getting to be quite boring. At some point during the summer, the villagers granted them a name, and the group of friends took it as their own. They called themselves the "Companions of the Relics". Now the first of the Companions was about to say his farewell, though he swore he would see them all again.

Salgor Bandago was ready to move on to other towns and other pubs in his search for brewing secrets. He swore to build his own inn someday, when he felt like settling down. The dwarf inquired of Katressa about employment as a Kashmer privateer: hunting brigands and tracking bounties. The Companions, through Cat, had received a handsome payment after bringing back the holy relic. After all, Lord Verantir Tessald was made aware of their efforts, and Kashmer's king compensated nobles for rewarding privateers who served their home. Korrelothar made sure to use his political weight with the enamored noble to see that the companions were rewarded rather than executed.

The dwarf was ready to try heading north first, towards Kashmer. Salgor's tough exterior never revealed a crack of sadness as he stood ready to leave. His oversized travel pack towered over his back. Some of its pockets were stuffed full with brew: a dwarven travel necessity. The other companions displayed wet eyes as they bid him a good journey. The last evening had been spent drinking and laughing the night away. The morning of his departure dawned solemn and quiet.

As they gave their goodbyes to Salgor, he leaned in close and gave each a tip on life. Some of his advice came straight out of taproom tales, the rest born from the warm heart of a dwarf warrior. When Salgor bent his head to whisper to Mel, he gave the gnome a special salute from one worshipper of Daerkfyre to another. Mel returned it with a smile. Salgor put on one last scowl and warned Mel. "Don't do anything to embarrass, Daerkfyre. Stand firm nay matter the foe."

"I'll stay strong!" Mel choked through tears.

The Companions watched as the oversized pack disappeared up the trail. Salgor never looked back.

Mel was the next to bid a tearful goodbye.

"I'm going home to face my family," Mel stated firmly. "I'm not looking for their acceptance anymore, nor do I care for their respect."

The other Companions of the Relics sat at the inn table with him as he explained his choice. The gnome who had always been so easygoing relayed his fears at going home, yet showed determination to face the family that exiled him. Mel continued, "I'm proud of who I am. I'm proud to wield magic. The only reason I'm going there is to flaunt that in front of all of them. They sent me away like I was an embarrassment and that their life would be better off without me. I'm going to show them my life turned out well, and that I have more respect for myself than for them!"

Trestan, Petrow and Cat patted his back and encouraged him with their blessings. They all wished for the best for Mel. Since his home forest bordered Troutbrook, they all expected him to return soon for a visit.

"I still want you all to know, you have been the best friends I have ever known." The gnome's lower lip trembled, as his eyes watered. "I've always worked hard to get to know people and look for respect, and you finally gave it to me. You take me for what I am: my faults, oddities, short stature and love of magic. You treat me as if I stand as tall as any of you, and you've been so kind to me. I'm sorry if I ever let you down. Know that my magic and abilities are always on your side. I'm glad to be one of the Companions of the Relics."

Mel was gone by the next evening, and everyone missed his endless conversations.

Trestan and Petrow still lived their daily routines in Troutbrook. Petrow worked at several chores as he continued to see Inedra on an almost daily basis. Trestan continued his work at the forge. Other than Petrow and Trestan, there was only one Companion not from Troutbrook. She yearned to travel again.

When Cat bid farewell, Trestan took her to Abriana's shrine in the woods. Many words passed between them, as Trestan had so much on his mind. Trestan still felt the strong need to follow the call of Abriana and honor his promise, "That seminary at Kashmer sounds like the place to go. I have so many questions and don't know how to go about them. I still have to figure when I can leave the forge."

Cat replied, "Of course, you must help your father. I suggest you make the trip before the snowfall."

Trestan self-consciously shifted a bit, "You won't miss me when I go? I still need to give you something special, but it's not ready yet. I also yearn for our times together. I will miss you terribly when you are traveling."

The half-elf offered a coy smile. "Your affection for me is plain upon your face. I also would like to explore these feelings between us. We will have time. Follow your calling, for it led you to save my life. Your time at the seminary will pass quickly enough. I am patient."

"What will you do?"

"Follow my own calling as a privateer," Cat patted her rapier. "I'll rid people of monsters and bandits, while Kashmer pays me for it. Such a job would also welcome the calling of Abriana's chosen."

Cat rode north to Kashmer. True to her word, she came back every few days to visit. Weeks went by with no word from Mel or Salgor, but Cat always came back.

The harvest season approached, and Hebden knew the time drew near for bidding farewells to his son again. The older smith observed Trestan's growth. The young man went off to Abriana's shrine every morning for prayers, though he always ran back to the forge on time and worked hard to help out. There was something forever changed in Trestan's eyes, newfound wisdom from his time adventuring. Trestan often took the Sword of the Spirit to a quiet place in the woods and practiced his swordplay. The young man never asked his father's permission, nor was there a need. Hebden had always suspected that Trestan had practiced, but now the young man openly professed his desire to learn the art of sword fighting.

During the late summer, an accident happened at the forge. Mikhael was helping out at the smithy when he stumbled and caught himself on the hot coals. Fire burned his hand, and Hebden's first reaction was to run to the temple and get a cleric. Instead, Trestan stepped forward and gripped Mikhael's wounded arm. The chosen of Abriana prayed out loud, summoning the miracle for the second time in Trestan's life. His divine powers completely restored the hand to normal. Mikhael and Hebden stood in awe of Trestan's gift. The young smith, after a moment of awkward silence, resumed his work and pounded away at a piece of metal as if nothing had ever happened.

Hebden talked to Trestan over the dinner table that night. "I can't ask you to stay and help me. You have a calling, something higher and bearing more purpose than working here as a smith."

Trestan looked into his father's eyes and nodded his understanding. Hebden continued, "I sent an inquiry to Abriana's seminary at Kashmer about a month ago. You have enough cash from your adventure to pay their housing fee and learn. You must follow your true path son, although I do regret seeing you leave again."

Trestan considered the words. His food sat unnoticed for some time. "I do feel that I have to go, but I hate to say goodbye. I hate leaving your side again."

Hebden smiled, "Son, I grew up just as you did. All my clothes are poor and patched. My hands will never lose their black stains. I accept my life now, but as a youth I wanted to run off for adventure and live a more exciting life. I reveled in the stories of brave men out to conquer the world, or save it from being conquered. I wanted to be the hero that fought back the villains and gave people a better life. You have that chance. Go see the world and what it has to offer, and come back often to visit. Know that your father is very proud of how you've grown."

Trestan and Hebden hugged, and tears flowed from the eyes of father and son. It was time for Trestan to leave.

342

*   *   *   *   *

The two riders halted their horses on the hill outside of the large city. Below them, Kashmer stretched almost to the limits of their vision. Tall towers and grand buildings stood out from a mass of streets going all directions. A few wide merchant streets crossed the center of the town, though courtyards, alleys, and open pavilions webbed about them. A large coliseum dominated one section, aged by centuries of use. Even outside the city perimeter, a temple or manor crowned every hill. The palette of the harvest season painted the landscape. An armada of boats sailed where the city met the sea. Their hull designs ranged between naval warships, cargo galleys, fishing ships, merchant traders, and the flagships of visiting foreign ambassadors.

"That city is so big. I've never seen anything like it. It makes Barkan's Crossing look like a village." Trestan remarked to his traveling companion.

Her hand came up and rubbed the back of his neck reassuringly. Cat smiled. "It is a big place, lots of happenings in the streets on a daily basis. I don't think you will get into the city much. You will be studying hard, maybe for some time."

Trestan could sense a touch of sadness in Cat's voice as she spoke. The half-elf had encouraged him to come to this place, but his studies would separate them for a time. Trestan turned his gaze away from the city, toward a large keep sharing the hill with them. The seminary dedicated to Abriana glistened in the sun, sparkling from its décor. Marble statues guarded the parapets alongside silver and gold fixtures. He saw corrals of horses, a large cathedral from which bells could be heard, a number of buildings housing the occupants of the keep, and throngs of people going about their daily business. A variety of people studied the teachings of the goddess, from peaceful monks and cleric healers to paladins who strove to defend what they loved. All of them gave up a portion of their lives to reflect and learn Abriana's tenets. For a moment, Trestan once again felt he risked giving up his life for this strange place. It made him nervous. He reminded himself that Abriana would not take away what he loved, and that she had given him a gift to assist in saving those that he cared about. The fear passed.

"Cat," Trestan looked down for a moment. His gaze returned to her eyes, though his own brown eyes revealed his heavy heart. "I will be studying inside those walls for a few years."

Cat patted her arm on his leg, nodding her head at his assessment. She didn't hide the sadness she felt at this parting. Trestan put his hand over hers and held it gently.

The young man leaned closer, "Will you be here when I am done? Promise me."

Her green eyes smiled back at him, and her raven hair tossed about in the breeze as she promised, "As long as it is within my means, I will be here when you are done. Stop doubting yourself, start believing. Focus your mind on your studies, and learn well the lessons."

Trestan smiled and looked back to the keep. Cat waited silently for him to say something more, but he didn't. Finally the adventuress could contain her curiosity no longer.

343

She adopted a demanding and yet playful tone. "Trestan Karok, how much longer do I have to wait!?"

"Oh?" Trestan assumed an innocent look on his face, but a hint of a smile revealed his bluff. "Wait for what?"

Cat gave him a playful slap. "For months now you hinted and promised a gift, and I avoided peeking in on the smithy when I knew you were working on something secret. Now where is my present? Don't keep me in suspense anymore!"

Trestan smiled, albeit nervously. He had indeed hoped for the right time, and now the moment was at hand. The chosen of Abriana reached into a large bag at his side and brought forth a golden treasure. Cat lost her breath when she saw what he had created with his own hands. Trestan offered it to her gently.

Humble as he was, his tone of voice seemed to apologize that it wasn't a better present than what he would have liked to have given her. "I remember when we were shopping in Barkan's Crossing, you said it was too much time and effort to mess with your hairstyle since it is often in a helmet, and that hair clasps and jewelry were easy options. So I made this for you to wear."

In awe, Cat took the object from his hands with her tender touch and brought it up to marvel before her eyes. Trestan continued with a reddened face, "I figured it would make a wonderful hair piece on you."

"Hair piece?" Cat spoke in disbelief, "That doesn't do this justice! Gods, Trestan, do you know what this is? This is a *Taef' Adorina*; it's an elvish tiara."

The half-elf ran her fingers over the item in her hands. It was a tiara shape, adorned with a thin, gold-wire framework stretched into elvish patterns. Charms hung from different places: symbols signifying the relationship between the giver and the receiver. A portion of the decorated tiara would hang down on the side of the face to cover the area between eyes and ears, and that too was decorated and woven into an elvish pattern.

Cat brought her gaze back to Trestan's red face. The shocked half-elf had joy written on her face. "This is something an elf gives to someone who owns their heart. To elves, this is very rare and special gift. Who taught you to make this?"

Trestan smiled, "Korrelothar did. He helped me make it."

Cat continued to look over the *Taef' Adorina* in her hands. She marveled at the knot patterns woven by the gold wires. She carefully looked over all of the charms set in it. "I see a unicorn horn, displayed under a rainbow." She smiled at the memory of what that meant. "And this one is...a waterfall? But it doesn't look like the one at Barkan's Crossing."

"That is the waterfall in the wilds near Troutbrook...." Trestan paused for a moment, "Where I first wanted to kiss you."

Tears formed at the edges of Cat's eyes. "I know what these are for: dwarvish axe with a mug, woodcutter's axe, a mouth smoking a pipe, a rapier crossed over a crossbow. This one must be you, a sword and smith hammer crossed over a heart. All our companions and the special moments of the journey commemorated as charms on the framework."

Cat cradled the gift. "The patterns and woven knots are familiar too, but I can't place them."

344

Trestan put a hand to his side and drew forth the Sword of the Spirit. He held the blade for Cat to see. Cat had been familiar with the elvish runes on the blade, but as she viewed it now, she paid more attention to an elvish decoration woven around the letters. There were knots and patterns at the base of the blade surrounding the runes, the same patterns which Trestan used to decorate the tiara.

Trestan put away the sword when Cat turned her attentions back to the tiara. At that moment though, a worry crept into the smith's mind. He remembered the last time he had given such a fine gift to a lady. Trestan nervously, but jokingly, stated, "Just don't let me ever catch you decorating your horse's mane with that."

Cat's look of shock was sincere, "Why would anyone treat such a wonderful gift that way? I love this, and will treasure it always."

With that, the beautiful half-elf set the tiara upon her brow. The gold complimented her wonderfully. Trestan had made the item just perfect, and it rewarded him to see how well she wore it. Katressa Bilil sat regally on her horse, tears in her eyes as she posed for Trestan with the crafted tiara on her head. The gift an elf gives to someone who owns his heart, and a precious gift indeed. She accepted it with all her heart.

Trestan and Cat bent closer together. Eyes locked, their bodies leaned in as their lips sought to join. They were very close when Cat's finger came up and halted Trestan's lips an inch from her own. Trestan listened as Cat whispered to him.

"I will be here, waiting for you when you are done. For you have my heart as well."

Cat moved her finger away. They reached for each other as they kissed deeply.

If you loved this book, then remember that authors live and prosper by good reviews on Amazon and Goodreads.

Follow Trestan and Cat's adventures and dive deeper into the plotline with the next installment: Trials of Faith.

Four years of study have honed Trestan's mind, heart and sword arm. With Cat at his side, he embarks on a holy quest to finish his training as a paladin. What he doesn't realize is that the quest will begin amidst the devastation of his home village.

The wizard Revwar and the dark cleric Savannah have returned with new allies. The relics that were once recovered will again be the subject of a renewed struggle. A pursuit will encompass two continents; including a chase in city streets, a deadly struggle above the clouds, and encounters deep within an unmapped wilderness where humans dare not tread.

The key to unlocking the mysterious history of the Earthrin Stones is found...buried in a dark page of Cat's past.

Appendix A – Notes on Magic, Miracles, and the Flow of the Supernatural

The world of Dhea Loral is known for the presence of "magic", as well as other phenomena not normally encountered in other mundane worlds. These phenomena all originate from a weave of supernatural energy that exists in the world, though they differ in how they interact with it. It is believed that this scattered essence is derived from the creation of the world and the continuous release of power by the gods in maintaining the land. The magical essence of the world is thus a residual energy given off by the gods' efforts. Different beings of the world can tap into this essence and control it in their own way. Several creatures were born spontaneously in this release of power, becoming a physical portion of the lattice of magic. It is important to learn the different expressions of this energy, as to how it relates to those who draw it from the world. "Magic" may be used as a general term for the powers and essence drawn from the sources listed below. It should be noted that there are types of magic that can not be so easily classified into any of these categories.

Arcanum/Arcana

Those who practice this type of magic call it "learned magic", merely because it is the one most noted for being based on study. Through years of experimentation and discovery the races were able to tap into a refined and sometimes devastating variety of powers. The general name for people who work this type of magic is a mage. This covers a broad array of classes and specialists that focus on the study of the arcane, many of which go by more specific names depending on their chosen field. Wizards, sorcerers, necromancers, conjurors and others all research the arcane arts and create prepared items to tap into the magic of the world. This method is generally highly organized, intellectual, and scientific in its approach. Some forms of arcana cross into the fringes of the other sources of magic.

Miracles

All supernatural energy that is directly granted by a deity is called a miracle. Clerics and paladins tap into the powers of their patrons and channel the flow into the real world. This form of energy saw only rare use before the Godswars from mortal hands. Since the time of the Covenant, miracles have become the sole way in which the gods manifest themselves in the world. The use of miracles is rarely referred to as "magic". The clerics who hear that term used in reference to their god-granted powers consider it as blasphemy. Miracles can be used for good or evil, depending on the intentions of the deity granting them.

Natura

349

This is a type of magic drawn from sources that are on a more primal level than arcana. It is often referred to as a spiritual elixir that flows from forms of life. Plants, animals, and spirits tend to give off their own energy, which is harnessed and controlled by those close to nature and the land. Some examples of the types of people who tap into natura are the deep woods druids, tribal mystics and spiritual shamans. There are those called greenmen, also known as feral warriors, who tap into this source as they call upon the essences of the land and animals. Medicines are often derived from the earth, and the ways of those who harness natura are very in tune with the wild world around them. When arcane magi create beings to fight for them, or perform duties for them, they are tapping into this same power of the spirits. It should be noted that there are many tribal shamans and mystics that are actually clerics tapping into divine miracles, so one should not get too hooked on the labels people apply to themselves. This type of magic is the oldest and simplest in the world.

Harmonic Web/Chi

Utilized in two different ways, this magic has earned two names for the same phenomenon. It is the belief that magic wraps about the world like a web, and can be tapped by feelings, voices, tunes or concentration. No books, scrolls, or mystical knowledge is needed; instead it is derived from mind focus, mental balance and mental discipline. Though arcana can be studied by many, and natura learned from mentors, the practice of this magic is hard to learn unless one is already a "prodigy". Minstrels, bards and skalds are examples of those who use voices and tunes to bring forth this kind of magic, by way of the harmonic web. The term Chi derives from the chiaso and martial artists that focus on it more as a type of discipline. In this latter group it does not manifest as external magic, instead focusing on augmenting mental and physical capabilities. Again there are some magi, notably mentalists, which also use this magic by utilizing their voices and the feelings of others.

Appendix B – Deities Commonly Worshipped in Dhea Loral

This is not a complete list of all the beings that hold governance over the world of Dhea Loral. It is a glance at some of the major powers that exert their influence over the land, people and natural events. The gods make possible all the little things that keep the world from falling into disharmony. They each have agendas carried out by worshippers residing in the world, for the gods themselves are forbidden to tread the realms as they once did. It should be noted that many gods exist under different names across various cultures and languages.

Abriana – Goddess of Love and Healing. She is the most loving goddess and a supporter of all that is good and wholesome in the world. She helps instill feelings in mortals of brotherly love, marital commitment, and care of the people. Many of her followers are pacifists and healers. There are others who do take up the call of arms, but only to fight for what they love and protect. Even those that become paladins are restricted from using weapons or incurring fighting on the first day of each month, as these days are sacred to Abriana.

Boyal – God of Justice. It is said when the Goddess of Death collects the souls of agnostics, unbelievers, and those who turned traitor to their god, she must bring them before Boyal for sentencing. Once that is done, she is only too happy to carry out the sentence or deliver the wayward soul to its fate. The clerics of this faith often find themselves on city councils, in courtrooms, or even libraries of official records. Boyal proclaims order as a paramount quality of civilization. The concept of law and rights, and how they apply to different people, is carefully studied. Many clerics go on pilgrimages to explore how the cultures of other lands express their laws.

The Codex – Book on the Philosophy of Good. Not a god by itself, it nevertheless has inspired a large following. This way of life is based on a literary work that champions a strong belief in the morals and principles that are known as "good". The original Codex was brought into existence with the help of several deities devoted to good causes, and it took a life of its own. People who devote themselves to this following are able to tap into clerical miracles just as if they were praying to a genuine god. There are many that serve to fulfill the moral requirements set forth in the book.

Daerkfyre – Dwarven god of Strength, Valor and Courage. Worshipped as one of the dwarven "battle gods", this deity favors strong warriors. Daerkfyre is often referred to with the extension "the Valorous". Often worshippers of this god are as strong and stubborn in the mind as they are with their muscles. Physical strength is a domain honored by dwarven miners and certain craftsmen. Warriors often pray to this god before battle. Weapons blessed by his clerics are exceptionally strong and durable.

351

Dalios – God of War, as well as the humans' God of Strength and Courage. This deity can be wildly unpredictable. At times he sets forth destruction and strife, though sometimes for the benefit of oppressed people. Regardless, this god is a major influence on events that shape the course of the world. His clerics are often eager to go into battle on either side of the lines, and sometimes they do meet across opposing armies. To these clerics, life is met by facing trouble in a straightforward type of manner. The clergy often spends their short lives seeking out glory amidst fighting for a cause. Dalios is believed to look over the world from a huge feasting hall, toasting those who struggle and fight for their beliefs.

Dawn – Goddess of Life and Rebirth. Closely related to Abriana, this goddess shares some of the same ideals. However, this deity views life as chaotic, with a bit of mystery. She creates and shapes new life, from babies to new species. Sometimes the new species can be deadly, but that is only to balance out and strengthen other forms of life. This goddess has a special abhorrence of the undead, and her clerics fight to rid the world of their existence. Due to her zeal for all kinds of life, many of her worshippers include people who feel more at home in nature than in civilized areas built upon stone.

DeLaris – Goddess of Death. Death can never be anything but frightening. She resides in one of the many Lower Worlds, but travels between them often and freely to carry out her tasks. Her most ardent followers in life may pass into the afterworld to become *Karet-Atriul*, otherwise known as Death Angels. These souls become harbingers and servants of her will, assisting the goddess with the many aspects of her position. She ferries the dead across the other worlds and homes of the gods. Those souls who were unfaithful, traitorous to a god, and untrue in their worship may find an eternity of torture or simply a boring, never-ending imprisonment. Some of her most powerful clerics can raise the dead back to life, but only to prove her power over death. Her clerics are not very strong with social ties, for they serve as a constant reminder to others of the dark fates that might befall them in the next world.

Foyul – God of Balance. Foyul works on the principal that too much influence by one side or force tends to imbalance the world. He walks a middle line between anarchy and order, good and evil. His followers come from all walks of life, all serving to sway the balance in their own way when needed. Foyul has few friends among the gods or men, as he tends to fight for all sides in order to not let any one force hold too much sway. His clerics may be evil or good, and may act for any number of good or bad intentions, striving to maintain the balance of the world.

Ganden – God of Honor, Duty, Service. This god has followers in many races. Those that feel fulfilled by a calling of decency to their fellow man and sacrifice for the sake of others fit into his followers. Those who break promises, or serve only themselves, fall out of favor to this deity. Ganden serves the other gods in the same way, carrying out honorable edicts and being of service to those that require aid. Often symbols of this god can be found with militias, honor guards, healers, and others who perform even menial services to others.

Juliustan – God of Storms and Cataclysms. Many races fear the name of this god, without a full understanding of his focus. On one hand, he strives to balance the natural forces of the world. This can only be done by allowing some of the pressure of the forces of nature to vent their wrath on occasion. He may hold back one storm, while allowing another to rage unchecked. On his other side, he also seeks to ease the suffering of the world's people through such terrible events. This aspect is apparent in his clerics. His followers bring relief to those who have been displaced by storms or cataclysms, and assist in rebuilding. People do not fully understand and tend to fear his name. Many blame him for catastrophes in the first place, and fear that it is somehow anger or wrath. His clerics believe the world would suffer worse destruction than the Godswars if Juliustan relaxed his control.

Kelor – God of Luck. Although the other gods maintain that followers must have faith, this god prefers blind chance more openly. He champions games of chance, gambling, and random fate. This god tilts the tables in the direction he prefers, so one never knows how chance will turn up. This god rivals Dalios in unexpectedly bringing down great warriors. Many adventurers worship him, or at least pray for his blessing. Clerics of this god often throw themselves at adventure, or raise funds for the church in gambling houses. This god excels in finding small ways to thwart big plans.

Krakus – God of the Sea. The water is home to many creatures, and the oceans and seas have their own unique biology. This god provides a home for some, and can bring down wrath on others with the power of water currents. Sailors pay homage to this god in return for passage over his domain. In time, Krakus can reshape the land with his currents, or smash cities in great waves, (and would do so more often, if not for the interventions of Juliustan). The influence of his domain resulted in several of his churches being built to float out on the water. His clerics have much influence over the element of water and some can walk over its surface.

Laedelious – Elven Goddess of Forests and Wildlands. Commonly referred to as the "Treemother", or "Lady of the Green", this goddess has worked through the elves to further the protection of nature. Due to her guidance, many elves build their cities within the trees and current topography, rather than cut down the woods. Many elves enjoy a certain harmony with the woodland creatures through their history with Laedelious. Though the race of man shapes the land around his needs, elves have learned to shape their civilizations and homes around the needs of nature. Although this goddess has many cleric followers, there are also a number of mystics that work in her name.

Mothrok – Goddess of Earth and Stone. Born of the element of earth, this goddess has a strong connection to earth and stone. She believes in the superiority of everlasting stone, and the plant life that flourishes from the ground. She sees animal life as a type of vermin that infests the planet on which Dhea Loral can be found. Given her perspective, one would think that she would have few followers. In actuality, Mothrok has many worshippers among the underground-dwelling races, and others that work with the land. Even goodly farmers spare prayers to her out of fear for their crops. As part of her control over the land, she has been known to bring forth the corpses buried within the ground and use them as undead abominations.

Nandorrin – God of Fire. Worshipped mostly by dwarven smiths, this god is also often seen as a smith. Whenever tales are heard of volcanoes running with lava, it is believed to be Nandorrin reforming part of the world. Many candle makers use his image or symbol on their work. Many wizards praise him for their destructive fire-based arcana. His clerics perform a lot of ceremonies around fire, and to an extent they can shape fire as well.

Noyugon – God of Knowledge and Learning. Often know as the "Lorekeeper", this god strives to preserve histories and knowledge, and is said to be a recorder of deeds for the gods themselves. He promotes academies and centers of learning. Needless to say, he does not have many followers outside of educated cultures.

Scriptum Verash – A Book on the Philosophies of Evil. Made by several dark gods, and by Foyul for the sake of balance, this tome is the exact opposite of The Codex. It details greed and lust, power and glory, and encourages the strong and cunning to take what they will. It is in every way a document of "evil", yet at the same time it also has a life of its own. These clerics practice in secret, with no room for honor or compassion. In the past they have lead armies filled with hate against enemies for no more reason than the cleric's own selfish needs.

Taekbol – God of Underworld. This dwarvish and gnomish god favors those who dwell under the ground, away from the light of the sun. This god also spreads gems and metals under the surface of the world, sometimes in competition with Mothrok's stone empire. Some human miners even claim worship to him.

Westrealei – Elven Goddess of Wind and Air. This goddess communicates with her followers by means of various flying creatures. Her own image is painted in the shape of a pegasus, whose head and neck is replaced by the upper half of a beautiful elven female. This elven deity is of the sky, and a force of nature. Elven arrows need to ride her winds to strike true to their targets. In this respect, a windy day is said to be a bad omen for going into battle, as the archers will have a harder time hitting their targets.

Yestreal – God of the Sun and Weather. This nature deity, worshipped by many who till the soil, exerts his influence on harvests and crops. Many times this puts him in direct competition with Mothrok for the success of farmers, but the two gods were once allied during the Godswars. The sunflower is often used as his symbol. His followers often come from agricultural regions, and are generally good at farming. Clerics of this god never condone weddings on rainy days, as they feel their god shuns the marriage. Elves also have numerous followers to this nature god.

Yurtash – God of Spirits. It is hard to define what spirits are to the common man, due to superstitions and drunken fireside chats. In short, spirits are creatures neither living nor dead that perform specific tasks in the world. They are the after images of once-living creatures. While the soul may depart to another world, a part of the spirit may remain in the world, trapped, only to be harnessed by magical means. Yurtash seems to store and nurture these lost energies of forgotten souls until they have a use in the world again. Mystics, greenmen and some arcane casters call upon the spirits in spells. Many of this god's clerics share the powers of mystics over these spirits.

Appendix C – The Calendar of Dhea Loral

The calendar of Dhea Loral is four hundred days long. That reflects the time it takes for one year to pass for the planet of Epos Goth. The calendar is divided into five seasons, with two months in each season, as follows…

Planting season: Primus, then Florum
Summer season: Jherad, then Doyal
Harvest season: Othgar, then Novak
Waning season: Tiquierum, then Norgrad
Winter season: Vientula, then Icethule

Each month is forty days long. Each week is ten days. The civilized societies of the land do tend to observe two-day weekends, however much work is still done on these days. The value of a weekend in Dhea Loral is seen more as a time for socializing and public events, but even on these days many merchants are still doing business. There is also a midweek day by which many government offices in the civilized lands take half of the day off. The evening on these days is usually reserved for balls, feasts, religious observations, or other relaxing endeavors. Note that many people do not observe such luxuries, as the struggle to work and survive has bred a strong work ethic into a number of cultures.

The New Season Day, which commemorates the start of the New Year, is held at the traditional end of winter. Usually it begins to snow in most of the lands by mid to late Norgrad, and by the first of Primus the snow is melting away.

The calendar is measured by an important date in Dhea Loral history. In a time when war was sweeping the lands, several immortals and demigods were taking sides. Several were trying to attain more power, while some defended the common man. Several gods lent their powers to affect the outcome as well. It was a dark time in the world when great civilizations fell and new governments arose. During the waning season of 1 BC, (Before Covenant), the fury of the demigods and the use and destruction of several artifacts led to the destruction of the last great empires. The winter season that followed was a struggle for survival for many races. Even those living in the vast cave and underground systems of the world, while not affected by the surface winter, were weak and foraging for meager foods. The major powers, those gods who exerted the most influence in the world, stepped in and forced an end to the conflict. On the first of Primus, in the year now called 1 AC, (After Covenant), the gods and demigods signed a pact regarding the involvement of the deities in the future of the world. Although the gods were capable of controlling the world much more directly, restrictions were placed and honored by all. In this way they voluntarily gave up several privileges, and bound their oaths. Even the most chaotic of gods can never break the Covenant.

This was more or less the start of the churches and clerics, at least in their modern day incarnation. Clerics are the necessary vessels through which the gods move the races,

356

although the gods retain the necessary powers over nature and magic to make the world run smoothly and stay in balance.

About the Author

Douglas was born on Nov. 28, 1971. He got the chance to live in many different places while he was growing up, courtesy of the assignments the US Army offered to his father. Too quiet and too shy for too long, there were always dreams of other worlds and places…and the desire to write about them. He got into fantasy role-playing games in his mid-teens. To this day he has friends whom he meets in tabletop role-playing games as well as online adventures. Many of his characters evolved in games, and each developed their own personality. *Inheritance of a Sword and a Path* is the second book he wrote, though the first he published. He finished the rest of the *Earthrin Stones* series and has moved on to other novels set in Dhea Loral…some of which reference the events in this book! *The Widow Brigade* started its reception earning ten straight 5-star reviews, including a recent widow who said it helped with her healing process.

He has been making appearances at local conventions and signing books for fans. Though Douglas expanded his entertaining to include game streams and recordings on YouTube and Twitch, his passion remains centered on his writing.

Douglas lives with his wife and two boys in Minnesota. He works in healthcare, serving people's needs at both hospitals and clinics depending on his rotation. When most people see him, he is wearing scrubs.

For more info, please see the author's website at **DheaLoral.com**

Sign up for his mailing list, also check out his social media:

Facebook – Dhea Loral
Twitter - @ThaminDheaLoral
YouTube - Thamin DheaLoral
Twitch: - Thamin_T

Want to experience more of the world of Dhea Loral? Explore the dwarf homelands through the eyes of revolutionary Duli! *The Widow Brigade* opened on Amazon with twelve critiques praising the story, and each giving it a perfect 5 stars! This story features strong women, in a fantasy setting, rebelling against the traditions of a male-dominated society.

"I felt the plot was well developed, well paced, and the motivations of the characters really drew me in, caring about what happened as the plot progressed. I felt the main character was not your typical shiny hero, or dastardly anti-hero. She just felt real. I highly recommend this book..." - Tom H

"This book is very well written and as always with his stories, the battle scenes are intense, with details that pull you in and fully immerse yourself in the story. The characters are well developed and allow you to enjoy loving and hating them." – Lockhart

Strangers thrown together, forced into service on a common quest, form a bond of camaraderie. Each seeks to find their focus in the world, amidst their private mysteries.

The half-orc savage, who takes pride in a company he no longer serves. The dusk-skinned archer, carrying a bow from her forgotten homeland. The dwarf who studies the past so he can create a future. The knight who pays fealty to no lord. The elf sorceress seeking knowledge, but what specific question is she trying to answer?

They will band together, seeking separate goals. How far will pilgrims travel to discover who they are?

-Pilgrims with Blades: Pressed into Service- (released Oct 2017)

Facing a crisis and looking for any excuse to strike in force against the orcs occupying the hills to their south, the city-state Kashmer conscripts privateers and adventurers into war. A band of strangers must learn to support and adapt to each other as a daring plan separates them from the main force in hostile territory. Each possess their own mystery, but without cooperation and trust, they will be doomed to failure.

Pressed into Service is the introduction to the bold Pilgrims with Blades series.

The Boxer series features non-chronological adventures in an alternate Earth history. It's a Steampunk Wild-West flavor mixed with the old 1930s adventure serials that inspired Indiana Jones. This short novella, (19,000 words), will take you into a new reality.

Brian "Boxer" DuWold is feeling outdated in a booming industrial age of electricity, magnetism, and stiff competition between steam and fossil fuel engines. The tough conman makes a living off gamblers, using prize-fighting rings or shooting matches. Few realize his livelihood supports his blind sister; unfortunately, the suits of the United Republic Agency use this leverage to their advantage.

The United Republic has seen a lot of technological advances since defeating the southern rebels in its Civil War years ago. Now, the territory of Texico has won its independence from Meztica, and is considering joining the UR. One hitch: the mad scientist who helped win the revolution for Texico is pursuing his own agenda, which includes a train full of chemical explosives steaming straight for the capital! The doctor is rumored to have zombie soldiers, steam war machines, and high-tech weapons at his disposal.

Boxer barely has time to grab his brass knuckles and six-shooter before URA men send him on a mission that one team has already failed. He's loaded into the most advanced biplane of his time and tasked to stop the train. It's time to buckle in for a wild ride of an adventure.

Thank you for supporting my passion! If you've been entertained by my story, please offer up a good review and/or a bunch of stars on Amazon or Goodreads! Follow my social media on my "About the Author" page and consider joining my mailing list. I hope you enjoyed sharing the paths of Dhea Loral with me. -*Douglas Van Dyke Jr*